About the Author

Born in Paris in 1947, Christian Jacq first visited Egypt when he was seventeen, went on to study Egyptology and archaeology at the Sorbonne, and is now one of the world's leading Egyptologists. He is the author of the internationally bestselling RAMSES and THE MYSTERIES OF OSIRIS series, and several other novels on Ancient Egypt. Christian Jacq lives in Switzerland.

The Judge of Egypt Trilogy

Beneath the Pyramid
Secrets of the Desert
Shadow of the Sphinx

CHRISTIAN JACQ

Translated by Sue Dyson

POCKET
BOOKS

London · New York · Sydney · Toronto

A CBS COMPANY

The Judge of Egypt Trilogy first published in Great Britain by Pocket Books, 2008
An imprint of Simon & Schuster UK Ltd

A CBS COMPANY

3 5 7 9 10 8 6 4 2

Simon & Schuster UK Ltd
1st Floor
222 Gray's Inn Road
London WC1X 8HB

www.simonandschuster.co.uk

Simon & Schuster Australia
Sydney

A CIP catalogue record for this book is available from the British Library

ISBN 978-1-84739-366-1

Typeset by Ellipsis Books Limited, Glasgow
Printed and bound by CPI Group (UK) Ltd, Croydon, CR0 4YY

Beneath the Pyramid

Lo, that which the ancestors predicted has come to pass: crime is everywhere, violence has invaded men's hearts, misfortune besets the land, blood flows, the thief grows wealthy, smiles have faded, secrets have been divulged, trees have been uprooted, pyramids have been desecrated, the world has sunk so low that a few madmen have seized control of the throne, and the judges have been driven away.

But remember respect for the Rule, the righteous succession of days, the happy time when men built pyramids and filled orchards with plenty for the gods, that blessed time when a simple mat provided all that a man could desire and made him content.

Predictions of the sage Ipu-Ur

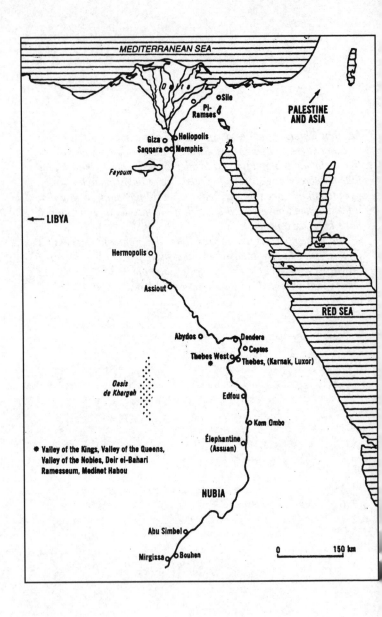

MEDITERRANEAN SEA

Delta

PALESTINE
AND ASIA

Sile

Pi-Ramses

Giza ○ ○Heliopolis
Saqqara ○○ ○Memphis

Fayoum

← LIBYA

RED SEA

Hermopolis ○

Assiout ○

Abydos ○   ○ Dendera
                  ○ Coptos
Thebes West ○   ○ Thebes, (Karnak, Luxor)
✦

Oasis
de Khargeh

Edfou ○

Kom Ombo ○

Éléphantine ○
(Assuan)

✦ Valley of the Kings, Valley of the Queens,
Valley of the Nobles, Deir el-Bahari
Ramesseum, Medinet Habou

NUBIA

Abu Simbel ○

Mirgissa ○○ Bouhen

0   150 km

Prologue

The moonless night had cast a veil of darkness around the Great Pyramid, and the group of soldiers who guarded it. In the distance, a desert fox slunk silently into the nobles' burial ground.

The only person permitted to enter the pyramid was the king, Ramses, who visited it once a year to pay homage to Khufu, his glorious ancestor. Rumour had it that the great king's mummy was housed in a gold sarcophagus, which was itself lavishly decorated. But no one would ever dare attack such a well-defended treasure. Only the reigning pharaoh could cross the monument's stone threshold and enter the labyrinth within. The guards would draw their bows at the slightest sign of trouble, bringing instant death to the curious or unwary.

Ràmses' reign was a happy one; Egypt was rich and peaceful, a shining example to the world. Pharaoh was seen as the messenger of light, the courtiers served him with respect, and the people glorified his name.

Dressed in coarse linen tunics, the five conspirators emerged from the workmen's hut where they had hidden during the day. They had gone over their plan a hundred times to make sure they had left nothing to chance. If they succeeded, sooner or later they would become masters of the country, and shape its destiny in their own image.

Silently they skirted the Giza plateau, casting fevered glances at the vast pyramid. A direct attack on the guards would be madness. Others before them had dreamed of seizing the treasure, but none had succeeded.

A month earlier, the Great Sphinx had been dug out of a sand drift which had accumulated during several recent storms. The giant monument, shaped like a pharaoh with a lion's body, was only lightly guarded, for it was known as the 'Living Statue', and the terror it inspired was enough to drive away evildoers.

The Sphinx's honour guard consisted of just five former soldiers. Two of them were fast asleep, propped up against the encircling wall facing the pyramids. They would not see or hear anything.

The lightest of the conspirators swiftly scaled the curtain wall, soundlessly strangled the sleeping soldier by the stone beast's right flank, then killed the guard by its left shoulder.

The other conspirators joined their companion. Killing the third guard, who was standing by the stele of Tuthmosis IV between the sphinx's front paws, would not be so easy. He was armed with a spear and a dagger, and was sure to defend himself.

One of the conspirators undressed and walked, naked, towards him.

He stared at her, aghast. This apparition must be one of the demons of the night who prowled around the pyramids, in search of souls to steal! Smiling, she approached him. Terrified, he sprang to his feet and brandished his spear. His arm was shaking. She halted.

'Get back, ghost!' he commanded. 'Leave me alone.'

'I shan't harm you. Let me kiss you.'

The guard could not tear his gaze from the woman's naked body, which gleamed white in the darkness. Hypnotized, he took a step towards her. A noose was suddenly flung about his neck and pulled tight. He dropped his spear, tried in vain to cry out, fell to his knees, and died.

'The way is clear,' she called.

'I'll get the lamps ready,' said one of the men.

The five conspirators stood beside the stele and consulted their map one last time, urging each other to continue despite the fear that racked them. They moved the stele aside, and there before their eyes was the mud seal that marked the position of the mouth of hell, the gateway to the bowels of the earth.

'So it wasn't just a legend.'

'Let's see if there really is a way in.'

Beneath the seal lay a flagstone, with a ring set into it. It took four of them to raise it. A very low, narrow corridor sloped steeply downwards into the depths of the earth.

'Quickly, the lamps!'

They filled dolerite cups with stone-oil, which was very greasy and burnt easily. Pharaoh forbade its use and sale, for the black smoke it produced brought sickness to the craftsmen who decorated temples and tombs, and soiled ceilings and walls. The sages had declared that this 'petroleum', as barbarians called it, was a harmful and dangerous substance; a malign secretion of the rocks filled with harmful vapours. But the conspirators could not have cared less.

Bent double, their heads often bumping against the limestone roof, they drove on deeper into the tunnel, towards the underground part of the Great Pyramid. No one spoke; they were all thinking about the sinister tale of a spirit which would break the neck of anyone trying to violate Khufu's tomb. And could they be sure this tunnel was taking them in the right direction? To mislead would-be thieves, false maps had been circulated; was theirs accurate?

They came up against a stone wall which they attacked with chisels; fortunately, the blocks were quite thin and pivoted easily. The conspirators slipped inside a vast chamber with an earthen floor. The room was about seven cubits high, twenty-eight long, and sixteen wide. In the centre was a well.

'The low chamber . . . We're inside the Great Pyramid!'

They had succeeded.

The long-forgotten passageway* did indeed lead from the sphinx to Khufu's giant monument, whose first chamber lay about sixty cubits below the base. It was here, within this evocation of the earth-mother's bosom, that the first resurrection rites had been carried out.

Now they must climb up a vertical shaft which led to the heart of the pyramid and joined a passage which began beyond the three granite plugs. The lightest of the five climbed up, using projecting rocks as hand- and footholds, and threw down a rope. One of the conspirators almost fainted for lack of air; his companions took him to the great gallery to get his breath back.

The sheer majesty of the place dazzled them. What architect had been mad enough to build such a structure, defying the centuries? According to Ramses' own master craftsmen, no one would ever again achieve such a feat.

One of the men was so overwhelmed that he wanted to give up; but the leader of the conspirators forced him on with a violent shove in the back. Giving up when they were so close to their goal would be stupid, for they now knew that their map was absolutely accurate. One doubt remained: had the stone portcullises been lowered between the great gallery and the corridor leading to the king's chamber? If so, the way would be blocked and they would have to leave empty-handed.

'It's all right – the entrance is clear.'

The five conspirators stooped low and entered the king's chamber, whose lofty ceiling was formed from nine immense blocks of granite. This chamber housed the very heart of the empire, the pharaoh's sarcophagus. It lay upon a silver floor, which maintained the purity of the place.

They hesitated.

Up to now, they had behaved like explorers in search of an unknown land. True, they had committed three crimes for which they would

---

*The existence of this passageway, mentioned in ancient sources, remains a matter for conjecture.

have to answer before the court of the afterlife, but they had acted for the good of the country and the people, by preparing the way for a tyrant's overthrow. But if they opened the sarcophagus, if they stripped it of its treasures, they would be violating the eternity not of a mummified man but of a god and his body of light. They would sever their last link with a thousand-year-old civilization in order to bring about a new world which Ramses would never accept.

They were torn between a desire to run away, and a sensation of great well-being. Air entered the pyramid through two channels cut into the north and south walls; and an energy rose up from the floor, imbuing them with some unknown strength. So this was how Pharaoh regenerated himself: by absorbing the power created by the stone and the monument's shape.

'We haven't much time.'

'We ought to leave now.'

'Certainly not.'

Two of the conspirators went over to the sarcophagus, then the third, and then the last two. Together, they lifted off the lid and laid it on the floor.

In the sarcophagus lay a radiant mummy covered with gold, silver and lapis lazuli, a mummy so noble that the looters could not bear to look into its eyes. Furiously, their leader tore off the golden mask; his acolytes seized the gold collar and the scarab, which lay where the heart had been. They took the lapis lazuli amulets and the sky-iron adze, the carpenter's tool that was used to open the mouth and eyes in the otherworld. But these marvels seemed almost derisory compared with the gold cubit symbolizing the eternal law that Pharaoh alone guaranteed.

Most precious of all was a small case in the form of a dove's tail. Inside it lay the Testament of the Gods. This text bequeathed Egypt to Pharaoh, and instructed him to keep the country happy and prosperous. When he celebrated his jubilee, he would be obliged to show the testament to the court and the people, as proof of his rightful kingship. If he could not produce it, sooner or later he would be compelled to abdicate.

By desecrating the pyramid's shrine, the conspirators had disrupted the principal energy centre and disturbed the radiance of the *ka*, the intangible power which animated every form of life. Soon misfortunes and calamities would rain down upon the land. Gradually, injustice would spread through the provinces, and more and more voices would be raised against Pharaoh until they became a destructive flood.

Lastly, the thieves seized a box filled with ingots of sky-iron, a rare metal as precious as gold. It would be used to complete their plan.

All they now had to do was leave the Great Pyramid, hide their booty, and weave their web.

Once safely back outside, before going their separate ways, they took an oath. Anyone who got in their way was to be killed: that was the price of power.

1

After a long career devoted to the art of healing, Branir was enjoying a peaceful retirement at his home in Memphis.

The old doctor was sturdily built and broad-chested, with elegant, silver hair framing a face whose stern appearance belied his kindliness and dedication. His natural nobility had impressed itself on everyone from the humble to the mighty, and no one could remember a single occasion when he been treated disrespectfully.

Branir was the son of a wig maker. He had left the family business to become a sculptor, painter and artist, and one of Pharaoh's master craftsmen had summoned him to the temple at Karnak. During one of the craftsmen's banquets, a stone cutter had fallen ill; instinctively, Branir had treated him with magnetism, snatching him from the jaws of certain death. The temple's own doctors had been quick to recognize his exceptional talent, and Branir had been trained by renowned physicians before beginning his work. Deaf to the court's pleas and uninterested in honours, he lived only to heal the sick.

However, now he was travelling to a small village near Thebes, and not to practise his craft. He had another mission to carry out, one so delicate that it seemed doomed to failure; but he would not give up until he had tried everything.

Branir ordered the bearers to set down his chair close to a tangled thicket of tamarisk trees. He felt a lump rise in his throat when he saw his home village once again, nestling in the heart of a palm grove. The air and sun were gentle; he watched the peasants at work and listened to the tune a flute player was piping.

An old man and two youths were breaking up clumps of earth in the high fields, turning Branir's thoughts to the season when the annual Nile flood deposited its fertile silt upon the land. The seed was trodden in by herds of pigs and flocks of sheep. Nature had endowed Egypt with untold riches, for this was the gods' beloved country.

Branir continued on his way. At the entrance to the village, he passed a team of placid oxen, and a man squatting outside one of the earthen houses, milking a cow. The old doctor smiled as he remembered the herd of cows he had once looked after; beasts with names like Good Advice, Pigeon, Sun-Water and Happy Flood. He had almost forgotten these simple scenes, this serene, unsurprising way of life, in which a man was simply one among many. Tasks were repeated over and over again, as they had been for centuries, and the Nile waters rose and fell, marking the rhythm of passing generations.

Suddenly, a powerful voice shattered the tranquillity summoning the people to a session of the village court. Nearby, a woman was loudly protesting her innocence, but the man in charge of maintaining order in the village kept a firm grip on her arm.

The court convened in the shade of a sycamore tree. Over it presided Pazair, a twenty-one-year-old judge who had the complete trust of all the village elders. Ordinarily, the elders would have appointed a middle-aged man with plenty of experience, who could answer for his decisions with his possessions if he was rich, and with his life if he had nothing worth seizing. Consequently, there were few candidates for the job of judge, even in a small country village. Any magistrate found to be at fault was punished more severely than a murderer; justice demanded it.

Pazair had had no choice. Because of his strong character and his uncompromising integrity, the elders had elected him by unanimous decision. Although he was very young, he had soon proved his competence by conducting each case with extreme care.

He was a tall man and rather thin, with chestnut hair and a broad, high forehead. His green eyes, flecked with brown, were bright and alert, and he impressed everyone with his serious manner; neither anger nor tears nor attempts at seduction perturbed him. He listened, scrutinized evidence, often investigated and checked witnesses' statements himself, and did not reach a decision until long and patient enquiries had been carried out. The villagers were sometimes astonished by his thoroughness, but they congratulated themselves on his love of truth and his talent for settling differences. Many feared him, knowing that they could not hope for compromise or indulgence from him; but none of his decisions had ever been challenged.

The jurors sat on either side of Pazair. There were eight in all: the village headman and his wife, two farmers, two craftsmen, an elderly widow and the scribe in charge of irrigation. All were over fifty.

The judge opened the court session with prayers to the goddess Ma'at, whose Rule earthly justice must strive to mirror. Then he read out the charge against the young woman. One of her friends accused her of stealing a spade belonging to her husband. In accordance with ancient law, there were no lawyers to act as intermediaries. Pazair asked the accuser to state her grievance clearly, and the defendant to present her defence. The former spoke calmly, the latter with such vehemence that Pazair ordered her to quiet herself.

He asked, 'Did anyone witness the crime?'

'I did,' replied the accuser.

'Where do you think the spade is now?'

'Hidden in her house.'

The accused woman denied the charge again with an energy which impressed the jurors. Her sincerity seemed obvious.

'We shall carry out a search immediately,' declared Pazair.

'You have no right to enter my house,' said the woman angrily.

'Do you confess you're guilty?'

'No! I'm innocent.'

'Lying in court is a serious offence.'

'She's the one who's lying.'

'If she is, she will be severely punished.' Pazair turned to the accuser and looked her straight in the eye. 'Do you still maintain that she stole the spade?' he asked.

She nodded.

The court moved off, following the scribe in charge of dealing with village disputes. The judge carried out the search himself. He found the spade in the cellar, wrapped in rags and hidden behind oil jars.

The guilty woman collapsed in tears. In accordance with the law, the jurors sentenced her to give her victim twice what she had stolen: in other words, two new spades. Moreover, lying under oath carried a sentence of forced labour for life, or even death in a criminal case. She was sentenced to work for several years, unpaid, on the lands of the local temple.

As the jurors were dispersing, Pazair heard someone ask, 'Will the judge grant me an audience?'

He could hardly believe his ears. That voice . . . Surely it couldn't be . . . ? He swung round. 'It *is* you!'

Branir and Pazair embraced.

'What on earth are you doing here?' asked Pazair.

'I have returned to my roots.'

'Let's go and sit down.'

The two men sat down on two low seats in the shade of a tall sycamore. On one of its sturdy branches hung a goatskin filled with fresh water.

'Sitting here brings back many memories, doesn't it?' said Branir. 'This is where, after your parents died, I told you your secret name, the "Seer, He Who Sees Far into the Distance". The Council of Elders was right to give you that name. What more could anyone ask of a judge?'

'And what a splendid celebration there was! I was circumcised, the village gave me my first official kilt, I threw away my toys, ate roast duck and drank red wine.'

'The boy quickly became a man.'

'Too quickly?'

'Everyone has his own pace. You have youth and maturity in the same heart.'

'You're the one who taught me everything.'

'You know that's not true,' said Branir. 'You taught yourself.'

'You taught me to read and write, you introduced me to the law and let me devote myself to it. Without you, I'd have been a peasant and would have been quite happy tilling my little piece of land.'

'No, you wouldn't. You're a different kind of man; the greatness and the happiness of a country depend upon the quality of its judges.'

'Living a just life,' said Pazair with a sigh. 'It's a daily battle, and no one could ever claim that he always wins.'

'But you want to – that's the most important thing.'

'The village is a haven of peace – today's sad business is an exception.'

'You've been made overseer of the wheat granary, haven't you?'

'The headman wants me to be appointed steward of Pharaoh's field, to prevent disputes at harvest time. The job doesn't tempt me; I hope he fails.'

'I'm absolutely certain he will.'

'Why is that?'

'Because the future holds something very different for you.'

'You intrigue me.'

'I have been entrusted with a mission,' said Branir.

'By the palace?'

'No, by the court of justice at Memphis.'

'Have I done something wrong?'

'On the contrary, for the last two years the inspectors of country judges have been writing highly favourable reports about you. You have just been appointed to the province of Giza, to replace a magistrate who died recently.'

'Giza? But that's so far away!' protested Pazair.

'It's only a few days by boat. You're to live in Memphis.'

Giza! The most famous place in all Egypt, site of the Great Pyramid of Khufu, which was the mysterious energy centre on which the harmony of the entire country depended.

'I'm happy, here in my village. I was born here, I grew up here, I work here. Leaving would be too great a wrench.'

'I supported your appointment, because I believe Egypt needs you. You aren't a man to put your own preferences first.'

'Is the decision irrevocable?'

'No, you can refuse.'

'I need time to think.'

'The body of a man is vaster than a grain store; it is filled with countless answers. Choose the right one, and leave the others locked up.'

Pazair walked towards the riverbank; at this moment, his life hung in the balance. He hated the thought of abandoning his daily routine, the quiet joys of the village and the Theban countryside, and losing himself in a great city. But how could he refuse Branir, the man he revered above all others? He had sworn to answer his mentor's call, no matter what the circumstances.

A great white ibis was striding majestically along the riverbank. Halting, it plunged its long beak into the mud, and turned its gaze on the judge.

'The sacred bird of Thoth has chosen you,' declared the gravelly voice of Pepy the shepherd, who was stretched out in the reeds. 'You have no choice.'

Pepy was a short-tempered seventy-year-old, with no great fondness for human company. As far as he was concerned, being alone with the animals was the pinnacle of happiness. Refusing to take orders from anyone, he wielded his gnarled staff with skill, and was adept at hiding in the papyrus forests whenever the tax collectors descended upon the village like a flock of sparrows. Pazair had given up summoning him before the court. The old man had taken it upon himself to punish anyone who mistreated a cow or a dog, and, in view of this, the judge chose to regard him as a kind of assistant.

'Look at the ibis and mark it well,' stressed Pepy. 'Its stride is the length of one cubit, the symbol of justice. May your conduct also be upright and exact. You're going to leave, aren't you?'

'How do you know that?'

'The ibis is flying up into the sky. It has chosen you.'

The old man stood up. His skin was tanned by the wind and the sun; he wore nothing but a kilt made from reeds. 'Branir is the only honest man I know,' he said. 'He never tries to deceive you or do you harm. When you live in the town, beware of officials, courtiers and flatterers: there is death in their words.'

'I don't want to leave the village.'

'And what about me? Do you think I want to go and look for the goat that's strayed?' Pepy vanished into the reeds.

The black and white bird flew away. Its great wings flapped to a rhythm it alone knew; it was heading north.

When Pazair went back to Branir, the old doctor read the answer in Pazair's eyes, and smiled. He said, 'Be in Memphis at the beginning of next month. You'll stay with me until you take up your post.'

'You aren't leaving already, are you?'

'I no longer practise medicine much, but a few sick people still need my services. I, too, wish I could have stayed longer.'

The chair and its bearers disappeared into the dust of the road.

The headman hailed Pazair, and told him, 'We've got a delicate matter to deal with: three families all claim they own the same palm tree.'

'I know. The dispute has lasted for three generations. Entrust it to my successor; if he doesn't manage to settle it, I'll deal with it when I get back.'

'Get back? You mean you're leaving the village?'

'The government has summoned me to Memphis.'

'And what about the palm tree?'

'Let it grow.'

2

Pazair checked that his travelling bag was in good condition. It was made of leather, and had two wooden poles which he stuck in the ground to hold it upright. When it was full, he would carry it on his back.

What was he going to put into it, apart from a rectangle of fabric for a new kilt, a cloak, and the all-important mat? The mat was made from woven papyrus strips, and could serve as a bed, a table, a carpet, a wall hanging, a screen, or as packaging for precious objects. Its last use would be as a winding-sheet to wrap its owner's dead body. Pazair's mat was very hard-wearing; in fact it was his finest item of furniture. As for his goatskin water-bag, it kept water cool for hours.

Hardly had he opened his travelling bag when a sandy-coloured mongrel rushed up to sniff at it. Brave was three years old, a mixture of greyhound and wild dog. He was longlegged, with a short snout, curly tail and drooping ears which pricked up at the slightest sound; and he was devoted to his master. Although he loved long walks, he did not hunt much and preferred his food cooked.

'We're leaving, Brave.'

The dog looked nervously at the bag.

'We'll walk, and then take the boat to Memphis.'

The dog sat down and waited for the bad news.

'Pepy's made you a collar. He's greased the leather and stretched it thoroughly. It'll be perfectly comfortable – really it will.'

Brave looked less than convinced, but grudgingly accepted the collar, which was pink, green and white and studded with nails. If another dog or a wild beast tried to seize him by the neck, he would be well protected. Pazair had added a finishing touch with an inscription in hieroglyphs: 'Brave, companion of Pazair'.

The dog gulped down a meal of fresh vegetables, but did not

take his eyes off his master. He sensed that this was not the time for play.

Led by the headman, the villagers took their leave of the judge; some wept. They wished him good fortune, and gave him two amulets, one representing a boat and the other a pair of sturdy legs. These would protect the traveller, who must pray to God each morning to preserve the talismans' power.

Pazair picked up his sandals. He did not put them on, for like his fellow countrymen he walked barefoot, using the precious footwear only when he entered someone's home and had washed the dust from his feet. He checked that the leather toe straps and soles were in good condition, put the sandals in his bag, then turned and left the village without a backward glance.

Just as he was setting off along the narrow, winding road which overlooked the Nile, a soft muzzle touched his right hand.

'Way-Finder, you've escaped!' he exclaimed. 'I must take you back to your field.'

The donkey was not listening. Holding out his right hoof for Pazair to take, he began to bray. The judge had rescued him from a brutal peasant who was beating him with a stick because he had chewed through his tether.

Way-Finder had a marked penchant for independence, and the strength to carry the heaviest loads. The animal was well aware that he was worth as much as a good cow or a fine coffin. He had a keen sense of direction, and could easily find his way around the maze of country roads. Often he went from place to place on his own, delivering foodstuffs. Although sober and placid, he would not sleep unless he was by his master's side.

'I'm going a long, long way away,' said Pazair. 'And you wouldn't like Memphis.'

The dog rubbed himself against the donkey's right foreleg. Way-Finder understood Brave's signal and turned sideways on, eager to receive his master's travelling bag.

Gently, Pazair took hold of the donkey's left ear. 'Who is the stubbornest creature in the world?'

With a rueful smile he gave up, and Way-Finder proudly took his place at the head of the little procession, instinctively taking the most direct route to the landing stage.

Under the rule of Ramses, travellers could use the roads and tracks without fear. On their journeys they encountered Pharaoh's messengers and postal officials; and if they needed to, they could ask for help from the guards on patrol. Egypt had come a long way since the days of terror when bandits roamed the land, robbing rich and poor alike. Ramses ensured that public order was respected, for without it happiness was impossible.*

Way-Finder walked sure-footedly down the steep slope that led to the river, as though he knew his master was planning to take the boat for Memphis. The trio boarded the craft, and Pazair paid the fare with a piece of fabric. While the animals slept he gazed out at Egypt, which poets had compared to an immense ship whose high sides were formed by chains of mountains. Hills and tall rock faces towered protectively over the fields. Plateaux bisected by valleys rose up here and there, between the black, fertile, generous earth and the red desert where dangerous forces roamed.

Pazair longed to go back to the village, and never leave it again. This journey into the unknown made him uneasy, robbing him of confidence in his own abilities. Only Branir could have persuaded him to accept this appointment, and no promotion could restore the peace of mind that he had lost. Now Pazair felt as though he were heading towards a future which might be beyond his power to control.

Pazair was stunned.

Menes the unifier had created Memphis, the largest city in Egypt.† It was the country's administrative capital, and was known as the 'Balance of the Two Lands'. Whereas the southern city of Thebes was devoted to tradition and the cult of Amon, Memphis, which stood at the junction of Upper and Lower Egypt, looked out towards Asia and the civilizations around the great sea to the north.

The judge, the donkey and the dog disembarked at the port of Perunefer, whose name meant 'Good Journey'. The docks were a hive of activity, with hundreds of cargo boats of all sizes unloading their wares; the goods were taken to immense warehouses, which were guarded and managed with the greatest care. Running parallel to the Nile was a canal, worthy of the builders of the Old Kingdom whose pyramids dominated the nearby plateau. The stone-lined canal allowed boats to travel in safety, and ensured that foodstuffs and raw materials could be transported whatever the season.

The three travellers headed for the northern district where Branir lived. As Pazair crossed the city centre he marvelled at the famous

---

*People travelled a good deal in ancient Egypt mostly on the Nile, though they also used country roads and desert paths. Pharaoh had a duty to guarantee travellers' safety.

†Menes was the pharaoh who first united the two lands of Upper and Lower Egypt. His name means the 'Stable One'.

Temple of Ptah, god of craftsmen, and passed by the military zone. This was where weapons were made and warships built. Here, the elite divisions of the Egyptian army were trained; they lived in vast barracks, between arsenals filled with chariots, swords, spears and shields.

To the north and south were granaries packed with barley, spelt and other types of grain. The granaries stood alongside the Treasury buildings, which contained gold, silver, copper, fabrics, unguents, oil, honey and other valuable things.

The sheer size of Memphis made the young countryman's head spin. He was sure he'd never find his bearings in this maze of streets and alleyways, this proliferation of districts with names like Life of the Two Lands, the Garden, the Sycamore, Crocodile Wall, the Fortress, the Two Mounds and College of Medicine. Brave seemed unsure of himself and kept close to his master's side, but the donkey went calmly on his way, guiding his two companions through the craftsmen's district, where stone, wood, metal and leather were worked in little shops which opened on to the street. Pazair had never seen so many pots, vases, dinner plates and domestic utensils.

The judge encountered many foreigners: Hittites, Greeks, Canaanites and Asiatics from various little kingdoms. They were relaxed and talkative, decking themselves in lotus garlands and declaring that Memphis was a garden of plenty. They were even able to celebrate their religious rites in temples dedicated to the god Baal and the goddess Astarte, whose presence Pharaoh tolerated.

Pazair asked a weaving-woman for directions, and was reassured to learn that the donkey had not led him astray. The judge noted that the nobles' sumptuous homes were mixed in with the little houses belonging to the common people. Tall porticoes, guarded by gatekeepers, opened on to flower-lined paths leading to two- and three-storey houses.

At last they reached Branir's house. It was delightfully attractive with its white walls, its lintel painted with red poppies, and decorations of cornflowers, perseas and greenery round its windows. A door opened on to a garden where two palm trees grew, shading the little house's terrace. True, the village was a very long way away, but the old doctor had succeeded in preserving a country atmosphere in the heart of the city.

Branir was standing on the threshold. 'Did you have a good journey?' he asked.

'Yes, but the donkey and the dog are thirsty.'

'I'll take care of them. Here is a basin of cool water, so that you can wash your feet, and some bread sprinkled with salt to welcome you.'

Pazair walked down a flight of steps into the first room, where he meditated before a small niche containing the statuettes of the ancestors. Then he continued into the reception room, whose ceiling was supported by two painted columns; the walls were lined with storage cupboards and chests, and there were mats on the floor. The remaining accommodation consisted of a workshop, a bathroom, a kitchen, two bedrooms and a cellar.

Branir invited his guest to climb the staircase up to the terrace, where he had set out cool drinks, accompanied by dates stuffed with honey and sweet pastries.

'I feel lost,' confessed Pazair.

'I'd be astonished if you didn't. A good dinner, a decent night's sleep, and you'll be ready for the investiture ceremony tomorrow.'

'Tomorrow? Why does it have to be so soon?'

'Cases are piling up.'

'I'd have liked time to get used to Memphis.'

'Your enquiries will make you do that. Here's a gift, since you haven't yet taken up your new post.'

Branir handed Pazair a copy of the book that was used to instruct scribes, teaching them how to behave correctly in all circumstances and have proper respect for the hierarchy of beings. At the top were the gods, goddesses, transfigured spirits, Pharaoh and the queen; then the king's mother, the tjaty, the council of wise men, senior judges, leaders of the army and the scribes of the House of Books. These were followed by a multitude of officials, from the director of the Treasury to the man in charge of the canals, and Pharaoh's representatives abroad.

Pazair unrolled the book a little way and read, 'A man with violence in his heart can never be anything but a trouble-maker, nor can a man who does not know when to stop talking. If you want to be strong, become the craftsman of your own words and fashion them, for, in the hands of a man who knows how to use it well, language is the most powerful weapon of all.' As he rolled it up again, he said sadly, 'I'm missing the village already.'

'You'll miss it for the rest of your life.'

'Why was I summoned here?'

'Your own conduct determined matters.'

Pazair slept little and badly, with his dog at his feet and his donkey lying beside his head. Events were moving too quickly, giving him no time to find his balance. Caught in a whirlpool, he had lost his usual points of reference and – in spite of his reluctance – he must embark upon an adventure into the unknown.

Waking at dawn, he washed, cleansed his mouth with natron,* and

*A natural compound of carbonate of soda and bicarbonate of soda.

ate breakfast with Branir, who afterwards took him to one of the best barbers in the city. As they sat on three-legged stools facing each other, the barber moistened Pazair's skin, and covered it with an oily foam before wielding his copper razor with consummate skill.

Dressed in a new kilt and a loose, diaphanous shirt, his body perfumed, Pazair looked fit to face the ordeal.

'I feel as if I'm in disguise,' he confided to Branir.

'Appearances are unimportant, but they shouldn't be neglected. Learn how to handle the tiller so that the tide of days doesn't carry you away from justice, whose practice safeguards a country's balance. Be worthy of yourself, my son.'

3

Pazair followed Branir into the Ptah district, which lay in the southerly part of the ancient, white-walled citadel. Although the young man was happy about the fate of the donkey and the dog, he was less sure about his own.

Not far from the palace stood several government buildings, whose entrances were guarded by soldiers. The old doctor spoke to an officer, who disappeared for a few moments before returning with a senior judge, the tjaty's delegate.

'I am happy to see you again, Branir,' he said. 'So this is your pupil.'

'Pazair is very nervous.'

'That is quite understandable, given his age. Is he ready to take up his new duties nevertheless?'

Pazair cut in, 'You need have no doubt of it.'

The judge frowned. 'I shall take him from you now, Branir. We must proceed with the investiture.'

The old doctor's warm smile gave his pupil the courage he still lacked. Whatever the difficulties might be, he would do Branir credit.

Pazair was shown into a small, rectangular room with bare white walls. The judge invited him to sit down on a mat, facing the court, which comprised himself, the governor of the province of Memphis, an official from the administration secretariat, and a senior priest of Ptah. All four men wore heavy wigs and full-skirted kilts. Their faces were unreadable, devoid of emotion.

'You are in the place where "the evaluation of difference"* is carried out,' announced the judge, who was in charge of the justice system. 'Here, you will become a man unlike others, a man who has been called to judge his fellow men. Like your colleagues in Giza province, you will carry out enquiries, preside over the local courts under your

*The expression is used in the *Book of the Dead* for distinguishing the just from the unjust.

jurisdiction, and refer matters to your superiors when they exceed your scope. Do you promise to do these things?'

'I promise.'

'Are you aware that your word, once given, cannot be taken back?'

'I am.'

'Let the court proceed, according to the commandments of the Rule, and judge the future judge.'

The governor of Memphis said in solemn, measured tones, 'Which jurors will you call upon to make up your court?'

'Scribes, craftsmen, guards, experienced men, respectable women, widows.'

'How will you intervene in their deliberations?'

'I shall not. Each juror will speak without being influenced, and I shall respect each one's opinion in making my judgment.'

'In all circumstances?'

'There is only one exception: if a juror is found to be corrupt. In such a case I would immediately halt the trial in progress and have the juror charged.'

'How must you act when a crime has been committed?' asked the administration official.

'I must carry out a preliminary investigation, document everything that happens in the case and give the information to the tjaty's office.'

The priest of Ptah placed his right arm across his chest, with his closed fist touching his shoulder. He said, 'No act will be forgotten, when you are judged in the afterlife; your heart will be laid upon the scales and weighed against the Rule. In what form has the law been passed down to us?'

'There are forty-two provinces and forty-two rolls of the law; but its spirit was not written down and must not be. Truth can only be passed on orally, from the master's mouth to the disciple's ear.'

The priest smiled, but the tjaty's deputy was not yet satisfied. He asked, 'How would you define the Rule?'

'Bread and beer.'

'What does that mean?'

'Justice for all, great or small.'

'Why is the Rule symbolized by an ostrich feather?'

'Because it is the means of communication between our world and the world of the gods. The feather is the rectrix, the rudder that determines both the direction of a bird's flight and the direction a human being will take. The Rule, the breath of life, must remain in men's lungs and drive evil from their hearts and bodies. If justice disappeared, wheat would no longer grow, rebels would seize power and festivals would no longer be celebrated.'

The governor stood up and placed a block of limestone in front of Pazair. 'Lay your hands upon this white stone,' he said.

The young man did so. His hands were steady.

'Let it bear witness to your oath. It will remember for ever the words you have spoken, and will be your accuser if you betray the Rule.'

The governor and the administration official stood on either side of the judge.

'Stand up,' ordered the tjaty's deputy. 'Here is the ring that bears your seal,' he said. He handed Pazair a rectangular plaque attached to a ring which the young man slipped on to the middle finger of his right hand. The flat surface of the gold plaque was inscribed, '*Judge Pazair*'. 'Documents upon which you place your seal will be official and you will bear responsibility for them. Do not use that ring lightly.'

The judge's accommodation was on the southern outskirts of Memphis, halfway between the Nile and the western canal and south of the Temple of Hathor. The young man, who had been expecting an imposing place, was cruelly disappointed: the government had allocated him only a small, two-storey house.

Sitting fast asleep on the doorstep was a sentry. Pazair tapped him on the shoulder, and he awoke with a start.

'I would like to go in,' said Pazair.

'The office is closed.'

'I am the judge.'

'I doubt that – he's dead.'

'I am Pazair, his successor.'

'Pazair? Oh yes, that's right. Iarrot, the scribe to the court, gave me your name. Have you got proof of your identity?'

Pazair showed him the seal ring.

'My job was to watch this place until you arrived. Now I'm done here.'

'When will I see Iarrot?'

'I've no idea. He's sorting out a tricky problem.'

'What kind of problem?'

'The wood for heating. It's cold in Memphis in winter, but last year the Treasury refused to deliver wood to this office because the request hadn't been submitted in triplicate. Iarrot has gone to the records office to sort things out. I wish you good luck, Judge Pazair; you certainly won't get bored here in Memphis.' And the sentry went on his way.

Slowly, Pazair pushed open the door of his new domain. The office was quite a large room, filled with cupboards and chests laden with tied or sealed papyrus scrolls. The floor was covered in a suspicious layer of dust. Pazair did not hesitate to tackle this unexpected peril. Despite the dignity of his office, he seized a stiff broom and swept the dust away.

Next, the judge drew up a list of the contents of the archives: land registry and tax documents, reports, complaints, notes relating to accounts and the payment of salary in grain, baskets or fabrics, letters, lists of employees . . . his duties covered widely diverse areas.

The largest cupboard contained all the essential materials a scribe needed: palettes with hollows for red and black ink, cakes of solidified ink, pots, bags of powdered pigments, bags for brushes, scrapers, adhesives, stone pestles, linen strings, a tortoise shell for mixing, a clay baboon representing Thoth, the master of hieroglyphs, limestone shards for rough notes, clay, limestone and wooden tablets. Everything was of good quality.

A small acacia-wood chest contained an extremely precious object: a water clock. The little vase, shaped like a truncated cone, was graduated inside, according to two different scales, with twelve notches; water flowed out through a hole at the bottom of the clock, and in this way the hours were measured. No doubt the scribe must have deemed it necessary to keep a check on the amount of time spent at his place of work.

One thing needed to be done straight away. Pazair picked up a fine reed brush, dipped the tip into a water pot, and let a drop fall on to the palette he was going to use. He murmured the prayer all scribes recited before writing: 'Water from the ink pot for your *ka*, Imhotep.' That was how they venerated the creator of the first pyramid, who was a designer of buildings, a doctor, an astrologer and the model for all those who practised hieroglyphs.

The judge climbed up to his official living quarters on the first floor. They had been empty for a long time. Pazair's predecessor, who preferred to live in a little house on the edge of the city, had neglected to look after the three rooms, which were occupied by fleas, flies, mice and spiders.

The young man was not discouraged. He felt he had the skills he needed for this particular battle. In the country, homes often had to be cleansed and unwelcome guests driven away.

After obtaining the necessary ingredients from local traders, Pazair set to work. He sprinkled the walls and the floor with water in which he had dissolved natron, then followed this with a layer of pulverized charcoal, mixed with the *bebet* plant,* whose strong smell drove away insects and vermin. Finally, he mixed incense, myrrh, cinnamon and

Inula graveolens.

honey, and burnt the mixture; the fumes would both purify the house and make it smell nice. To acquire these expensive ingredients, he had got himself into debt and had spent most of his next salary.

Worn out, he unrolled his mat and lay down on his back. Something bothered him and kept him awake: the seal ring. But he did not take it off. Pepy the shepherd was right: he no longer had a choice.

4

The sun was already high in the sky when Iarrot's heavy step sounded outside the office. A rather large man, he had a florid, veined complexion and podgy cheeks, and wherever he went he swung his stick to the rhythm of his stride. It was a special walking stick, inscribed with his name – indicating that he was an important person, worthy of respect. Iarrot was a self-satisfied forty-year-old with a young daughter who was the cause of all his woes. Each day, he argued with his wife about how to bring up the child whom he did not wish to displease for any reason whatever. The house echoed to the sound of their quarrels, which were becoming more and more violent.

To his great surprise, he found a workman mixing plaster with crushed limestone to make it whiter. As he watched, the man checked its quality by pouring it into a limestone cone, then filled in a hole on the front wall of the judge's house.

'I did not order any work to be done,' said Iarrot angrily.

'Ah, but I did. What's more, I'm doing it without delay.'

'On whose authority?'

'I am Judge Pazair.'

'But . . . but you're so young!'

'Are you by any chance Iarrot?'

'I am indeed.'

'The day is already well advanced.'

'Yes, that's true. I was delayed by family problems.'

'Are there any urgent cases?' asked Pazair, continuing with his plastering.

'Just one. A complaint from a man who owns a building company. He had bricks, but no donkeys to transport them. He accused the donkey hirer of sabotaging his building site.'

'It's been sorted out.'

'How?'

'I saw the donkey hirer this morning. He will pay damages to the builder and will transport the bricks first thing tomorrow; we have avoided a court case.'

'And you're a . . . plasterer, too?'

'Only a very modest amateur. Our budget is rather small, so in the majority of cases we shall have to manage by ourselves. What else?'

'You are expected to attend a re-count of livestock.'

'Won't the specialist scribe suffice?'

'The master of the estate, Qadash the tooth doctor, is convinced that one of his employees is stealing, and has asked for an investigation. Your predecessor delayed it as long as possible – to tell you the truth, I can well understand why. If you like, I'll find reasons for delaying it still more.'

'That won't be necessary. By the way, do you know how to handle a broom?'

Iarrot gaped. The judge handed him one.

Way-Finder was happy to smell the country air again. He trotted along briskly with the judge's materials, while Brave scampered about, chasing a few birds out of their nests. As usual, Way-Finder had listened carefully when the judge told him that they were going to Qadash's estate, which was two hours' walk from the Giza plateau, and lay to the south; the donkey had set off in the right direction.

Pazair was warmly welcomed by the estate steward, who was only too happy to greet a competent judge at last, one who wanted to resolve a mystery which was making the oxherds' lives a misery. Servants washed Pazair's feet and gave him a new kilt, promising to wash the one he was wearing, while two small boys fed the donkey and the dog. Qadash was informed of his arrival, and a platform was hastily erected, topped off by a red and black canopy with columns in the shape of lotus stems. Pazair and the scribe of the herds waited beneath it, shaded from the sun.

Qadash arrived, holding a long staff in his right hand. Servants followed, carrying his sandals, his parasol and his armchair; girls played the tambourine and the flute, and young peasant women presented him with lotus flowers.

He was about sixty, with a mass of white hair. He was tall, with a prominent nose criss-crossed with blue veins, a low forehead, high cheekbones and rheumy eyes, which he wiped frequently. Pazair was astonished by the redness of his hands; doubtless the man suffered from poor circulation of the blood.

Qadash regarded him suspiciously. 'So you're the new judge?'

'At your service. It's good to see that the peasants are happy when the owner of the estate has a noble heart and a firm grip on the reins of power.'

'You will go far, young man, if you respect the great.' Qadash was richly dressed. A kilt pleated at the front, a cat-skin corselet, a seven-string necklace of blue, white and red pearls, and row upon row of bracelets gave him an air of pride.

'Let's sit down,' he suggested.

He lowered himself into his painted wooden armchair, and Pazair sat down on a cube-shaped seat. In front of him and the scribe of the herds were small, low tables, designed to hold their writing materials.

'According to your declaration,' Pazair reminded him, 'you possess one hundred and one head of cattle, seventy sheep, six hundred goats and the same number of pigs.'

'Correct. At the time of the last count, two months ago, there was an ox missing. Now, my animals are very valuable; even the thinnest one could be exchanged for a linen tunic and ten sacks of barley. I want you to arrest the thief.'

'Have you conducted your own investigation?'

'That is not my line of work.'

The judge turned to the scribe of the herds, who was seated on a mat, and asked, 'What did you write in your registers?'

'The number of animals I was shown.'

'Whom did you question?'

'No one. My job is to write things down, not question people.'

Pazair could not draw anything more out of him. Irritated, he took from his basket a sycamore tablet covered with a fine layer of plaster, a sharpened reed brush and a water pot, in which he prepared some black ink. When he was ready, Qadash signalled to the head oxherd, who tapped the enormous lead ox on the neck and began leading the procession of animals past the platform. The ox moved forward slowly, followed by his heavy, placid fellows.

'Splendid, aren't they?' said Qadash.

'You must congratulate the men who rear them,' advised Pazair.

'The thief must be a Hittite or a Nubian – there are too many foreigners in Memphis.'

'Isn't your name of Libyan origin?'

Qadash did not hide his annoyance very well. 'I have lived in Egypt for a long time and I belong to the best society – isn't the wealth of my estate proof of that? I have treated the most famous members of court, you know. You should remember your place.'

The animals were accompanied by servants carrying fruit, bunches of leeks, baskets of lettuces and vases of perfume. Evidently this was not a simple re-count; Qadash wanted to dazzle the new judge and show him the extent of his fortune.

Brave had slipped silently under his master's chair and was watching the animals go past.

'Which province are you from, Judge?'

'I am the one conducting the investigation.'

Two yoked oxen passed the platform; the older one lay down on the ground and refused to go any further.

'Stop playing dead,' said the oxherd. The beast looked at him fearfully, but did not move.

'Beat him,' ordered Qadash.

'One moment,' ordered Pazair, stepping down from the platform.

He stroked the ox gently and, with the oxherd's help, encouraged it to get it back on its feet. Reassured, it stood up. Pazair went back to his seat.

'What a sensitive soul you are,' commented Qadash sarcastically.

'I detest violence.'

'Isn't it necessary from time to time? Egypt had to fight against the invader, and men died for our freedom. Would you condemn them?'

Pazair concentrated on the procession of animals; the scribe of the herds counted. At the end of the count, there was indeed one ox missing as the owner had claimed.

'This is intolerable!' roared Qadash, his face turning purple. 'People are stealing from me on my own lands, and no one will denounce the guilty party!'

'Your animals must be marked.'

'Of course.'

'Summon the men who applied the marks.'

There were fifteen of them. The judge questioned them one after the other, and kept them separate so that they could not talk to each other.

'I have identified your thief,' he announced when he had finished.

'Who is it?'

'Kani.'

'I demand that the court be convened immediately.'

Pazair agreed. He chose as his jurors an oxherd, a woman who looked after the goats, the scribe of the herds and one of the estate guards.

Kani, who had made no attempt to escape, came freely up to the platform, and looked the furious Qadash straight in the eye. The accused man was short and heavy-set, with deeply lined brown skin.

'Do you admit your guilt?' asked Pazair.

'No.'

Qadash struck the ground fiercely with his walking stick. 'Punish this insolent thief immediately!'

'Be quiet,' ordered Pazair. 'If you cause a disturbance, I shall halt the court proceedings.'

Angrily, Qadash turned away.

'Kani, did you mark an ox with Qadash's name?' asked Pazair.

'Yes.'

'That animal has disappeared.'

'It escaped from me. You'll find it in a neighbouring field.'

'Why were you so careless?'

'I'm a gardener, not a cowherd, and my real work is irrigating small patches of ground. All day long I carry a yoke on my shoulders, and empty heavy jars of water on to the fields. Even in the evening I can't rest; I must water the most delicate plants, maintain the irrigation channels, reinforce the banks of earth. If you want proof, look at the back of my neck; you'll see the scars of two abscesses. That's a gardener's complaint, not a cowman's.'

'Why did you change your occupation?'

'Because Qadash's steward caught me when I was delivering vegetables. I had to take care of the oxen and abandon my garden.'

Pazair summoned witnesses, and established that Kani was telling the truth. The court acquitted him, and the judge ordered that, as compensation, the runaway ox should become his property and Qadash must give him a large quantity of food in exchange for the working days he had lost.

The gardener bowed before the judge, and Pazair saw deep gratitude in his eyes.

'Compelling this peasant to work for you is a serious offence,' he reminded Qadash.

Blood rose to the man's face. 'I'm not responsible! I knew nothing about it. Punish my steward – he deserves it.'

'You know what the punishment is: fifty strokes of the stick and demotion to the status of a peasant.'

'The law is the law.' Qadash bowed briefly, and went back to his house.

When the steward was brought before the court, he did not deny his guilt. He was convicted, and the sentence was carried out on the spot.

When Judge Pazair left the estate, Qadash did not come to say goodbye.

5

Brave was asleep at his master's feet, dreaming of a feast, while Way-Finder, who had breakfasted on fresh forage, was acting as a sentry outside the office. Inside, Pazair had been hard at work since dawn, studying the current cases. The mass of difficulties did not overwhelm him. On the contrary, he was determined to make up for lost time and leave no loose ends.

Iarrot arrived in the middle of the morning, looking dishevelled.

'You seem rather depressed,' commented Pazair.

'Another argument with my wife – she's unbearable. I married her so that she could prepare tasty meals for me and now she's refusing to cook. Life's becoming impossible.'

'Are you considering divorce?'

'No, because of my daughter. I want her to become a dancer, but my wife has other plans, which I won't agree to. Neither of us will give in.'

'I fear that is something of a stalemate.'

'So do I. Did your investigation at Qadash's estate go well?'

'I'm just putting the final touches to my report. The ox was found, a gardener acquitted and the steward convicted. In my opinion, Qadash was at least partly responsible, but I can't prove it.'

'Leave him well alone,' said Iarrot. 'He has influential friends.'

'Are his customers rich?'

'He has treated the most famous mouths, but malicious gossips say that he's lost his touch and that it's better to avoid him if you want to keep healthy teeth.'

Brave growled; his master stroked him and he stopped. On first acquaintance, the dog seemed not to like the scribe much.

Pazair applied his seal to the papyrus containing his conclusions about the matter of the stolen ox. Iarrot marvelled at the fine, regular hieroglyphs; the judge wrote without the slightest hesitation, expressing his thoughts clearly.

'Surely you didn't implicate Qadash, did you?' asked the scribe.

'Of course I did.'

'That's dangerous.'

'What are you afraid of?'

'I don't know.'

'Be more precise,' said Pazair.

'Justice is so complex . . .'

'I don't agree. On one side there is the truth, on the other, falsehood. If you give in to the latter, even to the tiniest degree, justice no longer reigns.'

'You talk like that because you're young. When you've got a bit of experience, your opinions will be less clear-cut.'

'I hope not. In my village, many people put that argument to me, but I find it worthless.'

'You're ignoring the weight that important people carry.'

'Is Qadash above the law?'

Iarrot gave a sigh. 'You seem intelligent and brave, Judge Pazair. Don't pretend not to understand.'

'If the ruling classes are unjust, the country will rush headlong to its ruin.'

'They'll crush you like the others. Be content to resolve the problems put to you, and refer delicate matters to your superiors. Your predecessor was a sensible man, who knew how to avoid traps. You've been given a fine promotion; don't spoil it.'

'I was given this appointment because of my methods, so why should I change them?'

'Make the most of your opportunities without disturbing the established order.'

'The only order I know is the order of the Rule.'

Annoyed, the scribe said, 'You're running full tilt towards a precipice!' He tapped himself on the chest. 'Don't say I didn't warn you.'

'Tomorrow, you are to deliver my report to the provincial government.'

'As you wish.'

'One detail puzzles me. I don't doubt your zeal, but are you the only person I have working for me?'

Iarrot seemed embarrassed. 'In a way, yes.'

'What is that supposed to mean?'

'There's a man called Kem . . .'

'What does he do?'

'He's a guard officer. It's his job to make the arrests you order.'

'An important role, I'd have thought.'

'Your predecessor didn't have anybody arrested. If he suspected someone of being a criminal, he referred the case to a higher jurisdiction. Kem gets bored in the office, so he goes out on patrol all the time.'

'Am I to have the privilege of meeting him?'

'He comes here from time to time. Don't be under any illusions: he's a hateful man. I'm afraid of him. Just don't expect me to say anything unpleasant to him.'

Re-establishing order in my own office isn't going to be easy, thought Pazair. He reached for more papyrus and saw that there was not much left.

'Where do you get papyrus?' he asked.

'From Bel-Tran, the best maker in Memphis. His prices are high, but the papyrus is excellent and never wears out. I can recommend him.'

'Just reassure me on one point, Iarrot. Is that recommendation completely free of self-interest?'

'How dare you!'

'My mind was wandering.'

Pazair examined the recent complaints; none seemed serious or urgent. Then he moved on to the list of personnel he was to control and the appointments he was to approve; a mundane administrative task which required him simply to add his seal.

Iarrot sat down, his left leg bent underneath him, and the other raised in front of him; with a palette under his arm and a reed pen tucked behind his left ear, he washed brushes as he watched Pazair.

'Have you been at work long, Judge?' he asked

'Since dawn.'

'That's very early.'

'A village custom.'

'A . . . daily custom?'

'My master taught me that one day's negligence was a catastrophe. The heart cannot learn unless the ear is open and the mind alert. What better way to achieve such a state than through good habits? If we fail, the monkey dozing inside us starts dancing, and the shrine is deprived of its god.'

The scribe's tone darkened. 'That's not a very pleasant life.'

'We are the servants of justice.'

'About my hours of work—'

'Eight hours a day,' cut in Pazair, 'with six days' work to be followed by two rest days, and between two and three months' annual holiday, including the various festivals.* Are we in agreement?'

Iarrot nodded. He understood that, although the judge had not pressed the point, he must make an effort to be more punctual.

---

*The usual working pattern for Egyptians.

One brief report interested Pazair. The head of the guards at the Sphinx in Giza had just been transferred to the docks. This was a brutal downturn in the man's career: he must have committed a serious offence. No such offence was mentioned, contrary to usual custom, but the head provincial judge had placed his seal upon the document. All it now lacked was Pazair's seal, since the soldier resided within his area of jurisdiction. A mere formality, which he could have carried out without thinking.

'The post of head of the guards at the Sphinx is a coveted one, isn't it?'

'There's no lack of candidates,' agreed Iarrot, 'but the current post-holder puts them off.'

'Why?'

'He is an experienced soldier, with a remarkable service record, and he's a brave man, too. He guards the Sphinx with immense diligence, although that old stone lion is impressive enough to take care of its own defence. Who would think of attacking it?'

'So his is a prestigious post, it would seem.'

'Absolutely. The head guard recruits other veterans, to ensure that they have a small, regular income, and the five of them take charge of the night watch.'

'Did you know he'd been transferred?'

'Transferred? Is this a joke?'

'Here is the official document.'

'That's very surprising indeed. What has he done wrong?'

'That's exactly what I was wondering. The report doesn't say.'

'Don't worry about it. It's probably a military decision whose logic we don't understand.'

In the street, Way-Finder gave the special bray that signalled danger. Pazair got to his feet and went out. He found himself face to face with an enormous baboon, which its master was holding on a leash. With their aggressive eyes, massive head and broad torso covered in a cape of fur, baboons had an unchallenged reputation for ferocity. It was common for a wild beast to succumb to their blows and bites, and lions had been seen to run away at the approach of a troop of enraged baboons.

The creature's master, a Nubian with bulging muscles, was as impressive as the animal itself.

'I hope you're holding him securely,' said Pazair.

'This guard baboon* is at your service, Judge Pazair, as am I.'

---

*An impressive police baboon can be seen arresting a thief on a bas-relief from the tomb of Tepemankh, now in the museum at Cairo.

'You must be Kem.'

The Nubian nodded. 'People around here are talking about you. They say you stir things up a lot, for a judge.'

'I don't much care for your tone of voice.'

'You'll have to get used to it.'

'Certainly not. Either you show me the respect due to a superior, or you resign.'

The two men stared at each other for a long time; the judge's dog and the guard's baboon did the same.

'Your predecessor left me free to do as I pleased,' said Kem.

'I shall not.'

'You're making a mistake. By walking through the streets with my baboon, I deter thieves.'

'We shall see. What is your service record?'

'I must warn you, my past is a dark one. I belonged to the corps of archers in charge of guarding one of the fortresses in the Great South. Like many young men in my tribe, I signed on for the love of Egypt. I was happy for several years, but then, without intending to, I stumbled on gold-trafficking among the officers. The senior officers wouldn't listen to me, and I killed one of the thieves, my direct superior, in a brawl. At my trial I was sentenced to have my nose cut off. This one is made of painted wood – I'm not afraid of blows in the face any more. However, the judges recognized my loyalty, which is why they gave me this job. If you want to check, you'll find my details in the records at the army offices.'

'Very well, let's go there.'

Kem had not been expecting this reaction. While the donkey and the scribe guarded the office, Pazair and Kem headed for the administrative centre of the armed forces accompanied by the baboon and the dog, who continued to eye each other warily.

'How long have you lived in Memphis?' asked Pazair.

'A year,' replied Kem. 'I miss the south.'

'Do you know the man in charge of guarding the Sphinx at Giza?'

'I've met him two or three times.'

'Does he seem trustworthy to you?'

'He's a famous soldier – even at my fortress we'd heard of him. You don't give such a prestigious post to just anyone.'

'Is it dangerous?'

'Not in the least. Who would attack the Sphinx? It's a guard of honour, whose members' chief duty is to stop the monument being buried in the sand.'

Passers-by stepped aside when they saw the quartet; everyone knew how swiftly the baboon could react, sinking its teeth into a thief's leg or breaking his neck before Kem had time to intervene. When those two were on patrol, evil intentions evaporated into thin air.

'Do you know where he lives?'

'He has an official residence, near the main barracks.'

'My idea was a bad one. Let's go back to the office.'

'Don't you want to check my details?'

'It was his details I wanted to look at; but that won't get me any further. I shall expect you tomorrow, at dawn. What is your baboon's name?'

'Killer.'

6

At sundown, the judge closed the office and took Brave for a walk on the banks of the Nile. Ought he to persevere with this insignificant case, which he could close by putting his seal to it? Obstructing a mundane administrative procedure seemed rather nonsensical. But was it really mundane? Through contact with nature and animals, a countryman develops keen intuition. Pazair had such a strange, almost worrying, feeling about the case that he decided to carry out an investigation, no matter how brief, so that he wouldn't later regret approving the transfer.

Brave was a playful dog, but he didn't like water. He trotted a good distance from the river, where cargo vessels, fast sailing ships and small boats were passing by. Some people were sailing for pleasure, others delivering goods, or on a journey. Not only did the Nile feed Egypt, but it also provided her with an easy, rapid means of travelling around.

Large boats, with experienced crews, were leaving Memphis and heading for the sea; some were undertaking long expeditions to unknown lands. Pazair did not envy them; their fate seemed cruel to him, since it carried them far from a land which he loved down to its last grain of sand: every field, every hill, every desert track, every village. All Egyptians feared dying in a foreign land; the law stated that their bodies should be repatriated, so that they could live out eternity in the company of their ancestors, and under the gods' protection.

Brave whined; a lively little green monkey had just splashed his hindquarters with water. The mortified dog shook himself and bared his teeth in annoyance; scared, the little joker leapt into the arms of its mistress, a young woman aged around twenty.

'He's not a bad dog,' said Pazair, 'but he hates getting wet.'

'My monkey is well named: Mischief is always playing jokes, especially on dogs. I do try to reason with her, but it does no good.'

The woman's voice was so sweet that it calmed Brave, who sniffed her leg and licked it.

'Brave!' said Pazair.

'Let him be. I think he's adopted me, and that makes me happy.'

'Will Mischief accept me as a friend?'

'Come closer and find out.'

Pazair was rooted to the spot: he dared not step forward. In the village, a few girls had hung around him, but he had paid them no attention because, absorbed in his studies and learning his trade, he had had no time for love trysts or feelings. Practising law had made him mature for his age, but faced with this woman he felt completely defenceless.

She was beautiful. As beautiful as a spring dawn, an unfolding lotus bud, a sparkling wave upon the Nile waters. She was a little shorter than he, with light brown hair, a gentle, open face, a direct gaze and eyes of summer blue. Round her slender neck she wore a necklace of lapis lazuli; on her wrists and ankles were cornelian bracelets. Her linen robe disclosed glimpses of firm, high breasts, shapely flanks and long, slender legs. Her feet and hands were delightfully delicate and elegant.

'Are you afraid?' she asked, surprised.

'No – no, of course not.'

Approaching her would mean seeing her at close quarters, breathing in her perfume, almost touching her . . . He didn't dare.

Realizing that he wasn't going to move, she took three steps towards him and held the monkey out to him. With a trembling hand he stroked its brow, and in return Mischief scratched his nose with a nimble finger.

'That's her way of showing you're a friend.'

Brave did not protest; a truce had been concluded between the dog and the monkey.

'I bought her in a market where Nubian wares were on sale. She seemed so unhappy, so lost, that I couldn't resist.'

There was a strange object on her left wrist. Pazair couldn't help staring at it.

'Does my portable clock intrigue you?* I need it for my work. My name is Neferet, and I'm a doctor.'

Neferet, the Beautiful, the Perfect, the Complete. What other name could she possibly have had? Her golden skin seemed unreal; each word she spoke was like one of those enchanting songs heard at sunset in the countryside.

'May I ask your name?' she said.

---

*Egypt invented the first kind of watch, a portable water clock, which was used only by specialists (such as astronomers and doctors) who needed to be able to calculate time.

It was unforgivable. By not introducing himself, he was displaying inexcusable bad manners. 'It's Pazair – I'm one of the provincial judges.'

'Were you born here?'

'No, in the Theban region. I've only just arrived in Memphis.'

'I was born down there, too!' She smiled with delight. 'Has your dog finished his walk?'

'Oh, no. He's tireless.'

'Shall we walk together? I need some air – I've had a very tiring week.'

'Are you practising already?'

'Not yet; I am finishing the fifth year of my studies. First, I learnt how to prepare remedies, using plants and other ingredients. Then I worked as an animal doctor at the temple in Dendera. I was taught how to check the purity of the sacrificial animals' blood, and how to treat all sorts of animals from cats to cattle. Mistakes were severely punished: we were beaten with the rod, just as the boys were.'

Pazair winced at the thought of such tortures being inflicted on such a delightful body.

'Our old teachers' strictness is the finest education there is,' she assured him. 'Once the ear on your back has been opened, you never forget your lessons again. Next, I studied and practised a variety of specialist treatments: of the eyes, the stomach, the anus, the head, the hidden organs, the liquids dissolved in the humours and surgery. After that I was admitted to the medical school at Sais, where I was given the title of "attendant to the sick".'

'What will you do when you finish your training?'

'I could be a specialist, but that's the lowest rung of the ladder – I'll have to make do with that if I can't practise general medicine. A specialist sees only one aspect of sickness, a limited manifestation of the truth. A pain in a specific place doesn't mean that you know where the problem comes from. A specialist can make only a partial diagnosis. Becoming a general practiser is the true ideal of the doctor, but the standards that must be met are so high that most people give up.'

'Is there anything I can do to help you?'

'Thank you, but I must face my teachers alone.'

'I hope you succeed,' said Pazair.

They walked across a carpet of cornflowers where Brave was romping about, and sat down in the shade of a red willow.

'I've talked a great deal,' she said ruefully. 'I'm not usually like that. Are you the sort of person who attracts confessions?'

'They're part of my job. Thefts, late payments, contracts of sale, unjust taxes, slanders and a thousand other offences – they're what I deal with all the time. It's up to me to make enquiries, check witness statements, reconstruct the facts and arrive at a judgment.'

'What a huge responsibility!'

'Well, yes, but so is your profession. You love to heal, I love to see justice done; to do less than our utmost would be treason.'

'I hate taking advantage of circumstances, but . . .'

'Don't worry about that. Please tell me what the problem is.'

'One of my suppliers of herbs has disappeared. He's a rough-and-ready fellow, but honest and skilful. I and a few of my colleagues reported him missing recently. Perhaps you could speed up the search?'

'Of course I will. What's his name?'

'Kani.'

'Kani!'

'Do you know him?'

'He was forcibly conscripted by the steward on Qadash's estate. Yesterday, he was released, so there shouldn't be any further problems.'

'Was that your doing?'

'I carried out the investigation and passed judgment.'

She kissed him on both cheeks. Pazair, who was not a dreamer by nature, felt as if he had been transported to one of the paradise gardens reserved for righteous souls.

'Qadash,' said Neferet. 'Do you mean the famous tooth doctor?'

'That's right.'

'He used to be very good, they say, but he should have retired a long time ago.'

The green monkey yawned and curled up on Neferet's shoulder.

'I must go,' said Neferet. 'I've really enjoyed talking to you. We'll see each other again, I expect. And thank you with all my heart for saving Kani.'

She didn't walk, she danced; her step was light, her whole being radiant. Pazair stayed under the red willow for a long time, engraving deep into his memory every small movement she had made, every glance, every nuance of her voice.

Brave laid his right paw on his master's knee.

'You understand, don't you?' said Pazair. 'I've fallen madly in love.'

7

Kem and Killer were waiting at the agreed meeting place.

Pazair greeted Kem and asked, 'Have you decided whether to take me to see the head guard of the Sphinx?'

'I am yours to command.'

'I don't care for that tone of voice any more than the other one. Irony is just as offensive as defiance.'

The comment touched the Nubian on the raw. 'I'm not going to bow the knee to you.'

'Just do your job well and we'll get on fine together.'

The baboon and his master stared fixedly at Pazair; both pairs of eyes were full of suppressed rage.

'Let's go,' said Pazair calmly.

It was early morning, and the narrow streets were coming to life. Housewives were chatting, water carriers were distributing their precious burden, craftsmen were opening their shops. Seeing Killer, the crowd quickly parted to let them through.

The guard lived in a house similar to Branir's, but less attractive. On the doorstep, a little girl was playing with a wooden doll, but when she saw Killer she took fright and ran back inside, howling.

Her mother emerged immediately, and said angrily, 'Why are you scaring my child? Take that monster away.'

'Are you the wife of the head of the Sphinx's guard?' asked Pazair.

'What right have you to ask?'

'I am Judge Pazair.'

The young man's serious expression and the baboon's menacing appearance convinced the woman to calm down and be more polite.

'He doesn't live here any more. My husband's a former soldier, too – the army gave us this house.'

'Do you know where he's gone?'

'I met his wife when she was moving out, and she seemed upset. She said something about a house in the south of the city.'

'That's rather vague. Didn't she say whereabouts in the south?'

'I've told you all I know.'

The baboon strained at its leash. The woman recoiled and pressed herself back against the wall.

'She really said nothing more?'

'No, nothing, I swear!'

Since Iarrot had to take his daughter to her dancing class, Pazair gave him permission to leave the office in the middle of the afternoon. In return, he promised to deliver the reports of the cases the judge had dealt with to the provincial government headquarters. In only a few days, Pazair had sorted out more problems than his predecessor had done in six months.

When the sun went down, Pazair lit several lamps. He wanted to be rid of a dozen tax disputes, all of which he had resolved in favour of the taxpayer. All, that is, except one, which concerned a ship owner called Denes. The head provincial judge had written a note on the document: 'File. No further action.'

Taking Way-Finder and Brave with him, Pazair set off to visit Branir, whom he had not had a chance to consult since taking up his post. On the way, he pondered the curious fate of the senior guard who had left a prestigious post and lost his official house. What was hidden in this swarm of little irritations? Pazair had asked Kem to track the ex-soldier down. Pazair would not approve the transfer until he had questioned the man.

Brave kept scratching his right eye. Pazair examined it and saw that it was inflamed. Branir would know how to treat it.

The lamps were lit in Branir's house; he liked to read at night, when the sounds of the city had ebbed away. Pazair pushed open the front door, stepped down into the entrance hall and halted in astonishment. Branir was not alone. He was talking to a woman whose voice the judge recognized immediately. Her, here!

Brave slipped through his master's legs, went over to the old doctor and asked to be stroked.

'Pazair!' said Branir. 'Come in.'

Shyly, the judge accepted the invitation. He had eyes only for Neferet, who was sitting on the floor in front of Branir. Between her index finger and thumb she held a linen thread, at the end of which a small diamond-shaped piece of granite was swinging to and fro.*

'This is Neferet, my best pupil. My dear, this is Judge Pazair. Now that the introductions have been made, will you take a little cool beer?'

---

*A pendulum. Dowsing rods are also known to be able to find water in the desert. We know that certain pharaohs, such as Seti I, were great practitioners of this art.

'Your best pupil . . . ?'

'We've already met,' she said with an amused smile.

Pazair thanked his lucky stars; seeing her again filled him with joy.

'Neferet will soon have to take the final test before she can practise her art,' Branir explained, 'so we're repeating the dowsing exercises she'll have to use to help her make her diagnosis. I'm convinced she'll be an excellent doctor, because she knows how to listen – someone who knows how to listen will act wisely. Listening is better than anything. There is no greater treasure. It is the gift of the heart.'

'A knowledge of the heart is the doctor's secret, isn't it?' asked Neferet.

'That's what will be revealed to you if you are judged worthy.'

'I'm tired,' she said. 'I'd like to go home and rest.'

'Then you must.'

Brave scratched his eye again, and Neferet noticed.

'I think he's in pain,' said Pazair.

The dog let Neferet examine him. 'It's nothing serious,' she said when she'd finished. 'A simple eye lotion will cure it.'

Branir went and fetched it for her; eye infections were common and there were plenty of remedies. This one acted instantly. Brave's eye became less swollen as soon Neferet applied the lotion. For the first time, Pazair was jealous of his dog. He tried to think of a way of keeping Neferet here, but had to be content with wishing her goodbye as she left.

Branir poured out some excellent beer, which had been made the previous day.

'You look tired,' he said. 'You must have a great deal of work to do.'

'I came up against a man called Qadash.'

'Ah yes, the tooth doctor with the red hands. He's a tormented man – and he's more malicious than he seems.'

'I think he's guilty of forcing a peasant to work on his estate.'

'Can you prove it?'

'No. That's merely my opinion.'

'Be conscientious in your work. Your superiors won't forgive a lack of precision.'

There was a pause while Pazair absorbed the warning. Then he asked, 'Do you often give Neferet lessons?'

'I'm passing on all my knowledge to her, for I have total confidence in her.'

'She was born in Thebes, she told me.'

'She's the only daughter of a locksmith and a weaving-woman. It was when I was treating them that I got to know her. She asked me a thousand questions, and I encouraged her budding vocation.'

'A woman doctor . . . Won't she meet all sorts of obstacles?'

'She's as brave as she is gentle. There'll be enemies as well as obstacles. For instance, the head doctor at court hopes she'll fail, and she knows it.'

'He'll be a formidable opponent.'

'She knows that, too. But one of her great strengths is her determination.'

'Is she married?' asked Pazair casually.

'No.'

'Betrothed?'

'There's nothing official, as far as I know.'

Pazair spent a sleepless night. He couldn't stop thinking about Neferet, hearing her voice, smelling her perfume, dreaming up a thousand and one plans for seeing her again, without finding a satisfactory one. And the same worry kept recurring again and again: was she indifferent to him? He had detected no signs of attraction in her, only a polite interest in his work. Even justice took on a bitter taste. How could he go on living without her? How could he bear her absence? Never had Pazair thought that love could be such a torrent, capable of bursting its banks and flooding his entire being.

Brave saw how upset his master was and lavished affectionate looks on him, but he knew his affection was no longer enough. Pazair reproached himself for making his dog unhappy. He wished he could have been content with Brave's unclouded friendship, but he could not resist Neferet's eyes, or her limpid face, or the whirlpool into which she had drawn him.

What was he to do? If he kept silent, he was condemning himself to suffer. But if he told her he loved her he risked rejection and despair. He must persuade her, charm her – but what could he possibly offer her? He was only a minor local judge with no money.

The sunrise did not calm his torment, but prompted him to lose himself in his work. He fed Brave and Way-Finder, and left them to guard the office, for he was sure Iarrot would be late. Armed with a papyrus basket containing tablets, a case of brushes and prepared ink, he headed for the docks.

There were several boats at the quayside; the sailors were unloading them themselves, under the direction of an officer. After positioning a gangplank in the forward part of the boat, they balanced poles on their shoulders, hung bags and baskets from them, then walked down the slope. The strongest men were carrying heavy bundles on their backs.

Pazair asked the officer, 'Where can I find Denes?'

'The owner? He's everywhere.'

'Do the docks belong to him?'

'Not the docks, no, but an awful lot of boats do. He's is the most important carrier in Memphis, and one of the richest men in the city.'

'Is there any chance I might meet him?'

'He only stirs himself when a really big cargo comes in. Go to the central dock. One of his largest vessels has just berthed.'

The boat was indeed large – about a hundred cubits long – and could carry more cargo than a whole donkey caravan could. She was flat-bottomed, and made of many carefully hewn planks, put together like bricks; the ones on the edges of the hull were very thick and bound together with leather strips. A sizeable sail had been hoisted on a three-legged mast, which could be lowered and was firmly braced. The captain, a crusty fifty-year-old, was ordering his men to drop the round anchor.

When Pazair tried to step aboard, a sailor barred his way. 'You're not a member of the crew.'

'I am Judge Pazair.'

The sailor stood aside, and the judge crossed the gangplank and climbed up to the captain's cabin.

'I should like to see Denes,' he said.

'Denes?' snorted the captain. 'Here, at this hour? Surely you're not serious?'

'I have here a properly drawn-up complaint.'

'About what?'

'Denes is levying a tax on unloading boats which don't belong to him, which is illegal and unjust.'

'Oh, that old story! That's an owner's privilege, and the government turns a blind eye to it. Every year there's another complaint. It's unimportant: you can throw it in the river.'

'Where does he live?'

'In the largest house behind the docks, beside the entrance to the palace quarter.'

Without his donkey, Pazair found it rather difficult to find his way around. Without Kem's baboon, he had to confront large gatherings of gossips, in heated discussions around strolling merchants.

Denes's immense house was surrounded by high walls, and the impressive entrance was guarded by a porter armed with a staff. Pazair introduced himself and asked to be admitted. The porter called a steward, who took the request to his master, returning for the judge ten minutes later.

Pazair scarcely had time to savour the beauty of the garden, the charming boating-lake and the sumptuous flower beds, for he was taken directly to Denes, who was about to have his breakfast in a vast hall with four pillars and walls decorated with hunting scenes.

The ship owner was about fifty years old, a massive man, heavily built, with a square, rather coarse face fringed by a narrow white beard. He was sitting in a deep, lion-footed chair, and one servant was hurriedly anointing him with fine oil, while a second trimmed his fingernails, a third did his hair, a fourth rubbed his feet with scented ointment and a fifth told him what there was for breakfast.

'Judge Pazair,' said Denes. 'What favourable wind blows you to me?'

'A complaint.'

'Have you had breakfast? I haven't had mine yet.'

Denes sent away the servants. Two cooks immediately entered, bearing bread, beer, a roast duck and some honey-cakes.

'Help yourself, Judge,' he said.

'Thank you, but no.'

'A man who doesn't eat a hearty breakfast won't have a good day.'

'A serious accusation has been made against you.'

'I'm astonished to hear it.' Denes's voice lacked nobility. Sometimes it tended towards the shrill, betraying a nervousness which contrasted with his rather dignified, aloof bearing.

'You have been levying an unjust tax on unloading, and you are suspected of levying an illegal tax on the people who live on the riverbanks by two state landing stages you often use.'

'They're old customs – don't worry about them. Your predecessor attached no more importance to them than the head provincial judge did. Forget about all that and have a slice or two of duck.'

'I'm afraid I can't forget about it.'

Denes stopped eating. 'I haven't time to bother about this. Go and see my wife. She'll soon convince you that you're fighting a losing battle.'

The ship owner clapped his hands, and a steward appeared.

'Take the judge to the lady Nenophar's office,' and with that Denes went back to his breakfast.

Nenophar had a statuesque figure and a petulant manner. She dressed in the height of fashion, and was wearing an impressive black wig with heavy tresses, a turquoise pectoral, an amethyst necklace, expensive silver bracelets and a long dress adorned with green pearls. She owned vast, productive lands, several houses and twenty or so farms, and was a successful businesswoman, whose team of agents sold large quantities of products in Egypt and Syria. She also managed the royal storehouses, inspected the Treasury and was steward of fabrics at the palace.

Despite her success, she had succumbed to the charms of Denes, who was much less wealthy than she was. Considering him a poor manager, she had put him in charge of shipping goods. Her husband travelled a good deal, supported a huge network of relatives, and indulged in his favourite pastime – debating endlessly over a good wine.

Nenophar looked disdainfully at the young judge who had dared to venture into her domain. She had heard that this peasant had taken the place of the recently deceased judge, with whom she had been on excellent terms. No doubt he was paying her a courtesy visit: a good opportunity to tell him what was what.

He was not handsome, but he had a certain attraction; his face was fine-featured and serious, his gaze deep. She noted with displeasure that he did not bow as an inferior should do before his betters.

'I believe you have only just been appointed to Memphis?' she said.

'That is correct.'

'Congratulations. The post promises a brilliant career. Why did you wish to speak with me?'

'Regarding a tax which has been wrongfully levied and which—'

'I'm aware of it – as is the Treasury.'

'Then you will agree that the complaint is well-founded.'

'It's issued every year and cancelled immediately. I have an acquired right to the money.'

'That is not in accordance with the law – still less with justice.'

'You should be better informed about the extent of my offices. As a Treasury inspector, I myself cancel this kind of complaint. The country's business interests mustn't suffer because of an outdated legal case.'

'You are exceeding your rights.'

'Those are fine words, but they're meaningless. You know nothing about life, young man.'

'Please do not speak to me with such familiarity,' said Pazair. 'Must I remind you that I am questioning you officially?'

Nenophar did not take the warning lightly. A judge, no matter how junior, did not lack for powers.

She said, 'Have you settled in well in Memphis?'

Pazair did not reply.

'I've heard that your house isn't very comfortable. As you and I shall necessarily become friends, I could rent you a pleasant house at a very reasonable rate.'

'I am quite content with the accommodation allocated to me.'

A fixed smile appeared on Nenophar's lips. 'This complaint is ridiculous, believe me.'

'You have acknowledged the facts.'

'But you can't contradict your superiors!'

'If they are wrong, I shall not hesitate for a moment.'

'Be careful, Judge Pazair. You aren't all-powerful.'

'I am well aware of that.'

'Are you determined to examine this complaint?'

'I shall summon you to my office.'

'Please leave.'

Pazair bowed and obeyed.

In a fury, Nenophar burst into her husband's apartments, where she found Denes trying on a new pleated kilt.

He asked, 'Have you put the little judge firmly in his place?'

'No, I haven't, you idiot. He's as uncooperative as a wild animal.'

'You're very pessimistic. Let's give him some presents.'

'There's no point. Instead of preening yourself, do something about him. We must bring him to heel as a matter of urgency.'

8

'That's it over there,' announced Kem.

'Are you sure?' asked Pazair in astonishment.

'There's no doubt about it. That's definitely his house.'

'How can you be certain?'

The Nubian smiled fiercely. 'Tongues loosen when people see Killer. When he shows his teeth, even the dumb find their voices.'

'Those methods—'

'Are effective. You wanted a result and you've got one.'

The two men gazed around. They were in the great city's most miserable district. People had enough to eat, as they did everywhere in Egypt, but many of the hovels were dilapidated, and their cleanliness left something to be desired. This was where Syrians lived when they were looking for work, together with peasants who had come to Memphis and quickly been disillusioned, and widows with only a pittance to live on. It certainly wasn't wasn't a fitting home for the senior guard of Egypt's most famous sphinx.

'I'm going to question him,' said Pazair.

'This isn't a very safe place. You shouldn't go alone.'

'As you wish.'

In amazement, Pazair saw doors and windows slammed shut as they walked past. Hospitality, which was so dear to the hearts of Egyptians, seemed to have no place in this enclave. The baboon was on edge, and moved forward with jerky steps, while Kem kept a constant watch on the roofs.

'What are you afraid of?' asked Pazair.

'Archers.'

'Why should someone try to kill us?'

'You're carrying out an investigation, and if we have ended up here, it's because the matter is a shady one. If I were you, I'd give up.'

The palm-wood door looked solid. Pazair knocked. They heard someone moving around inside, but no one answered.

'Open the door. I am Judge Pazair.'

Silence fell. Forcing entry to a home without authorization was a crime; the judge wrestled with his conscience.

'Do you think your baboon . . . ?' he asked tentatively.

'Killer is on oath. His food is provided by the government, and we must answer for his actions.'

'Theory sometimes differs from practice.'

'Fortunately,' agreed the Nubian.

The door did not hold out for long. Pazair was astonished by Killer's strength – it was a good thing he was on the side of the law.

The two small rooms were in pitch darkness, because of mats slung across the windows. There was a beaten-earth floor, a chest for linen, another for crockery, a mat for sitting on and a few toiletries. This was a modest home, but clean.

In a corner of the second room crouched a small, white-haired woman, dressed in a dark-brown tunic.

'Don't hit me,' she pleaded. 'I didn't say anything, I swear I didn't!'

'Don't be afraid,' said Pazair. 'I want to help you.'

She accepted the judge's hand, and stood up. Suddenly, her eyes filled with terror. 'The monkey! He'll tear me to ribbons!'

'No, he won't,' Pazair reassured her. 'He's a guard baboon. Now tell me, are you the wife of the senior guard of the Sphinx?'

'Yes,' she said in a tiny, scarcely audible voice.

Pazair invited her to sit down on the mat and sat down opposite her.

'Where is your husband?'

'He's . . . he's gone on a journey.'

'Why did you leave your official house?'

'Because he was dismissed.'

'I am dealing with the matter of his transfer,' explained Pazair. 'The official documents don't mention his dismissal.'

'Perhaps I'm wrong.'

'What's happened?' asked the judge gently. 'Please understand that I'm not your enemy. If I can help you, I shall.'

'Who sent you?'

'Nobody. I am making enquiries on my own initiative, so as not to make a decision when I don't understand what's going on.'

The old woman's eyes became moist with tears. 'Do you really mean that?'

'I promise you – on the life of Pharaoh.'

'My husband is dead.'

'Are you certain?'

'Some soldiers told me. They assured me that he'd be buried properly, and they ordered me to leave my home and come and live here. I shall have a small pension until I die, as long as I keep silent.'

'What were you told about how he died?'

'That it was an accident.'

'I must know the truth.'

'What does it matter?'

'Let me take you somewhere safe.'

'No,' she said. 'I shall stay here and wait for death. Now go, I beg you.'

Nebamon, head doctor to the Egyptian court, was justly proud of himself. Although in his fifties, he was still a very handsome man; the list of his feminine conquests would continue to grow for a long time yet. Laden with titles and marks of honour, he spent more time at receptions and banquets than in his consulting room, where ambitious young doctors worked for him. Weary of other people's sufferings, Nebamon had chosen an entertaining and lucrative speciality: beauty. Lovely ladies often wished to have a flaw or two removed so as to remain delectable and make their rivals turn pale with jealousy. Only Nebamon could restore their youth and preserve their charms.

He was dreaming of the magnificent stone gateway which, as a mark of Pharaoh's favour, would decorate the entrance to his tomb; the king himself had painted the uprights dark blue, to the great envy of the courtiers who dreamt of such a privilege. Fawned upon, rich and famous, Nebamon treated foreign princes, who were happy to pay very high fees. Before agreeing to accept them as patients, he made extensive enquiries, and he granted consultations only to patients with benign illnesses which were easy to treat. A failure would have tarnished his reputation.

A scribe announced the arrival of Neferet.

'Show her in.'

The young woman had angered Nebamon by refusing to join his team. Her refusal still rankled, and he was set on revenge. If she acquired the right to practise, he would see that she had no power or influence and that she was distanced from the court. Some claimed that she had a real instinct for medicine, and that her talent with the pendulum enabled her to be both quick and accurate, so he would give her one last chance before declaring war and condemning her to a life of mediocrity. Either she would obey him, or he would break her.

Neferet bowed and said, 'You summoned me.'

'I have a proposition for you.'

'I'm leaving for Sais the day after tomorrow.'

'I am aware of that, but your services won't be needed for long.'

Neferet was really very beautiful. Nebamon dreamt of having a delicious young mistress like her, one he could show off in the best society. But her natural nobility and the brightness that radiated from her prevented him from paying her those few stupid compliments which were ordinarily so effective. Seducing her would be difficult, but particularly exciting.

'My patient is an interesting case,' he continued, 'a woman of the middle rank, from a large, quite well-off family with a good reputation.'

'What is the matter with her?'

'Her husband demands that she reshape those parts of her body he doesn't like. Certain curves will be easy to alter – we shall simply remove some fat here and there in accordance with the husband's instructions – and to slim her thighs and cheeks and dye her hair will be child's play.'

Nebamon did not add that he had already received his fee of ten jars of unguents and rare perfumes: a fortune which made failure unthinkable.

He turned on all his charm. 'I'd be delighted if you would work with me on this, Neferet – you have a very steady hand. Moreover, I'd write an extremely favourable report, which would be useful to you. Will you see my patient?'

Without giving Neferet time to reply, he went to an inner door and fetched the lady Silkis into the room.

Silkis hid her face in her hands. 'I don't want anyone to look at me,' she said in the voice of a scared child. 'I'm too ugly.'

Her body was well hidden under a loose robe, but it was clear she had quite ample curves.

'What food do you like?' asked Neferet.

'I . . . I don't really pay much attention.'

'Do you like cakes?'

'Very much.'

'It would help if you didn't eat so many of them,' said Neferet with a gentle smile. 'May I examine your face?'

This gentleness overcame Silkis's reticence; she let her hands drop. True, her doll-like face was a bit pudgy, but it certainly didn't inspire horror or disgust.

'You look very young,' said Neferet.

'I'm twenty.'

'Why don't you accept yourself as you are?'

'My future husband's right, I'm hideous. I'll do absolutely anything to please him.'

'Isn't this going too far?'

'He's so strong – and I've promised.'

'Couldn't you persuade him he's mistaken?'

Nebamon was furious. 'It is not for us to judge our patients' motivations,' he snapped. 'Our role is to meet their wishes.'

'I refuse to make this young woman suffer for no good reason.'

'Leave the room!'

'With pleasure.'

'You're making a big mistake behaving like this, you know.'

'I believe I'm being faithful to the doctor's ideal.'

'You know nothing, and you'll have nothing! Your career is finished.'

Iarrot gave a little cough.

Pazair looked up. 'Is there a problem?'

'It's a summons.'

'For me?'

'Yes. The Judge of the Porch wants to see you immediately.'

In front of the royal palace, and also in front of each temple, stood a wooden porch where a judge dispensed justice. He heard complaints, distinguished truth from falsehood, protected the weak and saved them from the powerful.

At the palace, the judge sat in some state. The porch was held up by four pillars and backed on to the front of the palace. It was large, four-sided and at its far end lay the audience chamber. When the tjaty went to see Pharaoh, he always spoke first with the Judge of the Porch, whose firmness of character and forthright way with words were known to everyone.

A summons from him must be obeyed immediately. Pazair laid down his brush and palette and set off at once.

When he got there, the audience chamber was empty. The Judge was seated on a chair of gilded wood, and his expression was decidedly frosty.

'Are you Judge Pazair?'

The young man bowed respectfully. Coming face to face with the most senior judge in the province was nerve-racking. This abrupt summons to see him did not augur well.

'You have made a stormy start to your career,' commented the Judge. 'Are you satisfied?'

'I shall never be that. My dearest wish has always been that people would become wise and judges' offices would disappear, but that childish dream is beginning to fade.'

'I have heard a great deal about you, although you have not been in Memphis long. Are you fully aware of your duties?'

'They are my whole life.'

'You get through a lot of work, and quickly, too.'

'Not enough for my liking. Once I have a better understanding of the difficulties of my task, I shall be more effective.'

'"Effective"? What do you mean by that?'

'Dispensing the same justice to all. Is that not our ideal and our rule?'

'No one would disagree with that.'

The Judge's voice had grown hoarse. He got to his feet and paced up and down. 'I did not care for your comments regarding Qadash.'

'I suspect him of wrongdoing.'

'Where is the proof?'

'As I made clear in my report, I have not found any, which is why I have not begun proceedings against him.'

'In that case, why this pointless attack?'

'To draw your attention to him. You probably know more about him than I do.'

Angry, the Judge stopped in his tracks. 'Be careful, Judge Pazair! Are you insinuating that I am withholding information?'

'That's the last thing I mean. If you consider it necessary, I shall continue my enquiries.'

'Never mind about Qadash. Why are you persecuting Denes?'

'In his case, the offence is flagrant.'

'Wasn't the complaint against him accompanied by a recommendation?'

'Indeed it was: "File. No further action." That's why I dealt with it as a priority. I have sworn to resist such practices with my last scruple of strength.'

'Are you aware that I am the author of that . . . recommendation?'

'A great man must lead by example, not benefit from his wealth to exploit humble folk.'

'You are forgetting the economic necessities.'

'The day they take precedence over justice, Egypt will be condemned to death.'

The Judge of the Porch was shaken by the retort. In his youth, he had himself uttered opinions like that, and with the same fervour. Then difficult cases had come along, promotions, necessary compromises, arrangements, concessions to people of high rank, middle age . . .

He asked, 'What are you accusing Denes of?'

'You know that.'

'Do you think his behaviour justifies convicting him?'

'The answer is obvious.'

The Judge could hardly tell Pazair that he had just spoken with Denes and that the ship owner had asked him to dismiss the young man. He said, 'Are you determined to continue your enquiry?'

'Yes, I am.'

'Do you know that I can send you back to your village within the hour?'

'Yes.'

'And that doesn't alter your point of view?'

'No.'

'Are you impervious to all reason?'

'This is a crude attempt at influencing the law. Denes is a cheat, and he's benefiting from privileges he doesn't deserve. His case comes within my jurisdiction, so why should I neglect it?'

The Judge thought for a moment. Ordinarily, he would have dismissed the young man on the spot, in the absolute belief that he was serving his country, but Pazair's stance had brought back many memories. He could see himself in this young judge who so wanted to do his duty without fear or favour. The future would destroy Pazair's illusions, but was he wrong to attempt the impossible?

'Denes is a rich and powerful man, and his wife is a famous businesswoman. Thanks to them, goods are transported regularly and efficiently. What is the point of disrupting that system?'

'Don't cast me in the role of the accused. If Denes is found guilty, cargo boats will still sail up and down the Nile.'

After a long silence, the Judge of the Porch sat down again. 'Carry out your duties as you see fit, Pazair.'

9

For two days, Neferet had been meditating in a room at the famous Sais medical school, in the Delta, where would-be doctors faced an ordeal whose nature had never been revealed. Many failed. In a country where people often lived to eighty, the authorities were determined to recruit only worthwhile members.

Would the young woman realize her dream as she struggled against evil? She would experience many defeats, but would never give up fighting suffering. But she still had to satisfy the demands of the medical court at Sais.

A priest brought her dried meat, dates, water and some medical papyri which she read over and over again; some of the ideas were starting to get mixed up in her head. Wavering between anxiety and confidence, she took refuge in meditation, gazing out at the vast orchard of carob trees that surrounded the school.*

As the sun was setting, the Keeper of the Myrrh, who specialized in cleansing and purifying buildings, came to find her. He took her to the workshop and presented her to several of his colleagues. In rapid succession they required Neferet to make up a prescription, to prepare remedies, to evaluate the good and ill effects of a drug, to identify complex substances, and to relate in detail how plants, gum-resin and honey were gathered. Several times she was severely taxed and had to dig deep into the recesses of her memory.

At the end of an examination lasting five hours, four of the five voted in her favour. The fifth explained why he had not: Neferet had made a mistake over two doses. Ignoring her tiredness, he demanded to question her again. If she refused, she would have to leave Sais.

Neferet met the challenge. Without departing from her usual sweetness of character, she submitted to her opponent's attacks. And he was the first to yield.

*The carob fruit, a pod containing sugary juice, was seen by the Egyptians as the perfect embodiment of sweetness.

She received no praise or congratulations, but was simply told she might withdraw. She went to her room and fell asleep as soon as she lay down on her mat.

The examiner who had so sorely taxed her awoke her at dawn. 'You have the right to continue,' he said. 'Are you willing to do so?'

'I'm at your disposal.'

'You have half an hour to wash and have breakfast. I warn you, the next trial is a dangerous one.'

'I'm not afraid.'

'Take time to think while you wash and eat.'

In half an hour he returned and escorted her to the workshop. On the threshold he repeated his warning and said, 'Don't take my words lightly.'

'I don't, but I shan't withdraw.'

'Very well. Take this.' He handed her a forked stick. 'Go into the workshop and prepare a remedy using the ingredients you will find there.'

Neferet went in, and he closed the door behind her. On a low table were phials, small dishes and jars. In the furthest corner, under the window, lay a basket with a lid. The weave was sufficiently open for her to see the contents as she approached it.

She recoiled in horror: a horned viper. Its bite was fatal, but the venom provided the base for very effective remedies against severe bleeding, nervous conditions and heart problems. So she understood what was expected of her.

Taking a deep breath, she reached out a steady hand and lifted the lid. The viper was wary, and did not come out of its lair immediately. Neferet stood absolutely still, concentrating hard, watching as it eventually slithered over the rim of the basket and away across the ground. The snake was as long as a man's arm and moved fast; the two horns jutted menacingly from its head.

Neferet gripped her stick with all her strength, moved to the left of the snake, and prepared to try to pin its head in the fork of the stick. For a split second she closed her eyes; if she failed, the viper would climb the stick and bite her. She struck.

The snake writhed furiously: she had succeeded. She knelt down, and seized it behind its head. She would make it spit out its precious venom.

On the boat carrying her home to Thebes, Neferet had had little time to rest. Several doctors had pestered her with questions on their respective specialities which she had practised during her studies.

Neferet adapted well to new situations, and didn't falter in even the most unexpected circumstances. She accepted whatever the world threw at her, and the differences between people; and took little interest in herself, concentrating instead on gaining a deeper understanding of the powers and the mysteries. She preferred being happy, of course, but adversity did not daunt her: through it all, she sought for the future joy that was hidden beneath the unhappiness. Not for a moment did she hate the men who had treated her so badly; as she saw it, they were building and proving the solidity of her vocation.

It was a real pleasure to see Thebes again. The sky seemed bluer than in Memphis, the air softer and smoother. One day she would come back to live here, close to her parents, and would once again walk in the countryside where she had spent her childhood. She thought of her monkey, which she had entrusted to Branir, hoping that the little creature would respect her old master and cause less mischief.

When Neferet reached the temple enclosure, behind whose high walls several shrines had been built, two shaven-headed priests opened the gate to allow her in. Here, in the domain of the goddess Mut, whose name meant both 'Mother' and 'Death', doctors were inaugurated.

The High Priest greeted her and said, 'I have received the reports from the school at Sais. If you wish, you may continue.'

'I do.'

'The final decision does not belong to human beings. Gather your thoughts, for you are about to appear before a judge who is not of this world.'

The priest fastened a cord with thirteen knots around Neferet's neck and told her to kneel.

'The doctor's secret,'* he said, 'is knowledge of the heart; from it visible and invisible vessels lead to every organ and every limb. Because of that, the heart speaks throughout the body. When you examine a patient by placing a hand on his head, the nape of his neck, his arms, his legs, or some other part of his body, seek first of all the heart's voice and rhythm. Be sure that it is solidly based, that it does not move from its proper place, that it does not fade and that it dances as it should. Know that a network of channels pervades the body and that they carry subtle energies, as well as air, blood, water, tears, sperm or faecal matter. Make sure that the vessels and the lymph are pure. When illness arises, it reveals a disorder of the energy; beyond the effects, look for the cause. Be honest with your patients and give them one of the three possible diagnoses: an illness which I know and which I shall

---

*The text called *The Doctor's Secret* was known by all practising doctors and formed the basis of their craft.

cure; an illness which I shall fight; an illness against which I can do nothing. Now go towards your destiny.'

The temple was silent.

Sitting back on her heels, with her hands on her knees and her eyes closed, Neferet waited. Time no longer existed. She was calm, in control of her anxiety. She had absolute trust in the brotherhood of physician-priests who, since Egypt's earliest days, had consecrated the vocation of healers.

Two priests helped her to her feet. Before her, a cedar-wood door swung open; it led into a shrine. The two men did not accompany her. Outside herself, beyond fear and hope, Neferet entered the dark, oblong chamber.

The heavy door closed behind her.

Immediately, Neferet sensed a presence: someone was crouching in the gloom, watching her. Her arms taut at her sides, her breathing laboured, she refused to yield to her fear. Alone, she had made it this far; alone, she would defend herself.

Suddenly, a ray of light shone down from the temple roof and lit up a diorite statue leaning against the far wall. It represented the goddess Sekhmet walking forward, the terrifying lion goddess who, at the end of each year, tried to destroy humanity by sending forth hordes of evil vapours, sicknesses and harmful germs. They scoured the earth, trying to spread misfortune and death. Only doctors could counter the formidable goddess, who was also their patron; she alone taught them the art of healing and the secret of remedies.

Neferet had often been told that no mortal being could look into Sekhmet's face on pain of losing their life. She ought to have lowered her eyes, turned her face away from the extraordinary statue, the furious face of the lioness,* but she confronted it.

Neferet looked straight at Sekhmet. She prayed to the goddess to make clear her vocation, to enter the very depths of her heart and to judge it true. The ray of light grew stronger, lighting up the whole of the stone figure, whose power overwhelmed the young woman.

Then a miracle happened: the terrifying lioness smiled.

The College of Doctors at Thebes had assembled in a vast pillared hall with a large pond at its centre.

---

*The Arabs were so terrified by this statue, which they called the 'Ogress of Karnak', that they did not destroy it. It can still be admired today in one of the shrines of the Temple of Ptah.

The High Priest approached Neferet. 'Is it your firm intention to heal the sick?'

'The goddess witnessed my oath.'

'What one recommends to others one must first apply to oneself.' He presented her with a cup filled with a reddish liquid. 'Here is a poison. After drinking it, you will identify it and make your diagnosis. If it is correct, you will have recourse to the right antidote. If it is wrong, you will die and the law of Sekhmet will have saved Egypt from a bad doctor.'

Neferet accepted the cup.

'You are free to refuse to drink, and to leave this assembly.'

Slowly, she drank the bitter liquid, already trying to work out what it was.

Followed by weeping women, the funerary procession passed along the temple enclosure and headed towards the river. An ox hauled the sledge on which the sarcophagus was laid.

From the temple roof, the High Priest and Neferet watched the game of life and death. She was worn out, and savoured the sun's caress on her skin.

The High Priest said, 'You will feel cold for a few hours more, but the poison will leave no trace in your body. Your speed and accuracy greatly impressed all my colleagues.'

'Would you have saved me if I had been wrong?'

'No, because he who cares for others must be pitiless with himself. As soon as you have recovered, you will return to Memphis to take up your first post. On your path, you will find many obstacles. A healer as young and gifted as you will arouse a good deal of jealousy. Don't be blind or naive.'

Swallows played in the sky above the temple. Neferet thought of her mentor, Branir, the man who had taught her everything and to whom she owed her life.

10

Pazair was finding it more and more difficult to concentrate on his work: he saw Neferet's face in every hieroglyph.

Iarrot brought him a pile of clay tablets. 'Here's the list of the craftsmen taken on at the weapons workshops last month. We must check that none of them has ever been convicted of a crime.'

'What's the quickest way to find out?' asked Pazair.

'Consult the registers at the main prison.'

'Could you deal with it?'

'Not until tomorrow – I must go home now, because I'm organizing a birthday party for my daughter.'

Pazair smiled. 'Enjoy yourself.'

Once the scribe had left, he re-read the document he had drawn up summoning Denes and notifying him of the charges. It swam in and out of focus before his eyes. It was no good: he was too tired. He fed Way-Finder, who then lay down in front of the office door, and went out for a walk with Brave. His steps led him into a quiet area, near the scribes' school where the country's future elite learnt their craft.

The sound of a door slamming shattered the silence. This was followed by shouts and snatches of music, in which he heard a flute and a tambourine. The dog's ears pricked up; intrigued, Pazair halted. The argument was turning nasty, with threats giving way to blows and cries of pain. Brave, who hated violence, presssed close against his master's leg.

About a hundred paces from where Pazair was standing, a young man in a fine scribe's outfit climbed the school wall, jumped down into the alleyway and ran full pelt towards him, shouting the words of a bawdy song. As he ran though a ray of evening sunlight, the judge glimpsed his face.

'Suti!' he exclaimed.

The fugitive stopped in his tracks and turned round. 'Who called my name?'

'Apart from me, there's no one here.'

'There soon will be: they're after my hide. Come on, we'd better run for it.'

Pazair accepted the invitation. Brave was delighted and galloped alongside. The dog was astonished at the two men's lack of stamina when, ten minutes later, they stopped to get their breath back.

'Suti, is it really you?' panted Pazair.

'It really is – and you're really Pazair! Come on. One final effort and we'll be safe.'

The trio took refuge in an empty warehouse on the banks of the Nile, far from the area where armed guards patrolled.

'I was hoping we'd meet again soon,' said Pazair, 'but in rather happier circumstances.'

'Oh, these circumstances are absolutely wonderful, I assure you! I've just escaped from that prison.'

'Prison? The great Memphis scribes' school?'

'I'd have died of boredom there.'

'But when you left the village five years ago, you said wanted to become a scholar.'

'I'd have said anything if it got me the chance to explore the city. The only wrench was leaving you – you were my only friend among all those peasants.'

'We were happy there, though, weren't we?'

Suti stretched out on the ground. 'There were some good moments, you're right. But we've grown up. Enjoying myself in the village, living real life, that wasn't possible. I was always dreaming of Memphis.'

'And has your dream come true?'

'At first I was patient. I studied and worked and read and wrote and listened to the teachings that open up the spirit – what a bore! Fortunately, I soon started frequenting alehouses.'

'Those places of debauchery?' said Pazair reproachfully.

'Don't moralize.'

'But you loved books even more than I did.'

'Ah, books and wise maxims! I've had my ears battered by them for the last five years. Do you want me to play teacher, too? "Love books as you love your mother, for nothing surpasses them; the books of the sages are pyramids, and the writing case is their child. Listen to the advice of those who are wiser than you, and read their words, which live on in books. Become a learned man; be neither lazy nor idle, but store knowledge in your heart." I recite the lessons well, don't I?'

'Very well.'

'They're just mirages for blind men.'

Pazair looked at him curiously. 'What happened this evening?'

Suti burst out laughing. The restless, boisterous boy, the life and soul of the village, had become a man of impressive stature. His hair was long and black, his face open, his gaze direct, and when he spoke there was pride in his voice. It was as though an all-consuming fire burnt inside him.

'I organized a little celebration.'

'At the school?'

'Of course. Most of my fellow students are dull, sad and characterless. They needed to drink some wine and beer and forget their precious studies. We played music, we got drunk, we threw up and we sang. Even the most dedicated students were wreathed in flower garlands and banging tambourines on their bellies.' Suti sat up. 'These little pleasures annoyed the masters in charge, and they came bursting in armed with clubs. I defended myself, but my comrades denounced me. I had to run away.'

Pazair was appalled. 'You'll be expelled.'

'Good. I wasn't meant to be a scribe. Never harm anyone, never worry them, never leave them in poverty and suffering – I'm going to leave that ideal world to the sages. I'm burning for adventure, a great adventure.'

'What sort of adventure?'

'I don't know yet – no, that's not right, I do know: the army. I shall travel and discover other lands, other peoples.'

'You'll be risking your life,' warned Pazair.

'It'll be all the more precious to me, after the danger. Why spend all your time guarding your life when death will destroy it anyway? Believe me, my friend, we must live from day to day and take pleasure where we find it. We're less than the butterflies; let's at least find out how to fly from flower to flower.'

Brave growled.

'Someone is coming,' said Pazair. 'We must go.'

'My head's spinning.'

Pazair stretched out an arm and Suti used it to help himself to his feet.

'Lean on me,' said Pazair.

'You haven't changed, have you? You're still a rock.'

'You're my friend. I'm your friend.'

They left the warehouse, walked along its side and entered a maze of little streets.

'Thank you. They won't find me now.' The night air had sobered Suti up. 'I'm not a scribe any longer. What about you? What do you do?'

'I hardly dare tell you.'

'Are the authorities looking for you?'

'Not exactly.'

'Are you a smuggler?'

'Not that either.'

'You rob honest folk, then!'

'I'm a judge.'

Suti stopped, took Pazair by the shoulders and looked him in the eye. 'You're playing a joke on me.'

'I couldn't if I tried.'

'That's true, you couldn't. A judge . . . By Osiris, that's unbelievable! Do you have guilty people arrested?'

'I have that right.'

'Are you a junior or a senior judge?'

'A junior one, but in Memphis. Come home with me – you'll be safe there.'

'Aren't you breaking the law?'

'No one has lodged a complaint against you.'

'Supposing they had?'

'Friendship is a sacred law. If I betrayed it, I'd be unworthy of my office.'

The two men embraced.

'You can always count on me, Pazair,' said Suti fervently. 'I swear it on my life.'

'I know. That day in the village, when we mixed our blood, we became more than brothers.'

'Tell me, do you have guards answering to you?'

'Two, a Nubian and a baboon, each as fearsome as the other.'

'You're giving me the shivers.'

'Don't worry; the school will be content with expelling you. But try not to commit any serious crimes – those would be outside my jurisdiction.'

'It's so good to see you you again, Pazair!'

Brave bounded around Suti, who challenged him to a race, much to the animal's joy. Pazair was delighted that they liked each other. Brave had good judgment and Suti had a big heart. True, Pazair didn't approve of the way he thought or the way he lived his life, and feared his friend might lead him into regrettable excesses; but he knew that Suti had criticisms of him. By joining forces, they would discover many truths about each other's nature.

The donkey seemed to approve of Suti and allowed him to enter Pazair's house. The young man did not tarry in the office, whose papyri and tablets brought back bad memories, but climbed straight up to the upper floor.

'It's no palace,' he remarked, 'but at least the air's breathable. Do you live here alone?'

'Not entirely. I have Brave and Way-Finder to keep me company.'

'I was talking about women.'

'I'm overwhelmed with work, and—'

'Pazair, my friend, don't tell me you're still . . . chaste?'

'I'm afraid so.'

'We'll soon put that right. I'm certainly not chaste any more. In the village I had no luck with girls, because there were always nosy old women on the lookout. Here in Memphis, it's paradise!

'I made love for the first time with a little Nubian girl who'd already had more lovers than she had fingers. When pleasure overwhelmed me, I thought I was going to die of happiness. She taught me how to caress her, to wait for her moment of pleasure, and how to get my strength back so that we could play games which no one lost.

'My second woman was betrothed to the school gate-keeper, but before becoming a faithful wife she wanted to sample a boy who was scarcely out of his teens. Her appetite almost wore me out. She had magnificent breasts, and buttocks as beautiful as islands in the Nile before the flood. She taught me delicate arts, and we had lots of fun together.

'Next, I enjoyed the company of two Syrian girls in an ale-house. There's no substitute for experience, Pazair; their hands were as soft as balm and even their feet could make me shiver just by brushing my skin.'

Suti burst out laughing again. Pazair couldn't maintain even a shred of dignity, and joined in his friend's happiness.

'I'm not boasting,' said Suti, 'but it would be quite a job to list all my conquests. I can't help myself – I just can't resist the warmth of a woman's body. Chastity is a shameful ailment which must be dealt with energetically. First thing tomorrow, I shall take charge of your case.'

'Well . . .'

A malicious glint appeared in Suti's eyes. 'You aren't refusing, are you?'

'My work, all those cases . . .'

'You were never any good at lying, Pazair. You're in love, and you're saving yourself for your sweetheart.'

'I'm usually the one who makes the accusations.'

'It's not an accusation. Personally I don't believe in undying love, but anything's possible with you – you being a judge and my friend at the same time proves that. So what's this marvel called?'

'I . . . She doesn't know anything. I'm probably just fantasizing.'

'Is she married?'

'Surely you're not thinking of—'

'Oh yes I am. My list of conquests doesn't contain a good wife. I won't force anyone, for I do have some morals, but if the chance presents itself I won't turn it down.'

'The law punishes adultery.'

'Only if it notices. In love, apart from frolics the most important quality is discretion. I shan't torture you about your intended. I shall find everything out by myself, and if necessary I shall give you a hand.' Suti lay down on a mat and tucked a cushion beneath his head. 'Are you really a judge?'

'You have my word.'

'In that case, I could do with a bit of advice.'

Pazair had been expecting something like this; he called upon Thoth, in the hope that the offence Suti had committed would come within his jurisdiction.

'It's a stupid story,' said his friend. 'I seduced a young widow last week. She's about thirty, with a lithe body and delicious lips . . . She'd had the misfortune to be mistreated by her husband, whose death was a godsend. She was so happy in my arms that she entrusted me with a little business deal: trading a sucking-pig at the market.'

'She owns a farm?'

'No, just a poultry yard.'

'What did you exchange the pig for?'

'That's the problem: nothing. The poor beast was roasted during our little celebration tonight. Usually, I'd be sure my charm would do the trick, but my widow's a bit of a miser and very much attached to her inheritance. If I go back empty-handed, I'm liable to be accused of theft.'

'Is there anything else?'

'Oh, nothing much, just a few debts here and there. The pig's my main worry.'

'Sleep well.' Pazair stood up.

'Where are you going?'

'Down to the office to consult a few documents. I'm sure there must be a solution.'

11

Suti didn't like getting up early, but he had to leave Pazair's house before dawn – his friend had to pour a jar of cold water over his head to wake him up. Pazair's plan seemed excellent, although it carried a few risks.

Suti reached the town centre, where the great market was being set up. Peasants and their womenfolk came here to sell country produce in a clamour of haggling and debate. Soon the first customers would start arriving. He slunk between the stalls and crouched down a short distance from his target, an enclosure filled with poultry. The prize he wanted to win was indeed there: a superb cockerel.*

The young man waited until his prey came within his grasp, then made a grab for its neck, gripping it so swiftly that it made no sound. The undertaking was hazardous: if he was caught, prison beckoned. Of course, Pazair had not chosen this particular trader at random; the man had been convicted of fraud, and should have paid his victim the value of a cockerel. The judge had not reduced the punishment, simply altered the procedure a little. Since the victim was the government, Suti was acting in its place.

Stuffing the cockerel under his arm, he headed for the young woman's farm. She was feeding her hens.

'I've got a surprise for you,' he announced, producing the fowl.

She was delighted. 'He's superb! You've done a good deal there.'

'It wasn't easy, I must confess.'

'I'm not surprised: a cockerel like that is worth at least three sucking-pigs.'

'When love guides a man, he can be persuasive.'

She set down her bag of grain, took the cockerel and put him in with the hens. She said, 'You're very persuasive, Suti. I can feel a gentle heat rising up within me, and I'd love to share it with you.'

---

*The Egyptians regarded the cockerel not as the king of the poultry yard but as a rather stupid creature, too concerned with its own importance.

'How could I refuse an invitation like that?'

Locked in a passionate embrace, they made their way to the widow's bedroom.

Pazair felt ill: listless and lacking his usual energy. Sluggish and drowsy, he could no longer find consolation even in reading the great ancient authors who had once enchanted his evenings. He had managed to hide his despair from Iarrot the scribe, but he could not hide it from Branir.

'You're not ill are you, Pazair?'

'It's nothing. I'm just tired, that's all.'

'Perhaps you oughtn't to work quite so hard.'

'I feel as if I'm being buried in cases.'

'You're being tested, to find out your limits.'

'They've already been passed.'

'Not necessarily. Supposing overwork isn't the reason why you aren't yourself?'

Pazair did not reply; he just looked gloomy.

'My best pupil has succeeded,' said Branir.

'Do you mean Neferet?'

'She passed the trials, in both Thebes and Sais.'

'So she is a doctor now.'

'Indeed she is, to our great joy.'

'Where will she practise?'

'To begin with, in Memphis. I have invited her to a modest celebration at my house tomorrow evening, to celebrate her success. Will you join us?'

Denes ordered his bearers to set down his travelling chair before the door of Pazair's office. The magnificent chair was painted blue and red, and had dazzled passers-by. However delicate the coming meeting might prove, it was unlikely to be as trying as his recent argument with his wife. Nenophar had accused her husband of being simple-minded, useless and no better than a sparrow,* because his attempt to influence the Judge of the Porch had proved utterly futile.

Denes had ridden out the storm and tried to justify himself, pointing out that his tactics usually resulted in total success. Then why, demanded his wife, had the judge refused to listen to him this time? Not only was he not transferring the new little judge, but he had even authorized him to send out a properly drafted summons, as

*Because of its perpetual agitation and its tendency to flock, the sparrow was considered a symbol of evil.

though Denes were any common citizen of Memphis! It was all because of Denes's lack of perspicacity that the two of them found themselves reduced to the level of suspects, subject to the ill will of a judge with no future, who had come up from the provinces determined to ensure that the law was observed to the letter. Since Denes was so brilliant at business discussions, let him charm Pazair and have the court case stopped!

Their large house had rung with Nenophar's shouts for a long time. She could not bear to be thwarted. Besides, bad news spoilt her complexion.

Way-Finder barred the entrance to the judge's office. When Denes tried to elbow the donkey out of his path, it bared its teeth.

He leapt back. 'Get that animal out of my way,' he ordered.

Iarrot emerged from the office, and pulled the beast's tail; but Way-Finder never obeyed anyone but Pazair. Denes skirted round the donkey at a distance so as not to soil his expensive clothes.

Pazair was studying a papyrus. 'Please be seated,' he said.

Denes looked around for a chair, but found none of them to his liking. 'You must admit, Judge Pazair, I am being very accommodating in responding to your summons.'

'You had no choice.'

'Must a third party be present?'

Iarrot got to his feet, ready to leave. 'I'd like to go home early. My daughter—'

'Scribe, you are to take notes when I tell you to.'

Iarrot huddled in a corner of the room, hoping that his presence would be forgotten. Denes would not allow himself to be treated like this without retaliating. If he carried out reprisals against the judge, the scribe would be caught up in the whirlwind.

'I am very busy, Judge Pazair,' said Denes. 'You were not on the list of meetings I had arranged for today.'

'But you were on mine.'

'We should not clash head-on like this. You have a small administrative problem to resolve, and I want to be rid of it as quickly as possible. Why don't we come to an understanding?' Denes used his most conciliatory voice. He knew how to talk to people on their own level and flatter them. Then, when their attention wandered, he struck the decisive blow.

'You are digressing.'

'I beg your pardon?'

'We are not discussing a business transaction.'

'Allow me to tell you a little story. A disobedient goat left the herd, where he was safe, and ran off. A wolf threatened him. When he saw its jaws opening, he declared, "Lord Wolf, I shall no doubt provide you with a feast, but before that happens I could entertain you. For example, I can dance. Don't you believe me? Play the flute, and you'll see." The wolf was in a playful mood, and agreed. The goat's dance alerted the dogs, who charged at the wolf and made it run away. The wild beast admitted its defeat; I am a hunter, he thought, and I played at being a musician. Too bad for me.'*

'What is the moral of your tale?'

'Every man must know his own place. When you try to play a role you aren't familiar with, you run the risk of making a mistake you will bitterly regret.'

'You impress me,' said Pazair.

'I am glad. Shall we leave it there?'

'In the land of fables, yes.'

'You're more understanding than I thought. You won't be stuck in this pathetic office for long. The Judge of the Porch is a good friend of mine. When he knows that you have handled the situation with tact and intelligence, he will consider you for an important post. If he asks for my opinion, it will be very favourable.'

'It is good to have friends.'

'In Memphis, it's essential – you're on the right path.'

Nenophar's anger had been unjustified; she feared that Pazair was not like other men, but she was wrong. Denes knew plenty of others like him: apart from a few priests, hidden away in temples, their only goal was to further their own interests.

Denes turned away from the judge and made ready to leave.

'Where are you going?' asked Pazair.

'To meet a boat which is arriving from the South.'

'We have not quite finished.'

The ship owner turned back.

'Here are the charges: exacting an unjust levy and a tax not prescribed by Pharaoh. The fine will be a heavy one.'

Denes turned white with anger. 'Have you gone mad?' he hissed.

'Write this down, scribe: "Insulting a magistrate".'

Denes turned on Iarrot, tore the tablet from his hands and trampled it underfoot. 'Don't you do any such thing!'

'Destroying materials belonging to the forces of law,' observed Pazair. 'You are making matters worse for yourself.'

'That's enough!'

'You will need this papyrus. Written on it, you will find the legal

---

*This fable is a classic. Aesop took his inspiration from Egyptian fables, which were also embodied in the work of La Fontaine.

details of the case and the size of the fine. Do not fail to pay, or a police record will be opened in your name at the main prison.'

'You are nothing but a young goat, and you will be eaten alive.'

'In your story, it was the wolf who lost.'

When Denes stormed across the office, Iarrot hid behind a wooden chest.

When Pazair reached Branir's house, he found it decorated with wreaths of flowers.

The old doctor was putting the finishing touches to a delicious meal. He had taken the roes from female grey mullet and, following a traditional recipe, washed them in lightly salted water before pressing them between two planks and drying them in the fresh air. He was also going to grill sides of beef, and serve them up with a purée of beans. The menu would be completed by figs and cakes, not forgetting a fine wine from the Delta.

'Am I the first to arrive?' asked Pazair.

'Help me set the table.'

'I attacked Denes head-on. My evidence is rock solid.'

'What sentence have you given him?'

'A heavy fine.'

Branir frowned. 'You've made a formidable enemy.'

'I applied the law.'

'Be careful.'

Pazair had no time to protest: the sight of Neferet made him forget Denes, Iarrot, the office and all his cases.

She wore a pale-blue dress with straps that left her shoulders bare, and had lined her eyes with green kohl. At once frail and reassuring, she lit up her host's home.

'Am I late?' she asked.

'Not at all,' said Branir. 'You gave me time to finish cooking. The baker has just delivered fresh bread, so now we can sit down to eat.'

Neferet had slipped a lotus flower into her hair; Pazair could not take his eyes off her.

'I am thrilled by your success,' said Branir. 'As you're a doctor now, I give you this talisman. It will protect you as it has protected me – wear it always.'

'But what about you?'

'At my age, demons no longer have any hold on me.'

He placed a fine gold chain around the young woman's neck. On it was suspended a magnificent turquoise.

'This stone,' he said, 'came from the mines of the goddess Hathor, in the Eastern desert. It keeps the soul young and the heart joyful.'

Neferet bowed before her master, her hands clasped in a sign of veneration.

'I would like to congratulate you, too,' said Pazair, 'but I don't know how.'

'The thought alone is enough.' She smiled.

'And I should like to give you a modest gift.'

He presented her with a bracelet of coloured pearls. Neferet took off her right sandal and slipped her bare foot through the bracelet, which she fastened round her ankle.

'Thank you,' she said. 'I feel prettier now.'

Those few words gave Pazair an insane hope: for the first time, he felt that she had noticed he existed.

The meal was a friendly one. Relaxed now, Neferet talked about some aspects of her difficult traning, though she was careful not to divulge any secrets. Branir assured her that nothing had changed since his young days. Pazair picked at his food, but devoured Neferet with his eyes and drank in her words. In the company of his mentor and the woman he loved, he spent an evening of utter happiness, shot through with flashes of anxiety: would Neferet reject him?

While Pazair worked, Suti took the donkey and the dog for walks, made love with the owner of the poultry yard, went off in search of new, rather promising, conquests, and revelled in the bustling life of Memphis. He was discreet, and did not annoy his friend very much – he had not slept at his house once since that first evening. Pazair had proved intractable on only one point: drunk with the success of his sucking-pig 'exchange', Suti had mentioned that he would like to repeat it. The judge was adamantly opposed. Suti's mistress was proving generous, so he didn't press the point.

The baboon's massive bulk loomed up, filling the door-way. Almost as tall as a man, it had a head like a dog and the teeth of a wild beast. Its arms, legs and belly were white, while its shoulders and back were covered in reddish fur. Behind the baboon stood Kem.

'There you are at last,' said Pazair.

'The investigation was long and difficult. Has Iarrot gone out?'

'His daughter's ill. What have you found out?'

'Nothing.'

'What do you mean, "nothing"? That's unbelievable.'

The Nubian fingered his wooden nose, checking that it was securely in place. 'I consulted my best informants. No one knows anything about the guard's death. I was constantly referred back to the commander of the guards, as if everyone was acting on orders.'

'Then I shall go and see him.'

'I wouldn't advise it. He doesn't like judges.'

'I shall try to be pleasant.'

Mentmose, the guards' commander, had two houses, one at Memphis, where he lived most of the time, and the other at Thebes. He was short and fat with a round face, and inspired confidence in people; but his pointed nose and nasal voice belied his affable appearance.

Mentmose was a bachelor. Since his youth, he had thought only of his career and the honours it could bring him. Luck had served him in the form of a succession of opportune deaths. Just as he was destined to become overseer of canals, the official in charge of his province's security had broken his neck falling off a ladder and, although Mentmose had no special qualifications, he was swift in putting himself forward, and obtained the post.

Profiting skilfully from his predecessor's work, he soon forged himself an excellent reputation. Some men would have been content with this promotion, but he was devoured by ambition, and now thirsted for the command of the river guards. Alas, the post was held by an enterprising young man beside whom Mentmose looked unimpressive. But the inconvenient fellow had drowned during a routine operation, leaving the field free for Mentmose, who had applied immediately, with the support of numerous relatives. He was chosen over other candidates who were better qualified but less adept at strategy, and had continued to apply his proven method: taking the credit for other people's efforts and deriving personal benefit from them.

Although he already held high rank in the security guards, he dreamt of attaining the highest position, but that was completely out of reach because the incumbent was a vigorous, middle-aged man who had known nothing but success. His only failure proved to be an unfortunate chariot accident as a result of which he died, crushed beneath the wheels. Naturally, Mentmose put himself forward immediately and was successful, despite noteworthy opponents. He was particularly skilful at displaying himself and his service record to best advantage.

Once he had reached the pinnacle of success, Mentmose was determined to remain there, so he surrounded himself with second-rate men, who were incapable of replacing him. As soon as he detected a strong personality, he sent him away. Working away in the shadows, manipulating individuals without their realizing it, and plotting intrigues: these were his favourite pastimes.

He was studying the list of appointments to the desert guards when his steward announced the arrival of Judge Pazair. Ordinarily, Mentmose referred junior judges to his subordinates, but this one interested him – after all, he had got the better of Denes, whose fortune normally enabled him to buy anyone. The young judge would soon meet his downfall, falling victim to his own illusions, but perhaps Mentmose could derive some advantage from his youthful zeal. The fact that he was bold enough to inconvenience the commander of the guards was proof of his determination.

Mentmose received Pazair at his home, in the room where he displayed his decorations, gold collars, semi-precious stones and staves of gilded wood.

'Thank you for seeing me,' said Pazair.

'I am devoted to assisting justice. Are you enjoying yourself here in Memphis?'

'I must speak with you about a strange matter.'

Mentmose ordered his steward to serve the finest beer and gave instructions that he was not to be disturbed.

'What is it?'

'I cannot ratify a transfer without knowing what has become of the person concerned.'

'That is indeed true. Who is the person?'

'The former head of guards of the Sphinx at Giza.'

'Isn't that an honorary post, reserved for former soldiers?'

'In this case, the ex-soldier has been sent away.'

'Has he committed a serious crime?'

'There is no mention of it in my documents. What's more, the man was forced to leave his official house and take refuge in the poorest part of town.'

Mentmose seemed annoyed. 'That is indeed strange.'

'There is something more serious. His wife, whom I have questioned, says her husband is dead, but she has not seen his body and does not know where he is buried.'

'Why is she so sure he's dead?'

'Soldiers told her – and they also ordered her to keep silent if she wished to receive a pension.'

Mentmose slowly drank a cup of beer. He had been expecting to hear about the Denes case, instead of which he was being told of an unpleasant enigma. 'A remarkably quick and efficient enquiry, Judge Pazair. Your growing reputation is well deserved.'

'I intend to continue.'

'How?'

'We must find the body and discover the cause of death.'

'Yes, you're right.'

'Your help will be vital. Being in charge of the guards in the towns and villages, on the river and in the desert, you can easily facilitate my investigations.'

'Unfortunately that won't be possible.'

'I'm surprised you should say that. Why not?'

'Your information is too vague. Besides, at the heart of this matter we have an ex-soldier and a group of soldiers – in other words, the army.'

'I know, and that's why I am asking for your help. If you ask for explanations, the military authorities will be obliged to respond.'

'The situation is more complicated than you realize. The army sets great store by its independence from the guards. I'm not accustomed to trespassing on its ground.'

'And yet you know it well.'

Mentmose waved a hand airily. 'Merely exaggerated rumours,' he said. 'But I fear you may be setting out on a dangerous journey.'

'I cannot leave a death unexplained.'

'I agree with you.'

'What do you advise me to do?'

Mentmose thought long and hard. This young judge wasn't going to back down, and manipulating him would certainly not be easy. It would take time and study to discover his weak points and use them wisely.

Eventually he said, 'Go and see the man who appointed the veterans to their honorary positions: General Asher.'

12

The shadow-eater* moved like a cat in the night, soundlessly avoiding obstacles, sliding along walls and melting into the shadows. No one saw or suspected anything.

The poorest part of Memphis was slumbering. Here, there were no porters or watchmen as there were outside wealthy people's homes. Face hidden beneath a wooden jackal mask,† the shadow-eater slipped into the house belonging to the senior guard's wife.

All orders were obeyed without question – it was a long time since the last vestiges of emotion had drained from that black heart. Like a human falcon,‡ the shadow-eater loomed up out of the darkness, deriving strength from it.

The old woman awoke with a start. The horrific sight took her breath away. She let out a terrible cry and collapsed, stone dead. The killer had not even needed to use a weapon or disguise the crime. The loose-tongued woman would speak no more.

General Asher punched a novice soldier hard on the back, and the lad collapsed into the dust of the parade ground.

'That's what sluggards deserve,' sneered the general.

An archer stepped forward from the ranks. 'He committed no offence, sir.'

'You talk too much. Leave the exercise immediately. Fifteen days confined to barracks, followed by a long spell in a southern fortress will teach you discipline.'

The general ordered the men to run for an hour with their bows, quivers, shields and food bags on their backs; when they left on

*An Egyptian expression meaning 'assassin'.

†The type of mask worn by priests playing the parts of the gods when celebrating rituals.

‡An Egyptian expression corresponding to our 'werewolf'.

campaign, they would encounter tougher conditions. If one of the soldiers halted, exhausted, Asher would grab him by the hair and force him to start running again – any man who failed to do so would rot in a cell.

Asher had enough experience to know that ruthless training was the only path to victory: every suffering endured, every action mastered, gave the fighter a better chance of survival. After a colourful career on the battlefields of Asia, Asher, a hero famed for his exploits, had been appointed Steward of the Horses, officer in charge of recruits, and training officer at the main barracks in Memphis. With a savage joy, he carried out this last office for the last time. From now on – his new appointment had been officially confirmed the previous day – he would be free of its onerous duties. As Pharaoh's emissary to foreign countries, he would pass on royal orders to the elite garrisons posted at the borders, act as charioteer to His Majesty, and fulfil the role of standard-bearer at the king's right hand.

Asher was a small man, of unpleasant appearance: the hair on his head was close-cropped, while that on his shoulders was stiff, black and thick. He had a broad chest and short, muscular legs. A scar ran across his chest from shoulder to navel, a reminder of the sword blade that had almost ended his life. Laughing uncontrollably, he had strangled his attacker with his bare hands. His deeply lined face was reminiscent of a rat's.

After spending this last morning at his favourite barracks, Asher's thoughts were turning to the banquet that had been organized in his honour. He was heading for the washrooms when an officer came up to him.

'Forgive me for bothering you, General, but a judge would like to speak with you.'

'Who is he?'

'I've never seen him before.'

'Send him away.'

'He claims it is urgent and serious.'

'Why does he want to see me?'

'It's confidential. He says it doesn't concern anyone but you.'

'Very well. Bring him here.'

Pazair was brought to the central courtyard where the general was standing, his hands crossed behind his back. To his left, recruits were exercising to develop their muscles; to his right, archers were busy at target practice.

'What is your name?' asked Asher.

'Pazair.'

'I detest judges.'

'What do you have against them?'

'They stick their noses into everything.'

'I am making enquiries about a man who has disappeared.'

'That is not possible in regiments under my command.'

'Not even in the Sphinx's honour guard?'

'The army is still the army, even when it is taking care of its former soldiers. The Sphinx has been guarded without fail.'

'According to his wife, the former head guard is dead, and yet the authorities are asking me to authorize his transfer.'

'Then authorize it. One does not argue with the authorities' directives.'

'In this case, I must.'

The general's voice rose to a roar. 'You are young and inexperienced. Get out of here.'

'I am not under your command, General, and I want to know the truth about this guard. You appointed him to his post, did you not?'

'Be very careful, little Judge. It is not wise to cross swords with General Asher.'

Pazair stood his ground. 'You are not above the law.'

'You don't know who I am. One more false move, and I'll crush you like an insect,' and Asher marched off, leaving Pazair alone in the middle of the courtyard.

His reaction puzzled the judge. Why was he so vehement if he had nothing to be ashamed of?

As Pazair was leaving by the barracks gate, the archer who had been placed under close arrest hailed him. 'Judge Pazair?'

'What do you want?'

'Perhaps I can help you. What are you looking for?'

'Information about the former head guard of the Sphinx.'

'His military records are filed in the barracks record office. Follow me.'

'Why are you doing this?'

'If you find firm evidence against Asher, will you charge him?'

'Without hesitation.'

'Then come with me. The keeper of the records is a friend of mine, and he hates the general, too.'

The archer and the keeper of the records spoke briefly.

'To consult the barracks records,' said the keeper, 'you'd need authorization from the tjaty's office. I shall leave the office for a quarter of an hour, just long enough to go and get something to eat from the mess. If you're still here when I get back, I'll have to raise the alarm.'

Five minutes to understand the filing system, another three to find the right papyrus scroll, the rest to read the document, memorize it, put it back into its case and then disappear.

Back in his office, Pazair thought over what he had read. The head guard's career had been exemplary, with not a single blot on his record. The end of the papyrus offered an interesting piece of information: the man had headed a squad of four men, the two oldest posted by the sphinx's flanks, the other two at the base of the great ramp leading to the pyramid of Khufu, inside the enclosure. Since Pazair now had their names, he could question them and probably obtain the key to the enigma.

Kem came in, scowling. 'She's dead.'

'Who are you talking about?'

'The guard's widow. I patrolled in that area this morning, and Killer sensed that something was wrong. The door of the house was ajar. I found her body.'

'Any traces of violence?'

'None at all. She succumbed to old age and grief.'

Pazair asked Iarrot to check whether the army would take care of the funeral arrangements; if not, the judge would defray the costs himself. Although he might not have been responsible for the poor woman's death, he had caused her anxiety in her final days.

'Have you made any progress?' asked Kem.

'Decisive progress, I hope – although General Asher gave me no help at all. Here are the names of the four guards commanded by the missing man. Obtain their addresses.'

Iarrot arrived just as the Nubian was leaving.

'My wife is persecuting me,' grumbled Iarrot, who looked crestfallen. 'Yesterday, she refused to make dinner. If things go on like this, she'll soon be barring me from her bed. Fortunately, my daughter's dancing better than ever.'

Muttering as he worked, he sulkily filed away tablets with bad grace. 'Oh, I almost forgot,' he said. 'I investigated the craftsmen who want to work at the weapons workshops. Only one interests me.'

'A criminal?'

'A man mixed up in an illegal trade in amulets.'

'But has he ever been convicted of anything?'

Iarrot's face took on a look of smug satisfaction. 'It should interest you. He's a jobbing carpenter. He used to be employed as a steward on Qadash's land.'

Pazair managed to enter Qadash's waiting room, not without some difficulty. He sat down next to a small man with a tense expression.

His black hair and moustache, lustreless skin and long, dry face dotted with moles lent him a sombre, rather repellent, look.

The judge greeted him. 'Waiting's difficult, isn't it?'

The little man nodded.

'Are you in a lot of pain?'

He replied with a vague wave of the hand.

'This is my first attack of toothache,' said Pazair. 'Have you ever been treated by a tooth doctor before?'

Qadash appeared. 'Judge Pazair! Are you in pain?'

'Unfortunately, yes.'

'Do you know Sheshi?'

'I don't have that honour.'

'Sheshi is one of the most brilliant inventors at the palace – he has no rivals when it comes to creating new things. I order medicated plasters and fillings from him, and he has just suggested an innovation to me. Don't worry, I shan't be long.'

Qadash's manner was ingratiating, as though he were greeting a long-standing friend. If this fellow Sheshi remained as uncommunicative as he had been up to now, his conversation with the doctor was liable to be brief. Indeed, it was no more than ten minutes before Qadash came and escorted the judge into his office.

'Sit down on this folding chair and lean your head back.'

'He doesn't say much, your inventor.'

'He's a rather reserved fellow, but very upright, a man you can count on. What's the trouble?'

'A sort of generalized pain.'

'Let's have a look.'

Using a mirror to reflect a ray of sunlight, Qadash examined Pazair's teeth. 'Have you consulted anybody before?'

'Only once, in the village. A travelling tooth doctor.'

'I can see a tiny speck of decay. I shall stabilize the tooth with an effective filling: terebinth resin,* Nubian earth, honey, grains of millstone, green eye drops and fragments of copper. If it becomes loose, I shall bind it to the neighbouring molar with gold wire . . . No, that won't be necessary. You have sound, healthy teeth. From now on, take care of your gums. To prevent inflammation, I shall prescribe you a mouthwash composed of colocynth, gum, aniseed and the cut fruits of the sycamore; you must leave it outside for one whole night so that it becomes impregnated with dew. You must also rub your gums with a paste made from cinnamon, honey, gum and oil.

*The terebinth is a pistachio tree which yields a resin used in medicine and in ritual ingredients.

And don't forget to chew plenty of celery. Not only is it good as a tonic and an appetizer, but it also strengthens the teeth. Now, let's talk seriously. Your teeth did not need urgent treatment. Why were you so eager to see me?'

Pazair stood up, glad to escape from the dentist's diverse array of instruments. 'About your steward.'

'I dismissed that useless idiot.'

'I mean the previous one.'

Qadash washed his hands. 'I don't remember him.'

'Try harder.'

'No, really . . .'

'Are you by any chance a collector of amulets?'*

Although carefully washed, the dentist's hands remained red. 'I have a few, as everyone does, but I don't attach much importance to them.'

'The most beautiful ones are very valuable.'

'I expect they are.'

'Your former steward was interested in them – he even stole a few especially fine specimens. Which is what worries me. Could it be that they were stolen from you?'

'There are more and more thieves, since there are more and more foreigners in Memphis. Soon, this town will no longer be Egyptian. With his obsession with probity, the tjaty is the man chiefly responsible. Pharaoh has such trust in him that no one can criticize him – you even less than others, since he is your superior. Fortunately, your humble position in the government means you won't have to meet him.'

'Is he so daunting?'

'He's impossible. Judges who forgot that have been dismissed, but they had all committed offences. By refusing to expel foreigners under the pretext of justice, the tjaty is causing the country to decay. Have you arrested my former steward?'

'He tried to get work at the weapons workshops, but a routine check revealed his past. It's an unfortunate story to tell the truth: he sold amulets stolen from a workshop, was denounced and dismissed by the successor you chose.'

'Whom was he stealing for?'

'He doesn't know. If I had the time, I'd investigate; but I don't have any leads and there are so many other matters occupying me.

*Figurines, most often made of faience, representing the gods, symbols like the cross of life or the heart, etc. The Egyptians liked to carry them to protect themselves from harmful forces.

The main thing is that you did not suffer from his misdeeds. Thank you for attending to me, Qadash.'

Mentmose had summoned his principal colleagues to his home; this working meeting would not be mentioned in any official document.

He summed up their reports on Judge Pazair. 'No hidden vices, no illicit passions, no mistress, no network of relatives ... You have drawn me a portrait of a demi-god. Your enquiries have proved fruitless.'

'His spiritual father, a man called Branir, lives in Memphis, and Pazair often goes to his house.'

'An old retired doctor, inoffensive and without power.'

'He used to have the ear of the court,' objected an officer.

'He lost it long ago,' replied Mentmose sarcastically. 'No one's life is free from shadows – and that applies to Pazair as much as to anyone else.'

'He devotes himself to his work,' said another officer, 'and does not flinch in front of characters like Denes or Qadash.'

'A judge with integrity and courage? Whoever would believe in such a fairytale? Work harder and bring me back something more believable.'

When the men had gone, Mentmose went outside and stood beside the lake where he liked to fish, and pondered deeply. He had the unpleasant feeling that he was not in control of this elusive, formless situation, and was afraid he might make a mistake which would tarnish his own reputation.

Was Pazair an innocent, lost in the maze of Memphis, or truly an uncommon individual, determined to forge ahead irrespective of dangers or enemies? Whichever was the case, he was doomed to failure.

There remained a third, extremely worrying, possibility: that the little judge was an emissary sent by someone else, some devious courtier at the head of a plot in which Pazair was simply the visible part. Furious at the idea that the man dared to defy him on his own territory, Mentmose called for his steward and ordered him to prepare his horse and chariot. He felt a burning desire to go into the desert and hunt hares. Killing a few terrified creatures would relax his over-stretched nerves.

13

Suti's right hand slid back up his mistress's back, stroked her neck, slid back down again and caressed her bottom.

'Again,' she purred.

The young man did not need to be asked twice. He loved giving pleasure. His hand became more insistent.

'No . . . I don't want to.'

Suti went on, slyly. He knew his companion's tastes and satisfied them unreservedly. She pretended to resist, then turned over and slid her legs apart to welcome in her lover.

'Are you pleased with your cockerel?' he asked some time later.

'The hens are delighted. You are an absolute godsend, my darling.'

Overwhelmed with pleasure, the young widow prepared a hearty lunch and made him promise to return the following day.

As night was falling, and after he had slept for two hours at the port in the shade of a cargo vessel, he went to Pazair's house. The judge had lit the lamps, and was sitting on the floor writing, with his dog at his side. Way-Finder allowed Suti to pass and in return he stroked the donkey.

'I'm afraid I need you,' said the judge.

'An affair of the heart?'

'I very much doubt it.'

'It's not to do with the guards, though, is it?'

'I'm afraid it is.'

'That's interesting. Can I know more, or are you sending me out blind?'

'I have set a trap for a tooth doctor named Qadash.'

Suti gave an admiring whistle. 'He's a famous man! He only treats rich people. What's he done?'

'His behaviour intrigues me. I ought to have used Kem, but he is busy elsewhere.'

'Can I do a little burglary?'

'Don't even think of it! Just follow Qadash if he leaves his house and behaves strangely.'

*

Suti climbed up into a persea tree. From there, he had a good view of the front door of the Qadash's house and the back entrance. He was not unhappy to be out on this restful evening. Alone at last, he could enjoy the night air and the beauty of the sky. After the lamps were extinguished and silence fell once again over the great house, a silhouette slipped out by way of the stable door. The man wore a cloak, but the white hair and profile definitely belonged to the man Pazair had described.

It was easy to follow him. Although wary, Qadash walked slowly and did not turn round. He headed for a district which was being rebuilt. Former government buildings which had fallen into disrepair had been demolished, and piles of bricks obstructed the roadway. Qadash walked round a mountain of debris and disappeared. Suti climbed up it, taking care not to dislodge any bricks and so betray his presence. Once he reached the top, he spotted a fire, round which three men were standing. One of them was Qadash.

They took off their cloaks and revealed that they were naked, save for leather sheaths hiding their penises; each wore three feathers in his hair. Brandishing a short staff made of jet in either hand, they danced and pretended to attack each other. Qadash's partners were younger than he was, and they sprang about, shouting like wild men. Although he found it difficult to keep up, Qadash joined in with gusto.

The dance lasted for more than an hour. Then, suddenly, one of the actors took off the leather sheath and revealed his manhood. His friends immediately did the same. As Qadash was showing signs of tiredness, they gave him palm wine to drink before leading him into a new frenzy.

Pazair listened attentively to Suti's account.

'That's strange,' he said.

'You don't know Libyan customs,' said Suti. 'That kind of celebration is typical.'

'What do they hope to achieve?'

'Virility, fertility, the ability to seduce women. As they dance, they acquire new energy. Qadash seems to find it difficult.'

'So he must feel his powers are waning.'

'From what I saw, he has reason to to. But there's nothing illegal in what they did, is there?'

'Basically, no. But this man claims to hate foreigners, yet hasn't forgotten his Libyan roots and indulges in customs which the members of polite society, whom he treats, would strongly disapprove of.'

'Have I at least been useful?'

'Invaluable.'

'Next time, Judge Pazair, send me to spy on women dancing.'

*

Using their powers of persuasion, Kem and his baboon combed every inch of Memphis and its suburbs, to trace the four men who had been guards at the Sphinx.

The Nubian did not speak to the judge until Iarrot had left; he did not trust the scribe. When Killer entered the office, Brave hid under his master's chair.

'Any problems?' asked Pazair.

'I have their addresses.'

'I trust you got them without using of violence?'

'Not even a trace of it.'

'First thing tomorrow, we shall question them.'

'They've all disappeared.'

Pazair laid down his brush in astonishment. When he had refused to ratify that mundane administrative document, he had never imagined that he was lifting the lid on a cauldron full of mysteries.

'Where have they gone? Do you know?'

'Two have left to live in the Delta, two in the Theban region. I have the names of the villages.'

'Pack your travelling bag.'

Pazair spent the evening at Branir's house. On his way there, he had the feeling he was being followed. He slowed his pace, and turned round two or three times, but saw no further trace of the man he thought he had glimpsed. No doubt he had been mistaken.

Sitting opposite Branir, on the terrace of his flower-covered house, he savoured a cup of cool beer and listened to the breath of the great city as it dozed off to sleep. Here and there, lights indicated people who liked to stay up late, or busy scribes still at work.

In Branir's company, the world came to a halt. Pazair would have loved to hold on to this moment like a jewel, keep it safe in the palm of his hand, and prevent it from dissolving into the blackness of time.

'Has Neferet received her posting yet?' he asked.

'Not yet, but it should come any day now. She is staying in a room at the medical school.'

'Who makes the decision?'

'An assembly of doctors, led by the head physician, Nebamon. Neferet will be given a post that is not too taxing, then the difficulty will be increased as she gains experience. You seem rather sombre, Pazair. Anyone would think you'd lost your love of life.'

Pazair outlined the facts. 'A good many disturbing coincidences, wouldn't you say?'

'What is your theory?'

'It's too soon to have one. A crime has been committed – I'm sure of that. But what sort of crime, and how serious? I'm worried, perhaps without reason. Sometimes I wonder if I should go on, but I cannot take responsibility, however small, unless it is in full agreement with my conscience.'

'The heart devises plans and guides the individual; as for the personality, it retains what has been gained and preserves what the heart sees.'*

'My personality won't be weak. I shall explore what I have uncovered.'

'Never lose sight of Egypt's happiness. Pay no attention to your own well-being. If your actions are righteous, they will come back to you many times over.'

'If we tolerate a man's disappearance without question, if an official document is as good as a lie, does that not threaten Egypt's greatness?'

'You're right to be worried.'

'If your spirit is with mine, I shall confront the most fearsome dangers.'

'You don't lack courage, but be more clear-sighted and be careful to avoid certain obstacles. Confronting them head-on will only wound you. Go round them, learn to use your opponent's strength. Be as supple as a reed and as patient as granite.'

'Patience is not my strong point,' said Pazair.

'Build yourself, as an architect works his raw material.'

'Do you advise me not to go to the Delta?'

'You have made your decision.'

Nebamon looked most impressive in his robe of pleated linen with its coloured fringes. Haughty and beautifully groomed, he opened the plenary session in the great hall at the Memphis medical school. Ten renowned physicians, none of whom had ever been found guilty of the death of a patient, were about to appoint the young, newly qualified doctors to their first posts. Ordinarily these decisions were made in a spirit of benevolence and did not lead to arguments. And this time, too, the task would be swiftly carried out.

'Now for the case of Neferet,' said one of the doctors. 'She has received glowing reports from Memphis, Sais and Thebes. It is said she has a brilliant, even exceptional, gift.'

'Yes, but she's a woman,' objected Nebamon.

'She isn't the first.'

'Neferet is intelligent, I admit, but she lacks stamina. Experience may well prove too much for her theoretical knowledge.'

---

*Branir is passing on to his pupil the words of the sages. These words were collected together as maxims, in the text known as *Teachings*.

'She has passed through numerous training courses without faltering,' a doctor reminded him.

'During training, the students have tutors,' said Nebamon smoothly. 'When she's alone with the patients, she may lose her footing. Her capacity for resilience worries me; I cannot help wondering if she has taken a wrong decision in following our path.'

'What do you suggest?'

'A rather severe trial and difficult patients. If she overcomes the difficulties, we shall congratulate ourselves. If not, we shall learn from it.'

Without raising his voice, Nebamon received his colleagues' assent. He was about to give Neferet the most unpleasant surprise of her budding career. When he had broken her, he would pick her up out of the ditch and take her back into his fold, grateful and submissive.

Neferet was devastated, and felt like going off on her own to weep.

Hard work did not daunt her, but she had not expected to be placed in charge of a military hospital, where sick and wounded soldiers were treated on their return from Asia. Thirty or more men were stretched out on mats. Some were on the point of death, others were delirious, some incontinent. The officer responsible for health in the barracks had not given the young woman any instructions; he had simply left her there. He was obeying orders.

Neferet pulled herself together. Whatever the cause of this punishment might be, she must do her job and take care of these unfortunate men. After examining the barracks' medical stores, she began to feel more confident. The most urgent task was to ease severe pain. She crushed roots of mandragora to extract a potent substance which served as both an analgesic and a narcotic. Then she mixed scented dill, date juice and grape juice, and boiled the result in wine. For four consecutive days, she would give the sick men this potion to drink.

She called to a young recruit who was cleaning the barracks' courtyard. 'You're going to help me.'

'Me? But I—'

'I'm appointing you my orderly.'

'The commander—'

'Go and see him immediately, and tell him that thirty men are going to die if he refuses to let you help me.'

The commander gave his permission. He did not care for the cruel game in which he had been forced to participate.

When the new recruit entered the hospital, he almost fainted.

Neferet comforted him, and told him, 'Raise their heads gently so that I can pour the remedy into their mouths. Then we shall wash them and clean the room.'

To begin with, the lad closed his eyes and stopped breathing; but, reassured by Neferet's calm demeanour, he forgot his disgust and was happy to see that the potion took effect quickly. Shouts and moans died down; several soldiers fell asleep.

One of the less seriously ill grabbed Neferet's leg as she gave him his medicine.

'Let go of me,' she ordered.

'Certainly not, my beauty – I'm not letting a prize like you escape me. I'm going to give you pleasure.'

The orderly let go of the patient's head, which fell back heavily on to the ground, and knocked him out with a punch. The man's grip slackened, and Neferet freed herself.

'Thank you,' she said.

'Weren't you afraid?'

'Of course I was.'

'If you want, I'll give them all the same sleeping draught.'

'Only if it's necessary.'

'What's wrong with them?'

'They've got dysentery.'

'Is it serious?'

'It's an illness which I know and which I shall cure.'

'In Asia, they drink stagnant water. I'd rather sweep the barracks.'

As soon as everywhere was perfectly clean, Neferet gave her patients potions based on coriander, to calm their spasms and purify the intestines. Then she crushed pomegranate roots with brewer's yeast, filtered the result through fabric and let it rest for a whole night. The yellow fruit, filled with bright red pips, produced a remedy which was effective against diarrhoea and dysentery.

Neferet treated the most acute cases with a clyster made from honey, fermented vegetable matter, sweet beer and salt, which she introduced into the anus with a copper horn. Five days of intensive treatment produced excellent results. Cow's milk and honey, the only foods she allowed, finished the job of putting the patients back on their feet again.

Nebamon was in a very good mood when he arrived to inspect the barracks' health facilities six days after Neferet had taken up her post. He pronounced himself satisfied, and decided to finish off his inspection with the dysentery cases in the hospital. The young woman would be exhausted and at the end of her tether. She would beg him to grant her another post and would agree to work in his team.

A recruit was sweeping the floor of the infirmary, whose door stood wide open. A draught of fresh air was purifying the room, which was empty and whitewashed.

'I must be mistaken,' said Nebamon to the recruit. 'Do you know where Doctor Neferet is working?'

'First office on your left.'

He found her writing names on a papyrus.

'Neferet, where are the patients?'

'Convalescing.'

'That's impossible!'

'Here is the list of patients, the types of treatment used, and the dates when they left the hopsital.'

'But how . . . ?'

'I must thank you for entrusting me with this task, which has enabled me to check how well our medicine works.' She spoke without animosity, with a gentle light in her eyes.

'I think I have made a mistake,' said Nebamon.

'What do you mean?'

'I'm an idiot.'

'That's not what people say.'

'Listen to me, Neferet . . .'

'You shall have a complete report first thing tomorrow. Will you be kind enough to notify me about my next post as quickly as possible?'

Mentmose was in a fury. In the great house, not one servant would dare move until his anger had been appeased.

During periods of extreme tension, his head seethed, and he scratched himself until he drew blood. At his feet lay shreds of papyrus, the miserable remains of his subordinates' reports, which he had torn up.

Nothing.

No consistent evidence, no notorious faults, no hints of malpractice: Pazair was behaving like an honest – and therefore dangerous – judge. Mentmose was not in the habit of underestimating his opponents. This one belonged to a formidable breed and would not be easy to thwart. No decisive action could be taken until he had an answer to one question: who was manipulating Pazair?

14

The wind swelled the broad sail of the single-masted boat as it sailed through the watery expanses of the Delta. The pilot steered the vessel with skill, making use of the current, while his passengers, Judge Pazair, Kem and Killer, rested in the cabin at the centre of the deck; their luggage was stowed on the roof. At the prow, the captain sounded the depth of the water with a long pole and gave orders to the crew. The eye of Horus, which was drawn on the prow and on the poop, protected the boat on its journey.

Pazair emerged from the cabin and leant over the rail, gazing out at the countryside, which he was seeing for the first time. How far away the valley was, with its fields tightly enclosed by two deserts. Here, the river divided into branches and canals, irrigating towns, villages, palm groves, fields and vines. Hundreds of birds – swallows, hoopoes, white herons, crows, larks, sparrows, cormorants, pelicans, wild geese, ducks, cranes and storks – flew across a soft blue sky, dotted here and there with clouds. The judge felt as though he were looking at a sea filled with reeds and papyrus; on mounds which stood clear of the water, thickets of willow and acacia protected single-storey whitewashed houses. Surely this must be the primordial marsh the old authors had spoken of, the earthly incarnation of the ocean which surrounded the world and from which the new sun emerged each day.

Men hunting hippopotamus signalled to the boat to change direction. They were pursuing a male, and had wounded it. It had just dived, and there was a risk that it would surface again suddenly and overturn a boat, even a sizeable one. The monster would fight fiercely for its life.

The captain did not ignore the warning; he chose to take 'the waters of Ra', which formed the easternmost branch of the Nile, leading in a north-easterly direction. Close to Bubastis, the city of the goddess Bastet, whose symbol was a cat, he directed the boat into the 'channel of gentle water', along Wadi Toumilat, towards the Bitter Lakes; the wind was blowing hard. To the right, beyond a pool where buffalo were bathing, was a hamlet, sheltered by tamarisk trees.

The boat tied up and the gangplank was thrown down. Pazair, who was not a good sailor, swayed as he walked down it. At the sight of Killer, a group of children ran away. Their cries alerted the peasants, who came to deal with the new arrivals, brandishing pitchforks.

'You have nothing to fear. I am Judge Pazair, and my companions represent the guards.'

The pitchforks were lowered, and the judge was taken to the village headman, a grumpy old man.

'I would like to speak with the ex-soldier who returned home a few weeks ago.'

'That will be impossible on this earth.'

'Is he dead?'

'Some soldiers brought back his body. We buried him in our burial ground.'

'What did he die of?'

'Old age.'

'Did you examine the body?'

'It was mummified.'

'What did the soldiers say to you?'

'They weren't very talkative.'

Exhuming a mummy would have been sacrilege. Pazair and his companions got back on the boat and left for the village where the second ex-soldier lived.

'You'll have to walk across the marsh,' said the captain. 'There are dangerous islets around there, and I must keep well out from the bank.'

The baboon did not like the water. Kem talked to it at length and managed to persuade it to venture along a path he had opened up in the reeds. The monkey was anxious and kept turning round, darting glances to right and left. The judge strode impatiently ahead, towards little houses clustered together at the top of a mound. Kem watched the animal's reactions carefully. It was confident in its own strength, and would not behave like this without good reason.

Killer let out a loud cry, knocked over the judge and seized the tail of a small crocodile which was slithering along in the muddy water. Just as the reptile opened its mouth, he pulled it backwards. The 'great fish', as the river folk called it, was quite capable of ambushing sheep and goats which came down to drink in the pools and killing them.

The crocodile struggled, but it was too young and too small to resist the fury of the baboon, which plucked it out of the mud and hurled it several paces away.

'Thank him,' Pazair told the Nubian. 'I predict promotion for him.'

The village headman was sitting on a low chair with a sloping seat and a rounded back, nicely settled in the shade of a sycamore tree. He was enjoying a copious meal of poultry, onions and a jug of beer, which had been arranged in a flat-bottomed basket.

He invited his guests to share the food. Killer, whose heroic deed was already the talk of the marshes, tore eagerly at a chicken thigh with his teeth.

'We are looking for a former soldier who has come to live out his retirement here,' said Pazair.

'Alas, Judge, all we have seen of him is his mummy. The army took charge of transporting the body, and paid the costs of burial. Our burial ground is modest, but eternity there is as happy as anywhere else.'

'Were you told the cause of his death?'

'The soldiers didn't say much, but I demanded to know. An accident, apparently.'

'What kind of accident?'

'That's all I know.'

On the boat taking him back to Memphis, Pazair could not conceal his disappointment. 'A total failure: the head guard has vanished, two of his men are dead, and the other two have probably been embalmed too.'

'Then you won't be setting out on another journey?' asked Kem.

'I must. I want to set the record straight.'

'I shall be happy to see Thebes again.'

'What do you think of all this?'

'That the fact that these men are dead is preventing you from discovering the key to the mystery – and so much the better.'

'Don't you want to know the truth?'

'When it's too dangerous, I'd rather not. The truth has already cost me my nose, and now it could rob you of your life.'

When Suti came home at dawn, Pazair was already at work, his dog at his feet.

'Didn't you sleep? Nor did I. I need some rest. My poultry keeper's wearing me out – she's insatiable and wants to try absolutely everything. I've brought some hot-cakes; the baker has just made them.'

Brave was the first to be fed; then the two friends had breakfast together. Although he was half-dead for lack of sleep, Suti saw that Pazair was deeply troubled.

'Either you're tired, or something is seriously worrying you. Is it something you can't resolve?'

'I can't talk about it.'

'Not even to me? It must be really serious.'

'I'm floundering, but I'm certain I've stumbled upon a criminal matter.'

'What is it? A murder?'

'Probably.'

'Be careful, Pazair. Crimes like that are rare in Egypt. Shouldn't you let sleeping dogs lie? You might annoy some important people.'

'That comes with the job.'

'Doesn't crime come under the tjaty's jurisdiction?'

'Provided it is proven.'

'Whom do you suspect?'

'I know only one thing for certain: soldiers have been involved in a plot. Soldiers who must be under the command of General Asher.'

Suti whistled admiringly. 'You're aiming high! A military plot?'

'I'm not ruling it out.'

'What's it for?'

'I don't know.'

'I'm your man, Pazair.'

'What do you mean?'

'I am seriously intending to enlist in the army. I shall swiftly become an excellent soldier, an officer – perhaps a general. In any case, a hero. I shall find out everything about Asher. If he's guilty of something, I shall find out, and then you'll find out, too.'

'It's too risky,' said Pazair.

'No, it's exciting. At long last, the adventure I've been dreaming of! And what if the two of us end up saving Egypt? If you mention military plots, you're really saying that a section of the army is planning to seize power.'

'That's a fine plan, Suti, but I'm not yet sure if the situation is that desperate.'

'What do you know about it? Tell me what to do.'

A charioteer officer, accompanied by two archers, arrived at Pazair's office towards the middle of the morning.

The man was curt but polite. 'I am here to regularize a transfer which was submitted to you for approval.'

'Are you referring to the former head of the Sphinx's guard?'

'I am.'

'I refuse to place my seal upon it before he has appeared before me.'

'My orders are to take you to where he is, in order to bring an end to the matter.'

Suti was sound asleep, Kem was on patrol, and Iarrot had not yet arrived. Pazair dismissed all thoughts of danger. What organized body, even the army, would dare make an attempt on a judge's life? He agreed to climb into the officer's chariot after stroking Brave, whose eyes were full of anxiety.

The vehicle sped out of Memphis and set off along a road which skirted the fields and plunged into the desert. There towered the pyramids raised by the pharaohs of the Old Kingdom, surrounded by magnificent tombs bearing witness to the genius of painters and sculptors.

The step-pyramid at Saqqara, the work of Djoser and Imhotep, loomed over the countryside; its gigantic stone steps formed a staircase to the heavens, enabling the king's soul to climb up to the sun and descend to earth. Only the top of the monument was visible, for a thick wall with a single carefully guarded gate hid it from the outside world. Within the great inner courtyard, Pharaoh would experience the rites of regeneration when his powers waned.

Pazair breathed in great lungfuls of the desert air, which was sharp and dry; he liked this red earth, this sea of burnt rocks and yellow sand, this void filled with the voices of the ancestors. Here, a man was stripped of all but the essentials.

'Where are you taking me?'

'We've arrived.'

The chariot halted before a house with tiny windows, far from all habitation; several sarcophagi were leaning against the wall. The wind raised clouds of sand. Not a single small tree or flower was visible; in the distance, there was nothing but pyramids and tombs. A rocky hill blotted out any view of the palm groves and fields. On the fringes of death, at the heart of solitude, the place seemed utterly abandoned.

'It's here.'

The officer clapped his hands.

Intrigued, Pazair got down from the chariot. The place was ideal for an ambush, and no one knew where he was. He thought of Neferet; to die without revealing his love for her would haunt his soul eternally.

The door of the house creaked open. A thin man appeared on the threshold. His skin was very white, his face and hands endlessly long and his legs frail. His thick black eyebrows joined above his nose; his thin lips seemed devoid of blood. There were brownish stains on his goatskin apron.

His dark eyes stared at Pazair. The judge had never encountered eyes like them before; their gaze was intense, glacial, as sharp as a blade. He resisted it.

'Djui is the official embalmer,' explained the lieutenant charioteer.
The man bowed his head.

'Follow me, Judge Pazair.'

Djui stood aside to allow the officer to pass, followed by the judge, who entered the embalming workshop where Djui mummified bodies on a stone table. Iron hooks, obsidian knives and sharpened stones hung on the walls; on shelves, there were pots of oil and unguents, and sacks filled with natron, which was vital for embalming. In accordance with the law, the embalmer had to live outside the town; he belonged to a feared caste, made up of wild, silent men.

The three men began walking down the steps that led to an immense cellar. They were worn and slippery. Djui's torch flickered. On the ground lay mummies of varying sizes. Pazair shivered.

'I have received a report concerning the former head guard of the Sphinx,' explained the officer. 'You were sent the request for transfer in error. He has died as a result of an accident.'

'A terrible accident, indeed.'

'What makes you say that?'

'Because it killed at least three men, maybe more.'

The officer shrugged. 'I don't know about that.'

'How did the accident happen?'

'I don't know the exact details. The head guard was found dead and his body was brought here. Unfortunately, a scribe made a mistake; instead of ordering his burial, he requested a transfer. It was a simple administrative error.'

'What about the body?'

'I wanted to show it to you, so as to put an end to this regrettable matter.'

'Mummified, of course?'

'Of course.'

'Has the body been placed in the sarcophagus?'

The officer looked at the embalmer, who shook his head.

'Then the final rites have not yet been celebrated,' concluded Pazair.

'That is true, but—'

'Then show me this mummy.'

Djui led the judge and the officer into the depths of the cave. He pointed out the head guard's body, which was standing upright in an alcove, wrapped in bandages. It bore a number written in red ink.

The embalmer presented the officer with the label which would be fixed on to the mummy.

'All that remains is for you to affix your seal,' the officer told Pazair.

Djui stood behind Pazair. The light flickered more and more.

'Ensure that this mummy remains here, Officer, and in this condition. If it disappears, or if anybody damages it, I shall hold you personally responsible.'

15

'Can you tell me where Neferet is working?' asked Pazair.

'You seem preoccupied,' commented Branir.

'It's very important,' said Pazair. 'I may have obtained material proof, but I can't do anything with it unless I have the help of a doctor.'

'I saw her last night. She has overcome an epidemic of dysentery and cured thirty soldiers in less than a week.'

'Soldiers? What job was she given?'

'Nebamon was trying to bully her.'

'I'll beat him senseless.'

'Is that really in accordance with the duties of a judge?'

'That bully deserves to be punished.'

'He was only exercising his authority,' Branir pointed out.

'You know that's not true. Tell me the truth: what new ordeal has that useless idiot subjected her to?'

'It seems he has mended his ways. Neferet is working at the Temple of Sekhmet, creating new remedies and potions.'

Near the Temple of Sekhmet, workshops processed hundreds of plants which were used as the basis for prescribed preparations. Daily deliveries guaranteed the freshness of the potions, which were sent out to doctors in towns and in the countryside. Neferet was supervising, making sure that the prescriptions were properly made up. Compared to her previous post, this was a step backwards. Nebamon had presented it to her as a compulsory phase and a time of rest before taking care of the sick again, and, ever professional, the young woman had not protested.

At noon, they all left the workshop and went to eat in the communal dining room. Colleagues chatted easily about new remedies, and lamented their failures. Two specialists were talking to Neferet, who was smiling. Pazair was certain they were paying court to her.

His heart beat faster; he plucked up the courage to interrupt them. 'Neferet?'

She stopped. 'Were you looking for me?'

'Branir told me about the injustices you suffered. They revolt me.'

'I was happy to be able to cure people. The rest is unimportant.'

'I need your help.'

'Are you ill?'

'I have a delicate enquiry which entails the involvement of a doctor. A simple expert opinion, nothing more.'

Kem drove the chariot with a steady hand; Killer crouched down, trying not to look at the road. Neferet and Pazair stood side by side, their wrists tied to the shell of the vehicle with leather straps, to prevent them falling out. As the chariot ran over bumps in the road, their bodies were jolted together. Neferet seemed not to notice, but Pazair felt a joy that was as secret as it was intense. He wished that this short journey could be endless and that the road could get worse and worse. When his leg touched Neferet's he did not move it away; he was afraid she'd rebuke him, but no rebuke came. Being so close to her, smelling her perfume, believing that she accepted this contact . . . the dream was sublime.

Two soldiers were on guard outside the embalmer's workshop.

'I am Judge Pazair. Let us pass.'

'Our orders are clear: nobody comes in. The place has been requisitioned.'

'No one may resist the law. Are you forgetting that we are in Egypt?'

'Our orders—'

'Stand aside.'

The baboon moved forward and bared its teeth; it stood on its hind legs, its eyes staring and its arms bent, ready to spring. Little by little, Kem slackened the chain.

The two soldiers gave in. Kem kicked open the door.

Djui was sitting on the embalming table, eating dried fish.

'Take us downstairs,' ordered Pazair.

Kem and Killer searched the darkened room suspiciously while the judge and the doctor went down into the cellar, lit by Djui's torch.

'What a horrible place,' whispered Neferet. 'And I love the air and the light so much.'

'To be honest, I'm not very comfortable, either.'

The embalmer walked down the staircase with his usual speed, not missing his footing once.

The mummy had not been moved; Pazair could see that no one had touched it.

'Here is your patient,' he said. 'I shall unwrap him under your directions.'

The judge took off the bandages carefully, revealing an amulet in the shape of an eye, placed on the mummy's forehead. There was a deep wound to the neck, undoubtedly caused by an arrow.

'There's no need to go any further. In your opinion, how old was this man?'

'About twenty,' replied Neferet.

Mentmose was wondering how to resolve the press of animals and vehicles that was making the daily lives of Memphis's citizens so difficult: too many donkeys, too many oxen, too many chariots, too many itinerant vendors, too many people chattering, all clogging up the narrow streets and blocking the flow of traffic. Every year he drew up decrees, each one less practicable than the last, and did not even bother submitting them to the tjaty. All he did was promise improvements which nobody believed would ever happen. From time to time, an influx of guards quietened frayed tempers. A street would be unblocked for a few days by a ban on stopping animals or carts, those who infringed the ban would be fined, and then bad habits would once more regain the upper hand.

Mentmose made sure his subordinates felt the weight of responsibility, and was careful not to give them the means to eliminate the problems. By remaining above the hurly-burly and plunging his colleagues into it, he preserved his own excellent reputation.

When Judge Pazair's arrival was announced, he emerged from his office to greet him in the waiting room. Little niceties like that made a good impression.

The judge's sombre face did not augur well.

'I have an extremely busy morning,' said Mentmose, 'but I am at your disposal.'

'I consider that essential.'

'You seem shaken.'

'I am.'

Mentmose scratched his forehead. He took the judge into his office, sending away his personal scribe. Tense, he sat down on a fine chair with feet in the shape of a bull's hooves. Pazair remained standing.

'I'm listening,' said Mentmose.

'A charioteer officer took me to see Djui, the official army embalmer. He showed me the mummy of the man I have been looking for.'

'The former Sphinx guard? Then he really is dead?'

'That's what they tried to make me believe, anyway.'

'What do you mean?'

'As the final rites had not been celebrated, I unwrapped the upper part of the mummy under the direction of Doctor Neferet. The body is that of a man of about twenty who was killed by an arrow. It is clearly not the body of the former soldier.'

Mentmose looked thunderstruck. 'That's unbelievable!'

'What is more,' the judge continued imperturbably, 'two soldiers tried to stop me entering the embalming workshop. When I came out, they had disappeared.'

'What is the chariot officer's name?'

'I don't know.'

'That's a serious omission.'

'Don't you think he'd have lied to me?'

On second thoughts, Mentmose agreed. He asked, 'Where is the body?'

'At Djui's house – he's guarding it. I shall draw up a detailed report, which will include witness statements from Doctor Neferet, the embalmer and my guard, Kem.'

Mentmose frowned. 'Are you satisfied with Kem?'

'His conduct is exemplary.'

'His past hardly speaks in his favour.'

'He helps me most effectively.'

'Don't trust him.'

'Let us get back to the mummy.'

Mentmose detested this type of situation, in which he was not master of the game. 'My men will go and fetch it and we shall examine it. We must find out who the man was.'

'We must also know if we are in the presence of a death resulting from a military engagement or from a crime.'

'A crime? Surely you don't think . . . ?'

'For my part, I am continuing my enquiries.'

'In what direction?'

'I am sworn to silence.'

'Are you defying me?'

'That is an ill-chosen question.'

'I am as lost as you are in this muddle. Shouldn't we work together?'

'I consider it more important for justice to be independent.'

Mentmose's anger made the walls of his headquarters shake. Fifty senior officials were dismissed that very day, and deprived of numerous benefits. For the first time since he had attained the summit of power, he had not been correctly informed. Such a failure cast a damning light on his system. But he would not allow himself to be struck down without fighting back.

Alas, the army seemed to have instigated these manoeuvres, the reasons for which remained beyond his comprehension. Advancing into that territory carried risks Mentmose would not run. If General Asher, whose recent promotions had rendered him untouchable, was the mastermind, there was no chance of striking him down.

Giving the little judge free rein presented many advantages. He would involve no one but himself and would, with all the zeal of youth, take virtually no precautions. He ran the risk of forcing open forbidden doors and infringing laws he did not know existed. By following his tracks, Mentmose could exploit the results of his enquiries while remaining in the shadows. It was as good as making an ally of him, until the day when he no longer needed him.

One irritating question remained: why had this drama been staged? Whoever was behind it had underestimated Pazair, believing that the strangeness of the place, its stifling climate and the oppressive presence of death would prevent the judge from examining the mummy closely, and would induce him to leave after placing his seal upon it. The result had in fact been the opposite: far from losing interest in the matter, Pazair was even more determined to resolve it.

Mentmose tried to reassure himself: the disappearance of one humble ex-soldier, the holder of an honorary post, wasn't going to topple the state! No doubt it was just a petty crime, committed by a soldier who was being protected by some senior military man – probably Asher or one of his acolytes. That was the line of enquiry that ought to be pursued.

16

On the first day of spring, Egyptians honoured the dead and also their own ancestors. As the mild winter drew to a close, the nights became suddenly cool because of the gusty desert wind. In all the great burial grounds, families venerated the memory of the dead by laying flowers in the shrines of their tombs, which opened on to the outside world.

There was no stark frontier between life and death, and so the living feasted with the departed, whose souls entered the flames of lamps. The darkness was filled with light, celebrating the meeting of this world with the world beyond. At Abydos, the sacred city of Osiris where the mysteries of resurrection were celebrated, the priests placed little boats on the tops of the tombs, representing the journey towards paradise.

After lighting sacred lamps in all the main temples at Memphis, King Ramses headed for Giza. He prepared to enter the great pyramid alone, as he did on the same day each year, and meditate before the sarcophagus of Khufu. At the heart of the immense monument, the pharaoh was nourished with the power he needed to unite the Two Lands of Upper and Lower Egypt, and make them prosper. He would gaze upon the builder's golden mask and gold cubit, which provided him with inspiration. When the time came for his regeneration ritual, he would lift up the Testament of the Gods and display it to the country.

The full moon shone down upon the plateau where the three pyramids stood.

Dressed only in a simple white kilt and broad gold collar, Ramses arrived at the outer wall of Khufu's monument, which was guarded by handpicked soldiers. The guards bowed and drew back the bolts. The king passed through the gate and began climbing the sloping walkway, which was paved with limestone flags. Soon, he would reach the Great Pyramid's entrance, whose secret mechanism was known only to Pharaoh.

This encounter with immortality affected the king more intensely with each year that passed. Without the vital energy the rites provided, Pharaoh could not carry out the exhausting task of ruling Egypt.

Slowly, Ramses climbed up to the great gallery and entered the sarcophagus chamber. Not even in his worst nightmare would he have dreamt that the country's energy centre could be transformed into a sterile hell.

Down at the docks, everyone was celebrating the feast day: the boats were decorated with flowers, beer flowed freely, sailors danced with bold-eyed girls, and itinerant musicians entertained the large crowds. Pazair had taken Brave for a short walk, and was retreating from the hubbub when a familiar voice hailed him.

'Judge Pazair! Surely you're not leaving already?'

From the midst of a crowd of revellers Denes's square, bearded face emerged. The ship owner jostled his way through the throng and joined the judge. 'What a beautiful day,' he said. 'Everyone's having fun and forgetting their cares.'

'I don't care for the noise.'

'You're too serious for your age.'

'It's difficult to change the way we are.'

'Life will take care of that.'

'You seem very cheerful.'

'Business is good,' said Denes. 'My cargoes arrive on time, my men obey me without question. What is there to complain about?'

'It seems you don't bear grudges.'

'You did your duty – I can't hold that against you. And besides, there's the good news.'

'What good news?'

'Because this is a feast day, several minor sentences have been annulled by the palace. It's an old Memphis custom, which had more or less fallen into disuse. I'm lucky enough to be one of the beneficiaries.'

Pazair turned pale. He could not conceal his anger. 'How did you contrive that?'

'I told you, it's the festival, just the festival. In the document you drew up, charging me, you forgot to specify that my case was not to be eligible for clemency. Play the game, Pazair. You've won, and I haven't lost.' Denes tried hard to make Pazair share his good humour. 'I'm not your enemy, Judge. In business, we sometimes pick up bad habits. My wife and I think you were right to teach us a lesson, and we shall learn from it.'

'Do you truly mean that?'

'I do. Forgive me, but I must go now – someone's waiting for me.'

Pazair was mortified. He had been impatient and vain, in such a hurry to see justice done that he had neglected the letter of the law. He turned to go, but found his way blocked by a military parade led by the triumphant General Asher.

Mentmose sat at his desk, looking confident and very much at his ease. 'The reason I summoned you here, Judge Pazair,' he said, 'is to tell you the results of my enquiries. The mummy you found is that of a young recruit killed in Asia during a skirmish. He was hit by an arrow and died instantly. Because of a similarity in names, his case was confused with that of the Sphinx's head guard. The scribes responsible claim it wasn't their fault. No one tried to mislead you. We thought there was a conspiracy, when in fact it was merely incompetence. You look sceptical, but you needn't be. I've checked every point.'

'I don't doubt your word.'

'I'm glad to hear it.'

'Nevertheless, the guard still hasn't been found.'

'That is strange, I agree. Perhaps he's in hiding, trying to escape some army disciplinary matter?'

'Two veterans who were serving under him died in an "accident".' Pazair emphasized the last word.

Mentmose scratched his head. 'What's suspicious about that?'

'The army ought to have a record of the incident, and you ought to have been informed.'

'Not at all. That sort of incident isn't my concern.'

Pazair tried to drive Mentmose into a corner. According to Kem, Mentmose was quite capable of orchestrating this affair in order to carry out a vast purge of his own administrative staff, certain members of which were beginning to criticize his methods.

'Aren't we over-dramatizing the situation?' asked Mentmose. 'The whole affair's just a chain of unfortunate circumstances.'

'Two ex-soldiers and the wife of the head guard are dead, and he himself has disappeared. Those are the facts. Couldn't you ask the military authorities to send you their report on the . . . accident?'

Mentmose stared at the end of his writing brush. 'That would be considered highly undesirable. The army doesn't like interference from the civilian security forces.'

'Then I'll attend to it myself.'

The two men took leave of each other with glacial politeness.

'General Asher has just left on a mission abroad,' an army scribe told Pazair.

'When will he be back?'

'That's a military secret.'

'Whom should I see, in his absence, to obtain a report on the accident that occurred recently at the Great Sphinx?'

'I can certainly help you. Oh, I almost forgot. General Asher entrusted me with a document which I was to send you. As you're here, I shall hand it to you in person. You must sign the register.' He handed Pazair a papyrus scroll.

Pazair removed the linen tie that kept the papyrus rolled up, and began to read. The text related the regrettable circumstances leading to the deaths of the head guard and his four men, following a routine inspection. The five had climbed on to the head of the Sphinx, to check that the stone was in good condition and identify any damage caused by sandstorms. One of them, in a moment of clumsiness, had slipped and dragged his companions down with him. The four ex-soldiers had been buried in their home villages, two in the Delta, two in the south. As for the head guard's body, because of his honorary position, it had been kept in an army shrine and would receive long, careful embalming. On his return from Asia, the general himself would lead the funeral ceremonies.

Pazair signed the register, confirming that he had indeed received the document.

'Is there anything else I can help you with?' asked the scribe.

'Thank you, but there's nothing more.'

Pazair wished he hadn't accepted Suti's invitation. Before enlisting, his friend wanted to celebrate the event in the most famous ale-house in Memphis. The judge thought constantly of Neferet, of the sun-bright face that lit up his dreams. Lost among the gleeful revellers, Pazair had no interest in the naked Nubian dancing girls or their supple bodies.

The customers sat on soft cushions, with jars of wine and beer lined up in front of them.

'You don't touch the girls,' explained Suti, beaming all over his face. 'They're here to excite us. Don't worry, Pazair, the lady of the house provides an excellent contraceptive made from crushed acacia thorns, honey and dates.'

Everyone knew that acacia thorns contained an acid which destroyed the fertile power of sperm, and from their earliest amorous trysts adolescents used this simple means of devoting themselves safely to pleasure.

About fifteen young women, veiled in diaphanous linen, came out of the small bedrooms that led off the central room. They were heavily made up, with lips painted red and eyes accentuated with kohl, and wore lotus flowers in their loose hair. Heavy bracelets jingled at their wrists and ankles as they approached their delighted guests. Couples formed instinctively and disappeared into the bedrooms, each one screened from the next by curtains.

As Pazair had rejected offers from two delightful dancers, he remained alone with Suti, who did not want to leave him on his own.

Then another woman appeared: Sababu, the owner of the ale-house. She was about thirty, and was naked save for a heavy wig of blonde ringlets and a belt of shells and coloured pearls. They clinked together as she danced slowly and played the lyre. Suti gazed in fascination at her tattoos, a lily on her left thigh, close to her pubis, and the god Bes above the black fleece of her sex – this one was designed to drive away venereal diseases. Sababu was more fascinating than even the most beautiful of her girls. Flexing her long, smooth legs, she danced slowly and lasciviously to the rhythm of the music. Her skin was freshly oiled, surrounding her with an enchanting perfume.

When she approached the two men, Suti could not control his passion.

'I like you,' she told him, 'and I think you like me too.'

'I can't desert my friend.'

'Leave him be. Can't you see he's in love? His soul is not here. Come with me.'

She led Suti into the largest bedroom. She sat him down on a low bed, covered with multicoloured cushions, knelt down and kissed him. He made to take her by the shoulders, but she pushed him away gently.

'There's no hurry – we have all night. Learn to hold back your pleasure, to make it grow in your belly, to savour the fire that flows through your blood.' She took off her belt of shells and lay down on her stomach. 'Massage my back.'

Suti played the game for a few seconds, but then, inflamed by the sight of her wonderful body, the touch of her perfumed skin, he could restrain himself no longer. Seeing how intense his desire was, Sababu stopped resisting him. Covering her in kisses, he made ardent love to her.

'You pleased me a lot. You aren't like most of my clients – they drink too much and get flabby and soft.'

'Not to pay homage to your charms would be a sin against the spirit.'

Suti caressed her breasts, attentive to her least reaction. Thanks to her lover's knowledgeable hands, Sababu was rediscovering long-forgotten sensations.

'Are you a scribe?' she asked.

'Soon I shall be a soldier, but before becoming a hero I wanted to have the sweetest of adventures.'

'In that case, I must give you everything.'

Using the lightest touch of her lips and tongue, Sababu reawakened Suti's desire. Their bodies joined once again, and for a second time they cried out together in pleasure.

Afterwards they lay gazing into each other's eyes, while they got their breath back.

'You have seduced me, my ram,' said Sababu, 'for you adore making love.'

'Is there any illusion more beautiful than this one?'

'And yet you're very real.'

Suti put his arm round her. 'How did you become the owner of an ale-house?'

'Because I despise false nobles and so-called great men. They say fine words, but they're hypocrites – really they're just like you and me, ruled by the demands of their sex and their passions. If you only knew . . .'

'Tell me.'

'Would you steal away my secrets?'

'Why not?'

Despite her experience, and all the men whose bodies she had known, handsome and ugly, Sababu could not resist her new lover's caresses. He awoke in her the will to avenge herself against a world which had so often humiliated her.

'When you are a hero,' she said, 'will you be ashamed of me?'

'Certainly not! I'm sure you've had lots of famous men as lovers.'

'You're right about that.'

'You must have some amusing stories to tell.'

She laid a slender finger on the young man's mouth. 'Only my private journal knows about them. It ensures my peace.'

'You write down the names of your clients?'

'And their habits and their confidences.'

'It must be an absolute treasure house.'

'If I'm left in peace, I shan't use it. When I am old, I shall read over my memories again.'

Suti rolled over on top of her. 'I'm still curious. At least give me one name.'

'No, I can't.'

'Just for me.'

The young man kissed her nipples. She shivered with pleasure.

'One name, just one,' he pleaded.

'He's known as a model of virtue. When I divulge his vices, his career will be at an end.'

'What's his name?'

'Pazair.'

Suti flung himself off Sababu's gorgeous body. 'What have you been told to do?'

'Spread rumours.'

'Do you know him?'

'I've never even seen him.'

'Yes you have.'

'What?'

'Pazair's my best friend. He's here, this very evening, but all he thinks of is the woman he loves and the cause he's defending. Who told you to smear his name?'

Sababu was silent.

'He's a judge,' Suti went on, 'the most honest judge in Egypt. Don't tell any more lies about him. You're powerful enough not to have to worry if you stop.'

'I can't promise anything.'

17

Pazair and Suti sat side by side on the banks of the Nile, watching the birth of the day. Vanquishing the darkness, the new sun sprang forth from the desert, turned the river to blood, and made the fish leap for joy.

'Are you really serious-minded?' asked Suti.

'Whatever are you accusing me of?' asked Pazair in surprise.

'A judge who's over-fond of debauchery is liable to find his mind gets clouded.'

'You're the one who dragged me into that ale-house. While you were fooling around, I was thinking about my cases.'

'About your beloved, more like.'

The river sparkled. Already, the bloody hue of dawn was fading, to be replaced by the golden tones of early morning.

Suti went on, 'How many times have you been to that pleasure house?'

'You must have been drinking.'

'So you've never met Sababu before?'

'Never.'

'And yet she was ready to tell anyone who'd listen that you're one of her best customers.'

Pazair turned pale, not so much because, if the story got about, his reputation as a judge would be tarnished for ever, but because of what Neferet would think of him.

'She's been bribed to do it!' he exclaimed.

'Exactly.'

'By whom?'

'Our love-making was so good that she took a liking to me. She told me about the plot she's mixed up in, but not who's behind it. But if you ask me the ringleader's easy to identify: those methods are absolutely typical of Mentmose.'

'I shall defend myself.'

'There's no need. I persuaded her to keep her mouth shut.'

'Let's not deceive ourselves,' said Pazair. 'The first chance she gets, she'll betray us both.'

'I'm not so sure. That girl has morals.'

'Allow me to be sceptical.'

'In certain circumstances, a woman does not lie.'

'All the same, I want to speak to her.'

Shortly before noon Pazair arrived, with Kem and Killer, at the door of the ale-house. A young Nubian girl hid in fright under a pile of cushions; one of her colleagues, who was less easily scared, dared to face the judge.

'I would like to see the owner,' he said.

'I'm just one of her girls, and—'

'Where is the lady Sababu? Don't lie to me. If you do, you'll be sent to prison.'

'But if I tell you, she'll beat me.'

'And if you don't, I'll charge you with obstructing justice.'

'I haven't done anything wrong.'

'No, and you haven't been charged yet. So tell me the truth.'

'She's gone to Thebes.'

'Did she leave an address?'

'No.'

'When is she coming back?'

'I don't know.'

So Sababu had chosen to run away and hide. From now on, the judge would be in danger if he made the slightest mistake. Someone was lurking in the shadows, plotting against him. Someone – probably Mentmose – had paid Sababu to destroy his good name, and to save herself she wouldn't hesitate to denounce him. The judge owed his temporary safety only to Suti's powers of seduction.

Sometimes, mused Pazair, debauchery was not entirely reprehensible.

After long reflection, Mentmose took a decision which would have weighty consequences: he would ask Tjaty Bagey for a private audience. Nervously, he rehearsed his declaration several times in front of a copper mirror, trying out different facial expressions. Like everyone else, he knew the tjaty's reputation for intransigence. Bagey was sparing with his words, and loathed wasting his time. His office obliged him to hear all petitions, wherever they came from, so long as they were well-founded; but anyone who wasted time, lied, or falsified the facts would live to regret it bitterly. Face to face with the tjaty, every word and every gesture counted.

Mentmose went to the palace in the late morning. At seven o'clock,

Bagey had spoken with the king, then given instructions to his principal colleagues and consulted the reports that had arrived from the provinces. Next, he had held his daily audience, to deal with the numerous matters that other courts had been unable to resolve. Before eating a frugal lunch, the tjaty would consent to a few personal meetings, if urgency demanded it.

He received Mentmose in an austere office whose spartan decor scarcely matched the grandeur of his rank: it contained only a chair, a mat, some storage chests and papyrus cases. A visitor would have thought he was in the presence of a simple scribe, if Bagey had not been wearing his grand robe and collar of office.

Tjaty Bagey was sixty years old, a tall, stooping, stiff-bodied man with a long face, prominent nose, curly hair and blue eyes. His hands were those of an artist, slender and elegant. He had never taken part in any sports; his skin reacted badly to the sun. After working as a craftsman, he had become first a teacher of writing, then an expert in geometry, renowned for his great thoroughness.

In time he had come to the notice of the palace, which had appointed him in succession head geometrician, senior judge of the province of Memphis, Judge of the Porch and finally tjaty. Many courtiers had tried in vain to catch him out. Feared and respected, Bagey belonged to a long line of great statesmen who, since the days of Imhotep, had kept Egypt on the right path. If he was sometimes criticized for the severity of his judgments and the inflexibility with which they were applied, no one could say that they were not well thought-out.

Up to now, Mentmose had confined himself to obeying the tjaty's orders and taking care not to displease him. This meeting made him nervous.

The tjaty was tired, and seemed half asleep. 'I'm listening,' he said. 'Be brief.'

'It's not that simple—'

'Then simplify it.

'Several ex-soldiers have been killed in an accident, falling off the Great Sphinx.'

'Tell me about the official enquiry.'

'The army carried it out.'

'Any anomalies?'

'There don't seem to be. I haven't looked at the official documents, but—'

'But your contacts have informed you of the contents. That is somewhat irregular.'

Mentmose had been afraid the tjaty might take that line. 'These are old customs.'

'They must be changed. If there's nothing amiss, why are you here?'

'It's about Judge Pazair.'

'Is he unworthy to be a judge?'

Mentmose's voice became more nasal. 'I'm not accusing him of anything, it's just that his conduct worries me.'

'Does he not respect the law?'

'He's convinced that the disappearance of the head guard, a former soldier with an excellent reputation, took place in peculiar circumstances.'

'Has he any proof?'

'No, none. I have the feeling that this young judge wants to stir things up so that he can make a reputation for himself. I find such an attitude deplorable.'

'I'm delighted to hear it,' said Bagey. 'Regarding the basic facts of the case, what is your opinion?'

'Oh, my opinion is of little value.'

'On the contrary. I am eager to know it.'

A trap yawned before Mentmose. He had a horror of committing himself one way or the other, for fear of taking a firm stance which might be criticized.

The tjaty opened his eyes. His cold blue gaze pierced Mentmose's soul.

Mentmose said, 'It seems unlikely that there's any mystery about the deaths of those unfortunate men, but I don't know enough about the matter to be definite about it.'

'If the head of Memphis's security guards himself has doubts, why should a judge not do so too? It is not his first duty to accept received opinions.'

'Of course,' murmured Mentmose.

'Incompetent people are not appointed in Memphis. Pazair was undoubtedly noticed because of his good qualities.'

'Indeed, Tjaty, but the atmosphere of a great city, ambition, too much power . . . The young man may carry too great a responsibility.'

'We shall see,' declared Bagey. 'If he does, I shall dismiss him. In the meantime, we shall allow him to continue. I am relying on you to assist him.' Bagey leant his head back and closed his eyes again.

Convinced that the tjaty was watching him through closed eyelids, Mentmose stood up, bowed and left. He would vent his anger on his servants.

Kani was sturdily built, with sun-browned skin. He arrived at Pazair's office just after dawn, and sat down outside the closed door, next to Way-Finder. Kani dreamt of owning a donkey. It would help him to carry heavy loads and relieve his back, which was worn out from the weight of the jars he used for watering the garden. Way-Finder listened attentively while Kani talked to him of days that were always the same, of his love for the earth, of the care he took when digging the irrigation channels, of his pleasure at seeing the plants flourish.

His confidences were interrupted by the sound of Pazair's brisk footsteps.

'Kani, did you want to see me?'

The gardener nodded.

'Come in.'

Kani hesitated. The judge's office scared him, as did the city. Far from the countryside, he felt ill at ease. Too much noise, too many nauseating smells, too many blocked horizons. If his future had not hung in the balance, he would never have ventured into the narrow streets of Memphis.

'I got lost ten times,' he explained.

'Are you having more problems with Qadash?'

'Yes.'

'What is he doing now?'

'I want to leave, and he won't let me.'

'Leave?'

'This year my garden produced three times more vegetables than the stipulated quantity, so I'm entitled to become an independent worker.'

Pazair nodded. 'That is certainly the law.'

'Qadash says it isn't.'

'Describe your piece of ground to me.'

Nebamon received Neferet in the shady gardens of his sumptuous home. Sitting under a blossoming acacia tree, he drank pink wine while a servant fanned him.

'Beautiful Neferet, how glad I am to see you.'

The young woman was primly dressed and wearing a short wig in the old style.

'You look very severe today,' said Nebamon. 'Isn't that dress long out of fashion?'

'You interrupted me in my work. Why did you summon me here?'

Nebamon told his servant to leave. Sure of his own charm, and convinced that the delightful setting would enchant Neferet, he had decided to offer her one last chance.

'You don't like me much, do you?' he said.

'Please answer my question.'

'Enjoy this lovely day, this delicious wine, the paradise we are living in. You are beautiful and intelligent, with a greater gift for medicine than the best-qualified of our doctors. But you have neither fortune nor experience, and without my help you'll vegetate in a village. At first, your moral strength will enable you to overcome the ordeal; but once you reach maturity you will regret your much-vaunted purity. A career cannot be built on idealism, Neferet.'

Arms folded, the young woman gazed silently across the garden to the small lake, where ducks were flapping among the lotus flowers.

'You will learn to love me,' Nebamon went on, 'and the way I conduct my affairs.'

'Your ambitions are no concern of mine.'

'You would make a worthy wife for Pharaoh's head doctor.'

'Don't deceive yourself.'

'I know a great deal about women.'

'Are you sure of that?'

Nebamon's charming smile hardened. 'Don't forget that I control your future.'

'My future is in the gods' hands, not yours.'

Nebamon rose to his feet, his expression grim. 'Leave the gods aside, and pay attention to what I say.'

'Don't rely on it.'

'This is my final warning.'

'May I return to my work?'

'According to the reports I have just received, your knowledge of preparing remedies is thoroughly inadequate.'

Neferet kept her composure. Unfolding her arms, she stared into her accuser's eyes and said, 'You know very well that isn't true.'

'The reports are quite clear.'

'Who wrote them?

'Men who value their jobs and deserve to be promoted for their vigilance. If you cannot prepare complex remedies, I cannot allow you to become part of an elite body. You know what that means, don't you? It will be impossible for you to progress in the medical profession. You will stagnate, unable to use the best that the workshops produce – they answer to me, and you will be denied access to them.'

Neferet said angrily, 'You are condemning sick people to death.'

'You are to refer your patients to more competent colleagues. When you can no longer bear the meaninglessness of your life, you will come crawling back to me.'

Denes's travelling chair was set down in front of Qadash's house while Pazair was speaking to the door keeper.

'Have you got toothache?' asked the door keeper.

'No, it's a legal problem.'

'You're lucky – I've got receding gums. Is Qadash in trouble with the law?'

'No,' said Pazair. 'It's just a simple detail which needs sorting out.'

The dentist with the red hands greeted his two clients, and asked, 'Who shall I start with?'

'Denes is your patient. As for me, I wish to speak to you about Kani.'

'My gardener?'

'Not any more. His work gives him the right to independence.'

'Rubbish! He's my employee and that's how he'll stay.'

'Place your seal upon this document.'

'I refuse.' Qadash's voice was unsteady.

'In that case, I shall instigate court proceedings against you.'

Denes intervened. 'Let's not lose our tempers. Let the gardener leave, Qadash; I'll find you another one.'

'It's a question of principle,' protested Qadash.

'A good compromise is better than a bad court case. Forget about Kani.'

With bad grace, Qadash followed Denes's advice.

Sekhem was a small town in the Delta, surrounded by wheat fields; its college of priests was devoted to the mysteries of the god Horus, the falcon whose wings were as vast as the skies.

Neferet was received by the High Priest, a friend of Branir, whom she had told about her exclusion from the official body of doctors. The priest allowed her to enter the shrine containing a statue of the jackal-headed god, Anubis, who had revealed the secrets of mummification and opened the gates of the afterlife to the souls of the righteous. He transformed inert flesh into a body composed of light.

Neferet walked round the statue. On the pillar at its back she found a long text in hieroglyphics, a treatise on the treatment of infectious diseases and the purification of lymph. She engraved it in her memory. Branir had decided to instruct her in a healing art to which Nebamon would never have access.

It had been an exhausting day. Pazair was relaxing, enjoying the peaceful evening on Branir's terrace. Brave, who had watched over the office all day, was also taking a well-deserved rest. The dying light crossed the sky and reached the very edges of the horizon.

'How is your investigation going?' asked Branir.

'The army's trying to snuff it out. What's more, someone's plotting against me.'

'Who's behind all this?'

'I can't help suspecting General Asher.'

'You mustn't have preconceived ideas.'

'I can't make any more progress because I'm being smothered under a mass of administrative documents which have to be dealt with straight away. This sudden increase is probably due to Mentmose. I was planning to go to Thebes, but I had to give up the idea.'

'Mentmose is a dangerous man. He's destroyed many people's careers to strengthen his own.'

'At least I've made one man happy – Kani the gardener. He's become a free worker and has already left Memphis for the South.'

'He used to supply me with medicinal plants. An awkward character, but he loves his work. No doubt Qadash objected to your involvement?'

'He listened to Denes's advice and bowed before the law.'

'He had no choice,' said Branir drily.

'Denes claims he has learnt his lesson.'

'He's first and foremost a businessman.'

'Do you think he really has turned over a new leaf?'

'Most men act in their own best interests.'

After a pause, Pazair asked, 'Have you seen Neferet lately?'

'Nebamon is still trying to keep his hold over her. He asked her to marry him.'

Pazair froze. Brave raised concerned eyes to his master's face. 'Did she refuse?'

'Neferet is gentle and loving, but no one will force her to act against her will.'

'She did refuse, didn't she?'

Branir smiled. 'Can you imagine Nebamon and Neferet as a couple, even for a moment?'

Pazair could not hide his relief. Reassured, the dog went back to sleep.

'Nebamon wants to force her into submission,' Branir went on. 'On the basis of false reports, he has declared her incompetent and expelled her from the body of qualified doctors.'

Pazair clenched his fists. 'I shall discredit those reports.'

'You'd have no chance of winning. A lot of doctors and remedy makers are in Nebamon's pay, and will uphold their lies.'

'She must be desperate.'

'She has decided to leave Memphis and set herself up in a village near Thebes.'

18

'We're going to Thebes after all,' Pazair told Way-Finder.

The donkey greeted the news with satisfaction, but when Iarrot saw the preparations for the journey, he was worried.

'Will you be gone long?' he asked.

'I don't know.'

'Where can I reach you if I need to?'

'Just put the cases to one side for me.'

'But—'

'And do try to be punctual. Your daughter won't suffer if you are.'

Kem lived near the workshops where weapons were made. He had an apartment in a two-storey building containing ten two- and three-roomed apartments. Today was his rest day, so Pazair hoped to find him at home.

The baboon opened the door, its eyes unblinking.

The main room was full of knives, spears and slingshots. Kem looked up from the bow he was repairing.

'What are you doing here?' he asked.

'Is your travelling bag packed and ready?'

'I thought you'd decided not to go.'

'I've changed my mind.'

'I'm at your command.'

Slingshot, spear, dagger, club, cudgel, axe, rectangular wooden shield: Suti had wielded all these weapons for three days with great dexterity. He had shown the assurance of an experienced soldier, and had drawn grudging admiration from the officers charged with training the recruits.

At the end of the trial period, the candidates for the military life were gathered together in the great courtyard of the main barracks in Memphis. On one side were stables containing horses, which observed the spectacle with curiosity; in the centre was an enormous reservoir of water.

Suti had visited the stables. They were built on pebbled pavements criss-crossed with channels along which dirty water could run away. The horsemen and charioteers pampered their charges, seeing that they were well-fed, clean and beautifully groomed, and had the best possible living conditions. The young man also approved of the soldiers' living quarters, which were shaded by a row of trees.

But he remained allergic to discipline. Three days of orders and being shouted at by junior officers had destroyed his taste for uniformed adventure.

The recruitment ceremony took place according to strict rules. First, an officer addressed the volunteers and tried to persuade them to enlist by describing the joys that awaited them in the army. Security, respectability and a comfortable retirement featured among the main benefits. Bearers held aloft the standards of the principal regiments dedicated to the gods Amon, Ra, Ptah and Set. A royal scribe got ready to register the names of the men enlisting. Behind him stood baskets piled high with food; the generals were hosting a banquet, with ample supplies of beef, poultry, vegetables and fruit.

'What a fine life we're going to have,' whispered one of Suti's companions.

'Not me.'

'Aren't you enlisting?'

'I prefer freedom.'

'You're mad. According to the captain, you have the best chance of promotion of any of us. You'd get a good posting straight away.'

'I'm looking for adventure, not slavery.'

'I'd think carefully if I were you.'

A messenger from the palace hurried across the courtyard, carrying a papyrus. He showed it to the royal scribe, who stood up and issued a few brief orders. In less than a minute all the gates of the barracks had been closed.

Murmurs rose from the ranks of volunteers.

'Quiet!' ordered the officer who had given the speech. 'We have just received orders. By Pharaoh's decree, you are all enlisted. Some will join provincial barracks, others will leave tomorrow for Asia.'

'It must be a state of emergency or a war,' said Suti's companion.

'I don't give a damn.'

'Don't be a fool. If you try to run away, you'll be treated as a deserter.'

That argument carried weight. Suti weighed up his chances of getting over the wall and disappearing into the neighbouring streets: they were non-existent. He was no longer at the scribes' school, but in a barracks full of archers and spear throwers.

One by one, the conscripted men walked past the royal scribe, whose welcoming smile had been replaced by an expression of cold efficiency.

'Suti . . . excellent results. Posting: Asian army. You are to be an archer, alongside the officer commanding the corps of charioteers. You leave tomorrow at dawn. Next.'

Suti saw his name written down on a tablet. Now desertion was impossible, unless he spent the rest of his life abroad and never saw Egypt or Pazair again. He was condemned to become a hero.

'Will I be under General Asher's command?' he asked.

The scribe looked up in annoyance. 'I said: next.'

Suti was given a shirt, a tunic, a cloak, a breastplate, leather leg-protectors, a cap, a small two-edged axe, and a long acacia-wood bow, thick at its centre and tapering towards the ends. It took great strength to draw, and could shoot arrows a hundred paces in a straight line, or two hundred in an arc.

'What about the banquet?' he asked the supply officer.

'Here is some bread, a pound of dried meat, some oil and some figs. Eat, drink some water from the tank, and get some sleep. Tomorrow, you'll be eating dust.'

On the boat on which Pazair and Kem travelled south, all talk was of Ramses' decree, which had been spread abroad by many heralds. Pharaoh had ordered that all the temples were to be purified, that lists were to be made of all the country's treasures and grain reserves, that offerings to the gods were to be doubled and that a military expedition was to be sent into Asia.

Rumour had multiplied these measures, and there was talk of imminent disaster, armed disturbances in the towns, rebellion in the provinces and an impending Hittite invasion. Like the other judges, Pazair must ensure that public order was maintained.

'Wouldn't it have been better to stay in Memphis?' asked Kem.

'Our journey won't take long. The village headmen will tell us that the two ex-soldiers were killed in an accident, and have already been mummified and buried.'

'You don't sound very optimistic.'

'Five men fell to their deaths: that's the official version.'

'But you don't believe it.'

'Do you?'

'What does that matter? If war's declared, I'll be called up again.'

'Ramses is advocating peace with the Hittites and the Asian princedoms.'

'They'll never give up their plans to invade Egypt,' said Kem.

'But our army's too strong for them.'

'Then why this Asian expedition and these extreme security measures?'

'I'm puzzled, too. Perhaps the problem's to do with internal security.'

'The country is rich and happy, the king is loved by his people, everyone has enough to eat, and the roads are safe. There's no threat of unrest.'

'I agree, but Pharaoh seems to think somewhat differently.'

The air whipped their cheeks. The sail had been lowered, and the boat was using the current. Dozens of other boats were sailing up and down the Nile, obliging the captain and his crew to be permanently watchful.

Not long after they had passed Meidum, a fast boat belonging to the river guards caught up with them, and ordered them to slow down. A guard grabbed the rigging and jumped on to the deck.

'Is Judge Pazair among the passengers?' he asked.

'Yes, here I am.'

'I must take you back to Memphis.'

'Why?'

'A complaint has been lodged against you.'

Suti was the last man up and dressed. The officer in charge of the barrack room ordered him to hurry and make up for lost time.

The young man had been dreaming of Sababu, of her caresses and her kisses. She had shown him undreamt-of paths to ecstasy, which he was determined to explore again before too long.

Watched enviously by the other recruits, Suti climbed into a war chariot, driven by an impressively muscular officer aged about forty.

'Hold on tight, my lad,' he advised Suti.

Scarcely had Suti slipped his left wrist into a retaining strap when the officer whipped his horses into a gallop. The chariot was the first one to leave the barracks and head north.

'Have you fought before, youngster?'

'I've fought scribes, sir' said Suti.

'Did you kill them?'

'I don't think so.'

'Don't worry, I'm going to offer you much better fare.'

'Where are we going, sir?'

'Straight to the enemy. We cross the Delta, follow the coast, and then come up against the Syrians and the Hittites. I think this decree's a splendid one. It's a long time since I trampled on one of those barbarians. Draw your bow.'

'Aren't you going to slow down?'

'A good archer can hit his target even in the worst conditions.'

'What happens if I miss?'

'I'll cut your retaining strap and send you tumbling down into the dust.'

'Sir, why are you so ruthless?'

'Ten Asian campaigns, five wounds, two Golden Fly awards for bravery, congratulations from Ramses himself – is that enough for you?

'There's no room for error?'

'Either you win or you lose,' said the officer. 'Now, instead of talking, hit that acacia over there, that one in the distance.'

Becoming a hero was going to be be more difficult than Suti had realized. He took a deep breath, drew his bow as far as it would go, forgot the chariot, the jolting and the bumpy road. The arrow shot up into the sky, described a graceful arc, and plunged into the trunk of the tree, which the chariot passed at top speed.

'Well done, young lad!'

Suti let out a long sigh. 'How many archers have you thrown into the dust, sir?' he asked.

'I've stopped counting – I loathe amateurs. This evening I'll buy you a drink.'

'In the tent?'

'Officers and their assistants are allowed to go to the inn.'

'And ... what about women?'

The officer gave Suti a hearty thump on the back. 'You were born to be in the army, my lad. After the wine, we'll have a little game or two with the women, which will empty our purses.'

Suti kissed his bow. Luck hadn't deserted him after all.

Pazair sat in his office, brooding. He had underestimated his enemies' capacity to strike back. On one hand, they wanted to stop him leaving Memphis and making enquiries in Thebes; on the other, they wanted to have him dismissed, so as to put an end to his investigations once and for all. So Pazair had indeed stumbled upon a murder – or, rather, upon several.

Alas, it was too late now to do anything about them. Just as he had feared, Sababu, acting under Mentmose's instructions, had accused him of debauchery. The governing body of judges would condemn Pazair for leading a dissolute life, which was incompatible with his office.

Kem came in, his head hanging low.

'Have you found Suti?' asked Pazair.

'He's been conscripted into the army fighting in Asia.'

'Has he left?'

'Yes, as an archer on a war chariot.'

'So the only witness who can prove my innocence is out of reach.'

'I could take his place.'

'No, Kem. It would be shown that you weren't at Sababu's ale-house, and you'd be convicted of perjury.'

'I hate seeing you slandered like this.'

'I was wrong to lift the veil that's been hiding these crimes.'

'If no one, not even a judge, can tell the truth, what's the point of living?'

Pazair was touched by the Nubian's concern, and said, 'I shan't give up, but I shall have to find proof.'

'They'll find a way to silence you.'

'I shan't let them.'

'I'll be right beside you, and so will Killer.'

The two men embraced.

The case was heard under the wooden porch in front of the palace, two days after Pazair's return. It was heard so quickly because of the accused man's position: if a judge was suspected of breaking the law, the case required immediate investigation.

Pazair had not hoped for indulgence on the part of the Judge of the Porch, but he was stunned by the sheer extent of the plot when he saw the members of the jury: Denes and Nenophar, Mentmose, a scribe from the palace and a priest from the Temple of Ptah. His enemies were in the majority, and, if the scribe and the priest were their allies, perhaps unanimous.

The Judge of the Porch sat at the back of the audience chamber, wearing a pleated kilt, his head shaven, his expression cold. At his feet lay a sycamore-wood cubit, signifying the presence of Ma'at. The jurors sat on his left; to his right was a clerk. Behind Pazair were many onlookers.

'Are you Judge Pazair?' began the Judge of the Porch.

'I am. I officiate at Memphis.'

'And your staff includes a scribe named Iarrot?'

'It does.'

'Bring forward the accuser.'

An alliance between Iarrot and Sababu? Pazair would never have foreseen that. So he had been betrayed by his closest colleague.

But the woman who stepped into the audience chamber was not Sababu but a short, heavily built brunette with an unattractive face.

'You are the wife of Iarrot the clerk?' asked the Judge.

'I am indeed,' she replied, in a bitter, rather stupid voice.

'Set out your accusations. And remember that you are speaking under oath.'

'My husband drinks beer – far too much beer, especially in the evenings. For a week now, he's been insulting me and beating me in the presence of our daughter. She's afraid, the poor child. I've been hit; a doctor has seen the marks.'

'Do you know Judge Pazair?'

'Only by name.'

'What do you ask of the court?'

'That my husband and his employer, who is responsible for his morals, are sentenced. I want two new dresses, ten sacks of grain and five roasted geese. Twice that, if Iarrot starts beating me again.'

Pazair was astounded.

'Bring forward the principal defendant,' ordered the Judge.

Iarrot obeyed, shamefacedly. His face even redder than usual, he presented his defence. 'My wife provokes me, and she refuses to cook my meals. I didn't mean to hit her – it was an unfortunate reaction. You must understand that I work very hard for Judge Pazair. The hours are dreadful, and there are so many cases to deal with that there really ought to be another scribe.'

'Would you object to that, Judge Pazair?'

'Those statements are untrue. We do indeed have a lot of work, but I have respected Iarrot's situation, accepted his family problems, and allowed him to vary his working hours.'

'Are there any witnesses who can confirm what you say?'

'People who live in the area, I suppose.'

The Judge of the Porch turned to Iarrot. 'Are we to call them, and do you dispute what Judge Pazair has said?'

'No . . . no, I don't. But all the same, I wasn't entirely in the wrong.'

'Judge Pazair, did you know that your clerk was beating his wife?'

'No.'

'You are responsible for your employees' moral standards.'

'I do not deny that.'

'Through negligence, you omitted to check Iarrot's moral character.'

'I had no time to do so.'

'Negligence is the only correct term.'

The Judge of the Porch had Pazair at his mercy. He asked the main participants if they wished to speak again; only Iarrot's agitated wife repeated her accusations.

The jury convened.

Pazair felt almost like laughing. Being condemned because of a domestic dispute – who could have imagined it? Iarrot's spinelessness and his wife's stupidity were unforeseen traps, which his adversaries were making the most of. The legal niceties would be respected, and he would be dismissed without the need for recourse to violence.

The jury's deliberations lasted less than an hour.

The Judge of the Porch announced the outcome, his expression as sour as ever.

'By unanimous decision, Iarrot the clerk is found guilty of bad conduct towards his wife. He is sentenced to give the victim what she asks for and to receive thirty strokes of the rod. If he offends again, a divorce will be immediately pronounced, with him as the guilty party. Does the accused protest against the sentence?'

Iarrot was only too happy to have escaped so lightly – the law dealt severely with brutes who mistreated women – and bared his back for punishment. He whimpered and snivelled under the rod; afterwards, a guard took him away to the local hospital.

The Judge of the Porch continued, 'By unanimous verdict, Judge Pazair is acquitted. The court advises him not to dismiss his scribe but to give him a chance to mend his ways.'

Mentmose merely acknowledged Pazair with a nod; he was in a hurry, as he was sitting on another jury which had been convened to judge a thief.

Denes and his wife – the latter wearing a many-coloured dress which was the talk of Memphis – offered the young judge their congratulations.

'It was a grotesque accusation,' said Nenophar emphatically.

'Any court would have acquitted you,' said Denes. 'We need judges like you in Memphis.'

'That's true,' agreed Nenophar. 'Business can only develop in a peaceful, just society. Your steadfastness impressed us greatly – my husband and I admire men of courage. From now on, we shall consult you if there are any legal problems in the way we conduct our business.'

19

After a swift and uneventful journey, the boat carrying Judge Pazair, Way-Finder, Brave, Kem, Killer and a few other passengers, came within sight of Thebes. Everyone fell silent.

On the left bank stood the holy temples of Karnak and Luxor. Behind high walls, sheltered from unworthy eyes, a small number of men and women worshipped the gods night and day, beseeching them to remain upon the earth. Acacias and tamarisks shaded the rows of stone rams leading to the huge pillared gateways that led into the temples.

This time, the river guards had not intercepted the boat. Pazair was to see his native province again; since he had left, he had endured trials, had been toughened up and, above all, had found love.

Neferet had not been out of his thoughts for an instant. He had lost his appetite, and was having more and more trouble concentrating; at night, he kept his eyes open, hoping to see her emerge from the darkness. His distraction was plunging him deeper and deeper into a void which was eating him away from the inside. Only the woman he loved could cure him, but could she understand his sickness? Neither gods nor priests could give him back his taste for life, no triumph could drive away his pain, no book could calm it.

Thebes, the city where Neferet was hiding, was his last hope.

Pazair was disheartened and no longer had any faith in his investigation: the plot had been woven perfectly. Whatever his suspicions, he would not reach the truth. Just before leaving Memphis, he had learnt that the head guard of the Sphinx had been buried, because, as General Asher's mission in Asia had no time limit, the military authorities had thought it best not to defer the funeral ceremonies. Was it really the guard's body in the tomb, or was it another corpse? Was the missing man still alive, hidden somewhere? Pazair would never know.

The boat tied up, just before the temple at Luxor.

'We're being watched,' said Kem quietly. 'A young fellow up in the bows. He was the last one to embark.'

'Let's see if he follows us – we can lose him in the town.'

The man did indeed follow them.

'Do you think he's one of Mentmose's men?' asked Kem.

'Probably.'

'Do you want me to get rid of him for you?'

'I've got a better idea.'

The judge headed for a main guard post, where he was greeted by a fat official whose office was filled with baskets of fruit and pastries.

'You were born in this region, weren't you?' the official asked.

'Yes, in a village on the west bank. I've been appointed to Memphis, where I had the privilege of meeting your superior, Mentmose.'

'And now you've come back.'

'Only for a short stay.'

'Business or pleasure?'

'I'm looking into the wood tax.* My predecessor left me some incomplete and rather obscure notes on this vital point.'

The fat man swallowed a few raisins. 'Is Memphis short of firewood?'

'Not at all. The winter was mild, and we didn't use up all our reserves. But I'm not sure that the rota of branch cutters is being managed properly – there are too many Memphites, and not enough Thebans. I'd like to consult your lists, village by village, in order to identify the people who are defrauding the system. Some don't want to collect small sticks, brush-wood and palm fibres and carry them to the sorting and redistribution centres. It's time to take action, don't you think?'

'Indeed, indeed.'

The official had had a letter from Mentmose, alerting him to Pazair's arrival and describing the judge as formidable, keen and over-curious. In place of that daunting individual, the fat man found a pernickety man preoccupied with minor details.

'The respective quantities of wood provided by the North and South speak volumes,' continued Pazair, 'and at Thebes the dried tree stumps aren't being correctly cut. Is there an illegal trade?'

'It's possible.'

'Please be good enough to register the object of my investigation locally.'

'I'll see to it.'

When the fat man received a visit from the young guard charged with following Pazair, he told him of the conversation. The two agreed that the judge had lost his original motivation and was sinking into routine. This sensible attitude would spare them a great deal of trouble.

*

*Wood was quite a rare material in Egypt, so its value was considerable.

The shadow-eater was wary of the monkey and the dog, perceptive creatures which could sense evil intentions, and spied on Pazair and Kem from a distance.

By giving up following them, the young guard – who was no doubt one of Mentmose's men – had made the task easier. If the judge got close to his goal, the shadow-eater would have to take action; otherwise, observation would be enough.

The orders were quite clear, and the shadow-eater never disobeyed orders. No one would be killed unless it was absolutely necessary. It was Pazair's persistence that had led to the death of the head guard's wife.

After the incident at the Sphinx, the ex-soldier had taken refuge in the little village on the west bank where he had been born. He would spend a happy retirement there, after his loyal service in the army. The story of the accident suited him perfectly. At his age, why should he fight a battle that was lost from the outset?

Since his return, he had repaired the bread oven and taken on the job of baker, much to the villagers' satisfaction. After ridding the grain of its impurities by sieving it, the women broke it up on the millstone and crushed it in a mortar, using long-handled pestles. This produced a coarse flour, which was then refined several times. The women then moistened it, producing a dough to which they added yeast. Some used a wide-necked jar to knead the dough, while others laid it out on a flagstone, angled to make it easier for the water to run off.

The baker then stepped in, baking the simplest loaves on hot coals and the more elaborate ones in an oven made of three vertical stone slabs covered by a horizontal slab, under which the fire was lit. He also used perforated moulds for cakes and stone platters, on which he placed the dough, to prepare round or oblong loaves, or hotcakes. Sometimes he shaped it into little animals, which the children loved.

He had forgotten the sounds of fighting and the cries of the wounded. The song of the flames was sweet to him, and he loved the softness of hot loaves. He still had the authoritarian nature of a military man, though. When he was heating the platters, he drove away the women and would allow no one near him but his assistant, a sturdy lad of fifteen, his adopted son, who would succeed him.

This morning the boy was late. The baker was getting annoyed, when he heard footsteps on the paved floor of the bakery. He turned round.

'I'm going to . . . Who are you?'

'I'm here to take your assistant's place. He has a bad headache.'

'You don't live in the village.'

'I work with another baker, half an hour from here. The headman of the village told me to come.'

'Very well. Then help me.'

The oven was deep, so the baker had to lean his head and shoulders inside in order to push the maximum number of moulds and loaves right to the back. His assistant held on to his hips, so as to pull him back out if anything went wrong.

The ex-soldier thought he was safe, but the shadow-eater knew that this very day Judge Pazair was to visit the village. He would find out the baker's true identity and would interrogate him. The shadow-eater had no choice. He seized the baker by his ankles, lifted them off the ground, and pushed him deep inside the oven.

The entrance to the little town was deserted. Not one woman stood at her front door, not one man dozed under a tree, not a single child was playing with a wooden doll. Pazair was certain that something unusual had happened, and he told Kem to stay where he was. The baboon and the dog looked around in all directions.

Pazair hurried down the main street, which was lined with single-storey houses.

Every inhabitant was gathered round the bakery oven. People were shouting, jostling each other, and calling upon the gods. A young lad was explaining for the tenth time that he had been knocked unconscious as he came out of his house on his way to work. He blamed himself for the terrible accident to his adoptive father, and was weeping copiously.

Pazair pushed through the crowd. 'What has happened?' he asked.

'Our baker has just died in the most horrible way,' replied the village headman. 'He must have slipped and fallen into his oven. Usually, his assistant holds on to his legs to prevent such a thing happening.'

'Was he an ex-soldier who recently returned from Memphis?'

'He was indeed.'

'Was anyone present when this ... accident happened?'

'No. Why are you asking all these questions?'

'I am Judge Pazair, and I came here to question the unfortunate man.'

'What about?'

'That is not important.'

A hysterical woman seized Pazair's arm. 'It was the night demons who killed him, because he agreed to deliver bread – our bread – to Hattusa, the foreign woman who rules the harem.'

The judge pushed her gently aside, but she went on, 'If your job is to see that justice is done, avenge our baker and arrest that she-devil!'

Pazair and Kem ate their lunch in the countryside, beside a well. Killer delicately peeled some sweet onions. He was beginning to accept the judge's presence, and to be less aggressive. Brave feasted on fresh bread and cucumber, while Way-Finder munched fodder.

Edgily, the judge hugged a goatskin bag of fresh water. 'One accident and five dead men! The army lied, Kem. Its report was falsified.'

'It could be a simple administrative error.'

'No, it's a murder, another murder.'

'There's no proof. The baker had an accident – it's happened before.'

'A murderer got here before us, because he knew we were coming to the village. No one should have found the fourth guard, no one should have taken an interest in this matter.'

'Don't look into it any further. What you've unearthed is probably a settling of scores between soldiers.'

'If justice gives up, violence will rule in Pharaoh's place.'

'Isn't your life more important than the law?'

'No,' said Pazair.

'You're the most single-minded man I've ever met.'

How wrong the Nubian was! Pazair could not drive Neferet from his thoughts, even in these moments of high drama. Following this last murder, which had confirmed that his suspicions were well-founded, he ought to have been concentrating on his investigation. Instead, love, as strong as the south wind, had swept away all his resolution. He stood up and leant against the well, his eyes closed.

'Do you feel ill?' asked Kem.

'It will pass.'

'The fourth guard was still alive until a little while ago,' Kem reminded him. 'What about the fifth?'

'If we could question him, we'd solve the mystery.'

'I'm sure his village isn't far away.'

'We shan't go there.'

The Nubian smiled. 'At last you're seeing reason.'

'We shan't go because we're being followed and someone will get there before us. The baker was murdered because we came here. If the fifth guard is still in the land of the living, we'll condemn him to death if we carry on like this.'

'Then what do you suggest?'

'I don't know yet. For the moment, we shall return to Thebes. The person or persons watching us will think we are straying from the right path.'

Pazair examined the results of the previous year's wood tax. The fat official opened up his archives and guzzled carob juice. It was obvious that the little judge was of no account. While Pazair consulted large numbers of accounting tablets, the Theban official wrote a letter to Mentmose, reassuring him that the young man was not going to ruffle any feathers.

Despite the comfortable room he had been provided with, Pazair spent a sleepless night, torn between the obsessive desire to see Neferet again and the need to continue his enquiries. To see her again, even though she was indifferent to him; to continue his enquiries, even though the matter was already dead and buried.

Sensing his master's turmoil, Brave lay down next to him. The dog's warmth gave him the energy he needed. Pazair stroked the dog, thinking of the walks he had taken along the Nile when he was a carefree young man; he'd then been convinced he was going to lead a peaceful existence in his village, where life followed the rhythm of the seasons.

Destiny had seized him like a merciless bird of prey. If he gave up his mad dreams – Neferet, the truth – would he regain his peace of mind?

He lied to himself in vain. Neferet would be his only love.

Dawn brought him a glimmer of hope. There was one man who might be able to help him.

So he went to the quayside, where a large market was held each day. As soon as the foodstuffs had been unloaded from the boats, the sellers laid them out on their little stalls. Men and women ran open-air shops selling a wide variety of foods, fabrics, clothes and a thousand and one other things.

Under the reed awning of one stall, some sailors were drinking beer and ogling the pretty housewives as they came to see what was new. A fisherman, sitting in front of a plaited reed basket containing Nile perch, exchanged some fine fish for a small pot of unguent. A pastry cook bartered cakes for a necklace and a pair of sandals, while a grocer swapped beans for a broom. Each transaction involved much haggling before a compromise was reached. If the debate centred on the weight of the goods, the matter was referred to a scribe with a set of scales.

At last, Pazair saw him.

As he had thought, Kani was there, selling chickpeas, cucumbers and leeks.

The baboon suddenly pulled at its leash with unexpected force and hurled itself on a thief whom nobody had noticed stealing two succulent lettuces. The monkey sank its teeth into the offender's thigh and he, roaring with pain, tried in vain to fight off his attacker. Kem intervened so that Killer did not rip the flesh to shreds, and the thief was handed over to two guards.

'You're always coming to my rescue, Judge,' remarked the gardener.

'I need your help, Kani.'

'In two hours I'll have sold everything. We'll go to my house then.'

The vegetable garden was bordered by cornflowers, man-dragora and chrysanthemums. Kani had created neat beds for each type of vegetable: beans, chickpeas, lentils, cucumbers, onions, leeks, lettuces, fenugreek. At the far end of the garden was a palm grove, protecting it from the wind; to its left were a vineyard and an orchard. Kani delivered most of his produce to the temple and sold his surplus at the market.

'Are you happy with your new life?' asked Pazair.

'The work's as hard as ever, but at least I'm reaping the rewards. The steward at the temple likes me.'

'Do you grow medicinal plants?'

'Come with me.'

Kani showed Pazair his proudest creation: a bed of simples, curative herbs and plants from which remedies could be made. Purple loosestrife, mustard, pyrethrum, pennyroyal and camomile were just a few examples.

'Did you know that Neferet is living in Thebes?' asked Pazair.

'Oh no, Judge, not now. She has an important job in Memphis.'

'Nebamon dismissed her from it.'

Intense anger showed in Kani's face. 'He dared . . . that crocodile dared!'

'Neferet no longer belongs to the official body of doctors and no longer has access to the great medicinal workshops. She must confine herself to a village and send seriously ill patients to more highly qualified colleagues.'

Kani almost pawed the ground in his fury. 'That's shameful, unjust!'

'You could help her.'

The gardener looked up questioningly. 'How?'

'If you supply her with rare and expensive medicinal plants, she'll be able to prepare remedies and cure her patients. We'll all fight to restore her reputation.'

'Where is she?'

'I don't know.'

'I'll find her,' said Kani determinedly. 'Is that what you wanted me to do?'

'No.'

'Then what is it?'

'I'm looking for a man who used to be in the Sphinx's honour guard. He's returned to his home, on the west bank, to live out his retirement. He is in hiding.'

'Why?'

'Because he has a secret. If he talks to me, his life will be in danger. I was going to speak to one of his fellow guardsmen, who had become a baker, but he was killed in an accident.'

'What do you want me to do?'

'Find him. Then I shall act – with the utmost discretion. Someone's watching me, so if I search for the man myself, he'll be murdered before I can speak to him.'

'Murdered!' echoed Kani.

'I shan't conceal the gravity of the situation, or the risks you'll be running.'

'You're a judge, so can't you –'

'I have no proof, and I'm involved in a matter which the army has covered up.'

'But what if you're wrong?'

'When I hear the guard's testimony – if he's still alive – all doubts will be dispelled.'

'I know the towns and villages on the west bank very well.'

'Be very careful,' warned Pazair. 'The murderer kills without hesitation and doesn't care about losing his soul.'

Kani smiled and said, 'Just this once, allow me to be the judge.'

At the end of every week, Denes held a reception to thank the captains of his cargo boats and a few senior officials who were especially willing to sign shipping, loading and unloading permits. Everyone loved the splendour of the vast garden, with its lakes and its aviary full of exotic birds. Denes went from one guest to another, exchanging friendly words and asking after their families, while Nenophar strutted about.

This evening, the atmosphere was less cheerful than usual. Ramses' decree had caused anxiety among the ruling elite. Some suspected others of having confidential information and keeping it to themselves. Denes, flanked by two colleagues whose business he was planning to absorb after buying up their boats, greeted a rare guest: Sheshi. He spent most of his life in the most secret workshop at the palace, and had little time for fraternizing with the nobility. A short man, with a sombre, rather unattractive face, he was said to be skilful and modest.

'Your presence honours us, dear friend,' said Denes.

A half-smile twitched on Sheshi's lips.

'What was the outcome of your latest experiments? Mum's the word, of course, but everyone's talking about them. They say you've created an extraordinary fusion of metals that will enable us to make unbreakable swords and spears.'

Sheshi shook his head doubtfully.

'Ah, obviously it's a military secret. Well, do your best to succeed. With what's in store for us . . .'

'What does that mean?' asked another guest.

'If Pharaoh's decree is to be believed, a fine old war. Ramses wants to crush the Hittites and rid us of the Asian princelings who are always rebelling against us.'

'But Ramses loves peace,' objected the captain of a merchant vessel.

'That may be the official position, but his actions speak differently.'

'That's very worrying.'

'Not at all,' said Denes. 'Who and what is there for Egypt to fear?'

'Some people are saying the decree shows that Ramses' power is weakening.'

Denes burst out laughing. 'Ramses is the greatest of all and he will remain so. Let's not turn a minor incident into a tragedy.'

'All the same, we ought to check our food reserves.'

Nenophar cut in, 'It's obvious what ought to be done: prepare for a new tax and fiscal reform.'

'Rearmament has to be financed,' added Denes. 'If he wanted to, Sheshi could tell us about it, and justify Ramses' decision.'

All eyes were turned on Sheshi, but he said nothing.

Ever the accomplished hostess, Nenophar guided her guests to a pavilion where refreshments were being served.

Mentmose took Denes by the arm and led him aside. 'Your problems with the law are over, I hope?'

'Pazair didn't press the point. He's more reasonable than I thought. He's young and full of ambition, certainly, but there's nothing wrong with that, is there? You and I both went through that stage, before we became leading citizens.'

Mentmose frowned. 'His whole personality . . .'

'It will improve with time.'

'You're an optimist.'

'No, a realist. Pazair is a good judge.'

'And an incorruptible one, according to you.'

'An incorruptible and intelligent judge who respects those who observe the law. Thanks to men like him, business is prosperous and the country is at peace. What more could anyone want? Believe me, dear friend, you should look favourably upon Pazair's career.'

'That's valuable advice.'

'There'll be no malpractice from him.'

'That's certainly an important point.'

'But you still have reservations.'

'He sometimes alarms me a bit. He doesn't seem to appreciate subtlety.'

'That's just his youth and inexperience,' said Denes. 'What does the Judge of the Porch think of him?'

'He agrees with you.'

'You see!'

The news Mentmose had received from Thebes by special messenger confirmed what Denes said. Mentmose need not have worried for nothing: the judge was concerned merely with the wood tax and the honesty of those paying it.

Perhaps he ought not to have alerted the tjaty so soon. But one could never take too many precautions.

20

Going on long country walks with Way-Finder and Brave, consulting documents in the government offices, drawing up an accurate list of those liable to pay the wood tax, inspecting villages, having administrative discussions with headmen and landowners. That was how Pazair spent his days in Thebes.

Each day ended with a visit to Kani, and each day the gardener's head hung low, and Pazair could tell that he had found neither Neferet nor the fifth ex-soldier.

A week passed. The officials in Mentmose's pay sent him routine reports about the judge's activities. Kem simply patrolled the markets and arrested thieves. Soon it would be time to return to Memphis.

Pazair crossed a palm grove, took an earthen track beside the irrigation channel, and went down the steps leading to Kani's garden. When dusk approached, Kani tended his medicinal plants, which needed regular careful attention. He slept in a hut after spending part of the night watering the plants.

The garden was deserted.

Surprised, Pazair walked round it, then tried the door of the hut. It was open. He sat down on a low wall and watched the sun go down. The full moon turned the river to silver. As time passed, anxiety clutched at his heart. Perhaps Kani had identified the fifth guard. Perhaps he had been followed. Perhaps . . . Pazair reproached himself for involving the gardener in an investigation that was beyond his skill. If something bad had happened to Kani, he would consider himself chiefly responsible.

Even when he felt the cool air of night on his shoulders, the judge did not move. He would stay there until dawn, and then he would know Kani wasn't coming back. Teeth clenched, muscles aching, Pazair deeply regretted his actions.

A boat was coming across the river.

Pazair got up and ran to the bank. 'Kani!'

The gardener moored the boat to a stake, and slowly climbed up the slope.

'Why are you so late back?' asked Pazair.

'Are you shivering?'

'Yes, I'm cold.'

'The spring wind makes people ill. Let's go into the hut.'

The gardener sat down on a tree stump, his back propped against the wooden wall, and Pazair sat on a tool chest.

'Any news of the guard?'

'No, still nothing.'

'Were you in any danger?'

'Never. I buy rare plants here and there, and I gossip with the old folk.'

Pazair asked the question that was burning on his lips. 'What about Neferet?'

'I didn't see her, but I know where she's living.'

Sheshi's workshop occupied three large rooms in the basement of a building attached to the barracks. The regiment lodged there contained only support soldiers who built earthworks. Everyone thought Sheshi worked at the palace, but he carried out his real research in these discreet surroundings. To outward appearances, there were no particular security measures, but anyone who tried to walk down the staircase into the basement would be roughly intercepted and questioned.

Sheshi had been recruited by the palace because he was exceptionally knowledgeable about the resistance of materials. Originally a bronze worker, he had continually sought better ways of handling raw copper, which was vital for manufacturing stone-cutters' chisels. Because of his success and dedication, he had been promoted again and again. The day he had provided remarkably good tools to cut stone blocks for Ramses' Temple of a Million Years, his reputation had reached the ears of the king.

Sheshi had summoned his three principal colleagues, all of them mature and experienced. Lamps with smokeless wicks lit the basement. Slowly and meticulously, Sheshi set out the papyri on which he had noted down his latest calculations.

The three men waited uneasily. His silence did not augur well, even though it was usual for him not to say very much. This sudden and urgent summons was not at all like him.

The little man turned his back on the others and asked, 'Which one of you talked?'

No one replied.

'I shall not repeat my question.'

'It has no meaning.

'When I was at a reception, a prominent citizen talked about new fusions of metals and new weapons.'

'That's impossible! Whoever says that is lying to you.'

'I heard it myself. Now, who talked?'

Once again, the question was met with silence.

'Even if the information spread abroad is incomplete, and therefore inaccurate, my trust has been betrayed.'

'You mean —'

'I mean that you're all dismissed.'

Neferet had chosen the poorest, most isolated village in the Theban region, which lay on the fringes of the desert. It was poorly irrigated, and its inhabitants suffered from a higher than usual incidence of skin diseases. The young woman was neither sad nor downcast, though; she was happy to have escaped from Nebamon's clutches, even if she had given up a promising career in return for her freedom. She would care for the poorest people with whatever means she had, and she would be content with a solitary life in the country. When a hospital boat went downriver to Memphis, she would go and see Branir. He knew her, and would not try to change her mind.

On only the second day after her arrival, Neferet had cured the most important person in the village, a man who specialized in fattening geese and who suffered from an irregular heartbeat. A long massage and manipulation of his spine had swiftly put him back on his feet. The cure was thought miraculous, and Neferet had become the heroine of the village.

The peasants asked her to advise them on how to fight the enemies of harvests and orchards, notably grasshoppers and crickets, but she preferred to fight another plague, which seemed to her to be at the root of the villagers' skin problems: flies and mosquitoes. Their abundance was explained by the presence of a stagnant pool which had not been drained for three years. Neferet had it dried out, advised all the villagers to cleanse and fumigate their houses, and treated the bites with loriot fat and applications of fresh oil.

The only patient who caused her concern was an old man with a worn-out heart. If his condition worsened, he would have to go to the hospital in Thebes – there'd be no reason for it if only she had certain rare plants she needed.

She was tending the old man at his bedside when a small boy came to tell her that a stranger had arrived and was asking questions about her.

Even here, Nebamon would not leave her in peace! Now what was he accusing her of? What failure was he going to have her judged guilty of? She must hide. The villagers would keep silent, and the emissary would go away again.

Pazair sensed that the villagers were lying and that they knew the name Neferet, despite their silence. The isolated village feared any intrusion; most of the doors closed in his face.

He was about to give up and leave when he saw a woman heading for the rocky hills.

'Neferet!' he called.

She turned, saw him, and came back towards him. 'Judge Pazair, what are you doing here?'

'I want to speak with you.'

The light of the sun shone out of her eyes. The country air had bronzed her skin. Pazair wanted to reveal his feelings to her, pour out his heart, but he could not say a single word.

She said, 'Let's go up to the top of that little hill.'

He would have followed her to the ends of the earth, to the bottom of the sea, to the heart of darkness. To walk beside her, to sit down next to her, to hear her voice, were intoxicating joys.

'Branir told me what happened,' he said when they were settled. 'Do you want to lodge a complaint against Nebamon?'

'It would be no use. Many doctors owe their careers to him and would testify against me.'

'I'll charge them with perjury.'

'There are too many of them, and, anyway, Nebamon would stop you.'

Despite the gentle spring warmth, Pazair shivered. He could not suppress a sneeze.

'Have you caught a chill?' she asked.

'I spent the night out of doors, waiting for Kani to come back.'

'Kani the gardener?'

'He's the one who found you. He lives in Thebes, and is tending his own garden there. Here's your chance, Neferet: he produces medicinal plants, and knows how to grow even the rarest ones.'

'You mean I could set up a workshop here?'

'Why not? You have all the necessary knowledge of medicines. Not only could you treat serious illnesses, but your reputation would be restored.'

'I have little appetite for beginning that struggle again. I'm content with my current situation.'

'Don't waste your gifts. Do it for the sick.'

Pazair sneezed again.

'Shouldn't we attend to you first? The treatises say that a spring wind breaks the bones, shatters the skull and hollows out the brain. I must prevent that disaster.'

Her smile, which was utterly free of irony, delighted him.

'Will you let Kani help you?' he asked.

'He's stubborn. If he's made his mind up, I can't stop him. Let us deal with this emergency first: a cold is a serious ailment. I'll put palm juice into your nostrils and then, if that doesn't work, mother's milk and aromatic gum.'

The cold grew worse. Neferet took the judge into her modest house in the centre of the village. He was developing a cough, so she prescribed him natural sulphur of arsenic, which the country people called 'that which makes the heart blossom'.

'We must try to stop it getting worse. Sit down on this mat and don't move.'

She gave instructions without raising her voice, which was as gentle as her gaze. Pazair hoped that the chill would last a long time and that he'd have to stay as long as possible in this humble room.

Neferet mixed sulphur of arsenic, resin and the leaves of antiseptic plants, crushed them and reduced the whole to a paste, which she heated. She spread it out on a stone which she placed in front of the judge, then covered it with an upturned pot with a hole in the bottom.

'Take this reed,' she told her patient. 'Place it in the hole and breathe through the nose and mouth alternately. The inhalation will relieve your symptoms.'

Pazair would not have minded if it failed, but the treatment worked. The congestion was reduced, and he breathed more easily.

'No more shivers?' she asked.

'No, but I feel rather tired.'

'For a few days, I advise you to eat rich, rather fatty foods, red meat and plenty of fresh oil on your food. A little rest would also do you good.'

'I can't rest.

'What brings you back to Thebes?'

He wanted to cry out, 'You, Neferet, only you,' but the words wouldn't come. He was certain that she could sense his passion, and waited for her to give him a chance to open his heart, for he dared not shatter her peace with a madness she would undoubtedly deplore.

Instead, he said, 'Perhaps one crime, perhaps several.'

He sensed that she was troubled by the drama, even though she was not involved in it. Had he the right to involve her in this affair, whose true nature he himself did not know?

'I trust you unreservedly, Neferet, but I don't want to burden you with my worries.'

'You're bound to secrecy, aren't you?'

'Yes, until I formulate my conclusions.'

'Murders . . . would those be your conclusions?'

'My firm personal belief.'

'But it's many years since a murder was committed!'

'Five ex-soldiers, who formed the honour guard to the Great Sphinx, were supposed to have died in a fall from its head during an inspection. An accident: that's the army's official version. One them actually survived and was hiding in a village on the west bank, where he was working as a baker. I wanted to question him, but when I got there he really was dead – another "accident". Mentmose is having me followed as if I were a criminal because I am carrying out an investigation. I'm lost, Neferet. Forget everything I've told you.'

'Do you want to give up?'

'I have a keen love of truth and justice. If I give up, I'll destroy myself.'

'Can I help you?'

A different fever filled Pazair's eyes. 'If we could talk from time to time, I'd feel braver.'

'A chill can have side effects and they should be carefully watched. Several more consultations will be necessary.'

21

The night at the inn was as pleasurable as it was exhausting. Suti indulged himself with slices of grilled beef, aubergines in cream sauce, an abundance of cakes, and a superb forty-year-old Libyan woman who had fled her own country and now entertained Egyptian soldiers. How lustily she laughed as she bent her body into unbelievable positions. The chariot officer had not lied: one man was not enough for her. Although Suti had always considered himself the most energetic of lovers, he was obliged to make a tactical withdrawal and pass the baton to his superior officer.

When the chariot set off next morning, Suti could hardly keep his eyes open.

'You'll have to learn how to do without sleep, my lad. Don't forget that the enemy will attack when you are tired. Now, I've a piece of good news for you. We're to be the vanguard of the vanguard – the first blows struck will be ours. If you want to be a hero, you're in luck.'

Suti clutched his bow to his chest.

The chariot ran along the King's Walls, a series of formidable fortresses built along Egypt's north-eastern frontier by the sovereigns of the Middle Kingdom, and constantly improved upon by their successors. It was well named, for it was in effect a huge wall stretching from the ocean shore to Iunu. The fortresses were linked by visual signals, and the system prevented invasion attempts by sand-travellers* or Asiatic peoples.

The King's Walls housed both permanent garrisons of soldiers, experienced in watching the borders, and customs officials. No one entered or left Egypt without giving their name and the reason for their journey; traders had to state the nature of their merchandise and pay a tax. The border guards turned back undesirable foreigners, and people

---

*Like the Libyans, the Bedouin were permanent troublemakers whom the Egyptians had been fighting since the earliest dynasties. In ancient times, they were known as 'sand-travellers'.

were not allowed to pass until their documents had been carefully scrutinized by an official from the capital. As Pharaoh's stele proclaimed, 'Anyone who crosses this border becomes one of my sons.'

The chariot officer presented his papers to the commander of a fortress whose sloping walls were surrounded by ditches. Archers were stationed on the battlements, and lookouts in the towers.

As he did so, he looked around and commented, 'The guard's been reinforced.'

Ten armed men surrounded the chariot.

'Dismount,' ordered the commander of the guard post.

'Are you joking?'

'Your documents aren't in order.'

The officer gripped the reins tightly, ready to whip his horses into a gallop. Spears and arrows were aimed at him.

'Dismount immediately.'

He turned to Suti. 'What do you think, youngster?'

'There'll be better battles to fight, sir.'

They stepped down.

'Your documents don't bear the seal of the first fort of the King's Walls,' said the commander. 'You'll have to turn back.'

'We are already late.'

'Rules are rules.'

'Couldn't we discuss this?' asked the officer.

'Very well. In my office – but don't get your hopes up.'

The discussion was brief. The officer left the office at a run, leapt into the chariot and galloped off along the road to Asia. The wheels squeaked, sending up a cloud of dust.

'Why the hurry, sir?' asked Suti. 'Everything's been settled now.'

'Well, more or less. I hit that idiot hard, but he may wake up sooner than I planned – that kind of stubborn fool has a hard head. I put our documents in order myself. In the army, youngster, you have to know how to improvise.'

The next few days of the journey were peaceful. Lengthy periods were spent travelling, caring for the horses, checking equipment, sleeping under the stars, stocking up on food in small towns where the officer contacted an army messenger or a member of the secret services. Their job was to inform the main body of the forces that there was nothing to halt their progress.

The wind turned, and became biting.

'Spring in Asia is often cold,' said the officer. 'Put your cloak on.'

'You seem on edge, sir.'

'Danger's coming. I can scent it, like a dog. How much food have we got?'

'Enough flat cakes, meatballs, onions and water for three days.'

'That should be enough.'

The chariot entered a silent village; there was no one in the main square. Suti's stomach knotted up.

'Don't panic, youngster. They may be in the fields.'

The chariot advanced very slowly. The officer snatched up a spear and looked around him with a practised eye. He halted before the official building where the military representative and interpreter were billeted. It was empty.

'The army won't get our report, so it'll know something serious has happened. A rebellion, most likely.'

'Are we going to stay here, sir?'

'I'd rather go on. Why? Wouldn't you?'

'That depends,' said Suti.

'On what?'

'Where's General Asher?'

'How do you know about him?'

'He's famous in Memphis. I'd like to serve under him.'

'Then you really are in luck. He's the one we're to join up with.'

'Do you think he evacuated this village?'

'Certainly not.'

'Then who did, sir?

'The sand-travellers. They're the vilest, most fanatical and deceitful people. Raiding, pillaging, taking hostages, that's their strategy. If we don't wipe them out, they'll bring ruin to Asia, to the peninsula between Egypt and the Red Sea, and to all the surrounding provinces. They're willing to form an alliance with any invader, they despise women as much as we love them, and they spit on beauty and the gods. I'm not afraid of them, but I dread them, with their ragged beards, their turbans and their long robes. Always remember, youngster, they're cowards: they strike from behind.'

'Do you think they killed all the villagers?'

'Probably.'

'Then General Asher's isolated, sir, cut off from the main army.'

'He may be.'

Suti's long black hair danced in the wind. Despite his solid build and powerful torso, the young man felt weak and vulnerable. 'Sand-travellers between him and us. How many, do you think?'

The officer shrugged. 'Ten, a hundred, a thousand . . .'

'Ten I can deal with. A hundred, I'm not so sure.'

'A thousand, youngster, that's the number for a real hero. You're not thinking of deserting me, I hope?'

The chariot set off again, the horses galloping towards the entrance to a ravine bordered by vertical cliffs. A tangle of bushes grew out of the rock, leaving only a narrow way through.

The horses whinnied and reared; the officer calmed them.

'Sir, they can sense something's wrong,' said Suti.

'So can I, lad. The sand-travellers are hiding in the bushes. They'll try to slash the horses' legs with axes, bring us down, slit our throats and cut off our testicles.'

'If you ask me, the price of heroism is too high.'

'Thanks to you, we shan't run much risk. An arrow into each bush, a good gallop, and we'll win.'

Suti swallowed. 'Are you sure about that?'

'Why? Aren't you? Just don't think about it too much.'

The officer shook the reins, and the horses leapt forward into the ravine. Suti had no time to be afraid; he let fly one arrow after another. The first two landed in empty bushes, but the third pierced the eye of a sand-traveller who fell out of the bush with a cry of pain.

'Keep it up, youngster,' shouted the officer.

His hair standing on end and his blood turned to ice, Suti aimed at each bush, turning to right and left with a speed he would have thought himself incapable of. The sand-travellers fell, wounded in the belly, the chest, the head.

The exit from the ravine was blocked by a barrier of stones and tree roots.

'Hold on tight, lad, we're going to jump it!'

Suti stopped firing and gripped the edge of the chariot. Two enemies he hadn't been able to shoot hurled their axes at the Egyptians.

At full speed, the two horses leapt over the barricade at its lowest point. The roots scratched their legs, and a stone broke the spokes of the right wheel, while another made a hole in the right side of the shell. For a moment, the chariot swayed, but with a final effort the warhorses cleared the obstacle.

The chariot raced on for some time before slowing down. Tossed about, dazed, barely keeping his balance, Suti hung on to his bow. At last, panting, covered in sweat and with foam on their muzzles, the horses halted at the foot of a hill.

The officer collapsed over the reins; there was an axe buried between his shoulder blades.

'Sir!' Suti tried to lift him up.

'Remember, youngster, cowards always attack from behind.'

'Don't die, sir!'

'Now you're the only hero.'

The officer's eyes closed, and he stopped breathing.

For a long time, Suti held the body tightly. Never again would the officer fight, urge him on, attempt the impossible. Suti was alone, lost in a hostile country, he, the hero, whose praises could be sung only by a dead man.

Suti buried the officer, taking care to fix the place in his memory. If he survived, he would come back for the body and return it to Egypt. There was no crueller destiny, for a child of the Two Lands, than to be buried far from his homeland.

Turning back meant going through the ravine again; going on meant the risk of meeting more enemies. But he chose the second option, hoping he'd soon be able to make contact with General Asher's soldiers – assuming they hadn't all been wiped out.

The horses were rested enough to continue. Suti picked up the reins and drove off. If there was another ambush, he would not be able to drive the chariot and use his bow at the same time. His throat tight, he followed a stony track which ended at a dilapidated hovel. He grabbed his sword and jumped down. Smoke was coming out of a rudimentary chimney.

'Come out of there!' he shouted.

On the threshold there appeared a wild-looking young woman dressed in rags, with dirty hair. She was brandishing a rough knife.

'Don't be afraid,' he said. 'Put the knife down.'

The woman looked too frail to put up a fight, and Suti wasn't afraid of her. But when he drew close, she threw herself at him and tried to plunge the blade into his heart. He dodged aside, but felt a burning pain in his left upper arm. Maddened, she struck again. He disarmed her with a kick, then overpowered her and pushed her to the ground. Blood trickled down his arm.

'Calm down, or I'll tie you up.'

She struggled like a fury. He turned her over and knocked her out with a blow to the nape of the neck. His relationships with women, as a hero, were taking a turn for the worse. He carried her into the hovel, whose single room had a floor of beaten earth, filthy walls, miserable furniture and a hearth covered with soot. Suti laid down his pathetic prisoner on a tattered mat, and bound her wrists and ankles with rope.

Suddenly, exhaustion overcame him. He sat down with his back to the chimney breast and his head in his hands, and began to shake all over.

The place's filth repelled him. Behind the house was a well. He filled jars, washed his wound, and then cleaned the room. When he'd finished, he looked down at the woman and said thoughtfully, 'You could do with a good wash, too.'

He threw some water over her, and she awoke and started screaming in rage. The contents of another jar silenced her cries. When he took off her dirty dress, she started wriggling like a snake.

'I don't want to rape you, you silly girl!'

Could she understand what he meant? She submitted. Standing up, naked, she seemed to enjoy the wash. When he dried her, she almost smiled. Without its layer of dirt and grease, her hair was fair, which surprised him.

'You're pretty. Have you ever been kissed?'

From the way she parted her lips and moved her tongue, Suti realized that he was not the first.

'If you promise to be good, I'll untie you.'

Her eyes pleaded with him. He took off the rope which bound her feet, stroked her calves, her thighs, and placed his mouth upon the golden curls of her sex. Her body arched like a bow. Once her hands were free, she embraced him.

Suti had slept for ten dreamless hours. Then his wound started to hurt, and he awoke with a start and went outside.

She had stolen his weapons, cut the chariot reins and chased the horses away. No bow, no dagger, no sword, no boots, no cloak. The chariot would sink uselessly into the mud where it stood in the rain, which must have been pouring down for hours. The hero, reduced to the status of an idiot fooled by a madwoman, could do nothing but walk north. In rage, he kicked the chariot to pieces so that it would not fall into enemy hands.

Dressed in nothing but a plain kilt, and laden like a mule, Suti walked through continuous rain. In a bag, he had some stale bread, a piece of chariot-shaft bearing the officer's name, a couple of pitchers of fresh water and the tattered mat. He crossed a pass, walked through a pine forest and slithered down a steep slope ending in a lake, which he skirted.

The mountains were becoming inhospitable. After a night spent in the shelter of a rock which protected him against the east wind, he climbed a slippery path and ventured into an arid region. His food stocks were exhausted, and he began to suffer from thirst.

As he was taking a few mouthfuls from a stagnant pool, Suti heard branches crack. Several men were coming. He crawled away and hid behind the trunk of a giant pine tree.

Five men were pushing a prisoner, his hands bound behind his back. Their leader, a short man, seized him by the hair and forced him to kneel. Suti was too far away to hear what he said, but the tortured man's cries soon shattered the calm of the mountains.

One against five, and without weapons ... Suti had no chance of saving the luckless man.

The torturer rained blows upon the prisoner, interrogated him, beat him again, then ordered his men to drag the prisoner to a cave. After a final interrogation, he slit the man's throat.

When the murderers had gone, Suti stayed still for over an hour. He thought of Pazair, of his love of justice and his idealism. How would he have reacted to this barbarism? He did not know that, so close to Egypt, there was a lawless world where human life had no value.

He forced himself to go down to the cave, though his legs almost gave way beneath him as the dying man's cries echoed in his head. The tortured man's soul had fled. To judge from his kilt and general appearance, he was an Egyptian, probably a soldier from Asher's army who had fallen into rebel hands. Suti dug him a grave with his bare hands, inside the cave.

Shocked and exhausted, he continued on his way, putting himself in the hands of destiny. If he came face to face with the enemy, he would no longer have the strength to defend himself.

When two helmeted soldiers hailed him, he collapsed onto the damp earth.

A tent. A bed, a cushion beneath his head, a blanket. Suti sat up.

The point of a knife forced him to lie down again, and a voice said, 'Who are you?'

The questioner was an Egyptian officer, with a deeply furrowed face.

'My name's Suti, and I'm an archer in the corps of charioteers.'

'Where have you come from?'

He related everything that had happened.

'Can you prove that?'

'In my bag there's a piece of the chariot, with my officer's name on it.'

'Tell me again what happened to him.'

'The sand-travellers killed him, I buried him.'

'You ran away, didn't you?'

'Of course I didn't! I killed a good two dozen of them with my arrows.'

'When did you enlist?'

'At the beginning of the month.'

'Barely a fortnight, and you're already an elite archer!'

'It's a gift.'

'I believe in training, not gifts. Why don't you tell me the truth?'

Suti threw back the blanket. 'It *is* the truth.'

'You killed your officer, didn't you?'

'You're mad!'

'A long stay in a prison cell will straighten out your ideas.'

Suti ran towards the way out. Two soldiers seized his arms, and a third punched him in the belly and knocked him out with a blow to the back of the neck.

'We were right to take care of this spy,' said the officer. 'He'll sing like a bird.'

22

Sitting at a table in one of Thebes' busiest taverns, Pazair steered the conversation towards Hattusa, one of Ramses' diplomatic wives. She was a daughter of the Hittite emperor, and was named after her birthplace, the capital of the Hittite empire. When a peace treaty was concluded with the Hittites, Pharaoh had married the princess as a pledge of his sincerity. She had been placed in charge of the harem at Thebes, and lived a life of luxury there.

Inaccessible and invisible, Hattusa was highly unpopular. Many rumours surrounded her: she was said to practise evil magic, to be in league with the demons of night, and to have refused to appear at major festivals.

'It's because of her,' claimed the tavern keeper, 'that the price of ointments has doubled.'

'How is she responsible for that?'

'She has vast numbers of attendant ladies, who spend all day making themselves look beautiful. The harem uses an incredible amount of high-quality unguents, buys them at inflated prices and makes the price rise. It's the same with oil. When are we going to be rid of the foreigner?'

No one spoke up in Hattusa's defence.

Luxuriant plants and flowers surrounded the buildings that made up the harem on the east bank of Thebes. The palaces were served by a canal whose abundant water irrigated several gardens reserved for elderly and widowed ladies of the court, a large orchard, and a flower-filled park where spinning and weaving women relaxed.

Like other Egyptian harems, the Theban one contained many workshops, schools of dancing, music and poetry, and a centre for producing aromatic herbs and beauty products. Specialists worked in wood, enamels and ivory. Superb linen dresses were made and sophisticated flower arrangements created.

Always bustling with activity, the harem was also an educational centre for the training of Egyptians and foreigners destined for senior government posts. Alongside elegant ladies decked with dazzling jewellery were craftsmen, teachers and managers whose job was to ensure that the residents received ample fresh food.

Judge Pazair arrived early in the morning at the main palace. His status enabled him to get past the guards and speak to Hattusa's steward, who passed on the judge's request to his mistress. To the steward's surprise, she did not reject it.

The judge was shown into a four-pillared room whose walls were decorated with paintings of birds and flowers. Many-coloured floor tiles added to the room's charm. Hattusa was sitting on a gilded wooden throne, while two maids bustled around her with pots and spoons of make-up, and boxes of perfume. Their mistress's morning toilette concluded with the most delicate operation of all, the adjustment of the wig and the replacement of any defective curls with false locks of hair.

At thirty years old, the Hittite princess was radiant and haughty. She sat gazing at her beauty in a mirror whose handle was shaped like a lotus stem.

'A judge in my apartments so early in the morning. I'm curious. Why have you come here?'

'I would like to ask you a few questions, my lady.'

She put down the mirror and dismissed her attendants. 'Will a private conversation suit you?'

'Perfectly.'

'A little entertainment at last! Life in this palace is so boring.'

With her very white skin, long slender hands and black eyes, Hattusa was at once alluring and disturbing. Mischievous, sharp-tongued and quick-witted, she showed no mercy to those who spoke to her, and took pleasure in pointing out their weaknesses, be they faults in speech, clumsiness or physical imperfections.

She looked Pazair up and down. 'You aren't the most handsome man in Egypt, but a woman could fall in love with you and remain faithful. Impatient, passionate, idealistic ... you're a collection of serious defects. And you are so serious, almost sombre – so much so that it ruins your youthfulness.'

'Will you permit me to question you, my lady?'

'An audacious move! Are you aware of your impudence? I am one of the wives of the great Ramses, and could have you dismissed within the hour.'

'You know very well that that is untrue. I would defend my cause before the tjaty's court, and you would be charged with abusing your power.'

'Egypt is a strange country. Not only do its inhabitants believe in justice, but they actually respect it and see that it is put into practice. The miracle won't last, of course.'

Hattusa picked up her mirror and examined the curls of her wig, one by one. 'If your questions amuse me, I'll answer them.'

'Who delivers fresh bread to you?'

The Hittite's eyes widened in astonishment. 'You're worrying about my bread?'

'To be precise, about the baker on the west bank who wanted to work for you.'

'Everyone wants to work for me. My generosity is well known.'

'And yet the common people dislike you.'

'The feeling is mutual. The common people are stupid here, as they are elsewhere. I am a foreigner, and proud to remain so. I have dozens of servants at my feet because the king has entrusted me with the running of this harem, the most prosperous of all.'

'My lady, please tell me about the baker.'

'See my steward – he'll tell you. If this baker has delivered any bread here, you'll know about it. Why is it so important?'

'Are you aware of an incident which occurred near the Great Sphinx at Giza?'

'What are you hiding, Judge Pazair?'

'Nothing vital, my lady.'

'This game is as boring as festivals and courtiers. The only thing I want is to go home. It would be amusing if the Hittite armies crushed your soldiers and invaded Egypt – a splendid revenge! But I shall probably die here, the wife of the most powerful king in the world, a man I've seen only once on the day when our marriage was sealed by diplomats and jurors in order to ensure our peoples' peace and happiness. Who cares about my happiness?'

'Thank you for your help, my lady.'

'It is for me to bring this audience to an end, not you.'

'I did not mean to offend you.'

'You may leave.'

Hattusa's steward told Pazair that he had indeed ordered bread from an excellent baker on the west bank, but none had been received.

Puzzled, Pazair left the harem. In accordance with his usual practice, he had tried to follow up even the smallest clue, even if it meant annoying one of the greatest women in the kingdom.

Was she somehow mixed up in the plot? It was yet another question with no answer.

The mayor of Memphis's assistant opened his mouth in panic.

'Relax,' advised Qadash. He had not hidden the truth: the molar would have to come out. Despite his intensive treatment, he had not been able to save it.

'Open wider.'

True, Qadash's hand might not be as steady as it had once been, but it would continue to prove his talent for a long time to come. After numbing the man's mouth, he moved on to the first phase of the extraction, positioning his pincers round the tooth.

His grip was imprecise and shaky, and he cut the gum, but pressed on regardless. But he had lost his nerve and did not manage the operation well; and when he tried to get the roots out, he caused heavy bleeding. Hurriedly he seized a drill, placed the pointed end in a hole in a block of wood, and rotated it fast until it produced a spark. As soon as the flame was sufficiently large, he heated a lancet and cauterized the wound.

The mayor's assistant left the surgery with a painful, swollen jaw, and did not thank the tooth doctor. Qadash had lost an important client who would be sure to blacken his name.

He was at a crossroads. He would not admit that he was getting old, or accept that he must give up his craft. True, dancing with the Libyans gave him comfort and a passing revival of his flagging energy, but that was no longer enough. The solution was so near and yet so far!

Qadash must use other weapons, perfect his technique, demonstrate that he was still the best.

Another kind of metal: that was what he needed.

The ferry was pulling away from the bank. Pazair made a huge leap, and landed on the loose boards of the flat-bottomed boat, which was crammed with people and animals.

The ferry travelled continuously between the two banks and, though it was a short crossing, people on board exchanged news and even made business deals. A restless ox jostled him with its hindquarters and pushed him against the woman next to him, who turned her back on him.

'I beg your pardon,' he said.

She did not reply, and covered her face with her hands.

His interest caught, Pazair looked at her more closely. 'You're Madam Sababu, aren't you?'

'Leave me alone.'

In a plain brown dress and maroon shawl, and with her hair untidy, Sababu looked like a pauper.

'There are a few things we need to talk about.'

'I don't know you. Go away.'

'Remember my friend Suti? He persuaded you not to smear my name.'

Terrified, she hurled herself towards the side of the boat.

Pazair seized her arm and held her back. 'The Nile flows dangerously fast here. You might drown.'

'I can't swim.'

Children jumped onto the bank as soon as the ferry arrived. They were followed by donkeys, oxen and peasants. Pazair and Sababu were the last to disembark. He was still holding her by the arm.

'Why won't you leave me alone? I'm just a simple serving woman, I—'

'That's a ridiculous defence. Now, be honest. Didn't you tell Suti I was one of your regular clients?'

'I don't understand.'

'I am Judge Pazair – remember?'

She tried to run away, but he held her fast, and said, 'Be sensible.'

'You're frightening me.'

'You tried to destroy me.'

She burst into tears. Somewhat embarrassed, he let go of her. She might be an enemy, but her distress moved him.

'Who gave you the order to slander me?' he asked.

'I don't know.'

'You're lying.'

'I'm not. One of his men contacted me.'

'A guards officer?'

'How should I know? I don't ask questions.'

'How were you paid?'

'By being left in peace.'

'And why are you helping me now?'

She gave a wan smile. 'Because I have many memories of happy days. My father was a country judge – I adored him. When he died, I couldn't bear to stay in my village and I moved to Memphis. I went from one bad encounter to another and eventually became a prostitute – a rich, respected prostitute, mind you. I was paid to obtain confidential information on the men who visited my ale-house.'

'Paid by Mentmose – am I right?'

'You can draw your own conclusions. I've never sullied the name of a judge, and out of respect for my father's memory I spared you. If you're in danger, that's too bad for you.'

'Aren't you afraid of reprisals?'

'My memories protect me.'

'What if the man who employs you isn't worried by that threat?'

She lowered her eyes. 'That's why I left Memphis and hid here. Because of you, I've lost everything.'

'Did General Asher ever come to your ale-house?'

'No.'

'The truth will out, I promise you.'

'I don't believe in promises any more.'

'Trust me.'

She look up at him again. 'Why do they want to destroy you, Judge?'

'I'm investigating an accident at Giza. The official report says that five men from the Sphinx's honour guard died there.'

'I haven't heard anything about it.'

His attempt had failed. Either she knew nothing, or she was keeping her mouth shut.

Suddenly, she clutched her left shoulder and gave a cry of pain.

'What is the matter?' he asked.

'I suffer badly from rheumatism. Sometimes I can't move my arm at all.'

Pazair did not hesitate. She had helped him, and now he must help her.

Neferet was treating a donkey foal with a wounded foot when Pazair introduced Sababu to her. The prostitute had promised the judge to conceal her identity.

'Neferet,' said Pazair, 'I met this woman on the ferry. She has a bad pain in her shoulder. Can you do anything?'

Neferet washed her hands carefully. 'Have you had this pain long?'

'More than five years,' replied Sababu aggressively. 'Do you know who I am?'

'A sick person whom I shall try to cure.'

'I am Sababu, a prostitute and the owner of an ale-house.'

Pazair went white with horror.

Neferet, however, was unmoved. She said, 'The frequency of sexual relations and the company of partners of dubious cleanliness may be the causes of your illness.'

'Examine me,' said Sababu, and she took off her dress. Underneath, she was naked.

Pazair didn't know where to turn; he wished the ground would open up and swallow him. Neferet would never forgive this insult. He was a prostitute's client – that was the revelation he was offering her. It would be as ridiculous as it would be pointless to deny it.

Neferet felt the shoulder, traced the line of a nerve with her finger, detected the energy points and checked the curve of the shoulder blade.

'It's serious,' she pronounced. 'The rheumatism has already caused deformity. If you don't look after yourself, you'll lose the use of your arm.'

Sababu's arrogance vanished. 'What . . . what must I do?'

'First, you must stop drinking alcohol. Next, each day you must drink a tincture of willow bark. Finally, you must receive a daily application of a balm made from natron, white oil, terebinth resin, oliban, honey and the fat of hippopotamus, crocodile, silurid fish and grey mullet. Those are expensive things, and I haven't got them. You must consult a doctor in Thebes.'

Sababu put on her clothes.

'Don't waste any time,' advised Neferet. 'The disease seems to be progressing rapidly.'

Mortified, Pazair accompanied the prostitute to the entrance to the village.

'Am I free to go?' she asked.

'You broke your word.'

'It may surprise you, but sometimes I have a horror of lying. And lying to a woman like that would be impossible.'

When she had gone, Pazair sat down in the dust beside the road. His naivety had led him to disaster. In an unexpected way, Sababu had at last fulfilled her mission; he felt broken. He, the honest judge, would be seen in Neferet's eyes as a prostitute's accomplice, a hypocrite, a dissolute man.

Sababu of the good heart, Sababu who respected judges and her father's memory, Sababu who had not hesitated to betray him at the first opportunity. Tomorrow, she would sell him to Mentmose – if she hadn't done so already.

Legend had it that those who drowned received the mercy of Osiris when they appeared before the court of the afterlife. The Nile waters purified them. He had lost his beloved, his good name, his ideals . . . The thought of suicide attracted him.

He felt a hand on his shoulder.

'Is your cold better?' asked Neferet.

He dared not move. 'I'm sorry.'

'What for?'

'That woman . . . I swear to you that—'

'You brought a sick woman to me. I hope she'll get treatment soon.'

'She was meant to ruin my reputation, but claims she stopped before any harm was done.'

'A prostitute with a heart of gold?'

'That's what I thought.'

'Why should anyone blame you for that?'

'I went to Sababu's ale-house with my friend Suti, to celebrate his enlistment in the army.'

Neferet did not take her hand away.

'Suti's a wonderful person,' he went on, 'with inexhaustible energy. He adores wine and women, wants to become a great hero, defies all restraint. He and I are friends for life, friends until death. While Sababu was entertaining him in her room, I stayed outside, thinking about my investigation. I beg you to believe me.'

'I'm worried about one of my patients, an old man. He must be washed and his house cleansed. Will you help me?'

23

'Get up.'

Suti dragged himself out of the cell where he had been locked away. Although dirty and famished, he had passed the time singing bawdy songs and thinking about the wonderful times he had spent in the arms of beautiful Memphis women.

'Step forward.'

The soldier giving the orders was a mercenary. A former pirate, he had left that adventurous life and joined the Egyptian army because it offered its soldiers such a comfortable retirement. He wore a pointed helmet, carried a short sword, and was completely lacking in feeling.

'Are you the one called Suti?'

The young man was slow to respond, so the mercenary hit him in the stomach. Although bent double, Suti did not kneel.

'You're proud and sturdy,' said the soldier. 'They say you fought the sand-travellers, but I don't believe it myself. When you kill an enemy, you cut off his hand and present it to your superior officer. I think you ran away like a frightened rabbit.'

'With a piece of shaft from my chariot?'

'You got that from pillaging. You say you were an archer. Well, we're going to check that.'

'I'm hungry.'

'We'll see about that later. A real warrior can go on fighting even when he's utterly exhausted.'

The man took Suti to the edge of a wood and handed him a heavy bow. The upper surface was coated with horn, the back with bark. The bowstring was an ox tendon covered with linen fibres, stopped by knots at either end.

'Target at a hundred paces, on the oak tree right in front of you. You have two arrows to hit it.'

When he drew the bow, Suti thought the muscles in his back were going to rip. Black dots danced before his eyes. He must maintain the right pressure, load the arrow, aim, forget what was at stake, visualize the target, become the bow and the arrow, fly through the air, sink into the heart of the tree.

He closed his eyes and fired.

The mercenary walked forward a little way. 'Almost in the centre.'

Suti picked up the second arrow, drew the bow again and aimed at the soldier.

'That is very unwise.' The mercenary dropped his sword.

'I told the truth,' insisted Suti.

'All right, all right!'

The young man let the arrow fly, and it plunged into the target, just to the right of the previous one.

The soldier breathed again. 'Who taught you how to handle a bow?'

'It's a gift.'

'Down to the river with you, soldier. Wash and dress and get something to eat.'

Equipped with a bow made of his favourite acacia wood, boots, a woollen cloak and a dagger, and properly fed and washed, Suti appeared before the commander of the hundred or so footsoldiers. This time, the officer listened to him attentively and made detailed notes.

He told Suti, 'We're cut off from our bases and from General Asher. He's encamped three days' march from here, with an elite force. I'm sending two messengers south, so that the main army can move more quickly.'

'Is there a rebellion?'

'Two Asian princelings, an Iranian tribe and some sand-travellers have formed an alliance. Their leader is an exiled Libyan called Adafi. He is the prophet of a vengeful god, and has decided to destroy Egypt and mount the throne in Ramses' place. Some say that he's a puppet, others that he's a dangerous madman. He favours surprise attacks, and takes no account of treaties. If we stay here we'll be slaughtered. But between us and Asher is a well-defended fort. We're going to attack it and take it.'

'Have we got any chariots?'

'No, but we've got several ladders and a wheeled tower. What we didn't have until now was a really good archer.'

Pazair had tried to talk to her ten times – no, a hundred times. But he had confined himself to lifting an old man, laying him down under a palm tree out of the wind and sun, cleaning his house and helping Neferet. He was on the alert for any sign of disapproval, any condemnatory look. But she was absorbed in her work, and seemed indifferent.

The previous evening, he had gone to see Kani, whose investigations were continuing. Kani was very careful, but he had visited most of the villages and talked to dozens of peasants and craftsmen. There was no trace of an ex-soldier who had returned from Memphis. If the man did indeed live on the west bank, he was well hidden.

When they had finished cleaning the old man's house, Pazair told Neferet, 'In about ten days' time, Kani will bring you the first consignment of medicinal plants.'

'The headman has allocated me an abandoned house on the edge of the desert. I shall be able to see my patients there.'

'What about water?'

'A channel will be dug as soon as possible.'

'And what are your quarters like?'

'They're small, but clean and pleasant.'

'Yesterday Memphis, today this forgotten place.'

Neferet smiled. 'Here, I have no enemies. There, it was war.'

'Nebamon won't rule over the doctors for ever.'

'That's for destiny to decide.'

'One day you'll be restored to your rightful status.'

'What does that matter? Now, you never told me how your cold is.'

'The spring wind doesn't agree with me.'

'You must have another inhalation.'

Pazair yielded. He loved to hear her preparing the antiseptic paste, kneading it and spreading it on the stone before covering it with the pot. Whatever she did, he adored.

Pazair's bedchamber had been searched from top to bottom. Even his mosquito net had been torn down, rolled into a ball and thrown on the wooden floor. His travelling bag had been emptied, his tablets and papyri strewn everywhere, his mat trampled on, and his kilt, tunic and cloak torn to bits.

Pazair knelt down and searched for clues. But the burglar had not left a single trace behind him.

He went and lodged a formal complaint with the fat official, who was astounded and outraged.

'Do you suspect anyone?'

'Yes, but I daren't say anything.'

'Please!'

'I was followed.'

'Did you identify the person?'

'No.'

'Can you describe him?'

'No, I can't.'

'That's a pity,' said the official. 'Finding the culprit won't be easy.'

'I quite understand.'

'I and all the other guard posts in the province have received a message for you. Your scribe is looking everywhere for you.'

'Why?'

'He doesn't say. He asks you to return to Memphis as quickly as possible. When will you leave?'

'Well . . . tomorrow.'

'Would you like an escort?'

'Kem will be quite enough.'

'As you wish, but be careful.'

'Who would dare attack a judge?'

The Nubian was armed with a bow, arrows, a sword, a club, a spear and a wooden-framed shield covered in ox skin; in other words, he carried all the usual weapons of a dedicated officer, ready to deal with tricky situations. Killer was happy with just his teeth.

'Where did all these weapons come from?' asked Pazair.

'The traders in the market bought them for me. One by one, my baboon arrested every member of a band of thieves who have been running wild for more than a year. The merchants wanted to thank me.'

'Did you get permission for them from the Theban guards?'

'They've been listed and numbered, and everything's in order.'

'There's a problem in Memphis, and we must go back. Any news of the fifth soldier?'

'Not a whisper in the market,' said Kem. 'Have you discovered anything?'

'No, nothing.'

'He must be dead, like the others.'

'Then why was my room searched?'

'I don't know,' said Kem, 'but I shall stick closer to you than a flea.'

'Don't forget you're under my command.'

'My duty is to protect you.'

'If I think it necessary. Wait for me here, and be ready to leave.'

'At least tell me where you're going.'

'I shan't be long.'

The wind was changing, and spring was becoming gentle and warm. Soon the sandstorms would begin, forcing people to take refuge in their homes for several days at a time. Everywhere, nature was flourishing.

Neferet was treated almost like a queen in her village. For the little community, having the benefit of a doctor's services was a priceless gift. Her smiling authority worked miracles; both children and adults listened to her advice and no longer feared illness.

She was very strict about the rules of cleanliness, which everyone knew but which were sometimes neglected. Hands must be washed frequently, particularly before meals, bodies must be washed every day, and feet before entering a house. The mouth and teeth must be purified, hair cut and body hair shaved regularly, and she advocated the use of ointments, creams and deodorants based on carob. Both rich and poor used a paste made from sand and fat; when added to natron, it cleaned and disinfected the skin.

At Pazair's urging, Neferet agreed to go for a walk beside the Nile.

'Are you happy here?' he asked.

'I think I'm useful.'

'I admire you a lot.'

'There are other doctors who deserve your admiration more than I do.'

'I've got to leave Thebes straight away. I've had a message from my scribe, Iarrot, saying I've been recalled to Memphis.'

'Because of this strange case?'

'Iarrot didn't say.'

'Have you made any progress?'

'We still haven't found find the fifth soldier, and we would have done if he had a regular job on the west bank. My investigation has reached a dead end.'

'Will you come back?' asked Neferet.

'As soon as I can.'

'You're worried, aren't you?'

'My room was searched.'

'To make you drop the case?'

'Someone thought I had a vital document. Now they know I haven't.'

'Aren't you taking too many risks?'

'Because of my incompetence, I'm making too many mistakes.'

'Don't be so hard on yourself. You've done nothing you need regret.'

'I want to put right the injustice that's been done to you.'

'You'll soon forget me.'

'I shan't – ever.'

She smiled, touched. 'Youthful promises are blown away by the evening breeze.'

'Mine aren't.' Pazair stopped, turned to her, and took her hands. 'I love you, Neferet. If you only knew how much I love you . . .'

Anxiety filled her eyes. 'My life is here, yours is in Memphis. Fate has decreed it.'

'I don't care about my career. If you love me, nothing else matters.'

'Don't be childish.'

'You are my happiness, Neferet. Without you, life is meaningless.'

She gently withdrew her hands. 'I need time to think, Pazair.'

He longed to take her in his arms, to hold her so tightly that no one could part them. But he must not shatter the fragile hope contained in her reply.

The shadow-eater watched Pazair's departure. The judge was leaving Thebes without having spoken to the fifth soldier, and was not taking away any compromising documents. The search of his room had revealed nothing.

The shadow-eater had not found the man, either. But he had had one small success: the soldier had been living in a small town to the south of the city, where he planned to set himself up as a repairer of chariots. Panicked by the baker's death, he had disappeared, and neither the judge nor the shadow-eater had managed to track him down. He knew he was in great danger, so he would hold his tongue.

Reassured, the shadow-eater decided to take the next boat for Memphis.

24

Tjaty Bagey had pains in his legs, which felt heavy and were so swollen that his ankle bones were all but invisible. He put on broad-fitting sandals with loose straps, but had no time for any other treatment. The more he stayed sitting in his office, the worse the swelling became, but the service of Egypt gave no scope for rest or absence.

His wife, Nedyt, had rejected the large official house outside the city that Pharaoh granted the tjaty, and Bagey had gone along with her decision, for he preferred the town to the country. Although at the pinnacle of government, he had not made himself rich: his duty came before his own prosperity. So they lived in a modest house in the centre of Memphis, watched day and night by guards. The tjaty of the Two Lands enjoyed perfect security; never in the entire history of Egypt had a tjaty been assassinated or even attacked.

Nedyt had found her husband's rise to power difficult to bear. Disadvantaged by being plain, short and plump, she refused to appear in society or attend official banquets. She longed for the days when Bagey had occupied an obscure post with limited responsibilities. Back then, he had come home early, helped her in the kitchen and had time to pay attention to his son and daughter.

As he walked to the palace, the tjaty's thoughts turned to his children. His son had originally been a carpenter, but his laziness had come to the attention of his master. As soon as he was told, Bagey had had the lad dismissed from the workshop and punished him by making him prepare rough bricks. Pharaoh had considered the decision unjust, and had reprimanded the tjaty, saying he was too strict with his own family. A tjaty must be careful not to favour his own, but to do the opposite was equally bad.* So Bagey's son had risen to become a checker of baked bricks. He had no other ambition; his only passion was playing board games with other lads of his own age.

---

*There is a case of a tjaty who was dismissed from his post because, out of fear of being accused of favouritism, he had been unjust towards those close to him.

Bagey was better pleased with his daughter. She was not attractive but her manners and behaviour were excellent, and she hoped one day to enter the temple as a weaver. Her father would not offer her any help; she must succeed by her talents alone.

When he reached his office, the tjaty was tired. Instead of sitting at his desk, he sat down on a low seat, slightly curved towards the centre, made of plaited cords in a fish-scale pattern. Before his daily meeting with the king, he must read the reports received from the various government secretariats. His back hunched and his feet aching, he had to force himself to concentrate.

His personal scribe interrupted him. 'I'm sorry to disturb you, Tjaty.'

'What is it?'

'A messenger from the Asian army has arrived with a report.'

'Summarize it for me.'

'General Asher's regiment has been cut off from the main body of our troops.'

'A rebellion?'

'Yes, by Adafi the Libyan, two Asiatic princelings and some sand-travellers.'

'Them again! Our informers have let themselves be caught off guard.'

'Are we to send reinforcements?'

'I shall consult His Majesty immediately.'

The king took the matter very seriously. He gave orders for two new regiments to leave for Asia, and the main army to move forward more quickly. If Asher had survived, he must wipe out the rebels.

Since the proclamation of the decree about security measures, the tjaty no longer knew where to turn to apply Pharaoh's instructions. Thanks to his efficient management, it would only take a few months to draw up an inventory of Egypt's wealth and her various reserves; but his emissaries would have to question the high priest of each temple and the governor of each province, draw up an impressive body of accounts and ensure that there were no mistakes. The king's demands had provoked an undercurrent of hostility, so Bagey, who was considered the one really responsible for this inquisition, would have to pour oil on troubled waters and calm numerous angry officials.

By late afternoon, Bagey had received confirmation that his instructions had been carried out to the letter. The garrison at the King's Walls was already on permanent alert, and from tomorrow its size would be doubled.

*

At the encampment, the evening was a sombre one. Tomorrow, they would attack the rebel fort in order to break through and try and establish a link with General Asher. The attack promised to be difficult. Many men would not be returning home.

Suti ate with the oldest soldier, a warrior who had been born in Memphis. He would be directing operations using the wheeled tower.

'In six months' time, my lad,' he said, 'I'll have retired. This is my last Asian campaign. Here, eat some of this fresh garlic. It'll purify your blood and stop you catching a chill.'

'It would go down better with a little coriander and some good wine.'

'We'll have a feast after our victory. Usually we eat well in this regiment. We often get beef and cakes, and quite fresh vegetables, and plenty of beer. In the old days, soldiers stole food all over the place, but Ramses forbade it and expelled the thieves from the army. I've never stolen from anybody. They'll give me a house in the country, a bit of land and a serving woman. I shan't pay many taxes and I can pass on my property to anyone I choose. You were right to sign on, lad: your future's assured.'

'As long as I get out of this hornets' nest alive.'

'Don't worry, we'll demolish that fort. But make sure you watch your left. Male death comes from that side, female from the right.'

'Hasn't the enemy got any women?'

'Oh yes, and brave ones, too.'

Suti decided that he'd watch both his left and his right – and he'd remember his back as well, as his chariot officer had told him to.

The Egyptian soldiers threw themselves into a wild dance, whirling their weapons above their heads, and pointing them skywards to ensure a favourable outcome and the courage to fight to the death. According to established custom, the battle would take place one hour after dawn. Only sand-travellers attacked without warning.

The old soldier stuck a feather in Suti's long black hair, and told him, 'It's the custom, for elite archers, and it represents the feather carried by the goddess Ma'at. With her help, your heart will be brave and your aim true.'

The footsoldiers, led by the former pirate carried the ladders. Suti climbed into the siege tower alongside the old man, and ten men pushed it towards the fort. The artificers had built a rough and ready earthen track, which enabled the wooden wheels to turn without too much difficulty.

'To the left,' ordered the old soldier.

The ground levelled out. Enemy archers fired from the battlements of the fort. Two Egyptians were killed, and an arrow just missed Suti's head.

'Now it's your turn, lad.'

Suti drew his horn-handled bow. If fired in a sweeping arc, his arrows could travel more than two hundred paces. Pulling back the bowstring as far as it would go, he concentrated hard, breathed out and let go.

A sand-traveller toppled from the battlements, shot through the heart. This success wiped away the footsoldiers' fear, and they ran straight at the enemy. When they were some hundred paces from their goal, Suti changed weapons. With his acacia-wood bow, which was more accurate and less tiring to use, he was able to make every arrow count, and he cleared half the battlements. Soon, the Egyptians were able to put up their ladders.

When the tower was no more than twenty paces from its objective, Suti's companion fell, an arrow in his belly. The tower speeded up and bumped against the walls of the fort. While his comrades were leaping onto the battlements and forcing their way inside the fortifications, Suti bent over the old soldier.

The wound was clearly mortal, but the old man raised his head a little and gasped, 'You'll have a fine retirement, my lad, just you see ... I was just unlucky.' His head lolled on his shoulder.

The Egyptians used a battering-ram to force open the gate; and the ex-pirate finished off the remains with his axe. Their opponents ran about in panic and disarray. The local princeling jumped on his horse and rode down the Egyptian officer who demanded his surrender. This unleashed a furious onslaught by the Egyptians, who gave no quarter.

While the fort was being set on fire, a fugitive clad in rags escaped from the conquerors' watchful gaze and fled towards the forest. Suti ran off in hot pursuit, and grabbed the tattered tunic, which ripped and came away in his hand.

It was a woman, young and comely. The very one who had robbed him.

Although naked, she kept running. To the accompaniment of his fellow soldiers' laughter and shouts of encouragement, Suti brought her down. She was terrified, and struggled long and hard. When she grew quiet, he picked her up, tied her hands and covered her with the remains of her pitiful dress.

'She belongs to you,' declared a soldier.

The few survivors, hands on heads, had abandoned their bows, shields, sandals and cudgels. According to the sacred texts, they had lost their souls and their names, and been drained of their sperm. The victors seized bronze dishes, oxen, donkeys and goats, burnt down the barracks, the furniture and fabrics. Nothing remained of the fort but a heap of charred rubble.

The former pirate came up to Suti. 'Our commander's dead, and so is the soldier in charge of the tower. You're the bravest of us, and a fine archer, you must take command.'

'But I'm a raw recruit.'

'You're a hero. We all agree that without you we'd have failed. Lead us north.'

Suti gave in, and agreed. He told the men to question the prisoners and to treat them properly. During the questioning, they established that the instigator of the rebellion, Adafi, had not been among the troops in the fort.

When they set off northwards, Suti marched at the head of the column, his bow in his hand. His prisoner walked beside him.

'What's your name?' he asked.

'Panther.'

Her beauty fascinated him. She was wild, with blonde hair, eyes like burning coals, a superb body and alluring lips. Her voice was warm and enchanting.

'And where are you from?'

'Libya. My father was one of the walking dead.'

'What do you mean?'

'In a raid, his skull was smashed open by an Egyptian sword. He should have died then, but he didn't. He was taken prisoner and worked as a farm labourer in the Delta. He forgot his language and his people and became an Egyptian. I hated him so much that when he did die I didn't even go to his funeral. I took up the fight in his place.'

'Why do you hate us?'

The question surprised Panther. 'We've been enemies for two thousand years!' she exclaimed.

'Wouldn't it be a good idea to arrange a truce?'

'Never!'

'I shall try to persuade you.'

Suti's charm was not entirely ineffective. Panther grudgingly raised her eyes to his, and asked, 'Am I to be your slave?'

'There aren't any slaves in Egypt.'

A soldier gave a shout of warning, and everyone flung himself to the ground. On the crest of a hill, the bushes were moving. A pack of wolves emerged, looked at the travellers, then continued on their way. Much relieved, the soldiers gave thanks to the gods.

'I'll be rescued,' declared Panther.

'Don't rely on anyone but yourself.'

'I'll betray you at the first opportunity.'

'Honesty's a rare virtue. I'm beginning to like you.'

She retreated into sulky silence.

They marched for two hours across stony terrain, then followed the bed of a dried-up river. His eyes glued to the rocky escarpments, Suti watched for the slightest sign of trouble.

When ten Egyptian archers barred their way, they knew that they were safe at last.

Pazair arrived at his office at about eleven o'clock in the morning, and found the door shut.

'Go and find Iarrot,' he told Kem.

'With Killer?'

'With Killer.'

'What if he's ill?'

'Bring him to me within the hour, no matter what state he's in.'

Kem hurried off.

When Iarrot arrived, red-faced and with swollen eyes, he explained in a whining voice, 'I was resting after an attack of indigestion. I took some cumin seeds in milk, but I still felt sick. The doctor told me to drink an infusion of juniper berries and take two days off work.'

'Why did you bombard Thebes police with messages for me?'

'Because of two emergencies.'

The judge's anger abated. 'What are they?'

'First, we've run out of papyrus. Second, checks have been made on the granaries under your jurisdiction. According to the note from the authorities, half the grain reserves are missing from the main store.' Iarrot lowered his voice. 'An enormous scandal is in the offing.'

The priests presented the first harvested grain to Osiris and offered bread to the goddess of harvests. Afterwards, a long procession of people carrying baskets of the precious foodstuff set off towards the grain stores, singing, 'A happy day is born for us.' They climbed steps leading to the grain stores' roofs, some of which were rectangular and others cylindrical, and emptied their treasures through a skylight which was closed by a trapdoor. A door at the foot of the building enabled the grain to be removed.

The overseer of the granaries greeted the judge coldly.

'The royal decree obliges me to check the grain reserves,' said Pazair.

'A specialist scribe has already done so for you.'

'What did he find?'

'He didn't tell me,' said the overseer. 'That concerns you alone.'

'Have a long ladder put up against the front of the main granary.'

'Must I repeat myself? A scribe has already checked.'

'Are you defying the law?'

At once, the overseer became less hostile. 'I'm only thinking of your safety, Judge Pazair. Climbing up there is dangerous, and you aren't used to doing such things.'

'So you don't know that half your reserves has disappeared?'

The overseer gaped at him in horror. 'What a disaster!'

'Have you any explanation?'

'Vermin – it must be.'

'Controlling vermin is your main responsibility, is it not?'

'I delegate the task to the health officials – they're the ones to blame.'

'Half the reserve,' said Pazair thoughtfully. 'That's an enormous quantity.'

'When you get vermin—'

'Put up the ladder.'

'It's pointless, I assure you. Besides, that's no job for a judge.'

'When I place my seal on the official report, you will be responsible before the law.'

Two workers brought a long ladder and leant it against the front of the grain store. Uneasily, Pazair climbed up; the rungs creaked, and it was not as stable as he might have wished. When he was halfway up, it swayed.

'Hold it steady!' he ordered.

The overseer looked around, as if seeking a means of escape, but Kem laid a hand on his shoulder and Killer crouched down beside his legs.

'Do as the judge says,' advised the Nubian. 'You wouldn't want an accident to happen, would you?'

They held the ladder firmly. Reassured, Pazair continued his climb. He reached the top, sixteen cubits above the ground, pushed across a latch, and opened the trapdoor. The store was full to bursting.

'That's unbelievable!' gasped the overseer when Pazair told him. 'The man who checked lied to you.'

'Or you were both involved,' suggested Pazair.

'Oh no, Judge! I've been deceived, you can be sure of that.'

'I find it difficult to believe you.'

The baboon growled and bared its teeth.

'He hates liars,' said Kem.

'Keep that creature under control,' quavered the overseer.

'I can't control him at all when a witness annoys him.'

The overseer hung his head. 'He promised me a rich reward if I backed up what he said. We were going to steal the grain that was supposed to be missing, and make a fine profit. Since the crime didn't actually take place, will I be able to keep my job?'

Pazair worked late. He drew up a document dismissing the overseer, added supporting arguments, and searched in vain among the lists of officials for the man who had checked the grain reserves. No doubt he had given a false name, but he would have to be found before the overseer was formally dismissed. Thefts of grain did happen occasionally, but theft on such a large scale as this was unheard of. Was it a single act, limited to one store in Memphis, or a sign of widespread corruption? If the latter, that would justify Pharaoh's surprising decree. The king was counting on the judges to re-establish equity and righteousness. If everyone acted justly, whether his office be humble or important, evil would soon be eliminated.

In the flame of the lamp, he saw Neferet's face, her eyes, her lips. At this hour of the night, she would be asleep. Was she dreaming of him?

25

Accompanied by Kem and Killer, Pazair took a fast boat to the largest papyrus plantation in the Delta, which was run by Bel-Tran under authorization from the king. In the mud and swamps, the plants with the tufted leaves and three-sided stems could grow to a height of twelve cubits and form dense thickets. The parasol-shaped flowers grew in tight clumps, crowning the precious plant.

The woody roots were used to make furniture; the fibres and bark to make mats, baskets, nets, cables, ropes and even sandals and kilts for the poorest folk. As for the spongy sap which flowed copiously beneath the bark, it underwent special treatment to become Egypt's famous papyrus, which was the envy of the world.

Bel-Tran was not content to let nature take its course, so on his immense estate he had cultivated papyrus to increase production and export a portion of it. For every Egyptian, the verdant stems symbolized youth and vigour; the goddesses' sceptres were shaped like papyrus stems, and temple pillars were stone representations of the plant.

A broad path had been opened up through the thickets. Pazair encountered naked peasants carrying heavy bales on their backs. They chewed the tender shoots of the papyrus, drank the juice and spat out the pulp. In front of the large warehouses where the material was kept dry in wooden cases or in terracotta pots, specialists were carefully washing selected fibres, before spreading them out on mats or planks.

The sections, which were a little less than a cubit long, were cut lengthways, and laid out in two layers, one on top of the other at right angles. Other skilled workers covered the whole arrangement with a damp cloth and struck it repeatedly with a wooden mallet. At last came the delicate moment when the strips of papyrus must stick together as they dried, without the addition of any other substance.

'Magnificent, isn't it?'

The stocky man who addressed Pazair had a round, moon-shaped head, and black hair smoothed down with balm. He was heavily built, with plump hands and feet, yet he seemed full of energy, almost agitated.

He hitched up his kilt and adjusted his fine linen shirt. Although he bought his clothes from the finest weaver in Memphis, they always seemed too small, too large or too loose.

He went on, 'I'm honoured that you should visit me, Judge Pazair. My name is Bel-Tran. I am the owner of this estate.'

'I'd like buy some papyrus,' said Pazair.

'Come and see my finest specimens.'

Bel-Tran led him into the warehouse where he kept his best papyri, in rolls made up of about twenty sheets, and unrolled one.

'Look at this splendid example. See how finely made it is, and what a wonderful shade of yellow. None of my competitors has succeeded in matching it. One of the secrets is the time it is exposed to the sun, but there are many other important points – on which my lips are sealed.'

Pazair touched the end of the roll. 'It's perfect.'

Bel-Tran did not conceal his pride. 'I made it for the scribes who copy out the ancient *Words of Wisdom** and add to them. The palace library has ordered a dozen like this for next month. I also supply papyri for copies of the *Book of Going Forth by Day*, which are placed in tombs.'

'Your business seems to be flourishing.'

'It is indeed, as long as I work night and day. But I'm not complaining – I love my work. Providing a basis for texts and hieroglyphs is vital work, isn't it?'

'My funds are limited. I can't afford such beautiful papyri.'

'I can provide some which aren't so fine, but are still of excellent quality. Their strength is guaranteed.'

The judge was happy with the goods, but the price was still too high.

Bel-Tran scratched the back of his neck. 'I like you very much, Judge Pazair, and I hope the feeling is mutual. I love justice, for it is the key to happiness. Will you allow me the pleasure of giving you this consignment?'

'I'm touched by your generosity, but I'm afraid I can't accept.'

'But I insist.'

'Any gift, in any form, would be classed as corruption. If you will allow me time to pay, it must be noted down and registered.'

'Very well, then. I've heard that you have no hesitation in attacking important merchants who don't respect the law. That's very brave.'

'It's simply my duty.'

'In Memphis recently, traders' moral standards have tended to decline. I assume Pharaoh's decree will stop this worrying development.'

---

*Collections of maxims, passed on from generation to generation.

'My colleagues and I will use it to do so, though I know little of Memphite morals.'

'You'll soon get used to them. These last few years, competition between merchants has been rather fierce, and they've been happy to deal one another severe blows.'

'Have you suffered any?'

'Yes, like everyone else. But I fight back. At first, I was employed as an accounting assistant on a large estate in the Delta, where papyrus was poorly exploited. My salary was tiny and I toiled night and day. I suggested improvements to the owner of the estate, and he accepted them, and raised me to the rank of accountant. I'd have been happy to go on the way I was, but I had some bad luck.'

The two men left the warehouse and walked along the flower-lined path which led to Bel-Tran's house.

'May I offer you a drink? I'm not trying to corrupt you, I assure you.'

Pazair smiled. He could tell that the man wanted to talk, so he said, 'You said you had some bad luck. What happened?'

'It was rather humiliating. I'd married a woman older than myself, from Elephantine; we got on well, despite a few minor squabbles. I usually got home late from work, but she accepted that. One afternoon, I took sick – overwork, probably – and had to be taken home. My wife was in bed with the gardener. At first I wanted to kill her, then I wanted to have her tried for adultery, but . . . the punishment's very heavy.* I made do with a divorce, which was pronounced immediately.'

'It must have been very painful for you.'

'I was deeply hurt, and I consoled myself by working twice as hard. The estate owner offered me a piece of land which no one wanted. Using a system of irrigation which I devised myself, I made it pay: the first harvests were a success, prices were good, and my customers were happy – and the palace noticed me! I was overwhelmed to become a supplier to the court. I was granted the marshes which you crossed to get here.'

'Congratulations.'

'Hard work is always rewarded. Are you married?'

'No.'

'I risked trying it again, and I'm glad I did.' Bel-Tran swallowed a pastille made from oliban resin and aromatic reeds from Phoenicia, a mixture which sweetened the breath. 'I'll introduce you to my young wife.'

---

*Adultery was considered a serious offence, for it represented a betrayal of a promise, and marriage rested on mutual trust.

*

The lady Silkis was terrified of seeing her first wrinkle appear. So she had procured some oil of fenugreek, which smoothed and freshened the skin. The perfumier separated pods and seeds, prepared a paste and heated it. The oil rose to the surface. Carefully, Silkis smeared her face with a paste made from honey, red natron and northern salt, then massaged the rest of her body with powdered alabaster.

Thanks to Nebamon's skill, her face and her body had been made more slender, according to her husband's wishes. She felt she was still too heavy and a little on the plump side, but Bel-Tran didn't criticize her for her voluptuous thighs. Before welcoming him for a substantial lunch, she painted her lips with red ochre, smoothed a gentle cream over her cheeks, and lined her eyes with green kohl. Then she rubbed her scalp with an antiseptic lotion containing beeswax and resin, which prevented the appearance of white hairs.

Silkis looked in the mirror and was satisfied with her reflection. She put on a wig made from perfumed locks of real hair. Her husband had given her this little treasure on the birth of their second child, a boy.

Her serving-woman announced the arrival of Bel-Tran and a guest. In panic, Silkis snatched up her mirror again. Would Bel-Tran think she looked attractive enough, or criticize a flaw she hadn't noticed? She had no time to re-do her make-up or change her dress.

Nervously, she went out of her bedchamber.

'Silkis, my darling,' said Bel-Tran, 'this is Judge Pazair, from Memphis.'

The young woman smiled, with respectable modesty and shyness.

'We entertain many buyers and experts on papyrus making,' Bel-Tran went on, 'but you're our first judge. It's a great honour.'

A serving woman brought beer, which had been kept cool by the large jars in which it was stored. She was followed by two children, a little red-haired girl and a small boy who looked like his father. They greeted Pazair, then ran to Bel-Tran, clamouring for his attention.

'Ah, these children,' said Bel-Tran. 'We adore them, but sometimes they're exhausting.'

Silkis agreed with a nod. Fortunately, her confinements had been straightforward and had not spoiled her body, thanks to long periods of rest. She hid a few rebellious curves under a full dress of fine linen, discreetly decorated with little red fringes. Her earrings, which were ornamented with ivory, had been imported from Nubia.

Pazair was invited to sit down on a chair made from papyrus.

'Original, isn't it?' said Bel-Tran. 'I like new things. If people like the design, I shall start selling it.'

Pazair marvelled at the layout of the house. It had ten rooms, all dimly lit – Silkis feared the sun, for it reddened her skin – and was laid out in a long line, very low, without a terrace because, said Bel-Tran, 'I suffer from vertigo. But come, Judge, and sit under this canopy, where we'll be sheltered from the heat.'

'Do you like Memphis, Judge?' asked Silkis.

'I preferred my village.'

'Where do you live?'

'Above my office. My quarters are a bit cramped, and since I took up my post there has been no shortage of cases to investigate. Documents are building up so fast that in a few months I shall be crowded out.'

'That's easily put right,' said Bel-Tran. 'One of my best business contacts is the official responsible for storing documents at the palace. He's the person who allocates space in state warehouses.'

'I wouldn't want to take advantage.'

'You won't. You're bound to meet him sooner or later, and sooner would be better, that's all. I'll give you his name, and you can sort it out.'

Pazair drank a little more of his beer. It was delicious.

'This summer,' said Bel-Tran, 'I'm going to open a papyrus warehouse near the weapons workshops. Delivery to government secretariats will be much faster.'

'Then your new premises will come under my jurisdiction.'

'I'm delighted to hear it. If I'm any judge of character, your controls will be thorough and effective, and that will help to establish my reputation firmly. Despite all the opportunities that come up, I loathe fraud – quite apart from anything else, you always get caught red-handed sooner or later. Egypt does not like fraudsters. As the proverb says, "A lie finds no ferry and will not cross the river."'

'Have you heard anything about an illegal trade in grain?' asked Pazair.

'When the scandal breaks, there'll be some severe sentences.'

'Who's involved?'

'All I know is that there are rumours that part of the harvest stored in the granaries is being stolen by certain people for their own profit. Just rumours, as I say, but they're persistent.'

'Haven't the authorities investigated?'

'Yes, but without success. But to more pleasant matters. Will you stay and have lunch with us?'

'I don't want to cause any inconvenience.'

'My wife and I would love to have you.'

Silkis leant forward and smiled her agreement.

Pazair enjoyed an excellent lunch: goose liver, herb salad and olive oil, fresh peas, pomegranates and pastries, the whole accompanied by a red Delta wine dating from the first year of Ramses' reign. The children ate on their own, but clamoured for cakes.

'Are you planning to start a family, Judge?' asked Silkis.

'My work keeps me very busy,' replied Pazair.

'Ah,' said Bel-Tran, 'but having a wife and children is surely the goal of every man's life. There's no greater happiness.'

Thinking herself unnoticed, the little girl stole a pastry.

Her father seized her by the wrist. 'You shall have no games and no walk this afternoon.'

The child burst into floods of tears and stamped her feet.

'You're too strict,' protested Silkis. 'It's not so very serious.'

'Having everything you want and yet stealing is a terrible thing.'

'Didn't you do the same, when you were a child?'

'My parents were poor but I never stole a thing from anyone, and I won't let my daughter steal, either.'

The child wept even more bitterly.

'Take her away,' said Bel-Tran.

Silkis obeyed.

'Ah, the trials of bringing up children! But there are more joys than pains, thanks be to the gods.'

After the meal, Bel-Tran showed Pazair the batch of papyrus sheets he planned to supply him with. He proposed strengthening the edges and adding a few rolls of a lower quality and whitish colour, to be used for rough work.

The two men took a cordial leave of each other.

Mentmose's bald head turned red, betraying an anger he could scarcely contain. 'These are rumours, Judge Pazair, nothing but rumours.'

'And yet you did investigate.'

'Merely as a matter of routine.'

'And you found nothing?'

'Nothing at all. No one would dare steal wheat from a state grain store – it's a grotesque idea! And why are you bothering yourself with this matter?

'Because the grain store is under my jurisdiction.'

Mentmose calmed down a little. 'So it is. I'd forgotten. Have you got proof?'

'The best of all: written evidence.'

Mentmose read the document. 'The checker noted that half the reserves had been used up. What's unusual about that?'

'The store is absolutely full – I saw it with my own eyes.'

Mentmose stood up, turned away and looked out of the window. 'This note is signed.'

'Yes, but it's a false name. It isn't on the list of accredited officials. You're best placed to find this elusive character, aren't you?'

'You have questioned the overseer of the granaries, I presume?'

'He claims not to know the real name of the man he dealt with, and to have seen him only once.'

'Do you think he's lying?'

'Perhaps not.' Despite Killer's presence, the steward had said nothing more, so Pazair believed he was telling the truth.

'There must be a lot of people involved.'

'There may be.'

'Judging by the evidence, the overseer's behind it all.'

'Perhaps, but I don't trust the evidence.'

'Hand the overseer over to me. I'll make him talk.'

'That's out of the question,' said Pazair.

'Then what do you suggest?'

'That a permanent and discreet watch is kept on the store. When the thief and his accomplices come for the grain you'll catch them red-handed, and then you'll be able to get the names of everyone involved.'

'But won't they have been alerted by the overseer's dismissal?'

'Quite. So he must continue in his post for the time being.'

'It's a complicated and risky plan.'

'I don't think so. But if you have a better one, I'll accept it.'

'I shall do what is necessary.'

26

Branir's house was the only haven of peace where Pazair's torments lessened. He had written a long letter to Neferet, declaring his love for her once again, and begging her to answer with her heart. He felt guilty for troubling her, but he could not hide his passion. Henceforth, his life was in Neferet's hands.

Branir laid flowers before the busts of the ancestors in the first room of his house. Pazair meditated at his side. Cornflowers with green calyxes and yellow persea flowers struggled against oblivion and enabled the sages to live longer in the paradise of Osiris.

Once the ceremony was over, master and pupil went up to the terrace. Pazair loved this time of day, when the light was dying, only to be reborn in the brightness of night.

Branir looked at him closely. 'You're shedding your youth like a worn-out skin. It was happy and peaceful, but now you must make a success of your life.'

'You know everything about me.'

'Even the things you don't confide to me?'

'It's pointless trying to hide anything from you. Do you think she'll accept me?'

'Neferet never play-acts. She will act in accordance with the truth.'

Pazair's throat tightened with strain. 'Perhaps I've gone mad.'

'There is only one act of madness: coveting what belongs to other people.'

'I was forgetting what you taught me: to increase one's intelligence through righteousness, deliberation and precision, never thinking of one's own happiness, but always acting so as to enable men to make their way in peace, temples to be built and orchards to blossom for the gods.* My love is burning me up, and I can't help feeding its flames.'

'That's good. Travel to the very ends of your being, to the point

*These words were inscribed on stelae of the sages, placed inside temples.

where you will never again turn back. May the heavens permit you never to stray from the right path.'

'I'm not neglecting my duties, though,' said Pazair.

'Any news of the Sphinx affair?'

'I've reached a dead end.'

'Is there no hope of progress?'

'Only if I find the fifth guard, or if Suti finds out something about General Asher.'

'That's a rather slender hope.'

'I know. But I shan't give up, even if I have to wait several years before I get any more clues. Don't forget, I have proof that the army lied. Officially, five guards were killed, but one of them lived and became a baker in Thebes.'

'The fifth guard is alive,' declared Branir, as confidently as if he could see the man nearby. 'Don't give up, for misfortune is roaming the land.'

There was a long silence. Branir's solemnity had shaken Pazair. The old doctor had the gift of second sight; sometimes he perceived a reality which was as yet invisible to others.

'I shall soon leave this house,' said Branir eventually. 'The time has come for me to live in the temple, and end my days there. The silence of the gods of Karnak will fill my ears, and I shall converse with the stones of eternity. Each day will be more serene than the last, and I shall move towards old age, which prepares a man to appear before the court of Osiris.'

Pazair protested, 'But I still need you to teach me!'

'What advice can I give you? Tomorrow, I shall take up the staff of old age and walk towards the Beautiful West, from whence no man returns.'

'If I really have uncovered a formidable sickness afflicting Egypt, and if it is possible for me to fight it, your moral authority will be essential to me. Your actions could prove decisive. Please wait a little, I beg of you.'

'Whatever happens, this house will belong to you as soon as I have retired to the temple.'

Sheshi lit the fire with date kernels and charcoal, placed a horn-shaped cooking pot on the flames and kindled them with the aid of his bellows. He tried one more time to perfect a new method of fusing metal, by pouring the molten substance into special moulds. He had an exceptional memory, and never wrote anything down for fear of being betrayed. His two assistants, strong, tireless fellows, were capable of keeping the fire going for hours on end by blowing down long, hollow stems.

The unbreakable weapon would soon be ready. Equipped with swords and spears which could withstand any test, Pharaoh's soldiers would shatter the Asian enemy's helmets and pierce their armour.

Shouts and the sounds of a struggle interrupted his reflections. Sheshi opened the workshop door and came up against two guards, who held a man with white hair and red hands in an iron grip. He was panting like a worn-out horse, his eyes were streaming, and his kilt was torn.

'He got into the metal stores,' explained one of the guards. 'We spotted him, and he tried to run away.'

Sheshi recognized Qadash, but did not show the slightest surprise.

'Let me go, you brutes!' demanded Qadash.

'You're a thief,' replied the senior guard.

What crazy notion had Qadash taken into his head? For a long time he had dreamt of having celestial iron with which to manufacture his instruments, so that he would become an unrivalled tooth doctor. He had lost his head over that private dream, forgetting the conspirators' plan.

'I shall send one of my men to the office of the Judge of the Porch,' announced the officer. 'We need a judge here within the hour.'

For fear of drawing suspicion to himself, Sheshi dared not oppose this plan of action.

Dragged out of bed in the middle of the night, the Judge of the Porch's scribe did not consider it necessary to wake his master, who was very particular about his sleep. He consulted the list of judges, and chose the last name on it, a man called Pazair, who, since he was the lowest in the hierarchy, probably needed to learn his craft.

Pazair was not asleep. He was daydreaming of Neferet, imagining her close to him, tender and reassuring. He would tell her about his cases, and she would tell him about her patients. Together they would share the respective burdens of their work, and enjoy a simple happiness which was reborn with each day's sun.

Way-Finder started braying and Brave barked. Pazair got up and opened the window. An armed guard showed him the order issued by the Judge of the Porch's scribe. Pazair threw a short cape about his shoulders, and followed the guard to the barracks.

At the top of the stairs leading down to the basement stood two soldiers, their spears crossed. They moved them aside to allow the judge to pass, and Sheshi met him at the door of his workshop.

'I was expecting the Judge of the Porch,' said Sheshi.

'I'm sorry to disappoint you, but I was given the task. What has happened?'

'An attempted theft.'

'Do you suspect anyone?'

'The guilty man has been arrested.'

'Then I can hear the facts and proceed to the committal, and he can be tried without delay.'

Sheshi looked embarrassed.

'I must question him,' said Pazair. 'Where is he?'

'In the corridor, on your left.'

The culprit was sitting on an anvil, under armed guard. He started when he saw the judge.

'Qadash!' exclaimed Pazair. 'What are you doing here?'

'I was taking a walk near the barracks, when I was attacked and brought to this place by force.'

'That isn't true,' protested the guard. 'He got into a storeroom, and we caught him.'

'You're lying! I shall lodge a complaint against you for assault.'

'But there are several witnesses, and they all accuse you,' Sheshi reminded him.

'What does this storeroom contain?' asked Pazair.

'Metals, mainly copper,' said Sheshi.

Pazair asked Qadash, 'Are you short of metals to make your instruments?'

'No. This is all a silly misunderstanding.'

Sheshi went over to Pazair and whispered a few words in his ear.

'As you wish,' said Pazair, and the two of them went into the workshop.

'The work I'm doing here requires the utmost discretion,' said Sheshi. 'Could you arrange for the case to be heard in secret?'

'Certainly not.'

'But in special cases—'

'Don't say any more, please.'

'Qadash is an honourable, wealthy man. I can't understand why he did it.'

'What is the nature of your work here?' asked Pazair.

'It's to do with making weapons. I'm sure you understand.'

'There's no specific law for your line of work. If Qadash is accused of theft, he'll defend himself as he wishes and you'll have to appear.'

'And I'll have to answer questions?'

'Of course.'

Sheshi stroked his moustache. 'In that case, I'd rather not lodge a complaint.'

'That is your right.'

'Above all, it's in the interests of Egypt. Indiscreet ears, in court or elsewhere, would be disastrous. I'll leave Qadash to you – as far as I'm concerned, nothing has happened. As for you, Judge, do please remember that you're sworn to secrecy.'

Pazair left the barracks with Qadash. As they went, he told him, 'No charge has been brought against you.'

'Well I want to bring one.'

'Unfavourable witnesses, your unaccountable presence here at a strange time, the suspicion of theft: they all add up to a damning case against you.'

Qadash coughed, hawked and spat. 'Very well, I give up.'

'But I don't.'

'Pardon?'

'I don't mind getting up in the middle of the night, and investigating in whatever conditions I have to, but I will not be taken for a fool. Tell me exactly what you were doing there, or I shall charge you with insulting a judge.'

Qadash spoke with great embarrassment. 'Top-quality copper – perfectly pure. I've been longing for some for years.'

'How did you hear about this warehouse?'

'The officer in charge of the barracks is a client of mine – and a loose-tongued one at that. He boasted, and I took my chance. Barracks never used to be so well guarded.'

'You decided to steal.'

'No, I was going to pay! I was going to exchange the metal for several fat oxen – the soldiers love them. And my instruments would have been wonderful, so light and precise. But that little man with the moustache was so cold. It was impossible to come to an arrangement with him.'

'Not everyone in Egypt is corrupt.'

'Corrupt?' said Qadash. 'What on earth are you talking about? Just because two individuals do a deal, that doesn't necessarily mean it's an illegal one. You have a very pessimistic view of the human race.' And he went off, grumbling to himself.

Pazair walked on in the darkness. Qadash's explanation had not convinced him. A store of metals, in a barracks . . . the army again. And yet this incident seemed linked not to the soldiers' disappearance but to the distress of a soul in torment, a tooth doctor who could not accept that his skills were failing.

The moon was full. According to legend, a hare armed with a knife lived on it; he had a warlike spirit, and cut off the heads of the shadows. Pazair would happily have taken him on as a scribe. The night-sun waxed and waned, filling with light and then emptying itself of it; the airborne boat would carry his thoughts to Neferet.

*

Nile water was famous as an aid to digestion. It was light, and brought harmful humours out of the body. Some doctors believed that its healing powers came from the medicinal herbs that grew on the banks and passed on their virtues to the tide. When the annual flood was unleashed, it carried pieces of vegetation and mineral salts with it. The people filled thousands of jars with the water, which stayed fresh and did not spoil.

Nevertheless, Neferet checked last year's reserves. If she thought the contents of a vessel were tainted, she threw in a sweet almond: twenty-four hours later, the water would be clear and delicious. Some jars were three years old and still excellent.

Reassured, she turned to watch the washerman at work. At the palace, this task was given to a trusted man, for the cleanliness of one's clothes was considered essential – the same was true in any community, large or small. After washing and wringing out the clothes, the man had to strike them with a wooden beater, then shake them and hang them on a rope strung between two poles.

'Are you by any chance ill?' asked Neferet.

'Why do you ask?'

'Because you have no energy. The washing has been grey for several days.'

'Ah, this is a difficult job,' said the washerman. 'Women's soiled linens are the worst.'

'Water alone isn't enough. Use this cleanser and this perfume.'

Gruffly, disarmed by her smile, the washerman accepted the two jars.

Neferet went next to the grain stores. To stave off attacks by insects, she emptied wood ash into the stores, a cheap and efficient means of purification. A few weeks from the flood, she would safeguard the cereals.

While she was inspecting the last compartment in the granary, she received a new delivery from Kani: parsley, rosemary, sage, cumin and mint. Dried or reduced to powder, the herbs would be used as the basis for some of the remedies she prescribed. The potions had relieved the old man's pain, and he was so happy to be remaining among his own people that his health was improving.

In spite of the doctor's discretion, her successes had not gone unnoticed. Her reputation grew quickly through word of mouth, and many peasants from the west bank came to consult her. She never sent anyone away, and took as much time as was necessary over each case. After exhausting days, she often spent part of the night preparing pills, ointments and poultices, helped by two widows who had been chosen for their attention to detail. After a few hours' sleep, dawn brought another procession of patients to her door.

She had not imagined her career being like this, but she loved to heal. Seeing joy return to an anxious face rewarded her amply for her efforts. Nebamon had done her a service by forcing her to develop her skills among the most humble folk. Here, the fine words of a society doctor would have failed; the ploughman, the fisherman, the mother, all wanted to be cured quickly and cheaply.

When she grew tired, the little green monkey, which she had brought from Memphis, cheered her with her games. Mischief reminded Neferet of her first meeting with Pazair, so entire, so uncompromising, at once disturbing and attractive. What woman could live with a judge whose vocation took precedence over everything else?

When Neferet got back to her workshop, ten bearers were depositing baskets outside, while Mischief bounded from one to the next. Neferet looked in the baskets: they contained willow bark, natron, white oil, oliban, honey, terebinth resin, and large quantities of various types of animal fat.

'Is all this for me?' she asked in astonishment.

'Are you Neferet the doctor?'

'Yes.'

'Then this is yours.'

'But these things cost . . .'

'It's all been paid for.'

'Who by?'

'Don't know – all we do is deliver. Sign this receipt, please.'

Neferet duly wrote her name on a wooden tablet. She was stunned and delighted. Now she could make up complex prescriptions and treat serious illnesses without anyone else's involvement.

When Sababu entered Neferet's house at sunset, Neferet was not surprised. She said, 'I was expecting you.'

'You guessed?' asked Sababu.

'The balm for your rheumatism will soon be ready. I have all the ingredients.'

Sababu no longer looked like a pauper. Her hair was decorated with scented reeds, and she wore a necklace of lotus flowers fashioned from cornelian. Her linen robe, which was transparent from the waist down, openly displayed her long legs.

She said, 'I want to be treated by you, and only by you. The other doctors are charlatans and thieves.'

'Isn't that a bit harsh?'

'I know what I'm saying. Your price will be my price.'

'Your gift is magnificent. I now have enough expensive ingredients to treat hundreds of cases.'

Sababu smiled. 'Mine first, though.'

'Have you made your fortune?'

'I've set up in business again. Thebes is a smaller town than Memphis, and its spirit is more religious and less worldly, but the rich citizens like ale-houses and their pretty inhabitants just as much. I took on a few young women, rented a pretty house in the centre of town, paid the head of the city guards his due, and opened the doors of an establishment whose name was soon well known. You have the proof of that in front of you.'

'You're very generous.'

'Don't deceive yourself. I just want to be looked after well.'

'Will you follow my advice?'

'To the letter. I run the ale-house, but I no longer entertain clients.'

'I'm sure you have no shortage of invitations.'

'I am willing to give a man pleasure but not vice versa, so I'm inaccessible.'

Neferet blushed.

'Doctor, don't say I've shocked you?'

'No, of course not.'

'You give a great deal of love, but do you receive any?'

'The question's irrelevant.'

'Don't tell me,' said Sababu, amused, 'you're still a virgin. It'll be a lucky man who seduces you.'

'Lady Sababu, I—'

'Lady? Me? You're joking!'

Neferet said firmly, 'Close the door and take off your dress. Until you're completely cured, you must come here each day and I'll apply the balm.'

Sababu undressed and lay down on the massage slab. 'Doctor, you deserve to be truly happy, too.'

27

Strong currents made the river dangerous, so Suti slung Panther over his shoulder.

'Stop struggling,' he said. 'If you fall off, you'll drown.'

'You just want to humiliate me.'

'Do you want to find out?'

She stopped struggling. Suti waded into the waist-deep water, supporting himself on boulders as he made his way across.

The water got still deeper, and he told Panther, 'Climb on my back and put your arms round my neck.'

'I can nearly swim.'

'You can finish learning later.'

Once, he slipped and Panther cried out. When he resumed his swift and agile progress, she clung even more tightly to him.

'Make yourself light and kick your legs,' he said.

Suti had a moment of panic as a wild wave covered his head, but he withstood it and reached the opposite bank.

Once there, he drove a stake into the ground, tied a rope to it and threw the other end of the rope across to the other riverbank, where a soldier fixed it firmly in position. Had she wanted, Panther could have run away.

The survivors of the attack and General Asher's detachment of archers crossed the river. The last footsoldier, sure of his own strength, foolishly let go of the rope. Weighed down by his weapons, he hit a rock just below the surface, and sank beneath the water, unconscious.

Suti dived in.

As if delighted to have captured two victims at once, the current grew stronger. Swimming underwater, Suti spotted the soldier. He slid his hands under the man's arms, stopped him sinking any further and tried to lift him up. The drowning man came to his senses, elbowed his rescuer in the chest and was swept away by the water. Suti's lungs were burning, and he was forced to abandon him and fight his way back to land.

'It wasn't your fault,' said Panther as she rubbed him dry.

'I don't like death.'

'He was only a stupid Egyptian.'

He slapped her.

Shocked, she threw him a look of hatred. 'No one's ever treated me like that.'

'More's the pity.'

'Do they beat women in your country?'

'Women have the same rights and duties as men. Now that I think of it, you didn't deserve more than a smacked bottom.' He rose threateningly.

'Get away from me!'

'Are you sorry for what you said?'

Panther's lips remained resolutely shut.

The sound of galloping horses diverted Suti. Soldiers came running out of their tents, and he snatched up his bow and quiver.

'If you want to go, go,' he told Panther.

'You'd find me and kill me.'

He shrugged.

'A curse on all Egyptians!'

The hoofbeats heralded not a surprise attack but the arrival of General Asher and his men. Already the news of the victory at the fort had spread.

The former pirate embraced Suti. 'I'm proud to know a hero. Asher will give you at least five donkeys, two bows, three bronze spears and a round shield. You won't be a simple soldier for long. You're brave, my boy, and that isn't common, even in the army.'

Suti rejoiced. At last he was approaching his goal. It was up to him to find a way of extracting information from the general's entourage and spot the fatal flaw. He would not fail; Pazair would be proud of him.

A huge man wearing a helmet hailed him: 'Are you the one they call Suti?'

'He's the one.' The pirate nodded. 'He enabled us to take the enemy fort and risked his life trying to save the man who drowned.'

'General Asher has promoted you to chariot officer. First thing tomorrow, you will help us to pursue that scum Adafi.'

'You mean he's been put to flight?'

'He's as slippery as an eel. But the rebellion's been crushed, and in the end we shall get our hands on that coward. Dozens of good men died in the ambushes he set. He kills at night like some deadly predator, corrupts the tribal chiefs, and thinks of nothing but stirring up trouble. Come with me, Suti. The general wants to decorate you himself.'

Although he loathed these ceremonies, in which one man's vanity simply exacerbated another man's boastfulness, Suti agreed. Seeing the general face to face would be compensation for the dangers he had run.

The hero walked between two ranks of enthusiastic soldiers, who banged their helmets against their shields and roared the victor's name. From a distance, General Asher did not look at all like a great warrior: he was short and stiff, more like a scribe who had been worn down by the minutiae of government.

Suti came to an abrupt halt a few yards from him.

Immediately, somebody gave him a shove in the back. 'Go on. The general's waiting for you.'

'Don't be afraid, my lad.'

White-faced, the young man advanced.

Asher took a step towards him. 'I am happy to meet the archer whose praises everyone is singing. Chariot Officer Suti, I hereby award you the Golden Fly for bravery. Keep this jewel. It is the proof of your courage.'

Suti bowed and accepted the award. His comrades crowded round and congratulated him. They all wanted to see and touch the decoration, which was coveted by every soldier. One or two of them noticed that the hero's thoughts seemed to be somewhere else, no doubt a result of high emotion.

When he returned to his tent, after a drinking session sanctioned by the general, Suti became the brunt of bawdy jibes. Surely beautiful Panther had different assaults in store for him?

Suti stretched out on his back. His eyes were open, but unseeing. Panther dared not speak, and huddled far away from him. She thought he looked like a demon who had been deprived of blood and was yearning to drain it from a new victim.

General Asher . . . Suti could not get the general's face out of his mind. It was the face of the very man who had tortured and murdered an Egyptian, a few yards from Suti's hiding place.

General Asher, a coward, a liar and a traitor.

The morning light shone through the bars of a high window, lighting up one of the hundred and thirty-four pillars in the immense chamber. The master builders had created the country's largest stone forest in the temple at Karnak, decorated with ritual scenes in which Pharaoh was shown making offerings to the gods. The vivid colours were revealed only at certain times; you had to live there for an entire year to follow the path of the sun's rays as it lit pillar after pillar, unveiling secret rites scene by scene.

Two men were conversing as they walked slowly along the central aisle, which was bordered by stone lotus flowers with outspread petals. The first was Branir, the second the High Priest of Amon, a man of seventy whose duty it was to govern the gods' sacred city, watch over its wealth and lead the priestly hierarchy.

'I have heard of your request, Branir. You, who have guided so many young people onto the path of wisdom, now wish to withdraw from the world and dwell within the inner temple.'

'That is my wish. My eyes are growing weak, and my legs are reluctant to walk.'

'Old age does not seem to handicap you so very much.'

'Appearances can be deceptive.'

'Your career is far from over,' said the High Priest.

'I have passed on everything I know to Neferet, and I no longer see patients. As for my house in Memphis, I have already willed it to Judge Pazair.'

'Nebamon has not exactly encouraged Neferet, has he?'

'He makes her undergo harsh tests, but he does not know her true nature. Her heart is as strong as her face is gentle.'

'Pazair is a native of Thebes, is he not?'

'Indeed.'

'You seem to have total trust in him.'

'He has fire within him.'

'Flames can destroy,' pointed out the High Priest.

'But if they are controlled they illuminate.'

'What role have you in mind for him?'

'Destiny will take care of that.'

'You understand people so well. To retire early would deprive Egypt of your gift.'

'A successor will emerge,' said Branir.

'You know, I'm thinking of retiring, too.'

'Your responsibilities are very heavy.'

'And they get heavier by the day. Too much administration, not enough meditation. Pharaoh and his council have accepted my request. In a few weeks, I shall move to a little house on the eastern bank of the sacred lake, and devote myself to the study of the ancient texts.'

'Then we shall be neighbours.'

'I fear not. Your house will be much more impressive.'

'What do you mean?'

'I mean that you, Branir, are my designated successor.'

Denes and Nenophar had accepted Bel-Tran's invitation. The man was but newly rich and his ambitions were all too clear but, nevertheless, the papyrus maker could no longer be called a nobody. His business acumen, his capacity for work and his skills had made him a man of the future. He had even received the approval of the palace, where he had influential friends. Denes could not allow himself to neglect a trader of this ilk, so he had persuaded his annoyed wife to attend the party given by Bel-Tran to celebrate the opening of his new premises in Memphis.

The annual flood looked likely to be good. The fields would be properly irrigated, everyone would have enough to eat, and Egypt would export wheat to her protectorates in Asia. Memphis the magnificent overflowed with riches.

Denes and Nenophar travelled to the party in a superb high-backed chair carried by forty sturdy bearers. It was equipped with a stool on which their feet rested, and also boasted elegant carved arm rests and a canopy to protect them from wind, dust and dazzling sunlight. The bearers moved quickly, watched by open-mouthed passers-by. The poles were so long and there were so many pairs of legs that the ensemble was immediately nicknamed the 'Millipede'. The bearers sang, 'We prefer a full chair to an empty one,' as they thought of the large fees they would receive.

Dazzling other people justified the expense. Denes and Nenophar were the envy of the other guests, who had gathered around Bel-Tran and Silkis. No one in Memphis could remember ever seeing such a wonderful chair. Denes swept away the compliments with a wave of his hand, and Nenophar deplored the lack of gilding.

All the business folk of Memphis were celebrating Bel-Tran's admission to the narrow circle of men of power. The door was ajar. Now it was up to him to push it open and prove his worth decisively. The opinions of Denes and his wife would carry considerable weight; no one had entered the elite band of traders without their assent.

Bel-Tran was nervous. He greeted the new arrivals immediately, and introduced them to Silkis, who had been ordered not to open her mouth. Nenophar looked her up and down disdainfully.

Denes surveyed his surroundings. 'Is this a warehouse or a trading house?'

'Both,' replied Bel-Tran. 'But later, if all goes well, I shall expand and separate the two functions.'

'That's an ambitious project.'

'Don't you approve?'

'Gluttony isn't an asset in business. One can so easily get a stomach ache.'

'Fortunately, I have an excellent appetite and perfect digestion.'

Nenophar lost interest in the conversation and went off to talk with old friends. Her husband knew that she had given her verdict; she found Bel-Tran unpleasant, vain and inconsistent. His high hopes would crumble like bad limestone.

Denes said to his host, 'Memphis is less welcoming than it seems; remember that. On your estate in the Delta you reign unchallenged. Here, you will encounter all the difficulties of a large city, and you may wear yourself out in useless activity.'

'You're pessimistic.'

'Follow my advice, dear friend. Each man has his limits. Don't go beyond yours.'

'To be frank,' said Bel-Tran, 'I don't yet know what they are. That's why I'm so enthusiastic about this new venture.'

'There are several long-established makers and sellers of papyrus in Memphis, and they've always given complete satisfaction.'

'I shall try to surprise them by offering better-quality products.'

'Isn't that rather boastful?'

'I have confidence in my work and I don't understand your . . . advice.'

'I am thinking only of your interests. Accept reality, and you'll avoid many disagreeable experiences.'

'Perhaps you should be more concerned about your own interests.'

Denes's thin lips turned white. 'Precisely what do you mean by that?'

Bel-Tran tightened the belt of his long kilt, which had a tendency to slip down. 'I've heard stories of offences and court cases. Your businesses no longer look as attractive as they used to.'

Their voices had risen, and many of the guests turned to listen.

'Those accusations are slanderous and uncalled-for,' said Denes furiously. 'My name is respected throughout Egypt, whereas no one's ever even heard of you.'

'Times are changing,' retorted Bel-Tran.

'Your malicious gossip and your slanders don't even deserve a reply.'

'What I have to say, I say out loud for all to hear. I leave insinuations and illegal dealing to others.'

'Are you accusing me?' demanded Denes.

'Why? Do you feel guilty?'

Nenophar took her husband's arm. 'We've stayed here quite long enough.'

'Be careful, Bel-Tran,' advised Denes angrily. 'One bad harvest and you'll be ruined.'

'I've taken precautions.'

'Your dreams are no more real than mirages in the desert.'

'Won't you be my first customer? I'll devise a range of products and prices especially for you.'

'I'll think about it.'

The opinions of those present were divided. Denes had got the better of many optimists, but Bel-Tran seemed sure of his own strength. The duel was set fair to be exciting.

28

Suti's chariot headed down a difficult path which ran alongside the foot of a rocky cliff. For a week, General Asher's troops had been chasing the last few rebels in vain. In the end, thinking the region pacified, the general gave the order to return.

Though he himself was now flanked by an archer, Suti was silent and stern-faced as he concentrated on driving the chariot. Panther had been granted special treatment: she was riding a donkey, whereas the other prisoners had to endure a forced march. Asher had granted this privilege to the hero of the campaign, and no one found fault with it.

The Libyan girl still slept in Suti's tent, but she was bewildered by the transformation in him. Ordinarily so ardent and expansive, he had withdrawn into a strange sadness. In the end, unable to contain herself any longer, she said, 'You're a hero, you'll be celebrated, you'll be rich, and yet you look as though you've been defeated. I want to know why.'

'A prisoner has no right to want anything.'

'I shall fight you all my life, as long as you are fit to fight back. Don't tell me you've lost your taste for life?'

'Stop asking all these questions and be quiet.'

Panther took off her tunic.

Naked, she threw back her blonde hair and danced, turning slow circles before him, displaying every facet of her body. Her hands traced her curves, brushed her breasts, her hips, her thighs. Her supple body swayed with an innate grace.

Sensual as a she-cat, she moved forward, but he did not react. She unfastened his kilt, kissed his body and lay down on top of him. She was delighted to see that the hero's vigour had not diminished. However much he might try to resist, he still desired her. She slid down her lover's body and kindled his lust with burning kisses.

Afterwards, as they lay quietly together, she asked, 'What will become of me?'

'In Egypt you'll be free.'

'Aren't you going to keep me with you?'

'One man wouldn't be enough for you.'

'Get rich, and I'll put up with it.'

'You'd be bored as a respectable woman. Besides, don't forget your promise to betray me.'

'You defeated me, and I shall defeat you.'

She continued to caress him with the low, seductive sound of her voice. Lying on her belly, with her hair tumbling about her shoulders and her legs apart, she beckoned him. Suti entered her with renewed ardour, only too aware that this devil-woman must be using magic to reawaken his desire like this.

'You aren't sad any more, are you?' she said.

'Don't try to read my heart.'

'Then talk to me.'

'Tomorrow, when I stop the chariot, dismount from your donkey, come to me and do as I say.'

'The right wheel's squeaking,' Suti told his archer.

'I can't hear anything.'

'I have very sharp hearing. That squeak might mean trouble. We'd better check.'

Suti was at the head of the column. He drove off the roadway and turned the chariot slightly, so that it faced a path which led into a wood.

'Let's have a look.'

The two men dismounted from the chariot. Suti knelt down and examined the suspect wheel.

'It's bad,' he said 'Two spokes are on the point of breaking.'

'Can we repair them?'

'We'll wait until the army carpenters get here.'

The carpenters marched at the rear of the column, just behind the prisoners. When Panther dismounted from her donkey and went over to Suti, there were plenty of bawdy comments from the soldiers.

'Get in,' Suti told her.

He knocked the archer down, seized the reins and drove the chariot at top speed down the path and into the woods. No one had time to react. The hero's bemused comrades-in-arms wondered why he was deserting.

Even Panther was astonished. 'Have you gone mad?' she asked.

'I have a promise to keep.'

An hour later, the chariot halted at the place where Suti had buried his officer after the sand-travellers killed him. Although horrified, Panther helped him to dig up the body. Suti wrapped it in a large linen cloth and bound the ends tightly with cord.

'Who is he?' asked Panther.

'A true hero, who shall rest in his own land, close to his own people.' Suti did not add that General Asher would probably not have given him permission to do this.

As he was finishing his sombre task, the Libyan girl cried out. Suti swung round, but was unable to avoid the bear claws that tore open his left shoulder. He fell, rolled over and tried to hide behind a rock. The enraged bear stood six cubits tall. It was both heavy and agile, and it was hungry. It let out a terrifying roar which sent all the birds fluttering into the air in panic.

'My bow and arrows, quickly!' shouted Suti.

Panther threw them to him. She dared not leave the fragile protection of the chariot. Before Suti could use his weapons, the bear's paw came down a second time, and tore his back open. He fell face down on the ground, covered in blood, and lay very still.

Panther shouted again, attracting the bear's attention. It bore down on her; there was no escape.

Suti heaved himself to his knees. A red mist veiled his eyes. Summoning up the last of his strength, he drew his bow and fired at the brown shape. Hit in the flank, the bear turned, dropped down on to all fours and charged at its attacker. As he lost consciousness, Suti fired again.

The head doctor at the military hospital in Memphis had given up hope. Suti's wounds were so deep and so numerous that he ought not to have survived. Soon the pain would kill him.

According to Panther, he had killed the bear with an arrow in its eye, but had succumbed to a last swipe of its claws. Panther had dragged his bleeding body to the chariot and, with a superhuman effort, hauled it inside. Then she had lifted the officer's corpse aboard. Touching a dead body disgusted her, but Suti had risked his life to bring it back to Egypt.

Fortunately, the horses had proved docile. Instinctively they retraced their steps and guided Panther, rather than having to be driven. The corpse of a charioteer officer, a dying deserter and a foreign fugitive: that was the strange sight that had greeted General Asher's rearguard.

Thanks to Panther's explanations and the identification of the dead officer, the facts had been established. The officer, because he had died on the field of honour, had been posthumously decorated and then mummified in Memphis; Panther had been put to work as an agricultural worker on a large estate; and Suti had been congratulated on his courage and condemned for his lack of discipline.

Kem tried to explain this complicated story to Pazair.

'Suti's here, in Memphis?' asked Pazair in amazement.

'The rebellion has been crushed, and Asher's victorious army has returned. The only thing they didn't do is catch the leader, Adafi.'

'When did Suti arrive?'

'Yesterday.'

'Then why hasn't he come home?'

The Nubian turned away, discomfited. 'He can't travel.'

The judge was annoyed. 'And what, exactly, does that mean?'

'He's wounded.'

'Seriously?'

'His condition is—'

'Tell me the truth.'

'His condition is critical.'

'Where is he?'

'At the military hospital – if he's still alive.'

'He's lost too much blood,' said the head doctor. 'Trying to clean and stitch the wounds would be madness. We'll have to leave him to die in peace.'

'Is that the best you can do?' demanded Pazair furiously.

'It's the only thing. That bear tore him to ribbons. His resilience is amazing, but he has no chance of surviving.'

'Can he be moved?'

'Of course not.'

Pazair made a decision: Suti was not going to die in a communal ward. 'Bring me a litter.'

'Surely you aren't going to move a dying man?'

'I'm his friend and I know what he wants: to die in his own village. If you deny him that wish, you'll be responsible before him and before the gods.'

The doctor did not take the threat lightly. A discontented spirit would become a ghost, and ghosts took their revenge pitilessly, even on head doctors.

'Very well, then,' he said. 'But you must sign this form.'

During the night, Pazair dealt with twenty minor cases which would keep Iarrot busy for three weeks. If Iarrot needed to contact him, he was to send his messages to the main court in Thebes. Pazair would dearly have liked to consult Branir, but the old man was in Karnak, preparing for his retirement.

Just after dawn, Kem and two orderlies laid Suti on a litter, carried him to the river and laid him down in the comfortable cabin of a light boat.

Pazair stayed at his side throughout the voyage, holding Suti's right hand in his own. Once, for a few moments, he thought Suti awoke and gripped his hand slightly, but it was only an illusion.

Pazair found Neferet in her workshop, seeing her patients.

'You're my last hope,' he said. 'The army doctor refused to operate on Suti. Will you examine him?'

She explained to the patients waiting under the palm trees that she must leave to deal with an emergency. She selected a number of pots of remedies, and Kem carried them to the boat for her.

'What did the army doctor say?' she asked.

'His wounds are very deep.'

'How did he withstand the journey?'

'He was unconscious all the time, though there was a moment when I thought I felt him stir.'

'Is he strong?'

'As strong as a stele.'

'Has he had any serious illnesses?'

'No.'

Neferet's examination lasted more than an hour. When she left the cabin, she look grave but determined. 'I shall do all I can to fight this illness,' she said. 'The risks are very great, but if I do nothing he'll certainly die, whereas if I cleanse his wounds he at least has a chance.'

She began towards noon. Pazair acted as her assistant, and passed her the knives and drugs as she asked for them. To ensure that Suti remained unconscious, she used a preparation of silica mixed with opium and mandragora root; the mixture was reduced to powder and administered in small doses. When she started working on a wound, she dissolved the powder in vinegar. This produced an acid which she collected in a stone horn and applied locally, to reduce the pain. She checked how long the substances worked by consulting the clock she wore on her wrist.

Using knives and fine blades made from obsidian, which was sharper than metal, she cut into the flesh. Her movements were precise and steady. She reshaped the flesh, brought the edges of each wound together and stitched them with a very fine thread made from the intestines of oxen; the many stitches were then strengthened with adhesive linen strips.

After five hours, Neferet was exhausted but Suti was still alive. She had put fresh meat, fat and honey on the most serious wounds. First thing next morning, she would change the dressings, which were made from gentle, protective vegetable matter, and both prevented infection and hastened the formation of scar tissue.

Three days passed. Pazair did not leave Suti's bedside for a moment.

On the third day, Suti stirred, then awoke, and was able to take some water and honey.

'You're going to live, Suti!'

'Where am I?' he asked weakly.

'On a boat, near our village.'

'You remembered that I wanted to die here.'

'You aren't going to die, you're going to get well. Neferet operated on you.'

'Your betrothed?'

'A remarkable surgeon and the best doctor in the world.'

Suti tried to sit up, but he cried out in pain and fell back.

'You mustn't move,' said Pazair.

'Me, unable to move . . .'

'Be patient – just for a little while.'

'That bear tore me to shreds.'

'Neferet sewed you up again, and you'll soon get your strength back.'

Suti's eyes rolled and Pazair was afraid he was going to collapse, but he gripped Pazair's hand tightly.

'Asher,' he said, panting with rage. 'I've got to live so that I can tell you about that murderer.'

'And so you shall, but you must keep calm.'

'You've got to know the truth, Judge. You've got to see that justice is respected in this country.'

'I'll listen, but don't exhaust yourself – please.'

Reassured, Suti lay back again. He said, 'I saw General Asher torture and murder an Egyptian soldier. Asher was with Asiatic men, the rebels he claimed to be fighting.'

Pazair wondered if fever had made his friend delirious, but Suti spoke steadily, hammering home each word.

'You were right to suspect him, and I've brought you the proof you needed.'

'Not proof, a witness statement,' Pazair corrected him.

'Isn't that enough?'

'He'll deny everything.'

'My word's as good as his!'

'As soon as you're well enough, we'll think of a plan. Until then, not a word to anyone.'

'I shall live. I shall live so that I can see that coward condemned to death.' Suti grimaced with pain. 'Are you proud of me, Pazair?'

'You and I speak with one voice.'

Neferet's reputation was spreading all over the west bank. Her successful treatment of Suti impressed her colleagues so much that some asked her to treat their most difficult cases. She agreed to do so, so long as she could benefit the village that had welcomed her, and obtain Suti's admission to the hospital at Deir el-Bahri. The authorities there agreed to accept him. He was not only a hero of the battlefield but also something of a medical miracle, whose case was becoming a shining light among doctors.

At the temple at Deir el-Bahri* people worshipped Imhotep, the greatest doctor of the Old Kingdom. A shrine had been hollowed out of the rock and dedicated to him. Doctors meditated there and sought their ancestor's wisdom, which was vital to the practice of their craft. A few patients were admitted to live in this magnificent place while they regained their strength; they strolled along the colonnades, marvelled at the relief carvings depicting Hatshepsut's exploits, and walked in the gardens, where they breathed in the aromatic resin of the incense trees brought from the mysterious land of Punt, in north-eastern Africa. Copper pipes linked pools to underground drainage systems and brought healing water, which was collected in vessels also made of copper. Suti drank about twenty cups a day, to prevent infection and other complications. Thanks to his prodigious vitality, he would heal swiftly.

Pazair and Neferet walked down the long, flower-lined ramp that linked the terraces of Deir el-Bahri.

'You have saved him,' said Pazair.

'I was lucky, and so was he.'

'Will there be any lasting ill effects?'

'Only a few scars.'

'They'll just add to his charm.'

The burning sun was climbing to its zenith. They sat down in the shade of an acacia tree, at the bottom of the ramp.

'Have you thought about what I said?' asked Pazair nervously.

She was silent. Her answer would bring him either happiness or misery. Life had come to a halt in the noonday heat. In the fields, the peasants were eating their lunch in the shade of reed huts where they would stretch out for a long nap. Neferet closed her eyes.

'I love you with all my being, Neferet. I want to marry you.'

'A life together . . . Are we capable of such a thing?'

'I shall never love another woman.'

'How can you be so certain? The pains of love are soon forgotten.'

'If you knew me better . . .'

'I know how serious you are – that's what frightens me.'

'Are you in love with someone else?'

*It was built on the west bank by the great queen-pharaoh Hatshepsut.

'No.'

'I couldn't bear that.'

'Are you jealous?'

'More than I'd thought possible.'

'You think I'm your ideal woman,' said Neferet doubtfully, 'faultless, endowed with all the virtues.'

'You aren't a dream.'

'Yes, you dream me. One day you'll wake up and you'll be disappointed.'

'I see you here and alive, I breathe in your perfume, you're close to me. That isn't an illusion.'

'I'm afraid. If you're wrong – if we're both wrong – the pain will be terrible.'

'You'll never disappoint me.'

'I'm not a goddess. When you realize that, you won't love me any more.'

'It's no use trying to discourage me,' said Pazair. 'The moment we met, the moment I first saw you, I knew you would be the sun of my life. You're as radiant as sunlight, Neferet – no one can deny the light that shines in you. My life belongs to you, whether or not you want it.'

'You're talking nonsense. You must think what it would be like for us living far apart. Your career will be in Memphis, but mine will be in Thebes.'

'My career doesn't matter.'

'Don't give up your vocation – you'd never let me give up mine, would you?'

'You have only to ask, and I will,' said Pazair.

'That would be absolutely untrue to your nature.'

'All I want is to love you more each day.'

'Don't you think you're being rather excessive?'

'If you refuse to marry me, I shall die.'

'Blackmailing me is unworthy of you.'

'That isn't what I meant. Please, Neferet, will you marry me?'

She opened her eyes and looked at him sadly. 'It would be wrong to deceive you.'

She walked lightly and gracefully away. Despite the heat, Pazair was frozen to the core.

29

Suti was not the kind of man who could endure the peace and silence of the temple gardens for long. The pretty priestesses did not take care of the patients, but remained far out of their reach, and Suti's only contact was with a gruff orderly, whose job was to change his dressings.

Within a month of the operation, he was bursting with impatience. When Neferet examined him, he could barely keep still.

'I'm better,' he insisted.

'Not completely,' she said, 'but you've certainly made a remarkable recovery. The stitches haven't given way, the wounds have scarred over, and there's no infection.'

'Then can I leave here?'

'Only if you take things slowly.'

He kissed her on both cheeks. 'I owe you my life, and I'm grateful. If you ever need me, I'll come running – you have my word as a hero.'

'You must take a jar of healing water with you and drink three cupfuls a day.'

'Can I start drinking beer again?'

'Yes, and wine, too – in small doses.'

Suti took a deep breath and stretched out his arms. 'It's so good to be alive again! All those hours of pain . . . Only women can wipe them out.'

'Aren't you ever going to marry one?'

'May Hathor protect me from that disaster! Me, with a faithful wife and a tribe of squalling brats? A mistress, and then another, and another – that's my wonderful fate. They're all different, and each one has her own secrets.'

'You seem very different from your friend Pazair,' Neferet remarked with a smile.

'Don't be deceived by him. He may look reserved but he's passionate, perhaps even more than I am. If he's summoned the courage to speak to you . . .'

'He has.'

'Don't take his words lightly.'

'He frightened me.'

'Pazair will love only once in his whole life. He's one of those men who fall madly in love and stay mad all their lives. Women can't understand them – a woman needs time to grow accustomed, to take time before committing herself. Pazair's a raging torrent, not a slow-burning fire, and his passion will never weaken. He's clumsy, and often too timid or too hasty, but his sincerity is absolute. He's never even had a flirtation or an amorous adventure, because he's capable only of one great love.'

'But what if he's mistaken?'

'He'll believe in his ideal right to the end. Don't hope for any concessions.'

'But can you understand why I'm afraid?'

'In love, reasoned argument's futile. I wish you happiness, whatever decision you make.'

Suti could understand why Pazair felt as he did. Neferet's beauty was radiant.

He had stopped eating, and sat at the foot of a palm tree like a grieving mourner, his head resting on his knees. He could no longer have told you if it was day or night. He looked so much like a block of stone that even the children did not taunt him.

'Pazair! It's Suti.'

There was no reaction.

'You're convinced that she doesn't love you.' Suti sat down next to his friend, and leant back against the tree. 'There'll never be another woman for you. I know. I can't share in your unhappiness, and I shan't try to console you. All you have left is your mission.'

Pazair was silent.

'Neither of us can let Asher win. If we give up, the court of the afterlife will condemn us to the second death, and we'll have no defence for our cowardice.'

Still the judge did not move.

'All right, then, starve to death thinking about her. I'll fight Asher by myself.'

At this, Pazair came out of his trance and looked at Suti. 'He'll destroy you.'

'Every man has ordeals to face. You can't bear Neferet's indifference. With me, it's the face of a murderer haunting my dreams.'

'I'll help you.' Pazair tried to stand up, but his head started spinning, and Suti had to steady him.

'I'm sorry,' said Pazair, 'but—'

'Don't say anything – you've told me often enough not to waste my breath. The important thing is to make you fit and well again.'

The two men took the ferry, which was as full as ever. Pazair had managed to nibble some bread and onions. The wind whipped at his face.

'Look at the Nile,' advised Suti. 'That's true nobility. Compared to the river, we're nothing.'

The judge gazed at the clear water.

'What are you thinking about, Pazair?'

'As if you didn't know.'

'How can you be sure she doesn't love you? I've spoken with her, and—'

'It's no use.'

'A drowned man may be blessed by the gods, but he's still drowned. And you've sworn to bring Asher to justice.'

'Without you, I'd give up.'

'Because you're no longer yourself.'

'Actually, it's only now that I really am myself. Now I know what real loneliness is.'

'You won't always feel like this.'

'You don't understand.'

'Time will heal you.'

'It won't change a thing.'

As soon as the ferry reached the bank, the other passengers disembarked in a noisy crowd, driving their donkeys, sheep and oxen, before them. The two friends let them pass, then went ashore themselves.

'We must go back to Memphis,' said Suti.

'Why are you in such a hurry?'

'I want to see Asher again. Why don't you tell me what you've found out so far?'

In a flat voice, Pazair did so.

Suti listened closely. 'Who followed you?' he asked when Pazair had finished.

'I have no idea.'

'Are those the sort of methods Mentmose uses?'

'They may be.'

Suti thought for a moment, then said, 'Before we leave Thebes, let's go and see Kani.'

Pazair made no objection. He was indifferent, detached from reality. Neferet's refusal was gnawing away at his soul.

Kani now had several people working for him, and the part of the garden devoted to vegetables was a hive of activity. Kani himself was tending the medicinal plants. His sun-tanned skin was more deeply lined than ever, and he moved slowly, weighed down by the weight of a large yoke bearing two water pots. No one else was privileged to water his favourite plants.

When Pazair introduced Suti, Kani stared at him and asked, 'He's your friend?'

'Yes. You can talk freely in front of him.'

'I've kept on searching for the soldier. Carpenters, joiners, water carriers, washermen, peasants – I haven't missed out a single trade. There is one small clue: our man spent a few days repairing chariots before he disappeared.'

'That's a big clue,' Suti corrected him. 'It means he must be alive.'

'Let's hope so.'

'But he may have been murdered since then, of course.'

'Either way, I can't find him.'

'Go on looking,' said Pazair. 'He's still in the land of the living.'

Could anything be sweeter than a Theban evening, when the north wind brought coolness to the canopies and pergolas where people drank beer as they watched the sunset? Tiredness melted away, tormented souls were soothed, and the beauty of the goddess of silence filled the crimson western sky. Ibis soared through the gathering dusk.

'Neferet, I'm leaving for Memphis tomorrow,' said Pazair

'Because of your work?'

'Suti witnessed a crime. It's safer for you if I don't say any more than that.'

'Is it really that dangerous?'

'The army's involved.'

'Then you be careful, too,' said Neferet.

'What do you care about what happens to me?'

'Don't be bitter. I want you to be happy.'

'You're the only person who can make me happy.'

'You are so uncompromising, so—'

'Come with me.'

'I can't. I'm not lit by the same flame as you. You have to accept that I'm different, that I can't do things in haste.'

'It's all very simple: I love you and you don't love me.'

'No, it is not all very simple. Day doesn't follow night with brutal suddenness, nor does one season succeed another abruptly.'

'Are you offering me a shred of hope?'

'If I promised you anything, I'd be lying.'

'You see?'

'Your feelings are so fierce, so impatient. You can't ask me to respond equally passionately.'

'Don't try to justify yourself.'

'I can't see clearly into my own heart, so how can I offer you anything with certainty?'

'If I leave alone, we'll never see each other again.'

With that, Pazair walked slowly away, hoping for words which did not come.

Pazair found that Iarrot had managed, by avoiding all responsibility, not to make any major errors. The district was quiet, and no serious crimes had been committed. Mentmose had sent a message summoning Pazair, so, after sorting out a few details, Pazair went to see him.

Mentmose's smile was broader than usual. 'My dear Judge,' he said, 'I'm delighted to see you again. You've been away?'

'An unavoidable absence.'

'The area under your jurisdiction is one of the most peaceful. Your reputation is bearing fruit: people know that you give no quarter where the law is concerned. But – and I don't wish to offend you – you look tired.'

'It's nothing.'

'Good, good.'

'Why did you want to see me?'

'On account of a delicate and . . . regrettable matter. I followed your plan to the letter regarding the grain store, although, if you remember, I doubted that it would work. Between you and me, I was right.'

'Has the overseer run away?'

'No, no – I have no complaint on his account. He wasn't there when the incident happened.'

'What incident?'

'Half the contents of the store were stolen during the night.'

Pazair gaped at him. 'Are you joking?'

'I'm afraid not. It is the sad truth.'

'But your men were watching the grain store.'

'Yes and no. There was a serious brawl not far away, and they had to intervene urgently – they can't be blamed for that. When they got back, they discovered the theft. And now, surprisingly, the state of the store matches the overseer's report!'

'Do you know who the thieves are?'

'We have no serious leads.'

'Any witnesses?'

'The area was deserted,' said Mentmose, 'and the theft was efficiently carried out. It won't be easy to identify the thieves.'

'I assume your best men are dealing with the matter?'

'You can rely on me for that.'

'Between ourselves, Mentmose, what is your opinion of me?'

'Well . . . I think you're a very conscientious judge.'

'Will you credit me with a little intelligence?'

'My dear Pazair, you underestimate yourself!'

'In that case, you will know that I cannot believe a word of your story.'

Silkis, who was in the grip of one of her frequent attacks of anxiety, was receiving attentive care from a specialist in disturbances of the mind, an interpreter of dreams. His consulting room was painted black and no light was permitted to enter. Each week, she lay down on a mat, told him her nightmares and asked for his advice.

The dream reader was a Syrian who had been settled in Memphis for many years. His clients were mainly noble ladies and well-off middle-class women, so his fees were very high – after all, using his grimoires, his 'keys to dreams',* and his practised flattery, he gave regular peace and comfort to the poor weak-minded creatures.

The interpreter insisted that the treatment must be open-ended; people never stopped dreaming. He alone could tell the meaning of the images and phantasms that disturbed a sleeping brain. He was very careful, and rejected the advances of most of his love-starved patients, yielding only to widows who had kept their looks.

Silkis gnawed her nails.

'Have you argued with your husband?' asked the dream reader.

'Yes, about the children.'

'What did they do wrong?'

'They told lies. But that's not such a terrible crime. My husband gets angry, I defend them, and voices are raised . . .'

'Does he hit you?'

'Sometimes, but I defend myself.'

'Is he pleased with the changes in your body?'

'Oh yes! He eats out of my hand most of the time. I can make him do what I want, as long as I don't interfere in his business affairs.'

'Are you interested in them?'

'Not in the least. We're rich – that's all that matters.'

'After the last argument, what did you do?'

'What I always do. I shut myself away in my bedchamber and I cried. Then I went to sleep.'

'Did you have a long dream?'

'The same images as always. First, I saw a mist rising up from the

---

*Some keys to dreams have been discovered; they indicate the nature of dreams and provide interpretations.

river. Something – a boat, I thought – tried to pass through it. Then the sun made the mist melt away. The thing wasn't a boat, it was a gigantic phallus – and it was coming right at me. I turned aside and tried to hide in a house on the banks of the Nile. But it wasn't a building, it was a woman's sex, which attracted and terrified me at the same time.'

Silkis was panting.

'Be careful,' advised the dream reader. 'According to the key of dreams, seeing a phallus means there's going to be a theft.'

'And what about a woman's sex?'

'That means poverty.'

In great alarm, Silkis rushed to the warehouse, where she found Bel-Tran talking to two embarrassed-looking men.

'Forgive me for disturbing you, my darling,' said Silkis, 'but I had to warn you. Someone's going to steal from you and we are in danger of ending up in poverty.'

'Your warning comes too late. These men are boat captains, and they have just told me there are no boats available to transport my papyri from the Delta to Memphis. Our warehouse will stand empty.'

30

Pazair tried to calm Bel-Tran down. 'What do you want me to do?' he asked.

'I want you to take action against people impeding the proper flow of goods. Papyri are piling up, but I can't deliver them to the people who ordered them.'

'As soon as a boat's available—'

'There'll never be one.'

'Are you alleging deliberate ill-will?'

'If you investigate, you'll soon prove it. Meanwhile, every hour that passes brings me closer to ruin.'

'Come back tomorrow. I may have some evidence by then.'

'I shan't forget what you're doing for me.'

'Not for you, Bel-Tran, for justice.'

The mission amused Kem, and amused Killer even more. Armed with a list of ship owners provided by Bel-Tran, they asked each one why he had refused. Garbled explanations, regrets and obvious lies confirmed that Bel-Tran was right. At the far end of a dock, at about the time when people took their afternoon nap, Kem turned his attention to a boat owner who was usually well-informed.

'Do you know Bel-Tran?' asked Kem.

'I've heard of him.'

'There are no boats available to transport his papyri.'

'So it seems.'

'And yet yours is at the quayside, empty.'

Killer opened his mouth wide, showing his big, sharp teeth.

'Keep that animal under control!' said the man.

'Just tell me the truth and we'll leave you in peace.'

'Denes has hired all the boats for a week.'

Late that afternoon, Judge Pazair observed the proper procedures by questioning the ship owners himself and requiring them to show him their contracts of hire.

Every single one bore the name of Denes.

*

Sailors sang and shouted to each other as they unloaded food, jars and furniture from a sailing-barge. Carpenters were repairing a sail, stone cutters reinforcing a landing stage. Another cargo boat was preparing to leave for the south.

There were few oarsmen to be seen; almost all the deck was taken up with cabins for storing the goods. The helmsman, who steered using a special oar, was already in position. All that was missing was the man who stood at the bow, sounding the depth of the water at regular intervals with a long staff. Denes was standing on the bustling quayside, talking to the captain, when Pazair, Kem and Killer arrived.

'May I speak to you?' asked Pazair.

'With pleasure, but later.'

'Forgive me for insisting, but I'm in a hurry.'

'Not in such a hurry that you'd delay the departure of a boat, I hope.'

'I'm afraid I am.'

'Why?'

Pazair unrolled a papyrus a good two cubits long. 'Here is the list of offences you have committed: forced hiring, intimidating boat owners, attempting to control the hiring of boats, and impeding the proper movement of goods.'

Denes looked at it. The accusations were drawn up with absolute precision and according to the rules.

'I dispute your interpretation of the facts, which is unbalanced and overdramatic. If I've hired a lot of boats, it's because I've got some exceptionally large cargoes.'

'What are they?'

'Oh, various materials.'

'That's too vague.'

'In my line of work, it's wise to foresee the unforeseeable.'

'Bel-Tran's business is suffering because of you.'

'There you are! I warned him that his ambition would lead to failure.'

'In order to break your control of hiring boats, which is incontestable, I am exercising the right of requisition.'

'As you wish. Take any barge from the western quay.'

'This one here will suit me very well.'

Denes stepped in front of the gangplank and shouted, 'I forbid you to touch it.'

'I shall pretend I did not hear that. Obstructing the law is a serious offence.'

The ship owner said more moderately, 'Be reasonable. Thebes needs this load.'

'Bel-Tran has lost trade because of your actions, and justice requires that you offer him restitution. He is willing not to bring a complaint against you, so as not to jeopardize your future relations. However, because of the delay he has an enormous amount of stock to deliver. This barge will only just be big enough.'

Pazair, Kem and Killer climbed aboard. Not only did the judge wish to give Bel-Tran justice, but he was also following his intuition.

Several cabins, made from planks with holes to allow free circulation of air, contained horses, oxen, bullocks and calves. Some were moving about freely, others were tied to rings fixed to the deck. Other cabins – simple shells made from light wood covered with a roof – contained stools, chairs and pedestal tables.

Aft, a large hold held some thirty portable grain stores.

Pazair called Denes over. 'Where did this wheat come from?'

'From warehouses.'

'Who delivered it to you?'

'Ask the cargo master.'

When questioned, the man produced an official-looking document bearing an indecipherable seal. Why, Pazair wondered, should he have taken care to look at it, since the goods were so ordinary? According to a province's needs, Denes transported grain all year round. The reserves in the state silos prevented any famine.

'Who gave the shipping order?' asked the judge.

The cargo master did not know. Pazair went back to Denes, who took him straight to his office in the port.

'I have nothing to hide,' insisted Denes edgily. 'All right, I tried to teach Bel-Tran a lesson, but it was only a joke. Why are you so interested in my cargo?'

'That is an official secret.'

Denes' records were well kept, and he was only too eager to produce the relevant slate tablet.

The shipping order came from Hattusa, Ramses' diplomatic wife.

Thanks to General Asher, calm had returned to the Asian princedoms. Once again, he had proved his perfect knowledge of the terrain. Two months after his return, in high summer, while a favourable flood was depositing fertile silt upon the two banks, a magnificent ceremony was staged in his honour. For Asher had brought back a tribute of a thousand horses, five hundred prisoners, two thousand sheep, eight hundred goats, four hundred oxen, forty enemy chariots, hundreds of spears, swords, breastplates and shields, and two hundred thousand sacks of grain.

The elite troops, royal guard and desert guards were gathered before the royal palace, along with representatives of the four regiments of Amon, Re, Ptah and Set, comprising the chariot corps, footsoldiers and archers. Not a single officer was absent. The Egyptian armed forces were displaying their might and celebrating their most decorated senior officer. Ramses would hand him five gold collars and proclaim three days of celebration throughout the land. Asher was becoming one of the most important people in the state, the king's armed fist and the country's bulwark against invasion.

Suti, too, was at the celebration. The general had granted him a new chariot for the parade, without requiring him to purchase the shell and shaft as most officers had to; three soldiers would take care of the two horses.

Before the procession, the general congratulated Suti. He said, 'Go on serving Egypt like that, young man, and I promise you you'll have a brilliant future.'

'I wouldn't be able to enjoy it, sir.'

'I'm surprised to hear that.'

'Until we've captured Adafi, I shan't rest easy.'

'There speaks a brilliant and generous-spirited hero,' said Asher warmly.

'I keep wondering, how did he manage to escape? After all, sir, we were scouring the whole region for him.'

'He's a sly scoundrel.'

'It's almost as if he guessed our plans.'

General Asher's brow furrowed. 'You've answered your own question. There must be a spy in our ranks.'

'Sir, there can't be.'

'Take it as a fact. Don't worry: my staff and I will attend to the problem. You can be certain that Adafi won't stay free for long.'

Asher patted Suti's cheek, then turned his attention to another fellow.

He had shown no sign of being disturbed by the insinuation, and for a moment Suti almost wondered if he was wrong. But then he saw the horrible scene again, crystal-clear in his memory. He had been naive to hope the traitor's mask would slip.

Pharaoh's long speech was summarized and proclaimed in every town and village by heralds. As supreme commander of the army, he guaranteed peace and kept a careful watch on the borders. The four great regiments, twenty thousand strong, would protect Egypt from any threat of invasion. The charioteers and the footsoldiers, many of whom were Nubian, Syrian or Libyan, set great store by the happiness of the Two Lands, and would defend them against all attackers, even their own former countrymen. The king would not tolerate any lack of discipline, and the tjaty would carry out his instructions to the letter.

As a reward for his good and loyal services, General Asher was made responsible for instructing the officers who trained the troops who gathered secret information in Asia. His experience would be valuable: already a standard-bearer at the king's right hand, from now on the general would be consulted on all tactical and strategic options.

Pazair picked up legal papyri and put them down again, filed documents he had already filed, gave Iarrot contradictory orders, and forgot to take Brave for walks. Iarrot no longer dared ask him a question, because the answer was always oblique.

Every day Pazair was bombarded with demands from Suti, who was growing more and more impatient and could not bear to see Asher at liberty. The judge had no firm plan to offer, but he had ruled out doing anything in haste and had made his friend promise not to do anything rash. Attacking the general without proper preparation could only end in failure.

Suti could see that Pazair was not very interested in what he had to say. Lost in his own painful thoughts, he was slowly fading away.

Pazair had thought that his work would absorb him and make him forget Neferet, but he'd been wrong: instead, being far from her only increased his distress. Aware that time would make things worse, he decided to become a shadow. After bidding farewell to Brave and Way-Finder, he left Memphis and walked westwards, towards the Libyan desert. He had not had the courage to confide in Suti, for he knew what his friend's arguments would be and had not the strength to counter them. Giving love and not receiving it had made his life agony.

Pazair walked beneath the raging sun on the burning sand. He climbed a hillock and sat down on a stone, gazing into the vastness around him. The sky and the earth would close in upon him, the heat would dry him out, the hyenas and the vultures would destroy his remains. In neglecting his tomb, he would insult the gods and condemn himself to suffer the second death, which forbade resurrection; but to spend all eternity without Neferet would be the worst of all punishments.

Absent from his own body, indifferent to the wind and the biting grains of sand, Pazair sank into nothingness. Empty sun, unmoving light . . . it was not so easy to die. He kept absolutely still, convinced that he must soon sink into the final sleep.

When Branir laid a hand upon his shoulder, he did not react.

'This is a tiring walk, at my age. When I got back from Thebes I was planning to rest, but you've compelled me to come and find you in the desert. Drink a little of this.' He held out a goatskin water bag.

Pazair hesitated, then took it, put the spout to his parched lips and drank. 'Refusing would have been an insult, but I shan't yield to you on anything else.'

'You have great resistance, your skin is not burnt and your voice is almost steady.'

'The desert will take my life.'

'It will refuse to give you death.'

Pazair trembled. 'I shall be patient.'

'Your patience will be futile, for you are a liar.'

The judge started. 'You, my master, you —'

'The truth is often painful.'

'I haven't gone back on my word.'

'You've forgotten something. When you accepted your first post, in Memphis, you swore an oath to which a stone bore witness. Look at the desert around us. That stone has become a thousand, and each one reminds you of the sacred promise you made before the gods, before men and before yourself. You know very well, Pazair, that a judge is not an ordinary man. Your life no longer belongs to you. Spoil it, lay it waste, it is unimportant; but a man who breaks his sacred oath is condemned to wander among the hate-filled shades that rip each other apart.'

Pazair stared at his master. 'I cannot live without her.'

'You must fulfil your office as a judge.'

'Without joy and without hope?'

'Justice is nourished not by feelings but by righteousness.'

'I can never forget Neferet, even for a moment.'

'Tell me about your inquiries.'

The enigma of the Sphinx, the fifth guard, General Asher, the stolen wheat: Pazair related the facts, concealing neither his doubts nor his uncertainties.

'You, a new and inexperienced judge at the bottom of your profession, have been entrusted by destiny with matters of exceptional importance. They go far beyond you – and may involve the future of Egypt. Are you really so shameful as to neglect them?'

'Very well,' said Pazair wearily, 'I'll take action, since you demand it.'

'It's your office that demands it. Do you think mine is any easier?'

'You'll soon be enjoying the peace of the covered temple.'

'Not its peace, Pazair, but its entire life. Against my wishes, I have been appointed High Priest of Karnak.'

Pazair's face lit up. 'When will you receive the golden ring?'

'In a few months' time.'

For two days, Suti had been looking for Pazair all over Memphis. He knew his friend was desperate enough to end his own life.

At last Pazair reappeared in his office, his face burnt by the sun. Suti forced him to share a long drinking session, filled with talk about childhood memories.

Next morning they bathed in the Nile, but were unable to ease their pounding headaches.

'Where were you hiding?' asked Suti.

'I was meditating in the desert. Branir brought me back.'

'What have you decided?'

'Even if the road is dull and grey, I shall respect my oath as a judge.'

'Happiness will come one day, you'll see.'

'You know it won't.'

'We'll fight the battle together,' said Suti. 'Where are you going to start?

'Thebes.'

'Because of her?'

'I shall never see her again. I must investigate an illegal trade in wheat and also find the fifth guard. His testimony will be vital.'

'What if he's dead?'

'Thanks to Branir, whose pendulum is never wrong, I'm sure he's in hiding.'

'It may be a long search.'

'Watch Asher, study what he does, and try to find a weak spot.'

Suti's chariot threw up a cloud of dust. As he drove, he bellowed a bawdy song about women's infidelity. He was optimistic: Pazair might have lost his zest for life, but he'd never break his word. At the first opportunity, Suti would introduce him to a carefree damsel who would drive away his melancholy.

Asher would not escape justice. Suti must give him what he deserved.

The chariot passed between two boundary stones, marking the entrance to the estate. The heat was so oppressive that most of the peasants were resting in the shade, but in front of the farmhouse there was uproar: a donkey had just thrown off its load.

Suti halted, jumped down, and pushed away the donkey driver, who was brandishing a stick, ready to punish the animal. Suti steadied the frightened animal by holding its ears, and stroked it to calm it down.

'You should never hit a donkey,' he said.

'What about my sack of grain? Didn't you see him drop it?'

'It wasn't his fault,' cut in a young lad.

'Then whose was it?'

'The Libyan girl's. She likes sticking thorns in his backside.'

'That one!' said the donkey driver. 'She deserves the stick ten times over.'

'Where is she?' asked Suti.

'Near the pond. If you try and catch her, she climbs up into the willow tree.'

'I'll deal with it.'

As soon as Suti approached, Panther scrambled up the tree and stretched out on one of the largest branches.

'Come down,' he ordered.

'Go away! It's because of you that I'm reduced to slavery.'

'I almost died, if you remember, and I've come to set you free. Jump down into my arms.'

She did so without hesitation. Suti was knocked over, hit the ground hard and grimaced.

Panther traced his scars with her fingertip. 'Do other women reject you now?'

'I need a devoted nurse for a little while. You can massage me.'

'But you're all dusty.'

'I hurried, because I was so eager to see you again.'

'Liar!'

'You're right,' he said, 'I should have washed.'

He got up, scooped her into his arms, ran to the pool and dived in, locked in a passionate embrace.

Nebamon was trying on the official wigs his attendant had prepared. He didn't like any of them: too heavy, too complicated. It was becoming more and more difficult to follow the fashion. He was overwhelmed by the demands of rich ladies determined to preserve their charms by reshaping their bodies, and, as if that weren't enough, he had to preside over government commissions and to get rid of candidates who might want to succeed him. He wished he had a woman like Neferet at his side. His failure with her still rankled.

His private scribe bowed before him. 'My lord, I have the information you wanted.'

'Is she in poverty and distress?

'Not exactly.'

'Has she abandoned medicine?'

'Quite the reverse, my lord.'

'Are you mocking me?'

'She has set up a workshop in a small village, where she prepares her own remedies, she has carried out operations, and she has won the approval of the authorities in Thebes. Her fame is growing by the day.'

'That's insane! She has no money? How can she procure rare and expensive ingredients?'

The scribe smiled. 'I think you'll be pleased with me, my lord.'

'Why?'

'I followed a tortuous trail. Has the reputation of one Sababu reached your ears?'

'Didn't she keep an ale-house in Memphis?'

'The most famous of all. She left it suddenly, although it brought in a tidy profit.'

'What is the connection with Neferet?'

'Sababu not only receives treatment from her but also provides her with funds. The whore offers Theban customers pretty young girls, and then uses the money she makes money from this trade to support her favourite doctor. Isn't that an affront to morality?'

'A doctor financed by a prostitute . . . At last I have her!'

31

'Your reputation does you credit,' Nebamon told Pazair. 'Wealth doesn't impress you and you aren't afraid to attack the privileged – in short, justice is your daily bread and integrity is second nature to you.'

'That is the very least required of a judge.'

'Indeed, indeed; and that's also why I have chosen you.'

'Should I be flattered?'

'I'm counting on your probity.'

Ever since childhood, Pazair had disliked seducers, with their forced smiles and calculated attitudes. Nebamon annoyed him intensely.

Nebamon lowered his voice to a whisper, so as not to be heard by Iarrot. 'A terrible scandal is about to break, one which could devastate my profession and bring shame upon all doctors.'

'You will have to be more explicit.'

Nebamon gave a meaning look at Iarrot; Pazair nodded his consent, and the scribe withdrew.

'Complaints, courts, administrative slowness . . . Can't we avoid all these irritating formalities?'

Pazair said nothing.

'You want to know more, which is quite normal. May I count on your discretion?'

The judge waited.

'One of my pupils, Neferet, made bad mistakes, for which I punished her. At Thebes, she was supposed to be prudent, and defer to more competent colleagues. She has greatly disappointed me.'

'Are you saying she's made more mistakes?'

'Yes, and they're more and more serious. She treats patients without consulting someone more experienced, she provides out-of-season remedies, and she's set up a private workshop in which she makes the remedies herself.'

'Is that illegal?'

'No, but she had no money with which to do all this.'

'The gods must have looked kindly on her.'

'Not the gods, Judge Pazair. It was a woman of ill repute, Sababu, an ale-house proprietor from Memphis.'

Nebamon waited, grave-faced, for an expression of anger, but Pazair seemed unmoved.

'The situation is very worrying,' he went on. 'One day, someone will discover the truth and respectable doctors will be tainted.'

'Yourself, for example?'

'Absolutely, since I was Neferet's teacher. I can't tolerate such a risk any longer.'

'I sympathize, but I can't see what my role is in all this.'

'Discreet but firm action would get rid of this . . . unpleasantness. Sababu's ale-house is in your sector, and she's working in Thebes under a false identity, so you have ample reason to charge her. Threaten Neferet with very heavy penalties if she continues as she is – the warning will reduce her to her proper place as a village doctor. Of course, I don't expect you to help for nothing. A career has to be built: I am well placed to help you progress within the ranks of judges.'

'I'm aware of that.'

'I knew we'd understand each other. You're young, intelligent and ambitious, unlike so many of your colleagues, who are so insistent on the letter of the law that they lose sight of common sense.'

'What happens if I fail?'

'I'll bring a complaint against Neferet, you'll preside over the court, and between us we'll choose the jurors. But I hope we can avoid that – be as persuasive as you can.'

'I'll make every effort.'

Nebamon, relaxed now, congratulated himself on a job well done. He had judged the judge correctly. He said, 'I'm glad I knocked at the right door. Between people of quality, it's easy to smooth over difficulties.'

Divine Thebes, where he had known happiness and misery. Enchanting Thebes, where the splendour of dawn matched the magic of evening. Implacable Thebes, where destiny had brought him back in search of a truth that was as difficult to catch as a frightened lizard.

It was on the ferry that they met.

She was returning from the east bank, and he was crossing to the village where she practised. He had feared she'd avoid him, but she didn't.

He said, 'I meant what I said. This meeting should never have happened.'

'Haven't you forgotten me a little by now?'

'Not for a single moment.'

'You're torturing yourself.'

'What does that matter to you?'

'Your pain saddens me,' said Neferet. 'Do you really think it necessary to make it worse by seeing each other again?'

'I'm speaking to you now purely as a judge.'

'Why? Have I been accused of something?'

'Yes, of accepting gifts from a prostitute. Nebamon is demanding that you confine your activities to the village and that you refer all serious cases to your colleagues.'

'And if I don't?'

'He'll try to have you convicted of immorality – in other words, he'll try to stop you practising.'

'Is his threat one I should take seriously?'

'Nebamon is a man of considerable influence.'

'I escaped from him, and he can't bear to be defied.'

'Are you sure you don't want to give up?'

'What would you think of me if I did?'

'Nebamon's relying on me to persuade you.'

'He doesn't know you.'

'Fortunately for us. Do you trust me?'

'Unreservedly.'

There was a warmth in her voice which thrilled him. Was she emerging from her reserve, looking at him in a new, less distant way?

'Don't be afraid, Neferet. I'll help you.'

He accompanied her to the village, wishing the earthen track might never end.

Although still forced to take endless precautions because of the Nubian and his monkey, the shadow-eater felt reassured. Judge Pazair's journey seemed entirely private. Far from looking for the fifth guard, he was paying court to the lovely Neferet.

The shadow-eater was beginning to believe that the guard had died of natural causes, or else had fled so far to the south that nothing more would ever be heard of him; either way, the only thing that mattered was his silence. But the shadow-eater was cautious, and would continue to watch the judge.

Killer was uneasy.

Kem looked around, but could see nothing unusual. Peasants and their donkeys, workmen repairing the dykes, water carriers. And yet Killer could sense danger.

On the alert now, the Nubian drew closer to Pazair and Neferet. For the first time, he fully appreciated the judge's worth. The young man was forged from idealism, at once strong and fragile, realistic and dreamy; but righteousness guided him. He could not by himself wipe out the evil in human nature but he would fight it to the last, and in doing so he gave hope to the victims of injustice.

Kem would have preferred him not to embark on such a dangerous venture, which was sure to break him sooner or later; but how could he reproach him when so many poor souls had been murdered? As long as the welfare of simple folk wasn't scorned, as long as a judge didn't grant special privileges to the great merely because of their wealth, Egypt would continue to flourish.

Neferet and Pazair did not speak. He was dreaming of taking a walk like this one day when, hand in hand, they would be content to be together. They walked in step, as though they were a couple. He stole moments of impossible happiness, clung to a dream more precious than reality.

Neferet walked with a quick, light step; her feet seemed barely to brush the ground and she moved tirelessly. He revelled in the priceless privilege of accompanying her, and he would have offered himself to her as her humble, zealous servant, had he not been obliged to stay a judge in order to defend her against the coming storms. Was he imagining it, or did she seem less reticent towards him? Perhaps she needed this double silence. Perhaps, if he didn't speak of it, she would grow accustomed to his love.

They went to the workshop, where Kani was sorting medicinal plants.

'The crop was excellent,' he said.

'It may have been for nothing,' said Neferet sadly. 'Nebamon wants to stop me.'

'If poisoning people wasn't illegal . . .'

'He'll fail,' declared Pazair. 'I shall stand in his way.'

'He's deadlier than a viper,' said Kani. 'He'll bite you, too.'

'Is there any news?' asked Pazair.

'The temple priests have granted me a large piece of land to cultivate. I'm going to be their official supplier.'

'You deserve it, Kani,' said Pazair warmly.

'I haven't forgotten our investigation. I was able to talk to the scribe who keeps records of employees, and he said no ex-soldier from Memphis has been taken on in the workshops or on the farms in the last six months. Every ex-soldier has to register with the scribes or lose his rights, which would mean condemning himself to poverty.'

'Yes, but our man's so afraid that he prefers poverty to living in the light of day.'

'What if he's gone into exile?'

'No. I'm convinced he's in hiding somewhere on the west bank.'

Pazair was in the grip of warring emotions. One moment he felt light, almost joyful; the next he was sombre and depressed. Having seen Neferet, feeling her closer, more friendly, brought him back to life; admitting that she would never be his wife plunged him into despair. Fortunately, though, fighting for her, for Suti and Bel-Tran, prevented him from dwelling on his feelings all the time. Branir's words had put him in his place: a judge's first duty was to others, and today it was his duty to see Hattusa.

It was a feast day in the Theban harem: they were celebrating the success of the Asian expedition, the greatness of Ramses, the consolidation of peace and the fame of General Asher. Weaving women, musicians, dancing girls, specialists in enamel, governesses, hairdressers and floral designers strolled in the gardens and chatted as they ate sweet pastries. In the shade of a pavilion, fruit juices were served. The guests admired one another's jewellery, and exchanged jealous remarks behind one another's backs.

Pazair felt out of place, but he managed to approach Hattusa. In her beauty she outshone all the other women of the court. She was an expert in the arts of beauty, and showed great scorn towards those with less than perfect make-up. She aimed equally cutting remarks at the flatterers who surrounded her.

'Aren't you the little judge from Memphis?' she asked when she saw Pazair.

'If you will permit me to disturb you for a moment, my lady, I would be most grateful for a private audience.'

'What a lovely idea! These social events bore me. Let us walk to the lake.'

Everyone wondered who this modest-looking judge was, and how he could conquer the most inaccessible of princesses like this. Hattusa had probably decided to play with him, then throw him away like a broken doll. People had lost count of her extravagances.

White and blue lotus flowers mingled on the surface of the water, rippled by a light breeze. Hattusa and Pazair sat down on folding stools, beneath a sunshade.

'People will talk, Judge Pazair. We are hardly respecting etiquette.'

'I know that will please you.'

'Have you a taste for the splendours of my harem?'

'My lady, is the name Bel-Tran familiar to you?'

'No.'

'What about Denes?'

'Again, no. Is this an interrogation?'

'I need your testimony, my lady.'

'These people don't belong to my household, as far as I know.'

'An order, issued by you, was sent to Denes, the largest ship owner in Memphis.'

'That means nothing to me. Do you think I interest myself in such details?'

'The hold of the boat, which was to unload here, was full of stolen grain.'

'I'm afraid I don't understand.'

'My lady, the boat, the grain, and the shipping order bearing your seal have all been seized.'

Hattusa's eyes flashed. 'Are you accusing me of theft?'

'I would be grateful for an explanation.'

'Who sent you?'

'Nobody.'

'You mean you're acting on your own initiative? I don't believe you.'

'Indeed I am, my lady.'

'People are trying to undermine me again, and this time they're using the services of an ignorant, compliant little judge!'

'Slandering a judge is punishable by strokes of the rod.'

'You're insane! Do you know to whom you're speaking?'

'To a lady of very high rank, who is as subject to the law as is the humblest peasant woman, and who is implicated in a theft of grain belonging to the state.'

'I couldn't care less.'

'Implicated doesn't mean guilty, my lady. That's why I'm asking for your explanation.'

'I shan't demean myself by giving one.'

'If you're innocent, what have you to fear?'

'How dare you cast doubt on my integrity!'

'My lady, the facts oblige me to do so.'

'You have gone too far, Judge Pazair, much too far.'

In fury, she rose to her feet and strode away. Courtiers scattered, worried by an anger whose consequences they were bound to suffer.

The most senior judge of Thebes, a ponderous, middle-aged man who was a close friend of the High Priest at Karnak, received Pazair three days later. He took time to examine the various documents pertaining to the case.

'Your work is exemplary in all respects,' he said when he had finished.

'As this is beyond my jurisdiction,' said Pazair, 'I'm leaving it to you to pursue. But if you think I ought to take action, I'm willing to convene a court.'

'What is your personal feeling about all this?'

'The illegal grain traffic has been proven. Denes doesn't seem to be involved.'

'What about Mentmose?'

'He probably knew something, but I can't tell how much.'

'And the lady Hattusa?'

'She refused to give me any explanation at all,' said Pazair.

'That's most unfortunate.'

'Her seal cannot be removed.'

'True, but who placed it there?'

'She did. It's her personal one, which she wears as a ring. Like all important people in the kingdom, she's never parted from it.'

'We're moving into dangerous territory, Judge Pazair. Hattusa may not be popular in Thebes – she's too haughty, too critical, too authoritarian – but even if he shares that opinion Pharaoh will be obliged to defend her.'

'Stealing food, the people's food, is a serious crime.'

'I agree, but I should like to avoid a public trial which might harm Ramses. As you yourself said, the investigation is not finished yet.'

Pazair tensed.

'Do not worry, my dear colleague; as the senior judge of Thebes, I have no-intention of losing your case in the middle of a pile of dusty records. I should simply like a little more support for the accusation, since the accuser will be the state itself.'

'Thank you for making these details clear. As for the public trial . . .'

'It would be preferable, I know, but is your first desire for truth or for the head of the lady Hattusa?'

'I feel no special hostility towards her.'

'I shall try to persuade her to talk to you, and will send her an official summons, if necessary. We must let her be mistress of her own destiny. If she's guilty, she'll pay.'

Pazair thought the senior judge seemed sincere. With relief, he asked, 'Do you need my cooperation?'

'For the moment, no. In any case, you have been urgently recalled to Memphis.'

'By my scribe?'

'No, by the Judge of the Porch.'

32

Nenophar's anger showed no signs of abating. How could Denes have behaved so stupidly? He had judged this man badly, as usual, and had thought Bel-Tran would crumble without putting up a fight. The result was catastrophic: a forthcoming court case, a cargo boat requisitioned, suspicion of theft and the triumph of that young crocodile of a judge.

'Your record is truly remarkable,' she said acidly.

Denes was undaunted. 'Have some more grilled goose – it's excellent.'

'You're leading us to public shame and failure.'

'Don't worry, our luck will change.'

'Luck perhaps, but not your stupidity!'

'One boat is out of action for a few days – what does that matter? The load has been transferred, and will soon arrive in Thebes.'

'And what about Bel-Tran?' said Nenophar.

'He isn't lodging a complaint. We've reached an understanding. Instead of war between us, there'll be cooperation, and we'll both benefit from that. He isn't big enough to take our place, and he's learnt his lesson. We shall even be shipping a portion of his stock – at the right price.'

'There's still the accusation of theft.'

'It can't go any further, because there are plenty of documents and witnesses to prove my innocence. Besides, I really wasn't involved. Hattusa used me.'

'And what about Judge Pazair's charges?'

'Ah, yes,' said Denes, 'them. They're awkward, I admit.'

'So we shall lose a case, lose our good name as well, and have to pay heavy fines.'

'We haven't reached that stage yet.'

'Do you believe in miracles?'

'If I organize them myself, why not?'

*

Silkis was quivering with joy. She had just received an aloe, an immensely long stem crowned with yellow, orange and red flowers. Its juice contained an oil with which she would rub her genitals in order to prevent inflammation, and which could be used to treat the skin ailment that had covered her husband's legs with red lumps. Silkis would also apply a paste made from egg whites and acacia flowers.

When Bel-Tran heard that he had been summoned to the palace, he was stricken with an attack of itching. Braving the discomfort, he set off anxiously.

While she waited, Silkis prepared the soothing balm.

Bel-Tran returned home in the early afternoon, and in reply to her anxious look he told her, 'We aren't returning to the Delta immediately. I shall appoint a local man to take charge there.'

'Has our papyrus-making authorization been withdrawn?'

'Quite the reverse. I was most warmly congratulated on my management and expansion of the business to Memphis. The palace has actually been watching my activities for two years.'

'Then who's trying to harm you?'

'Nobody. It seems that the head of the Granaries secretariat has been following my rise and wondered how I would react to success. As he's seen me working harder and harder, he's called me to his side.'

Silkis was entranced. The head of the Granaries secretariat fixed taxes, collected them in kind, oversaw their redistribution in the provinces, headed a body of specialist scribes, inspected provincial collection centres, drew up lists of revenues and sent them to the Double House, where the kingdom's finances were administered.

'Called you to his side? You mean . . . ?'

'I've been appointed principal treasurer of the granaries.'

'That's wonderful!' She threw her arms round his neck. 'Are we going to be even richer?'

'Probably, but business will take up a lot more of my time. I'll be spending short periods in the provinces and will have to do as my superior orders. You shall take charge of the children.'

'I'm so proud! You can rely on me.'

When Pazair reached his office, he found Iarrot sitting next to Way-Finder in front of the door, which had been sealed shut.

'Who did this?' asked Pazair.

'Mentmose himself, on the orders of the Judge of the Porch.'

'Why?'

'He refused to tell me,' said Iarrot.

'That's against the law.'

'What could I do? I couldn't fight him.'

Pazair went immediately to see the Judge of the Porch, who kept him waiting for over an hour before receiving him. When he was admitted, the Judge's opening words were, 'So here you are at last, Judge Pazair. You're away from your office a great deal.'

'On business matters.'

'Well, you're going to have a rest. As you have no doubt seen, you are suspended from your office.'

'May I ask why?'

'Because of your youthful carelessness. Being a judge doesn't place you above rules and regulations.'

'Which ones have I broken?'

The Judge's voice became fierce. 'The rules of taxation. You have failed to pay your taxes.'

'But I haven't received any notification,' protested Pazair.

'I took it to your office myself three days ago, but you weren't there.'

'But I have three months in which to pay.'

'In the provinces, but not in Memphis. Here, you have only three days, and that time has expired.'

Pazair was dumbfounded. 'Why are you doing this?'

'Out of simple respect for the law. A judge must set an example, and you have not done so.'

Pazair swallowed the anger bubbling up inside him – attacking the Judge of the Porch would only make matters worse. But he couldn't help saying, 'You're persecuting me.'

'No grand words, now. I must compel late payers to set their affairs in order, whoever they may be.'

'I'm ready to settle my debt straight away.'

'Let's see now . . . Two sacks of grain.'

Pazair was very relieved that the amount was so low.

'But the fine, that's a different matter. Let's say . . . one fat ox.'

Pazair rebelled. 'That's disproportionate!'

'Your office obliges me to be severe.'

'Who's behind all this?'

The Judge of the Porch pointed to the door of his office. 'Go.'

Suti had promised himself that he would gallop to Thebes, break into the harem and make the Hittite confess. From what Pazair had said, she must be the one behind this ridiculous punishment. Ordinarily, there was no arguing with taxation, and complaints were as rare as fraud. By attacking Pazair from this angle, and using the rules applying to large towns, she had reduced the judge to silence.

Pazair, aware of how his friend felt, said, 'I strongly advise you against heroics. You'd lose your position as an officer, and would have no credibility during the trial.'

'What trial? You no longer have the authority to convene one.'

'Do you think I've given up already?'

'Almost.'

'Almost . . . yes, you're right, but not altogether. This attack is too unjust.'

'How can you stay so calm?'

'Hardship helps me think,' said Pazair, 'and so does your hospitality.'

As a charioteer officer, Suti had a house with four rooms, fronted by a garden where Way-Finder and Brave slept all they liked. Panther had, without enthusiasm, taken charge of the cooking and cleaning – fortunately, Suti often interrupted her to lead her off into other, more entertaining activities.

Pazair hardly left his room. He went over the various aspects of his main cases again and again, indifferent to the amorous exploits of his friend and his beautiful mistress.

'Thinking, thinking,' grumbled Suti. 'And what do you get from all this thinking?'

'Thanks to you, we may perhaps be moving forward a bit. Qadash tried to steal copper from a barracks where Sheshi has a secret workshop.'

'Making weapons?'

'Without a doubt.'

'Isn't he one of General Asher's favourites?'

'I don't know. But Qadash's explanation didn't convince me. Why was he wandering around there? According to him, the officer in charge of the barracks told him about Sheshi – that should be easy for you to check.'

'I'll take care of it.'

Pazair fed his donkey, took his dog for a walk, then ate the midday meal with Panther.

'You scare me,' she confessed.

'Why? I'm not exactly terrifying, am I?'

'You're so serious all the time. Haven't you ever been in love?'

'More deeply than you can imagine.'

'Good. You're different from Suti, but your friendship means everything to him, and he's told me about your problems. How are you going to pay the fine?'

'Frankly, I'm wondering that, too. If I have to, I'll work in the fields for a few months.'

Panther was scandalized. 'A judge, working as a peasant?'

'I grew up in a village. I don't mind sowing, ploughing and reaping.'

'Well, I'd steal the ox. After all, taxation is the biggest thief of all.'

'Temptation is always there – that's why we have judges.'

'And you're honest?'

'I try to be.'

'Why are those people trying to destroy you?'

'It's to do with power.'

'Is there something rotten in the kingdom of Egypt?'

'We're no better than other men, but at least we know it. If rottenness exists, it will be cleansed.'

'By you?'

'With Suti's help. And if we fail, others will replace us.'

Panther rested her sulky chin on her fist. 'In your place, I'd let myself be corrupted.'

'When a judge commits a crime, it's a step towards war.'

'My people like fighting, yours don't.'

'Do you think that's a weakness?'

The black eyes flamed. 'Life's a battle I want to win, and I don't care how I do it or what it costs.'

Suti drained half a pitcher of beer with gusto. He was sitting astride the low garden wall, enjoying the last rays of the setting sun. Pazair sat cross-legged on the ground, stroking Brave.

'Mission accomplished,' said Suti. 'The commander of the barracks was flattered to welcome a hero of the last campaign. What's more, he has a loose tongue.'

'What are his teeth like?'

'Excellent – he's never been Qadash's patient.'

Suti and Pazair shook hand jubilantly. They had just uncovered a magnificent lie.

'And that's not all,' said Suti.

'Don't keep me in suspense.'

Suti grinned.

'Do I have to beg?'

'A hero must have a modest triumph. The warehouse contains top-quality copper.'

'I know.'

'What you don't know is that, immediately after being questioned, Sheshi had an unmarked chest moved elsewhere. It must have contained something very heavy, because four men could only just carry it.'

'What men? Soldiers?'

'Sheshi's personal guards.'

'Where did they take it?'

'I don't know. But I shall find out.'

'What would Sheshi need in order to make unbreakable weapons?'

'The rarest and hardest material is iron.'

'I agree. If we're right, that's the treasure Qadash was after. A tooth doctor with iron instruments . . . he thought they'd give him his skills back. All we have to do now is find out who told him about the hiding place.'

'How did Sheshi behave when you questioned him?'

'He was remarkably discreet. He didn't even lodge a complaint.'

'That's rather odd. He ought to have been delighted that a thief had been caught.'

'Which means . . .'

'. . . that they're accomplices.'

'But we've no proof,' said Pazair.

'Sheshi told Qadash about the iron, and he tried to steal part of it for his own use, but got caught. Sheshi didn't want him to appear in court because he'd have had to testify.'

'The workshop, the iron, the weapons – everything points to the army. But why should Sheshi, who's always so close-mouthed, confide in Qadash? And how does a tooth doctor get involved in a military conspiracy? It's absurd.'

'We may not have got everything right, but we're on the right track.'

'No, I think we're straying off the track.'

'Don't be a defeatist,' said Suti. 'The key person is Sheshi. I'll watch him day and night, I'll question his household, I'll break through the wall that this discreet, unassuming man has built round himself.'

'If only I could do something.'

'Just be patient for a while.'

Pazair looked up. Hope shone again in his eyes. 'Have you thought of something?'

'I shall sell my chariot.'

'You can't. You'd be dismissed from the army.'

Suti punched the wall. 'We've got to get you out of this mess – and soon. What about Sababu?'

'You mustn't even think of such a thing! A judge's debt paid by a prostitute? The Judge of the Porch would strike me from the roll of judges.'

Brave stretched out his paws and looked up at his master with trusting eyes.

33

Brave loathed water, so he kept a safe distance from the riverbank. Having run until he was out of breath, he paused, sniffed around, ran back to his master and then ran off again. The area around the irrigation channel was deserted and silent. Pazair thought of Neferet and tried to interpret every small sign in his favour. Had she or had she not shown a new kindness towards him? At the very least she had agreed to hear him out.

Behind a tamarisk tree, a shadow moved. Brave took no notice so, reassured, Pazair continued his walk. Thanks to Suti, the investigation had moved forward; but would he be able to take it any further? A junior judge with no experience was at his superiors' mercy: the Judge of the Porch had reminded him of that fact in the most brutal way.

Branir had comforted his pupil and told him that, if necessary, he would sell his house to enable Pazair to pay his debt. It had to be paid. The Judge of the Porch's actions must not be taken lightly, because he was stubborn and relentless, and quite happy to attack young judges in order to shape their characters.

Brave stopped in his tracks, sniffing the wind.

The shadow emerged from its hiding place and walked towards Pazair. The dog growled, but his master held him back by his collar.

'Don't be afraid, there are two of us.'

Brave nuzzled Pazair's hand.

It was a woman, a slender woman, her face concealed by a piece of dark cloth. She walked confidently and stopped a couple of paces from Pazair.

Brave froze.

'You have nothing to fear,' she said, and she removed her veil. It was Hattusa.

'The night is mild, my lady,' said Pazair, 'and conducive to meditation.'

'I wished to see you alone, away from all witnesses.'

'Officially, you're at Thebes.'

'You're very perceptive.'

'Your vengeance had the desired effect, my lady.'

'My vengeance?'

'I have been suspended, as you wished me to be.'

'I don't understand,' she said.

'My lady, please don't make fun of me.'

'On the name of Pharaoh, I have done nothing against you.'

'To use your own words, I went too far, didn't I?'

'You made me angry, it's true, but I admire your courage.'

'Are you saying you acknowledge that I had reason to do what I did?'

'One piece of proof will be enough for you. I have spoken with the senior judge of Thebes.'

'And what was the result?'

'He knows the truth, and the incident is closed.'

'It isn't for me, my lady.'

'Is your superior's opinion not good enough for you?'

'In this case, no.'

'That's why I'm here. The senior judge assumed – rightly, it seems – that my visit would be necessary. I'm going to tell you the truth, but first I require your promise of silence.'

'I cannot accept any restrictions.'

'You're so inflexible,' complained Hattusa.

'Were you hoping for a compromise?'

'You don't like me very much, and neither do most of your fellow countrymen.'

'You should say, "our fellow countrymen". You're Egyptian now.'

'None of us can ever forget our origins. I'm concerned with the fate of the Hittites who were brought here as prisoners of war. Some have virtually become Egyptian, others find it difficult to survive. It's my duty to help them, so I used wheat from the store in my harem for them. My steward told me our reserves would be exhausted before the next harvest. He suggested an arrangement with one of his colleagues in Memphis, and I gave my assent. Therefore I take full responsibility for that transfer.'

'Was Mentmose informed, my lady?'

'Of course. Feeding hungry people didn't seem criminal to him.'

What court would convict her? It would accuse her only of an administrative offence, which in any case would be blamed on the two stewards. Mentmose would deny everything, Denes would be exonerated, and Hattusa wouldn't even appear before the court.

'The senior judge of Thebes and his counterpart in Memphis have put the documents in order,' she added. 'If you feel the procedure is illegal, you are free to act. The letter of the law was not respected, I grant you, but surely the spirit is more important?'

She was fighting him on his own ground.

'My poor compatriots don't know where the food they receive comes from, and I don't want them to find out. Will you grant me that privilege?'

'It seems to me that the case has been dealt with in Thebes.'

She smiled. 'They say your heart is made of stone. Are they wrong?'

'I wish it were.'

Reassured, Brave started trotting about and sniffing the ground.

'One last question, my lady: have you met General Asher?'

She stiffened, and her voice became harsh. 'The day he dies, I shall rejoice. May the demons of hell devour the man who slaughtered my people.'

Suti was living the good life. Following his exploits, and because of his wounds, he had been granted several months of rest before returning to active service.

Panther played the submissive wife, but the wildness of her lovemaking proved that her temperament had scarcely softened. Each evening the joust began again; sometimes she was the radiant victor, and complained of her partner's softness. The following evening, Suti would make her surrender. The game enchanted them, for they took pleasure together and knew how to provoke each other while skilfully stimulating each other's bodies. She repeated that she would never fall in love with an Egyptian, and he declared that he loathed barbarians.

When he announced that he was going to be away for an unspecified time, she threw herself at him and hit him. He flattened her against a wall, prised her hands off him, and gave her the longest kiss they had ever shared. She quivered like a she-cat, rubbed herself against him, and made him want her so violently that he took her standing up, without letting her go.

'You shan't go away,' she said.

'It's a secret mission.'

'If you go, I shall kill you.'

'I'll come back.'

'When?'

'I've no idea.'

'You're lying! What is this mission?'

'It's secret.'

'You haven't any secrets from me.'

'Don't presume too much.'

'Take me with you. I can help you.'

Suti had not considered that possibility. Spying on Sheshi would undoubtedly be long and boring; besides, in some circumstances it would indeed help if there were two of them.

'If you betray me, I shall cut off one of your feet.'

'You wouldn't dare.'

'Once again, you're wrong.'

Picking up Sheshi's trail took only a few days. In the mornings, he worked in the palace workshops, alongside the best inventors in the kingdom. In the afternoons, he went to an outlying barracks, not emerging until dawn. Suti heard only good things about Sheshi: he was hard-working, skilful, discreet, modest. The only criticisms were that he was too quiet and self-effacing.

Panther soon got bored. There was no movement and no danger, and she had to be content with waiting and watching. The mission offered little of interest. Suti himself grew discouraged. Sheshi saw no one and was wholly absorbed in his work.

The full moon lit up the Memphis sky. Panther slept, draped across Suti. This would be their last night's watch. Suddenly, Sheshi appeared in the barracks' doorway.

Suti shook Panther awake and whispered, 'There he is.'

'I'm sleepy.'

'He seems worried about something.'

Sulkily, Panther looked. 'It's nearly dawn,' she said. 'He's just going to the workshop.'

Sheshi came out into the courtyard, mounted a donkey and let his legs hang down slackly. The beast moved off.

'It's finished for us,' said Suti. 'Sheshi's a blind alley.'

But Panther suddenly looked astounded. 'Where was he born?' she demanded.

'In Memphis, I think.'

'Sheshi's no Egyptian.'

'How do you know that?'

'Only a sand-traveller would ride a donkey like that.'

Suti's chariot halted in the courtyard of the frontier post, which was not far from the marshes of the town of Pitom. He entrusted his horses to a groom and ran to see the scribe in charge of immigration.

It was here that sand-travellers who wished to come and live in Egypt underwent detailed questioning. At certain times, no one was allowed in. In many cases, the request sent by the scribe to the authorities in Memphis was rejected.

'I'm Charioteer Officer Suti.'

'I've heard of you.'

'Can you give me some information about a sand-traveller who became a naturalized Egyptian, probably a long time ago?'

'That's rather irregular. Why do you want to know?'

Suti looked down in embarrassment. 'An affair of the heart. If I could persuade my betrothed that he isn't of Egyptian stock, I think she'd come back to me.'

'Very well,' said the scribe with a smile. 'What's his name?'

'Sheshi.'

The scribe consulted his records.

'I have one Sheshi,' he said eventually. 'He is indeed a sand-traveller, originally from Syria. He arrived at the frontier post fifteen years ago, and as Egypt and her neighbours were at peace, we let him enter.'

'There was nothing suspicious about him?'

'He had no dubious associates, and he'd never been in any military action against Egypt. The commission gave a favourable answer after three months' investigation. He took the name of Sheshi and found work in Memphis as a metal worker. The checks carried out during his first five years in Egypt didn't reveal any irregularity. It looks as though he's forgotten his origins, but I wish you luck anyway with your betrothed.'

Pazair and Branir were sitting on the terrace of Branir's house, with Brave asleep at his master's feet. With his last scruple of strength, Pazair had again refused Branir's offer to sell the house, even though the old man had tried hard to persuade him. Selling the house would be too great a wrench for Branir.

They sat in silence for a while, then Pazair asked, 'Are you certain the fifth guard is still alive?'

'If he were dead, I'd have felt it when I used my pendulum.'

'He's given up his pension and taken refuge in anonymity, so he'll have to work to survive. Kani was methodical and thorough, but he couldn't find him.'

Pazair went to the edge of the terrace and gazed down at Memphis. Suddenly the great city's peace seemed threatened, as if some sly danger were spreading out across it. If Memphis were stricken, first Thebes would yield, then the entire country. Feeling ill, he sat down again.

'You feel it too, don't you?' said Branir.

'It's horrible.'

'And it's getting stronger.'

'Are we the victims of some illusion?'

'You felt the evil in your flesh. At first, a few months ago, I thought it was just a nightmare. But it came back more and more often, and each time it was stronger and more oppressive.'

'What is it?'

'A plague whose nature we don't yet know.'

Pazair shivered. The feeling of illness faded, but his body retained the memory of it.

A chariot drew up outside the house, and Suti leapt out and raced up the steps to the terrace.

'Sheshi's a naturalized sand-traveller! Do I deserve a beer? Forgive me, Branir, I didn't greet you properly.'

Pazair handed his friend a drink, which he gulped down gratefully.

'I had time to think as I was travelling back from the frontier. Qadash is Libyan, Sheshi's a Syrian sand-traveller, Hattusa's a Hittite – foreigners, all three of them. Qadash has become a respectable tooth doctor, but he takes part in lewd dances with his countrymen. Hattusa hates her new life and keeps all her affection for her own people. Sheshi, the loner, takes part in strange research. There's your conspiracy! And Asher is behind them, manipulating them.'

Branir said nothing. Pazair wondered if Suti really had just given them the solution to the puzzle that had been tormenting them.

After a few more moments' thought, Pazair said, 'You're jumping to conclusions. How can there be a link between Hattusa and Sheshi, or between her and Qadash?'

'The link is their hatred of Egypt.'

'She hates Asher even more,' said Pazair.

'How do you know?'

'She told me, and I believe her.'

'Don't be so naive, Pazair. Those objections are childish. Be objective, and you'll soon see the truth. Hattusa and Asher devise the plots and then Qadash and Sheshi put them into action. The weapons Sheshi's developing won't go to the army.'

'Do you mean there'll be a rebellion?'

'Hattusa wants an invasion, and Asher's organizing it.'

Suti and Pazair both turned to Branir, eager to hear his opinion.

'Ramses' power hasn't weakened,' said the old man. 'Any attempt of that kind seems bound to fail.'

'And yet preparations are being made for it,' said Suti. 'We must act now – nip the conspiracy in the bud. If we start legal action, they'll take fright and know they've been unmasked.'

'But,' said Pazair, 'if our accusations are deemed to be unfounded and defamatory, we'll be heavily punished and they'll have free rein. We must strike hard and accurately. If we had the fifth guard with us, General Asher's credibility would be destroyed.'

'Are you going to wait for disaster to strike?' demanded Suti.

'Give me a night to think.'

'A night? Take all year if you want! You can't convene a court any more.'

'I'll say it once more, and this time,' said Branir, 'Pazair cannot refuse. I shall sell my house, and Pazair must pay his debts and return to office as soon as possible.'

Pazair walked alone through the darkness. Life had taken him by the throat, forcing him to concentrate on the ins and outs of a conspiracy whose seriousness seemed to grow from one hour to the next. All he wanted to think about was the woman he loved, who was out of his reach. He could renounce happiness, but not justice.

His suffering was making him more mature; a force, deep inside him, refused to be extinguished. A force he would use to serve those he loved.

The moon, the 'Fighter', was a knife which cut through the clouds, or a mirror which reflected the beauty of the gods. He asked it for power, praying that his gaze might be as all-seeing as that of the night-sun.

His thoughts returned to the fifth guard. What trade would a man pursue if he wanted to go unnoticed? Pazair ran through the occupations of the people who lived on the west bank of Thebes, and eliminated them one by one. From butcher to seed sower, all had links with the general population, and Kani would have found out about him sooner or later.

Except one.

Yes, there was one trade, at once so solitary and so visible that it formed the most perfect mask.

Pazair lifted his eyes to the sky, a lapis-lazuli vault pierced with doors in the form of stars, through which the light passed. As if he had managed to gather in that light, he now knew where to find the fifth guard.

34

Bel-Tran's new office was huge and light, and he would have four specialist scribes permanently at his disposal. He was positively radiant in a brand-new kilt and a short-sleeved linen shirt which didn't really suit him. He had enjoyed his success as a trader, but wielding public power had attracted him ever since he learnt to read and write. Because of his modest birth and scant education, it had seemed out of reach. But his hard work had proved his worth in the eyes of the government, and he was determined to use his energies in its service.

After greeting his staff and emphasizing his preference for order and punctuality, he turned to the first matter assigned to him: a list of people who were late paying their taxes. Bel-Tran always paid his on time, so he read the list with a certain amusement. A land owner, an army scribe, a man who ran a carpenters' workshop and ... Judge Pazair! The tax scribe had noted the amount owing and the size of the fine, and Mentmose himself had affixed the seals to the judge's door.

Bel-Tran went to see Iarrot and asked where the judge was living. When he reached Suti's house, he found only Suti and Panther there. Pazair had just left for the port, from which light boats sailed between Memphis and Thebes.

Bel-Tran was just in time to catch him. 'I have learnt of your difficulties,' he said.

'It was an oversight on my part.'

'It's blatantly unjust. The fine is grotesque in comparison with the offence. Seek redress through the courts.'

Pazair shook his head. 'I'm in the wrong. The case would last a long time, and all I'd gain would be a reduction in the fine and countless enemies.'

'The Judge of the Porch doesn't seem to like you very much.'

'It's his custom to put young judges to the test.'

'You helped me when I was in difficulties; I'd like to do the same for you. Will you let me pay your debt?'

'I appreciate your offer, but I can't accept it.'

'Then will you accept a loan – interest free, of course? At least let me not make a profit out of a friend.'

'But how can I repay you?'

'Through your work. In my new position as head of the Granaries secretariat, I shall often need to call upon your skills. I'll leave you to calculate how many consultations are worth two sacks of grain and a fat ox.'

'I think we'll be seeing a lot of each other,' said Pazair.

'Here's a document showing you can pay all that's due.'

Bel-Tran and Pazair embraced warmly.

The Judge of the Porch was making preparations for the following day's audience. A sandal thief, a disputed inheritance, compensation for an accident: simple cases which could be sorted out quickly. Then came an entertaining visitor.

'Pazair! Have you changed your profession, or have you come to pay what you owe?' The Judge laughed at his own joke.

'The latter.'

Still laughing, the Judge looked more closely at Pazair, who was perfectly serious.

'That's good, you have a sense of humour. This career isn't for you, you know. Later, you'll thank me for my severity. Go back to your village, marry a good peasant woman, give her two children, and forget about judges and justice. It's too complex a world. I know men, Pazair.'

'I congratulate you.'

'Ah, so you have returned to your senses.'

'Here is confirmation that my debt has been paid.'

The Judge stared at the document in utter amazement.

'The two sacks of grain have been deposited outside your door, and the fat ox is recovering its strength in your official stables. Are you satisfied?'

Mentmose looked ill-tempered. His face was red, his features pinched, his voice nasal and his impatience evident.

'I'm receiving you simply out of good manners, Pazair. Today, you're no more than a citizen outside the law.'

'If that were so, I'd no longer be permitted to disturb you.'

Mentmose looked up. 'What does that mean?'

'Here is a document signed by the Judge of the Porch. Everything is now in order with the tax authorities. He even considered that my fat ox exceeded the norm and granted me a tax credit for next year.'

'How did you ... ?'

'I should be obliged if you would remove the seals from my door with all possible speed.'

'Of course, my dear Judge, of course! Naturally I tried to defend you in this unfortunate matter.'

'I don't doubt it for a moment.'

'Our future collaboration . . .'

'Augurs extremely well. There's just one thing: as regards the stolen wheat, everything has been settled. I'm fully informed about the matter now – but of course you knew all about it before I did.'

Restored to office, and with his mind much eased, Pazair boarded a fast boat for Thebes. Kem accompanied him, and Killer slept beside them.

'You've surprised me,' said the Nubian. 'Most people would have been crushed by what you've been through.'

'I was lucky.'

'Force of will, more like. A will so strong that people and events bend to it.'

Pazair smiled. 'You credit me with powers I haven't got.'

The boat sailed on, taking him closer to Neferet. Nebamon would soon demand results, but she would never rein in her activities. A confrontation was inevitable.

The boat berthed at Thebes late in the afternoon. Pazair sat down on the bank, away from passers-by. The sun was sinking, tingeing the Peak of the West rosy pink; the flocks were returning from the fields, to the melancholy sound of flutes.

The last ferry carried only a few passengers. Kem and Killer stood at the back. Pazair went over to the ferryman. The man wore an old-fashioned wig which hid half his face.

'Stay as you are,' ordered the judge.

The ferryman remained hunched over the tiller.

'We need to talk; you're safe here. Answer without looking at me.'

Who paid any attention to the ferryman? Everyone was in a hurry to get to the other bank, talking, dreaming, never glancing at the man in charge of the ferry. He was content with little, lived apart, and had no contact with the general population.

'You're the fifth soldier, the only survivor of the Sphinx's honour guard.'

The ferryman didn't protest.

'I'm Judge Pazair and I need to know the truth. Your four comrades are dead, probably murdered, and that's why you're in hiding. There must be something mortally serious behind so many killings.'

'How do I know you're who you say you are?'

'If I wanted to kill you, you'd already be dead. Trust me.'

'That's easy for you—'

'No it isn't – far from it. Now tell me, what terrible event did you witness?'

'There were five of us, five ex-soldiers. We guarded the Sphinx at night. It was a risk-free job, completely honorary, before we retired. I and a colleague were sitting outside the wall that surrounds the stone lion, and as usual we'd fallen asleep. He was woken by a noise and he woke me. I was sleepy, and I calmed him down. But he was anxious and insisted, so we went to see. We walked inside the wall and found the body of one of our men by the Sphinx's right flank, then another on the other side.' He stopped a lump in his throat. 'And then there were these terrible moans – I still hear them. I found our commander lying between the Sphinx's paws. There was blood flowing from his mouth, and he could hardly speak.'

'What did he say?'

'He'd been attacked and he'd defended himself.'

'Who attacked him? Did he say?'

'A naked woman, and several men. "Foreign words in the darkness": those were his last words. My comrade and I were afraid. Why all the violence? Should we warn the soldiers on guard at the Great Pyramid? My comrade was against it, because he thought it would cause trouble for us – we might even be accused ourselves. The three others were dead . . . He said it was better to keep quiet, pretend we'd seen nothing, heard nothing. In the end I agreed, and we went back to our posts. When the day guard relieved us at dawn, they discovered the bodies. We pretended to be horrified.'

'Were you punished at all?' asked Pazair.

'No. We were just sent into retirement in our home villages. My comrade became a baker, and I was planning to repair chariots. But when he was murdered, I had to go into hiding.'

'He was murdered? Why do you say that?'

'He was a very careful man, especially with fire. I'm certain he was pushed. The tragedy at the Sphinx is pursuing us. We weren't believed. Someone thinks we know too much.'

'Who questioned you at Giza?'

'A senior officer.'

'Has General Asher contacted you at all?'

'No.'

'Your testimony will be decisive during the trial.'

'What trial?' asked the ferryman.

'The general approved a document certifying that you and your fellow guards were killed in an accident.'

'Good, that means I no longer exist.'

'If I could find you, others will. But if you testify, you'll be free again.'

The ferry arrived at the riverbank.

'I . . . I don't know. Leave me in peace.'

'It's the only way – for your comrades' memory and for yourself.'

'Tomorrow morning, on the first ferry, I'll give you my answer.'

The ferryman jumped onto the bank and wound a mooring rope round a stake. Pazair, Kem and Killer went ashore and walked off.

'Watch that man all night,' said Pazair.

'What about you?'

'I'll sleep at the nearest village, and come back at dawn.'

Kem hesitated. He didn't like the idea. If the ferryman had talked, Pazair was in danger, and Kem couldn't guard both men at once. He decided to guard Pazair.

The shadow-eater had watched the ferry cross the river, bathed in the setting sun. The Nubian was at the back, the judge next to the ferryman. That was strange. Side by side, they looked at the other bank. There were few passengers, and plenty of room, so why this closeness, unless it was so that they could talk?

A ferryman . . . the most visible yet unnoticeable of trades.

The shadow-eater jumped into the water and crossed the Nile, swimming with the current. When he reached the other side, he remained crouching in the reeds for a long time, watching. The ferryman slept in a wooden hut.

Neither Kem nor Killer was anywhere to be seen, but the shadow-eater waited a little longer, to be certain that no one was watching the hut. Then he sneaked inside and slipped a leather strap round the neck of the sleeping man who awoke with a start.

'If you move, you die,' growled the murderer.

The ferryman was helpless. He raised his right arm in submission. The shadow-eater loosened the strap a little, and said, 'Who are you?'

'The . . . the ferryman.'

'One more lie and I'll strangle you. Are you an ex-soldier?'

'Yes.'

'Where did you serve?'

'In the Asian army.'

'What was your last posting?'

'The Sphinx's honour guard.'

'Why are you hiding?'

'I'm afraid.'

'Afraid of what?'

'I . . . I don't know.'

'What is your secret?'

'I haven't got one!'

The leather strap bit into his flesh.

Half-choked, he managed to say, 'An attack, at Giza. Killings. The Sphinx was attacked, and my comrades died.'

'Who was the attacker?'

'I didn't see.'

'Did the judge question you?'

'Yes.'

'What did he ask?'

'The same as you.'

'And what did you tell him?'

'He threatened me with court, but I didn't say anything. I don't want any problems with the law.'

'Then what did you tell him?'

'That I was a ferryman, not a soldier.'

'Good.'

The leather strap was removed and, greatly relieved, the soldier rubbed his painful neck. The shadow-eater knocked him out with savage blow to the forehead, then dragged him out of the hut and down to the river. He held the ferryman's head under the water for a long time. When he left, the corpse was floating beside the ferry. Just another run-of-the-mill drowning accident.

Neferet was preparing a potion for Sababu. As the prostitute was now taking proper care of herself, her illness had abated. Full of energy again, and free from the burning attacks of rheumatism, she had asked Neferet's permission to make love with the porter at her ale-house, a strapping young Nubian.

'May I disturb you?' asked Pazair.

'I was coming to the end of my day's work.'

Neferet looked drawn.

'You work too hard,' he said.

'It's just tiredness, that's all. Is there any news of Nebamon?'

'He hasn't shown his hand yet.'

'It's probably the calm before the storm.'

'I'm afraid you may be right.'

'And how is your investigation going?' asked Neferet.

'It's taking great strides forward, although for a while I was suspended by the Judge of the Porch.'

'Tell me about it.'

He told her of his misfortunes while she washed her hands and tidied her workshop.

'You're surrounded by friends. Our master Branir, Suti, Bel-Tran – that was great good luck.'

'Do you feel lonely here?'

'The villagers do all they can to help, but I can't ask anyone for advice. Sometimes it's a heavy burden.'

They sat down on a mat outside, facing the palm grove.

'You look worried,' said Neferet.

'I've just found a vital witness. You're the first person to know.'

Neferet did not look away. In her eyes he saw interest, if not affection.

'You might be prevented from making more progress, mightn't you?'

'I don't care. I believe in justice as you believe in medicine.'

Their shoulders touched. Pazair held his breath. As if she were unaware of this chance contact, Neferet did not draw away.

'Would you go so far as to sacrifice your life to find the truth?' she asked.

'If I had to, without hesitation.'

'Do you still think of me?'

'Every moment of every day.'

His hand brushed Neferet's, rested on it, lightly, imperceptibly.

'When I'm tired,' she said, 'I think of you. Whatever happens to you, you seem indestructible and you keep on going.'

'That's only on the surface – I'm often full of doubts and fears. Suti accuses me of being naive. For him, the only thing that counts is adventure. As soon as he's threatened with routine, he's ready to commit any kind of madness.'

'Do you dislike it too?'

'No. It's an ally.'

'Can a feeling last for years and years?'

'A whole lifetime, if it's more than a feeling, a commitment of the whole being, a certain paradise, a communion nourished by daybreaks and sunsets. If love fades, it's really no more than a conquest.'

She leant her head on his shoulder, her hair brushing his cheek, and said, 'You have a strange power, Pazair.'

It was only a dream, as fleeting as a shooting star in the Theban night, but it lit up his life.

He spent a sleepless night in the palm grove, gazing up at the stars. He tried to preserve the brief moment when Neferet had lowered her guard before sending him away and closing her door. Did it mean she felt a degree of tenderness for him, or had it been simply the result of tiredness? At the idea that she might accept his presence and his love, even without sharing his passion, he felt as light as a spring cloud and as ardent as a swelling flood. It was almost dawn before he slept.

When he awoke, Killer was sitting a few paces away, eating dates and cracking open the kernels.

'Killer? What are you—'

'I decided to make sure you were safe,' said Kem from behind him. 'To the river, quickly!'

Day was breaking when they got there. A crowd had gathered on the bank.

'Stand aside,' ordered Pazair.

A fisherman had brought in the body of the ferryman, which he had found floating down river.

'Perhaps he couldn't swim,' said a woman.

'He must have slipped,' said another.

Ignoring these and other comments, Pazair examined the body.

'This was murder, not an accident,' he declared. 'There is the mark of a ligature on his neck, and a bruise from a violent blow on his forehead. He was strangled and knocked unconscious before being drowned.'

35

Pazair was in a cold rage. The ferryman's body, which had been carried to the nearest guard post, had been the subject of a misleading report by a petty local official who, for fear of being demoted, refused to admit that a crime had taken place on his territory, and declared that the ferryman had drowned. According to him, the injuries on the man's neck and forehead were accidental. Pazair could do nothing but express his grave reservations.

Before leaving for the north, he had seen Neferet for only a few moments. Many patients had been occupying her attention since early morning, so the pair had restricted themselves to a few polite words and an exchange of looks, in which he was sure he saw encouragement and support.

Laden with papyrus, brushes and palettes, Way-Finder guided his master and his master's friends through the outskirts of Memphis. If he made a mistake Suti could correct it, but the animal lived up to his name. Kem and Killer completed the procession, which headed for the barracks where Sheshi had his workshop. Early in the morning, he worked at the palace; the coast was clear.

Suti was jubilant. At last his friend had decided to take action.

In the barracks, which was some distance from the main military establishments in Memphis, there was no sign of life. Not one soldier at weapons drill, not one horse being exercised.

Suti went off to talk to the sentry stationed at the entrance; he found there was none. Cautiously, they entered the building, which was rather dilapidated.

Two old men were sitting on a stone wall. Pazair went over to them and asked, 'Which army corps is stationed here?'

The older man guffawed. 'The regiment of veterans and walking wounded, my lad! We've been billeted here until we're packed off to the provinces. Farewell Asian roads, forced marches, inadequate rations. Soon I'll have a little garden, a housekeeper, fresh milk and good vegetables.'

'Who's in charge here?'

'He's in that building over there, behind the well.'

The officer, when Pazair found him, looked very weary. 'We don't get many visitors,' he said.

'I'm Judge Pazair, and I wish to search your storehouses.'

'Why?'

'A man named Sheshi has a workshop here.'

'Sheshi? Don't know him.'

Pazair described him.

'Oh, him,' said the officer. 'He comes here in the afternoon and spends the night here, that's right. Orders from on high. I just carry them out.'

'Open up the room for me.'

'I haven't got a key.'

'Take me there.'

A stout wooden door prevented anyone entering Sheshi's underground workshop. On a slate tablet, Pazair noted down the year, month, day and time of his visit, together with a description of the place.

'Open the door,' he told the officer.

'I have no authority to do that.'

'I'll take full responsibility.'

Suti helped the officer to force the wooden lock with a spear, and Pazair and Suti entered, while Kem and Killer stood guard.

The workshop looked well equipped, with its hearth, furnaces, stocks of charcoal and palm bark, moulds and copper tools. Everything was tidy and clean. After a quick search, Suti found the mysterious chest that had been brought here from the other barracks.

'I'm as excited as a virgin with his first girl!' he crowed.

'Just a moment,' said Pazair.

'We can't stop now, not when we're so close to our goal.'

'I'm writing my report: condition and location of suspect object.'

Hardly had Pazair finished writing when Suti removed the lid from the chest.

'Iron,' he said, 'iron ingots – and not just any iron, either.' He felt the weight of an ingot, pressed it, licked it and scratched it with a nail. 'This doesn't come from the volcanic rocks in the Eastern desert. It's the legendary iron they used to tell tales about in the village: sky-iron.'

'From rocks that fall from the sky,' agreed Pazair.

'It's worth a fortune.'

'This is the iron the priests use in the House of Life to make the metal ropes up which Pharaoh ascends to the heavens. How can Sheshi possibly have got it?'

Suti was fascinated. 'I knew of it, but I never thought I'd actually hold it in my hand.'

'It doesn't belong to us,' Pazair reminded him. 'It'll be needed in the trial. Sheshi must explain where it came from.'

At the bottom of the chest lay a carpenter's adze made of sky-iron. An adze was used to open a mummy's mouth and eyes when the mortal body had been brought back to life through resurrection rituals and was transformed into light. Neither Pazair nor Suti dared touch it. If it had been dedicated to the gods, it was endowed with supernatural powers.

'We're being ridiculous,' said Suti stoutly. 'It's only metal.'

'You may be right, but I'm not taking any risks.'

'Then what do you suggest we do?'

'Wait here until Sheshi arrives.'

When Sheshi saw the door to his workshop standing open, he spun round and tried to run away. He ran straight into the Nubian, who pushed him inside. Killer went on calmly eating raisins, which Kem knew meant that none of Sheshi's allies was lurking nearby.

'I'm glad to see you again,' said Pazair. 'You have a taste for moving about.'

Sheshi's gaze fell on the chest. 'Who gave you permission to do that?' he demanded.

'It has been confiscated.'

Sheshi exercised all his self-control and stayed icily calm. 'Confiscation is an unusual procedure,' he remarked.

'So are your activities.'

'I have the use of this workshop in addition to my official one.'

'You seem to like working in army barracks.'

'I'm developing the weapons of the future, so the army authorized me to work here. If you check, you'll find that these premises are known about and my work is encouraged.'

'I'm sure it is, but you won't succeed by using sky-iron. That is for temple use only – and so is the adze hidden at the bottom of the chest.'

'It isn't mine.'

'Were you aware of its existence?'

'No. Somebody must have put it there without my knowledge.'

'That's not true,' cut in Suti. 'You ordered the chest's transfer yourself. You thought you'd be safe from prying eyes in this forgotten corner.'

'Have you been spying on me?' said Sheshi angrily.

'Never mind that,' said Pazair. 'Where did you get this iron?'

'I refuse to answer your questions.'

'In that case, you're under arrest for theft, receiving stolen goods, and obstructing an official investigation.'

'I shall deny everything, and you'll have no case.'

'Either you come with us calmly, or I shall tell Kem to bind your hands.'

'I shan't run away.'

The interrogation meant that Iarrot had to work overtime while his daughter, the finest dancer in her class, was giving a performance in the main square. To make matters worse, he had little to do, because Sheshi wouldn't answer any questions and remained stubbornly silent, sitting upright on a mat.

Pazair asked patiently, 'Who are your accomplices? One man alone could not have stolen iron of this quality.'

Sheshi looked at him through half-closed eyelids. He seemed as impregnable as a fortress on the King's Walls.

'Who entrusted you with this precious material? And why? When your research bore fruit, you dismissed the men who worked for you, using Qadash's attempted theft as an excuse to accuse them of incompetence. That meant there were no further checks on your activities. Did you make that adze, or did you steal it?'

Still the man did not answer. Suti would have liked to beat him, but Pazair would have intervened.

'You and Qadash have been friends for a long time, haven't you?' said Pazair. 'He knew about your treasure, and tried to steal it. Unless, of course, it was all a charade so that you could appear to be a victim and remove all inconvenient witnesses from your workshop.'

Sheshi kept silent. He knew Pazair could not use violence on him.

'Despite your silence, I shall find out the truth.'

The prediction did not worry Sheshi.

Pazair asked Suti to tie the suspect's hands and attach them to a ring fixed into the wall. When that had been done, Pazair turned to Iarrot.

'I'm sorry,' he said, 'but I must ask you to watch him.'

'Will it take long?'

'We'll be back before nightfall.'

The palace at Memphis was a government institution made up of dozens of departments, where a multitude of scribes worked. The inventors answered to an overseer of royal workshops, a tall, dried-out man of around fifty, who was openly astonished by the judge's visit.

'My assistant is Charioteer Officer Suti, who bears witness to my accusations,' said Pazair.

'What accusations?'

'One of your subordinates, Sheshi, has been arrested.'

'Sheshi? That's impossible! There must be some mistake.'

'Do your people use sky-iron?'

'Of course not,' exclaimed the overseer. 'It's so rare that it's reserved for ritual use in temples.'

'Then how do you explain the fact that Sheshi has a large quantity of it?'

'There must have been a mix-up.'

'Does he have specific duties?'

'He works directly for those in charge of making weapons, and it's his duty to check the quality of the copper used. I can vouch for Sheshi's honesty, the thoroughness of his work and his worth as a man.'

'Do you know that he has a secret workshop in an isolated barracks?'

'He had proper authorization from the army.'

'Signed by whom?' asked Pazair.

'By some of the senior officers who get specialists to develop new weapons. Sheshi's one of the specialists.'

'But the use of iron was not provided for.'

'There must be a simple explanation.'

'If so, he won't tell us what it is.'

'Sheshi's never been talkative,' said the overseer. 'He's a rather taciturn fellow.'

'Do you know where he hails from?'

'He was born in the Memphis region, I think.'

'Could you check that?'

'Is it important?'

'It might be.'

'I must consult my records.'

The search lasted more than an hour.

'I was right,' said the overseer. 'Sheshi comes from a small village to the north of Memphis.'

'Given the nature of his work, you checked, of course.'

'The army took charge of that, and found nothing unusual. The controller's seal was affixed, according to the rules, and the department employed Sheshi without any worries. I expect you to release him in the very near future.'

'The charges against him are multiplying. To theft, he's added lying.'

'Judge, aren't you being rather excessive? If you knew Sheshi better, you'd know that he's incapable of dishonesty.'

'If he's innocent, the trial will prove it.'

*

Iarrot was sobbing on the doorstep under the cynical gaze of Way-Finder. Suti took the scribe by the shoulders and shook him. Pazair looked inside his office and saw that Sheshi was gone.

'What happened?' he asked.

'He came here, he demanded my statement of charges, he saw two shortened paragraphs which made it illegal, he threatened me with reprisals, freed the suspect. He was right, so I had to give in.'

'Who are you talking about?'

'Mentmose.'

Pazair read the statement of charges. Iarrot had indeed failed to note down Sheshi's titles and offices, or to state that the judge himself was conducting a preliminary enquiry without the involvement of a third party. The case was therefore null and void.

A ray of sunlight filtered through the crossbars of a stoneframed window and lit up Mentmose's head, which was shiny with perfumed lotion.

Smiling, he greeted Pazair with forced enthusiasm. 'We live in a wonderful country, don't we, my dear Judge? No one can be subjected to the severity of an excessive law, since we watch over the citizens' well-being.'

'"Excessive" seems to be a fashionable word. The overseer of the palace workshops also used it.'

'He can hardly be blamed. While he was consulting his records, he sent word to me of Sheshi's arrest. I went immediately to your office, convinced that a regrettable mistake had been made. That was indeed the case, so Sheshi was freed immediately.'

'My scribe's failings are not in question,' admitted Pazair, 'but why are you so interested in Sheshi?'

'His work is of great value to the army. Like his colleagues, he's under my direct supervision, so he cannot be questioned without my agreement. I'd like to think you were unaware of that fact.'

'The accusation of theft removes Sheshi's partial immunity.'

'The accusation is unfounded.'

'A procedural error doesn't alter the validity of the complaint.'

Mentmose grew solemn. 'Sheshi is one of our finest experts in weaponry. Do you really think he'd risk his whole career in such a stupid way?'

'Do you know what the stolen object is?'

'What does it matter? I don't believe Sheshi stole it. Stop being so eager to gain yourself a reputation for righting wrongs.'

'Where have you hidden Sheshi?'

'Beyond the reach of a judge who exceeds his rights.'

Suti agreed with Pazair: the only option was to convene a court and put their all into it. Evidence and arguments would be decisive, provided the jurors had not been bribed by the opposition – Pazair could not reject the jurors wholesale, on pain of being removed from the case. The two friends were convinced that the truth, if proclaimed at a public trial, would penetrate even the dullest of minds.

When Pazair told his plan to Branir, the old doctor said, 'You're taking a lot of risks.'

'Is there a better way?'

'You must do as your heart tells you.'

'I think it's necessary to strike high, so as not to lose myself in secondary details. By concentrating on what is vital, I'll be better able to combat lies and cowardice.'

'You'll never be content with half-measures; you must have the full light of day.'

'Am I wrong, Branir?'

'This trial really needs a mature, experienced judge, but the gods have entrusted you with the task and you have accepted it.'

'Kem's guarding the chest of sky-iron. He's covered it with a plank and Killer's sitting on it. No one will get near it.'

'When will you convene the trial?'

'Within a week at the latest – because of the exceptional nature of the case, I shall speed up the procedures.' Pazair hesitated for a moment, then asked, 'Do you think I've identified the evil that's prowling round us?'

'You're getting close.'

'May I ask a favour of you?'

'Of course.'

'Despite your new appointment, will you be a juror?'

Branir gazed up at his patron planet, Horus, Bull of the Sky,* which was unusually bright tonight. 'Need you ask?'

---

*Saturn.

36

Brave could not get used to Killer's presence under his roof, but as his master tolerated it so did he. Kem spoke little, saying only that this trial was madness: however bold he might be, Pazair was too inexperienced to succeed. Although he understood the Nubian's disapproval, the judge continued to prepare himself, while Iarrot provided him with forms and registers, duly checked – the Judge of the Porch would be quick to exploit any irregularities.

Nebamon's arrival was hardly discreet: he was very elegantly dressed and wore a perfumed wig.

'I should like to speak with you privately, Judge,' he said. He seemed annoyed.

'I'm very busy.'

'It's urgent.'

Pazair abandoned a papyrus relating the trial of a nobleman accused of farming lands which did not belong to him; in the name of the king, despite his position at court – or, rather, because of it – his possessions had been confiscated and he had been sentenced to exile. He had appealed against the sentence, but it stood.

The two men walked into a quiet side street shaded from the sun. Little girls were playing with their dolls; a donkey passed, laden with baskets of vegetables; an old man was asleep on the doorstep of his house.

'We have misunderstood each other, my dear Pazair,' said Nebamon.

'Like you, I deplore the fact that Sababu continues in her distasteful profession, but there are no legal grounds for charging her. She pays her taxes and doesn't disturb public order. I have even heard it said that certain well-known doctors frequent her ale-house.'

'And what about Neferet? I asked you to persuade her to obey me.'

'And I said I'd do my best.'

'What a brilliant result you've achieved! One of my Theban colleagues was about to give her a post at the hospital in Deir el-Bahri, but fortunately I intervened in time. Do you realize how much offence she causes to approved doctors?'

'Well, at least you recognize her skills.'

'However gifted she may be, Neferet is on the fringes of medicine.'

'That isn't the impression I got.'

'I'm not interested in your impressions,' said Nebamon crossly. 'When one is trying to build a career, one must bow to the wishes of influential men.'

'You're right.'

'I'll give you one last chance, but don't disappoint me.'

'I don't deserve another chance.'

'Forget your initial failure and do something.'

'I'm wondering . . .' said Pazair.

'What about?'

'My career.'

'Follow my advice, and you'll have no further worries.'

'I'm content to be a judge.'

'I don't understand.'

'Leave Neferet alone,' said Pazair.

'Have you lost your mind?'

'Don't ignore my warning.'

'You're being very stupid,' said Nebamon. 'You're wrong to support a young woman who's going to fail most abjectly. Neferet has no future – and anyone who links his fate with hers will be swept away.'

'Your bitterness has clouded your mind.'

'No one has ever spoken to me like that! I demand an apology.'

'I'll try to help you.'

'Help *me*?'

'I can feel you sliding down towards failure.'

'You will live to regret those words!'

Denes was watching a cargo boat unloading. The crew were in a hurry, as they were due to leave again for the south the following morning, taking advantage of a favourable current. The cargo of furniture and spices was directed to a new warehouse which Denes had just acquired. Soon, he would buy up one of his fiercest competitors and swell the empire that he would bequeath to his two sons. Thanks to his wife's relatives, he was constantly strengthening his links with senior levels of government, so he wouldn't encounter any obstacles to his expansion.

The Judge of the Porch took a rare walk along the quayside. Leaning on a walking stick, because of an attack of gout, he approached Denes.

'Don't stand here, Judge, or they'll knock you over.'

Denes took the Judge by the arm and led him towards the part of the warehouse where the goods had already been stacked.

'Why this visit, Judge?' he asked.

'Dramatic events are in the offing.'

'Am I involved?'

'No, but you must help me to avert a disaster. Tomorrow, Pazair is presiding over the court. I could not refuse him, because he convened it according to all the rules.'

'Who's being charged?'

'He's kept the names of the accused and accuser secret. But rumour has it that state security is involved.'

'Then rumour's wrong,' said Denes. 'How could that little judge handle a case of such magnitude?'

'Beneath his reserved exterior, Pazair is a ram. He charges straight ahead, and no obstacle stops him.'

'Are you worried?'

'The man's dangerous. He carries out his duties as though they were a sacred mission.'

'You've known judges like him before, and they soon crumbled.'

'But this one is harder than granite,' said the Judge. 'I have already had occasion to put him to the test, and he's unusually resilient. In his place, a young judge who was preoccupied with his career would have withdrawn. Believe me, he's going to cause problems.'

'You're too pessimistic,' said Denes.

'Not this time.'

'Well, how can I help?'

'It's my task to appoint two jurors, since I have allowed Pazair to preside beneath the Porch. I have already chosen Mentmose, whose good sense will be vitally important to us. With you as well, I shall feel much more confident.'

'Tomorrow's impossible for me – there is a cargo of precious vases arriving, and I must check every single one. But my wife will be more than able to do what you want.'

Pazair took the summons to Mentmose himself.

'I could have sent my scribe, but our friendly relations oblige me to be more polite.'

Mentmose did not invite him to sit down.

'Sheshi will appear as a witness,' continued Pazair. 'As you're the only person who knows where he is, please bring him to the court. Otherwise, we'll have to send town guards out to look for him.'

'Sheshi's a reasonable man,' said Mentmose. 'I wish you were – then you'd give up this trial.'

'The Judge of the Porch considered it could be upheld.'

'You'll wreck your career.'

'A lot of people seem to be concerned about my career at the moment. Should I be worried?'

'When you've failed dismally, Memphis will laugh at you and you'll have to resign.'

'If you're chosen as a juror, don't refuse to hear the truth.'

'Me, sit on a jury?' Bel-Tran was astonished. 'I'd never have dreamt—'

'This is a very important trial, and its outcome is uncertain.'

'Do I have to do it?'

'Not at all. The Judge of the Porch is appointing two jurors, as am I, and four will be chosen from among leading citizens who have already officiated.'

'I confess I'm worried. Playing a part in a legal decision seems more difficult than selling papyrus.'

'You'll have to pronounce on the fate of a man.'

Bel-Tran took a long time to think. Eventually, he said, 'I'm moved by your trust in me. I'll do it.'

Suti made love with a fury which surprised Panther, even though she was accustomed to his ardour. He was insatiable and could not tear himself away from her, bombarding her with kisses and caresses.

Skilled in love, she knew how to be tender after the storm. 'Such violence,' she said, 'like a traveller who's about to leave. What are you hiding from me?'

'It's the trial tomorrow.'

'Are you afraid?'

'I'd prefer to fight with my bare fists.'

'Your friend scares me.'

'What do you have to fear from Pazair?'

'He'll spare no one, if the law demands it.'

'You haven't betrayed him, have you, without telling me?'

She threw him onto his back and lay across him. 'When will you stop being suspicious of me?'

'Never. You're a wild panther, the most dangerous of all species, and you've sworn a thousand times to kill me.'

'Your judge is more dangerous than I am.'

'You're the one who's hiding something, aren't you?'

She rolled onto her side, away from her lover. 'Perhaps.'

'I haven't interrogated you very well.'

'You know how to make my body speak.'

'But you're still keeping your secret.'

'If I didn't, would I be worth anything in your eyes?'

He threw himself on her and held her fast. 'Have you forgotten you're my prisoner?'

'Believe what you like.'

'When will you run away?'

'As soon as I'm a free woman.'

'That decision's up to me. I have to declare you as such to the authorities.'

'What are you waiting for?'

'Nothing. I'll do it straight away.'

Suti dressed in haste, putting on his finest kilt, and the collar on which hung the Golden Fly, and hurried to the government office.

He arrived just as the scribe was about to leave, long before the office was supposed to close. 'Come back tomorrow,' said the scribe.

'That's out of the question.'

Suti's tone was threatening. Moreover, the Golden Fly indicated that this powerfully built young man was a soldier, and soldiers often quickly resorted to violence.

'What do you want?' asked the scribe.

'An end to the conditional freedom of the Libyan woman Panther, who was granted to me during the last Asian campaign.'

'Do you guarantee her morality?'

'It's perfect.'

'What kind of work does she plan to do?'

'She's already worked on a farm.'

Suti completed the necessary formalities, wishing that he had made love to Panther one last time; his future mistresses might not be her equal. This would have happened anyway, sooner or later. It was better to cut the bonds before they became too strong.

On his way home, he recalled some of their amorous jousts, which had equalled the exploits of the mightiest conquerors. Panther had taught him that a woman's body was a paradise filled with moving landscapes, and that the pleasure of discovery could be constantly renewed.

The house was empty.

Suti wished he hadn't hurried. He'd have liked to spend the night before the trial with her, to forget tomorrow's battles, to sate himself on her perfume. He'd console himself with some old wine.

'Fill another cup,' said Panther, stealing up behind him and sliding her arms round his chest.

Qadash broke the copper instruments and threw them at the walls of his consulting room, which he had virtually destroyed. When he received the summons to appear before the court, a destructive madness had taken hold of him.

Without the sky-iron, he could no longer operate, because his hand shook too much. With the miraculous metal, he would have been like a god, rediscovering his youth and his skill. Who would respect him now? Who would boast of his marvellous work? People would talk of him in the past tense.

Could he delay his downfall? He must fight, refuse to become decrepit. Above all, he must disprove Judge Pazair's suspicions. If only he had the judge's strength, his dynamism, his determination! Making an ally of him was just a fantasy. The young judge must fall, and justice with him.

In a few hours, the trial would start. Pazair walked along the riverbank with Brave and Way-Finder. The dog and the donkey were content to wander along in the dusk after a good dinner, though they never lost sight of their master. Way-Finder walked in front, and chose the route.

Tired and tense, Pazair was assailed by questions. Was he wrong? Had he burnt his boats? Was he taking a path which led to the abyss? But these were shameful thoughts. Justice would take its course, as imperious as the course of the divine river. Pazair was not its master but its servant. Whatever the result of the trial might be, the veils would be lifted.

What would become of Neferet if he was dismissed? Nebamon would attack her even more determinedly, to prevent her practising. But fortunately Branir was watching over her. The future High Priest of Amon would admit her into the medical team at the temple, out of Nebamon's reach.

Knowing that she was protected from a miserable fate gave Pazair the courage he needed to confront the whole of Egypt.

37

The trial opened with the customary ritual words: 'Before the gate of justice, in the place where all complaints are heard, where truth is distinguished from lies, in this great square where the weak are protected and saved from the powerful.'* The court of justice backed onto the pillared gateway of the Temple of Ptah, and had been enlarged to accommodate a large number of dignitaries and common folk, all of them curious about the trial.

Judge Pazair, assisted by Iarrot, stood in the middle of the chamber. To his right was the jury. It was made up of Mentmose, Nenophar, Branir, Bel-Tran, a priest from the Temple of Ptah, a priestess from the Temple of Hathor, a landowner and a carpenter. The presence of Branir, who was regarded by many as a true sage, proved the gravity of the occasion. The Judge of the Porch sat on Pazair's left. He represented the legal hierarchy, and was there to ensure that the proceedings were conducted in the proper manner. The two judges, dressed in long white linen robes and plain, old-fashioned wigs, unrolled a papyrus relating the glory of the golden age when Ma'at, the harmony of the universe, had reigned unchallenged.

'I, Judge Pazair, declare this court in session. The accuser in this case is Charioteer Officer Suti, and the accused is General Asher, standard-bearer to the king and instructor to officers in the Asian army.'

A ripple of disbelief ran around the assembled throng. If their surroundings had not been so austere, many would have believed that this was a joke.

'I am Charioteer Officer Suti.'

The young man made a good impression on the crowd. He was handsome and confident, and did not look like a crank or an embittered soldier who had fallen out with his superior.

'Do you swear to tell the truth before this court?'

Suti read the words on the papyrus Iarrot handed him. 'By the

---

*This text was inscribed on the gate itself.

everlasting names of Amon and Pharaoh – whose power is more terrible than death – I swear to tell the truth.'

'Set forth your case,' said Pazair.

'I accuse General Asher of felony, high treason and murder.'

Exclamations of amazement and disbelief rose from the watching throng.

The Judge of the Porch cut in. 'Out of respect for Ma'at, I demand silence in court. Anyone who fails to observe it will be expelled immediately and heavily punished.'

The warning was effective.

'Officer Suti,' Pazair went on, 'have you any evidence to support these charges?'

'The evidence exists.'

'In accordance with the law,' said Pazair, 'I carried out an investigation. During it, I uncovered a number of strange facts, which I believe to be linked to the main accusation. I therefore put forward the theory that there is a conspiracy against the state and a threat to Egypt's safety.'

The tension increased. Those leading citizens who were seeing Pazair for the first time were astonished by the gravity of such a young man, by his firmness and the weight with which he spoke.

'I am General Asher.'

However famous he might be, Asher had had to appear before the court: the law did not permit substitutes or representatives. The small, rat-faced man came forward and took the oath. He had donned full fighting kit: a short kilt, leg protectors and a coat of mail.

'General Asher, how do you respond to your accuser?'

'Officer Suti, whom I appointed to his post myself, is a brave man – I decorated him with the Golden Fly. During the last Asian campaign, he achieved several remarkable things and he deserves to be recognized as a hero. I consider him a gifted archer, one of the best in our army. His accusations have no basis in truth. I reject them. No doubt this is simply a fleeting lapse of reason on his part.'

'So you consider yourself innocent?'

'I am innocent.'

Suti sat down at the base of a pillar, facing Pazair and a few paces from him. Asher did likewise, on the other side, near the jurors, who could easily see his facial expressions and the way he conducted himself.

'The role of this court,' said Pazair, 'is to establish the truth. If the crime is proved, the matter will be referred to the tjaty's court. I summon Qadash the tooth doctor.'

Qadash took the oath nervously.

'Do you admit that you tried to steal from an army workshop directed by the inventor Sheshi?'

'No, I do not.'

'Then how do you explain your presence there?'

'I had gone there to buy top-quality copper. The transaction didn't go well.'

'Who told you where the copper was?'

'The officer in charge of the barracks.'

'That is not true.'

'Yes, it is. I—'

'The court has his written statement. On that point, you have lied. Moreover, you have just repeated this lie after taking the oath, and have therefore committed the offence of perjury.'

Qadash trembled. A harsh jury would sentence him to forced labour in the mines; if they were lenient, the punishment might be a season working in the fields.

'I challenge your previous answers,' continued Pazair, 'and I ask you again: who told you about the copper?'

Qadash stood frozen to the spot, his mouth hanging open.

'Was it Sheshi?'

Qadash dissolved into tears. At a sign from Pazair, Iarrot led him back to his seat.

'I summon Sheshi the inventor.'

For a moment, Pazair thought Sheshi was not going to appear. But he had proved 'reasonable', as Mentmose put it.

The general asked permission to speak. 'I really am astonished. Surely this has become an entirely different trial?'

'In my opinion,' said Pazair, 'these persons are very much part of the matter we are dealing with.'

'Neither Qadash nor Sheshi has ever served under me.'

'Have a little patience, General.'

Thwarted, Asher watched Sheshi out of the corner of his eye. He seemed relaxed.

'Is it true that you work for the army in a workshop, developing new weapons?' asked Pazair.

'Yes,' said Sheshi.

'In reality, you have two jobs: one official, out in the open, in a palace workshop; the other much more discreet, in a workshop hidden in a barracks.'

Sheshi gave a brief nod.

'Following Qadash's attempt at robbery, you moved to new premises, but you did not bring charges against Qadash.'

'It seemed the most discreet solution.'

'As a specialist in metal alloys and foundry procedures, you receive materials from the army and keep an inventory of your stocks.'

'Of course.'

'Why have you been hiding ingots of sky-iron, which is reserved for religious uses, and an adze made of that metal?'

The question stunned the audience. Neither sky-iron nor sacred adzes ever left the precincts of the temple, and stealing them was punishable by death.

'I'm unaware of the existence of this treasure,' said Sheshi.

'Then how do you explain its presence in your workshop?'

'Someone is trying to do me harm.'

'Have you many enemies?'

'If I were convicted, my research would be interrupted and Egypt would suffer.'

'But you aren't a native Egyptian, are you?' said Pazair. 'You were born a sand-traveller.'

'I had forgotten.'

'You lied to the overseer of the workshops, and told him you were born in Memphis.'

'There was a misunderstanding. I meant that I felt like a true native of Memphis.'

Pazair turned to Asher. 'As was its duty, the army checked and corroborated your statement. Were the officials carrying out those checkes not under your authority, General?'

'It's possible,' murmured the general.

'Therefore you authorized a lie.'

'I didn't do it myself. It was an official under my command.'

'In law you are responsible for your subordinates' errors.'

'I admit that, but it's too trifling a matter to punish. Scribes make mistakes every day when they write their reports. Besides, Sheshi has become a true Egyptian. His profession proves the trust placed in him, and he has shown himself worthy of that trust.'

'The facts can be read another way. You have known Sheshi for a long time. You first met during your earliest campaigns in Asia. His gift for working with metal interested you, so you made it easy for him to enter Egyptian territory, glossed over his past, and helped him set out on his career making weapons.'

'That is pure speculation,' retorted Asher.

'The sky-iron is no speculation. What did you plan to use it for, and why did you obtain it for Sheshi?'

'That is a complete fabrication.'

Pazair turned to the jury. 'I would ask you to note that Qadash is Libyan, and Sheshi is a sand-traveller of Syrian origin. I believe that these two men are co-conspirators, with links to General Asher. They have been plotting for a long time, and were planning to take a decisive step forward by using sky-iron.'

'That's only your theory,' objected the general. 'You have not one shred of proof.'

'I admit that I have established only three reprehensible facts: Qadash's false testimony, Sheshi's false declaration, and your department's administrative shortcomings.'

The general folded his arms arrogantly. Thus far, Pazair was making himself look ridiculous.

'Now for the second part of my investigation,' Pazair went on, 'the matter of the honour guard at the Great Sphinx at Giza. According to an official document signed by General Asher, the five ex-soldiers forming the honour guard died in an accident, when they fell from the Sphinx. Do you confirm that, General?'

'I indeed placed my seal upon the report.'

'That version of the facts doesn't correspond with reality.'

Disconcerted, Asher unfolded his arms. 'The army paid for the funerals of those unfortunate men.'

'For three of them,' said Pazair, 'the head guard and two men from the Delta. I was unable to establish the exact cause of death. The other two were sent into retirement in the Theban region. They were certainly alive after the alleged accident.'

'That's very strange,' agreed Asher. 'May we hear what they have to say?'

'They are both dead now. The fourth soldier died in an accident – or was he in fact pushed into his own bread oven? The fifth was afraid and took refuge in the guise of a ferryman. He drowned – or should I say someone drowned him?'

'I object,' declared the Judge of the Porch. 'According to the report sent to my office, the local authorities believe it was an accident.'

'Whatever it was, at least two of the five soldiers did not die by falling from the Sphinx, as General Asher would have us believe. Moreover, the ferryman spoke to me before he died. His fellow guards were attacked and killed by an armed band comprising several men and a woman. They spoke in foreign tongues. That's the truth that the general's report concealed.'

The Judge of the Porch frowned. Although he detested Pazair, he could not cast doubt on a judge's words, spoken before the court and revealing a new fact of enormous importance.

Even Mentmose was shaken; the real trial was beginning.

The general defended himself vehemently. 'Each day I sign many reports without checking the facts myself, and I have very little to do with ex-soldiers.'

'The jurors will be interested to learn,' said Pazair, 'that Sheshi's workshop, where the chest containing the sky-iron was stored, was situated in a veterans' barracks.'

'What does that matter?' snapped Asher. 'The accident was investigated and verified by the army, and I simply signed the necessary document so that the funeral ceremonies could be organized.'

'Then you deny, under oath, that you knew of the attack on the honour guard at the Sphinx?'

'Yes, I certainly do deny it. And I also deny all responsibility, direct or indirect, in the deaths of those five unfortunate men. I knew nothing of this tragedy or subsequent events.'

The general defended himself with a conviction which would be looked upon favourably by the majority of the jury. True, the judge had brought a tragedy to light, but Asher could be blamed only for a second administrative error, not for one or more murders.

'Without calling into question the bizarre features of this case,' interposed the Judge of the Porch, 'I think that an additional investigation is essential. But we must surely cast doubt upon the statements made by the fifth guard, who may have made up a story to impress the judge.'

'A few hours later, he was dead,' Pazair reminded him.

'A sad coincidence.'

'If he was indeed murdered, someone wished to prevent him saying more, and to prevent him appearing before this court.'

'Even if we accept your theory,' said Asher, 'how am I involved? If I had checked, I would have seen, as you did, that the honour guard didn't die in an accident. At the time, I was busy preparing for the Asian campaign, and that was necessarily my first priority.'

Pazair had hoped, but without too much optimism, that the general would be less confident, but he was managing to parry the attacks and turn the most incisive arguments to his favour.

'I am Suti.' He rose, solemn-faced.

'Do you maintain your allegations?'

'I do.'

'Explain why.'

'During my first mission in Asia, after the death of my officer, who was killed in an ambush, I wandered through a troubled region, trying to find General Asher's regiment. I thought I was lost when I witnessed a terrible scene. An Egyptian soldier was tortured and murdered a few paces from me; I was too exhausted to help him, and his attackers were too numerous. One man carried out the interrogation, then slit the soldier's throat. That criminal, that traitor to his country, is General Asher.'

The general kept his composure. The shocked spectators held their breath. The jurors became suddenly grim-faced.

'Those scandalous words have no basis in truth,' declared Asher in a voice which was almost serene.

'Denying it is not enough,' said Suti hotly. 'I saw you, you murderer!'

'Please remain calm,' Pazair told him. 'This testimony proves that General Asher is collaborating with the enemy, and that is why the Libyan rebel Adafi remains uncaptured. His accomplice warns him in advance of our troop movements, and is planning an invasion of Egypt with him. The general's guilt leads us to believe that he is not innocent in the Sphinx affair. Did he have the five soldiers killed to try out the weapons made by Sheshi? An additional investigation will no doubt demonstrate this, linking together the various elements I have set out.'

'My guilt has not been proved in any way,' declared Asher.

'Do you cast doubt upon the words of Officer Suti?'

'I believe he's sincere, but he's wrong. According to his own testimony, he was utterly exhausted. No doubt his eyes deceived him.'

'The murderer's face is engraved in my mind,' declared Suti, 'and I swore that I would find him again. I didn't know then who he was. I identified him as General Asher at our first meeting, when he congratulated me on my exploits.'

'General, did you send out scouts into enemy territory?' asked Pazair.

'Of course,' replied Asher.

'How many?'

'Three.'

'And were their names registered at the Foreign Affairs secretariat?'

'That's the rule.'

'Did they all return alive from the last campaign?'

For the first time, the general looked uneasy. 'No. One of them died.'

'The one you killed with your own hands because he had realized what you were doing.'

'That's untrue. I'm not guilty.'

The jurors noticed that his voice was trembling.

'You, who are laden with honours,' said Pazair, 'who train officers, have betrayed your country in the most contemptible manner. It is time to confess, General.'

Asher gazed into the distance. This time, he was close to yielding. 'Suti is mistaken.'

'Send me back there with officers and scribes,' suggested Suti. 'I'll recognize the place where I buried the poor man. We'll bring back his body, he'll be identified, and we shall give him a worthy tomb.'

'I order an immediate expedition,' declared Pazair. 'General Asher will be held in the main barracks at Memphis, under close guard. He is to have no contact with the outside world until Suti returns. We shall then continue the trial and the jury will reach its verdict.'

38

The echoes of the trial could still be heard in Memphis. Some people already believed General Asher to be the worst kind of traitor, and praised Suti's courage and Judge Pazair's skill.

Pazair would have loved to consult Branir, but the law forbade him to speak to the jurors until the end of the case. He declined several invitations from leading citizens and locked himself away in his house. In less than a week, the expedition would return with the body of the scout murdered by Asher, and the general would be convicted and sentenced to death. Suti would be promoted to a senior rank. Above all, the plot would be dismantled and Egypt saved from a peril which came both from outside and from within. Even if Sheshi slipped through the net, the goal would have been reached.

Pazair had not lied to Neferet. He had not stopped thinking about her for a moment. Even during the trial, her face had haunted him. He had had to concentrate on every word so as not to sink into a dream in which she was the only heroine.

He had entrusted the sky-iron and the adze to the Judge of the Porch, who had immediately handed them over to the High Priest of Ptah. Working with the religious authorities, Pazair must establish where they came from. One thing worried him: why had no one reported their theft? Their exceptional quality hinted at a rich and powerful shrine, which was certainly the kind most likely to own them.

Pazair had granted Iarrot and Kem three rest days. Iarrot was eager to return home, where a new domestic drama had just broken out. His daughter was refusing to eat vegetables, and living solely on pastries. Iarrot could accept the whim, but his wife could not.

The Nubian did not leave the office. He didn't need rest and considered himself responsible for Pazair's safety. A judge might be untouchable, but it was vital to be careful.

When a shaven-headed priest tried to enter the building, Kem barred his way.

'I must give a message to Judge Pazair,' said the priest.

'Give it to me.'

'I must give it to him in person.'

'Wait here.'

Although the man was thin and unarmed, the Nubian felt uneasy.

He went into Pazair's office and told him, 'A priest wants to speak to you. Be careful.'

Pazair smiled. 'You see danger everywhere.'

'At least keep Killer with you.'

'As you wish.'

The priest entered, and Kem remained behind the door. Killer munched unconcernedly on a date stone.

'Judge Pazair, you're expected tomorrow at dawn, at the great gate of the Temple of Ptah.'

'Who wants to see me?'

'I have no other message.'

'What is the reason for this meeting?'

'I repeat, I have no other message. Please shave off all your bodily hair, abstain from sexual relations, and meditate before the ancestors.'

'I'm a judge. I have no intention of becoming a priest.'

'Do as I ask. May the gods protect you.'

Kem watched while the barber finished shaving Pazair.

'There you are,' said the man, 'smooth enough to enter holy orders. Are we losing a judge and gaining a priest?'

'It's simply a matter of cleanliness. Don't the nobility do the same on a regular basis?'

'You've become one of them, true enough. I like that. In the streets of Memphis, people can't stop talking about you. Who would dare attack all-powerful Asher? Today, tongues are loosening. Nobody liked him. There are rumours that he tortured recruits.'

Yesterday worshipped, today scorned. Asher had seen his destiny turned upside-down in a few hours. The most sordid rumours were circulating about him. Pazair took the lesson to heart: no one was safe from human baseness.

'If you aren't becoming a priest,' ventured the barber, 'you must be going to see a lady. Lots of women like well-shaven men who look like priests – or who *are* priests. All right, love isn't forbidden to them, but it must be exciting to consort with men who see the gods face to face. I have a jasmine and lotus lotion here; I bought it from the best perfume maker in Memphis. It will give your skin a pleasant scent for several days.'

Pazair accepted it. In so doing, he ensured that the barber would spread throughout Memphis the news that the most unbending judge in the city was also a charming lover. All that remained was to find out the name of the chosen woman.

After the barber had left, Pazair read a text dedicated to Ma'at. She was the venerable ancestor, the source of joy and harmony. Daughter of the Light, Light herself, she showed favour to those who acted in her name.

Pazair asked her to keep his life on the path of righteousness.

Cloistered priests, dressed in white linen, emerged from their dwellings on the edges of the lake, from which they took water to wash themselves each morning. In procession, they laid vegetables and bread on the altars, while the High Priest, acting in the name of Pharaoh, lit a lamp, broke the seal on the innermost shrine where the god lay, wafted incense, and spoke the words 'Awaken in peace.' At the same time, other high priests were carrying out the same ritual in other temples.

In one of the chambers of the inner temple, nine men had gathered. The tjaty, the bearer of the Rule, the overseer of the Double House, the official in charge of canals and director of water dwellings, the overseer of writings, the overseer of fields, the director of secret missions, the scribe of the land registry and the king's steward formed the council of the nine friends of King Ramses.

Each month, they met in this secret place, far from their offices and their staff. In the peace of the shrine, they enjoyed the quiet they needed for reflection. They felt the weight of their task more and more heavily since Pharaoh had issued his unusual orders, as if the empire were in peril. Each man must carry out a systematic inspection within his own department, to ensure the honesty of his most senior colleagues. Ramses had demanded swift results. Irregularities and laxness must be thoroughly dealt with, and incompetent officials dismissed. Each of the nine friends had noticed, during conversations with Pharaoh, that the king was preoccupied or even worried.

After a night of fruitful conversations, the nine men parted. A priest whispered a few words in Bagey's ear, and the tjaty headed for the doorway to the pillared hall. A young man was awaiting him there.

'Thank you for coming, Judge Pazair,' said Bagey. 'I'm the tjaty.'

Pazair, already impressed by his majestic surroundings, was even more impressed by this meeting. He, an insignificant judge from Memphis, had been granted the immense privilege of speaking alone with Tjaty Bagey, whose legendary strictness frightened even the most senior officials.

Bagey was taller than Pazair, with a long, austere face and a muffled, slightly hoarse voice. His tone was cold, almost abrupt.

'I wanted to see you here, so that our conversation would remain secret. If you consider it against the law, withdraw now.'

'Please continue, Tjaty. I'm listening.'

'Are you aware of the importance of the trial you are conducting?'

'General Asher is a great man, but I believe I have demonstrated that he is a criminal.'

'Are you certain of that?'

'Suti's testimony cannot be contested.'

'But he is your closest friend, is he not?' said Bagey.

'That's true, Tjaty, but our friendship doesn't influence my judgment.'

'That fault would be unforgivable.'

'I believe the facts have been established.'

'Isn't that for the jury to decide?'

'I shall bow to their decision.'

'In attacking General Asher, you're calling into question our defence policy in Asia. The morale of our troops will be damaged.'

'Tjaty, if the truth had not been discovered,' said Pazair, 'the country would have faced a much more serious danger.'

'Have there been attempts to impede your investigation?'

'The army threw obstacles in my way, and I'm certain that murders have been committed.'

'The fifth guard?'

'All five guards died violently, three at Giza, and the two survivors in their villages. That's my belief. It's for the Judge of the Porch to pursue the investigation, but . . .'

'But?'

Pazair hesitated. This was the tjaty himself standing before him. To speak lightly would be fatal; to hide his thoughts would be tantamount to lying. Those who had tried to mislead Bagey no longer served in his government.

'But, Tjaty, I am not altogether certain that he'll conduct it with the necessary determination.'

'Are you daring to accuse the most senior judge in Memphis of incompetence?'

'I have a feeling that the fight against darkness no longer attracts him. His experience makes him foresee so many worrying consequences that he prefers to remain in the background and not venture onto dangerous ground.'

'That's a harsh criticism. Do you think he's corrupt?'

'No, Tjaty, merely linked to important people he doesn't want to annoy.'

'We are a long way from justice.'

'It is not justice as I understand it, that's true.'

'If General Asher is convicted, he'll appeal,' said Bagey.

'That's his right.'

'Whatever the verdict, the Judge of the Porch will not remove you from this case and will ask you to pursue the instruction on points which are unclear.'

'Forgive me, Tjaty, but I doubt that.'

'You're wrong, for I shall give him the order. I want everything out in the open, Judge Pazair.'

'Suti got back yesterday evening,' Kem told Pazair.

'Then why isn't he here?'

'He's been detained at the central barracks.'

'That's illegal!'

Pazair hurried to the barracks, where he was received by the scribe who had commanded the expedition.

'I demand an explanation,' said Pazair.

'We went to the scene of the incident. Officer Suti recognized the place, but we searched in vain for the scout's body. I believed it fitting that Suti be placed under arrest.'

'That decision is unacceptable, as long as the current trial hasn't ended.'

The scribe agreed that that was true, and Suti was immediately freed.

The two friends embraced.

'Were you tortured?' asked Pazair.

'No. My travelling companions were all convinced of Asher's guilt, and our failure has plunged them into despair. Even the cave had been laid waste, to wipe out all traces.'

'And yet we told no one about it.'

'Asher and his allies took precautions. I was as naive as you, Pazair. We shan't be able to defeat him on our own.'

'For one thing, the trial is not lost yet; and for another, I have full powers.'

The trial recommenced the following day.

Pazair summoned Suti to give evidence.

'Please tell the court about your expedition to the scene of the crime.'

'In the presence of sworn witnesses, I saw that the corpse had gone. Someone had carefully destroyed the place.'

'That's grotesque.' Asher sniffed. 'The officer made up a story and now he's trying to justify it.'

'Do you maintain your accusations, Officer Suti?' asked Pazair.

'I did indeed see General Asher torture and murder an Egyptian.'

'Where is the body?' sneered Asher.

'You had it removed.'

'You think that I, general of the Asian army, would act like the vilest of criminals? Who could possibly believe that? The facts can be made to tell a very different story: you killed your chariot officer because you yourself are the sand-travellers' accomplice. And you are anxious to put the blame on someone else to vindicate yourself. Since there is no proof of either version of the story, the trick rebounds on its author. I therefore demand that you be punished.'

Suti clenched his fists. 'You're guilty and you know it. How dare you give instruction to our best troops when you viciously murdered one of your own men and led our soldiers into ambushes?'

Asher lowered his voice. 'The jurors will enjoy these increasingly ludicrous fabrications. Soon, no doubt, I shall be accused of wiping out the whole army.' His mocking smile won over the spectators.

'Suti is speaking under oath,' Pazair reminded him, 'and you recognized his worth as a soldier.'

'All the praise for his heroism has turned his head.'

'The disappearance of the body doesn't wipe out his testimony.'

'No, but you will agree, Judge, that it reduces its scope considerably. I, too, am testifying under oath. Is my word worth less than Suti's? If he did indeed see a murder, he has the wrong murderer. If he'll make a public apology to me here and now, I shall forget his fleeting madness.'

Pazair turned to Suti. 'Officer Suti, are you agreeable to that suggestion?'

'When I emerged from the hornets' nest that almost killed me, I swore to bring this most contemptible of men to justice. Asher is skilful: he fosters doubt and suspicion. And now he wants me to recant. I shall proclaim the truth to my last breath.'

'Faced with the blind stubbornness of a soldier who has lost his mind,' said Asher, 'I, general and royal standard-bearer, affirm my innocence.'

Suti wanted to rush at him and make him eat his words. But a hard stare from Pazair held him back.

'Does anyone here present wish to speak?' asked Pazair.

No one said a word.

'Then I invite the jury to consider its verdict.'

The jury sat in a chamber at the palace, the judge presiding over discussions which he was not allowed to enter into on either side. His role was to ensure that everyone had a chance to speak, to avoid confrontations and to maintain the dignity of the court.

Mentmose spoke first, with objectivity and moderation. A few specific points were added to what he had to say, but his conclusions were retained with no great changes. Less than two hours later, Pazair read the verdict and Iarrot noted it down.

'Qadash the tooth doctor is found guilty of perjury. Because the lie was not a serious one, and in view of his age and brilliant past, Qadash is sentenced to give one fat ox to the temple and a hundred sacks of grain to the veterans' barracks he disturbed by his intrusion.'

Qadash sighed with relief.

'Does Qadash wish to appeal or to reject this judgment?'

He rose. 'I accept it, Judge Pazair.'

'Sheshi is acquitted of all charges.'

The man did not even smile.

'General Asher is found guilty of two administrative errors, which did not prejudice the conduct of the army in Asia. Moreover, his excuses were found to be valid. He is therefore only given a warning, so that this kind of failure doesn't happen again. The jurors do not consider that the murder was properly and definitively established. General Asher is therefore not considered to be a traitor or a criminal, but Officer Suti's testimony cannot be qualified as defamatory. Since the jurors could not make a clear pronouncement because of the doubt surrounding several vital facts, the court asks that the investigation be continued, in order to establish the truth as quickly as possible.'

39

The Judge of the Porch was kneeling by a flower bed, watering a clump of irises which grew between some hibiscus bushes. He had been a widower for five years, and lived alone in his villa on the south side of the city.

He looked sternly up at Pazair, and asked, 'Are you proud of yourself, Judge? You have sullied the reputation of a general respected by everyone, sown confusion in people's minds, and have not even obtained victory for your friend Suti.'

'That was not my goal.'

'Then what was?'

'The truth.'

'Ah, the truth! Don't you realize it's harder to grasp than an eel?'

'But I unearthed the elements of a conspiracy against the state.'

'Stop talking nonsense. Why don't you help me to my feet and water the narcissi – gently, mind. That will make a change from your usual ruthlessness.'

Pazair did as he was bidden.

'Have you calmed our hero down?'

'No, he's as angry as ever.'

'What did he expect? To overthrow Asher with one mad gesture?'

'I believe Asher's guilty,' said Pazair, 'and so do you.'

'You're very indiscreet. That's yet another fault.'

'Did my arguments give you cause for concern?'

'At my age, nothing disturbs me any more.'

'I think the contrary is true.'

'I'm tired,' said the Judge, 'and no longer fit to carry out long investigations. Since you have begun, you can continue.'

'Am I to understand that—'

'You understand perfectly. I have taken my decision, and I shan't change my mind.'

*

The news was soon all round the palace and the official buildings: to everyone's surprise, Pazair was not being removed from Asher's case. Although he had not succeeded, the young judge had impressed many dignitaries by his thoroughness. Favouring neither the accuser nor the accused, he had not tried to hide the gaps in the evidence. Some had forgotten his youth and stressed his promising future, although it might be compromised because of who the accused was.

Undoubtedly Pazair had been wrong to give so much credit to the testimony of Suti, the hero of a day and a fanciful fellow. But if most people, after reflection, believed the general innocent, all agreed that Pazair had brought to light some disturbing facts. Even if the deaths of the five guards and the theft of the sky-iron were not linked to some imaginary conspiracy, they were nevertheless scandalous episodes which ought not to be forgotten. The state, the legal hierarchy, dignitaries and the common people all expected Judge Pazair to reveal the truth to them.

Suti did calm down somewhat when he learnt that Pazair was to continue his enquiries, and he tried to forget his disappointment in Panther's arms. He promised his friend that he wouldn't do anything without their first agreeing on a strategy. Although he had retained his status as a charioteer officer, he wouldn't be taking part in any missions before the final verdict.

The dying sun turned the desert sand and the stones in the quarries to gold; the workmen's tools had fallen silent, the peasants were returning to their farmhouses, and the donkeys were resting, relieved of their burdens. On the flat roofs of the houses in Memphis, people were enjoying the cool air while eating cheese and drinking beer.

Brave was stretched out on Branir's terrace, dreaming of the piece of grilled beef he had just eaten. In the distance, the pyramids on the Giza plateau formed triangles of absolute purity, marking the edges of eternity in the dusk. The country was falling peacefully asleep, as it did every evening in Ramses' reign.

'You overcame the biggest obstacle,' said Branir.

'It was a paltry success,' objected Pazair.

'You have been recognized as an honest, skilful judge, and you now have a chance to pursue the investigation without hindrance. Who could ask for more?'

'Asher lied, even though he was speaking under oath. Not just a murderer but a perjurer, too.'

'The jury didn't censure you. Neither Mentmose nor Nenophar tried to vindicate the general. They have set you on the road to your destiny.'

'The Judge of the Porch would have liked to remove me from the case.'

'Perhaps, but he has confidence in your abilities, and the tjaty wants reliable information on which to base his actions.'

'I may not be able to find any, because Asher took care to destroy the proof.'

'Your path will be long and difficult, but you can reach the goal. Soon, you'll have the support of the High Priest of Karnak and you'll have access to temple records.'

Pazair nodded. He was determined to investigate the theft of the sky-iron and the adze as soon as Branir took office.

Branir went on, 'You are your own master now. Distinguish justice from iniquity, and resist the advice of those who fail to do so in order to mislead people. This trial was only a skirmish; the true battle has yet to be fought. Neferet, too, will be proud of you.'

In the stars' light shone the souls of the sages. Pazair thanked the gods, who had permitted him to meet one in the world of men.

Way-Finder was a silent, thoughtful donkey. He rarely made a sound, but when he did, his braying was piercing enough to wake a whole street.

Pazair awoke with a start.

It was scarcely past dawn, but his donkey had definitely called to him. The judge opened the window.

Outside the house stood a crowd of some twenty people, among them Nebamon.

Nebamon shook his fist and shouted, 'Here are the finest doctors in Memphis, Judge Pazair! We are lodging a complaint against our colleague Neferet, for preparing unsafe medicines, and we demand her expulsion from the medical profession.'

Pazair reached the west bank of Thebes at the hottest time of the day. He requisitioned a town-guard chariot, whose driver was sleeping in the shade of an awning, and ordered him to drive quickly to Neferet's village. The sun reigned unchallenged, halting time in its tracks.

Neferet was neither at home nor at her workshop.

'Try the canal,' recommended an old man, rousing briefly from his doze.

Pazair abandoned the chariot, walked alongside a field of wheat, crossed a shady garden, set off along a path and at last reached the canal, where the villagers often bathed. He scrambled down the steep slope, passed through a curtain of reeds, and saw her.

He should have called to her, closed his eyes, turned away, but no words emerged from his lips and he was frozen to the spot by her entrancing beauty. She was naked, and swimming with natural grace, letting the current bear her along. She dived and resurfaced, and he saw that she was wearing a cap made from reeds and a necklace of turquoises.

When she saw him, she went on swimming. 'The water's wonderful,' she called. 'Come in and have a swim.'

Pazair took off his kilt and walked towards her, not even feeling the cool of the water. She reached out her hand to him and he took it, his whole being aflame. A wave brought their bodies into contact. When her breasts touched his chest, she didn't draw away. He dared to press his lips against hers and slip his arms round her.

'I love you, Neferet.'

'I shall learn to love you.'

'You're the first, and there will never be anyone else.'

Clumsily, he kissed her. Arm in arm, they returned to the riverbank and stretched out on a sandy beach, hidden in the reeds.

'I'm a virgin, too,' said Neferet.

'I want to offer you my life. First thing tomorrow, I shall ask for your hand in marriage.'

She smiled, conquered, abandoning herself to the moment. 'Make love to me. Make love to me now.'

He lay down on top of her, gazing into her blue eyes. Their souls and bodies united under the midday sun.

Neferet listened to her father's and mother's views. Neither of them was opposed to the marriage, but they wanted to see their future son-in-law before making their decision. True, she had no need of their consent, but she respected them and their approval meant a great deal to her. Her mother had a few reservations. Wasn't Pazair too young? And there were still doubts about his future prospects. Not to mention the fact that he was late, on the very day when he was asking for her daughter's hand.

Their concerns transmitted themselves to Neferet. A horrible thought entered her head: what if he had already stopped loving her? What if, contrary to everything he had said, he had wanted only a brief affair? No, that was impossible. His passion would be as everlasting as the mountain of Thebes.

At last he entered the modest dwelling. Neferet remained distant, as the solemnity of the moment required.

'Please forgive me; I lost my way in the maze of little streets. I confess I have no sense of direction – usually, my donkey guides me.'

Neferet's mother was astonished. 'You have a donkey?'

'Yes. His name is Way-Finder.'

'Is he young and in good health?'

'He's never been ill in his life.'

'What else have you got?'

'Next month, I shall have a house in Memphis.'

'Being a judge is a good job,' declared Neferet's father.

'Our daughter is young,' pointed out her mother. 'Couldn't you wait?'

'I love her, and want to marry her this very second.'

Pazair's manner was serious and determined. Neferet gazed at him with the eyes of a woman in love. Her parents yielded.

Suti's chariot hurtled through the gates of the main barracks in Memphis. The guards dropped their spears and threw themselves aside to avoid being run over. Suti jumped down from the moving vehicle, leaving the horses to continue galloping round the great courtyard. He ran up the staircase that led to the senior officers' quarters, where General Asher was staying. He dealt the first guard a sharp blow to the back of the neck, punched the second in the belly, and kicked the third in the testicles. The fourth had time to unsheathe his sword and wound him in the left shoulder; but the pain only intensified Suti's rage, and he knocked out his opponent with a double-fisted blow.

General Asher was sitting on a mat, with a map of Asia spread out in front of him. He turned to look at Suti. 'What are you here for?'

'To kill you.'

'Don't be a fool.'

'You may escape justice, but you won't escape me.'

'If you attack me, you won't leave this barracks alive.'

'How many Egyptians have you killed with your own hands?'

'You were exhausted,' said Asher, 'and your eyes deceived you. You made a mistake.'

'You know that isn't true.'

'Then let us come to an arrangement.'

'An arrangement?'

'A public reconciliation would be the most effective thing. I shall be confirmed in my position, and you'll be promoted.'

Suti rushed at Asher and grabbed him by the throat. 'Die, filth!'

Soldiers rushed in and surrounded the madman. They dragged him off the general, and rained blows upon him.

Asher was magnanimous enough not to lodge a complaint against Suti. He could understand his attacker's reaction, although he had the wrong culprit. In his place, he would have done the same. This behaviour cast Asher in a favourable light.

As soon as he returned from Thebes, Pazair did everything he could to free Suti, who was being held in the main barracks. Asher even agreed to waive the punishments for insubordination and insulting a superior officer if Suti resigned from the army.

'You'd better accept,' Pazair advised him.

'I'm sorry. I forgot my promise. Please forgive me.'

'With you, I'm always too soft-hearted.'

'You'll never be able to beat Asher.'

'I'm stubborn and determined, remember.'

'Yes, but he's cunning.'

'Forget the army.'

'I hate the discipline, anyway. I have other plans.'

Pazair dreaded to think what they might be. He said, 'Will you help me prepare for a celebration?'

'What are you celebrating?'

'My marriage.'

The conspirators met at an abandoned farm, making sure that none of them had been followed.

Since they had looted the Great Pyramid and stolen the symbols of Pharaoh's legitimacy, they had been content to observe. Recent events, however, had forced them to take decisions.

Only Ramses knew that his throne rested on shifting sands. As soon as his power faltered, he must celebrate his festival of regeneration, which would mean admitting to the court and the country that he no longer possessed the Testament of the Gods.

'The king's stronger than we thought.'

'Patience is our best weapon.'

'Yes, but time is passing.'

'What risks do we run? Pharaoh is bound hand and foot. He takes protective measures, and hardens his attitude towards his own government, but he can't confide in anyone. His character's strong but it's crumbling. The man's doomed – and he knows it.'

'We've lost the sky-iron and the adze.'

'That's just a tactical error.'

'I'm afraid. We should give up, put them back.'

'Don't be stupid.'

'We can't give up, not when we're so close.'

'Egypt's in our hands. Tomorrow, the kingdom and its riches will belong to us. Are you forgetting our great plan?'

'All conquests require sacrifices, this one more than any other. We mustn't let remorse stop us. A few corpses along the way are unimportant compared to what we're going to accomplish.

'Judge Pazair's a real danger, though. We're here now because of him.'

'He'll get bogged down.'

'Don't fool yourself. He's the keenest investigator in Egypt.'

'He doesn't know anything.'

'His conduct of his first major trial was masterly, and his instinct's often acute. He's already gathered damaging evidence; he might put us at risk.'

'When he arrived in Memphis he was alone, but now he has considerable support. If he takes one more step in the right direction, who is there to stop him? We should have prevented his rise to power.'

'It isn't too late.'

40

Suti was waiting for Neferet when the boat arrived from Thebes.

'You're so beautiful!' he exclaimed.

She laughed. 'Don't make me blush in front of a hero.'

'Now that I've seen you, I'd rather be a judge. Give me your travelling bag. I think Way-Finder will be happy to carry it.'

She asked anxiously, 'Where's Pazair?'

'He's cleaning the house and he hasn't finished yet, which is why I've come to meet you. I'm so happy for you both.'

'Are you fully recovered?'

'You're the best healer in the world. I've got all my strength back, and I'm planning to use it well.'

'And wisely, I hope?'

'Don't worry,' said Suti. 'And don't let's keep Pazair waiting. Since yesterday he's talked of nothing but headwinds, probable delays, and I don't know what other disasters that might stop you coming. Being that much in love stuns me.'

Way-Finder led the way.

The judge had given Iarrot a day's holiday, decorated the front of his house with flowers, and purified the interior. A delicate scent of oliban and jasmine filled the air.

Neferet's green monkey and Pazair's dog glared at each other, while he took her in his arms. The local inhabitants were always on the alert for unusual events, and soon realized what was going on.

'I can't help worrying about the patients I've left behind in the village,' said Neferet.

'They'll have to get used to another doctor. In three days' time, we're moving into Branir's house.'

'Do you still want to marry me?'

His answer was to lift her up and carry her across the threshold of the little house where he had spent so many nights dreaming of her.

Outside, there were shouts of joy. Since they were now living under the same roof, Pazair and Neferet had officially become man and wife.

After a night of celebration involving everyone in the district, they slept entwined until late morning. When he awoke, Pazair gazed at her lovingly. He had not thought that he could ever be so happy.

Eyes still closed, she took his hand and laid it upon her heart. 'Swear to me that we shall never be parted.'

'May the gods make us one and inscribe our love in eternity.'

Their bodies were so attuned that their desires were in perfect harmony. Beyond the pleasure of the senses, in which they revelled with adolescent fervour and hunger, they were already experiencing a spiritual union that would endure for all time.

'Well, Judge Pazair,' said Nebamon, 'when is the trial to begin? I understand that Neferet has returned to Memphis. She's therefore ready to appear before the court.'

'Neferet has become my wife.'

Nebamon frowned disapprovingly. 'That's very unwise. Her conviction will tarnish your name. If you value your career, you must divorce her quickly.'

'Are you still determined to make these accusations?'

Nebamon burst out laughing. 'Has love turned your brain?'

'Here is the list of medicines Neferet made in her workshop. The plants were supplied by Kani, gardener to the temple at Karnak. As you will see, everything she made is on the official list of permissible medicines.'

'You aren't a doctor, Pazair, and the testimony of this fellow Kani won't be enough to convince the jury.'

'Do you think Branir's testimony will?'

Nebamon's smile froze on his lips. 'Branir no longer practises. He—'

'He is the future High Priest of the temple at Karnak, and will testify in Neferet's favour. He is well known for thoroughness and honesty. He has examined the drugs that you call dangerous, and has found nothing amiss.'

Nebamon was furious. Branir's unrivalled prestige meant that his support would be of enormous benefit to Neferet. He said, 'I underestimated you, Pazair. You're a good tactician.'

'I simply use the truth to counter your wish to do harm.'

'Today you've won, it seems, but tomorrow you'll be brought down to earth.'

*

That night, while Neferet was asleep upstairs, Pazair worked late on a case in his office. He heard Way-Finder bray, which meant someone was coming.

He went to the door. There was no one about, but on the doorstep he found a scrap of papyrus. On it was scrawled: '*Branir is in danger. Come quickly.*'

Pazair dropped the papyrus and ran.

The surroundings of Branir's house seemed peaceful, but although it was late the door stood open. Pazair crossed the first room and saw his master sitting with his back against the wall and his head sunk on his chest. A blood-spattered spike of mother-of-pearl was embedded in his neck.

Pazair's heart stood still. Overwhelmed, he could hardly take in the truth: someone had murdered Branir.

Mentmose strode in, followed by several guards who surrounded Pazair.

'What are you doing here?' demanded Mentmose.

'I got a message saying Branir was in danger.'

'Show it to me.'

'I dropped it in the street, outside my house.'

'We'll check.'

'Why are you so suspicious?'

'Because I'm accusing you of murder.'

Mentmose woke the Judge of the Porch in the middle of the night. The Judge was astonished to see Pazair standing between two guards.

'Before making the facts public,' declared Mentmose, 'I want to consult you.'

'Why have you arrested Judge Pazair?'

'For murder.'

'Whom has he killed?'

'Branir.'

'That's absurd,' cut in Pazair. 'He was my master, and I venerated him.'

'Why are you so certain, Mentmose?' asked the Judge.

'We caught him almost in the act. He'd pushed a mother-of-pearl spike into Branir's neck – there wasn't much bleeding. When my men and I entered the house, he was standing over his victim.'

'That's a lie,' protested Pazair. 'I had just discovered the body.'

'Did you summon a doctor to examine the body?' asked the Judge.

'Yes. Nebamon,' said Mentmose.

Despite the terrible sadness in his heart, Pazair tried to think clearly. 'It's strange that you happened to be there at that time, with a squad of guards, Mentomose. How do you explain it?'

'A night patrol. From time to time, I go out with my men – it's the best way of knowing their difficulties and resolving them. We were lucky enough to catch a criminal red-handed.'

'Who sent you, Mentmose?' said Pazair. 'Who set this trap?'

His guards seized Pazair by the arms. The Judge took Mentmose aside and asked, 'Answer me, Mentmose: were you there by chance?'

'Not entirely. An anonymous message reached my office that afternoon. At nightfall, I stationed myself near Branir's house. I saw Pazair go in and followed almost immediately, but it was already too late.'

'Is his guilt certain?'

'I didn't see him stab his victim, but there's not much doubt about it.'

'Nevertheless, that small doubt is important. After the Asher scandal, such a drama . . . And accusing a judge, a judge serving under me!'

'Let justice do its duty,' said Mentmose. 'I've done mine.'

'One point is still unclear. What was his motive?'

'That's of minor importance.'

'By no means.' The Judge of the Porch seemed troubled.

'Detain Pazair secretly,' suggested Mentmose. 'Officially, he'll have left Memphis for a special mission in Asia, in connection with the Asher case. That's dangerous country – he might well meet with an accident, or be killed by bandits.'

'Mentmose, you wouldn't dare . . .'

'We've known each other a long time, Judge. Our only guide is our country's interest. You wouldn't want me to find out who sent the anonymous message. This little judge is causing a lot of trouble, and Memphis likes calm.'

Pazair interrupted them. 'You're wrong to attack a judge. I shall return and find out the truth. By the name of Pharaoh, I swear that I shall return!'

The Judge of the Porch closed his eyes and his ears.

Mad with worry, Neferet had alerted everyone in the district. Some had heard Way-Finder braying, but no one had any idea where Pazair had gone. Suti could find out nothing, and Branir's house was locked up. The only thing left to Neferet was to consult the Judge of the Porch.

'Pazair has disappeared,' she said.

The Judge looked astonished. 'The very idea! Don't worry. he's on a secret mission in connection with his investigation.'

'But where is he?'

'Even if I knew, I couldn't tell you. But he didn't give me any details, and I don't know where's he's gone.'

'He didn't say anything to me,' said Neferet.

'I'm glad to hear it. If he had, he would have deserved a reprimand.'

'But he left in the middle of the night, without a word.'

'No doubt he wanted to avoid a painful parting.'

'We were going to move to Branir's house the day after tomorrow. I wanted to speak to Branir, but he's on his way to Karnak.'

The Judge's voice grew solemn. 'My poor child, haven't you heard? Branir died last night. His former colleagues are going to organize a magnificent funeral.'

41

The little green monkey no longer played, the dog refused to eat, and the donkey's large eyes brimmed with tears. Devastated by the death of Branir and the disappearance of her husband, Neferet had lost the heart to do anything.

Suti and Kem came to her aid. They ran from barracks to barracks, from government office to government office, from official to official, to find out even the tiniest piece of information about Pazair's mission. But doors closed in their faces, and lips were sealed.

In her despair, Neferet realized just how much she loved Pazair. For a long time she had repressed her feelings, for fear of becoming involved too lightly, but his persistence had made them grow, day after day. She had become one with Pazair; parted, they would wither. Without him, life lost its meaning.

Accompanied by Suti, Neferet laid lotus flowers on the shrine at Branir's tomb. The master would never be forgotten. He was the guest of the sages, in communion with the reborn sun, which would give his soul the energy it needed to journey continually between the afterlife and the darkness of the tomb, where it would continue to shine forth.

Suti was too much on edge to pray. He left the shrine picked up a stone, and flung it into the distance.

Neferet laid a hand on his shoulder. 'He'll come back, I'm sure.'

'Ten times I've tried to corner that damned Judge of the Porch, but he's more slippery than an eel. 'Secret mission' – those are the only two words he knows. And now he's refusing to see me.'

'What are you going to?'

'Go to Asia and find Pazair.'

'But you don't know where he is.'

'I still have friends in the army.'

'And have they helped you?'

Suti lowered his eyes. 'Nobody knows anything. It's as if Pazair had vanished in a puff of smoke. Can you imagine how distressed he'll be when he learns of Branir's death?'

Neferet felt cold.

They walked away from the burial ground with heavy hearts.

Killer devoured a chicken leg greedily. Kem was worn out. He refreshed himself by washing in warm, scented water and putting on a clean kilt.

Neferet brought him a meal of meat and vegetables.

'I'm not hungry,' he said.

'How long is it since you had any sleep?'

'Three days – maybe more.'

'And you've learnt nothing?'

'Nothing at all. I've done everything I can, but my informers are all silent. I'm certain of only one thing: Pazair has left Memphis.'

'Then he must have gone to Asia.'

'Without telling you?'

From the roof of the High Temple of Ptah, Ramses gazed down upon the city, which was sometimes feverish and always joyful. Beyond its white walls lay the lush fields, fringed with deserts where the dead lived. After conducting ten hours of rituals, the king had chosen to be alone, to savour the invigorating evening air.

At the palace, at court, in the provinces, nothing had changed. The threat seemed to have moved further away, carried off by the river. But Ramses remembered the prophecies of the old sage Ipu-Ur, announcing that crime would spread, that the Great Pyramid would be desecrated, and that the secrets of power would fall into the hands of a few madmen, who were prepared to destroy a thousand-year-old civilization to serve their own interests and their madness.

As a child, reading the famous text under the guidance of his teacher, he had rebelled against this pessimistic vision; if he reigned, he would drive it away for ever! In his foolish vanity he had forgotten that no one, not even Pharaoh, could drive evil out of men's hearts.

Today, more alone than a traveller lost in the desert, despite the hundreds of courtiers who surrounded him, he must fight darkness so dense that it would soon hide the sun. Ramses was too clear-headed to be beguiled by illusions; this battle was lost in advance, since he did not know his enemy's face and so could not take action against him.

A prisoner in his own land, a victim doomed to the worst of all downfalls, his spirit haunted by an incurable evil, the greatest of Egypt's kings sank into the end of his reign as though into the murky waters of a marsh. His final dignity was to accept destiny without cowardly complaints.

When the conspirators met, they were smiling broadly. They congratulated themselves on their ruse, which had produced an excellent result. Fortune did indeed smile upon victors. If there had been a few criticisms about an individual's behaviour, or an incautious act, they were no longer relevant in this period of triumph, this prelude to the birth of a new state. The bloodshed was forgotten, the last traces of remorse wiped away.

Everyone had done his part, and no one had succumbed to Judge Pazair's assaults. By not yielding to panic, the group of conspirators had shown its unity, a precious treasure which must be preserved in the future, when power was distributed.

All that remained was to carry out one formality, so as to rid themselves of the ghost of Judge Pazair for ever.

In the middle of the night, Way-Finder's bray warned Neferet of a hostile presence. She lit a lamp, pushed open the shutter and looked down into the street. Two soldiers were knocking at her door.

They looked up at her. 'Are you Neferet?'

'Yes, but—'

'Please come with us.'

'Why?'

'Orders from our superiors.'

'And if I refuse?'

'We'll have to use force.'

Brave growled. Neferet could have called for help, woken her neighbours, but she calmed the dog, threw a shawl round her shoulders, and went downstairs. The presence of these two soldiers must be linked to Pazair's mission. What did her safety matter, if she was at last going to get some reliable information?

The trio crossed the sleeping town swiftly, and went to the central barracks. Once there, the soldiers handed Neferet over to an officer, who took her without a word to General Asher's office.

He was seated on a mat, surrounded by papyri, and his attention remained on his work.

'Sit down, Neferet,' he said.

'I would rather stand.'

'Would you like some warm milk?'

'Why have you summoned me at this peculiar hour?'

Asher's voice became aggressive. 'Do you know why Pazair went away?'

'He didn't have time to tell me.'

'He's so stubborn! He couldn't accept his defeat, and he wants to bring back this famous corpse – which doesn't exist! Why does he continue to pursue me with his hatred?'

'Pazair is a judge. He wants to find out the truth.'

'The truth was brought out during the trial, but he didn't like it. All that mattered was for me to be dismissed and dishonoured.'

'I'm not interested in your grievances, General,' said Neferet. 'Have you anything else to say?'

'Indeed I have.' Asher unrolled a papyrus. 'This report is marked with the seal of the Judge of the Porch; it has been checked. I received it less than an hour ago.'

'What does it say?'

'Pazair is dead.'

Neferet closed her eyes. She wanted to wither away like a lotus flower, to die in a single breath.

'There was an accident on a mountain path,' explained the general. 'Pazair didn't know the area but, with his usual imprudence, he set out on a mad venture.'

The words seared her throat, but Neferet had to ask, 'When will you bring his body home?'

'We're still searching for it, but I haven't much hope. In that region, the rivers are wild and the gorges inaccessible. I condole with your pain, Neferet. Pazair was a man of virtue.'

'Justice doesn't exist,' said Kem, laying down his weapons.

'Have you seen Suti?' asked Neferet anxiously.

'He'll wear out his feet with walking, but he won't give up until he finds Pazair – he's still convinced that he isn't dead.'

'And if . . . ?'

The Nubian shook his head.

'I shall continue the investigation,' she declared.

'It's no use.'

'Evil must not win.'

'It always wins.'

'No, Kem. If that were so, Egypt wouldn't exist. It was justice that founded this country, and it was justice that Pazair wished to see reigning. We have no right to surrender to lies.'

'I shall be at your side, Neferet.'

Neferet sat beside the canal, at the place where she had met Pazair for the first time. Winter was approaching, and the wind tugged at the turquoise hanging at her throat. Why had the precious talisman not protected him? Hesitantly, she rubbed the precious stone between her thumb and index finger, thinking of Hathor, the mother of turquoises and queen of love.

The first stars appeared, their light springing forth from the otherworld; she suddenly felt certain that her beloved was with her, as if the frontiers of death had been broken down. One wild thought became a hope: the soul of Branir, Pazair's murdered master, must be watching over his disciple.

Yes, Pazair would return. Yes, the Egyptian judge would drive away the darkness, and light would be reborn.

Secrets of the Desert

Great is the Rule, and lasting its effect; it has not been disrupted since the time of Osiris.

Iniquity is capable of gaining possession of the many, but evil shall never bring its undertakings to fruition.

Have no part in any plot against the human race, for God punishes such actions . . .

If you have listened to the maxims I have just told you, all your plans will proceed well.

The teachings of the sage Ptah-hotep: extracts
from maxims 5 and 38

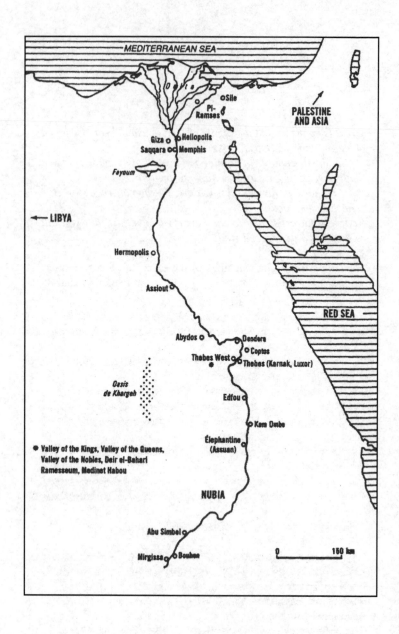

MEDITERRANEAN SEA

D e l t a

○ Sile

○ Pi-
Ramses

PALESTINE
AND ASIA

Giza ○ ●Heliopolis
Saqqara ○○ Memphis

Fayoum

← LIBYA

Hermopolis ○

Assiout ○

RED SEA

Abydos ○   ○ Dendera
                 ○ Coptos
Thebes West ○—
●   ○ Thebes (Karnak, Luxor)

Oasis
de Khargeh

Edfou ○

○ Kom Ombo

Éléphantine ○
(Assuan)

NUBIA

● Valley of the Kings, Valley of the Queens,
Valley of the Nobles, Deir el-Bahari
Ramesseum, Medinet Habou

Abu Simbel ○

Mirgissa ○ ○ Bouhen

0   150 km

1

The heat was so overpowering that the only creature to venture out into the sand-covered prison yard was a black scorpion. Deep in the desert between the Nile Valley and the Khargeh oasis, a week's march west of the holy city of Karnak, the prison housed persistent offenders who had been sentenced to back-breaking hard labour. When the temperature allowed, they maintained the track linking the valley to the oasis, along which caravans of donkeys travelled, laden with supplies.

For the tenth time, Judge Pazair presented his request to the camp's governor, a giant of a man who was quick to lash out at anyone who breached his iron discipline.

'I cannot go on getting preferential treatment like this,' said Pazair. 'I want to work like all the others.'

Pazair was a lean man, quite tall, with chestnut hair, a broad, high forehead and green eyes flecked with brown. Although his prison ordeal had banished all traces of his youthful energy, he still had a nobility which commanded respect.

'You aren't like the others,' said the governor.

'I'm a prisoner, too.'

'You haven't been sentenced, you're just being held secretly. For me, you don't even exist. No name in the register, no identification number.'

'That doesn't mean I can't break rocks.'

'Go back and sit down.'

The governor was wary of Pazair. The judge had astonished Egypt by organizing the trial of the famous General Asher. Asher had been accused by Pazair's best friend, Lieutenant Suti, of the torture and murder of an Egyptian scout, and of collaborating with the sand-travellers and with the Libyans, who were Egypt's hereditary enemies.

The unfortunate scout's body had not been found at the place Suti had indicated. So the jurors, who were unable to convict the general, had confined themselves to demanding an additional investigation. An investigation which was swiftly aborted, since Pazair had fallen into an ambush, and had been accused of murdering his spiritual father, the sage Branir, the designated High Priest of Karnak. Caught red-handed, he had been arrested and deported, with no regard for the law.

Pazair sat down on the burning sand. He thought constantly of his wife, Neferet. For a long time, he had believed that she would never love him; then happiness had come along, as blazing as a summer sun. A happiness which had been brutally shattered, a paradise from which he had been driven, without any hope of ever returning.

A hot wind began to blow. It turned the grains of sand into whirlwinds that whipped the skin. Pazair sat with a white cloth over his head and paid it no heed; he was reliving the stages of his investigation.

He had come from the provinces as a junior judge, quite lost in the great city of Memphis, and had made the mistake of being too conscientious, by studying a strange case in detail. He had uncovered the murders of five former soldiers who had been the honour-guard of the Great Sphinx at Giza, murders which had been made to look like an accident. He had also discovered the theft of a large quantity of sky-iron, which was strictly reserved for use in the temples, and a conspiracy involving important and influential people. But he had been unable to find conclusive proof of General Asher's guilt, or his intention to overthrow Egypt's great king, Ramses II.

Just when Pazair had obtained the full powers he needed to link these diverse elements together, disaster struck.

Pazair recalled every second of that terrible night: the anonymous message telling him Branir was in danger, his mad dash through the streets of the town, his discovery of Branir's body, a mother-of-pearl needle driven into the old man's neck. The arrival of the commander of the city guards, Mentmose, who had instantly treated the judge as a murderer, the sordid complicity of the Judge of the Porch, the most senior magistrate in Memphis. Pazair had been seized and held in absolute secrecy, and all he had to look forward to now was a lonely death. He had not even been able to make the truth known.

The plot had been very cleverly staged. With Branir's support, Pazair could have investigated within the temples and identified the people who had stolen the sky-iron. But his master had been killed, like the soldiers of the honour-guard, by mysterious attackers whose aims were still unknown. Pazair had learnt that a woman and men of foreign origin were among their number; consequently his suspicions had fallen upon Sheshi the inventor, Qadash the tooth-doctor, and the wife of Denes the ship-owner, a rich, influential and dishonest man; but he had not established anything for certain.

Pazair withstood the heat, the sandstorms and the bad food, because he wanted to survive, to hold Neferet in his arms and see justice blossom again.

What story had his superior, the Judge of the Porch, made up to explain Pazair's disappearance? What lies were people spreading about him?

Escape was an impossible dream, even though the camp opened on to the neighbouring hills. On foot, he would not get far. He had been imprisoned here so that he would die. When he was worn out, eaten away, when he had lost all hope, he would lose his mind, babbling incoherently like a poor madman.

Neither Neferet nor Suti would abandon him. They would not listen to lies or slander; they would search for him all over Egypt. He must hold fast, let time flow through his veins.

The five conspirators met once again at the abandoned farm. The atmosphere was joyful, for their plan was unfolding exactly as they had envisaged.

First, they had violated the Great Pyramid of Khufu and stolen the all-important insignia of power – the gold cubit and the Testament of the Gods, without which Ramses the Great was deprived of his rightful claim to the throne. Now they were getting closer to their goal with each day that passed.

From the Great Sphinx ran an underground passageway, enabling the conspirators to enter the pyramid. The murder of the honour-guard and the elimination of Judge Pazair were minor incidents which they had all but forgotten.

'The most important thing is still to be done,' declared one of the conspirators. 'Ramses is holding firm.'

'We mustn't be impatient.'

'Speak for yourself.'

'I speak for everyone; we need more time to consolidate the foundations of our future empire. The more tightly Ramses is bound hand and foot, powerless to act, knowing that he is heading for his own downfall, the easier our victory will be. He cannot tell anyone that the Great Pyramid has been desecrated and that the centre of spiritual energy, for which he alone is responsible, no longer functions.

'Soon his powers will be exhausted, and he will be forced to go through the regeneration ritual.'

'What will force him to do so?'

'Tradition, priests and himself. It is impossible for him to avoid that duty.'

'At the end of the festival, he must show the people the Testament of the Gods.'

'And the testament is in our hands.'

'Then Ramses will abdicate, and offer the throne to his successor.'

'The very successor we have designated.'

The conspirators were already relishing their victory. They would leave Ramses no choice, and he would be reduced to the status of a slave. Each member of the conspiracy would be rewarded according to his or her merits, and soon they would all occupy privileged positions. The greatest country in the world would belong to them; they would alter its structures, the way its government operated, and reshape it according to their own vision, which was radically opposed to that of Ramses, a prisoner of outdated values.

While the fruit was ripening, they would develop their network of contacts, sympathizers and allies. Crimes, corruption, violence . . . None of the conspirators regretted them. Such things were the price of power.

2

The setting sun was turning the hills a rosy hue. At this time of day Pazair's dog, Brave, and his donkey, Way-Finder, would be enjoying the food Neferet had prepared for them, after a long day's work. How many sick people had she healed? Was she still living in the little house in Memphis, where he had had his office on the ground floor, or had she returned to her village in the Theban region, to continue her work as a doctor far from the bustle of the city?

The judge's courage was weakening. He had dedicated his whole life to justice, but he knew now that it would never be meted out to him. No court would recognize his innocence. Besides, even if he did get out of prison, what future could he offer Neferet?

An old man, thin, toothless and with deeply lined skin, came over and sat down beside him. 'It's over for me,' he said with a sigh of relief. 'I'm too old. The governor's letting me off carrying stones. I'm going to do the cooking. Good news, isn't it?'

Pazair nodded.

'Why aren't you working?' asked the old man.

'They won't let me.'

'Who did you steal from?'

'Nobody.'

'Everyone's a hardened thief here – they've all committed lots of crimes. They'll never get out of this prison, because they broke their oath not to steal again. The courts take a dim view of people who don't keep their word.'

'Do you think they're wrong?'

The old man spat in the sand. 'That's a strange question! Are you on the side of the judges?'

'I am one.'

The old fellow could not have been more astounded if he had been told he was about to be set free. 'You're joking.'

'Do you really think I'd want to do that?'

'Good heavens . . . A judge, a real judge!' He stared at Pazair with a mixture of fear and respect. 'What did you do?'

'I was carrying out a major investigation, and people wanted to shut my mouth.'

'You must be mixed up in something very peculiar. As for me, I'm innocent. A disloyal colleague accused me of stealing some honey which actually belonged to me.'

'You're a bee-keeper?'

'I had hives in the desert – my bees gave me the best honey in Egypt. My competitors were jealous; they laid a trap and I fell into it. At the trial, I got angry. I rejected the verdict against me, asked for a second judgement and prepared my defence with a scribe. I was sure I'd win.'

'But you were convicted?'

'My competitors hid some things they'd stolen from a workshop in my house, and said it was proof that I'd stolen again. The judge didn't look any further.'

'He was wrong. In his place, I'd have examined the accusers' motives.'

'And what if you really were in his place? What if you showed that the so-called proof was false?'

'I'd have to get out of here first.'

The bee-keeper spat in the sand again. 'When a judge betrays his office, they don't keep him secretly in a camp like this one. They haven't even cut your nose off. You must be a spy, or something like that.'

'Whatever you say.'

The old man got up and walked away.

Pazair did not touch his daily ration of soup. He had lost the will to fight. What did he have to offer Neferet, other than disappointment and shame? It was better that she should never see him again, that she should forget him. She would retain the memory of a magistrate with an unshakeable faith, a man who was madly in love, a dreamer who had believed in justice.

He stretched out on his back and gazed up at the lapis-lazuli sky. Tomorrow, he would die.

White sails travelled up and down the Nile. At nightfall, the sailors liked to jump from one boat to another, as the north wind increased the boats' speed. Men were falling into the water, laughing, calling to each other.

A young woman was sitting on the riverbank, deaf to the rivals' shouts. Neferet had fair hair, a face of great purity and tenderness, summer-blue eyes, and was as beautiful as a lotus in bloom. She was calling upon the soul of Branir, her murdered master, and imploring him to protect Pazair, whom she loved with all her being. Pazair, whose death she could not accept, even though it had been officially proclaimed.

'May I speak with you for a moment?'

She turned her head. Close by stood Nebamon, the most senior doctor at Pharaoh's court. He was still a fine figure of a man at sixty. He was also her bitterest enemy – he had tried several times to destroy her career. Neferet loathed him. He was greedy for wealth and women, and used medicine to gain power over other people and as a means of making his fortune.

Nebamon's hot gaze roamed over Neferet, whose perfect, enticing curves could be glimpsed through her linen dress. Firm, high breasts, long, slender legs and delicate hands and feet were a delight for the eyes. Neferet was radiantly beautiful.

She said coldly, 'Be good enough to leave me alone.'

'You should be more friendly. I know something that will be of great interest to you.'

'Your intrigues are of no interest to me.'

'It's about Pazair.'

She could not hide her emotion. 'Pazair is dead.'

'That's not true, my dear.'

'You're lying!'

'I assure you I'm telling the truth.'

'What do you want from me? Must I beg for the truth?'

'Beg? No. I prefer you unbending and proud. What I have to tell you is this: Pazair is alive, but has been accused of murdering Branir.'

'That's . . . that's absurd! I don't believe you.'

'You should,' said Nebamon. 'Mentmose, commander of the city guards, has arrested him and is holding him secretly.'

'Pazair would never have killed Bramir.'

'Mentmose is convinced that he did.'

'People want to destroy him, ruin his reputation and stop him carrying on with his investigation.'

'That doesn't matter to me.'

'Why are you telling me this?'

'Because I am the only person who can prove Pazair's innocence.'

A shiver ran through Neferet's flesh, mingling hope and anguish.

'If you want me to take the proof to the Judge of the Porch, you must become my wife, Neferet, and forget your little judge. That is the price of his freedom. By my side, you will be in your rightful place. Now you are mistress of the game. Either you free Pazair or you condemn him to death.'

The thought of giving herself to Nebamon appalled Neferet, but if she refused his proposition she would become Pazair's torturer. Where was he being held, and what torments was he suffering? If she delayed too long, imprisonment would destroy him. Neferet had not confided in Suti, Pazair's loyal friend and spiritual brother: he would have killed Nebamon on the spot.

She decided to give in to his demand, on condition that she saw Pazair once more. Sullied and in despair, she would confess all to him before poisoning herself.

She looked up and saw Kem, a Nubian guard who had worked for Pazair, coming towards her. In Pazair's absence, he had continued to patrol Memphis with Killer, his formidable baboon, who specialized in arresting thieves by sinking his teeth into their legs.

Kem had had his nose cut off for being implicated in the murder of an officer who was guilty of trafficking in gold; but once his innocence and good faith had been recognized, he had become a guard officer. A false nose made of painted wood lessened the effect of the mutilation. Kem admired Pazair. Although he had no confidence in justice, he believed in the young judge's probity, which had been the cause of his death.

'I have a chance to find out where Pazair is,' Neferet told him gravely.

'In the kingdom of the dead, from which no one returns. Didn't General Asher send you his report, saying that Pazair had died in Asia, searching for proof?'

'That report was false. Pazair is alive.'

'Do you mean they lied to you?'

'Pazair has been accused of murdering Branir, but Nebamon has proof of his innocence.'

Kem took Neferet by the shoulders. 'Then he is saved!'

'On condition that I become Nebamon's wife.'

In rage, the Nubian drove his fist into the palm of his other hand. 'Suppose he's just playing games with you?'

'I want to see Pazair again.'

Kem tapped his wooden nose. 'You won't regret confiding in me.'

After the cooks and kitchen workers had left, Pazair slipped into the kitchen, a wooden frame covered with cloth. He would steal one of the pieces of flint used to light the fire, and cut his wrists. Death would be slow, but sure; in the full sunlight, he would slip gently into a pleasant stupor. In the evening, a passing guard would kick him and his corpse would roll over on the burning sand. During these last hours, he would live with the soul of Neferet, in the hope that its invisible presence would help him on his final journey.

Just as he was grasping the sharp stone, something hit him hard on the back of the neck and he fell to the ground, next to a cooking-pot.

The old bee-keeper was standing over him with a wooden club in his hand and a sarcastic smile on his face.

'So the judge becomes a thief!' he said loudly. 'What were you planning to do with that flint? Don't move, or I'll hit you! Shed your blood and leave this accursed place by the road of bad death! This is stupid of you, and unworthy of a good man.'

Then he lowered his voice to a whisper and said, 'Listen to me, Judge. I know a way out of here. I wouldn't have the strength to cross the desert, but you're young. I'll tell you, if you agree to fight my case for me and get my sentence overturned.'

Pazair came to his senses. 'It wouldn't be any use.'

'Are you refusing?'

'Even if I escape, I won't be a judge any more.'

'Become one again for me.'

'That's not possible. I'm accused of having committed a serious crime.'

'You? Never!'

Pazair rubbed his neck.

The old man helped him to his feet, and told him, still whispering, 'Tomorrow is the last day of the month. A cart drawn by oxen will come from the oasis, bringing food, and it'll go away again empty. Take your water-skin and get into the cart and hide while it drives off. When you see the first dry river-bed on your right, get out of the cart and climb up the river-bed until you reach the foot of the hill. You'll find a spring at the centre of a thicket of palm-trees there. Fill your water-skin, then walk towards the valley and try to meet up with the nomads. At least you'll have tried.'

For the second time, Nebamon had removed the rolls of fat from the lady Silkis, the young wife of Bel-Tran, a wealthy papyrus-maker and high official whose influence was steadily growing. For making women more beautiful in such ways, Nebamon charged enormous fees, which his patients paid without a murmur. Precious stones, fabrics, foodstuffs, furniture, tools, oxen, donkeys and goats had swollen his fortune, which now lacked only one priceless treasure: Neferet. Other women were equally beautiful, but she was the embodiment of a unique harmony in which intelligence was allied to charm, giving birth to an incomparable radiance.

How could she have fallen in love with a fool like Pazair? It was a piece of youthful madness, which she would have regretted all her life if Nebamon had not intervened.

Sometimes he felt as powerful as Pharaoh. After all, he knew secrets which saved or prolonged lives, he held sway over many doctors and remedy-makers, and it was he whom the highest men in the land begged for help to recover their health. His assistants might work in the shadows to produce the best treatments for him, but it was Nebamon, and no other, who would reap all the glory. And Neferet had a genius for medicine, which he was determined to exploit.

After the operation on Silkis, Nebamon was enjoying a week's rest at his house in the country, south of Memphis, where an army of servants satisfied his every wish. Abandoning lesser tasks to his medical team, which he controlled with a firm hand, he would prepare the list of forthcoming promotions on board his new pleasure-boat. He was eager to sample a white wine from the Delta, which came from his own vines, and his cook's latest dishes.

His steward came in, bowed, and informed him that he had a young and pretty visitor.

Intrigued, Nebamon went out to the gate of his estate. 'Neferet! What a delightful surprise. Will you have lunch with me?'

'I'm in a hurry.'

'You'll soon have a chance to visit my home, I'm sure. Have you by any chance brought me your reply?'

Neferet bowed her head.

Nebamon's heart leapt. 'I knew you'd see reason.'

'Give me time.'

'Since you've come here, you must have made your decision.'

'Will you grant me the privilege of seeing Pazair again?

Nebamon frowned. 'You are submitting yourself to a pointless ordeal. Save Pazair, but forget him.'

'I owe him one last meeting.'

'As you wish. But my conditions have not changed. First, you must prove your love to me. Then, and only then, I shall take action. Are we fully agreed?'

'I'm in no position to bargain.'

'I admire your intelligence, Neferet; it is equalled only by your beauty.'

He took her tenderly by the hand.

'No,' she said quickly, 'not here, not now.'

'Where and when, then?'

'In the big palm-grove by the well.'

'Is that place dear to you?'

'I often go there to think.'

Nebamon smiled. 'Nature and love make good bedfellows. Like you, I enjoy the poetry of the palm-trees. When?'

'Tomorrow evening, after sunset.'

'Very well. I accept that our first union will take place in darkness, but afterwards we shall be united in the full light of day.'

4

Pazair slid out of the cart as soon as he saw the dry river-bed winding up through the sand-dunes and rocks towards a steep, wind-ravaged hill. He dropped soundlessly out on to the sand, and the cart continued its journey through the dust and heat. The driver had fallen asleep, leaving the oxen to find their own way.

No one would bother to come after the fugitive, because he would have no chance of survival without water in the furnace-like heat of the desert. In due course, a passing patrol would bring back his bones. Barefoot and wearing only a threadbare kilt, he forced himself to walk slowly and to conserve his breath. Here and there, squiggles on the ground marked the passage of a sand viper, a fierce creature with a deadly bite.

Pazair imagined that he was walking with Neferet through verdant countryside, filled with birdsong and criss-crossed by canals; it made the landscape seem less hostile, his step lighter. He followed the dry river-bed to the foot of the hill, where he was greeted by the incongruous sight of three palm-trees.

He knelt down and began to scoop out a hole. A handspan beneath the cracked crust, the earth was damp: the old bee-keeper had told the truth. After an hour's digging, punctuated by a few brief pauses, he reached the water. He slaked his thirst, then took off his kilt, cleaned it with sand and used it to rub himself down. Then he filled the goatskin water-bag he had brought with him.

At nightfall, he set off eastwards. He could hear hissing all around him; the snakes emerged when the sun went down. If he stepped on one by accident, there would be no escape from a horrible death. Only a very learned doctor – like Neferet – knew how to cure their bite. The judge resolutely ignored the danger and went on, under the moon's protection. He revelled in the relative coolness of the night air. When dawn broke, he drank a little water, dug a hollow in the sand, covered himself with the loose sand and went to sleep, curled up in a ball.

When he awoke, the sun was beginning to sink. With his muscles aching and his head burning, he continued in the direction of the valley, so far away, so inaccessible. His reserves of water were exhausted, and he would have to rely on finding a well, surrounded by a circle of stones. In the immense space, sometimes flat, sometimes bumpy, he began to stagger. His lips were dry, his tongue swollen, and he was at the end of his strength. What was there left to hope for, save the intervention of a benevolent god?

Nebamon ordered his chair-bearers to set him down within earshot of the big palm-grove, and then sent them away. He was already savouring this marvellous night when Neferet would give herself to him. He would have preferred more spontaneity, but the methods used were of little importance. He had obtained what he desired, as usual.

The guards of the palm-grove were leaning against the tree-trunks, playing the flute, drinking cool water and talking. Nebamon set off along a wide path which forked to the left and led to the ancient well. The place was lonely and quiet.

She seemed to emerge from the sunset's glow, which turned her long linen dress orange.

Neferet was yielding to him. She, who was so proud, who had defied him, would obey him like a slave. When he had conquered her, she would become attached to him and would forget the past. She would acknowledge that only Nebamon could offer her the life she had dreamt of without realizing it. She loved medicine too much to hide any longer in a subsidiary role; becoming the wife of the highest doctor in the land was the most enviable destiny imaginable.

She did not move. He went forward.

'Will I see Pazair again?' she asked.

'You have my word.'

'You must have him set free.'

'That is my intention, if you agree to be mine.'

'Why are you so cruel? Be merciful, I beg of you.'

'Are you mocking me?'

'I'm appealing to your conscience.'

'You shall be my wife, Neferet, because that is what I have decided.'

'Give up that idea.'

He moved closer, stopping a single pace from his prey. 'I enjoy looking at you, but I want other pleasures, too.'

'Is destroying me part of those pleasures?'

'Freeing you from an illusory love and a second-rate existence.'

'One last time, please change your mind.'

'You belong to me, Neferet.' He reached out to seize her.

The moment he touched her, he was brutally dragged backwards and thrown to the ground. He looked up and saw a terrifying attacker: an enormous baboon with a wide-open mouth and foam-flecked lips. Its powerful left hand encircled the doctor's throat while its right grabbed his testicles and pulled. Nebamon let out a howl.

Kem set his foot on Nebamon's forehead. The baboon froze, but did not slacken its grip.

'If you refuse to help us, my baboon will castrate you. I won't have seen anything, and he won't feel the slightest remorse.'

'What do you want?' quavered Nebamon.

'The proof that Pazair is innocent.'

'No, I—'

The baboon gave a low growl, and its grip tightened.

'All right, all right!'

'Go on,' said Kem.

Nebamon panted, 'When I examined Branir's body, I saw that he'd died several hours or even a whole day earlier. The state of the eyes, the appearance of the skin, the mouth, the wound – the signs were unmistakeable. I wrote down my observations on a papyrus. Pazair wasn't caught in the act of committing murder; he was nothing but a witness. No serious charges could be brought against him.'

'Why did you suppress the truth?'

'It was too good an opportunity to miss – I could have Neferet at last.'

'Where is Pazair?'

'I . . . I don't know.'

'Oh yes you do.'

The baboon growled again. In fear for his life, Nebamon gave in.

'I bribed Mentmose not to kill Pazair – he had to be kept alive, if my plan was to succeed. The judge is being held secretly, but I don't know where.'

'Do you know who the real murderer is?'

'No, I swear I don't!'

Kem did not doubt the honesty of his answer. When the baboon carried out an interrogation, suspects did not lie.

Neferet closed her eyes and prayed, giving thanks to Branir's soul. The master had protected his pupil.

The Judge of the Porch dined frugally on figs and cheese. He had not slept well and had lost his appetite, and he had sent his servant away because he could no longer bear anyone near him. Why should he blame himself? All he had wanted was to save Egypt from turmoil. And yet his conscience did not rest easy. Never in all his long career had he departed from the Rule in this way.

Sickened, he pushed away the wooden bowl.

He could hear what sounded like someone moaning outside; according to magicians, ghosts came to torture unworthy souls. The judge swallowed hard and went out to see what it was.

To his astonishment he saw Kem dragging Nebamon along by the ear. The baboon was at his side.

Kem bowed and said, 'Nebamon wants to make a confession, Judge.'

The judge disliked Kem. He knew the big Nubian's violent past, disapproved of his methods and deplored the fact that he had been recruited into the guards. He said coldly, 'Nebamon is not acting of his own free will. His statement will be worthless.'

'I'm talking about a confession, not a statement.'

Nebamon tried to pull free. The baboon bit him in the leg, but did not sink its teeth right in.

'Be careful,' advised Kem. 'If you annoy him, he won't hold back.'

'Leave my house!' ordered the infuriated judge.

Kem pushed the doctor towards him. 'Hurry up, Nebamon. Baboons aren't patient creatures.'

'I have evidence relating to the Pazair case,' said Nebamon.

'Not evidence,' Kem corrected him. 'Proof of his innocence.'

The Judge of the Porch went pale. 'Are you trying to make fun of me?'

'The doctor is a serious and respectable man.'

Nebamon reached into his tunic and took out a rolled and sealed papyrus. 'This contains my written conclusions about Branir's body. The arrest of Pazair was a . . . miscalculation. I . . . forgot to send you this report.'

The judge took the document with no great enthusiasm. It felt like putting his hand into hot coals.

'We were wrong,' he lamented, 'and now for Pazair it is too late.'

'Perhaps not,' objected Kem.

'What do you mean? He's dead.'

The Nubian smiled. 'Another miscalculation, no doubt. Your good faith has been abused.'

Kem gestured to Killer to let go of Nebamon.

'Am I free to go?'

'Yes, go – quickly.'

Nebamon fled, limping. His leg bore the imprint of Killer's teeth, and he thought he could still see the animal's eyes shining red in the darkness.

The Judge of the Porch coughed. 'If you agree to forget these deplorable events, I can offer you a quiet, easy posting.'

'Don't do anything of the sort, Judge, or I won't restrain Killer. Soon the truth must be told – the whole truth.'

5

Pazair had dragged himself into the shade of an enormous rock, which had become detached from a natural pyramid. He was at the end of his strength: without water, he could go no further.

A cloud of dust rose up in the midst of the landscape of pale sand and black-and-white mountains. Looking out from his shelter, he saw two men on horseback.

They must be either desert guards or sand-travellers – except for caravans, no one ventured into these desert wastes. If they were desert guards, they would take him back to prison. If they were sand-travellers, they would do whatever they felt like at that moment: either torture him or enslave him. At the worst, Pazair would exchange prison for slavery. But perhaps . . . As the men rode nearer, he staggered out from behind the rock and collapsed on the sand.

They were sand-travellers: they wore brightly striped robes and had long hair and short beards. When they saw him, they stopped and stared in amazement.

'Who are you?' asked one of them.

'I escaped from the thieves' prison.'

The younger man dismounted and stared narrowly at Pazair. 'You don't look very strong.'

'I'm thirsty. Will you give me some water?'

'Water has to be earned. Get up and fight.'

'I can't, I'm not strong enough.'

The sand-traveller unsheathed a dagger. 'If you can't fight, you'll die.'

'I'm a judge, not a soldier.'

'A judge! Then you can't have come from the thieves' prison.'

'I was wrongfully accused. Someone wants to destroy me.'

The sand-traveller laughed. 'The sun's driven you mad.'

'If you kill me, you will be cursed in the afterlife. The judges of hell will cut your soul into pieces.'

'Nonsense!'

The older man stayed the younger man's hand. 'The Egyptians' magic is formidable. Let's get him back on his feet, and then we can make use of him as a slave.'

Panther was furious. The beautiful, bright-eyed Libyan girl was a sworn enemy of Egypt; she had fallen into the hands of the young chariot officer, who had become a hero following his first campaign in Asia. On a whim, he had given her back her freedom – not that it benefited her much, because she thoroughly enjoyed making love with him.

Panther lived for love. Deprived of Suti's, she was wasting away. Suti was tall and well-built, with a long face, a direct and honest gaze, and long black hair; ordinarily, his every move was invested with strength, elegance and seductive power. But her usually passionate and inventive lover had turned into a gloomy, wretched creature.

Suti had seen General Asher murdering one of his own scouts, but the court had been unable to convict the killer because the body had disappeared before witnesses could be brought to see it. Even when he was expelled from the army – for trying to strangle Asher – Suti had not lost his buoyant energy. But since the death of his friend Pazair he had withdrawn into silence, had stopped eating, and hardly even looked at her.

'When are you going to come back to life?' demanded Panther.

'When Pazair returns.'

'Pazair, always Pazair! Don't you understand? His enemies killed him.'

'We aren't in Libya. Killing is such a serious act that it condemns the perpetrator to utter destruction. A murderer doesn't come back to life.'

Panther shrugged impatiently. 'Forget all that nonsense. There's only one life, and it's here and now.'

'Forget a friend?'

'I'm a free woman and I won't live with a stone. If you stay like this, I shall leave.'

'Very well, go.'

She knelt down and put her arms round his waist. 'You don't know what you're saying.'

'If Pazair suffers, I suffer. If he's in danger, I feel his fear. You won't change that.'

Panther unfastened Suti's kilt; he didn't protest. She had never seen such a handsome, powerful, well-coordinated body. Since the age of thirteen, Panther had had many lovers; but none of them had satisfied her desires like this Egyptian, the sworn enemy of her people. She stroked his chest gently, then his shoulders, his nipples, his navel. Her light, sensual fingers contained the very essence of pleasure.

At last he reacted. Suddenly, almost sneeringly, he tore away the straps of her short dress. Naked now, she stretched out beside him, pressing her body against his.

'Just feeling you,' she said, 'being one with you, that's enough for me.'

'It isn't for me.'

He threw her on to her belly and took her. Triumphantly sensual, she accepted his desire as though it were the elixir of life, smooth and fiery.

From outside, someone called to Suti in a serious, commanding voice. Suti rushed to the window.

'Come with me,' said Kem. 'I know where Pazair is.'

The Judge of the Porch was laboriously watering the little flower-bed at the entrance to his house. As he got older, he found it more and more difficult to bend down.

'Can you help me?' asked a voice behind him.

The Judge turned round and recognized Suti: the former chariot officer had lost none of his impressiveness.

'Where is my friend Pazair?' demanded Suti.

'He is dead.'

'That's a lie.'

'An official report has been produced.'

'I don't give a curse for that.'

'You may not like the truth, but nothing can alter it.'

'The truth is that Nebamon has bought your conscience, and Mentmose's, too.'

The Judge of the Porch drew himself up. 'No, not mine.'

'Then tell me.'

The judge hesitated. He could have Suti arrested for insulting a judge and for verbal violence. But he was ashamed of his own behaviour. True, Judge Pazair frightened him: he was too determined, too passionate, set too much store by justice. But surely he, the old judge, broken by all the intrigues, had betrayed his youthful faith? The fate of his young colleague haunted him. Perhaps Pazair was already dead, having been unable to withstand the ordeal of prison.

'He's in the thieves' prison, near Khargeh oasis,' he whispered.

'Give me a warrant.'

'You ask a great deal.'

'Do it quickly – I haven't much time.'

*

Suti left his horse at the last staging-post, near the track that led to the oasis; only a donkey would be able to bear the heat, dust and wind. Armed with his bow, fifty arrows, a sword and two daggers, Suti felt sufficiently well armed to face the enemy, whoever that might be. The Judge of the Porch had given him a wooden tablet stating that he was under orders to bring Judge Pazair back to Memphis.

Kem had, very reluctantly, stayed with Neferet. Once Nebamon had recovered from his fright he would retaliate, and only Killer and his master could defend her properly. The big Nubian, although he badly wanted to take part in rescuing Pazair, had to admit that it was his duty to protect her against attack.

When her lover had said he was leaving, Panther flew into a rage. If he stayed away for more than a week, she hissed, she would deceive him with the first man she met and tell everyone how unfortunate she was. Suti had promised nothing, except that he would return with his friend.

The donkey carried water-skins and baskets filled with dried meat and fish, fruit and loaves which would keep for several days. The man and the animal would allow themselves little rest, for Suti was in a great hurry to reach his goal.

Within sight of the camp, a collection of miserable hovels scattered over the desert, Suti called upon the god Min, patron of caravan-leaders and explorers. Although he considered the gods beyond men's reach, in certain circumstances it was better to ensure their cooperation.

Suti woke the camp governor, who was asleep in the shade of a cloth awning and grumbled about being disturbed.

Suti ignored his protests and said, 'You are holding Judge Pazair here.'

'Don't know the name.'

'He isn't registered, I know.'

'I told you, I don't know him.'

Suti showed him the tablet. It brought no reaction at all.

'No Pazair here,' said the governor. 'Persistent thieves, no judge.'

'My mission is an official one.'

'Wait for the prisoners to come back, and see for yourself.' The governor went back to sleep.

Suti wondered if the Judge of the Porch had sent him up a blind alley, while having Pazair killed in Asia. Had he, Suti, been naive again?

He went over to the kitchen, to refill his water-bags.

The cook, a toothless old man, awoke with a start and asked, 'Who are you?'

'I've come to rescue a friend. Unfortunately, you don't look like Pazair.'

'What name did you say?'

'Judge Pazair.'

'What do you want with him?'

'To free him.'

'Really? Well, you're too late.'

'What do you mean?' demanded Suti.

The old bee-keeper explained in a low voice. 'With my help, he's escaped.'

'Him, in the middle of the desert? He won't last two days. What route did he take?'

'The first dried-up riverbed, the hill, the thicket of palm-trees, the spring, the rocky plateau, and then due east towards the valley. If he has a strong will to live, he'll succeed.'

'Pazair isn't very strong.'

'Then hurry up and find him – he's promised to prove me innocent.'

'But you're a thief, aren't you?'

'Not much of one, and a lot less than others. I just want to tend my bee-hives. Get your judge to send me back home.'

6

Commander Mentmose received the Judge of the Porch in his armoury, where he exhibited shields, swords and hunting trophies. The commander had a pointed nose, a nasal voice, and a bald, red scalp which often itched. Rather overweight, he followed a diet in order to keep a reasonable figure. Mentmose was cautious and cunning. He attended all the big receptions and had a large network of friends; he reigned unchallenged over all the different city guards companies in the kingdom. No one had ever been able to criticize him for making a mistake; he paid close attention to keeping up his reputation as an impeccable official.

He asked, 'Is this a private visit, my dear Judge?'

'A discreet one, as you always prefer.'

'That's how to ensure a long and peaceful career, isn't it?'

'When I had Pazair secretly detained, I set a condition,' said the judge.

'My memory must be going . . .'

'You were to discover the motive for Branir's murder.'

'Don't forget I caught Pazair red-handed.'

'Why should he have killed his master? The old man had been summoned to become High Priest of Karnak, and was therefore his most valuable supporter.'

Mentmose shrugged. 'Jealousy – or madness.'

'Don't treat me like a fool.'

'What does the motive matter to you? We've got rid of Pazair – that's the important thing.'

'Are you absolutely certain he's guilty?'

'As I told you, he was bending over Branir's body when I caught him. In my place, what conclusion would you have come to?'

'Yes, but the motive?'

'You admitted it yourself: a trial would have been very damaging – the country must respect its judges and have confidence in them. Pazair has a taste for scandal. Branir no doubt tried to calm him, and he lost his temper and stabbed the old man. Any jury would have condemned him to death. You and I were generous to him: we've kept his reputation intact. Officially, he died while on a mission. Isn't that the most satisfactory solution for him as well as for us?'

'Suti knows the truth.'

'How . . . ?'

'Kem made Nebamon talk. Suti knows Pazair is alive, and I told him where his friend is being held.'

To the judge's astonishment, Mentmose, who was generally regarded as a cool-headed man, reacted with fury.

'That's madness, utter madness! You, the most senior judge in the city, giving in to a disgraced ex-soldier! Kem and Suti can do nothing against us.'

'You're forgetting Nebamon's written statement.'

'A confession obtained under torture is invalid.'

'It was made well before that, and it's dated and signed.'

'Destroy it!'

'Kem made Nebamon write out a copy and have it witnessed by two servants on his estate. Pazair's innocence has been proven. During the hours leading up to the crime, he was working in his office. Witnesses will testify to that – I've checked.'

'Very well, but . . . Why on earth did you say where we're hiding him? There was no hurry.'

'To be at peace with my conscience.'

'With your experience, and at your age, you—'

'Exactly: at my age. The judge of the dead may call me at any moment. In the case of Pazair, I betrayed the spirit of the law.'

'You chose to further Egypt's interests, rather than concern yourself with the privileges of one person.'

'Your words don't deceive me, Mentmose.'

'Surely you aren't abandoning me?'

'If Pazair comes back . . .'

'People often die in the thieves' prison.'

For a long time, Suti had heard the sound of galloping horses. They were coming from the east, two of them, and they were approaching rapidly. Sand-travellers on a raid, on the lookout for easy prey.

Suti waited until they were within range, then drew his bow. He went down on one knee, took aim at the man on the left, and fired. Hit in the shoulder, the man toppled backwards. His comrade galloped towards the attacker. Suti adjusted his aim. The arrow sank into the top of the man's thigh. Roaring with pain, the sand-traveller lost control of his mount, fell off and knocked himself out on a rock. The two horses ran in aimless circles.

Suti laid the point of his sword against the throat of the first man, who was now back on his feet and staggering about.

'Where are you from?' he asked sternly.

'The tribe of sand-travellers.'

'Where are they camping?'

'Behind the black rocks.'

'Did you capture an Egyptian a few days ago?'

'Yes, a man who was lost in the desert – he claimed to be a judge.'

'What did you do with him?'

'Our leader's questioning him.'

Suti leapt on to the back of the sturdier horse, and held the other by the rudimentary reins the sand-travellers used. He left the two wounded men to fend for themselves.

He set off along a track bordered by stones. It got steeper and steeper, and the horses were blowing hard and bathed in sweat by the time they reached the summit of a hill, covered with a random scattering of stone blocks.

It was a sinister place. Between the burnt, blackish rocks were hollows where the sand swirled; they reminded him of the cauldrons of hell in which the damned were consumed, upside down.

At the foot of the hill was the nomads' camp. It was not very big, so there would be only comparatively few people there. The tallest and most brightly coloured tent, in the middle, must belong to the chief. Horses and goats were penned in an enclosure. Two sentries, one at the south and the other at the north, were keeping watch.

Suti waited for night to fall. It was against the rules of warfare to attack at night, but he reckoned that, since sand-travellers constantly criss-crossed the desert in search of victims to loot and pillage, they didn't deserve any respect. As soon as it was dark enough, he crawled forward silently, little by little, rising to his feet only when he was very close to the southern sentry, whom he felled with a blow to the back of the neck. Suti slunk through the darkness to the chief's tent, and slipped into it through an oval hole which served as a door. Tense and focused, he felt ready to unleash all his violence.

A totally unexpected sight met his eyes.

The chief was lying on a pile of cushions, listening to Pazair, who was sitting on the floor, apparently under no restraint.

The sand-traveller sat up and Suti pounced on him.

'Don't kill him,' cried Pazair. 'We were just beginning to understand each other.'

Suti flattened his adversary against the cushions.

'I asked the chief about his way of life,' explained Pazair, 'and tried to show him that he was doing wrong. My refusal to become a slave, even when threatened with death, astonished him. He wanted to know how our legal system works, and—'

'When you no longer amuse him, he'll tie you to a horse's tail and drag you across sharp stones until you're cut to pieces.'

'How did you find me?'

'How could I ever lose you?' Suti began binding and gagging the sand-traveller. 'Let's get out of here quickly. Two horses are waiting for us at the top of the hill.'

'What's the point? I can't go back to Egypt.'

'Follow me, instead of talking rubbish.'

'I haven't the strength.'

'You'll find it when you realize that you've been proved innocent and that Neferet is waiting impatiently for you.'

7

The Judge of the Porch did not dare look at Judge Pazair. 'You are free,' he declared in a broken voice.

The Judge of the Porch was expecting bitter reproaches, perhaps even a formal accusation. But Pazair simply stared at him.

'The charges have been dropped, of course. As to the rest, I beg you to be patient for a little while. I am working to resolve your situation as quickly as possible.'

'What about Mentmose?'

'He sends his apologies. He and I were both deceived . . .'

'And Nebamon?'

'He is not really guilty. It was a matter of simple administrative negligence. You were the victim of an unfortunate conjunction of circumstances, my dear Pazair. If you wish to lodge a complaint . . . ?'

'I shall think about it.'

'Sometimes it is important to know how to forgive.'

'Give me back my official status without any more delay.'

Neferet's blue eyes were like two precious stones, born at the heart of the golden mountains, in the land of the gods; at her throat hung a turquoise, protecting her from evil. A long white linen dress with straps accentuated her slender waist.

As he drew near her, Judge Pazair breathed in her perfume. Lotus and jasmine wafted from her satin skin. He took her in his arms, and they remained locked in an embrace for a long time, unable to speak.

'So you do love me a little bit?' he asked.

She pushed him away to look at him. He was proud, passionate, a bit mad at times, thorough, young and old at the same time, lacking superficial physical beauty, fragile but energetic. Those who thought him weak and easily defeated were very much mistaken. Despite his stern face, his high, austere forehead and his demanding nature, he had a taste for happiness.

'I don't ever want to be separated from you again,' she said.

He held her tightly for a moment, then released her. Life had a new energy, as powerful as the young Nile. And yet it was a life so close to death, in this immense burial ground at Saqqara where Pazair and Neferet were walking slowly along, hand in hand. They wanted to visit the tomb of their murdered master, Branir, straight away, to meditate there. For he had passed on the secrets of medicine to Neferet and encouraged Pazair to turn his vocation into reality.

Because of his occupation, the embalmer Djui lived apart from ordinary men. When they entered his workshop they found him sitting on the floor, his back against a whitewashed wall. He had a long face, thick black eyebrows joined above his nose, thin, bloodless lips, extraordinarily long hands and skinny legs. He was eating pork with lentils, even though this meat was forbidden during hot periods: he was uncircumcised and had no time for religious rules and regulations.

On the embalming table lay the mummy of an old man whose flank he had just cut into with an obsidian knife.

'I know you,' Djui said, looking up at Pazair. 'You're the judge who's investigating the deaths of the honour-guard.'

'Did you mummify Branir?' asked the judge.

'That's my job.'

'Did you notice anything unusual?'

'No, nothing.'

'Has anybody come to visit his tomb?'

'Not since the burial ceremony. Only the priest in charge of the funeral service has entered the shrine.'

Pazair was disappointed. He had hoped that the murderer, in the grip of remorse, might have come to beg his victim's forgiveness, in order to escape the punishments of the afterlife. But it seemed even that threat did not frighten the killer.

'Have you found out what you wanted to know?' asked Djui.

'I will.'

Shrugging indifferently, the embalmer sank his teeth into a slice of pork.

The stepped pyramid of King Djoser dominated the eternal landscape. Many tombs faced it, in order to share the immortality of the king, whose immense shade travelled up and down the gigantic stone staircase each day.

Usually, sculptors, hieroglyphic engravers and painters were to be found working on countless sites. Here, they were excavating a rock-tomb; there, another was being restored. Long lines of workmen hauled wooden sledges laden with blocks of limestone or granite, while water-carriers were on hand to slake the workers' thirst.

Today the site was deserted, for it was the day when people paid their respects to Imhotep, the master craftsman of the Step Pyramid. Pazair and Neferet walked between lines of tombs dating from the days of the first pharaohs, which were carefully maintained by one of Ramses' sons. Whenever someone's gaze alit on the names of the dead written in hieroglyphs, it brought them to life, shattering the obstacle of time. The power of the word was greater even than the power of death.

Branir's tomb was close to the Step Pyramid. It was built of fine white limestone brought from the quarries at Tura. The head of the funerary well, which gave access to the underground chambers where the mummy lay, had been blocked by an enormous stone slab, while the shrine remained open to the living, who could come to feast in company with the statue and pictures of the dead man, which had been endowed with his immortal energy.

The sculptor had created a magnificent image of Branir, immortalizing him as an old but sturdily built man with a serene expression. The main text, written in horizontal lines, hoped that the reborn Branir would be welcomed into the beautiful West; at the end of a tremendous journey he would arrive among his own people, his brothers the gods, would feed upon stars and be purified with water from the primordial ocean. Guided by his heart, he would walk along the perfect paths of eternity.

Pazair read out the words addressed to visitors to the tomb: '*You who live upon the earth and pass by this tomb, you who love life and hate death, speak my name that I may live, pronounce the offertory words for my sake.*'

'I shall find the murderer, master,' he promised.

Neferet had dreamt of a quiet happiness, far from quarrels and the demands of men's ambition. But her love had been born in the whirlwind, and neither she nor Pazair would ever know peace until the truth had been discovered.

When the darkness had been vanquished, the earth grew light. Trees and grass became green once more, birds flew from their nests, fish leapt out of the water, and boats sailed up and down the river. Pazair and Neferet emerged from the shrine, whose carved panels welcomed the first light of dawn. They had spent the night with the soul of Branir, whom they had sensed close by, vibrant and warm.

They would never be separated from him.

Now that the festival was over, the craftsmen were returning to the site. Priests were celebrating the morning rites, so as to perpetuate the memory of the dead. Pazair and Neferet walked along King Unas's long covered roadway, which led to a temple below, at the edge of the fields. A little laughing girl brought them dates, fresh bread and milk.

'We could just stay here and forget about crimes, the law and men,' said Pazair wistfully.

'You aren't becoming a dreamer, are you?'

'Someone wanted to get rid of me in the vilest way and he won't give up. Is it wise to embark on a war which is lost before it begins?'

'For Branir, the man we revere, we have a duty to fight without thinking of ourselves.'

'I'm only a junior judge. The powers that be will transfer me to a distant corner of some far-off province. They'll break me easily.'

'Surely you aren't afraid?'

'I've not much courage left. Prison was a terrible ordeal.'

She laid her head on his shoulder. 'We're together now. You have lost none of your strength – I know it, I can sense it.'

A gentle warmth washed over Pazair. The pain faded, his exhaustion ebbed away. Neferet was a sorceress.

'Each day for a month,' she said, 'you must drink water from a copper vessel. It is an effective remedy against weariness and despair.'

'Whoever laid that trap for me must have been someone who knew Branir would soon become High Priest of Karnak and would therefore be our most powerful supporter.'

'Who did you tell?'

'Only Nebamon – to impress him.'

'Nebamon? The man who held the proof of your innocence and was trying to force me to marry him!'

'I know. I made a terrible mistake. When he learnt of Branir's appointment, he must have decided on a double blow: kill Branir and have me accused of the crime.' A furrow appeared across Pazair's brow. 'But he isn't the only suspect. When Mentmose arrested me, it was obvious he had an understanding with the Judge of the Porch.'

'So the city's guards and magistrates were partners in crime.'

'A conspiracy, Neferet, a conspiracy bringing together men of power and influence. Branir and I were becoming inconvenient, because I had collected irrefutable evidence and he would have enabled me to carry my investigation to its conclusion. Why was the Great Sphinx's honour-guard wiped out? That's the question to which I must find the answer.'

'Don't forget the inventor Sheshi, the theft of the sky-iron, and that murderer General Asher.'

'I haven't. But I can't find a way of linking the suspects and their crimes.'

'Let us concern ourselves above all with Branir's memory.'

Suti insisted on celebrating his friend Pazair's return properly, by inviting the judge and his wife to a respectable Memphis tavern, where they enjoyed mature red wine, fine grilled lamb, vegetables in sauce, and unforgettable cakes. The life and soul of the party, he tried to make them forget Branir's murder for a few hours.

When he stumbled unsteadily back into his house, his head spinning, he bumped into Panther.

She grabbed him by the hair. 'Where have you been?'

'The prison.'

'Half drunk?

'No, completely drunk, but Pazair's safe and sound.'

'And what about me? Don't I get any attention?'

He seized her round the waist, lifted her off the ground and held her above his head. 'I've come back – isn't that a miracle?'

'I don't need you.'

'You're lying. Our bodies haven't finished exploring each other yet.'

He carried her into the bedchamber, laid her down gently on the bed, took off her short dress with the delicacy of an old lover, and entered her with the wild enthusiasm of a youth. She cried out in pleasure, unable to resist this longed-for attack.

When they were resting side by side, panting and sated, she laid her hand on Suti's chest. 'I said I'd be unfaithful to you while you were away.'

'And were you?'

'You'll never know. The doubt will make you suffer.'

'Don't deceive yourself. For me, the only things that matter are pleasure and the moment.'

'You're a monster!'

'Are you complaining?'

'Are you going to go on helping Judge Pazair?'

'We're blood-brothers.'

'Is he going to take his revenge?'

'He's a judge first and a man second. The truth matters more to him than his own feelings.'

'For once, listen to me. Don't encourage him and, if he persists, keep away.'

'Why do you say that?'

'He's attacking an enemy who's too strong for him.'

'What do you know about it?'

'I had a premonition.'

'What are you hiding from me?'

'Nothing – no woman could deceive you.'

Mentmose's office was like a buzzing bee-hive. He was rushing about, issuing orders which sometimes contradicted each other, urging his scribes to hurry up and transport the papyrus scrolls, wooden tablets and every small record accumulated since he took up his post. His eyes darting all over the place, he kept scratching his head and cursing his staff's slowness.

As he stepped out into the street to check that a cart had been loaded correctly, he bumped into Judge Pazair.

'My dear Judge,' he almost stammered.

'You're looking at me as if I were a ghost.'

'What an idea! I hope your health . . .'

'Prison life damaged it, but my wife will soon get me fit again.' Pazair looked at the bustle around him. 'Are you moving?'

'The Irrigation secretariat has predicted a very high annual flood. I must take precautions.'

'This district isn't vulnerable to flooding, surely?'

'It pays to be cautious.'

'Where are you moving to?'

'Er . . . my own house. It's only temporary, of course.'

'That is illegal. Has the Judge of the Porch been informed?'

'The dear judge is very tired – disturbing him would have been very inconsiderate.'

'I think you should stop this transfer of files until he has been informed.'

Mentmose's voice became nasal and shrill. 'You may be innocent of the crime you were accused of, but your position is still uncertain and it doesn't grant you authority to give me orders.'

'That's true, but yours obliges you to help me.'

The commander's eyes narrowed. 'What do you want?'

'To examine closely the mother-of-pearl needle that killed Branir.'

Mentmose scratched his head. 'In the middle of moving—'

'It is a piece of evidence, not an item from your archives. It must be held in a file, with the message that deceived me: "Branir is in danger, come quickly."'

'My men didn't find it.'

'And what about the needle?'

'Just a moment.'

Mentmose disappeared inside the office. Gradually, the hustle and bustle calmed down. Bearers carrying papyri laid their burdens in the carts and got their breath back.

Mentmose reappeared ten minutes later, looking sombre. 'The needle has disappeared.'

8

As soon as Pazair drank the healing water from a copper cup, Brave demanded his share. He had long legs and a curly tail, big floppy ears which pricked up at mealtimes, and a fine pink and white leather collar inscribed with the words *'Brave, companion of Pazair'*. The dog lapped up a cupful of the water, and so in turn did the judge's donkey, Way-Finder. Mischief, Neferet's green monkey, sprang on to the donkey's back, pulled the dog's tail and then hid behind her mistress.

'How can I possibly work in these conditions?'

'Don't complain, Judge. You have the privilege of being constantly cared for at home by a conscientious doctor.'

He planted a kiss on her neck, in the place where it made her shiver.

Neferet summoned up enough resolve to push him away. 'The letter,' she said firmly.

Pazair sat down on the ground, and unrolled a fine papyrus scroll. Given the importance of the message, he would write on only one side. To the left was the portion he had unrolled; to the right was the part on which he was going to write. In order to give additional formality to the text, he would write in vertical lines, separated by a straight line drawn in his best ink, with a reed pen whose point had been sharpened to perfection.

His hand was perfectly steady.

To Tjaty Bagey, from Judge Pazair.

May the gods protect the tjaty: may Ra illuminate him with his rays, Amon preserve his integrity, Ptah grant him coherence. I hope that your health is excellent, and that you continue to prosper. I am appealing to you in my capacity as a magistrate, in order to keep you informed regarding facts of exceptional gravity. Not only was I wrongly accused of murdering the sage Branir and deported to a thieves' prison, but the murderer's weapon has disappeared while in the possession of Mentmose, commander of the city guards.

*I am a district judge, and believe I have brought to light the
suspicious behaviour of General Asher and shown that the five
former soldiers who formed the Great Sphinx's honour-guard
were murdered.*

*The attack on me was an attack upon the entire legal system.
Someone attempted to get rid of me, with the active cooperation
of the commander of the guards and of the Judge of the Porch,
in order to suppress my inquiry and protect conspirators who
are pursuing an unknown goal.*

*My personal fate is of little importance, but I wish to identify
the guilty party or parties who killed my master. May I also be
permitted to state my anxieties as regards the country: if so many
atrocious deaths remain unpunished, surely crime and falsehood
will soon be the people's new guides? Only the tjaty has the
ability to tear up this evil by the roots. That is why I am begging
him to act, in the sight of the gods, and swearing upon the Rule
that what I say is true.*

Pazair dated the document, placed his seal upon it, rolled it up and
fastened it with a clay seal. He wrote his name and that of the recipient.
In less than an hour, he would hand it to a messenger who would
deliver it to the tjaty's office that same day.

When he had finished, he got to his feet and said worriedly, 'This
letter might mean exile for us.'

'Have faith. Tjaty Bagey's reputation has never been called into
question.'

'If we're wrong, we'll be parted for ever.'

'No, we won't, because I shall go with you.'

There was no one in Suti and Panther's little garden. The door of the
small white house was open, so Pazair went inside. Neither of them
was there, though it was late. It was almost sunset, so perhaps the
lovers had gone to take the air in the palm-grove by the old well?

Pazair crossed the main room to sit down and wait. As he did, he
heard a few sounds. They came not from the bedroom but from the
open-air kitchen, which was behind the house. It was clear that Panther
and Suti were working.

The Libyan was making butter, mixed with fenugreek and caraway,
which she would keep in the coolest part of the cellar. No water or
salt would be added, to prevent it turning brown.

Suti was making beer. Using barley flour, he had made a dough which
he kneaded and partly cooked in dishes arranged around the hearth. The
loaves would then be soaked in water sweetened with dates; after

fermentation, the liquid must be brewed and filtered, then transferred into a jar covered with clay, which was vital in order to keep it fresh.

Three jars had been placed in holes in a raised plank, and stoppers had been made from dried river-silt.

'Are you starting your own workshop?' asked Pazair.

Suti spun round. 'I didn't hear you! Yes, Panther and I have decided to make our fortune. She's going to make butter, and I shall brew beer.'

In irritation, Panther pushed away the greasy mass, wiped her hands on a brown cloth and disappeared without saying a word to the judge.

'Don't hold it against her – she's in a bad mood. Let's forget the butter. Fortunately there's the beer! Taste this for me.'

Suti lifted the largest jar out of its hole, removed the stopper, and put in place the pipe linked to a filter that would allow only liquid to pass through and would hold the pieces of dough in suspension.

Pazair took a mouthful, and almost choked. 'It's sour!'

'What do you mean, sour? I followed the recipe to the letter.' Suti took a sip, and spat it out at once. 'That's vile! I'm giving up making beer – it's no job for me. What have you been up to?'

'I've written to the tjaty.'

'A bit risky, isn't it?'

'It's essential.'

'You won't survive the next prison.'

'Justice will prevail.'

'Your gullibility is touching.'

'Tjaty Bagey will take action.'

'What makes you think he isn't corrupt and compromised like Mentmose and the Judge of the Porch?'

'Because he is Tjaty Bagey.'

'That old lump of wood is impervious to all feeling.'

'Perhaps, but he'll put Egypt's interests first.'

'May the gods hear you!'

'Tonight, I relived the horrible moment when I saw the needle sticking out of Branir's neck. It was a precious, expensive thing, which could be wielded only by an expert hand.'

'Have you got a new lead?'

'No, just an idea – and perhaps a futile one, at that. Would you mind paying a visit to the main weavers' workshop in Memphis?'

'Are you sending me on a mission?'

Pazair smiled. 'They say the women there are very beautiful.'

'Why don't you go yourself?'

'The workshop doesn't come under my jurisdiction. If I make the smallest mistake, Mentmose will pounce.'

*

Weaving was a royal monopoly, employing a large number of men and women. They worked at looms with low rails, comprising two rollers on which the threads were wound, and high rails, made up of a rectangular frame arranged vertically. The threads were wound round the upper roller, and the woven cloth round the lower one. Some pieces of fabric were more than forty cubits long.

Suti watched a man finishing off a length of braid for a noble's tunic, his knees drawn up to his chest, but paid closer attention to the young girls who were rolling linen fibres into balls. Their colleagues, who were no less charming, were arranging the warp threads on the upper roller of a loom which had been laid down flat, before interlacing the two sets of taut threads. Nearby, a spinner was shaping fibres into a thin, strong thread, using a stick with a wooden disc on the end, which she handled with stunning dexterity.

Suti did not pass unnoticed. Few women were indifferent to his lean face, direct gaze, long black hair, and blend of elegance and strength.

'What do you want?' asked the spinner.

'I'd like to speak to the overseer of the workshop.'

'The lady Tapeni only receives visitors who have been recommended by the palace.'

'Aren't there any exceptions?' whispered Suti.

Somewhat smitten, the spinner put down her staff. 'I'll go and see.'

The workshop was large, airy and clean, as the inspectors demanded. Light entered through rectangular skylights set below the flat roof, and air circulated by means of carefully placed oblong windows. The place was warm in winter and cool in summer. After an apprenticeship lasting several years, qualified weavers could command high pay, and there was no discrimination between men and women.

As Suti was smiling at a weaving-woman, the spinner reappeared and beckoned to him.

'Please follow me.'

The lady Tapeni, whose name meant 'mouse', was sitting in an immense room containing looms, bobbins, needles, spinning-staffs and other equipment needed for the practice of her craft. She was small and lively, with black hair, green eyes, and brown skin, and directed the workforce with military precision. Her apparent gentleness concealed an often tiresome authoritarianism. But the fabrics and clothes that emerged from her workshop were so beautiful that no one could criticize her methods. At the age of thirty, Tapeni was still unmarried and thought only of her profession. She viewed a family and children as obstacles to the pursuit of a career.

As soon as she saw Suti, she was afraid: afraid of falling stupidly in love with a man who had only to look at a woman to seduce her. But her fear was instantly transformed into another feeling, as exciting as she could wish for: the irresistible attraction of a huntress for her quarry.

She said in her most beguiling voice, 'How may I help you?'

'It's a ... private matter.'

Tapeni dismissed her assistants. The scent of mystery increased her curiosity tenfold. 'We're alone now.'

Suti walked around the room and halted in front of a row of mother-of-pearl needles laid on a cloth-covered plank.

'These are superb. Who has permission to use them?'

'Are you interested in the secrets of our craft?'

'Passionately.'

'Are you an inspector from the palace?'

'No, don't worry. I'm simply looking for someone who used this type of needle.'

'A runaway mistress?'

Suti smiled. 'Not necessarily.'

'Men use them, too. I hope you aren't ... ?'

'I can soon lay your fears to rest.'

'What's your name?' asked Tapeni, blushing.

'Suti.'

'And your profession?'

'I travel a great deal.'

'A merchant with a touch of the spy ... You're very handsome.'

'And you're very attractive.'

'Really?' Tapeni drew the wooden bolt across the office door.

'Are these needles found in every weaving-workshop?'

'Only the largest ones.'

'So the number of people who use them is limited.'

'Indeed.'

She went closer, walked round him, touched his shoulders. 'You're very strong. You must know how to fight.'

'I'm a real hero. Will you give me some names?'

'Perhaps. Are you in a hurry?'

'Yes, to identify the owner of a needle like these.'

'Be quiet for a moment – we can talk about it later. I'll help you, provided you're loving, very loving ...' Her lips touched Suti's.

After a moment's hesitation, he was obliged to respond to the invitation. Politeness was, after all, one of the intangible values of civilization. Not refusing a gift was one of Suti's moral imperatives.

Tapeni smoothed a pomade made from crushed acacia-seeds and honey over her lover's penis. Now that his sperm had been sterilized, she could enjoy his magnificent body without fear, forgetting the sound of the looms and the workers' complaints.

'Investigating on behalf of Pazair,' mused Suti to himself, 'brings nothing but danger.'

9

When Pazair reached his office he found Kem waiting for him outside, and the two men embraced warmly. The big Nubian was accompanied, as always, by Killer, whose gaze was so fierce that it frightened passers-by. Kem was moved to tears, which he tried to hide by rubbing his wooden nose.

'Neferet told me everything,' said Pazair. 'I know it's you I have to thank for my freedom.'

Kem cleared his throat. 'Killer was very persuasive.'

Pazair led the way inside. When they were seated in his office, he asked, 'Is there any news of Nebamon?'

'He's "resting" at home.'

'He'll attack again, I'm sure of it.'

'So am I. You must be more careful.'

'I will, so long as it doesn't stop me carrying out my duties as a judge. I've written to the tjaty: either he'll take charge of the enquiry and confirm me in my office, or he'll think my request impertinent and unacceptable.'

Red-faced, breathless and weighed down with armfuls of papyri, Pazair's scribe, Iarrot, came in. 'These are all the matters I dealt with while you weren't here. Am I to start work again?'

'I don't know what the future holds, but I detest leaving cases to wait. For as long as I'm not forbidden to do so, I shall set my seal on them. How is your daughter?'

'She is coming down with measles, and she has had a fight with an odious little boy who scratched her face. I've lodged a complaint against the parents. Fortunately, she's dancing better and better. But my wife . . . What a vicious woman!' Iarrot went on grumbling as he put the papyri into the right cases.

'I shan't leave my office until I have an answer from the tjaty,' said Pazair.

'I'll go and prowl around outside Nebamon's house,' said the Nubian.

Neferet and Pazair had decided never to live in Branir's house. No one should live in that place, where misfortune had struck. They would be content with the little official residence, half of which was taken up with the judge's files. If they were driven out, they would return to the Theban region.

Neferet rose earlier than Pazair, who liked to work late. After washing and putting on her face-paint, she fed the dog, the donkey and the monkey. Brave, who had a slight infection in his paw, was treated with Nile mud, which had antiseptic qualities and worked fast.

She placed her medical equipment on Way-Finder's back; the donkey had an instinctive sense of direction, and guided her through the narrow streets of the district where sick people required her services. They paid her by piling various types of food into the panniers that the donkey carried with obvious satisfaction. Rich and poor did not live in separate districts; leafy terraces rose above little houses of dried brick, huge houses surrounded by gardens stood alongside narrow alleyways crowded with animals and people. People called to each other, haggled and laughed, but Neferet had no time to participate in the discussions and celebrations.

After three days of hard struggle, she was at last succeeding in driving a bad fever from the body of a little girl, which had been invaded by the demons of the night. The patient could now drink milk from a wet-nurse, which was kept in a vase shaped like a hippopotamus; her heart was beating properly, and her pulse was regular. Neferet put a necklace of flowers round the child's neck and light earrings on her ears; her patient's smile was the best reward of all.

When she returned home, exhausted, she found Suti and Pazair there, deep in discussion. She greeted them, then went to wash and to put on fresh perfume.

'I saw the lady Tapeni, who oversees the main weaving-workshop in Memphis.'

'Did you learn anything?'

'A bit, and she's agreed to help me.'

'Have you found a promising line of investigation?'

'Not yet. A lot of people use that type of needle.'

Pazair looked down at his feet. 'Tell me, Suti, is Tapeni pretty?'

'She's not unattractive.'

'And was this first contact purely . . . friendly?'

'Tapeni's independent and affectionate.'

Neferet came back into the room, and poured drinks for them.

'This beer is safe,' said Pazair, 'which may not be true of your liaison with Tapeni.'

'Are you thinking of Panther? She'll understand that it's purely in the interests of the inquiry.' Suti kissed Neferet on both cheeks. 'Don't forget, you two: I'm a hero.'

Denes, a wealthy and famous ship-owner, loved to rest in the living room of his sumptuous Memphis house. The walls were painted with lotus-flowers, while the coloured tiles on the floor depicted fish frolicking in a pond. On small tables stood baskets of pomegranates and grapes. When he returned from the docks, where he oversaw the departure and arrival of his boats, he liked to eat salted curds and drink water which had been kept cool in a terracotta ewer. Stretched out on cushions, he was massaged by a servant-girl and shaved by his personal barber, who carefully trimmed the narrow white beard fringing his square, heavy face.

Denes stopped issuing orders when his wife, Nenophar, appeared, a striking figure dressed in the latest fashions. She owned three-quarters of the couple's fortune, so, during their frequent arguments, Denes felt it wise to give in.

That particular afternoon, there was no argument. Denes wore a glum expression and did not even listen to Nenophar as she angrily cursed the tax authorities, the heat and the flies.

When a servant showed in the tooth-doctor Qadash, Denes rose to greet him warmly.

Qadash was moist-eyed, with a low brow and jutting cheekbones. His nose bore a tracery of little purple veins looking fit to burst, and he constantly rubbed his hands, which were red because of poor circulation. Pazair had suspected him and his friend Denes of wrongdoing, and had investigated their activities, although he had not been able to prove their guilt.

Qadash's white hair was ruffled, and he was obviously in a state of great agitation. 'Pazair has come back,' he said, his voice shaking. 'What can have gone wrong? There was an official report saying he was dead!'

'Calm down,' urged Denes. 'He may be back, but he won't dare do anything against us. His imprisonment has broken him.'

'What do you know about it?' protested Nenophar, who was putting on her face-paint. 'That little judge is a determined man. He'll take his revenge.'

'I'm not afraid of him,' said Denes.

'Because you're blind – as usual!'

'Not at all. Now that you've been made steward of fabrics and a Treasury scrutineer, your court connections mean we can always keep track of what Pazair's doing.'

'Legal matters are kept quite separate from trade and finances,' she objected. 'And supposing he takes his case to the tjaty?'

'Bagey's as uncompromising as he is awkward. He won't let himself be manipulated by an ambitious judge who only wants to cause a scandal and thereby become better known.'

They fell silent as the steward announced Sheshi the inventor and showed him in. Sheshi was a small man with a black moustache, and a manner so withdrawn that he spent entire days in complete silence. He moved about like a shadow.

'I apologize for being late,' he said.

'Judge Pazair's alive and here in Memphis!' stammered Qadash.

'I know.'

'What does General Asher think about it?'

'He's surprised as we are. We were delighted when the judge's death was announced.'

'Who freed him?'

'Asher doesn't know.'

'What's he going to do?'

'He doesn't confide in me.'

'What about your new weapons?' asked Denes.

'Their development is continuing.'

'Is a military expedition planned?

'That Libyan warlord Adafi caused trouble near Gubla – a couple of villages rose in rebellion – but the appearance of a detachment of troops was enough to put a stop to it.'

'So Pharaoh still trusts Asher?'

'So long as Asher's guilt isn't proven, Ramses can hardly dismiss a hero whom he decorated himself and appointed chief instructor to the Asian army.'

Nenophar stroked her amethyst necklace. 'War and trade often make good bedfellows. If Asher says there's to be a campaign against Syria or Libya, let me know straight away so that I can change my trading-routes. You won't find me ungrateful.'

Sheshi bowed.

'You're all forgetting Pazair!' protested Qadash.

'He's just one man trying to fight forces which will soon crush him,' sneered Denes. 'We shall continue as planned.'

'But suppose he finds out?'

'We'll leave Nebamon to deal with him. After all, our brilliant doctor is the main person involved.'

Nebamon took ten hot baths a day in a large pink granite pool, which his servants filled with scented water. Then he smoothed a soothing ointment over his testicles; little by little, it took away the pain.

Kem's damned baboon had come close to castrating him. Two days after the attack, a crop of spots had afflicted the delicate skin on his testicles. Fearing that they would ooze pus, Nebamon had shut himself away in his most beautiful house, cancelling the operations he had promised to carry out to restore the ageing beauties of the court.

The more he hated Pazair, the more he loved Neferet. She had mocked him, it was true, but he did not bear her a grudge. Had it not been for that insignificant, obstinate little judge, she would undoubtedly have yielded and become his wife. Nebamon had never failed before, and this intolerable insult caused him actual physical pain.

His most valuable ally was still Mentmose. The position of the guards commander, who had destroyed the message that lured Pazair to Branir's house, was becoming very delicate. A detailed inquiry would show, at the very least, that he was incompetent. Mentmose, who had plotted throughout his career to obtain his current post, would not be able to bear being dismissed. So all was not lost.

With Mentmose in attendance, General Asher was himself directing exercises involving the elite soldiers, who would leave for Asia as soon as they received the order. He was short, with a rat-like face, close-cropped hair, a wiry black pelt covering his shoulders and his short legs, and a scar across his chest. Asher took real pleasure in seeing men suffer as they crawled through the sand and dust, laden with sacks filled with stones, and had to defend themselves against knife-wielding attackers. Those who failed, he killed without pity. Nor were the officers spared: they, too, had to demonstrate their physical prowess.

Asher turned to Mentmose. 'What do you think of these future heroes?'

The commander was wrapped up a woollen cloak; he could not bear the dawn chill. 'I congratulate you on them, General.'

'Half of these fools are unfit for service,' spat Asher, 'and the others are hardly better! Our army is too rich and too lazy. We have lost the taste for victory.'

Mentmose sneezed.

'Have you caught a chill?'

'No, I'm just tired – and worried.'

'About Judge Pazair?'

'Your help in the matter would be invaluable, General.'

'In Egypt, no one can attack the legal system. In other countries, we'd have more freedom of action.'

'It was officially reported that he'd died in Asia.'

'A stupid administrative error, for which I am not responsible. The court case Pazair brought against me came to nothing, and as you see I've kept my command. The rest doesn't interest me.'

'You should be more careful.'

'Why? The little judge has been disqualified, hasn't he?'

'The charges against him have been dropped. Couldn't the two of us come up with . . . a solution?'

'You're commander of the city guards, I'm a soldier. We shouldn't mix the two occupations.'

'But in both our interests—'

'My interests lie in keeping as far away from Pazair as possible. I must leave you now, Mentmose. My officers are waiting for me.'

10

The hyena crossed the southern outskirts of the city, gave its sinister cry, climbed down the riverbank and drank from the Nile. Children howled in fear. Their mothers hurried them inside and slammed their front doors. No one dared attack the animal, because it was so big and fierce – not even experienced hunters dared go near it. Once its thirst was slaked, the hyena went back into the desert.

Everyone knew the ancient prophecy: 'When wild beasts drink from the river, injustice will reign and happiness will flee the land.'

The people whispered, and their words spread from place to place until they reached the ears of Pharaoh Ramses. The Invisible One was beginning to speak: by manifesting himself in the form of a hyena, he was disowning the king in the eyes of all Egypt. In every province, people worried about the evil omen, and wondered about the legitimacy of the king's reign. Soon, Pharaoh would have to take action.

Neferet was sweeping the bedroom with a short-handled broom. Kneeling, she held it firmly and nimbly flicked the long tufts of reed fibres back and forth.

'There's been no answer from the tjaty,' said Pazair, who was sitting on a low chair, sorting out papyri for that day's work.

Neferet laid her head on his knee. 'Why do you torment yourself like this? Worry is eating away at you, sapping your strength.'

'I worry about what Nebamon may try to do to harm you.'

'Whatever he does, you'll protect me, won't you?'

He stroked her hair. 'In you, I have found everything I could ever desire. How beautiful this time is! When I sleep beside you, an eternity of happiness washes over me. By loving me, you have lifted up my heart. You are within it, you fill it with your presence. Never go far away from me. When I look at you, my eyes no longer need any other light.'

Their lips met as tenderly as if it were their first kiss.

Pazair was very late for work.

*

Neferet had loaded her remedies and equipment on to Way-Finder, and was about to set off on her rounds of the city, when a breathless young woman came running up to her.

'Wait! Please wait!' cried Silkis, wife of Bel-Tran.

Neferet drew the donkey to a halt.

'My husband wants to see Judge Pazair on a matter of great urgency.'

'Bel-Tran, a maker and seller of papyrus, had come to prominence because of his abilities as a manager and had been raised to the rank of head overseer of granaries, then deputy director of the Treasury. Pazair had helped him during a difficult period, and in return he had offered gratitude and friendship. Silkis, who was much younger than he, had been to see Nebamon, who had succeeded in making her face and her plump thighs slimmer. Bel-Tran set great store by displaying a wife comparable to the most beautiful women in Egypt, even at Nebamon's prices. Silkis had clear skin, and now that her features were more delicate she looked like a curvaceous adolescent.

'If he'll come with me now, I'll take him to the Treasury, where Bel-Tran will receive him before leaving for the Delta. But, first, I'd very much like to consult you yourself.'

'What's the matter?'

'I keep getting terrible headaches.'

'What do you eat?'

'A lot of sweet things, I have to admit. I adore fig-juice and pomegranate-juice, and I dip my pastries in carob-juice.'

'What about vegetables?'

'I don't like them so much.'

'Eat more vegetables and fewer sweetmeats, and your headaches should improve. And you must rub this into your forehead.'

Neferet handed her a jar of ointment made from reed-stems, juniper, pine-sap, laurel-leaves and terebinth resin, all crushed and reduced to a compacted mass to which fat had been added.

Silkis thanked her and said, 'My husband will pay you handsomely.'

'As he wishes.'

'Would you agree to become my doctor?'

'If you're happy with my treatment, why not?'

'My husband and I will both be very happy. May I take the judge to him now?'

'As long as you don't lose him.'

Bel-Tran had jet-black hair, which he smoothed down with scented pomade, and a round head. He was heavily built, with plump hands and feet. He spoke quickly and never stopped moving. He seemed unable to enjoy even a short rest, torn between ten different projects and a thousand cares.

The faster he worked, the more he was entrusted with thorny, complex cases. His prodigious memory for figures and his ability to add up at incredible speed made him indispensable. Only a few weeks after taking up office among the senior officials at the Treasury, he had been promoted and become one of the closest colleagues of the director of the House of Gold and Silver, in charge of the kingdom's finances. Everyone spoke of him in glowing terms; he was accurate, quick, methodical and a hard worker; he never seemed to sleep, and was always the first to arrive at the Treasury offices and the last to leave. People were predicting a dazzling career for him.

When his wife showed Pazair in, Bel-Tran was flanked by three scribes, to whom he was dictating administrative orders. He greeted the judge warmly, finished what he was doing, sent away the scribes and asked his wife to prepare an especially good midday meal.

'We have a cook, of course, Judge, but Silkis won't use any but the best foodstuffs and ingredients – she's fussy about that.'

'You seem very busy,' said Pazair.

'I hadn't realized my new duties would be so enthralling. But never mind that. Let's talk about you. You've been through a terrible ordeal. I wasn't told about it until so late that there was nothing I could do to help.'

'I don't hold it against you. Suti was the only person who could have got me out of that dreadful situation.'

'Who do you think are the guilty parties?'

'The Judge of the Porch, Mentmose and Nebamon.'

'The judge ought to resign,' said Bel-Tran angrily. 'Mentmose's case is more difficult because he'll swear he was deceived. Nebamon's gone to earth on his estate, but he's not a man to give up. And don't forget General Asher – he really hates you because during the trial you almost destroyed his reputation. He's still as powerful and influential as ever . . . Mightn't he be the one hiding in the shadows, pulling the strings?'

'I've written to the tjaty, asking him to pursue the inquiry.'

Bel-Tran nodded approvingly. 'A good idea.'

'He hasn't replied yet.'

'I'm sure Bagey won't see justice scorned like this. If your enemies attack you, they'll come up against him, too.'

'Even if he removes me from the case, even if I am no longer a judge, I shall find out who murdered Branir. I consider myself responsible for his death.'

'Whatever do you mean?'

Pazair shook his head. 'I've already said too much.'

'Don't torture yourself like this, my friend.'

'Accusing me of murdering him was the cruellest blow anyone could have dealt me.'

'But they failed, Pazair, and will again. I wanted to see you to assure you of my support. Whatever trials you may face in the future, I'm with you. Now tell me, wouldn't you like to move house, to somewhere a bit more spacious?'

'I'm waiting for the tjaty's answer.'

Even in his sleep, Kem stayed on the alert. He still had the hunter's instinct he had acquired during his youth in far-off Nubia. Many of his comrades had been over-confident and had died there in the grasslands, torn to shreds by a lion's claws.

He awoke with a start and felt for his wooden nose; sometimes he dreamt that the inert material had turned into living flesh. But this was no time for illusions; men were climbing the stairs. Killer was awake, too.

Kem lived surrounded by bows, swords, daggers and shields; so he armed himself in a moment, just as two guards broke down the door of his lodgings. He knocked out the first and Killer dealt with the second, but twenty more attackers followed them.

'Run away, Killer!' Kem shouted.

The baboon gave him a look which mingled bitter disappointment with the promise of vengeance. Then he escaped from the crowd, slipped through the window, jumped on to the roof of the house next door and vanished.

Kem struggled with every last bit of his strength, and the guards had great difficulty overcoming him. But at last they succeeded in throwing him down on his back, binding him tightly, and putting a rope round his neck.

At that point Mentmose came into the room. The commander himself put manacles on Kem's bound wrists.

'At last,' he said with a smile, 'we have the murderer.'

Panther crushed fragments of sapphire, emerald, topaz and haematite, sifted the powder through a fine sieve made of reeds, then poured it into a cooking-pot under which she had lit a fire of sycamore wood. She added a little terebinth resin to produce a luxurious unguent, which she shaped into a cone; she would use it to grease wigs, head-dresses and hair, and to perfume her whole body.

She was bending over her mixture when Suti came in.

'You cost me dear, you she-devil, and I still haven't found the way to make my fortune. I can't even sell you as a slave.'

'You've slept with an Egyptian woman.'

'How do you know that?'

'I can smell it. Her scent has soiled you.'

'Pazair entrusted me with a delicate investigation.'

'Pazair, always Pazair! Did he order you to betray me?'

'I had a conversation with a remarkable woman, who runs the largest weaving-workshop in the city.'

'What's so . . . remarkable about her? Her backside, her sex, her breasts, her—'

'Don't be coarse.'

Panther threw herself on her lover with such force that she flattened him against the wall and he could barely breathe.

'In your country it's illegal to be unfaithful, isn't it?'

'We aren't married.'

'Of course we are, because we're living under the same roof.'

'You're a foreigner, so we'd need a contract. I hate formalities like that.'

'If you don't finish with her at once, I'll kill you.'

Suti reversed the situation: it was her turn to be flattened against the wall.

'Listen to me carefully, Panther. No one has ever told me how to behave. If I have to marry another woman to fulfil my duties as a friend, I'll do it. Either you understand that, or you leave.'

Her eyes widened, but she did not shed a tear. She would kill him; that much was certain.

In his best script, Judge Pazair was preparing to write another message to the tjaty, further emphasizing the gravity of the facts and requesting urgent action on the part of Egypt's most senior judge.

At that moment, Mentmose entered his office, looking thoroughly pleased with himself. 'Judge Pazair, I deserve your congratulations!'

'Why? What have you done?'

'I have arrested Branir's murderer.'

Pazair looked at Mentmose, but did not move a muscle. 'The matter is too serious for joking,' he said coldly.

'I'm not joking.'

'What is his name?'

'Kem.'

'That's ludicrous!'

'The man's nothing but a brute. And remember his past: this isn't the first time he's killed.'

'Your accusation is extremely serious. On what evidence do you base it?'

'We have an eye-witness.'

'He must appear before me.'

Mentmose looked sheepish. 'Unfortunately, that's impossible – and pointless.'

'Pointless? What do you mean?'

'The trial has already been held and sentence pronounced.'

Pazair rose to his feet, speechless.

'I have here the relevant document, signed by the Judge of the Porch.'

Pazair read it quickly: Kem had been condemned to death, and thrown into a cell in the great prison. 'The witness's name isn't given,' he protested.

'It doesn't matter. He saw Kem kill Branir, and has declared so under oath.'

'Who is he?'

'Forget about him. The murderer will be punished, that's the important thing.'

'You must be losing your mental balance, Mentmose, or you wouldn't dare show me such a miserable document.'

The commander gaped at him. 'I don't understand.'

'The accused was not present when the judgement was handed down. That is illegal, and annuls the verdict.'

'I bring you the head of the guilty party, and you talk to me about legal quibbles!'

'No, about justice,' Pazair corrected him.

'Be reasonable for once! Some scruples are futile.'

'Kem's guilt has not been proven.'

'That matters little. Who'll regret the loss of one mutilated Nubian with a criminal background?'

If Pazair had not been bound by his dignity as a judge, he could not have contained the anger burning inside him.

'I have more experience of life than you,' Mentmose continued. 'Certain sacrifices have to be made. Your office obliges you to think first and foremost of Egypt, its well-being and security.'

'How did Kem pose a threat to those things?'

'Neither you nor I have any interest in lifting certain veils. Osiris will welcome Branir into the paradise of just souls, and the criminal will have been punished. What more could you want?'

'The truth,' snapped Pazair.

'That's just an illusion.'

'Without it, Egypt would die.'

'If you aren't careful it's you who'll die, Judge.'

*

Kem had no fear of death, but he missed Killer very much. After so many years working together, he regarded the animal as a brother, and now he could no longer exchange meaningful looks with it or take account of its intuition. Nevertheless, he consoled himself with the knowledge that Killer was still free. Kem was locked up in a low-ceilinged room like a cellar, in stifling heat. No proper trial, an immediate sentence, and a summary execution: this time he wouldn't escape from his enemies. Pazair wouldn't have time to intervene, and would be able only to mourn the Nubian's death, which Mentmose would portray as an accident.

Kem felt no warmth towards the human race. He regarded it as corrupt, vile and sly, fit only to serve as fodder for the monster who sat beside the scales of the last judgement, waiting to devour the damned. One of his few joys had been to know Pazair, whose conduct had affirmed the existence of a justice Kem had long since ceased to believe in. With Neferet, his companion for all eternity, the young judge had embarked on a battle that was lost before it began, without caring about his own fate. Kem would have liked to help him right to the end, until the final disaster, when falsehood would bear him away, as it always did.

The cell door opened.

Kem sat up and stuck out his chest: he wasn't going to present the torturer a picture of a broken man. Heaving himself up, he emerged from his prison into the sunlight, pushing away the arm reaching out to him.

Dazzled by the light, he thought his eyes were deceiving him. 'It can't be . . .'

Pazair cut the rope binding Kem's wrists. 'I overturned the charges, because many of the procedures followed were illegal. You are free, my friend.'

The big Nubian picked the judge up and hugged him, almost suffocating him. 'Haven't you got have enough troubles of your own, Pazair? You should have left me there in that dungeon.'

'Imprisonment seems to have weakened your mind.'

Kem looked around. 'Where's Killer?'

'He's run away.'

'He'll come back.'

'He was acquitted, too. The Judge of the Porch acknowledged that my protests were well founded, and disowned what Mentmose had done.'

'I shall wring Mentmose's neck.'

'Then you really would be guilty of murder. Besides, we've got better things to do – especially identifying the mysterious eye-witness who was the cause of your arrest.'

The Nubian raised his clenched fists to heaven. 'Leave that one to me!'

Pazair didn't reply. Instead, he handed Kem his weapons.

Kem felt a savage joy enter him as he was reunited with his bow, arrows, club and ox-hide-covered wooden shield.

'Killer isn't called that for nothing,' he added with a laugh. 'No guards will ever arrest him.'

Pharaoh Ramses stood before Khufu's looted sarcophagus and gathered his composure. His throat was tight and his chest ached, for the most powerful man in the world had become the slave of a band of murderers and thieves. By seizing the sacred emblems of kingship, and depriving him of the great state magic willed by the gods, they had rendered his power illegitimate and condemned him to abdicate, sooner or later, in favour of a plotter who would destroy the work that had been carried out over so many dynasties.

What the criminals were attacking was not just Pharaoh but the very ideal of government and the traditional values he embodied. If Egyptians were among the culprits, they had not acted alone; Libyans, Hittites or Syrians had almost certainly prompted them to this most evil of plans, so as to topple Egypt from its pedestal and open the country up to foreign influences, so much so that it would be dependent on on them.

The Testament of the Gods had been passed on and preserved intact from one pharaoh to the next. Today, impure hands held it and demon-like minds were manipulating it. For a long time Ramses had hoped that heaven would protect him and that the people would remain ignorant of what had happened – at least until he could think of a solution.

But the great king's star was beginning to wane.

The next Nile flood would be a poor one. Of course, the reserves in the royal granaries would feed the worst-affected provinces and no one would starve. But farmers would be forced to leave their fields, and people would whisper that the king could no longer ward off misfortune, unless he celebrated a festival of regeneration, during which the gods and goddesses would endow him with new energy, an energy reserved for the man who possessed the Testament legitimizing his reign.

Ramses pleaded for help from the Light that had given him birth; he would not give in without a fight.

11

Keeping a firm grip on the wooden handle of his razor, the barber drew the copper blade across Judge Pazair's cheeks, chin and neck. Pazair was sitting on a stool outside his house, next to Way-Finder, who watched the scene placidly, while Brave slept between the donkey's hooves and Neferet watched from the doorway.

Like all barbers, this one was talkative. 'If you're making yourself so handsome, you must have been summoned to the palace.'

'I see I can't hide anything from you.'

Pazair did not explain that he had just received an extremely brief response from the tjaty, summoning him without delay on this beautiful summer's morning.

'Promotion, is it?'

'I think that's unlikely.'

'May the gods look favourably upon you. After all, a good judge is their ally.'

'Yes, indeed he should be.'

The barber dipped his blade in a cup containing water mixed with natron. He drew back from his client, contemplated his work and delicately shaved a few rebellious hairs from underneath his chin.

'Ramses' officials have handed down some strange decrees these past few days. Why is he so set on re-affirming that he's our only defence against bad luck and disasters? No one in the land doubts that – well, almost no one. But there are rumours that his power is failing. The hyena drinking from the river, the poor flood, rain in the Delta at this time of year: all those things are tangible signs of the gods' disfavour. Some people think Pharaoh should celebrate a festival of regeneration so as to regain his full magical powers. What a splendid thing that would be! A fortnight's rest, free food, as much beer as anyone could want, dancing-girls in the streets. While the king was locked away in the temple with the gods, we'd have a fine old time!'

The royal decrees had puzzled Pazair: what secret enemy was Ramses afraid of? He had the feeling that the king was on the defensive, albeit the visible or invisible foe he was fighting remained unidentified. And yet Egypt was calm, and the only sign of instability was the mysterious conspiracy Pazair had dismantled, at least in part. But how could the theft of the sky-iron endanger Pharaoh's throne?

Of course, there was still General Asher, who Suti had sworn was a traitor and a secret ally of the Asians, and they were always on the alert for a chance to invade Egypt, the source of all wealth. But Asher held one of the highest military posts in the country, so would he really want to raise troops and rebel against the king? The idea seemed most unlikely. What the general cared about was his own career and privileges, not the burden of ruling, which he was wholly incapable of taking on.

Since Branir's murder, Pazair felt as if the ground under his feet was no longer solid. He was groping for answers in a void, felt jolted around like a load on a donkey's back. Although he had established a solid case against Asher and his probable accomplices, he could not see clearly, so obsessed was he with the martyred face of the man whom he had revered and whose life had been so brutally cut short.

'That's perfect,' pronounced the barber. 'You might mention my name at the palace – I'd love to shave a few of those courtiers.'

It was Neferet's turn to look Pazair over. His hair was combed, his body washed, perfumed, his white kilt was spotless. She could find no fault at all.

'Are you ready?' she asked.

'I shall have to be. Do I look nervous?'

'Not on the outside.'

'The tjaty's letter wasn't encouraging.'

'Don't expect any goodwill, and you won't be disappointed.'

'If he dismisses me, I shall demand that the investigation continues.'

'We shan't let Branir's murderer go unpunished.'

He was reassured by her smile, which expressed her inflexible will. 'I'm afraid, Neferet.'

'So am I. But we shan't draw back.'

The nine Friends of Pharaoh were dressed in heavy black wigs and long, white, pleated robes, belted at the waist. They had met during the morning, summoned by Tjaty Bagey. After a somewhat heated debate, they had reached a unanimous decision. Following detailed exchanges of views, the bearer of the Rule, the overseer of the white Double House, the official in charge of canals and director of water-dwellings, the overseer of writings, the overseer of fields, the head of secret missions, the scribe of the land registry and the king's steward had all adopted the tjaty's surprising proposal, which they had at first thought unrealistic or even dangerous. But the urgency of the situation and its dramatic nature justified a quick and unusual decision.

When Pazair was announced, the nine Friends filed into the great audience chamber, with its bare white walls, and took their seats on stone benches on either side of Bagey, who was sitting on a low-backed chair.

At his throat the tjaty wore an imposing copper heart, the only ritual jewel he allowed himself. Beneath his feet, a panther-skin symbolized the savagery that had been tamed.

Judge Pazair bowed before the august assembly, and kissed the ground. The icy expressions of the nine Friends did not bode well.

'Stand up,' ordered Bagey.

Pazair got to his feet, facing the tjaty. Bearing the weight of nine relentless pairs of eyes was a formidable ordeal.

'Judge Pazair, do you agree that only the practice of justice maintains the prosperity of our land?'

'That is my most profound belief.'

'If we do not act in accordance with justice, if it is considered to be a falsehood, rebels will lift up their heads, famine will strike and demons will roar. Is that also your conviction?'

'Your words express the truth as I live it.'

'I received your two letters, Judge Pazair, and handed them to this council so that each of its members might judge your conduct. Do you consider that you have been faithful to your mission?'

'I do not believe I have betrayed it. I have suffered in my flesh, and I have had the taste of despair and death in my mouth, but these sufferings are insignificant compared to the outrage inflicted upon the office of judge. It has been sullied and trampled underfoot.'

'When I tell you that the commander of the city guards, Mentmose, and the Judge of the Porch were appointed by this assembly, and with my approval, will you persist in your accusations?'

Pazair swallowed hard. He had gone too far. Even with strong evidence, irrefutable proofs, a junior judge ought not to attack leading citizens. The tjaty and his council would take the side of their close colleagues.

Summoning all his courage, he said, 'Whatever it may cost me, I shall uphold my accusations. I was unjustly deported, Mentmose made no serious attempt to find out what had really happened, and the Judge of the Porch rejected the truth in favour of lies. They wanted to get rid of me, so that the investigation into Branir's murder, the mysterious deaths of the Great Sphinx's honour-guard and the disappearance of the sky-iron would not be pursued. You, the nine Friends of Pharaoh, have heard this truth and will not forget it. Corruption has emerged from its lair and infected part of the state. If the sick limbs are not cut off, it will infect the entire body.'

Pazair did not lower his eyes; he met the tjaty's gaze, something few men had dared to do.

'Haste and intransigence lead even the best of judges astray,' observed Bagey. 'Which of these two paths would you follow: making a success of your life, or serving justice?'

'Why must they be opposed to each other?'

'Because the life of a man is rarely in accordance with the law of Ma'at.'

'Mine was dedicated to her under oath.'

The tjaty was silent for a long time. Pazair knew he was about to pronounce a sentence against which there could be no appeal.

At last Bagey spoke again. 'The bearer of the Rule, the king's steward and myself have examined the facts, asked questions and reached the same conclusions. The Judge of the Porch has indeed made serious mistakes. Because of his age, his experience, and the service he has given to the law, we sentence him to exile in the Khargeh oasis, where he will end his days in solitude and meditation. He will never return to the valley. Are you satisfied?'

'Tjaty, I cannot find satisfaction in a judge's misfortune.'

'Sentencing him is a duty.'

'The continuance of the investigation is another.'

'I am entrusting it to the new Judge of the Porch. You, Pazair.'

The judge went pale. 'But I am too young.'

'The office of Judge of the Porch does not require great age, but it does require the skill that this assembly recognizes in you. Do you fear the weight of this burden so much that you would refuse it?'

'I had not expected . . .'

'Destiny strikes in a moment, as swiftly as the crocodile that dives into the water. What is your answer?'

Pazair raised his clasped hands as a sign of respect and acceptance, and bowed very deeply.

'Judge of the Porch,' declared Bagey, 'you have no rights. All that counts is your duties. May Thoth guide your thoughts and direct your judgement, for only a god can save man from his baseness. Know your rank, be proud of it, but do not boast of it. Place your honour above the crowd, be silent and useful to others. Do not let go of the tiller-rope, be as a solid pillar in your office, love goodness, and hate evil. Offer no falsehood, be neither flippant nor confused, have no greed in your heart. Explore the depths of those you judge, by means of the eye of Ra, the celestial light. Hold out your right hand with the fingers spread.'

Pazair obeyed.

'Here is your ring, bearing your seal. It will authenticate the documents on which you place it. Henceforth, you will sit at the gates of the temple to dispense justice, and to protect the weak. You will ensure that order is respected throughout Memphis, and you will see that taxes are paid on time, fields are properly worked, and foodstuffs delivered. If necessary, you will sit in Egypt's highest court of justice. In all circumstances, do not be content with what you hear, and look deep into the secret depths of men's hearts.'

'Since you desire justice, who will deal with Mentmose, whose deceitfulness is unforgivable?' asked Pazair.

'Your investigation must set out his offences.'

'I promise you that I shall not yield to any passion, and that I shall take all the time necessary.'

The bearer of the Rule got to his feet. 'I confirm the tjaty's decision in the name of the council. From this moment on, Judge of the Porch Pazair will be recognized as such throughout Egypt. He will be granted a house, material goods, servants, offices and administrative staff.'

The overseer of the Double House also stood up. 'In accordance with the law, the Judge of the Porch will be responsible, on peril of losing all his possessions, for all unjust decisions. If reparations are due to someone who brings a charge, he will pay them himself, without recourse to public finances.'

The tjaty gave a sudden gasp of pain, and everyone turned to look at him. Bagey clasped his hand to his right side, gripped the back of his chair, tried in vain to hold himself upright, and fell to the ground, where he lay very still.

When Neferet saw Pazair running towards her, with his brow covered in sweat and anguish in his eyes, she thought he had fled from the palace.

'The tjaty has been taken ill.'

'Is Nebamon with him?'

'Nebamon isn't well, and none of his assistants dares do anything without his permission.'

The young woman fixed her portable clock to her wrist, and quickly loaded her remedies and equipment on to Way-Finder's back. The donkey set off along the right road.

When she reached the palace, she was shown into a private chamber where Bagey was lying on a cushioned couch. Neferet sounded him, listened to the voice of the heart in his chest, in his veins and in his arteries. She identified two currents, one heating up the right side of the body, the other chilling the left side. The illness was deep-seated and involved the whole body. Using her timepiece, she calculated the rhythm of his heart and the reaction times of his main organs.

The members of the court anxiously awaited her diagnosis.

'I know and can treat this illness,' she said. 'The liver is affected, the portal vein obstructed. The hepatic arteries and the bile duct, which link the heart to the liver, are in bad condition. They are no longer giving enough air and water and are sending out blood which is too thick.'

Neferet gave the patient an infusion of chicory to drink. This plant, with its large blue flowers which closed at noon, was grown in temple gardens. It had many curative powers; mixed with a little old wine, it was used to treat several afflictions of the liver and gall bladder. She magnetized the obstructed organ; before long, the tjaty sat up, looking very pale, and vomited.

Neferet told him to drink several cups of the chicory infusion, to keep doing so until he was able to keep the drink down; at last the patient's body was refreshed.

'His liver has been opened up and washed out,' she announced.

'Who are you?' asked Bagey.

'My name is Neferet, Tjaty, and I am a doctor and Judge Pazair's wife. You must be careful what you eat,' she added calmly, 'and drink chicory every day. To avoid another serious blockage, which would completely incapacitate you, you are to take a potion made from figs, grapes, sycamore fruit, bryony seeds, persea fruit, gum and resin. I shall prepare this mixture for you myself and it must be exposed to the dew and filtered in the early morning.'

'You have saved my life.'

'I did my duty, and we were fortunate.'

'Where do you practise?'

'In Memphis.'

The tjaty got to his feet. Although his legs felt heavy and he had a bad headache, he managed a few steps.

'It's vital that you rest,' said Neferet, helping him to sit down. 'Nebamon will—'

'You are the one who will treat me.'

Just one week later, Tjaty Bagey had entirely recovered. He gave the new Judge of the Porch a limestone stele, on which were engraved three pairs of ears, one pair coloured dark blue, one yellow, and the third pale green. This evoked the lapis-blue sky where the stars of the sages dwelt on high, the gold from which the gods' flesh was made, and the turquoise of love. In this way the duties of the most senior judge in Memphis were set out: to listen to plaintiffs, respect the will of the gods, and be benevolent but without weakness.

Listening was the basis of a child's upbringing, and the ability to listen remained a magistrate's most important quality. Serious and intensely focused, Pazair took the stele, and raised the limestone block to his eyes before all the judges of the great city, who had met to congratulate the new Judge of the Porch.

Neferet wept with joy.

12

The house allocated to the Judge of the Porch was situated at the heart of a modest district, made up of small two-storey white dwellings housing craftsmen and junior officials. The young couple marvelled at it: it had only just been finished, and no one had ever lived in it before. It had originally been meant for another official, but he would lose nothing by the change. It was a long building with a flat roof, and was made up of eight rooms whose walls were decorated with paintings of many-coloured birds frolicking in the papyrus forest.

At first, Pazair didn't dare go in. He lingered in the poultry-yard, where an employee was force-feeding geese; ducks were quacking in a pond dotted with blue lotus-flowers. In the shade of a hut, two boys who were supposed to be throwing grain for the poultry were fast asleep. The new master of the estate did not wake them. Neferet, too, was delighted to have such riches. She gazed at the fertile earth, aerated by worms whose casts made excellent manure for cereal crops. No peasant would kill worms, knowing that they ensured the fertility of the soil.

Brave was the first to scamper into the splendid garden, followed immediately by Way-Finder. The donkey lay down under a pomegranate-tree, whose beauty was the most lasting of all, since whenever a flower fell a new one opened. The dog preferred a sycamore-tree, whose rustling leaves evoked the sweetness of honey. Neferet caressed the slender branches and the ripe fruit, some red, some turquoise, and drew her husband towards her in the shadow of the tree, shelter of the sky goddess. In delight they gazed upon a path bordered by fig-trees imported from Syria, and a shelter built of reeds, from which they could watch the splendid sunsets.

Their peace did not last long; Mischief, Neferet's little green monkey, let out a cry of pain and leapt into her mistress's arms. Sheepishly she held out her paw, in which an acacia thorn was embedded. The wound must not be taken lightly; if the foreign body remained under the skin, it would eventually cause internal bleeding which defied many doctors.

Without needing to be told, Way-Finder got to his feet and came over to them. Neferet took a scalpel from her medical kit, took out the thorn with infinite gentleness, and smeared the wound with an ointment made from honey, colocynth, ground cuttlefish-bone and powdered sycamore-bark. If infection did develop, she would treat it with sulphur of arsenic. But Mischief's life hardly seemed in any danger; as soon as she was free of the thorn, she climbed up into a date-palm in search of ripe fruit.

'Shall we go inside?' suggested Neferet.

'Things are becoming serious.'

'What do you mean?'

'We got married, it's true, but neither of us owned anything then. The situation has changed.'

'Surely you aren't tiring of it already?'

'Never forget, Doctor, that I was the one who came along and tore you away from your peaceful life.'

'My memories are rather different; didn't I notice you first?'

'We should have been seated side by side, surrounded by a crowd of relatives and friends, and have chairs, clothing-chests, vases, toilet articles, sandals and goodness knows what else paraded in front of us. You would have been brought in a litter, dressed in ceremonial clothes, to the sound of flutes and tambourines.'

'I prefer it like this: the two of us alone together, without any noise or fuss.'

'As soon as we cross the threshold of this house we shall become responsible for it. The authorities would rebuke me if I didn't draw up a contract safeguarding your future.'

'Is that an honest proposition?'

'I'm conforming with the law. I, Pazair, bring all my possessions to you, Neferet, who will retain your name. Since we have decided to live together under the same roof, and so to be married, I will owe you reparation if we should ever separate. A third of all that we have acquired, from this day onwards, shall come to you as of right, and I must feed and clothe you. In all other matters, the court will judge.'

'I must confess to the Judge of the Porch that I am madly in love with a man and that I have the firm intention of remaining bound to him until my last breath.'

'Perhaps, but the law—'

'Hush! Let's go inside.'

'Before we do, one correction: it's I who am madly in love with you.'

Arm in arm, they crossed the threshold of their new life.

The first room, which was small and low-ceilinged, was reserved for the veneration of the ancestors. They meditated there for a long time, venerating the soul of Branir, their murdered master. Then they explored the reception chamber, the bedchambers, the kitchen, the washing areas with their terracotta pipes and a toilet equipped with a limestone seat.

They were hugely impressed by the bathing-room. On the limestone flagged floor, set in a corner were two brick benches on which serving-men and -girls stood to pour water on anyone who wanted a shower. Square tiles of limestone covered the brick walls, so that they were not exposed to the damp. A slight incline, leading to the opening of a deep-buried earthenware pipe, enabled the water to run away.

In the airy bedchamber a mosquito-net hung over a bed made of solid ebony, with feet in the shape of a lion's paws. On the sides was the jovial face of the god Bes, whose task was to guard people while they slept and give them happy dreams. Wide-eyed, Pazair lingered over the sleeping-frame, which was made from plaited ropes of vegetable fibres and was of an exceptional quality. The many cross-pieces had been positioned with perfect precision to support a heavy weight for many years.

At the head of the bed was a robe of the finest white linen, the bride's garment which would also be her winding-sheet.

Pazair said, 'I'd never have imagined sleeping in a bed like this, not even for a single night.'

'Why wait?' asked Neferet teasingly.

She laid out the precious robe on the sleeping-frame, took off her dress, and stretched out naked, happy to welcome Pazair's body on top of hers.

'This moment is so sweet,' he said, 'that I shall never forget it. By the way you look at me, you make it eternal. Don't ever leave me. I belong to you like a garden which you shall enrich with flowers and scents. When we form a single being, death no longer exists.'

But the very next morning, Pazair began to miss the little house he had lived in as a junior judge and to realize why Tjaty Bagey was content with a modest dwelling in the centre of city. True, there were plenty of reed brushes and besoms with which to clean the place thoroughly, but you still needed hands to wield them. Neither he nor Neferet had the time to do this work, and it was out of the question to ask the gardener or poultryman, who stuck strictly to their own jobs. No one had thought to employ a cleaning-woman.

Neferet and Way-Finder left early for the palace; the tjaty wished for a consultation before his first audience. Without a clerk, without a proper office, without servants, the Judge of the Porch felt completely lost, in charge of a domain which was too big for him. The sages had been quite right when they called the wife 'mistress of the house'.

The gardener recommended a woman in her fifties, who hired out her services to householders in distress; for six days' work, she demanded no less than eight goats and two new dresses! Bled white, certain that he was endangering the couple's financial stability, the Judge of the Porch was obliged to accept. Until Neferet returned, he would live in straitened circumstances.

Suti gazed at the new house in wonder, and prodded the walls. 'They feel real.'

'The building's new, but it's good quality.'

'I thought I was the greatest practical joker in Egypt, but you've outdone me by a thousand cubits. Who lent you this house?'

'The state,' replied Pazair.

'Surely you're not going to keep on claiming you're the new Judge of the Porch?'

'If you don't believe me, ask Neferet.'

'Ha! She's your accomplice.'

'Then go to the palace.'

Suti was shaken. 'Who appointed you?'

'The nine Friends of Pharaoh, led by the tjaty.'

'You mean that cold fish Bagey actually dismissed your predecessor, one of his esteemed colleagues, a man with a spotless reputation?'

'He had his faults. Bagey and the High Council acted according to the law.'

'It's like a miracle, a dream . . .'

'My request was heard by the full council.'

'But why appoint you to such an important post?'

'I've been thinking about that.'

'And what have you concluded?

'Suppose half of the High Council is convinced of Asher's guilt, and the other half isn't. Wouldn't it be a clever move to entrust an increasingly dangerous investigation to the judge who lifted the first veil? When the case is settled, one way or the other, it will be easy either to disown me or to congratulate me.'

'You aren't as stupid as you look,' said Suti, grinning.

'I'm not surprised or shocked by their decision; it's in accordance with Egyptian law. I began the matter, so it's up to me to finish it – if I didn't I'd be nothing more than an agitator. Besides, why should I complain? I've been given resources beyond my wildest hopes. Branir's soul is protecting me.'

'Don't rely on the dead. Kem and I will protect you much more effectively.'

'Do you think I'm in danger?'

'You're getting more and more exposed. The Judge of the Porch is usually an old, cautious man, determined not to take risks and to enjoy his privileged life to the full – in short, the complete opposite of you.'

'What can I do? Destiny has made its choice.'

'I may not be as mad as you are, but I'm pleased to hear that. You'll arrest Branir's murderer, and I shall enjoy removing Asher's head.'

Pazair smiled and then changed the subject. 'And how is the lady Tapeni?'

'She's a splendid mistress – no match for Panther, but what imagination! Yesterday afternoon, we fell out of bed at the crucial moment. An ordinary woman would have paused for a moment, but not her. I had to show I was her equal, even though I was underneath.'

'You have my admiration. On a less convivial note, what have you learnt from her?'

'It's obvious that you aren't an expert in seduction. If I ask too many direct questions, she'll close up like a night-flower at noon. We've begun to talk about the illustrious women who practise the art of weaving. Some are incredibly skilled with the needle. You and I are on the right track, I can feel it.'

Neferet came back at last, led by Way-Finder. Brave greeted the donkey with joyful barking, and the two companions ate together; one had a chunk of beef and the other had fresh fodder. Mischief wasn't hungry any more; her belly was so full of fruit she had stolen from the orchard that she was indulging in a long nap.

Neferet was radiant. Neither tiredness nor cares had any hold over her. Often, Pazair felt unworthy of his wife.

'How is the tjaty?' he asked.

'Much better, but he'll have to go on having treatment for the rest of his life. His liver and his bile duct are in a dreadful state, and I'm not sure I can prevent his legs and feet from swelling when he's tired. He ought to do a lot of walking and get some country air, not stay seated for whole days at a time.'

'You're asking the impossible. Did he say anything about Nebamon?'

'He's ill. Killer seems to have left his mark.'

'Ought we to feel sorry for him?'

A loud bray from Way-Finder interrupted them: he hadn't had enough to eat.

'I'm overwhelmed,' confessed Pazair. I did manage to take on a temporary cleaning-woman – at an extortionate rate – but I feel lost in this big house. We haven't got a cook, the gardener does only what he feels like, and I don't understand the first thing about all these different brushes. My files are all untouched, I haven't got a clerk, and I—'

Neferet kissed him.

13

Dressed in a kilt with a weighted panel at the front and a fine pleated shirt with long sleeves, Bel-Tran came to visit Pazair and Neferet in their new home.

He began by congratulating them both warmly. Then he said, 'This time, Pazair, I definitely am going to help you, and in the most direct way. I've been charged with reorganizing the central government offices. As Judge of the Porch, you are a priority.'

'That's very kind of you, but I can't accept any favours at all, no matter how small.'

'This isn't a favour. It's merely an arrangement, in accordance with the rules, which will enable you to have all your files to hand. We shall work side by side, in large, spacious premises. Please don't stop me pleading the cause of our common efficiency!'

Bel-Tran's rapid rise to power had amazed even the most world-weary members of the court, but no one criticized it. He would blow the dust off secretariats which had become mired in routine, get rid of lazy or incompetent officials, and face up to the thousand and one problems that arose from one day to the next. Endowed with infectious enthusiasm, he happily bullied his subordinates. Sons of noble families deplored his modest origins, but accepted that they must obey him or be sent back home. No obstacle daunted Bel-Tran: he took its measure, attacked it with an inexhaustible energy, and eventually overcame it. Whenever an insoluble difficulty presented itself, Bel-Tran was its inevitable recipient. To his great credit, he had even managed to sort out the wood tax, which large landowners – ignoring the public good – had for a long time escaped paying. On this occasion, Bel-Tran had not omitted to call on Pazair's judicious intervention once again.

Pazair saw that he had a powerful ally. Thanks to Bel-Tran, he would avoid many pitfalls and snares.

Bel-Tran turned to Neferet. 'Silkis is feeling much better. She's very grateful to you and considers you a friend.'

'How are her headaches?'

'Much less frequent. When they start, we apply your salve and it's remarkably effective. I'm afraid, though, that despite your warnings and those of the interpreter of dreams – like you, he told her not to eat too much sugar – she's still greedy. I hide the pomegranate juice and the honey but she secretly obtains carob-juice, or figs.'

'No medicine can replace willpower.'

Bel-Tran grimaced. 'May I consult you, too? For the last week, my ankles have been painful. I'm even finding it difficult to get my sandals on.'

Neferet examined his small, plump feet. 'Boil beef-fat and acacia-leaves, pound them into a paste and apply it to the sensitive areas. If that doesn't help, let me know.'

They paused for a moment as the cleaning-woman came to ask Neferet which room should be cleaned next. Neferet was adapting marvellously to her role as mistress of the house, and would soon set up her consulting-room in one of the ground-floor rooms.

At the palace her reputation was growing: curing the tjaty had brought her glowing praise which provoked envy among the court doctors, who were still paralysed by Nebamon's absence.

'This house is delightful,' observed Bel-Tran, nibbling a slice of watermelon.

Pazair smiled. 'Without Neferet, I'd have run away.'

'Don't be so unambitious, my dear Pazair! Your wife is an exceptional person. No doubt many people will be jealous of you.'

'Nebamon's jealousy is quite enough for me,' said Pazair.

'He won't stay quiet for long. You and Neferet humiliated him, and he'll be thinking of nothing but getting his revenge – though, admittedly, your new position will make that more difficult.'

'Let's talk of something else,' said Pazair. 'What do you think of the recent royal decrees?'

'They're very puzzling. Why does the king need to reaffirm a power which nobody's challenging?'

'The last annual flood was very low, a hyena came and drank from the river, several woman have given birth to malformed children . . .'

Bel-Tran snorted. 'Those are just the common folk's superstitions.'

'Perhaps, but superstitions can sometimes be very powerful.'

'It is up to the servants of the state to prove they're groundless. Now, tell me, are you going to resume your case against Asher and the investigation into the killing of the honour-guard?'

'Of course. They're the main reasons for my appointment.'

'A lot of people at the palace were hoping those unfortunate events would be forgotten. I'm delighted to see that they won't be – mind you, it's no more than I expected of you, with your courage.'

'Ma'at is a smiling but implacable goddess. The source of all happiness is within her, so long as she isn't betrayed. If I didn't seek the truth, I'd be unable to breathe.'

In a darker tone, Bel-Tran said, 'Asher's calmness worries me, too. He's a violent man, a doer of brutal deeds. Once he knew of your promotion, he ought to have reacted in some visible way.'

'Surely he has less room to manoeuvre now?'

'That's true, but don't celebrate too soon.'

'It isn't in my nature to do that.'

'You're no longer alone now, but your enemies have by no means vanished. Everything I learn, I shall tell you.'

For two weeks Pazair lived in a whirlwind. He consulted the Judge of the Porch's enormous archives, oversaw the separate filing of tablets made from clay, limestone and wood, draft legal documents, furniture inventories, official mail, sealed rolls of papyrus and scribes' materials. He consulted the list of his staff, summoned each scribe, oversaw the payment and adjustment of salaries, examined delayed complaints and corrected a host of administrative mistakes. Although he was surprised by the size of the task, he did not balk at it and quickly built up good relationships with his subordinates. Each morning, he conferred with Bel-Tran, whose advice was very valuable.

Pazair was sorting out a delicate land-registry problem when a scribe with a red face and thick features arrived.

'Iarrot!' exclaimed the judge. 'Where on earth have you been?'

'My daughter's going to become a professional dancer, that's definite. But my wife won't agree to it, so I'm having to get divorced.'

'When will you be coming back to work?'

'I don't belong here.'

'You couldn't be more wrong! A good scribe—'

'You're too important now. In these offices, scribes have to work set hours – and stick to them. That wouldn't suit me. I'd sooner take charge of my daughter's career. We'll travel from province to province and take part in village festivals, then obtain a contract with a well-established troupe. The poor little thing must be protected.'

'Is that your final decision?'

'You work too hard. You'll come up against interests which are too powerful for you. I'd rather give up my staff, official kilt and funerary stele while I still can, and live at a safe distance from dramas and quarrels.'

'Are you sure you really will escape them?'

'My daughter worships me and will always listen to me. I shall make her happy.'

*

Denes was enjoying his cherished victory. The fight had been taxing, and his wife had had to enlist all her relations to drive away their countless competitors, who were extremely bitter at their defeat. But it would be Denes and Nenophar who organized the banquet in honour of the new Judge of the Porch. The ship-owner's know-how and his wife's strength of belief had once more gained them the title of Master of Ceremonies for the whole of Memphis. Pazair's appointment had been such a surprise that it deserved a true celebration, at which the members of high society would vie with each other in elegance.

Pazair got ready without enthusiasm. 'I know this reception is going to bore me,' he complained to Neferet.

'But you're the honoured guest, my darling.'

'I'd rather spend the evening with you. My office doesn't mean I have to be involved in this kind of worldly activity.'

'We've refused all the purely social invitations from Memphis's leading citizens, but this one has an official aspect.'

'That man Denes doesn't miss a thing. He knows I suspect him of being part of the conspiracy, and he's playing the delighted host.'

'It's a good idea. He hopes to put you off your guard.'

'Do you think he'll succeed?'

Neferet's laughter enchanted him. How beautiful she was in that clinging dress, which left her breasts bare. Her black wig, with highlights of lapis-lazuli, set off her slender face, which bore hardly a trace of paint. She was the embodiment of youth, grace and love.

He took her in his arms. 'I wish I could lock you away.'

'Are you jealous?'

'If anyone so much as looks at you, I'll strangle him.'

'Judge of the Porch! How dare you suggest such a horrible thing?'

Pazair encircled Neferet's waist with a belt of amethyst beads, incorporating worked gold in the form of a panther's head. 'We're ruined, but you're the most beautiful woman in all the world.'

'This seems remarkably like an attempt at seduction.'

'You've unmasked me.' Pazair slid down the left strap of her dress.

'But we're already late,' she protested.

Before dressing for the banquet, Nenophar went to the kitchens, where her butchers had cut up an ox and were preparing the pieces, which they hung on a beam held up by forked posts. She picked out the joints to be grilled and those to be stewed, tasted the sauces, and made sure that several dozen roasted geese would be ready in time. Then she went down to the cellar, where her cellar-keeper showed her the chosen wines and beers. Reassured about the quality of the food and drink, Nenophar inspected the banqueting-hall, where serving-men and

-women were setting out gold cups, silver salvers and alabaster plates on low tables. The whole house was full of the delectable scent of jasmine and lotuses. The reception would be a memorable one.

An hour before the first guests were due to arrive, the gardeners picked fruit, which would be served fresh and full of flavour; a scribe noted down the number of jars of wine placed in the banqueting-hall, so as to prevent fraud. The head gardener checked that all the pathways were clean, while the gate-keeper tugged at his kilt and adjusted his wig. The latter was the estate's unbending guardian and would not allow in anyone whom he did not know or who did not have an invitation tablet.

As the sun got lower in the sky, preparing to sink behind the Peak of the West, the first couple presented themselves to the gate-keeper. He identified them as a royal scribe and his wife, and they were soon followed by the great city's elite. The guests strolled in the garden, which was planted with pomegranate-, fig- and sycamore-trees, and chatted as they stood around the ornamental lakes, under the pergolas or wooden canopies, or admired the flowers arranged at the junctions of the pathways. The presence of Tjaty Bagey, who never attended parties, and of all the Friends of Pharaoh impressed everyone: it was going to be an unforgettable evening.

At the precise moment when the sun's disc vanished, the servants lit lamps which filled the garden and the villa with light. Nenophar and Denes appeared on the threshold of the house. She wore a heavy wig, a white dress bordered with gold, a necklace of ten strings of pearls, gazelle-shaped earrings and golden sandals, while he sported a layered wig, a long pleated robe with a cape, and leather sandals ornamented with silver. They were the perfect fashionable hosts, happy to display their wealth in the avowed hope of arousing envy.

In accordance with protocol, the tjaty was the first to walk towards them. His legs were heavy, and he had confined himself to worn-out sandals, a full, inelegant kilt and a short-sleeved overshirt.

Nenophar and Denes knelt in delight.

'How hot it is,' grumbled the tjaty. 'Only the winter is bearable. A few moments in the sun, and my skin burns.'

'One of our lakes is at your disposal, should you wish to cool down before the banquet,' offered Denes.

'I can't swim and I loathe the water.'

Denes led the tjaty to the place of honour. The Friends of Pharaoh came in turn, then the senior officials, other royal scribes and assorted people who had had the good fortune to be invited to the year's most prestigious celebration. Be-Tran and Silkis were among these last; Nenophar greeted them distractedly.

'Is General Asher coming?' Denes whispered in his wife's ear.

'He's just sent his apologies – demands of work.'

'What about Mentmose?'

'He's ill.'

In the banqueting-hall, with its vine-decorated ceiling, the guests sat in comfortable armchairs padded with cushions. In front of them were pedestal tables bearing cups, plates and salvers. Three female musicians – a flautist, a harpist and a lute-player – played light, cheerful tunes.

Naked young Nubian girls moved about among the guests and placed little cones of perfumed pomade upon their wigs; as the cones melted, they gave off sweet smells and drove away insects. Each person was given a lotus-flower. A priest poured water on to an offertory table in the centre of the room, in order to purify the food.

Suddenly, Nenophar realised that the very people being celebrated weren't there. 'It's unbelievable that they should be so late!' she exclaimed to her husband.

'Don't worry about it. Pazair's no doubt working late on a case – he's obsessed with his work.'

'On an evening like this? Our guests are getting impatient. We must begin to serve the food.'

'Don't be so fretful.'

Hiding her anger, Nenophar asked the best professional dancing-girl in Memphis to perform earlier than planned. Twenty years old, and a pupil of Sababu, owner of the most respectable ale-house in the city, she wore only a belt of shells, which clinked together delightfully at each step. On her left thigh were tattoos of the god Bes, the laughing dwarf, guarantor of joy in all its forms. The dancer easily held the guests' attention; she would execute the most acrobatic moves until Pazair and Neferet arrived.

While the guests were nibbling grapes and thin slices of melon to stimulate their appetites, and Nenophar was getting more and more angry, she noticed a certain amount of activity around the gates of the estate. It was them – at last!

'Come in, quickly.'

'I'm extremely sorry,' apologized Pazair.

He could hardly explain that he'd been unable to resist the urge to undress Neferet, that his ardour had led him to tear one of the straps of her dress, that he'd managed to make her forget all about the banquet, and that their love was worth more than the most brilliant of invitations. Her hair in a mess, Neferet had had to choose a new dress in haste and almost drag Pazair out of their bed of pleasure.

The dancing-girl withdrew and the musicians stopped playing when the young couple crossed the threshold of the banqueting-hall. In a second, they were judged by dozens of pairs of eyes, without indulgence.

Pazair had not bothered about elegance: his short wig, bare torso and short kilt made him look like an austere scribe from the time of the pyramids. His only concession to his own time was a pleated front panel in his kilt, which slightly relieved his sober dress. The man, thought the guests, was living up to his reputation for thoroughness. Inveterate gamblers wagered on the date when he would, like everyone else, yield to corruption. Others, less enjoyably, contemplated the extensive powers of a Judge of the Porch, whose somewhat incongruous youth would inevitably lead him to fatal excess. And people criticized the decision of the old tjaty, who was increasingly absent-minded and too quick to delegate parts of his authority: many courtiers were urging Ramses to replace him with an experienced, active administrator.

Neferet did not provoke the same debates. A simple band of flowers round her hair, a broad necklace hiding her breasts, light earrings in the form of lotus-flowers, bracelets at wrist and ankle, a long dress of transparent linen which revealed more of her figure than it hid: the sight of her enchanted the most world-weary and sweetened the most bitter. To her youth and beauty were added the brilliance of an intelligence so lively that it was expressed, without the least haughtiness, in her laughing eyes. They were right: her charm did not exclude a strength of character which few people would ever succeed in shaking.

Why, the guests wondered, had she bound herself to a junior judge whose stern appearance promised nothing for the future? True, he had obtained an eminent post, but he would not be able to hold it for very long. The love-affair would die, and Neferet would choose a more glittering partner. Where the unfortunate Nebamon had failed, another would succeed. A few grand ladies in their middle years deplored such daring clothes being worn by the wife of a senior magistrate, unaware that she had no other dress to put on.

The Judge of the Porch and his wife took their places beside the tjaty. Servants hurried to bring them slices of grilled beef and smooth red wine.

'But I see your wife isn't with you, Tjaty,' said Neferet. 'I hope she isn't unwell.'

'No, it's simply that she never goes out. Her kitchen, her children and her home in the city are enough for her.'

'I'm almost ashamed to have accepted such a grand house,' confessed Pazair.

'You shouldn't feel that way. I refused the estate Pharaoh grants to the tjaty, but that's because I detest the countryside. I've lived in the same place for forty years, and I have no intention of moving. I love the city. Wide-open spaces, insects, fields as far as the eye can see – they leave me cold or drive me mad.'

'All the same,' Neferet told him, 'as a doctor I advise you to walk as much as possible.'

'I walk to and from my office.'

'You need more rest, too.'

'As soon as my children's futures are settled, I shall start working shorter hours.'

'Are you worried about them?'

'Not about my daughter, though I am disappointed. She entered the Temple of Hathor as an apprentice weaver, but she didn't like the life because the whole structure of the day is governed by ritual. She's now been taken on as accounting-scribe of grain for a farm and will make a career of that. My son is more difficult to handle. He's a brick-checker, but he loves gambling and loses half his pay at the gaming-board. Fortunately, he lives at home and his mother feeds him. If he's hoping I'll use my position to improve his own, he's going to be disappointed: I have neither the right nor the wish so to do. But don't let my tedious difficulties discourage you; having children is the greatest happiness of all.'

The excellent food and wines delighted the guests, who exchanged small-talk until the Judge of the Porch's short speech, whose tone surprised everyone.

'All that matters is my office, not the individual who occupies it for a time. My only guide will be Ma'at, goddess of justice, who lays out the path for this country's magistrates. If mistakes have been made recently, I feel responsible for them. So long as the tjaty grants me his trust, I shall fulfil my duties without regard for anyone's interests. Current cases will not remain secret, even if leading citizens are involved. Justice is Egypt's most precious treasure. I hope that each of my decisions will enrich it.'

Pazair's voice was strong, clear and trenchant. Anyone who still doubted his authority was enlightened. The judge's apparent youth would not be a handicap; on the contrary, it would give him indispensable energy, placed at the service of impressive maturity. Many changed their opinions; perhaps the reign of the new Judge of the Porch would not be so brief, after all.

Late in the night, the guests dispersed; Tjaty Bagey, who liked to retire early, was the first to leave. Everyone wished to greet Pazair and Neferet, and to congratulate them.

When they were free at last, they went out into the garden. The sound of voices caught their attention. As they drew near a thicket of tamarisks, they came upon Bel-Tran and Nenophar, locked in a fierce argument.

'I hope never to see you again in this house,' said Nenophar.

'Then you shouldn't have invited me.'

'Politeness obliged me to.'

'In that case, why are you so angry?'

'Not only are you persecuting my husband with a tax demand, but you have also abolished my post as scrutineer of the Treasury.'

'It was only an honorary one. The state paid you at a rate out of all proportion to the real work. I am setting to rights all government departments which were too free with their money, and I shall never permit such extravagance again. Be sure that the new Judge of the Porch will agree with my course of action, and that he would have done the same thing – with a punishment thrown in. Be grateful that you have escaped that.'

Nenophar scowled at him. 'A fine way to justify yourself! You're more ferocious than a crocodile.'

'Crocodiles clean the Nile and keep the numbers of hippos down. Denes ought to beware of them.'

'Your threats don't impress me. Cleverer plotters than you have come to grief.'

'Then I wish you good luck.'

Nenophar stormed away from Bel-Tran, who hurried to rejoin his impatient wife.

Pazair and Neferet greeted the dawn on the roof of their house. They thought of the happy day that was breaking and would light them with a love as sweet as a festival perfume. On earth as in the afterlife, when generations had been wiped away, he would deck his beloved wife with flowers and plant sycamores near the cool lake, where they would never tire of gazing at each other. Their unified soul would come to drink in the shade, nourished by the song of the leaves as they rippled in the wind.

14

Pazair was obsessed by the urgent need to put together a case which would prove Kem's innocence once and for all and give him back his dignity. In so doing, Pazair would identify Mentmose's secret witness and find the commander guilty of producing false evidence.

As soon as she arose, and before even kissing him, Neferet made him drink two big gulps of copper-water; an obstinate cold proved that the Judge of the Porch's lymph was still infected and fragile, following his imprisonment.

Pazair ate his breakfast too quickly and rushed to his office, where he was immediately besieged by an army of scribes brandishing a series of strident complaints from twenty small villages. Because of the refusal by an overseer of the royal granaries, oils and cereals – which were vital to the well-being of the inhabitants because the flood had been so meagre – had not been delivered. Using an obsolete ruling to justify himself, the petty official was mocking the hungry peasants.

With help from Bel-Tran, the Judge of the Porch devoted two long days to resolving this apparently simple matter without making any administrative errors. The overseer of granaries was transferred to control the canal serving one of the villages that he was refusing to feed.

Then another difficulty arose, a conflict between some fruit-growers and the Treasury scribes whose task was to assess their profits; to avoid an interminable case, Pazair himself went to the orchards, punished the individuals behind the fraud and rejected the unjustified accusations made by the taxation scribes. He understood ever more clearly the extent to which the country's financial equilibrium, which allied private individuals and business with state planning, was a miracle, ceaselessly renewed. It was up to the individual to work as he chose and, beyond a certain threshold, to harvest the rewards of his labour; it was up to the state to take care of irrigation, the safety of property and persons, the storage and distribution of food when the flood was inadequate, and all other tasks in the community's interests.

Realizing that he would be in difficulties if he did not regulate the use of his time, Pazair scheduled the 'Kem case' for the following week. As soon as the day was announced, a priest from the Temple of Ptah opposed it: it was an illomened date, the anniversary of the cosmic battle between Horus, the celestial light, and his brother Set, the storm.* On such a day it was better not to leave one's house and not to undertake a journey; of course, Mentmose would use the argument so as not to appear.

Pazair was annoyed with himself, and almost gave up when an obscure customs matter was submitted to him, implicating foreign traders. Once his momentary discouragement had passed, he began to read the file, then pushed it away. How could he forget the distress of the big Nubian, who was searching for Killer in the most obscure corners of the city?

On his way home that evening, Pazair stopped to buy some red Nubian flowers to make an infusion Brave enjoyed.†As he turned away from the flower-seller's stall, he was accosted by Mentmose.

The commander was clearly ill at ease, and his voice was unctuous as he said, 'I was badly deceived. But, deep inside, I always believed in your innocence.'

'Yet you still sent me to prison.'

'In my place, wouldn't you have done the same thing? The law must be pitiless towards judges, otherwise it will lose all credibility.'

'But in my case the judgement had not even been handed down.'

'An unfortunate combination of circumstances, my dear Pazair. Today destiny favours you, and we all rejoice at that. I have heard that you are planning to hold a trial, under the porch, concerning that regrettable Kem affair.'

'You're well informed, Commander. It only remains for me to set a date which, this time, will not be a day of ill omen.'

'Shouldn't we forget those regrettable incidents and put them behind us?'

'Forgetting is the beginning of injustice. The porch is the place where I must protect the weak and save them from the powerful.'

'Your Nubian is hardly weak.'

'But you are powerful, and you are trying to destroy him by accusing him of a crime he did not commit.'

---

*Papyri provide us with lists of 'auspicious days' and 'days of ill omen', which correspond to mythological events.
†It was karkade, which is still drunk in modern Egypt. The flowers are those of the hibiscus.

'Would you accept an arrangement which would prevent a great deal of unpleasantness?'

'What sort of arrangement?'

'Certain names might be mentioned ... And leading citizens set great store by their respectability.'

'What would an innocent man have to fear?'

'Rumours, tittle-tattle, ill-will, things like that.'

'Those things will hold no sway beneath the porch. You committed a serious offence, Commander.'

'I am the active arm of the law. Cutting yourself off from me would be a grave mistake.'

'I want the name of the eye-witness who accused Kem of having murdered Branir.'

Mentmose looked down. 'I made him up.'

'You certainly did not. You would not have put forward that argument if the person did not exist. I consider false testimony a criminal act, with the power to ruin a life. The trial will take place. It will shed light on your role as a manipulator, and will enable me to interrogate your famous eye-witness in Kem's presence. What is his name?'

'I refuse to give it to you.'

'Is he so highly placed?'

'I promised to tell no one. He took a lot of risks and doesn't wish his identity to be made public.'

'You refuse to cooperate in an investigation? You know the punishment for that.'

'You're mad! I'm not just a nobody, I'm the commander of the city guards.'

'And I am the Judge of the Porch.'

Suddenly Mentmose, whose face had turned brick-red and whose voice had grown very shrill, realized that he was no longer up against a junior provincial judge with a thirst for integrity, but was facing the highest judge in the city, who was moving, neither hastily nor slowly, towards his goal.

'Judge,' he said, 'I need time to think.'

'I shall expect you tomorrow morning, at my office. You will then reveal the name of your false witness.'

Although the banquet in honour of the Judge of the Porch had been a great success, and had much increased his prestige, Denes had stopped thinking about that lavish celebration. He was preoccupied with calming his friend Qadash, who was so agitated that he had begun to stutter. Pacing up and down, the tooth-doctor constantly fiddled with the wayward strands of his white hair. An influx of blood had turned his hands red, and the small veins in his nose looked ready to burst.

The two men had taken refuge in the furthest part of the pleasure-garden, well away from indiscreet ears. The inventor Sheshi, who joined them there, checked that no one could hear them, then sat down at the foot of a date-palm. Although the little man with the black moustache deplored Qadash's agitation, he shared his anxieties.

'Denes, your plan is a disaster,' said Qadash accusingly.

'All three of us agreed to use Mentmose, have Kem accused, and thus cool Judge Pazair's hot head,' Denes reminded him.

'And we failed – lamentably! I can't practise my profession because my hands are shaking so badly, and you have refused to let me use the sky-iron! When I agreed to join you, you promised me a post at the very pinnacle of the state.'

'First the post of principal doctor, in place of Nebamon,' said Denes reassuringly, 'then even greater things.'

'Farewell, beautiful dreams!'

'Not at all.'

'Have you forgotten that Pazair is Judge of the Porch, that he wants to stage a trial to clear Kem of all suspicion and force the eye-witness – namely, me – to appear?'

'Mentmose won't reveal your name.'

'I'm not so sure about that.'

'He's schemed his whole life long to get his present job. If he betrays us, he'll condemn himself.'

Sheshi nodded in agreement. Reassured, Qadash accepted a cup of beer.

Denes, who had eaten too much at the banquet, massaged his swollen belly. 'This commander of the guards is a useless idiot,' he groused. 'When we take power, we must get rid of him.'

'Too much haste would be dangerous,' said Sheshi, in a small, barely audible voice. 'General Asher is working away in the shadows, and I'm not unhappy with my latest results. Soon we'll have access to excellent weapons, and we'll also have control of the main weapons stores. Above all, we must not show our hand. Pazair is convinced that Qadash wanted to steal the sky-iron from me, and that we are enemies. He knows nothing about the links between us, and if we're careful he'll never find out. Thanks to Denes's public declarations, he believes that the army's aim is to make unbreakable weapons. Let us encourage him in that idea.'

'Can he really be that naive?' worried Qadash.

'Far from it. But a project of this size will draw his attention. What could be more important than a sword which can cut through helmets, armour and shields without breaking? With its aid, Asher will foment a conspiracy to seize power. That is the truth which will impose itself on the judge's mind.'

'It implies your complicity,' Denes pointed out.

'My obedience, as an expert, clears me of responsibility.'

'All the same I'm worried,' insisted Qadash, who had started pacing up and down again. 'Ever since he crossed our path, we've underestimated Pazair. And now he's Judge of the Porch!'

'The next storm will sweep him away,' prophesied Denes.

'And every day that passes is in our favour,' said Sheshi. 'Pharaoh's power is weakening, being eroded like a stone.'

None of the three conspirators noticed the presence of a witness who had not missed one word of the conversation. Perched high in a palm-tree, Killer was gazing fixedly at them with his red-rimmed eyes.

Appalled by Bel-Tran's bigoted, hostile attitude, Nenophar took immediate action. She summoned to her house the scribes who oversaw the financial affairs of the fifty wealthiest families in Memphis. Like herself, their patrons enjoyed a number of honorary positions which did not oblige them to do any work but which gave them access to confidential information and afforded them privileged contact with the highest levels of government. Nenophar explained the situation clearly to the scribes. In his frenzy of reorganization, Bel-Tran was abolishing these posts one after another. Since the beginning of its history, Egypt had always rejected the authoritarian excesses of this kind of jumped-up official, who was as dangerous as a sand viper. Everyone thoroughly approved of this passionate speech. One man was obliged to take the side of reason and justice: Pazair, the Judge of the Porch. So a delegation, made up of Nenophar and ten eminent representatives of the nobility, obtained an audience the very next morning.

No one arrived empty-handed: at the judge's feet they laid vases of ointment, precious fabrics and a chest full of jewels.

'Receive this homage to your office,' said the eldest man.

'Your generosity touches me, but I am obliged to refuse your gifts.'

The old scribe was highly indignant. 'Why is that?'

'Attempted corruption.'

'Nothing could not be further from our thoughts. I pray you, do us the honour of accepting them.'

'Take these gifts away and give them to your most deserving servants.'

Nenophar decided it was time she intervened. 'Judge of the Porch, we seek proper respect for Egypt's traditional society and values.'

'In that, you will find an ally in me.'

Reassured, she spoke warmly. 'Without any proper cause, Bel-Tran has abolished my honorary post as scrutineer of the Treasury, and is preparing to do similar harm to many members of the most respected families in Memphis. He is attacking our customs and our ancient privileges. We ask you to take action to stop this persecution.'

Pazair read out a passage from the Rule:

> *'You who judge, make no distinction between a rich man and a man of the people. Pay no attention to fine clothes, and do not disdain those who dress simply because of their modest resources. Accept no gifts from the man who possesses much, and be not prejudiced against the weak man or in his favour. Thus the country will have a solid foundation if you concern yourself only with the laws when handing down your sentence.'*

Although everyone knew these precepts, they still caused a stir.

'What does this reminder mean?' asked Nenophar in surprise.

'That I am fully aware of the situation and that I approve of what Bel-Tran is doing. Your "privileges" are hardly ancient, since they date only from the first years of Ramses' reign.'

'Are you daring to criticize what the king did?'

'He would urge you, as nobles, to take on new duties, not to derive profit from a title. The tjaty has made no objections to Bel-Tran's reorganization of the government secretariats. The early results are encouraging.'

'Surely you aren't hoping to impoverish the nobility?'

'No, I hope to give it back its true greatness, so that it may serve as an example to others.'

Bagey the rigorous, Bel-Tran the ambitious, Pazair the idealistic: Nenophar shuddered at the thought that these three were allies. Fortunately, the old tjaty would soon retire, the ambitious jackal would break his long teeth on a stone, and the honest judge would sooner or later succumb to temptation.

'Enough of this preaching,' she said. 'Which side are you taking?'

'Have I not made that clear?'

'No senior official has ever built a successful career without our cooperation.'

'Then I must resign myself to being the exception.'

'You will fail.'

Tapeni was insatiable. She did not have Panther's inimitable fervour, but she showed splendid imagination both in positions and in caresses. So as not to disappoint her, Suti was obliged to follow – and even anticipate – her initiatives. Tapeni felt a deep affection for the young man, for whom she reserved treasures of love. Brown-skinned, small, and highly excitable, she practised the art of the kiss, sometimes with refinement, sometimes with violence.

Fortunately, she was equally occupied with her work. Suti was grateful for the resulting periods of rest, which he used to reassure Panther and prove to her that his passion was undimmed.

After their latest bout of love-making, Tapeni put on her dress, and Suti adjusted his kilt.

'You're a very handsome man and a lusty stallion,' she purred.

'"Leaping gazelle" would suit you.'

'Poetry bores me, but your virility fascinates me.'

'And you know how to speak to it persuasively. But we've rather lost sight of the reason for my first visit.'

'The mother-of-pearl needle?'

'The very same.'

'Something as beautiful, rare and precious as that would only be handled by women of quality: the most highly skilled weavers.'

'Do you have a list of them?'

'Of course.'

'Will you let me have it?'

'Those women are my rivals. You're asking too much.'

Suti had been afraid she'd say something like that. 'How can I persuade you?'

'You're the man I've always wanted. In the evening, and at night, I miss you. I have to make love to myself while I think of you. This pain is becoming unbearable.'

'I could let you have one night, from time to time.'

'I want all your nights.'

'You mean you want—'

'Marriage, my darling.'

'I'm rather against the idea, on principle.'

'You'll have to give up your mistresses, get rich, live with me, wait for me, always be ready to satisfy my wildest desires.'

'There are more painful duties.'

'We shall make our union official next week.'

Suti did not protest; he would find a way of escaping this slavery. 'What about the weavers?'

Tapeni simpered. 'Have I your word?'

'I have only one.'

'Is this information really so important?'

'For me, yes. But if you refuse . . .'

She gripped his arm. 'Don't be angry.'

'You're torturing me.'

'I'm teasing you. Few noble ladies know how to use those types of needle perfectly and steadily, with the nimbleness and precision required. I have seen only three: the wife of the former overseer of canals is the best.'

'Where can I find her?'

'She is eighty years old, and she lives on the island of Elephantine, near Egypt's southern border.'

Suti frowned. 'What about the other two?'

'The widow of the director of granaries is small and frail. She used to be incredibly strong, but she broke her arm two years ago, and—'

'And the third?'

'Her favourite pupil who, despite her wealth, continues to make most of her dresses herself: the lady Nenophar.'

15

The hearing was due to begin halfway through the morning. Although he had still not found Killer, Kem had agreed to attend.

At daybreak, Pazair inspected the porch to which destiny had called him. Confronting Mentmose would not be easy: the commander might have been pushed into a corner, but he would not let himself be trussed up like a frightened hen. The judge was anxious that he might have to deal with a vicious reaction, typical of a high official who was ready to trample others underfoot to maintain his standing.

Pazair left the porch and gazed at the temple it backed on to. Behind the high walls experts in divine energy were working; although aware of human weaknesses, they refused to accept them as inevitable. Man was clay and straw; God alone built houses of eternity where the forces of creation dwelt, inaccessible for ever and yet present in the humblest flint. Without the temple, justice would have been no more than petty annoyances, the settling of accounts, domination by one caste; thanks to it, Ma'at held the tiller of the ship and watched over the weighing-scales. No individual could own the justice system; only Ma'at, whose body was as light as an ostrich-feather, knew the weight of deeds. It was the judges' task to serve her with all the love a child feels for its mother.

Mentmose suddenly loomed out of the fading darkness. Pazair, chilly despite the time of year, had thrown a woollen cape round his shoulders; the commander was content with a heavy robe, which he wore haughtily. At his belt hung a short-handled dagger with a slender blade. His eyes were cold.

Pazair said, 'You are up and about very early.'

'I have no intention of playing the role of the accused.'

'I have called you solely as a witness.'

'Your plan is simple: to crush me beneath more or less imaginary misdeeds. I remind you that, like you, I apply the law.'

'While forgetting to apply it to yourself.'

'An investigation cannot always be carried out with absolute virtue. Sometimes one has to get one's hands dirty.'

'Have you perhaps forgotten to wash them?'

'The time for moralizing is past. I warn you, do not choose a dangerous Nubian criminal over the commander of the guards.'

'There is no inequality in the eyes of the law: I have sworn an oath to that effect.'

'Who do you think you are, Pazair?'

'An Egyptian judge.'

Those words were spoken with such power and gravity that they shook Mentmose. He had had the misfortune to come up against a judge from ancient times, one of those men depicted on carved panels dating from the golden age of the pyramids, with their upright stance, respect for righteousness, love of truth and imperviousness to blame and praise alike. After so many years spent in the labyrinthine ways of high government, Mentmose had been convinced that that race of men would die once and for all with Tjaty Bagey. Alas, like a weed once thought destroyed, it had been reborn with Pazair.

'Why are you persecuting me?' he asked.

'You are not an innocent victim.'

'I was used and manipulated.'

'By whom?'

'I don't know.'

'Well, Mentmose! You're the best-informed man in Egypt, and you're trying to tell me that someone even more cunning than yourself wove the web that entrapped you?'

'If you want the truth, yes, that's it. You can see that it doesn't make me look good.'

'I'm still not convinced.'

'You should be. I know nothing about the reason for the honour-guard's deaths or about the theft of the sky-iron. Branir's murder gave me an opportunity – through that anonymous accusation – to get rid of you. I didn't hesitate, because I hate you. I hate your intelligence, your will to win through whatever the cost, your refusal to compromise. One day you would have attacked me. My last chance was Kem; if you'd accepted him as a scapegoat, we could have reached a truce.'

'Is your false eye-witness not the puppet-master, then?'

Mentmose scratched his head. 'There's certainly a conspiracy, and General Asher is the brains behind it, but I haven't been able to disentangle the threads. You and I have common enemies. Why don't we become allies?'

Pazair's silence seemed to augur well.

'Your obstinacy won't last long,' declared Mentmose. 'It has enabled you to climb high in the legal establishment, but don't play on it any more. I know life; take my advice, and you'll do well.'

'I'm thinking.'

'About time! I am prepared to put aside my hatred and regard you as a friend.'

'If you aren't at the centre of the conspiracy,' said Pazair pensively, 'it's much more serious than I realized.'

Mentmose was taken aback. He had hoped for a very different reaction.

'The name of your false witness is becoming an absolutely vital piece of evidence.'

'Don't insist on knowing it.'

'Then you will fall alone, Mentmose.'

'Would you dare accuse me —'

'Of conspiring against the safety of the state.'

'The jurors will never follow you!'

'We shall see. There are enough grievances to alert them.'

'If I give you the name, will you leave me in peace?'

'No.'

'You're mad!'

'I shall not give in to blackmail.'

'In that case, I have no further interest in talking to you.'

'As you wish. I shall see you later, in court.'

Mentmose's fingers tightened round the hilt of his dagger. For the first time in his career, he felt caught in a hunter's net. 'What future have you in mind for me?'

'The one you have chosen for yourself.'

'You are an excellent judge, I am a good officer. A mistake can be set right.'

'What is the false witness's name?'

Mentmose was not prepared to be disgraced alone. 'Qadash the tooth-doctor.' He watched for Pazair's reaction, but the judge said nothing so Mentmose was reluctant to leave. 'Qadash,' he repeated.

He turned on his heel, hoping the revelation would save him. He had not noticed an attentive witness, whose red eyes had not left him for a moment. Killer, perched on the roof of the porch, looked like a statue of the god Thoth. Seated, with his hands laid flat on his knees, he seemed to be meditating.

Pazair knew Mentmose had not lied. If he had, the baboon would have hurled itself on him.

The judge called to Killer. The baboon hesitated, then slid down the length of a column, landed in front of Pazair and held out its hand.

When it was reunited with Kem, the animal flung its arms round his neck and the man wept for joy.

*

Pazair could not help brooding. Surely Mentmose's confession proved that, since the very first days of his investigation in Memphis, Pazair had been drawn to one of the damned souls in the conspiracy? Qadash had not hesitated to bribe Mentmose in order to send the judge to prison. Caught in a dizzy spiral, the Judge of the Porch asked himself whether he might not be the instrument of a superior will, which was carving out its own path and forcing him to follow it, whatever happened.

Qadash's guilt led him to ask himself questions he must not answer hurriedly or without proof. A strange, sometimes unbearable, fire tormented him; in his haste to discover the truth, was he risking destroying it by burning his bridges?

Neferet decided to drag him away from his office and his cases. Paying no heed to his protests, she took him into the smiling solitude of the countryside.

A flock of quail flew over the fields and came down in the corn. Tired after a long migration, the leading bird had not seen the danger. Lying flat on their bellies on the ground, a group of hunters deployed a net with small mesh, while their assistants shook pieces of cloth to frighten the birds. They succeeded: the birds were captured in great numbers, to be roasted and enjoyed on the very best dinner-tables.

Pazair did not enjoy the sight. To see a creature, even a simple quail, deprived of liberty caused him real pain.

Neferet, who could sense every change in his mood, led him further into the countryside. They walked to a lake with calm waters, surrounded by sycamores and tamarisks, which a Theban king had created for his Great Royal Wife. According to legend, the goddess Hathor came to bathe there at sunset. Neferet hoped the sight of this paradise would bring the judge peace.

Her hopes were not realized.

'I'm wasting precious time,' complained Pazair.

'Is my company such a burden?'

'No, of course not. Forgive me.'

'You need some rest.'

'Qadash gives us the link to Sheshi and so to General Asher, hence to the murder of the honour-guard, and doubtless to Denes and his wife. The conspirators are among the highest dignitaries in the country. They want to seize power by creating a military plot and ensuring that only they have use of the new weapons. That's why they killed Branir, who would have allowed me to investigate the theft of the sky-iron from the temples. That's why they tried to kill me by accusing me of my master's murder. The affair is enormous, Neferet. And yet . . . I'm not sure that I'm right. I sometimes doubt my own words.'

She guided him along a path beside the lake. It was the middle of the afternoon, and the heat was overwhelming, so the peasants were dozing in the shade of the trees or huts.

Neferet knelt down on the bank and picked a lotus-bud, which she put in her hair. A silvery fish with a plump belly leapt out of the water and vanished in a shower of sparkling droplets. She waded into the water; once wet, her linen dress stuck to her and revealed her shapely form. She dived and swam with lithe grace, laughing as her hands followed the zigzag movement of a carp swimming ahead of her. When she emerged, her scent was intoxicating, heightened by her bathe.

'Won't you join me?' she asked.

Looking at her was so wonderful that Pazair had forgotten to move. He slipped out of his kilt while she took off her robe. Naked and entwined, they slid into a papyrus thicket, where they made love, aglow with happiness.

Neferet received a summons from Nebamon, and decided to obey it. Pazair was strongly opposed to her going: why should Nebamon summon her, if not to spring a trap and take his revenge? But she was adamant, and the best he could do was tell Kem and Killer to follow her, to ensure her safety. The baboon would slip into Nebamon's garden; if there was any threat to Neferet, it would take instant action.

Neferet was not in the least afraid. On the contrary, she was glad to know her worst enemy's intentions. Despite Pazair's misgivings, she had accepted Nebamon's condition that it be a private conversation between the two of them.

Nebamon's gate-keeper allowed the young woman to pass, and she set off along an avenue of tamarisks, whose many intertwined branches touched the ground; their fruit, with its long, sugary hairs, had to be gathered in the dew and dried in the sun. With the wood, valuable coffins could be made, similar to Osiris's, as well as staves to drive away the enemies of light. Surprised by the abnormal silence reigning over the vast estate, Neferet suddenly regretted not arming herself with such a stave.

Not a single gardener, not one water-bearer or servant ... The surroundings of the sumptuous house were deserted. Hesitating, Neferet crossed the threshold. The vast room reserved for visitors was cool, well ventilated, dimly lit by a few rays of light.

'Nebamon? I am here,' she called.

There was no answer. The house seemed abandoned. Had Nebamon returned to the city, forgetting his meeting? Uneasily, she began to look around the private apartments.

She found Nebamon lying asleep on his back in his large bed. The bedchamber's walls were decorated with ducks in flight and egrets at rest. His face was hollow-cheeked, his breathing shallow and irregular.

'I am here,' she repeated softly.

Nebamon awoke. Incredulous, he rubbed his eyes and sat up. 'You dared . . . I would never have believed it.'

'Are you really so formidable?'

He gazed at her slender form. 'I used to be. I longed for Pazair's death and your ruin. Knowing you were happy together tortured me; I wanted you at my feet, poor, begging for mercy. Your happiness destroyed mine. Why hadn't I been able to seduce you? So many others gave in – but you aren't like them.'

Nebamon looked much older, and his voice, once famous for its languorous inflexions, was halting.

'What is wrong with you? Are you ill?' asked Neferet.

'I am a wretched host. Would you like to try my pyramid-cakes stuffed with date preserve?'

'Thank you, but I'm not hungry.'

'And yet you love life and give yourself to it unstintingly. We would have made a splendid couple. Pazair is no match for you – you know that. He won't be Judge of the Porch for long, and you will seek a wealthy man instead.'

'Wealth isn't essential.'

'It is: a poor doctor cannot have a successful career.'

'And do your riches protect you from illness and pain?'

'I have a growth in one of my veins.'

'That isn't incurable. To ease the pain, I prescribe applications of sycamore-juice, extracted from the tree in early spring, before it bears its fruit.'

Nebamon nodded. 'An excellent prescription. You know the remedies for many infirmities, don't you?'

'But, in addition, you must have an operation. I shall create an incision with a sharpened reed, remove the tumour by heating it with fire, and cauterize the wound.'

'You'd be right so to do, if I were strong enough to withstand the operation.'

'Have you grown so very weak?'

'My days are numbered. That's why I have sent away those close to me and my servants. They all bore me. There must be turmoil at the palace. No one will take any decisions in my absence – the dolts who obey me so slavishly won't know which foot to put forward first. What a miserable farce! But seeing you again brightens my last days.'

'May I sound you?'

'Please do as you wish.'

She listened to the voice of his heart, which was weak and irregular. Nebamon was not lying: he was gravely ill. He remained motionless, breathing in Neferet's scent, savouring the gentleness of her hand on his skin, the softness of her ear on his chest. He would have traded his eternal life if only these moments could never end. But he no longer possessed such a treasure; the soul-eater was waiting for him at the foot of the scales of judgement.

Neferet straightened up and stepped back. 'Who is treating you?'

'I'm treating myself. I am, after all, the most respected doctor in the kingdom of Egypt.'

'What method are you using?'

'Contempt. I hate and despise myself because I cannot make you love me. My life was a series of successes – and of lies and shameful behaviour. I miss your face, the passion that should have brought you to me. I am dying from the lack of you.'

'I cannot leave you here alone.'

'Don't hesitate for a moment. Make the most of your good fortune. If I recovered, I'd become a brute again, and would never stop trying to kill Pazair and possess you.'

'A sick man deserves to be treated.'

'Will you do it?'

'There are other doctors in Memphis.'

'It must be you, no one else.'

'Don't be childish,' said Neferet firmly.

'Would you have loved me, if it hadn't been for Pazair?'

'You know the answer to that.'

'Lie to me, please!'

'I'll see that your servants come back this very evening. For now, I prescribe a light diet.'

Nebamon sat up. 'I swear to you that I took no part in any of the conspiracies your husband is investigating. I know nothing about the murder of Branir, the deaths of the honour-guard or General Asher's machinations. All I wanted was to send Pazair to prison and force you to become my wife. As long as I live, I shall have no other ambition.'

'You ought to give up chasing the impossible.'

'The wind will change, I'm sure of it.'

16

Panther was radiant as she caressed Suti's chest. He had made love to her with all the energy of a rising flood so potent that its tide sought to drown the mountains.

'Why are you so gloomy?' she asked.

'Oh, it's nothing important.'

'There are a lot of rumours flying round the town.'

'What about?'

'Ramses' luck. Some people claim it has turned. Last month there was a fire at the docks, there have been several accidents on the river, and some acacia trees were split in two by lightning.'

'Those are just trivial things.'

'Not for your fellow-countrymen,' said Panther. 'They're convinced that Pharaoh's magical power has run out.'

'So what? He'll celebrate a festival of regeneration, and the people will shout for joy.'

'What is he waiting for?'

'Ramses has an instinct for doing the right thing at the right time.'

'And what about your worries?'

'I told you, they aren't important.'

'It's to do with a woman, isn't it?'

'No, my investigation.'

'What does she want?'

'I've got to—'

'Marry her, with a proper contract! In other words, you're casting me off!' Hysterical, Panther leapt off the bed. She vented her rage by smashing several terracotta bowls and tearing apart a straw-seated chair.

'What's she like?' she demanded. 'Tall, short, young, old?'

'Small, with very dark hair – she isn't nearly as beautiful as you.'

'Is she rich?'

'Of course.'

'I'm not good enough for you – I have no money. You don't enjoy your Libyan whore any more, so you're turning respectable with your rich brunette!'

'I have to get some information out of her,' said Suti.

'And that means you have to get married?'

'It's only a formality.'

'And what about me?'

'Be patient for a little while. As soon as I've got what I want, I shall get a divorce.'

'And how will she take that?'

'For her this marriage is merely a whim. She'll soon forget me.'

'Don't do it, Suti. You're making a huge mistake.'

'I've got to do it.'

'Stop doing what Pazair wants!'

'The marriage contract has already been signed.'

Pazair, Judge of the Porch, the most senior judge in Memphis, whose moral authority was incontestable, was sulking like a thwarted child. He could not accept the efforts Neferet had made to help Nebamon. She had asked help from several other doctors, who had gone to the sick man's bedside, brought back his servants to the estate, and ensured that he was cared for and had people around him.

Pazair furiously resented all this. 'We shouldn't help our enemies,' he growled.

'How can a judge say such a thing?'

'He must.'

'I'm a doctor.'

'That monster tried to destroy both of us.'

'But he failed,' said Neferet. 'And now he's destroying himself, from the inside.'

'His illness does not wipe out his crimes.'

'You're right: it doesn't.'

'If you admit that, have nothing more to do with him.'

'I don't think about him at all, but I had to do my duty as a doctor.'

Pazair's grim expression relaxed a little.

'Surely you're not jealous?' she asked, smiling.

He drew her towards him. 'No one in the world is more jealous than I am.'

'Will you give me permission to treat a patient other than my husband?'

'If the law allowed me to, I'd forbid it.'

Brave, who had been watching them anxiously – any disagreement between his master and mistress made him unhappy – sat up on his haunches and offered his right paw to Neferet and his left to Pazair.

His acrobatic pose made them burst out laughing, and, reassured, the dog joined in with joyful barking.

In a towering rage, Suti pushed his way between two scribes, their arms full of papyri, barged into a clerk, and flung open the door of Pazair's office. He found the judge drinking a cup of copper-water.

Pazair took one look at his friend's dishevelled long black hair and asked, 'Is something wrong?'

'Yes, you!'

The judge got up and closed the door; there were fierce storms ahead. He said, 'Perhaps we should discuss this somewhere else.'

'Absolutely not! This place is precisely the reason I'm angry.'

'Why? Has it done you an injustice?'

'You've been sucked into the system, Pazair! You've swallowed the bait of titles and respectability. Look around you: petty scribes, narrow-minded officials, little minds preoccupied with their own advancement. You've forgotten our friendship, you're neglecting the investigation into General Asher, you've given up trying to find the truth – you're acting as though you don't believe me any more. But I tell you again, I saw Asher torture and kill an Egyptian, I know he's a traitor – and here you are, parading around like a courtier!'

'You've been drinking.'

'Bad beer, and far too much of it. I needed it. No one dares talk to you the way I do.'

'Subtlety isn't your strong point,' said Pazair, 'but I never thought you were stupid.'

'Don't insult me as well! Deny it if you can.'

'Sit down.'

'I won't be patronized!'

'Let's at least call a truce.'

Swaying slightly, Suti managed to sit down without losing his balance. 'It's no use trying to sweet-talk me. I've seen right through your game.'

'Then you're lucky. I've lost my way.'

Astonished, Suti blinked at him. 'What do you mean?'

'Take a closer look: I'm overwhelmed with work. In my district of Memphis, as a junior judge, I had a little time for investigation. Here, I have to answer a hundred pleas, deal with hordes of cases, calm the anger of some people and the impatience of others.'

'There you are, that's it, the trap. Resign, and follow me.'

'What are you planning to do?'

'To wring Asher's neck and cure Egypt of the sickness eating away at her.'

'You won't manage to cure Egypt.'

'Of course I will! If you kill the head of the conspiracy, there'll be no more sedition.'

'And what about Branir's murderer?'

Suti smiled ferociously. 'I was a good investigator, but I had to marry Tapeni.'

'I'm grateful for your sacrifice.'

'If I hadn't, she wouldn't have told me anything.'

'So now you're rich.'

'Panther's taken it badly.'

'A seducer like you should be able to cope with that.'

'Me, married! It's worse than a prison. As soon as possible, I'm getting a divorce.'

'Did the ceremony go well?'

'It took place in the strictest privacy – she didn't want anyone there at all. In bed she's uncontrollable, treats me like an inexhaustible sweetmeat.'

'And what about your investigation?'

'Only a few high-born weavers use the type of needle that killed Branir. Of them, the most skilled and the most remarkable is Nenophar. Her post as Treasury scrutineer may have been only honorary, but she's still steward of fabrics and she knows the craft extremely well.'

Nenophar. She was married to Denes the ship-owner, the bitterest enemy of Bel-Tran, Pazair's greatest supporter. And yet, as a member of the jury during the Asher case, she had not censured Pazair. Once again, the judge felt wrong-footed. Her guilt seemed evident, but his belief was not strengthened.

'Arrest her at once,' advised Suti.

'I can't. We've no proof.'

'The same as with Asher! Why do you always refuse to accept the evidence?'

'I don't, but the court would. To recognize a person as guilty of murder, the jurors require a flawless case.'

'But I married Tapeni to get you this information!'

'Try to get more.'

'You're getting more and more demanding, and you're losing yourself in a maze of laws which stop you facing reality. You won't accept the truth: that Asher is a traitor and a criminal who's trying to gain control of the Asian army, and that Nenophar murdered your master.'

'If that's true, why hasn't Asher made his move?'

'Because he's still stationing his men in the protectorates and in Egypt itself. As instructor to the Asian officers, he's creating a clan of scribes and soldiers who are devoted to him. Soon, with the help of his friend Sheshi, he'll have access to unbreakable weapons, and they'll enable him to face any army in the world without fear of defeat. Whoever controls those weapons will be able to govern the country.'

Pazair still wasn't convinced. 'If Asher tried to seize the throne, he'd never succeed.'

'This isn't the golden age, it's the reign of Ramses II. In our provinces, there are thousands of foreigners, and our dear compatriots think more about getting rich than about pleasing the gods. The old morality is dead.'

'Perhaps, but the person of Pharaoh is still sacred. Asher does not have that stature. No clan would support him – the whole country would reject him.'

That argument won the day. Suti admitted that his reasoning, although cogent for an Asian country, did not work for the Egypt of Ramses. A faction, even one with invincible weapons, could not force the temples – still less the people – to accept it. To govern the Two Lands, force was not enough. It required a magical being who could make a pact with the gods and cause a love of the afterlife to shine forth on earth. Laughable words to the ears of a Greek, a Libyan or a Syrian, but essential to those of an Egyptian; whatever his abilities as a strategist and plotter, Asher did not have those particular qualities.

'It's strange,' observed Pazair. 'We had three suspects in the murder of Branir: the exiled Judge of the Porch, who is dying of starvation; Nebamon, who has been struck down by a serious illness; and Mentmose, who's standing right at the edge of the abyss. Any one of them could have written the message summoning me to my master, and then set up the charade intended to incriminate me. And now you've added Nenophar to the list. The old judge seems unlikely: his behaviour was that of a worn-out, weak man, broken by his own compromises. Nebamon swore to Neferet that he was not involved in a conspiracy. And Mentmose, who's usually so skilful and sure of himself, now seems like a puppet, rather than the puppet-master. If we've been so utterly deceived by those three, surely we shouldn't be too hasty when it comes to Nenophar?'

'There it is, your conspiracy! Asher isn't content with his chosen soldiers. He needs support from the nobility and the rich, and he's got it from Nenophar and Denes, the wealthiest traders in Memphis. With their fortune, he'll be able to buy silence, consciences and cooperation. There are two brains behind this affair.'

'But Denes organized the banquet to celebrate my investiture.'

'Maybe so, but didn't he once try to buy you, too? When he failed, he fabricated a story which suited him. You became Branir's murderer, and Qadash became a witness to the murder so as to get rid of your faithful guard, Kem, once and for all.'

This time, despite Suti's drunkenness, Pazair found his reasoning persuasive. 'If you're right,' he said thoughtfully, 'our enemies are even more numerous and more powerful than we thought. Could Denes ever attain the stature of a pharaoh?'

'Of course not! He's much too full of himself, and he doesn't care in the least about other people. He's also too short-sighted: he can't see beyond his money and his own interests. Nenophar, on the other hand, is much more formidable than she seems. I think she might well be capable of establishing a regency. We aren't dreaming, Judge of the Porch! Five dead ex-soldiers, Branir's murder, several other murder attempts – Egypt hasn't known disruption like this for a lifespan. Your investigation is alarming people. You've got power, so use it. Your administrative chores can wait.'

'No, because they guarantee the country's stability and the people's daily happiness.'

'If the conspiracy succeeds, how much of all that will be left?'

Pazair grew tense as he thought about it. He stood up. 'Inactivity weighs you down, doesn't it?'

'A hero needs to do brave deeds.'

'Are you ready to face danger?'

'As ready as you are. I want to be there when Asher gets the punishment he deserves.'

Silkis's colic had reached alarming proportions. Fearing it might be dysentery, Bel-Tran had himself fetched Neferet to her in the middle of the night. The doctor gave the sick woman fragrant dill seeds; their sedative and digestive properties would ease the spasms. Used in an ointment, added to bryony and coriander, they relieved migraines. The fine umbelliferous plant with the yellow flowers would not be enough on its own, so painful was the diarrhoea; every quarter of an hour, therefore, Neferet made Silkis drink a full cup of carob-beer, made from the pods mixed with oil and honey. After only an hour of this treatment, Silkis's symptoms began to ease.

'You're a marvel,' she breathed.

Neferet smiled. 'Don't worry. You'll be better by tomorrow. Drink carob-beer for one week.'

'Are there likely to be any complications?'

'No. It was a simple case of food poisoning, though it might have become serious if not properly treated. For a few days, you must eat only cereals.'

Bel-Tran thanked Neferet warmly, then led her to one side. 'Is that true, or were you just reassuring her?'

'Don't worry, it's true.'

He thanked her again, and said, 'You must be tired. Won't you sit down and have something to eat?'

Neferet was glad of this short rest before another long day spent visiting more patients, both rich and poor. It would soon be dawn, so there was no point trying to go back to sleep.

'Since I entered the Treasury,' said Bel-Tran, 'I've suffered from terrible insomnia. While Silkis is asleep I work on the next day's files. Sometimes such a painful lump forms in the pit of my stomach that I'm almost paralyzed.'

'You're wearing yourself out with nervous strain.'

'The Double House never lets me rest. I accept what you say, Neferet, but isn't the same thing true of you? You run from one place to another, all over town, and you never refuse a request for help. You really belong elsewhere. The palace has no doctors of your skill and quality. By surrounding himself with second-rate ones, Nebamon created a void around himself. He drove you out of the doctors' organization because he was jealous of your skill.'

'The court's principal doctor decides on appointments – neither you nor I can do anything about them.'

'You cured the tjaty and several other important people. I shall gather their statements and present them to the doctors in charge of maintaining discipline. Even the stupidest of them will have to recognize your talent.'

'I have no stomach for a fight like that.'

'Pazair, as Judge of the Porch, can't intervene in your favour because he'd be accused of partiality. But I can. And I shall – I'll fight for you.'

Thebes was in uproar. The greatest city of southern Egypt, guardian of the country's most ancient traditions, was hostile to innovations which its northern rival, Memphis, accepted with too much readiness. Now Thebes was impatiently awaiting the announcement of the name of the new High Priest of Amon. He would reign over more than eighty thousand employees, sixty-five towns and villages, a million men and women working more or less directly for the temple, four hundred head of livestock, four hundred and fifty vineyards and orchards, and ninety ships. It was Pharaoh's task to supply the ritual objects – food, oil, incense, precious ointments and clothing – and to bestow gifts of land whose ownership would be marked with large stelae set at the edges of the fields, one at each corner. It was the High Priest's task to levy taxes on merchandise and on fishermen.

The High Priest ruled a state within a state; so the king must appoint a man whose fidelity and obedience to him were absolute, yet who was by no means an empty-headed person who lacked authority. Branir would have been a man of that stamp; his murder had put Ramses in a quandary. The day before the new High Priest's enthronement was due, his choice was still not known.

Pazair and Suti had gone to the temple at Karnak out of both curiosity and necessity. The High Priest of Ptah in Memphis had been consulted, but could provide no information about the theft of the sky-iron. The precious metal must originally have come from a Southern temple; only the High Priest of Amon could set the investigators on the right track. But what kind of person would Pazair be facing?

As Judge of the Porch, Pazair was admitted to the landing-stage, along with Suti, whom he presented as his assistant. A host of boats occupied the lake that had been created between the Nile and the temple; rows of trees kept the air cool.

The two friends, led by a priest, walked past the human-headed sphinx, whose eyes drove away unbelievers. Before each of these watchful guards, an irrigation channel carried the water to a ditch, about a cubit deep, where flowers grew. So the sacred way, leading from the outside world to the temple, was adorned with the most vivid, shimmering colours.

Pazair and Suti were allowed into the first great courtyard, where shaven-headed priests in linen robes were garlanding the altars with flowers. Whatever else might happen, worship must continue. The pure ones, the divine fathers, the servants of the god, the masters of the secrets, the enacters of rituals, the star-watchers and musicians were all attending to their occupations, which had been fixed by the Rule that had been in operation since the time of the pyramids. Only a few of these people lived permanently within the temple complex; the others officiated there for periods ranging from a week to three months. Twice a day and twice a night they carried out their ablutions, believing that inner purity must be accompanied by impeccable physical cleanliness.

The two friends sat down on a stone bench. The calm majesty of the place, the profound peace inscribed within the stones of eternity, made them forget their cares and questions. Here, life – delivered from the erosion of time – took on a different taste. Even Suti, who did not believe in the gods, felt his soul fulfilled.

The new High Priest of Amon received the insignia of his office from the king: a gold cane and two rings. Henceforth in charge of the wealthiest and largest of all Egypt's temples, he would see that its treasures were preserved. Each morning, he would open the double doors of the secret shrine, the region of light where Amon regenerated in the mystery of the East. He had taken an oath to observe the ritual, to ensure that offerings were replenished, and to take care of the divine dwelling where the creation of the first moments was kept in balance. Tomorrow, he would think about his many staff, including the head of his household, a head steward, scribes, secretaries and team-leaders; tomorrow, he would regret losing the tranquil life from which Pharaoh's decision had torn him away. In this most intense of moments, he thought about the main precept of the Rule:

Do not raise your voice in the temple: God detests shouting. May your heart be loving. Do not question God, wrongly or indirectly, for he loves silence. The silent one is like the tree that grows in the orchard: its fruits are sweet, its shade is agreeable, it grows green and ends its days in the orchard where it was born.

The High Priest meditated for a long time in the holy of holies, alone facing the innermost shrine which contained the god's statue. Never had he hoped to experience such an emotion, reducing to nothing his aspirations of yesterday and his derisory hopes. The robe of the First Servant of Amon stripped him of his humanity and made him a stranger to his own eyes. That mattered little, since he would no longer have the leisure to wonder about his own tastes or doubts.

The High Priest withdrew, walking backwards and wiping away his footprints. As soon as he had left the holy of holies, he would return to confront the universe of the temple.

Cheers greeted the appearance of the new High Priest on the threshold of the immense pillared hall built by Ramses. From now on, it would fall to him to open the way with his gold staff and to lead a peaceful army, devoted to the glory of Amon.

Pazair stared. 'That's incredible.'

'Do you know him?' asked Suti.

'It's Kani, the gardener.'

17

When the dignitaries paid him homage in the great courtyard, Kani halted for a long time in front of Pazair. The judge bowed. As their eyes met, the two men shared the same profound joy.

'I should like to consult you at the earliest opportunity,' said Pazair.

'You may come to see me this evening,' promised Kani.

The High Priest's palace, which stood close to the temple entrance, was an architectural and decorative marvel. The beauty of the paintings enchanted the eye, glorifying the presence of the gods in nature. Kani received Pazair in his private study, which was already full to overflowing with papyri.

They greeted each other with a warm embrace.

'I am very happy for Egypt,' said Pazair.

'I pray that you're right to be. The office I now hold was meant for Branir. He was a sage among sages – who can equal him? I shall honour his memory each morning, and offerings will be made to his statue, which has been erected inside the temple.'

'Ramses has chosen well.'

'I love this place, it is true, as if I'd always lived here. It's thanks to you that I'm here.'

'I did very little.'

'Perhaps,' said Kani, 'but your influence was decisive. However, I can tell that you're worried.'

'My investigation is proving to be extremely difficult.'

'How can I help you?'

'I should like to make inquiries in the temple at Kebet, to try to discover the origin of the sky-iron that was delivered to Sheshi the inventor, General Asher's accomplice. To implicate the first and prove the second's guilt, I must follow the trail back. Without your permission, that would be impossible.'

'Might priests be the criminals' accomplices?'

'It cannot be ruled out.'

'We shall not shirk our responsibilities. Give me one week.'

Pazair stayed in a little house beside the sacred lake of Karnak, and took part in the rites as a 'pure priest', his entire body shaven. Each day he wrote to Neferet, praising the splendour and peace of the temple. Suti, who would not sacrifice his long hair, took refuge with a lady friend he had encountered at a naval tournament. She was not yet married, and dreamt of Memphis; he devoted body and soul to entertaining her.

On the agreed day, the High Priest received the two friends in his audience chamber. Kani had already changed. Although his features were still those of the former gardener who specialized in medicinal plants, his face sunburnt and deeply lined, his bearing had become regal. In choosing him, Ramses had detected the humble man's great authority. He would need little time to adapt; already, in just a few days, Kani had become imbued with the majesty of his office.

Pazair introduced Suti, who was ill at ease in this austere place.

'It is indeed at Kebet that you must investigate,' said Kani. 'The experts in precious metals and rare minerals are answerable to the High Priest of the temple there. He was a miner before becoming a desert guard and then a priest, and if anyone can enlighten you as to the origin of this sky-iron, he can. Kebet is the departure-point for all the great expeditions to the mines and quarries, and he also has special responsibility for the gold road.'

'Is it possible that he himself might be implicated?' asked Pazair.

'According to the reports I've received, no. He both oversees and is overseen, and takes charge of deliveries of precious metals to all the temples in Egypt. Not once has he acted incorrectly in twenty years. Nevertheless, I have drawn up a written order which will give you access to the temple archives. To my mind, the fraud is taking place elsewhere. Perhaps you should look among the miners and prospectors.'

A strong wind tousled Suti's black hair as he stood at the prow of the boat, sailing towards Memphis. He was still furious, and indignant at Pazair's calm demeanour.

'Kebet, the desert, the treasures of the sands – it's crazy!'

'With the document Kani gave me, I can search the temple at Kebet from top to bottom.'

'That's ridiculous. The thieves aren't stupid enough to have left traces of their crime.'

'Your point of view seems reasonable. So—'

'So we ought to act like heroes and set off on an adventure, along with some fearless fellows who wouldn't hesitate to kill their grandmothers for a pittance! A while ago the experience might have tempted me, but I'm married, and—'

Pazair laughed. 'You, a staid middle-class husband!'

'Well, yes, I'd like to enjoy the benefits of Tapeni's wealth for a little while, in exchange for my good and loyal services. Besides, didn't you ask me to get more information out of her while I hold her in my arms?'

'It's not like you to live at a woman's expense.'

'Send your Nubian friend, Kem.'

'He'd be identified straight away. I shall follow the trail myself.'

'You're mad! You wouldn't last two days.'

'I survived the prison camp.'

'The men who search for minerals are used to almost dying from thirst, to enduring the burning sun, and to fighting scorpions, snakes and wild animals. Forget this idiocy.'

'The truth is my profession, Suti.'

Neferet was called urgently to Nebamon's bedside. Although three doctors were permanently in attendance, the sick man had lapsed into a coma after calling for her. Way-Finder agreed to act as her mount; he set off at a good pace for Nebamon's house.

As soon as Neferet arrived, Nebamon recovered consciousness. He had pains in his stomach, arms and chest. 'A heart attack,' Neferet diagnosed. She laid her hand on his chest, and magnetized him until the pain eased. She heated a root of bryony in oil and completed the potion with acacia-leaves, figs and honey.

'You must drink this four times a day,' she told him.

'How long do I have left to live?'

'Your case is serious.'

'You cannot lie, Neferet. How long?'

'Only God is master of our destiny.'

'I'm not interested in fine words. I'm afraid of dying, and I want to know how many days I have left, so I can have whores brought to me, and can drink my wine.'

'That is your choice.'

Nebamon grasped her arm. 'I'm still lying, Neferet. It is you I want. Kiss me, I beg you. Once, just once.'

She freed herself, as gently as possible.

His face was dripping with sweat, his complexion waxy. 'The judgment of the afterlife will be a severe one. My life was second-rate, but I was happy to be leader of the most illustrious doctors in

Egypt. All I lacked was a woman, a real woman, who could have made me less evil. Before meeting Osiris, I shall help Pazair, the man who defeated me. Tell him that Qadash bought my testimony with amulets, exceptional pieces which his former steward deals in. To pay such a price, the matter must be enormous. Enormous.'

That was Nebamon's last word. He died drinking in Neferet with his eyes.

Pazair remembered Qadash's corrupt steward, who had in fact already been implicated in trafficking the precious objects of which his employer was so fond. A fine lapis-lazuli amulet could be exchanged for a whole basket of fresh fish. All people, the living and the dead alike, wanted this magical protection against the forces of darkness. Amulets – in the shape of an eye, a leg, a hand, a staircase to the heavens, tools, a lotus-flower or papyrus-stem, or bearing images of the gods – were receptacles for positive energy. Many Egyptians, irrespective of age or social class, gladly wore them round their necks, in direct contact with the skin.

Qadash was beginning to look more and more important, so Pazair instructed his staff to track down the tooth-doctor's former steward. The investigations soon brought results: the steward had obtained a similar post on a large estate in Middle Egypt. An estate which belonged to a close friend of Qadash, Denes the ship-owner.

At the weekly audience the tjaty granted to his close colleagues, many subjects were debated. Bagey liked concise comments and detested people who rambled; his own conclusions were brief and not open to discussion. One scribe wrote them down, while another transformed them into administrative decisions to which the tjaty added his seal.

'Have you anything further to say, Judge Pazair?' asked Bagey.

'Only that we need a new commander of the city guards. Mentmose is unworthy of his office. His misdeeds are too serious to be pardoned.'

The tjaty's secretary was highly indignant. 'But Mentmose has given great service to the country. He has always been extremely conscientious about maintaining law and order in the city.'

'The tjaty knows my reasons,' replied Pazair. 'Mentmose has lied, falsified evidence and made a mockery of the law. Only the former Judge of the Porch has been punished. Why should his accomplice go free?'

'The commander can hardly be expected to be an innocent little lamb!'

'That is enough,' cut in Bagey. 'The facts are known and established, and there are no ambiguities in the case. Read the charges, scribe.'

They were overwhelming. Without exaggerating them, Pazair had brought all Mentmose's crimes out into the light.

'Does anyone still wish Mentmose to remain in his post?' inquired the tjaty, when the scribe had finished.

Not one voice was raised in Mentmose's favour.

'Mentmose is dismissed,' decided Bagey. 'If he wishes to appeal he shall appear before me, and if he is again found guilty he will be sent to prison. Let us proceed immediately to the appointment of his successor. Whom do you propose?'

'Kem,' said Pazair in a steady voice.

'That's outrageous!' protested one of the scribes, and others followed his lead.

'Kem has a great deal of experience,' Pazair went on. 'He has suffered what he regards as injustice, but he has always remained on the side of law and order. True, he is not fond of the human race, but he carries out his duties as rigorously as a priest.'

'A Nubian of low birth, a—'

'A man with practical experience, and with no illusions. No one will ever corrupt him.'

The tjaty put an end to the argument: 'Kem is appointed commander of the city guards of Memphis. If anyone objects, he may present his arguments to my court. If I consider them inadmissible, he will be sentenced for slander. The audience is at an end.'

In the presence of the Judge of the Porch, Mentmose handed Kem the official seal of the guards' commander, the ivory staff, crowned with a hand and known as the 'Hand of Justice', that symbolized his authority, and a crescent-moon-shaped amulet engraved with an eye and a lion, emblems of vigilance. Despite his appointment, the Nubian had refused to trade his bow, arrows, sword and club for the garb of a leading citizen.

Kem did not thank Mentmose, who was on the verge of apoplexy. No speeches were made. The wary Nubian tested the seal immediately, in case his predecessor had falsified it.

'Are you satisfied?' demanded Mentmose, almost choking.

'I bear witness that the tjaty's degree has been observed,' replied Pazair serenely. 'As Judge of the Porch, I hereby register the transfer of offices.'

'It was you who persuaded Bagey to dismiss me!'

'The tjaty acted in accordance with his duty. It is your own misdeeds which condemn you.'

'You . . . I should have . . .' Before Mentmose dared utter the word searing his lips, Kem's glare silenced him.

'Making a death threat is a crime,' said Kem sternly.

'I haven't made anything of the sort.'

'Don't try to do anything against Judge Pazair. If you do, I shall deal with you.'

'Mentmose, your new duties await you,' said Pazair. 'You would do well to leave Memphis as soon as possible.'

Mentmose had been appointed overseer of the Delta fisheries. From now on he would live in a small coastal town where the only plots he could hatch would be to do with calculating the price of fish, according to size and weight.

He tried to think of a stinging retort, but the sight of the imposing Nubian took his breath away.

Kem put away the 'Hand of Justice' and his official amulet at the bottom of a wooden chest, underneath his collection of Asian daggers. Delegating the administrative tasks to scribes who were accustomed to such fastidious work, he closed the door of Mentmose's office behind him, resolutely determined to make only brief appearances there. The streets, the fields and nature were and would remain his preferred workplace: you couldn't arrest criminals by reading papyrus scrolls. Then, taking Killer with him, he left the office and joined Pazair at the Nile landing-stage, delighted to be travelling with him. Their boat sailed as soon as they were aboard.

They disembarked at Khmun, city of the god Thoth, master of sacred language. Riding donkeys bred specially to carry important people, they passed through beautiful, peaceful countryside. It was sowing time. After the flood had abated, the earth, enriched with fertile silt, was given over to the ploughs and hoes which broke up the lumps of earth; sometimes the ploughman would find a fish trapped in a small pool left by the receding floodwaters.

The seed-sowers, their necks and heads garlanded with flowers, cast seeds on to the soil from little papyrus-fibre bags. Sheep, oxen and pigs then trampled on the seeds, pushing them down into the soil. The rams led their flocks on to firm ground; the shepherds wielded leather thongs, which they cracked occasionally to bring stragglers back to the flock. Once covered over, the seed would make Egypt into a fertile, rich land, by means of an alchemical process which mirrored the death and resurrection of Osiris.

Denes's estate was absolutely enormous: no fewer than three villages served it. In the largest one, Pazair and Kem drank goats' milk and sampled creamy fermented milk, salted and preserved in jars. They spread it on slices of bread, and then added fine herbs. The peasants used alum from the Khargeh oasis to curdle the milk without making it sour and for making very popular cheeses.

Their appetites satisfied, the two men walked to Denes's huge farm, which was made up of several groups of buildings: grain-stores, a cellar, wine-press, stables, sheds for livestock, poultry yard, bakery, butchery and workshops. After washing their feet and hands, they asked to see the steward of the estate. A groom went to fetch him from the stable.

As soon as the steward spotted Pazair, he tried to run for it. Kem did not move, but Killer leapt forward and brought the fugitive down in the dust. He sank his teeth into the steward's back, and the steward at once stopped struggling. Kem decided that this position was quite suitable for a detailed interrogation.

'I'm glad to see you again,' said Pazair. 'But you seem frightened to see us.'

'Get that monkey off me!'

'Who engaged you?'

'Denes the ship-owner.'

'On Qadash's recommendation?'

The steward hesitated, and Killer's jaws tightened. 'Yes – *yes!*'

'So he didn't hold it against you that you'd stolen from him,' said Pazair thoughtfully. 'Of course, there may be a simple explanation for that: Denes, Qadash and you are accomplices. Perhaps you tried to run away because you're hiding incriminating evidence here on the farm. I have drawn up a search warrant, which takes immediate effect. Will you help us?'

'Judge,' gasped the steward, 'you're making a mistake.'

Kem would happily have let Killer make the steward talk, but Pazair preferred a less rough, more methodical solution. The steward was pulled to his feet, tied up and placed under the guard of several peasants. They hated him because he had been a tyrant to them, and were more than happy to cooperate with the judge. They told him the steward had forbidden them to go into one particular storehouse, which was always kept locked by several wooden bolts. Kem forced them open with his dagger.

Inside were many ornate wooden chests of different sizes, some with flat lids, others with curved or triangular. The lids were all held in place by cords wound round two pegs, one on the side and the other on top. Taken together, this collection of furniture was worth a great deal. Kem cut the cords and they began to inspect the contents. In several sycamore-wood chests they found pieces of the very finest linen, robes and bedsheets.

'Lady Nenophar's treasure?' suggested Kem.

'We'll ask her for the scrolls recording when they left the workshops.'

The two men next opened some softwood chests veneered with ebony and decorated with panels in different kinds of valuable wood. Inside were hundreds of lapis-lazuli amulets.

'These are worth an absolute fortune!' exclaimed Kem.

'The work is so fine that it should be easy to find out where they were made.'

'I'll see to it.'

'Denes and his accomplices sell them for high prices in Libya, Syria, Canaan and other countries where Egyptian magic is valued. They may even offer them to the sand-travellers to make them invulnerable.'

'Isn't that tantamount to attacking the safety of the state?'

'Denes will deny it and accuse the steward.'

'Are you saying that, even though you're Judge of the Porch, you doubt the legal system can cope with all this?'

'Don't be so pessimistic, Kem. After all, we're here in an official capacity.'

Hidden under three flat-lidded chests, they found something unexpected which astounded them: a massive, gilded acacia-wood chest, about one cubit tall and a little less wide and deep. On its ebony lid were two ivory pegs, carved to perfection.

'This is worthy of a pharaoh,' murmured Kem.

'Anyone would think it was meant for a tomb.'

'In that case, we have no right to touch it.'

'I must make a list of the contents,' said Pazair.

'But wouldn't that be committing sacrilege?'

'No. There's no inscription on the chest.'

Kem allowed the judge to remove the string binding the ivory pegs to the ones on the sides. Pazair raised the lid slowly.

The flash of gold dazzled him. It was an enormous scarab made of solid gold. Beside it were a miniature sculptor's chisel made from sky-iron, and a lapis-lazuli eye.

'The eye of the Risen One,' he whispered, 'the chisel used to open his mouth in the otherworld, and the scarab laid in the place of his heart so that his metamorphoses may be eternal.'

On the belly of the scarab there had been a hieroglyphic inscription, but it had been so throughly hammered away that he could not decipher it.

'These things *were* made for a pharaoh,' said Kem, appalled, 'a pharaoh whose tomb has been looted.'

In the era of Ramses II, such a crime seemed impossible. Several centuries earlier sand-travellers had invaded the Delta and looted the burial-grounds, so, ever since Egypt's liberation from the Hyksos, pharaohs had been buried in the Valley of the Kings and their tombs were guarded night and day.

'Only a foreigner could have conceived such a monstrous plan,' Kem went on, his voice shaking.

Deeply troubled, Pazair closed the chest. 'We must take this treasure to Kani. It will be safe at Karnak.'

18

The High Priest of Karnak ordered the temple craftsmen to examine the chest and its contents. As soon as he had their findings, he summoned Pazair. The two men strolled together beneath a portico, shaded from the sun.

'I regret to say,' said Kani, 'that we cannot identify the owner of these marvels.'

'Was he a king?'

'The size of the scarab is worrying, but that on its own isn't enough to tell for certain.'

'Kem thinks a tomb has been looted.'

'That's most unlikely. The break-in would have been discovered – how could such a thing, the most hideous of all crimes, go unnoticed? It is more than five hundred years since it was committed. Nobody could possibly have suppressed the scandal. Ramses would have condemned the crime as beyond all hope of pardon, and the names of the guilty parties would have been destroyed in full view of the entire population.'

Kani was right, thought Pazair, and Kem's fears were unjustified.

'It's likely,' Kani went on, 'that these wonderful things were stolen from the workshops. Either Denes planned to sell them, or else he intended them for his own tomb.'

Knowing the ship-owner's vanity, Pazair was inclined towards the second solution.

'Have you investigated at Kebet yet?' asked Kani.

'I haven't had time, and I'm not sure what methods I should use.'

'Be very careful.'

'Have you learnt something new?'

'The goldsmiths of Karnak are certain that the scarab's gold comes from the mine at Kebet.'

Kebet, which lay a little to the north of Thebes, was a strange town. The streets were thronged with miners, quarrymen and desert explorers, some on the eve of departure, others back from a season in the hell of the burning, rocky wastes. Every man always promised himself that, next time, he would discover the richest vein. Caravan traders sold their wares, which they had brought all the way from Nubia, hunters brought back game to the temple and the nobles, and nomads tried to integrate into Egyptian society.

Everyone was waiting for the next royal decree, which would urge volunteers to take one of the many tracks leading to the quarries of jasper, granite or porphyry; to the port of Kosseir, on the Red Sea; or indeed to the turquoise deposits of Sinai. Men dreamt of gold, of secret or unexploited mines, of that flesh of the gods which the temple reserved for the gods and the pharaohs. The miners were closely watched, and had no chance of spiriting away large quantities of the precious metal. A thousand times, plots had been hatched to seize it; a thousand times, they had failed, because of the omnipresent special guards known as 'the All-Seeing Ones' and their ferocious, tireless dogs.

These were rough and pitiless men, who knew every last track, even the smallest dried-up riverbed, and who could find their way without difficulty in a hostile world where outsiders did not survive for long. Hunters of animals and men, they killed ibex, wild goats and gazelles, and recaptured fugitives who had escaped from prison. Their favourite prey was the sand-travellers who tried to attack caravans and rob travellers. Although the sand-travellers were numerous and well trained, the All-Seeing Ones gave them little opportunity to succeed in their cowardly attacks. If, by some misfortune, a group of more cunning sand-travellers did succeed, the desert patrols took on the assignment of catching them and wiping them out. It was many years since a looter had survived to boast of his exploits.

On his way to the great temple at Kebet, where the priests guarded age-old maps showing the locations of Egypt's mineral wealth, Pazair met a group of All-Seeing Ones and their dogs. They were herding along some prisoners, who had been mauled by the dogs.

He felt impatient and uneasy. Impatient to make progress and to know if Kebet would yield useful information; uneasy because he was afraid the temple's High Priest might be in league with the conspirators. Before doing anything, he must either banish this doubt or confirm it.

Kani's scroll of authorization was highly effective: as soon as it was read the gates opened one after another, and the High Priest received Pazair within the hour. The priest was elderly, stout and sure of himself; the dignity of his office had not wiped out his past as a man of action.

'What honours and attentions!' he said with irony, his harsh voice making his subordinates tremble. 'A Judge of the Porch authorized to search my modest temple? There is a mark of esteem I was not expecting. Is your detachment of guards about to invade this place?'

'I have come alone,' said Pazair.

The priest knitted his bushy eyebrows. 'I don't understand.'

'I wish for your help.'

'Here, as elsewhere, people have talked a great deal about the case you brought against General Asher.'

'What do they say?'

'The general has more supporters than opponents.'

'In which camp do you stand?'

'He's a villain!'

Pazair hid his relief. If the priest meant what he said, things were looking brighter. 'What makes you say that?'

'I'm a former miner and officer of the desert guards. For a year Asher has been trying to take control of the All-Seeing Ones – but as long as I live he won't do it.'

Pazair was sure the priest's anger was genuine. Relieved, he said, 'You are the only person who can perhaps help me regarding the theft of a large quantity of sky-iron. It was found in Memphis in the workshop of an inventor called Sheshi. Of course, he says that he didn't know it was there and that he was an innocent victim. But he is trying to make unbreakable weapons, probably on Asher's behalf, so he would need that special iron.'

'Whoever told you that was making fun of you.'

'Why?'

'Because sky-iron isn't unbreakable. It comes from rocks which fall from the sky.'

'Not unbreakable?'

'That story's spread far and wide, but a story's all it is.'

'Are the locations of these rocks known?'

'They fall all over the country, but I have a map. Only an official expedition, under the control of the desert guards, is allowed to collect sky-iron and bring it to Kebet.'

'A whole block of sky-iron has been stolen.'

'That's not very surprising. A band of looters probably stumbled on a rock whose position hadn't been mapped.'

'Would Asher use it?'

'What for? He knows sky-iron is reserved for ritual uses. By making weapons from it he'd lay himself open to serious trouble. On the other hand, selling it abroad – especially to the Hittites, who value it extremely highly – would earn him a fortune.'

Selling, speculating, trading . . . Those were the specialities not of Asher but of Denes, with his insatiable greed for money and possessions.

In the process, Sheshi would get his commission. Pazair had been wrong: the inventor was only playing the role of go-between, in Denes's schemes. However, Asher wanted to gain control of the desert guards.

'Have there been any thefts of precious metals from your stores?'

The High Priest smiled. 'I'm watched by an army of guards, priests and scribes, and I watch them – we watch each other. Did you by any chance suspect me?'

'Yes, I must confess I did.'

'I appreciate your honesty. Stay here a few days, and you'll see that theft is impossible.'

Pazair decided to trust him. 'Among the treasures acquired by a trafficker in amulets, I found a very large scarab made of solid gold – and the gold came from the mine at Kebet.'

The High Priest looked troubled. 'Who says so?'

'The goldsmiths of Karnak.'

'Then it's true.'

'I suppose such a precious piece would be listed in your archives?'

'What's the owner's name?'

'The inscription has been removed.'

'That's a pity. Since the most ancient times, each consignment of gold from the mine has been meticulously registered, and you'll find all the records in the archives. Its destination is given: which temple, which pharaoh, which goldsmith. Without a name, you won't be able to find out anything.'

'Do craftsmen work at the mine itself?'

'Not often, but from time to time goldsmiths have made things on the site of the mine. This temple is open to you; search it from top to bottom.'

'That won't be necessary.'

'I wish you good luck. And rid Egypt of that man Asher. He brings bad luck.'

If the High Priest of Kebet was innocent – and Pazair was convinced he was – Pazair would probably have to give up trying to find out where the sky-iron had come from. It must be at the heart of a new illegal trade by Denes, whose abilities in the field seemed unlimited. But it might be that the miners, goldsmiths or desert guards were stealing precious stones or metals on behalf of either Denes or Asher, or perhaps even for both of them. After all, the two allies were amassing a huge fortune which they intended using to fund an attack on Egypt's security. But Pazair still did not know what form that attack would take.

If he could prove that Asher was the head of a gang of gold thieves, the general would receive the most severe penalty the system permitted. The only way to get proof, he thought, would be if someone were to mingle with the prospectors and pretend to be one of them. Finding a man brave enough to do that would be difficult, if not impossible, because it would be very dangerous – he had only suggested it to Suti to provoke him.

The only solution was to get taken on himself, after persuading Neferet that he was justified in doing so.

Brave's barking gladdened his heart. The dog came charging madly towards him and stopped, panting, at the feet of his master, who lavished caresses on him. Knowing his donkey's tetchy nature, Pazair went to him immediately to prove his affection. Way-Finder's smiling eyes were his reward.

As soon as he took Neferet in his arms, Pazair could tell that she was tired and careworn. He asked her what had happened.

'It's serious,' she said. 'Suti's taken refuge in our house. For the last week, he has gone to ground in a bedchamber and he refuses to come out.'

'What's he done?'

'He won't speak to anyone but you. This evening he drank an awful lot.'

Sighing, Pazair went into Suti's room; Neferet followed silently.

'Here you are at last!' exclaimed Suti with great relief.

'Kem and I have unearthed vital clues,' said Pazair.

'If Neferet hadn't hidden me, I'd have been exiled to Asia.'

'Why? What crime have you committed?'

'Asher has accused me of desertion, insulting a superior officer, abandoning my post, losing official weapons, cowardice in the face of the enemy and slanderous denunciation.'

'You'll certainly win the case.'

'I certainly won't.'

'What do you mean?'

'When I left the army, I didn't complete the documents that freed me from further army service. The period for doing so has expired, and Asher – he's within his rights – has pounced on my negligence. Effectively, I'm a deserter and can be sent to a military prison.'

'That's annoying.'

'Annoying? I'm facing a year in a labour camp. Can you imagine how the general's scribes would treat me? I wouldn't get out alive.'

'I'll see what I can do.'

'No, Pazair, you mustn't,' said Suti. 'It's my own fault. You're Judge of the Porch – you can't go against the law.'

'We're blood brothers, aren't we?'

'But you mustn't suffer because of me. The trap was cleverly laid. There's only one thing to do: as you suggested, I'll become a prospector and vanish into the desert. I'll escape from Tapeni and Panther as well as Asher, and I might even make my fortune. The gold road! There's no finer dream.'

'Nor, as you said yourself, is there a more dangerous one.'

'I wasn't made for a sedentary life. The women will miss me, but I'm trusting in my luck.'

'We don't want to lose you,' objected Neferet.

Moved, he gazed at her. 'I'll come back – and I'll be rich, powerful and honoured. All the Ashers in the world will tremble at the sight of me and crawl at my feet, but I shall be merciless and trample them underfoot. I shall come and kiss you on both cheeks and gorge myself on the food and drink you'll have ready for me.'

'To my mind,' said Pazair, 'it would be better to have the feast straight away and give up your plan to be a drunkard.'

'I've never been so clear-headed. If I stay here, I'll be found guilty. And I'll take you down with me, because you're so stubborn that you'll insist on defending me and fighting for a lost cause. Then all our efforts will have been in vain.'

'Is it really necessary to take such a huge risk?' asked Neferet.

'Without drastic action, how can I get myself out of this mess? From now on the army is forbidden to me, and all that's left is the damned profession of gold-seeker. No, I haven't gone mad. This time I shall make my fortune. I can sense it, in my head, my fingers, my belly.'

'Is that your final decision?'

'I've been going round in circles for a week; I've had plenty of time to think. Even you won't change my mind.'

Pazair and Neferet looked at each other; he wasn't joking.

'In that case,' said Pazair, 'I've some important information for you.'

'About Asher?' asked Suti.

'Kem and I have uncovered an illegal trade in amulets, involving Denes and Qadash, and it's possible that Asher is involved in stealing gold. In other words, the conspirators are amassing money.'

'Asher a gold thief? Wonderful! That carries the death penalty, doesn't it?'

'If it can be proved.'

'You really are my brother, Pazair.' Suti hugged his friend warmly. 'I'll bring you that proof. Not only am I going to get rich, but I'll knock that murderer off his pedestal.'

'Don't get too excited. It's only a theory.'

'No, it's the truth, I'm sure it is.'

'If you insist on going ahead, I'm going to make your mission official.'

'In what way?'

'With Kem's agreement, you enlisted in the desert guards a fortnight ago. You'll be paid a wage.'

'A fortnight ago? You mean before Asher made his accusation?'

'Kem takes little notice of administrative formalities. Matters will be in order, that's the vital thing.'

'Let's have a drink,' demanded Suti.

'Get yourself a job with the miners,' advised Pazair, 'and don't tell anyone at all that you're a guard, unless you need to in order to save yourself from immediate danger.'

'Do you suspect anyone in particular?'

'Asher would like to take control of the desert guards, so he must have infiltrated spies or bought a few consciences – probably even among the miners. We'll communicate either by the official message service or by any other means that doesn't endanger you. We must keep each other informed as to the progress of our respective inquiries. My code-name will be ... Way-Finder.'

'If you admit you're a donkey, the path to wisdom isn't yet out of your reach.'

'I want a promise from you.'

'You have it.'

'Don't force your famous good luck. If danger becomes pressing, come back.'

'You know me.'

'Yes,' said Pazair drily, 'I do.'

'I'll be acting in secret, but you'll be an exposed target.'

'Are you trying to say I'll be running bigger risks than you?'

'If judges are becoming intelligent, this country may yet have a future.'

19

In the garden of his estate, Denes counted the dried figs and then counted them again. After checking several times, he came to the conclusion that some had been stolen. Eight were missing, according to the list prepared by the scribe in charge of his fruit trees. Furious, he summoned his staff and threatened them with terrible punishments if the guilty party did not confess. An old cook who valued her quiet life pushed forward a ten-year-old boy, the fruit-tree scribe's own son. The scribe was sentenced to ten strokes of the rod, and the boy to fifteen. Denes demanded strict absolute honesty; even the least of his possessions must be respected as such. In the absence of Nenophar, who was locked in a tussle with the financial secretariats to try to lessen Bel-Tran's influence, Denes was running his estate himself.

His anger had made him hungry, so he ordered roast pork, milk and soft cheese to be brought to him at once. His appetite suddenly vanished when his steward came and announced that the Judge of the Porch wished to see him. Nevertheless, he put on a cheerful expression and invited the judge to share his meal.

Pazair sat down on the low dry-stone wall enclosing the pergola and watched Denes closely. 'Why did you employ Qadash's former steward, who had been found guilty of dishonesty?'

'The scribe who sees to employing people made a mistake. Qadash and I were sure that the miserable wretch had left the province.'

'He did leave, it's true, but only to take charge of your largest farm, near Khmun.'

'He must have used a false name. You may be certain he'll be dismissed first thing tomorrow.'

'That won't be necessary,' said Pazair. 'He's in prison.'

Denes smoothed his thin fringe of beard, putting a few stray hairs back in place. 'In prison? What has he done?'

'Did you not know that he was a go-between for stolen goods?'

'A go-between? How dreadful!' Denes seemed indignant.

'He was involved in an illegal traffic in amulets stored in chests,' specified Pazair.

'On my property? On my farm? That's incredible – insane! I do ask you for the greatest discretion, my dear Judge. My reputation shouldn't suffer because of that despicable fellow's crimes.'

'So you're one of his victims?'

'He's deceived me in the vilest way. He must know I never go to that estate – my business affairs keep me in Memphis, and I've no great fondness for the provinces. I dare to hope he will be punished very severely.'

'Had you no idea what your steward was doing?'

'None at all. I've acted in all good faith.'

'Did you know that treasure was hidden on that farm?'

Denes looked astounded. 'Treasure now, is it? What kind of treasure?'

'That's confidential. Do you know where your friend Qadash is?'

'Yes. He's here. He was suffering from exhaustion, so I invited him to stay.'

'If his health permits, may I see him?'

With much annoyance, Denes sent a servant to fetch the tooth-doctor.

Arms waving, and unable to stand still, Qadash launched into a series of involved explanations in which he defended himself for having employed the steward on his estate, while at the same time arguing that he had later dismissed him. He answered Pazair's questions only with disjointed phrases. Either he was losing his mind or he was playing a game.

Eventually Pazair interrupted Qadash and said, 'I think I understand what you are saying: that neither of you knew anything, and that the traffic in amulets was operating without your knowledge.'

Denes congratulated the judge on his conclusions. Qadash walked away without another word.

'You must forgive him,' said Denes. 'His age, you know, and he's been overworking . . .'

'My investigation is continuing,' said Pazair. 'The steward is only a pawn. I shall find out who devised the game and fixed its rules. You may be sure that I'll keep you informed.'

'I would be much obliged.'

'I should like to speak with your wife.'

'I don't know what time she'll return from the palace.'

'I'll come back this evening.'

'Is that really necessary?'

'Absolutely.'

*

When Pazair arrived that evening, he was shown into Nenophar's workshop. He found her, her face carefully painted, indulging in her favourite activity, making new clothes. She was sewing the sleeve of a long dress.

'I'm tired,' she said irritably. 'Being bothered in my own home like this is very disagreeable.'

'As you can see, I am sorry.' He went a little closer. 'Your work is truly remarkable.'

'Are you impressed by my talent for needlework?'

'I'm fascinated.'

Nenophar seemed bewildered. 'What is all this about?'

'Where do the fabrics you use come from?'

'That is no one's concern but mine.'

'I'm afraid it is.'

Outraged, she abandoned her work and got to her feet. 'I demand an explanation.'

'At your farm in Middle Egypt, among a number of suspicious items we found dresses, bedsheets and pieces of linen. I assume they belong to you.'

'Have you any proof of that?'

'Not formal proof, no.'

'In that case, spare me your assumptions, and leave here at once.'

'I am obliged to do so, but I must stress one point: I am not deceived.'

At last Panther had finished. It had taken her two weeks to assemble the ingredients: hairs from a sick man who had died the previous day, a few grains of barley stolen from a child's tomb before it was closed, some apple-pips, blood from a black dog, sour wine, donkey's urine and sawdust. The potion would work quickly and well. Now she must ensure that her rival, either willingly or by force, drank the mixture. As consumed with love as ever, but never again able to respond to a man's passion, Tapeni would bore Suti and he would soon leave her.

Panther heard a soft noise. Someone had just passed through the small garden and entered the little white house.

She put out the kitchen lamp and armed herself with a knife. So that she-devil Tapeni had dared to come and confront Panther under her own roof, no doubt intending to murder her. She heard the intruder go into the bedchamber, open a travelling-bag and begin throwing things into it.

Panther crept through the house to the bedchamber door. Brandishing the knife, she hurled herself into the room.

'Suti!'

The young man spun round and saw her. Seeing the gleaming blade, he threw himself to one side. Panther dropped the knife.

'Have you gone mad?' He straightened up and seized her by the wrists. 'What the devil's that knife for?'

'To run her through.'

'Who are you talking about?'

'That creature you married.'

'Forget about her – and forget about me, too.'

Panther trembled. 'Suti . . .'

'As you can see, I'm leaving.'

'Where are you going?'

'On a secret mission.'

'You're lying! You're going back to her!'

He burst out laughing, let go of her, stuffed one last kilt into his bag, and threw it over his shoulder. 'Don't worry, she won't follow me.'

Panther grabbed her lover. 'You're frightening me. Tell me what's happened, please!'

'I'm regarded as a deserter and I must leave Memphis right away. If Asher gets his hands on me I'll be deported, and he'll make sure I don't come back.'

'Can't Pazair protect you?'

'I was careless and it's my own fault. If I succeed in doing what he has trusted me to do, I'll defeat Asher and come back.' He kissed her passionately.

'If you've lied to me,' she promised, 'I'll kill you.'

With the help of the temple priests, Kem investigated the most prestigious amulet workshops in Kebet, but found nothing. He left Thebes and took a boat to Memphis, where he carried out a similar investigation; it was equally disappointing.

It must mean, the big Nubian reflected, that the beautiful amulets being traded illegally did not come from a well-established workshop. So he questioned several informants, all of whom eyed Killer nervously. One of them, a dwarf of Syrian origin, agreed to talk, on condition that he received three sacks of barley and a donkey under three years old. Drafting a written request for the payment and following the proper procedure would have taken too long. So Kem paid for everything himself, and threatened to break the dwarf's ribs if he tried to lie. The dwarf said an illegal trade – he didn't know in what – had been operating for two years in the northern district of the city, near the naval boatyard.

For three days and nights, disguised as a water-carrier and with

Killer at his side, Kem observed the comings and goings around the boatyard. After the yard closed in the evenings, strange workers slipped down an alleyway with no apparent way out, and re-emerged before dawn, carrying closed baskets which they handed to a boatman.

On the fourth night, the pair set off down the alleyway. It ended in a panel made from reeds, which were covered with dried mud so that the panel looked like a wall. Followed by Killer, Kem charged at it and broke through.

They found themselves in a stuffy, low-ceilinged workshop where four craftsmen were working. Kem felled the nearest, Killer bit the second in the leg, and the third fled. The last, a short, pot-bellied, elderly man, stood rooted to the spot, hardly daring to breathe. In his hand was a magnificent lapis-lazuli Knot of Isis, which he dropped when Kem went towards him.

'Are you in charge?' demanded Kem.

The man nodded, too scared to speak.

Kem picked up the Knot of Isis. 'This is fine work – you're clearly no apprentice. Where did you learn your trade?'

'At . . . at the T-Temple of Ptah,' he stammered.

'Why did you leave?'

'I w-was expelled.'

'Why?'

The man hung his head. 'For theft.'

Kem looked around the workshop. Along the dried-mud walls were piled chests containing blocks of lapis-lazuli from the far-off mountainous regions. On a low table lay finished amulets; a nearby basket contained spoilt items and waste.

'Who's your employer?' asked Kem.

'I . . . I can't remember.'

'Come on, my brave fellow, lying is stupid. What's more, it infuriates my baboon – and he isn't called Killer for nothing, you know. I want the name of the man behind this illegal trade.'

'Will you protect me if I tell you?'

'You'll be safe in the thieves' prison.'

The fat man would be more than happy to leave Memphis, even to exchange it for the underworld. But he hesitated.

'I'm waiting,' said Kem grimly.

'Prison? Is there no way of avoiding it?'

'That depends on you, and above all on the name you give me.'

'He hasn't left any traces behind him, he'll deny everything, and my testimony won't be enough to convict him.'

'Don't bother yourself with the legal side of things.'

'Couldn't you just let me go?'

Hoping the Nubian would do nothing, the craftsman took a step towards the alleyway.

A huge, strong hand closed round his neck. 'The name – now!'

'It's Sheshi, Sheshi the inventor.'

Pazair and Kem walked along the canal, watching the cargo-boats. The sailors shouted to each other and sang, some leaving, others returning home. Everything spoke of Egypt's prosperity, happiness and peace.

And yet at night Pazair could not sleep: he sensed that tragedy was coming, though he could not identify the causes of the evil. He had told Neferet and, despite her natural optimism, she had had to admit that his fear was justified.

Pazair shook off his worries, and turned to Kem. 'You're right,' he said. 'The case against Sheshi would fail. He'd protest his innocence, and the word of a thief expelled from the temple would carry no weight.'

'But the man was telling the truth.'

'I don't doubt it.'

'The legal system,' grumbled the Nubian. 'What's the point of it?'

'Give me time. We now know of the bonds of friendship that link Denes to Qadash, and Qadash to Sheshi. Those three are definitely accomplices, and Sheshi – whose skill as an inventor must be very useful to them – is probably working for Asher as well. So we have four conspirators, responsible between them for quite a number of crimes. What we need now is for Suti to bring us proof of Asher's guilt. I'm convinced that Asher stole the sky-iron and that he's behind the traffic in precious things like lapis-lazuli, and perhaps even gold – his knowledge of Asian affairs would be a great advantage. Denes is an ambitious man, greedy for wealth and power; he's manipulating Qadash and Sheshi. And I'm not forgetting Nenophar, so skilled in handling the very kind of needle that killed Branir.'

'Four men and a woman. How can they threaten Ramses' reign?'

'That question torments me, but I cannot answer it. Why, if it was indeed the same people, did they loot a royal tomb? There are still so many uncertainties, Kem. Our work is far from complete.

'Despite my title,' Pazair went on, 'I shall continue to investigate alone. You're one of only three people I trust. I shall free you from all administrative work.'

'Yes, but . . .'

'What is it?'

'Be as careful as I am.'

'The only other people I trust are Suti and Neferet.'

'He's your blood brother, and she's your sister for eternity. If either betrays you, they will be damned on earth and in the afterlife.'

'Why are you so suspicious?'

'Because you're forgetting to ask one vital question: are there really only five conspirators, or are there more?'

At dead of night, her head covered with a shawl, she slipped silently into the warehouse where, in the name of her friends, she had arranged a meeting with the shadow-eater. She had been chosen, by the drawing of lots, to meet him and give him his instructions. Ordinarily, they would never have taken such a risk, but the urgency of the situation required both a meeting in person and the certainty that the orders would be understood perfectly. Dressed in a peasant-woman's coarse robe and papyrus sandals, and with her face thickly painted, she was sure she was unrecognizable and ran no risk of being identified.

The previous day, Denes had called an urgent meeting of his allies. The confiscation of the block of sky-iron was only a financial loss, but Pazair's discovery of the funerary items belonging to Pharaoh Khufu looked set to cause more serious difficulties. True, Pazair could neither identify the king, whose name had been carefully removed, nor understand that Ramses was obliged to keep silent about what was happening. Not one word could be spoken by the most powerful man in the world, who was locked in lonely solitude, unable to confess that he no longer possessed the symbols of government that gave his rule legitimacy.

Denes had advocated doing nothing – the judge's interference didn't frighten him – but the other conspirators had disagreed. Even if Pazair stood no chance of getting at the truth, he was causing them more and more problems in their various activities. Sheshi was the most vehement: he had just lost all his substantial future profits from his traffic in amulets. Determined, patient and thorough, the judge would eventually make a case, and one or more notables would be implicated, perhaps found guilty, or even imprisoned. If that happened, it would be a double blow. On one hand, the conspiracy would be severely weakened. On the other, Pazair's victims would publicly lose their integrity – which they would badly need on the day when Ramses abdicated.

The woman trembled when she heard someone say her name, then rejoiced. A delicious shiver ran though her, like the one she had felt when she stripped naked in front of the commander of the Great Sphinx's honour-guard at Giza. As she lured the commander towards her, she had made him drop his guard and opened the gates of death. It was her charms that had sealed their victory.

She knew nothing of the shadow-eater, except that he committed crimes to order, more for the pleasure of killing than for high fees. When she saw him, sitting there on a chest peeling an onion, she was both frightened and fascinated.

'You're late,' he said. 'The moon has passed the end of the port.'

'You must act again.'

'Who?'

'It will be a very delicate task.'

'A woman, a child?'

'A judge.'

'In Egypt, people don't murder judges.'

'You aren't to kill him, you're to cripple him.'

'Difficult.'

'What do you want?'

'Gold. And plenty of it.'

'You'll have it,' she promised.

'When?'

'Don't strike until you're certain of success. Everyone must be convinced that Pazair was the victim of an accident.'

'The Judge of the Porch himself? The amount of gold has just doubled.'

'We shan't tolerate failure.'

'Neither shall I. Pazair is well protected, so it's impossible to fix a specific time.'

'We can accept that. But the sooner the better.'

The shadow-eater got to his feet. 'There's just one more thing.'

'What?'

'Quick as a snake, he twisted her arm, just short of breaking it, and forced her to turn away from him. 'I want an advance.'

'You wouldn't dare!'

'An advance in kind.'

He lifted up her dress.

She did not scream, but hissed, 'You're mad!'

'And you're careless. Your face doesn't interest me, and I don't want to know who you are. If you cooperate, it'll be better for both of us.'

When she felt his manhood between her thighs, she stopped resisting. Making love to a murderer was more exciting than her usual frolics. She'd never tell anyone about this. Their coupling was quick and rough, just the way she liked it.

'Your judge won't bother you any more,' promised the shadow-eater.

20

Shade was provided by palm-, fig- and carob trees. Sitting in the garden after her noon meal, and before resuming work, Neferet savoured the silence. It was soon broken by her monkey leaping around with little cries of joy as it brought a fruit to its mistress. Mischief did not quieten until Neferet sat down again; reassured, the monkey slipped under her chair and watched Brave's comings and goings.

It was said that the whole of Egypt was like a garden, where Pharaoh's benevolent shade enabled the trees to flourish, both in the joy of morning and in the peace of evening. Ramses himself often supervised the planting of olive- or persea-trees. He loved to walk in flower-filled gardens and gaze upon orchards. The temples enjoyed the shelter of tall trees in which the birds – messengers of the gods – built their nests. The sages said that a troubled soul is a tree withering in its heart's drought; a calm soul, on the contrary, bears fruit and spreads a gentle coolness around it.

Neferet planted a sycamore seedling in the centre of a small trench; a porous jar, which conserved moisture, protected the young plant's roots. As they grew, the fragile container would burst apart, and the fragments of pottery would mix with the earth, adding strength to the soil. Neferet took care to reinforce the border of dried mud, designed to hold in moisture after watering.

Brave started barking, announcing Pazair's imminent arrival; well before the judge crossed the threshold, and no matter what time of day or night it was, the dog always sensed his master's approach. When he was away for a long time, Brave lost his appetite and no longer reacted to Mischief's provocation.

Forgetting the dignity of his office, the Judge of the Porch ran to his dog, which jumped up and decorated his clean kilt with two muddy footprints. The judge took it off and lay down on a mat, close to his wife.

'How gentle this sunshine is,' he said.

'You look exhausted.'

'I've had far more than the usual dose of troubles today.'

'Did you remember to take your copper-water?'

'I didn't have time to look after myself. My office wasn't empty for a single moment. Everyone in Egypt – from the footsoldier's widow to the scribe unable to gain advancement – wanted to see me.'

She lay down beside him. 'You aren't thinking clearly, Judge Pazair. Gaze upon your garden.'

'Suti's right. I'm trapped by this post. I want to go back to being a little village judge.'

'It isn't your destiny to go backwards. Has Suti left for Kebet?'

'He went this morning, with his weapons and his baggage. He promised me he'd return with Asher's head and a pile of gold.'

'Each day we must pray to Min, the protector of explorers, and Hathor, queen of the deserts. Our friendship will cross the space between us.'

'And what about your patients?' asked Pazair.

'A few of them are worrying me. I am waiting for some rare plants in order to make up my remedies, but the workshop at the central hospital has not responded to my orders.'

Pazair closed his eyes.

'There's something else worrying you, my darling, isn't there?' said Neferet.

'I can't hide anything from you. Well, yes, there is, and it concerns you.'

'Have I broken the law?'

'The position of principal doctor to the court has become vacant. As Judge of the Porch, I must examine the legal validity of the applications submitted to the council of specialists. I was obliged to accept the first one.'

'From whom?'

'Qadash. If he's chosen, the file Bel-Tran prepared in your favour will fall to the bottom of a rubbish pit.'

'Does he have any chance of success?'

'He presented a letter from Nebamon designating Qadash his preferred successor.'

'Is it a forgery?'

'Two witnesses have authenticated it and certified that Nebamon was sane when he wrote it. And who are those witnesses? Denes and Sheshi. Those villains aren't even hiding any longer!'

'My career doesn't matter. I'm happy simply to care for people – working as I do now is enough for me.'

'They'll try to stop you. And you'll be attacked in other ways, too.'

'Ah, but I'll have the best judge in Egypt to defend me.'

'Qadash ... I've been wondering for a long time about his exact role, and now the veil has been torn down. What are the principal doctor's duties?'

'To treat Pharaoh, appoint doctors and remedy-makers to the official body based at the palace, to receive and check poisons and dangerous medicines, to issue directives regarding public health and ensure they are applied after obtaining the agreement of the tjaty and the king.'

Pazair shook his head worriedly. 'If Qadash had powers like that . . . This is definitely the post he has been scheming for.'

'It isn't easy to influence the council of doctors who'll decide.'

'Don't deceive yourself. Denes will try to bribe them. Qadash is old, apparently respectable, has many years' experience, and – and Ramses suffers from only one notable ailment, toothache! This appointment is a phase of their plan. They must not succeed.'

'How can you stop them?'

'I don't know yet.'

'Are you afraid Qadash would harm Pharaoh's health?'

'No, that would be too risky.'

Mischief jumped on to Pazair's shoulder and pulled his hair. He yelped in pain and made a grab for her, but his hand closed on empty air. The monkey had already taken refuge under its mistress's chair.

'If that damned animal hadn't brought about our first meeting, I'd give it a good spanking.'

To gain forgiveness, Mischief climbed a date-palm and threw down some fruit, which Pazair caught in mid-air. Brave ran up and gulped it down.

When Pazair turned back to Neferet, she was looking sad.

'What's the matter?' he asked.

'I thought of a crazy plan.'

'What sort of plan?'

'I've given it up.'

'Tell me about it.'

'What's the use?' She nestled against him. 'I'd have liked . . . a child.'

'I think about it, too.'

'Is it what you want?'

'Yes, but until the light has been gained we'd be wrong to have a child.'

'I fought against that conclusion for a long time, but you're right.'

'Either I give up this investigation or we'll have to wait.'

'Forgetting Branir's murder would damn us as the vilest of people.'

He put his arm round her. 'Do you really need to keep that dress on when the air's so warm and gentle?'

The shadow-eater's task would not be easy. First, leaving his official post too often and for too long would draw attention to him. As he worked alone without accomplices, who might have denounced him at any time, and as he must get to know Pazair's habits and routine, he would have to be patient. Also, he had been ordered to turn the Judge of the Porch into an invalid, not to kill him, and to make the crime look like an accident, so that no investigation would be opened.

The execution of this plan presented enormous difficulties. So the shadow-eater had demanded three gold ingots, a fine fortune which would enable him to buy a farm in the Delta, and to set himself up and live a happy life there. In future he would kill only for pleasure, when the urge became irresistible, and would enjoy commanding an army of servants who were ready to satisfy his every whim.

As soon as he had the gold, he would set off on the hunt; he was excited at the idea of carrying out his masterpiece.

The oven had been heated until it was white-hot. Sheshi had arranged the moulds, into which the liquid metal would flow to form a large ingot. The temperature in the workshop was almost unbearable but Sheshi did not perspire, though Denes was bathed in sweat.

'I've got our friends' agreement,' said Denes.

'No regrets?'

'We have no choice.'

Denes took out of a fabric bag the gold mask and collar that had adorned the head and shoulders of Pharaoh Khufu's mummy. 'We can make two ingots out of these.'

'What about the third?'

'We'll buy it from Asher. His thefts of gold are expertly organized, but nothing escapes me.'

Sheshi gazed at the face of the man who had built the Great Pyramid. The features were stern and serene, extraordinarily beautiful. The goldsmith had created a feeling of eternal youth.

'This frightens me,' he confessed.

'It's only a funeral mask.'

'But the eyes . . . they're alive.'

'You're just imagining things. That judge has already cost us a fortune by seizing the block of sky-iron we wanted to sell to the Hittites and the gold scarab I was reserving for my tomb. Keeping the mask and collar has become too risky – besides, we need them to pay the shadow-eater. Hurry up.'

Sheshi obeyed Denes, as he always did. The sublime face and the collar disappeared into the furnace. Soon the molten gold would flow down a channel and fill the moulds.

'What about the gold cubit?' asked Sheshi.

Denes's face lit up. 'We could use it for the third ingot. So we needn't deal with Asher after all.'

Sheshi hesitated.

'It's better to get rid of it,' Denes went on. 'Let's keep only what's absolutely vital: the Testament of the Gods. Where it is, Pazair has no chance of finding it.'

Denes smirked when Khufu's royal cubit disappeared into the furnace. 'Before long, Sheshi, my fine fellow, you'll be one of the most important people in the kingdom. This evening the first part of the fee will be paid to the shadow-eater.'

The desert guard was a giant of a man. Two daggers with worn handles hung from the belt of his kilt. He never wore sandals; he had walked so often on stones that even an acacia-thorn could not pierce the thick soles of his feet.

'What is your name?' he demanded.

'Suti.'

'Where are you from?'

'Thebes.'

'Profession?'

'Water-carrier, linen-gatherer, pig-farmer, fisherman . . .'

An enormous short-haired dog with empty eyes sniffed the young man. It weighed as much as a grown man, and its back was covered with scars. Suti sensed that it was ready to spring at any moment.

'Why do you want to be a miner?'

'I like adventure.'

'Do you also like thirst, scorching heat, horned vipers, black scorpions, forced marches, and back-breaking work in narrow, airless galleries?'

'Every trade has its disadvantages.'

'You're taking the wrong path, my lad.'

Suti smiled as foolishly as possible. The guard let him pass.

In the queue waiting to sign on at the office, he cut a rather fine figure. His confident air and impressive muscles contrasted sharply with the sickly appearance of several of the other men, who were clearly unfit for the job.

Two elderly miners asked him the same questions as the guard, and he gave the same answers. He felt as though he were being examined like a fine-bred animal.

'An expedition is being organized. Are you available?'

'Yes,' said Suti. 'Where's it going?'

'In our job, you do as you're told and you don't ask questions. Half the new men fall by the wayside, and they have to do whatever they can to get back to the valley – we don't waste time on weaklings. We're leaving tonight, two hours before dawn. Here's your equipment.'

Suti was given a cane, a mat and a rolled-up blanket. With a piece of string, he tied the blanket and the mat round the cane, which was vital in the desert. By banging it on the ground as you walked along, you could frighten snakes away.

'What about water?' he asked.

'You'll be given your ration. Don't forget the most precious thing.'

Suti hung round his neck the little leather bag into which the happy discoverer would slip gold, cornelian, lapis-lazuli or any other precious stones. The contents of the purse would belong to him, as well as his pay.

'It doesn't hold much,' he commented.

'Many purses stay empty, boy.'

'Only inadequate men's.'

'You've got a lot to say for yourself. The desert'll soon teach you to hold your tongue.'

More than two hundred men had assembled at the eastern gate of the city, close to the trail. Most were praying to Min and making three vows: to return home safe and sound, not to die of thirst, and to bring back precious stones in their leather bags. Amulets hung at their necks. The most educated of them had consulted star-watcher, and some had withdrawn from the journey because the omens were unfavourable. To unbelievers and miscreants, the old hands had passed on the usual message: 'We leave without God for the desert, we return with him into the valley.'

The leader of the expedition, Ephraim, was a tall, bearded man with immensely long arms. His body was covered with so much stiff black hair that he looked like a bear. When they saw him, several would-be miners changed their minds; people said he was brutal and cruel.

He reviewed his men, lingering over each volunteer. 'Are you the one called Suti?'

'I have that good fortune.'

'It seems you're an ambitious fellow.'

'I haven't come here to collect pebbles.'

'While you're waiting, you can carry my bag.' He passed an enormously heavy bag to Suti, who hoisted it on to his shoulder.

Ephraim grinned. 'Make the most of it. Soon you won't look so proud.'

The men shook themselves into wakefulness before sunrise and walked until mid-morning, travelling deep into a bare, arid landscape.

Ephraim avoided the burning sand and kept to the paths, which were strewn with shards of rock as sharp as metal. The country fellows, ill prepared for this terrain, found their feet got cut to ribbons.

The first mountains took Suti by surprise. They seemed to form an impenetrable barrier, barring access to a secret land where the blocks of pure stone reserved for the gods' dwellings were formed. There a formidable energy was concentrated; the mountain gave birth to the rock, which was pregnant with precious minerals and did not unveil its riches except to patient, determined lovers. Fascinated, he laid down his burden.

A kick in the backside sent him tumbling into the sand.

'I didn't give you permission to rest,' said Ephraim sarcastically.

Suti got up.

'Clean my bag, and during the meal don't put it down on the ground. As punishment for disobeying me, you'll have no water.'

Suti wondered if he had been denounced, but then he saw that other volunteers were also being bullied. Ephraim liked to test his men by pushing them to the limit. A Nubian who made as if to raise his fist was promptly knocked unconscious and abandoned beside the track.

Late in the afternoon, they reached a sandstone quarry. Stone-cutters were removing blocks, which they marked with their team's special sign. Little grooves were cut out carefully along each vein, then round the desired block. The overseer used a mallet to insert wooden pegs into notches aligned with the aid of a rope, so as to detach the block from the mother rock without shattering it.

Ephraim hailed him. 'I'm taking a band of idle good-for-nothings to the mines. If you need a hand, just say so.'

'I wouldn't say no, but haven't they walked all day?'

'If they want to eat, they'll have to make themselves useful.'

'That's a bit irregular.'

'I'm the one who lays down the law.'

'Ten blocks need to be brought down from the top of the quarry. With thirty men, it wouldn't take long.'

Ephraim chose them, including Suti, from whom he retrieved his bag.

'Have some water and then start climbing.'

The overseer had built a slide but it had broken halfway down the slope, so the blocks had to be held back with ropes to that point, before they were freed and allowed to slide the rest of the way. A thick cable, held by five men on either side, was stretched horizontally in order to stop the blocks moving too fast. As soon as the slide was repaired, this would be unnecessary. But the overseer was behind schedule, and Ephraim's proposal would put that right.

The accident happened when the sixth block reached the cable too quickly. The men holding it back were tired, and could not slow it down. It hit the horizontal cable so hard that the workmen were flung aside, except for one middle-aged man, who fell on to the slide. He tried in vain to hold on to Suti's arm while two comrades hauled the young man backwards.

The unfortunate man's scream was soon stifled. The block crushed him, left the slide and shattered with a thunderous growl.

The overseer buried his face in his hands.

'Still, we've done half the work,' said Ephraim.

21

The ibex stag, whose chin was fringed with a short beard and whose two long, curved horns pointed to the sky, stood on an overhanging rock and gazed down at the miners making their way along beneath the burning sun. In the language of hieroglyphs, the ibex symbolized serene nobility acquired at the end of a life which had conformed to divine law.

'Look! Up there!' roared one of the miners. 'Kill it!'

'Shut up, you fool,' retorted Ephraim. 'That's the guardian of the mine. If we touch it, we'll all die.'

The stag scaled a near-vertical slope and, with a prodigious leap, disappeared on to the other side of the mountain.

Five days' forced march had exhausted the miners; only Ephraim seemed as fresh as at the outset. Suti was still strong, too; the inhuman splendour of the landscape renewed his strength. Neither Ephraim's brutality nor the exhausting conditions of the journey had dented his determination.

Having ordered the men to gather round, Ephraim climbed up on to a large rock, showing his authority over this band of good-for-nothings.

'The desert is immense,' he declared in his thunderous voice, 'and you're less than ants. You're forever complaining of being thirsty, like helpless old women. You aren't worthy of being miners and searching the bowels of the earth. Still, I've brought you here – the metals are worth more than you. When you cut into the mountain, you hurt it; it'll try to take its revenge by swallowing you up. Too bad for you if you're careless. Set up camp now. Work begins tomorrow at dawn.'

The workmen put up the tents, beginning with Ephraim's, which was so heavy that carrying it had worn out five men. It was carefully unrolled, put up under Ephraim's watchful eye, and stood in splendour at the centre of the camp. The meal was prepared, the ground was dampened to lay the dust, and the men slaked their thirst with water which had been kept cool in goatskins. Fortunately, there was no shortage of it, because a well had been dug near the mine.

Suti was dozing, when someone kicked him hard in the ribs.

'Get up,' ordered Ephraim.

The young man swallowed his anger and obeyed.

'Most of the men here have something to be ashamed of. What about you?'

'That's my secret.'

'Talk.'

'Leave me alone.'

'I hate people who keep secrets.'

'I deserted from my compulsory work for the state.'

'Where?'

'In my village, near Thebes. They wanted to take me to Memphis to clean out canals. I chose to run away instead, and try my luck as a miner.'

'I don't like the look of you,' said Ephraim. 'I'm sure you're lying.'

'I want to make my fortune and nobody, not even you, is going to stop me.'

'You annoy me, little man. I'm going to put you in your place. We'll fight, bare-knuckled.'

Ephraim chose an arbiter, whose role would consist of disqualifying either man for biting; anything else was permitted.

Without warning, Ephraim charged Suti, seized him round the chest, lifted him high, spun him round above his head and threw him. Suti hit the ground nearly ten paces away.

Grazed, and with a painful shoulder, the young man got up. Hands on hips, Ephraim looked at him contemptuously. The miners laughed.

Suti spat the sand out of his mouth. 'I'm ready for you now, so attack again if you're brave enough.'

Ephraim answered the challenge at once, but this time his long arms captured only empty air, as Suti dodged aside at the last moment. Suti regained some of his confidence. It seemed Ephraim knew only one hold, and was relying on his great strength to win. Even if the gods did not exist, Suti thanked them for having given him a turbulent childhood during which he had learnt to fight.

At least ten times, Suti avoided Ephraim's attacks. Ephraim got more and more angry, which tired him and made him stop thinking clearly. Suti could not afford to make a single mistake; if he got caught in a stranglehold, he'd be killed. Using all his speed and agility, he unbalanced Ephraim by hooking a foot through his leg, slid under the big man as he toppled, and used his opponent's own energy to trap him in a headlock. Ephraim crashed to the ground. Suti sat astride him and threatened to break his neck.

Ephraim punched the sand, accepting his defeat. 'All right, little man!'

'You deserve to die.'

'If you kill me, the desert guards will kill you.'

'I don't care. You won't be the first man I've sent to hell.'

Ephraim saw that he meant it. 'What do you want?'

'Swear that you won't torture the men any more.'

The miners were no longer laughing. They crowded round, hanging on every word.

'Hurry up, or I'll break your neck.'

'I swear, in the name of Min.'

'And before Hathor, Lady of the West. Say it.'

'Before Hathor, Lady of the West, I swear it.'

Suti relaxed his grip. Ephraim could not break an oath like that, sworn before so many witnesses. If he did, he would see his name destroyed for all eternity and would be condemned to utter destruction.

The miners shouted with joy. Two of them hoisted Suti on to their shoulders and carried him around in triumph.

When their excitement had abated somewhat, he spoke to them firmly.

'The leader here is Ephraim. He's the only one who knows the routes, the watering-places and the mines. Without him we'll never see the valley again, but if we obey him, and if he keeps his word, all will go well.'

Amazed, the bearded man laid a hand on Suti's shoulder. 'You're strong, little man, but intelligent, too.' He drew Suti aside. 'I've misjudged you.'

'I want to make my fortune.'

'We could be friends.'

'Perhaps, so long as it's useful to me.'

'It might be, little man.'

Women bearing offerings processed slowly into the palace of Princess Hattusa. Each wore a white dress held up by a strap which passed between her bare breasts, and an apron decorated with pearls, embroidered in the shape of a diamond. On their heads they wore wigs drawn into a horse-tail at the back, and they were so fresh and pretty that Denes felt his blood heating. When he was away from home he was always unfaithful to Nenophar with perfect and obligatory discretion. A scandal would discredit him, so he had no official mistress and was content with brief encounters which led nowhere. He did make love to his wife from time to time, of course, but in his eyes Nenophar's coldness justified his extra-marital adventures.

The steward of the harem came to see him in the garden. Denes thought of asking for a girl, but decided against it: a harem was a centre of trade and business, where the ruling spirit was work, not debauchery.

In his capacity as a ship-owner, Denes had requested an official audience with Ramses' Hittite wife. She received him in a four-pillared hall, with walls painted bright yellow. The floor was decorated with a mosaic of green and red squares.

Hattusa was seated on an ebony chair, with gilded arms and feet. With her black eyes, very white skin and long, slender hands, she had the strange charm of Asian women. Denes kept on his guard.

'This is an unexpected visit,' she observed acidly.

'I am a transporter of goods, Princess, and you run a harem. No one will be surprised by our meeting.'

'And yet you considered it dangerous.'

'The situation has changed drastically. Pazair has become Judge of the Porch, and he is thwarting my activities.'

'In what way does that concern me?'

'My lady, surely you have not changed your mind?'

'Ramses has spurned me, and he humiliates my people. I want vengeance.'

Satisfied, Denes stroked his white fringe of beard. 'You shall have it, Princess. Our goals are still identical. The king is a tyrant – and an incompetent one, at that. He is chained to outdated traditions and has no vision of the future. Time is working in our favour, but some of my friends are getting impatient, so we have decided to undermine Ramses' popularity even more.'

'Will that be enough to bring him down?'

Denes was on edge, and knew he must not say too much. The Hittite was only a temporary ally, who would have to be discarded as quickly as possible after the king's fall. 'Trust us. Our plan cannot fail.'

'Be careful,' warned Hattusa. 'Ramses is an experienced warrior, skilful and brave.'

'He is bound hand and foot.'

A gleam of excitement shone in Hattusa's eyes. 'Should I not know more about this?'

'My lady, that would be pointless and inadvisable.'

Hattusa frowned. Her suppressed anger made her even more delectable. 'What do you propose to do?'

'To disrupt the whole of Egypt's trade. At Memphis I shall have no difficulty, but at Thebes I shall need your help. The people will grumble, and Pharaoh will be held responsible. The weakening of the country's trade will shake his throne.'

'How many consciences have to be bought?'

'Not many, but they are expensive. The principal scribes who control the movement of goods must make repeated "mistakes". The resulting investigations will be long and complicated, and the disruption will take several weeks to set up.'

'My trusted men will take action.'

Denes had little confidence in this plan's effectiveness. Although it was a fresh blow against the king, it would have only limited consequences. But he had stilled Hattusa's mistrust.

'I have something else to tell you in strict confidence,' he said in a low voice.

'I'm listening.'

He went closer and spoke even more quietly. 'In a few months' time, I shall possess a large quantity of sky-iron.'

The Hittite's eyes betrayed her interest. Used for magical ends, the rare metal would be a new weapon against Ramses. 'What is its price?'

'Three gold ingots at the time of the order, three on delivery.'

'When you leave the harem, they will be in your baggage.'

Denes bowed. His allies would never know about this transaction, and the princess would never receive the sky-iron. The thought of selling something he did not have and making such an enormous profit filled him with glee. Keeping the princess waiting would be easy. If she got too impatient he would blame Sheshi – the inventor's servility had already been very useful.

Pazair and Neferet were dining with Bel-Tran and Silkis. The cook brought in a copper dish of grilled lamb chops, with delicious-looking fresh courgettes and peas, and laid it on the pedestal table in front of them. A serving-woman brought olives, radishes and a lettuce. Silkis prepared the seasoning herself, although she was wearing one of her best dresses and her most valuable earrings, discs decorated with rosettes and spirals.

'Thank you for accepting our invitation, my dear friends,' said Bel-Tran. 'To have both of you at our table is an honour.'

'There's no need for this formality,' protested the judge.

'I keep having a very strange dream,' Silkis said. 'I dreamt several times that I was drinking hot beer. I was so worried that I consulted the interpreter. His diagnosis frightened me. He said it means all my possessions are going to be stolen.'

'Don't worry so much,' advised Neferet. 'Dream-interpreters are often wrong.'

'May the gods hear you!'

'My wife is very worried,' said Bel-Tran. 'Couldn't you give her something to help?'

After the meal, while Neferet was prescribing calming herbal infusions for Silkis, Bel-Tran and Pazair strolled in the garden.

'I have so few opportunities to enjoy nature,' lamented Bel-Tran, 'because my work takes up more and more of my time. When I come home in the evening, my children are in bed. Not seeing them grow and not being able to play with them are painful sacrifices. Managing the granaries, my papyrus works, the Treasury secretariat . . . the days are just too short. Don't you feel the same way?'

'Yes, often. Being Judge of the Porch certainly isn't restful.'

'Are you making any progress in your investigation into General Asher?'

'It's moving on, little by little.'

'Something unexpected has happened, and I'm very worried about it. You know Princess Hattusa is a rather aggressive woman, and she hasn't forgiven Ramses for taking her away from her country.'

'She hardly bothers to hide her hostility.'

'Where will it lead? Opposing the king openly, or trying to conspire against him, would be suicidal. Nevertheless, she has just received a strange visit: from Denes.'

'Are you sure?'

'One of my colleagues thought he recognized him during a visit to the harem. He was so surprised that he checked, to make sure he wasn't mistaken.'

'Why is it so surprising for them to have met?'

'Hattusa has her own fleet of trading-ships. The harem is a state institution where a private ship-owner should have no role to play. If this was a friendly visit, what does it mean?'

Pazair thought for a moment. An alliance between the Hittite princess, the king's secondary wife, and one of the conspirators: Bel-Tran's revelation was certainly important. Could it be that Hattusa was the mastermind of the plot and Denes was her agent? The conclusion seemed too hasty. No one knew what they had talked about, though the mere fact that they had met indicated a meeting of interests, unlikely to be conducive to the kingdom's well-being.

'This collusion is suspicious,' emphasized Bel-Tran.

'Can we find out how far it goes?'

'I don't know. Are you thinking about preparations for an invasion from the north? It is true that Ramses has choked off the Hittites for the time being, but I doubt if they'll ever give up their dreams of expansion.'

'In that case, General Asher would be an essential link.'

The clearer the enemy's outline became, the more difficult the battle promised to be and the more uncertain the future.

*

That same evening, a messenger from the palace brought Neferet a letter marked with the seal of Queen Tuya, Ramses' mother: she wished to consult Neferet as soon as possible. Although she lived in strict seclusion, the Mother of Pharaoh was still one of the most influential people at court. Her pride made her detest mediocrity and pettiness; she gave advice rather than orders, and watched over the greatness of the country with jealous care. Ramses both admired and loved her, and since the death of his adored wife, Nefertari, had made his mother his principal confidante. Some said that he never took a decision without first consulting her.

Tuya ruled over a large household and had a palace in each large town. The one in Memphis was made up of about twenty rooms and a vast four-pillared hall where she received important guests.

A steward led Neferet to the queen's bedchamber.

Now aged sixty, Tuya was thin with piercing eyes, a slender, straight nose, prominent cheekbones and a small, almost square chin. She wore the ritual wig of her office, shaped like a vulture, its wings encasing her face.

She said, 'I have heard much of you, Doctor Neferet. Tjaty Bagey, who is not inclined to pay idle compliments, says you have worked miracles.'

'Majesty, I could show you a long list of failures, too. A doctor who boasts of his or her success should change to another calling.'

'I am unwell and I need your skill – Nebamon's assistants are ignorant.'

'What is troubling you, Majesty?'

'My eyes. Also, I have strong, stabbing pains in my belly, my hearing is poor, and my neck is stiff.'

Neferet easily diagnosed that the stabbing pains were caused by abnormal secretions from the womb. She prescribed fumigation with terebinth resin mixed with high-quality oil.

The eye examination worried her more: the rims of the queen's eyes were reddened and sore; there were small, hard pustules on the insides of her eyelids; and the queen complained of pressure within her eyes and occasional dimness of sight.

The queen saw that the doctor was concerned. 'Be frank with me,' she ordered.

'Majesty, these are sicknesses I know and can cure. But the treatment will take a long time and will require you to be meticulous in its application.'

When she rose in the morning, the queen must wash her eyes with a solution based on hemp, which was very effective against pressure within the eye. The same solution, with the addition of honey and applied locally as an ointment, would soothe the belly pains. Another remedy, whose principal agent was black flint, would remove the infection from the rims of her eyes, as well as the malign humours. To get rid of the pustules, the patient must apply to her eyelids a lotion made from ladanum, galenite, tortoise-bile, yellow ochre and Nubian earth. Lastly, using the hollow quill of a vulture, she must put drops into her eyes. Aloes, chrysocolla, colocynth-flour, acacia-leaves, ebony-bark and cold water would be mixed, reduced to a paste, dried and then mixed with water. The resulting lotion must spend a night in the open air, receive the dew, and be filtered. Besides using it as drops, the queen must use it in compresses applied to the eye four times a day.

'How old and weak I am,' she remarked. 'Having to spend so much time on myself displeases me.'

'You are unwell, Majesty. But if you take the time to care for yourself, you will recover.'

'I think I must obey you, whatever it costs me. Accept this, with my thanks.' Tuya handed the doctor a magnificent collar of seven strings of cornelian and Nubian gold beads; the two clasps were shaped like lotus-flowers.

Neferet hesitated. 'Majesty, will you not at least wait to see if the treatment brings results?'

'I am feeling better already.'

Tuya fastened the collar round Neferet's neck, and stood back to judge its effect. 'You are very beautiful, Doctor.'

Neferet blushed.

'What is more, you are happy. Those close to me tell me that your husband is an exceptional judge.'

'Serving Ma'at is the whole meaning of his life.'

'Egypt needs people like you and him.'

Tuya called for her cup-bearer, who brought sweet beer and succulent fruit. The two women sat down on low chairs padded with comfortable cushions.

The queen went on, 'I have followed Judge Pazair's career and investigations for some time. I was amused at first, then intrigued, and in the end appalled. His deportation was unjust and abominable. Fortunately, he has won a first victory: his position as Judge of the Porch enables him to pursue the struggle with greater means. Appointing Kem commander of the city guards was an excellent move, and Tjaty Bagey was right to approve it.'

These few sentences were not spoken by chance, Neferet knew. When she reported them to Pazair, he would be transported with joy; through Tuya, Pharaoh's closest advisers were approving his conduct.

'Ever since the death of my husband and my son's accession to the throne, I have watched over the country's happiness. Ramses is a great king: he has dispelled the threat of war, enriched the temples, and fed his people. Egypt remains the beloved land of the gods. But I am worried, Neferet. Will you be my confidante?'

'If you think me worthy of your trust, Majesty.'

'Ramses is more and more preoccupied, sometimes absentminded, as if he had suddenly aged. His character has changed. He seems to have lost interest in fighting, in resolving difficulty after difficulty, and making light of obstacles.'

'Could he be ill?'

'Apart from his toothache, he is still the most vigorous and tireless of men. But for the first time in his life he is wary of me, and I can no longer read his inner thoughts. That would not shock me if, as is his custom, he had told me his decision face to face. But he is wary of me, and I do not know why. Speak of it to Judge Pazair. I am afraid for Egypt, Neferet. So many murders in these last few months, so many enigmas unresolved, and the king distancing himself from me, his new taste for solitude . . . Pazair must continue his investigations.'

'Do you think, Majesty, that Pharaoh's reign is threatened?'

'He is greatly loved and respected.'

'But are there not rumours that good fortune is deserting him?'

'That always happens when a king has reigned for a long time. Ramses knows the solution: to celebrate a festival of regeneration, to strengthen his pact with the gods, and breathe joy back into the souls of his subjects. The rumours do not trouble me. But why has Pharaoh promulgated decrees restating his authority, which no one is challenging?'

'Could it be that an insidious evil is weakening his spirit?'

'If it were, the court would soon see its effects. No, his faculties are intact; and yet he has changed.'

Neferet sensed that she must not ask any more questions. It was for Pazair to weigh up these exceptional confidences and know how to make use of them.

Tuya changed the subject. 'I greatly appreciated your dignity when Nebamon died. He was worthless as a man, but he knew how to impose his personality. He showed rare injustice towards you, so I have decided to make recompense for what he did. He and I were in charge of the main hospital in Memphis, but he is dead, and I am not a doctor. Tomorrow a decree shall be published appointing you overseer of that hospital.'

22

Two servants emptied jars of lukewarm water over Pazair, who washed himself with a cake of natron. Afterwards, he brushed his teeth with a scented reed and rinsed with a mixture of alum and dill. He shaved with his favourite razor, which was shaped like a carpenter's chisel, and rubbed his neck with oil of wild mint to repel flies, mosquitoes and fleas. He rubbed the rest of his body with ointment based on natron and honey. If necessary, in the midday heat he would use a preparation made from carob and incense to prevent his sweat from smelling unpleasant.

As he finished his ablutions, the inevitable happened. He sneezed twice, five times, ten times. His cold had returned, his obstinate cold, again accompanied by coughing spasms, pains round his eyes, and buzzing in his ears. Admittedly it was his own fault: he was overworking, forgetting to take his medicine, and not getting enough sleep. But he certainly needed a new remedy.

Consulting Neferet wasn't easy, because she rose at six and left shortly afterwards for the hospital she now ran – he had hardly seen her for a week. Determined to do well in her new position, she was giving it her all, for she was now responsible for the largest centre of healing in Egypt. Queen Tuya's decree, approved immediately by the tjaty, had received the assent of all the doctors and remedy-makers at the hospital. The temporary administrator, who had been blocking the delivery of medicines to Neferet, had become a mere doctor's assistant, and now looked after bedridden invalids.

Neferet had told the scribes at the hospital that her vocation was healing, not administration, and had asked them to carry out the orders from the tjaty's office, which she had no intention of disputing. This had won most of them over to their new overseer, who worked closely with the different specialist doctors. Some patients who came to the hospital were very sick people whom town and country doctors had failed to cure, while others were well-off people who wanted treatment which would prevent the appearance or exacerbation of certain ailments.

Neferet paid a great deal of attention to the workshop where remedies were prepared and dangerous, poisonous substances were handled.

Since the pain round his eyes was getting worse and he had been left to his own devices, Pazair decided to go to the only place where he would get some attention: the main hospital. The gardens laid out in front of it were delightful. There was no hint of the suffering so close by.

A friendly nurse greeted the visitor. 'How can I help you?'

'It's an emergency. I would like to consult the hospital overseer, Doctor Neferet.'

'I'm afraid that won't be possible today.'

'Not even for her husband?'

'You are the Judge of the Porch?'

'I'm afraid so.'

'Please follow me.'

The nurse led him through a series of bathing-chambers furnished with three stone basins, the first for total immersion, the second for sitting baths, and the third for the legs and feet. Other places were reserved for sleep cures. Small, well-ventilated rooms housed patients who were watched over constantly by the doctors.

Neferet was checking the preparation of a remedy, and noting the coagulation time of a substance by consulting a water-clock. Two experienced remedy-makers were assisting her.

Pazair waited until she had finished before coming forward. 'May a patient have the benefit of your care?'

'Is it urgent?'

'An emergency.'

Barely keeping a straight face, she led him into a consulting-room. The judge sneezed loudly, at least ten times.

'Hmm, you weren't joking. Any difficulty in breathing?'

'I've had a whistling noise in my chest ever since you stopped taking care of me.'

'What about your ears?'

'The left one's blocked.'

'Are you feverish?'

'A little.'

'Lie down on the stone bench. I must listen to your heart.'

'You already know what it says.'

'We are in a respectable place, Judge Pazair. I must ask you to behave with proper decorum.'

While she sounded his heart, the Judge of the Porch remained silent.

'You were right to tell me. A new course of treatment is needed.'

In the workshop, Neferet used a dowsing-wand to choose the

appropriate remedy. It twitched in her hand when she passed it over a sturdy plant with broad, five-lobed leaves of pale green, and red berries.

'Bryony,' she said. 'It's a mortal poison, but used very much diluted it will eliminate the congestion and clear your breathing-passages.'

'Are you absolutely sure?'

'I'd stake my position on it.'

'Then give me some quickly. My scribes must be cursing me for being away so long.'

There was unheard-of uproar in the judge's offices. Scribes who were usually calm, who spoke quietly and never gesticulated, were shouting at each other, unsure what to do. Some said it was best to wait, in the judge's absence; others advocated exercising firmness – so long as they didn't have exercise it themselves; a third group demanded that the city guards be summoned. Broken tablets and torn papyri lay strewn across the floor.

Silence fell when Pazair arrived.

He looked around in astonishment. 'Have you been attacked?'

'In a manner of speaking,' replied an old scribe, aghast. 'We could not hold back the fury. Now she has invaded your office.'

Intrigued, Pazair crossed the huge room where the scribes worked and went into his own office. He found Panther kneeling on a mat, searching through the archives.

'Whatever has got into you?' he asked

'I want to know where you've hidden Suti.'

'Get up and leave my office.'

'Not until I know.'

'I shall not use force, but I shall summon Kem.'

That threat carried the day. She obeyed.

'We'll discuss this outside,' said Pazair.

She stalked out in front of him, watched with great interest by the scribes.

'Clear up this mess and get back to work,' he ordered them.

Pazair and Panther walked quickly and turned into a narrow, busy street. On a market day like this, buyers thronged around the peasants selling fruit and vegetables, in a great din of haggling. The judge and the Libyan escaped from the tide of humanity and took refuge in a deserted, silent alleyway.

'I want to know where Suti's hiding,' she insisted, on the verge of tears. 'Since he left, I can't think of anything but him. I forget to put on my perfume and paint my face. I've lost all sense of time, I just wander round the streets.'

'He isn't hiding. He's on a delicate and dangerous mission.'

'With another woman.'

'Alone, and without help from anyone – man or woman.'

'But he's married!'

'He thought the marriage necessary to his investigation.'

'I love him, Judge Pazair, I'm dying of love for him. Can you understand that?'

Pazair smiled. 'Better than you think.'

'Where is he?'

'I can't tell you that, Panther. If I did, I'd put him in danger.'

'You wouldn't – I swear it! I'd never, never tell another soul.'

Moved, and convinced of her love and sincerity, Pazair yielded. 'He has enlisted in a party of miners which left from Kebet.'

Glowing with happiness, Panther kissed him on the cheek. 'I shall never forget your help. If I have to kill him, you'll be the first person to know.'

The rumour spread through all the provinces, from north to south. At Pi-Ramses, Pharaoh's royal capital in the Delta, at Memphis and at Thebes, it quickly infected all levels of government and deeply troubled the officials responsible for carrying out the tjaty's instructions.

Before he could read the report by General Asher that had sparked the rumours, Pazair had to resolve a housing problem which was tearing a family apart: two cousins had bought the same piece of land from a dishonest seller. Pazair dealt with the case quickly – he ruled that the seller must repay twice his profit – and then turned to Asher's report on the state of the Egyptian army.

The general considered the situation in Asia unstable because of the constant cuts in the Egyptian forces that kept the peace there, and said the small princedoms would eagerly unite under the banner of the elusive Libyan warlord Adafi. The troops' weapons were of poor quality, because since the victory over the Hittites no one had paid any attention to improving them. As for the state of the barracks, even in the interior of the country things were bad: neglected horses, damaged chariots which had not been repaired, lack of discipline, poorly trained officers. In the event of an invasion, would Egypt be capable of repelling it?

The impact of such a report would, Pazair knew, be strong and long-lasting. He wondered what Asher was hoping to achieve by it. If the future proved Asher right, he would be seen as a clear-sighted prophet and would occupy a position of great strength, the position of a possible saviour of the country. And if Ramses gave him credit for analysing the problem correctly, Asher would insist that his demands be met; his influence would be strengthened accordingly.

Pazair thought of Suti. What arid track was he on at this hour of the day, hunting for virtually impossible evidence against the murderer who was trying to dictate the country's military strategy?

He summoned Kem, and said, 'Can you carry out a rapid investigation into the main barracks in Memphis?'

'In what respect?'

'The troops' morale, the state of their equipment, the health of both men and horses.'

'Easily, so long as I have an official reason.'

The judge suggested a plausible one: the search for a chariot which had knocked down several people and must bear signs of the accident. 'Do it quickly,' he urged.

As soon as Kem had left, Pazair hurried to the official residence of Bel-Tran, who was getting to grips with the inventory of grain harvests. The two men climbed up to the terrace of the building, away from indiscreet ears.

'Have you read Asher's report?' asked Pazair.

'It's horrifying.'

'Assuming it's accurate.'

'Do you think it isn't?'

'I suspect him of exaggerating the situation for his own benefit.'

'Is there any evidence of that?'

'We must gather it as quickly as possible.'

'Asher will be punished.'

'Perhaps not. If Ramses agrees with him, Asher will be have a free hand and will be seen as the saviour of Egypt. If that happens, no one will dare criticize him.'

Bel-Tran nodded his agreement.

'You wanted to help me,' said Pazair, 'and the time has come.'

'What do you need?'

'Information about our troops serving abroad, and on how much has been spent on weapons and military equipment over the last few years.'

'It won't be easy, but I'll try.'

On his return to his office, Pazair wrote a long letter to Kani, the High Priest of Karnak, asking him about the state of the troops stationed in the Theban region and of their equipment. The letter was written in a code based on the term 'medicinal plant', Kani's speciality, and entrusted to a reliable messenger.

'There's nothing much to report,' said Kem.

'A little more detail, please,' said Pazair.

'The barracks is calm, and the buildings and equipment are in good repair. I examined fifty chariots, and found that the officers keep them in excellent condition, as they do their horses.'

'What do they think of Asher's report?'

'They take it seriously, but they think it concerns all the barracks except theirs. By gaining their trust, I was able to inspect the one that lies furthest south of the city.'

'And what did you find?'

'Exctly the same thing: nothing to report. They also think Asher's criticism is well-founded – for other people.'

Pazair thanked Kem, and hurried off to see Bel-Tran. They met in the courtyard in front of the Temple of Ptah, where many people were chatting, indifferent to the priests' comings and goings.

'On the first point,' said Bel-Tran, 'I got conflicting information, because Asher is keeping to himself almost all information on the troops in Asia. Officially, the number of troops has been cut and there has been unrest again; but a scribe of the recruits assured me that the list of men in service hasn't changed. On the second point, it was easy to find out the truth, because the army records are kept at the Treasury. Spending has been the same for several years, and no lack of equipment has been reported.'

'So Asher lied.'

'His report is more subtle than that. He presents the facts in an alarmist manner, without actually stating too much. Many senior officers support him, and a number of courtiers are afraid of Hittite plots. They see Asher as a hero because he's giving people a much-needed jolt.'

Brave was curled up asleep at his master's feet. Pazair was sitting beside the pool, whose surface was covered with lotus-flowers. A breeze gently ruffled the dog's coat and the judge's hair. Neferet was consulting a medical papyrus which Mischief persisted in rolling up, despite her mistress's reprimands. The last glimmers of daylight bathed the garden in golden light; tits, robins and swallows were singing their evening songs.

'Our army in in an excellent state,' said Pazair. 'Asher's report is a web of lies, which he hopes will make the civilian authorities panic and will weaken the troops' morale. If he succeeds, that will make it easier for him to take control.'

'Why doesn't Ramses censure him?' asked Neferet.

'He trusts him, because of his past feats of arms.'

'Can anything be done about it?'

'I must give my findings to Tjaty Bagey, who'll pass them on to Pharaoh. They'll be countersigned not only by Kem but by Kani, whose answer I've just received. Both at Thebes and at Memphis, our military strength is intact. The tjaty will extend the checks to the whole country and then take action against Asher.'

'Then perhaps this is the end for Asher.'

'Let's not take that for granted. He'll protest, proclaim his good faith and his love for the country, will accuse his subordinates of having given him false information. But he'll be stopped in his tracks. And I'm hoping to take my advantage further.'

'How?'

'By confronting him.'

General Asher was supervising the elite chariot troops' exercise in the desert. There were two men in each chariot; the officer fired his bow at a moving target, while his assistant handled the reins, driving at top speed. Any man who was clumsy was expelled from the corps.

When Pazair arrived, two footsoldiers asked him to wait and not to venture on to the practice area: a stray arrow might hit an incautious passer-by.

At last Asher, covered in dust, gave the signal to rest, and walked unhurriedly over to Pazair.

'You don't belong here, Judge,' he said.

'There is no part of Egypt where I don't belong,' retorted Pazair.

Asher's ratlike face tightened with annoyance, and he scratched the scar that ran down his chest from shoulder to navel. 'I'm going to wash and change. Come with me.'

Asher and Pazair went to the bath-house for senior officers. While two soldiers poured warm water over the general's body, the judge opened his attack.

'I'm contesting your report.'

'On what grounds?'

'That much of it is inaccurate.'

'You aren't a soldier – your opinion's worthless.'

'It is a matter of facts, not opinions.'

'I refute them.'

'Without knowing what they are?'

'I can easily guess. You walked around two or three barracks, and were shown a few brand-new chariots and a handful of soldiers who are happy with their lot. You're ignorant and incompetent, and you were duped.'

'Is that how you would describe the commander of Memphis's city guards and the High Priest of Karnak?'

The question put the general in an awkward position. He dismissed the soldiers and dried himself.

'They're new to their posts, and as inexperienced as you are.'

'That's a feeble argument.'

'What are you looking for now, Judge Pazair?'

'Still the same treasure: the truth. Your report is false, and I have sent my comments and objections to the tjaty.'

'You dared—'

'It was not daring, it was a duty.'

Asher stamped his foot in anger. 'That was a stupid thing to do! You'll get your fingers burnt.'

'That is for Tjaty Bagey to judge.'

'I'm the expert!'

'Our military strength is not in decline, and you know it perfectly well.'

The general's jerky movements, as he donned his kilt, betrayed his tension. 'Listen to me, Pazair. What matters is the spirit of my report – the details are unimportant.'

'What does that mean?'

'A good general must foresee the future in order to ensure the defence of the country.'

'Does that justify making alarmist, unfounded claims?'

'You don't understand.'

'Is there perhaps a link with Sheshi's activities?'

'Leave him out of it.'

'I'd like to question him.'

'You can't. He's in hiding.'

'On your orders?'

'On my orders.'

'I'm afraid I must insist.'

Asher's voice became unctuous. 'If I wanted to get the attention of the king, the tjaty and the court by pointing out our weaknesses, it was with the aim of removing them and getting a final agreement for the making of a new weapon which will render us invincible.'

'Your naivety surprises me, General.'

Asher's eyes narrowed like a cat's. 'What are you insinuating?'

'Your famous weapon is no doubt an unbreakable sword made of sky-iron.'

'Swords, spears, daggers – Sheshi's working on the project day and night. I shall demand that he be given back the block kept in the Temple of Ptah.'

'So it belonged to him, then?'

'The important thing is that he uses it.'

'Some lies can deceive even the most sceptical people.'

'What do you mean?'

'Sky-iron isn't unbreakable.'

'You're mad!'

'Sheshi's lying, either to you or to himself. The priests at Karnak will confirm what I say. The ritual use of sky-iron made you dream, mistakenly. You wanted to acquire a weapon of such power that even the highest authority in Egypt would have to fall in with your wishes. But you've failed.'

The ratlike face displayed utter bafflement. Was Asher, wondered Pazair, realizing that he had been fooled by his own accomplice?

As soon as the judge had left the bath-house, the general picked up a terracotta jar of warm water and smashed it against a wall.

23

Suti unrolled his mat and spread it out on a flat stone. Wearily, he lay down on his back and gazed up at the stars. The desert, the mountains, the rocks, the mine, the stiflingly hot galleries where you had to crawl on your belly, scraping off your skin . . . Most of the men were grumbling and already regretting an adventure which was turning out to be more exhausting than lucrative. But Suti was in his element. Sometimes he was so absorbed by the landscape that he even forgot Asher. He, who loved the pleasures of the town, had no difficulty in forming a bond with this hostile region, as if he had always lived here.

In the sand to his left, he heard a characteristic swishing. A horned viper passed close to the mat, leaving an undulating trail behind it. On the first night Suti had played the snake's little game and had been afraid of it, but now he was used to it. He knew instinctively that he wouldn't be bitten; scorpions and snakes did not frighten him. An accepted guest in their domain, he respected their customs and worried less about them than about the blood-drinking sand-tick, from which some of the miners were suffering badly. Its bite was painful, and the flesh became sore and infected. Ephraim kept sandticks away by sprinkling himself with a lotion made from marigolds. Suti was simply lucky: the ticks weren't interested in him.

Despite an exhausting day, the young man could not sleep. He got up, and walked slowly towards a dry riverbed which was bathed in moonlight. Moving about alone at night in the desert was mad. Fearsome gods and fantastical animals were on the prowl, devouring unwary wanderers, whose bodies were never found. If anyone wanted to get rid of him, this was the perfect time and place.

A faint sound put him on the alert. At the bottom of the hollow, where the water bubbled during the stormy rains, an antelope with lyre-shaped horns was scraping away determinedly at the sand with its front hooves, looking for an underground spring. Another antelope came to join it; this one had very long horns, scarcely curved at all, and white fur. The two animals were the incarnation of the god Set, whose inexhaustible energy they possessed. They were not mistaken: soon they were lapping up the precious water, which welled up between two round stones. They were followed by a hare and an ostrich. Fascinated, Suti sat down. The animals' nobility and happiness were a secret sight whose memory he would cherish for all eternity.

He heard someone coming and looked round. It was Ephraim.

The big man laid a hand on Suti's shoulder. 'You love the desert, little man. But it's a vice and if you go on feeding it you'll eventually see the falcon-headed, lion-bodied monster, which no hunter can pierce with arrows or catch with a noose. Then it'll be too late for you. The monster will seize you in its claws and carry you off into the darkness.'

'Why do you hate Egyptians?'

'I'm of Hittite descent, and I'll never accept the Egyptians as my masters. Here, on these desert tracks, I'm the one who's master.'

'How long have you been leading teams of miners?'

'Five years.'

'Haven't you made your fortune yet?'

'You ask too many questions,' growled Ephraim.

'If you've failed, what hope have I got?'

'Who says I've failed?'

Suti smiled. 'That's reassuring.'

'Don't be too quick to rejoice.'

'But if you're rich, why go on sweating and slaving?'

'I hate valleys, fields and the Nile. Even if I was made of gold, I wouldn't leave my mines.'

'Made of gold . . . I like that expression. Up to now, you've had us explore worked-out mines.'

'You're observant, little man. What better training could there be? When the serious work begins, the toughest men will be ready to search the belly of the mountain.'

'The sooner the better.'

'You're in a mighty hurry.'

'Why wait?'

'Hundreds of men have set out on the gold road, but almost all of them have failed.'

'Aren't the seams of ore marked?'

'The maps belong to the temples and never leave there. And anyone who tries to steal gold is immediately arrested by the desert patrols.'

'Can't one evade them?'

'Their dogs are everywhere.'

'But you've got the map in your head, haven't you?'

The bearded man sat down next to Suti. 'Who told you that?'

'No one, don't worry. But you're not a man to keep valuable information anywhere else.'

Ephraim picked up a pebble and crushed it between his fingers. 'If you try to deceive me, I'll kill you.'

'How many times do I have to tell you that all I want is to get rich? I want an enormous estate, horses, chariots, servants, a pine-forest, a—'

'A pine-forest? There aren't any in Egypt.'

'Who's talking about Egypt? I can't stay in this damned country. I want to settle in Asia, in a princedom Pharaoh's army won't enter.'

'You're beginning to interest me, boy. You're a criminal, aren't you?'

Suti didn't answer.

'The guards are looking for you, and you're hoping to escape by hiding among the miners. But those guards are stubborn. They won't rest till they've hunted you down.'

'This time they won't take me alive.'

'Have you been in prison?'

'I'll never let them lock me up again.'

'Which judge is after you?'

'Pazair, the Judge of the Porch.'

Ephraim whistled admiringly. 'You're big game! When that judge dies, a lot of people like you will throw a gigantic party.'

'He never gives up.'

'Perhaps fate will be against him.'

'My purse is empty; I'm in a hurry.'

'I like you, little man, but I'm not taking any risks. Tomorrow we'll be digging for the real thing, and then we'll see what you're made of.'

Ephraim divided his men into two teams. The first, larger one was set to collecting copper, which was vital for making tools, especially stone-cutters' chisels. Broken up and washed, the metal was smelted on the site of extraction in rudimentary furnaces, then poured into moulds. Sinai and the deserts provided large quantities of copper, which still had, however, to be imported from Syria and western Asia, as the communities of builders were so fond of it. The army used it, too, blending it with tin to produce strong blades.

The second team, to which Suti belonged, was made up of only ten determined men. Everyone knew that the real difficulties were just beginning. In front of them was the entrance to a gallery, a hell-mouth opening on to depths which might conceal treasure. Round their necks the miners strung their leather purses, which would be filled to bursting if they struck lucky. They wore only leather kilts and covered their bodies with sand.

Who would go first? That was the best position, but also the most dangerous. Suti was pushed forward. He turned round and struck out. A general tussle followed. Ephraim interrupted it, picking up a small fighter by the hair and making him cry out in pain.

'You,' he ordered, 'take the lead. You'll need a torch.'

The men formed a line. The passageway was narrow and very steep, and the miners bent double, looking for footholds. Their eyes scanned the walls, searching for the glint of a precious metal whose nature Ephraim hadn't specified. The leader moved too fast and raised a cloud of dust; the second, half-choked, pushed him in the back. Caught off balance, he lost his footing and tumbled down the slope to a level area below, where the miners were able to stand straight.

'He's passed out,' said one of his comrades.

'So much the better,' retorted another.

After getting their breath back, in the stifling atmosphere, they went on into the belly of the mine.

'There! Gold!'

The discoverer was immediately joined by two envious competitors, who knocked him to the ground.

'Fool! It was just a shiny stone.'

Suti sensed menace at every step: the men behind him intended to get rid of him. With the sure instinct of a wild animal, he ducked at the very moment they attacked him, trying to smash his skull with a stone. The first attacker fell head over heels, and Suti broke his ribs with a kick.

'I'll kill the next one,' he swore. 'Have you gone mad? If we go on like this, none of us will get out alive. Either we kill each other now or we share everything.'

The able-bodied men chose the second solution.

The miners crawled on into another passageway. Feeling ill, two gave up. The torch, which was made of rags soaked in sesame oil, was handed to Suti, who had no hesitation in taking the lead.

Even further down, in the darkness, he saw a flash of light. His mouth watering, he speeded up, and at last touched the treasure.

'Copper! It's only copper.'

Suti was determined to make Ephraim tell the truth about his ill-gotten gains. As he squeezed back out of the gallery, he was instantly astonished by the abnormal silence hanging over the site. The miners had been drawn up into two rows, under the watchful eyes of ten desert guards and their enormous dogs. Their leader was none other than the big man who had questioned Suti before he signed on.

'Here are the others,' said Ephraim.

Suti and his comrades were made to stand in a line, including the wounded; the dogs growled, ready to bite. Each guard held a ring to which were attached nine leather thongs, enabling him to strike hard and fast.

'We're in pursuit of a deserter,' said the big man. 'He ran from work duty, and a complaint has been lodged against him. I believe he's hiding among you fellows. The rules of the game are simple. If he gives himself up, or you denounce him, the matter will be settled. But if you keep quiet we'll question you all, using the punishment ring – no one will be spared. We'll repeat the process as many times as necessary.'

Suti's eyes met Ephraim's. The Hittite would not try to deceive the guards: betraying Suti would consolidate his reputation with the forces of law and order.

'Have a little courage, men,' said Ephraim. 'The runaway has gambled and lost. We miners aren't a rabble of layabouts.'

No one stepped forward.

Ephraim went closer to his men. Suti had no chance of escape. The miners themselves would turn against him.

The dogs barked and strained at the leash. The guards waited calmly for their prey.

Ephraim grabbed the diminutive fighter again, and threw him at the feet of the guards' commander. 'Here's your deserter.'

Suti felt the weight of the giant's gaze on him. For a moment, he thought he'd challenge Ephraim's denunciation. But the suspect, under the threat of the dogs, was already babbling a confession.

'I still like you, little man.'

'You deceived me,' said Suti angrily.

'I put you to the test. Anyone who can get out of that abandoned mine can get out of any kind of trouble.'

'You should have warned me.'

'The test wouldn't have been conclusive. Now I know what you're made of.'

'The guards will be back for me before long.'

'I know, so we aren't staying here. As soon as I have all the copper the overseer at Kebet wants, I shall send three-quarters of the men back to the valley with it.'

'And then?'

'And then, with the men I've've chosen, we shall carry out an expedition which hasn't been authorized by the temple.'

'If you don't go back with your miners, the guards will be after you, too.'

'If I succeed, it'll be too late. This will be my last exploration.'

'Won't there be too many of us?'

'On the gold road you need bearers, for part of the journey. Usually, little man, I go back alone.'

Tjaty Bagey received Pazair in his office, just before he was due to go home for lunch. He sent away his secretary, and dipped his swollen feet in a stone basin of luke-warm salt water. Although Neferet's treatment meant his illness was no worse, the tjaty had not given up his wife's fat-laden cooking and was continuing to overload his liver.

Pazair was growing used to Bagey's coldness. The tjaty's long, stern, unattractive face and questioning eyes showed clearly that he was not interested in making people warm to him. On the walls of his office hung maps of the provinces, some of which he had drawn himself when he was a map-maker.

'You have set me no easy task, Judge Pazair. Ordinarily, a Judge of the Porch is content to fulfil his many duties without investigating in the field.'

'The seriousness of the case required it.'

'Shall I add that military matters are not within your remit?'

'The trial did not clear General Asher of all suspicion; I am in charge of pursuing the case. It is the man himself who interests me.'

'Why dwell on his report about the state of our troops?'

'Because it is a lie, as is proved by the irrefutable testimonies of the head of the Memphis guards and the High Priest of Karnak. When I convene a new trial, this document will add weight to the case. The general is still making a mockery of the truth.'

'Convene a new trial? Is that really what you intend to do?'

'Asher is a murderer. Suti, unlike the general, did not lie.'

'But Suti is in difficulty with the law.'

Pazair had been worried that the tjaty would raise that point.

Bagey had not raised his voice, but he seemed annoyed. 'Asher has lodged a complaint against him, and the charge is a serious one: desertion.'

'That charge cannot be substantiated,' objected the judge. 'Suti was taken on by the Memphis guards before he received the document – Kem's registers are quite clear on that point. That means that Suti the former soldier belongs to a state body, and that there has been no interruption of his career and no desertion.'

Bagey made notes on a clay tablet. 'I suppose you can prove your case?'

'Yes, I can.'

'What do you really think of Asher's report?'

'That it is intended to create confusion in order to make the general seem like the country's saviour.'

'Suppose he is telling the truth?'

'My first inquiries indicate precisely the opposite. I admit they've been limited in time and scope, but you, Tjaty, have the ability to reduce the general's arguments to nothing.'

The tjaty reflected.

Suddenly, Pazair was seized by a terrible doubt. Was Bagey in league with Asher? Was the image of the unbending, honest, incorruptible tjaty merely an illusion? If it was, the Judge of the Porch's career was about to come to an abrupt end, under some administrative pretext. At least he wouldn't have long to wait. Bagey's reply would tell him what to expect.

'Excellent work,' declared Bagey. 'Every day you justify your appointment and you surprise me. I was wrong to favour age in designating senior judges. However, I console myself by assuming that you are an exception. Your analysis of Asher's report is very worrying, and the support of Commander Kem and the High Priest of Karnak, even though both were only recently appointed, gives it a great deal of weight. Moreover, you stood firm in the face of my doubts. I shall therefore challenge the accuracy of the report and order a detailed inventory of our available weapons.'

Pazair waited until he was safely home and in Neferet's arms before he wept with joy.

General Asher sat down on the shaft of a chariot. The barracks was asleep, the sentries dozing. What had a country as powerful as Egypt to fear, united round its king and solidly built on ancestral values which not even the strongest winds had shaken?

Asher had lied, betrayed and murdered in order to become a powerful and respected man. He wanted to seal an alliance with the Hittites and the Asian princes, to create an empire of which Ramses himself would not have dared dream. The illusion had been shattered, because of one piece of ill fortune. He had been deceived for months: Sheshi had used him.

The great General Asher! Soon he would be a helpless puppet, unable to withstand Judge Pazair's repeated attacks. He had not even had the pleasure of having Suti locked up. Complaint rejected and report refused by the tjaty. The re-examination would lead to Asher's condemnation, and he would be sent to prison for damaging the troops' morale. When Bagey took hold of a matter, he became as fierce and stubborn as a hound gripping a bone between its teeth.

Why had Sheshi encouraged him to write that report? Dazzled by the idea of becoming a national hero, acquiring the stature of a statesman, gaining the people's loyalty, Asher had lost touch with reality. Through deceiving others, he had eventually deceived himself. Like Sheshi, he believed in the extinction of Ramses' kingdom, the mixing of the races, the overthrow of the traditions inherited from the age of the pyramids. But he had forgotten the existence of archaic men like Tjaty Bagey and Judge Pazair, servants of Ma'at, lovers of the truth.

Asher had suffered from being written off as a soldier of no account, whose future was already marked out, and who lacked ambition. The instructors had been very wrong about him. Classified in a category from which he could not escape, the general could no longer bear the army. He would either control it or destroy it. The discovery of Asia, of its princes skilled in trickery and lies, of its clans' constantly changing alliances, had prompted him to conspire and form bonds with Adafi, the leader of the rebellion.

A plaything in the hands of a trickster: his future glory was toppling into ridicule. But his false friends did not know that the wounded animal still had unsuspected resources. Ridiculous in his own eyes, Asher would rehabilitate himself by dragging down his allies with him.

Why had evil taken hold of him? He could have been content with serving Pharaoh, loving his country, and following in the footsteps of the generals who had been satisfied with carrying out their duty. But the taste for intrigue had wormed its way into him like a sickness, coupled with the desire to gain control of what properly belonged to other people.

Asher could not stand people who stepped out of their proper station, like Suti or Pazair. They diminished him and prevented him from blossoming. Some built, others destroyed; if he belonged to the latter category, were the gods not responsible for that? No one could alter their will.

As a man was born, so he died.

24

Eyes half-closed, tiny ears quivering, nostrils just above the surface of the water, the hippopotamus yawned. When another male bumped into him, he growled. These two huge crocodile-killers led the two main herds that shared the Nile south of Memphis. They loved swimming in deep water, where despite their bulk – each one weighed more than two chariots – they stopped looking ungainly and became almost graceful. They hated being disturbed when they were sleeping or resting, and were liable to open their jaws almost flat and then run the intruder through with canine teeth nearly a cubit long. Easily roused to anger, they yawned to frighten the adversary. Usually, they climbed up on to the riverbank at night and fed on fresh grass, which it took them a whole day to digest. During the day they enjoyed the sun on a sandy bank, far from human habitation, often going back into the water to protect their delicate skin.

The two battle-scarred males faced each other, baring their teeth. Then, abandoning their mutual hostility, they swam side by side to the bank. There madness overtook them, and they ravaged the crops in the fields, smashed the trees in the orchards, and spread panic among the farmers. A small child who did not dodge aside quickly enough was trampled and killed.

Twice, three times, the male hippos began again, while the females protected their young against crocodile attacks. Several village headmen appealed to the Memphis guards for help. Kem arrived and organized the hunt. The two males were killed, but other calamities struck the countryside: marauding flocks of sparrows, a plague of house-mice and field-mice, mysterious deaths of cattle, colonies of worms in the grain reserves – not to mention hordes of scribes fiercely determined to check the tax declarations. To fend off the bad luck, many farmers wore a fragment of cornelian on a necklace; the flame it contained defeated the harmful attacking forces.

Nevertheless, rumours spread apace. The red hippopotamus was becoming destructive because Pharaoh's protective magic was weakening. A poor annual flood was predicted, which surely proved that the king's power over nature was exhausted, and that he must renew his alliance with the gods by celebrating a festival of regeneration.

The weapons inspections and checks ordered by the tjaty took their course, but Pazair was still worried, because there had been no news from Suti. He had written to Suti in code, telling him that Asher's position was becoming untenable and that there was no point in taking big risks. In a few days, Suti's mission might even have become unnecessary.

Something else worried him, too. According to Kem, Panther had disappeared. She had left during the night, without telling her neighbours where she was going, and none of Kem's informants had spotted her in Memphis. Was it possible that, unhappy and deeply hurt, she had returned to Libya?

The festival of Imhotep, model of the sages and patron of scribes, gave the judge a rest day, which he devoted to treating his cold and cough with solutions of bryony and to thinking about his problems. Seated on a folding stool, he admired a large flower arrangement Neferet had created, binding together palm-leaf fibres, persea-leaves and masses of lotus-petals. Winding the carefully concealed cord required great dexterity. It was clear that Brave appreciated this work of art: he stood on his hind legs, put his paws on the table and tried to eat the lotus-flowers. Pazair called him off a dozen times, before presenting him with something more attractive in the form of a bone.

A storm was threatening. Heavy dark clouds, coming from the north, would soon block out the sun. Animals and people were becoming anxious, insects began to bite. The cleaning-woman was running about in all directions, and the cook had broken a jar. Everyone both longed for and feared the rain. It would be torrential, damaging the humblest houses and, in the areas close to the desert, forming torrents of mud and stones.

Despite the heavy demands of her work at the hospital, Neferet ruled her household with a smile and never raised her voice. The servants adored her, while they feared Pazair, whose stern appearance concealed shyness. True, he found the gardener rather lazy, the cleaning woman too slow and the cook greedy, but they all took pleasure in their work, so he held his tongue.

With a light brush, Pazair himself groomed Way-Finder, who found the stifling heat very trying. Cool water and fresh fodder cheered the donkey, who flopped down in the shade of a sycamore. Covered in sweat, Pazair felt in need of a wash. He crossed the garden, where the dates were ripening, walked along the wall separating it from the street, passed the poultry-yard, where the geese were honking, and entered the big house – he was at last beginning to get used to it.

The sound of voices indicated that the bathing-room was occupied. A young servant-girl, standing on a low wall, was pouring the contents of a water-jar on to Neferet's golden body. The lukewarm water slid over her silken skin, then ran away along a pipe whose opening was in the limestone paving covering the floor.

The judge sent away the girl and took her place.

'What an honour,' said Neferet, smiling. 'The Judge of the Porch in person. Would he be willing to massage me?'

'He is your most devoted servant.'

They went into the massage-room.

Pazair adored Neferet's slender waist, her sun-kissed sensuality, her firm, high breasts, her softly curved hips, her slender hands and feet. More in love with her every day, he could not decide whether to gaze at her without touching her or to drag her into a whirlpool of caresses.

She stretched out, face down, on a stone bench covered with a mat, while Pazair undressed and then selected aromatic oils; some of the phials and vases were made of glass in different colours, others of alabaster. He spread a little oil on his wife's back, and gently rubbed it in from her bottom to the nape of her neck. Neferet considered a daily massage very important. It eased tension, eased muscle spasms, calmed the nerves, and improved the circulation of energy into the organs, which were all linked to the tree of life where spinal marrow was formed, and also maintained balance and good health.

Pazair picked up a box in the shape of a naked girl swimming, pushing in front of her a duck with jointed wings; its body served as a container. Pazair scooped up some ontment, this time scented with jasmine, and smoothed it over Neferet's neck.

The shiver his touch produced did not escape him. His lips followed his fingers; Neferet rolled over and welcomed her lover.

The storm had still not broken.

Pazair and Neferet ate lunch in the garden, much to the delight of Brave, who careered round the little rectangular tables, made of reeds and papyrus stems, on which a servant-girl had set the cups, dishes and jars. The judge had tried in vain to train the dog not to beg during meals, but Brave had detected an ally in Neferet – anyway, how could his sensitive nose resist such delicious food?

'I'm feeling hopeful,' said Pazair.

'That's unusual for you.'

'Asher must not escape us. A murderer and a traitor . . . How can anyone soil himself like that? I never thought I'd have to fight against absolute evil.'

'You may encounter worse things than Asher.'

'Now you're being pessimistic.'

'I'd love simply to be happy, but I can feel that our happiness is being threatened.'

'Because of the investigation?'

'You're becoming more and more exposed. Do you really think Asher will let himself be struck down without fighting back?'

'I'm convinced he's only a minor player, not the leader of the conspiracy. He was deceived about the sky-iron – his accomplices lied to him.'

'He might have been play-acting.'

'No, I'm sure he wasn't.'

Neferet took her husband's hand. This simple contact was all they needed to communicate with each other. Neither the monkey nor the dog disturbed them, respecting the beauty of a moment when two people achieved a unity above and beyond themselves.

The cook shattered this paradise.

'It's happened again,' she complained. 'The chambermaid has filched the medallion of fish I was going to use to garnish your meal.'

Reluctantly, Neferet got up and went to investigate. The guilty servant, who had deprived the judge of his favourite delicacy, had hidden, well aware of the enormity of her crime. The cook called her in vain, then began to search the house.

Her scream frightened Brave, who hid under a table. Pazair ran to see what the matter was.

He found the cook crying as she bent over the chambermaid, who lay like a broken doll on the paved floor of the reception-chamber.

Neferet was already examining her. 'She's paralysed,' she said.

When the shadow-eater saw Judge Pazair come out of the house, he cursed his bad luck. He had prepared his attack with minute attention to detail, using all the information about Pazair's tastes that he had got from a talkative servant-girl. He had disguised himself as a fish-seller and had sold the cook a fine grey mullet and a little medallion with pink, appetising flesh.

To make the medallion, he had used the liver of a puffer-fish, which inflated itself with air when a predator threatened it. As well as the bones and the head, the liver contained a deadly poison. The shadow-eater had used only a tiny dose, so as to produce incurable paralysis.

A stupid, greedy girl had cost him certain success. He would have to try again and again, until he succeeded.

'We'll care for her at the hospital,' said Neferet, 'but there's no hope of improvement.'

'Do you know what caused it?' asked Pazair, in great distress.

'I would wager it was a fish.'

'Why?

'Because our cook bought a grey mullet and a medallion from a travelling fish-seller, who had both fresh and prepared fish. The medallion must have been made from poisonous fish.'

'That means the crime was premeditated.'

'The dose was calculated to cripple, not to kill. And you were the chosen victim. Nobody would murder a judge, would they? But they could stop him thinking and acting.'

Trembling, Neferet took refuge in Pazair's arms. She imagined him powerless, his eyes glazed, foam around his lips, his limbs motionless. Even like that, she would love him till death.

'He'll try again,' said Pazair. 'Did the cook give you a description of him?'

'Only a very vague one. An ordinary middle-aged man, not the sort you'd remember.'

'Then it wasn't Denes or Qadash. It might have been Sheshi, perhaps, or a killer in their pay. He made a big mistake in letting us know he exists. I shall set Kem on his trail.'

The council of doctors and remedy-makers charged with appointing the kingdom's new principal doctor received the first candidates to be approved by the law. They were an eye specialist, a doctor from Elephantine, Nebamon's former right-hand man, and Qadash.

Like his colleagues, Qadash answered questions about his methods, presented the discoveries he had made during his career, and disclosed his failures and their causes. He was questioned at length about his plans.

The votes were split, and no candidate achieved the required majority. A supporter of Qadash annoyed the council with his biased advocacy, and was sternly warned against following past practice: nobody would accept the sort of vote-fixing Nebamon had encouraged. The supporter admitted defeat.

A second round of voting brought the same result. The kingdom would therefore have to remain without a principal doctor.

'General Asher? Here?' asked Denes in surprise.

His steward confirmed that the general had arrived at the gates.

'Tell him— No, let him come in. But not here, in the stable.'

Denes took the time to do his hair and perfume his skin. He cut off two long white hairs, which spoiled the neatness of his narrow fringe of beard. It was very annoying to have to talk to that hidebound old soldier, but Asher might still be useful – notably as a scapegoat.

He found the general admiring a magnificent grey horse.

'A fine beast,' said Asher. 'Is it for sale?'

'Everything's for sale, General, that's the law of life. The world is divided into two categories: those who can buy, and the rest.'

'Spare me your homespun reasoning. Where is your friend Sheshi?'

'How should I know?'

'He's your most faithful ally.'

'I have dozens.'

'He's supposed to be working on making new weapons, under my supervision, but he hasn't been to the workshop for three days.'

'I am sorry, but your problems don't interest me very much.'

Asher barred Denes's way. 'You thought I was a fool who'd be easy to control, and Sheshi pushed me into a mantrap. Why?'

'Your imagination's running away with you.'

'If everything's for sale, sell me Sheshi. Name your price.'

Denes hesitated. One day he'd grow tired of Sheshi's servility, but this was not the time to get rid of him. He had another role in mind for his best supporter.

He said, 'You're asking a great deal, General.'

'Are you refusing?'

'There are the bonds of friendship to consider.'

'I've been stupid, but you don't know what I'm really capable of. You were wrong to make a fool of me.'

Qadash gesticulated wildly. His white hair standing on end, all the little veins on his nose straining fit to burst, he called upon the gods of sky, earth and the world between to bear witness to his misfortune.

'Calm down,' said Denes, embarrassed. 'Be like Sheshi.'

The inventor was sitting, sipping a sweet drink, on the floor in the darkest corner of the dining-chamber where the three men had eaten. The atmosphere was sinister. Nenophar was still trying to undermine Bel-Tran at court, but she was making scant progress and was getting more and more angry about it.

'Calm down? How do you explain your failure to have me made principal doctor?'

'It's merely a temporary setback.'

'But you bought the same doctors Nebamon did.'

'A simple misunderstanding. You can rely on me to remind them of our contract. At the next vote there'll be no unpleasant surprises.'

'I'm going to be principal doctor – you promised! Once I'm

appointed, we'll control all the drugs and poisons. We must have control of the country's health – it's essential.'

'It will fall into our hands, as will the other organs of power.'

Qadash hitched up the shawl wound round his body, covering his cat-skin corslet. 'Why hasn't the shadow-eater done something?'

'He needs more time.'

'Time, always time! I'm an old man, and I want to make the most of my new advantages.'

'Being impatient won't help us.'

'Sheshi,' said Qadash, 'what do you think? Oughtn't we to hurry?'

'Sheshi must stay in hiding,' explained Denes.

Qadash lost his temper. 'I thought we held the reins!'

'We do, but Asher's position is getting weaker. Judge Pazair challenged his report, and the tjaty is following up Pazair's findings.'

'That man Pazair again! When will we be rid of him?'

'The shadow-eater's dealing with that. But we've no need to hurry. People are grumbling more every day about Ramses.'

Sheshi took a sip of his drink.

'I'm tired,' confessed Qadash. 'You and I are already rich. Why do we need more?'

Denes pursed his lips. 'I don't quite understand you.'

'We could simply give up.'

'It's too late.'

'Denes is right,' said Sheshi.

Qadash rounded on him. 'Have you ever thought about being yourself, just once?'

'Denes commands, and I obey.'

'And supposing he leads you to ruin?'

'I believe in a new country, which only we are capable of building.'

'Those are Denes's words, not your own.'

'Are you saying you disagree with us?'

'Pah!' Qadash turned away sulkily.

'I grant you,' Denes said, 'that it's annoying to have supreme power within our grasp, and yet to have to wait. But you must admit that we're avoiding taking unnecessary risks and the mesh we've woven is indestructible.'

'Will Asher hunt me for long?' asked Sheshi anxiously.

'You're out of his reach – he's at bay.'

'But he's stubborn and vicious,' objected Qadash. 'Didn't he come to cause you trouble, even threaten you? Asher won't go down alone. He'll drag us down with him.'

'That is certainly what he intends to do,' agreed Sheshi, 'but he's deluding himself again. Don't forget, he doesn't hold a single key. By seeing himself as Egypt's saviour, he's doomed himself.'

'But you encouraged him, didn't you?' said Qadash.

'He was becoming a problem.'

'At least with him Judge Pazair has a bone to gnaw,' laughed Denes. 'There'll be a fight to the death between those two, and we must encourage them. The more ferocious the fight, the more blinded the judge will be.'

'But what if the general tries force against you?' asked Qadash. 'He already suspects that you're hiding Sheshi.'

'Can you imagine him attacking my house at the head of an army?'

Taking offence, Qadash grew sullen.

'We're like gods,' Denes assured him. 'We've created a river and no dam can stem its flow.'

Neferet was brushing the dog, while Pazair was reading a scribe's report littered with errors. Suddenly, his attention was caught by a bizarre sight. Ten paces away from him, on the rim of the lotus-pool, a magpie was attacking another bird, stabbing with its beak.

He put down the papyrus, and went and chased the magpie away. He found that its prey was a swallow, its wings spread out and its head covered in blood. The magpie had pecked out one of its eyes and torn open its head; spasms still racked its lacerated body. Pazair was horror-struck: the swallow was one of the forms Pharaoh's soul assumed when it rose up to heaven.

'Neferet, come quickly!'

She ran up. Like Pazair, she revered the beautiful bird, which bore two names, 'Greatness' and 'Stability'. Its joyful dances in the gold and orange light of the sunset made the heart sing.

Neferet knelt and picked up the wounded bird. In her warm, gentle hands it relaxed, glad to have found refuge.

'We can't save it,' she said sadly.

'I shouldn't have interfered.' Pazair was angry with himself for his thoughtlessness. Man ought not to interfere in nature's cruel game, or step between life and death.

The bird's claws sank into Neferet's hands, clinging to her as though to the branch of a tree. Despite the pain, she did not put it down.

Pazair was inconsolable: he had committed a crime against the spirit. He was unworthy to be a judge, because he had inflicted pointless suffering on a swallow, tearing it away from its destiny.

'Wouldn't it be better to kill it? If necessary, I—'

'You couldn't do it.'

'I'm responsible for its death-agonies. How can anyone ever trust me again?'

25

Princess Hattusa was dreaming of another world. She, who had been given to Egypt to seal the peace with the Hittites, was nothing but a deserted woman.

The wealth of her harem did not console her. She had hoped for love, for Pharaoh's warm affection, but instead had to live a lonelier and more frightening life than that of a recluse. The more her life was diluted in the waters of the Nile, the more she hated Egypt.

When would she again see Hattusa, the great Hittite capital after which she was named? It lay on a high plateau, at the far edge of an inhospitable landscape made up of ravines, gorges and steep mountains beyond arid plains – the terrain protected the city from attack. The city was a fortress, built from enormous blocks of stone, and it loomed over enclosed hillsides and valleys, a symbol of the pride and savagery of the first Hittites, who had been warriors and conquerors. Its ramparts followed the contours of the landscape, adapting themselves to the rocky peaks and spurs. By their very presence they repulsed invaders. As a child, the princess had run through the steep alleyways, stolen cups of honey placed on rocks to placate the demons, played ball with boys who vied with each other in skill and power.

In those days, she had not counted the hours.

Of all the foreign princesses who had come to live at the Egyptian court as tokens of alliance and in respect for treaties, not one had ever returned to her own country. Only the Hittite army could deliver Princess Hattusa from her gilded prison. She knew very well that neither her father nor her family had given up their plans to seize the Delta and the Nile valley, to turn Egypt into a colony of slaves and a gigantic grain-store. She must eat away at the country's foundations, undermine it from inside, weaken Ramses and impose herself as regent. Many women had reigned in the past, and it was a woman who had inspired the war of liberation from the Hyksos invaders in the north of the country. Hattusa had no other choice: by freeing herself, she would offer her people the most wonderful victories.

Denes had not realized that in offering her the sky-iron he was strengthening her belief and her powers. Among the Hittites, anyone who owned sky-iron obtained the favour of the gods. There was no better way of communicating with them than through this treasure from the depths of space. As soon as she had the block in her possession, Hattusa would have it made into amulets, necklaces, bracelets and rings. She would dress herself in sky-iron, would look like the daughter of the fire-stones that tore through the clouds.

Denes was a pretentious idiot, but he would be useful. Disrupting Egypt's trade was a severe blow to Ramses' prestige; but there was another, even more effective, way to open up the road to conquest.

Hattusa was preparing to fight the decisive battle. She must persuade one man, just one, in order to split Egypt apart and thus open a breach into which the Hittites would pour.

At noon, the Temple of Amon in Karnak was dozing. Of the three offertory rituals that the High Priest celebrated in the king's name, the mid-morning ritual was the shortest. It consisted simply of venerating the closed innermost shrine containing the divine statue, which had been brought back to life at the dawn ceremony, and ensuring that the invisible power made fertile the immense stone vessel that guaranteed the world's harmony.

Kani the gardener, though he was now High Priest of the Temple of Amon and the third most important official in the country after Pharaoh and the tjaty, had lost none of his peasant ways. Some of the haughtier scribes, who had been educated at the best schools in the country, looked down on his lined skin and callused hands, but he ignored them and ruled the men with the same care he gave to his plants. And, despite the heavy demands of the daily rituals and administration, he allowed no one else to take charge of the garden where he grew medicinal plants.

To everyone's surprise, Kani had gained the support of the whole priesthood, which was notoriously difficult to charm. He had no time for acquired privileges, and was determined that the temple's estates should be prosperous and the divine service maintained in respect of the Rule. Since he knew no method of achieving this but hard work and the love of a job well done, that was the method he applied. His words, which could be somewhat earthy, often shocked scribes accustomed to more delicacy, but he never spared himself when it came to work, and knew how to impose his will. There had been no serious opposition to him. Despite all the gloomy predictions, Karnak obeyed him and Ramses' courtiers never failed to commend him on his excellent choice.

That was all nonsense, in Hattusa's eyes.

The king, the supreme tactician, had avoided appointing someone with a strong personality who might have clashed with him. Ever since the reign of Akhenaton, relations between Pharaoh and the High Priest of Amon had been tense. Karnak was too wealthy, too powerful, too big; the god of victories reigned there. True, the king appointed the High Priest, but once in his post the latter always tried to extend his power. The day a schism appeared between a High Priest, master of the South, and a king reduced to reigning only over the North, Egypt would be doomed.

Kani's appointment was her opportunity to achieve just that. A man of the people, a peasant, would soon grow intoxicated by luxury and wealth. Having become king of a temple, he would aspire to govern the provinces of Middle Egypt, then the whole country. He did not know it yet, but Hattusa was certain of it. It was up to her to reveal Kani to himself, to arouse in him an all-consuming ambition, to seal an alliance against Ramses. No lever could be more effective than the High Priest of Amon.

Hattusa had dressed simply, without a necklace or jewels; austerity suited the immense pillared hall where the High Priest had agreed to receive her. No one would have been able to distinguish Kani from the other priests, had he not been wearing the gold ring that was the emblem of his office. With his shaven head and broad chest, he was far from elegant. The princess congratulated herself on her appearance: he must dislike coquetry.

'Shall we walk?' he suggested.

'This place is magnificent.'

'It either crushes us or raises us up.'

'Ramses' builders and craftsmen are geniuses.'

'They express the will of Pharaoh, as do you and I.'

'I am only his secondary wife, part of his diplomacy.'

'You symbolize peace with the Hittites.'

'I am not fulfilled by being a symbol.'

'Do you wish to withdraw into the temple? The priestesses of Amon would welcome you gladly. Since the death of Nefertari, the Great Royal Wife, they feel they have lost a mother.'

'I have other, more ambitious plans,' said Hattusa.

'Do they concern me?'

'To the highest degree.'

'As you can see, I am surprised.'

'When Egypt's destiny hangs in the balance, surely the High Priest of Karnak should not remain indifferent?'

'That destiny is in Ramses' hands.'

'Even if he holds you in contempt?'

'I did not receive that impression.'

'Because you do not know him – his duplicity has deceived many people. To him, the office of High Priest of Amon is an inconvenience, and he sees no solution, in the short term, except to oust the holder and occupy it himself.'

'But he does so already,' Kani pointed out. 'Pharaoh is the sole intermediary between the gods and his people.'

'I am not concerned with the worship of the gods. Ramses is a tyrant, and your powers hinder him.'

'What are you suggesting?'

'That Thebes and its High Priest should refuse to accept this dictatorship.'

'To oppose Pharaoh is to deny life.'

'You come from a modest background; I am a princess. Let us be allies. We shall have the ear of both the people and the court. We shall create another Egypt.'

'Setting South and North against each other would break the country's backbone and cause paralysis. If Pharaoh no longer links the Two Lands, misery, poverty and invasion will be our lot.'

'It is Ramses who is leading us to that disaster, and only you and I can avert it. If you help me, you'll become very rich.'

'Lift up your head, Princess, and look around you,' said Kani. 'There is no wealth in the world greater than to gaze upon the gods, who live for ever in these stones.'

'You are Egypt's last hope. If you do not act, Ramses will lead the country to ruin.'

'You are a disappointed woman, bent on vengeance. Unhappiness oppresses you, and you wish to ruin your adopted land. To divide Egypt, break its backbone, turn it into a Hittite province ... Is that what you secretly want?'

'What if it is?'

'That would be high treason, Princess. The judges would demand the death penalty.'

'You are missing your chance to save Egypt.'

'At the heart of this temple neither chance nor mischance exists, only the service of the gods.'

'You are wrong.'

'If it is wrong to be loyal to Pharaoh, this world no longer deserves to exist.'

Hattusa had failed. Her lip trembled. 'Will you denounce me?'

'The temple loves silence. Silence the voice of destruction within yourself, and you will know peace.'

The swallow clung to life. Neferet had settled it in a basket lined with straw, safe from cats and other predators. She dripped a little water into its damaged beak. Unable to feed itself, let alone fly, the bird was becoming used to her presence, and was unalarmed when she took its basket out into the garden so that it might feel the sun's warmth.

Pazair was still angry with himself for his stupid interference.

'Why don't you question Nenophar again?' asked Neferet. 'Serious suspicions have fallen on her.'

'She's the official steward of fabrics, and an excellent needlewoman, I know, but I can't see her murdering Branir in cold blood. She's haughty, loud, sure of herself, full of her own importance—'

'Or perhaps just an accomplished actress?'

'I agree. And she's also physically strong.'

'Didn't the murderer attack Branir from behind?'

'Yes, that's right.'

'Then accuracy mattered more than strength – plus having a good knowledge of the body, so as to strike in the right place.'

'Nebamon is still the best suspect.'

'Before he died he told me the truth. He wasn't guilty.'

'If I summon Nenophar before a court, she'll deny the charge and will be acquitted. All I have is some worrying clues, not proof. Questioning her again would bear no fruit. She'd protest her innocence, call upon her many relations and friends to support her, and submit a complaint of harassment. I need something new.'

'Have you told Kem about the attempted poisoning?'

'He and Killer are watching me day and night – they take it in turns to sleep.'

'Can't he send guards to protect you?'

'I've already suggested that, but he doesn't trust them.'

'You won't stop him protecting you, will you?' asked Neferet anxiously.

'Sometimes it's highly inconvenient.'

'Judge of the Porch, your duties take precedence over your convenience.'

'Do you think I'm behaving like an old man?'

She considered for a moment. 'That's a matter which ought to be examined carefully. We'll see, tonight, if—'

He caught her in his arms, lifted her and carried her indoors. 'This old man will marry you as many times as he has to. Why wait until tonight?'

*

The Judge of the Porch held his seal over the papyrus. Since the early morning, the seal had given authorization to a huge number of documents relating to the proper conduct of agricultural works, controls on property revenues, and the delivery of goods. Pazair read quickly and could get the gist of a report in a few seconds.

This one shocked him. 'Five days' delay for a delivery of fresh fruit?'

'That's correct,' said a scribe, nodding.

'It's unacceptable. I refuse to approve this. Have you set a fine?'

'I sent the necessary documentation to my colleague in Thebes.'

'What was his reply?'

'It hasn't arrived yet.'

'Why not?'

'They're overwhelmed by similar delays.'

'This chaos has been going on for over a week, and nobody told me!'

The scribe began to stammer an excuse. 'There were more important inquir—'

'More important? Dozens of villages are at risk of running out of fresh food. It seems unimportant to you only because of the size of your belly!'

Thoroughly discomfited, the scribe laid a pile of papyri on the judge's mat. 'There have been other delays, too, in the delivery of other goods. We've just had warning of a very alarming one: no fresh vegetables from Middle Egypt will reach the Memphis barracks for ten days.'

Pazair blanched. 'Can you imagine the soldiers' reaction? To the docks, quickly!'

Kem himself drove the chariot alongside the canal that ran parallel to the Nile, with its warehouses and granaries, and drew up at the docks where goods arrived. The instant the chariot stopped, Pazair leapt out and ran to the office where fresh produce was registered.

Inside, a small boy was fanning two sleepy scribes.

'What are our stocks of fruit and vegetables?' demanded Pazair.

'Who are you?' asked one of the scribes.

'The Judge of the Porch.'

The two men jumped to their feet in horror, and bowed very low.

'Forgive us, Judge,' said the scribe. 'For several days we've had no work at all, because the deliveries have been disrupted.'

'Where are the boats being delayed?'

'Nowhere. They arrive at Memphis, but not with the right cargoes. Today, the largest fruit-boat was carrying stones. What can we do?'

'Is it still at the quayside?'

'It is leaving again soon, bound for Thebes.'

Pazair and Kem, accompanied by Killer, crossed a naval boatyard, and reached the port, where a seagoing vessel was about to leave for Cyprus. On the fruit-boat, the sails were being hoisted. The judge stepped on to the gangplank.

'Just a moment,' said Kem, holding him back by the arm.

'We must hurry.'

'I have a bad feeling.'

The baboon was sitting up very straight, its nostrils drawn in.

'I'll go first,' said Kem firmly.

When they got aboard, he saw why Killer was upset. Among the cases on deck was a cage, and behind its wooden bars a panther was pacing up and down. The animal, which a sailor told them had been captured in the Nubian desert, was magnificent.

'Where's the captain?' asked Pazair.

A man of around fifty, with a low brow and a heavy frame, left the tiller and came towards them. 'I'm about to cast off my moorings,' he shouted. 'Get off my boat.'

'City guards,' said Kem. 'I'm acting on orders from the Judge of the Porch, here present.'

The captain lowered his voice. 'All my documents are in order, although the dock offices won't accept my load of stones.'

'Weren't they expecting vegetables?'

'Yes, but I was requisitioned.'

'Requisitioned?' Pazair was astonished. 'By which secretariat?'

'I have to obey the scribes. I don't want any trouble.'

'Show me your ship's records.'

While Pazair was examining them, Kem had a chest opened. It did indeed contain stones destined for the temple sculptors.

The records noted a big cargo of fresh fruit, which had been loaded on the eastern bank of Thebes, requisitioned in the middle of the river by naval scribes, and unloaded at Thebes west. The boat had then sailed north, to the quarries of Gebel el-Silsila, where it had taken on a cargo of chests of stone ordered by – Karnak! In accordance with its first instructions, the boat had headed for Memphis, where the captain had been refused permission to unload the stones because they were not the cargo specified.

Deeply suspicious, Kem examined the contents of several other chests. All were filled with blocks of stone.

The shadow-eater had been following Pazair since the morning. The presence of Kem and Killer complicated a task which was already extremely difficult. He must devise a new plan and wait for a moment when their vigilance slackened.

Ah! Here was an opportunity: the panther.

Aboard the cargo-boat, Pazair was deep in discussion with the captain, while Kem and Killer were inspecting the hold. A group of sailors were going aboard, taking rations for the crew. The shadow-eater tagged on to them, got aboard and hid behind the mainmast. As soon as he was sure he had not been spotted, he crawled towards the cage.

One by one, he pulled out four of the five bars imprisoning the animal. As if it realized his intention, the panther froze, ready to spring for freedom.

Pazair was getting furious. 'Where is the seal of the river guards?' he asked the captain for the third time.

'They forgot to put it on, they—'

'Do not leave Memphis.'

'But I've got to. I have to deliver these stones.'

'I am taking away your ship's journal to examine it in detail.' The judge headed for the gangplank.

As he passed the cage, the shadow-eater removed the fifth bar and lay down flat on the deck.

At the sound of Pazair's footsteps, the panther sprang out of the cage and crouched, snarling, at the top of the gang-plank. Fascinated and afraid, Pazair gazed deep into its eyes. He saw no hatred there: it would attack him simply because he was an obstacle in its way.

A ferocious howl made the whole crew jump. Killer shot out of the hold and leapt between the panther and the judge. Mouth gaping, eyes bright red, hair on end, arms swinging like a prize-fighter's, the baboon defied its opponent.

In the grasslands, even a hungry panther abandoned its kill when a group of baboons threatened it, but this one defiantly bared its teeth and unsheathed its claws. The baboon jumped up and down excitedly.

Dagger in hand, Kem stepped to Killer's side. He would not leave his best officer to fight alone.

At that, the panther retreated and slunk back into its cage. Kem went slowly forward and, keeping his eyes firmly on it, replaced the bars one by one.

'Over there!' shouted a sailor. 'There's a man running away!'

The shadow-eater had escaped from the boat by sliding down a mooring-rope on to the quay, and was disappearing round the corner of a dockside building.

'Can you describe him?' Pazair asked the sailor.

'Sorry, no. All I saw was the vague shape of a man running away.'

Pazair thanked Killer by placing his hand in the powerful, velvety paw. The baboon had calmed down now; there was pride in its eyes.

'Somebody tried to kill you again,' said Kem.

'I don't think so. I think they wanted me to be badly wounded. You'd have dragged me out of the panther's claws, but in what state?'

'As commander of the city guards, I'd like to lock you up in your house.'

Pazair smiled. 'As Judge of the Porch, I'd set myself free on the grounds of unlawful arrest. Still, the fact that our enemies are acting like this proves that we're moving in the right direction.'

'I'm afraid for you.'

'I must go forward. What else can I do?'

Kem took something out of his pouch. 'This will help you.' It was the stopper from a jar. 'There are ten like this in the lower hold: the captain's wine reserve. The inscriptions identify the owner of the cargo.'

The hieroglyphics were hastily scrawled but readable. They said, '*Harem of Princess Hattusa*'.

26

The captain of the cargo-boat confessed, without having to be asked, that he was indeed working for Princess Hattusa. Not content either with the material evidence or with this declaration, Pazair continued his investigation in more depth.

Kem questioned the regional commanders of the river guards. It seemed that none of them had given the order to requisition a consignment of fruit and vegetables at Thebes, which was why the official seal was not on the ship's journal.

Pazair summoned the captain again. 'You lied to me.'

'I was afraid.'

'Of whom?'

'Of the law, of you, and especially of her.'

'Princess Hattusa?'

'I've been in her service for two years. She's generous, but very demanding. She ordered me to do what I did.'

'Do you realize that you have disrupted the delivery of fresh food?'

'If I hadn't obeyed I'd have been dismissed. And I wasn't the only one – others did the same.'

Two scribes each took down the captain's statement and Pazair read both copies, making sure they were identical. The captain agreed that they were accurate.

Tense and anxious, the judge sent a message to Bel-Tran, asking for a meeting.

They met in the potters' district, where craftsmen with skilful hands and agile feet made a thousand and one vessels, from tiny ointment vases to large jars for holding dried meat. Many pupils watched closely as a master-potter worked, before taking their own turn at the wheel.

'I need your help again,' said Pazair.

'My position isn't easy,' said Bel-Tran. 'Nenophar's waging a veritable war against me. She's trying to form a group of courtiers to demand my dismissal, and some of them have the tjaty's ear.'

'Bagey will judge the case on its merits.'

'Yes, but I have to spend my evenings checking the accounting scrolls, so that no one can find even the slightest irregularity in my work.'

'What weapons is Nenophar using?'

'Lies and insinuations. I know how powerful they can be, but all I can do in response is work harder.'

Pazair smiled. 'I've just uncovered some facts which may help you.'

'What are they?'

'There's been disruption of the trade in fresh foodstuffs.'

'Was it simply an administrative error?'

'No, it was deliberate.'

'But if the people don't get the food they need,' said Bel-Tran, aghast, 'they may stop working, or perhaps even riot!'

'Don't worry, I've identified the culprit.'

'Who is it?'

'Princess Hattusa.'

Bel-Tran adjusted his kilt. 'Are you sure?'

'My file contains proof and written statements.'

'This time she's gone too far. But attacking her would call the king into question.'

'Would Ramses let his people go hungry?'

'The question is meaningless. But would he let his wife, symbol of peace with the Hittites, be convicted?'

'She has committed a serious crime. If high-born people can evade the law, Egypt will become a land of compromises, privileges and lies. I shall not suppress the matter, but without an official complaint from the Treasury the princess will block the case.'

Bel-Tran did not hesitate for long. 'It may cost me my career, but you shall have your complaint.'

Ten times that day, Neferet moistened the swallow's beak. The bird turned its head towards the light; the doctor stroked it and spoke to it, desperate to save its life.

Pazair returned late, exhausted. 'Is it still alive?'

'It seems in less pain.'

'Is there any hope at all?'

'In all honesty, no. Its beak is still closed, and it's gently slipping away. We've become friends.' She looked at him more closely. 'Why are you so worried?'

'Princess Hattusa is trying to starve Memphis and the villages in the region.'

'That's absurd! How could she possibly succeed?'

'Through corruption, by playing on the government's inertia. But it is indeed absurd: there are too many levels of control. She must have lost her mind. The Treasury is lodging a complaint, through Bel-Tran, and I'm leaving for Thebes to lay charges against the princess.'

'Aren't you forgetting Branir, Asher and the conspirators?'

'Perhaps not, if Hattusa is Denes's ally.'

'Bringing a case against the most famous general in Egypt, then against a royal wife . . . You're no ordinary judge, Pazair!'

'And you're no ordinary woman. Do you approve of what I'm doing?'

'Yes, but it may be dangerous. What will you do to protect yourself?'

'Nothing. I must question her, and present the charges. Then I shall pass the matter to the tjaty; he wouldn't accept a slapdash case.'

'I love you, Pazair.'

They kissed.

Neferet, though, was still anxious. 'Your enemies have tried poison and then a wild panther. What will they try next?'

'I don't know, but don't worry. Kem and I will be travelling on a boat belonging to the river guards.'

Before dinner, he paid a visit to the swallow. To his great surprise, it raised its head. The injured eye had scarred over, and the little body quivered with more energy.

Amazed, Pazair dared not move. Neferet took some straw and laid it under the bird's feet, to serve as a perch. The swallow gripped it.

Suddenly, with stunning energy, it beat its wings and took flight.

Instantly, from all corners of the sky, came a dozen of its fellows; one of them kissed it, like a mother rediscovering her child. Then a second, a third and the whole flight, mad with joy. The community of swallows danced above Neferet and Pazair, who could not hold back their tears.

'Look! They're reunited,' breathed Pazair.

'You were right to tear it away from death. Now it's living among its own kind. What does it care for tomorrow?'

The sky was a radiant blue, the sun reigning over all.

At the prow of the boat, Pazair gazed admiringly at his country. He thanked the gods for allowing him to be born on this magic soil, in this land of contrasts between cultivated fields and desert. Beneath the crowns of the palm-trees flowed the benevolent waters of the irrigation channels, and peaceful villages of white houses sheltered in the trees' shade. The golden corn gleamed, the green of the palm-groves charmed the eye. Wheat, linen and fruit were born out of the black earth, which had been cultivated by generations of peasants. Acacias and sycamores vied in beauty with tamarisks and perseas; on the banks of the Nile, far from the landing-stages, papyrus and reeds throve. In the desert sand, plants sprang up at the first sign of rain, and the depths preserved the sky-water for weeks on end, in springs which could be detected with a dowsing-rod. The Delta and its fertile expanses, the valley with the sacred river cutting its way between the arid mountains and the barren plateaux, enchanted the soul and put man in his rightful place in creation, after animals, minerals and plants, according to the sages' teachings. Only the human race, in its vanity and madness, tried from time to time to distort life; that was why the goddess Ma'at had offered it law, so that the twisted staff might be made straight.

'I think you're wrong to do this,' said Kem.

'Surely you don't think the princess is innocent?' asked Pazair.

'You'll get your fingers burnt.'

'My case is watertight.'

'Perhaps, but what will it be worth in the face of a royal wife's denials? I wonder if you aren't actually helping the rabble trying to destroy you. Can you imagine how angry Hattusa will be? Even Bagey won't be able to protect you.'

'She is not above the law.'

'A fine thought – and a laughable one.'

'We shall see.'

'Where do you get such confidence from?'

'From my wife's eyes, and just recently from the flight of a swallow.'

Without warning, a fierce wind sprang up, and unexpected whirlpools churned the Nile's waters. At the prow of the boat, the man who sounded the river with a long staff could no longer do so. The sudden storm took the sailors by surprise, and they were slow to reduce sail: the yards broke, the mainmast twisted, and the rudder stopped responding to the tiller. Steering an erratic course, the boat hit a sandbank. They dropped the stern anchor, a heavy stone block which would hold the the vessel steady in the strong current. People were running about on deck; Kem re-established calm with his powerful voice. With the captain, he assessed the damage and gave orders to proceed with repairs.

Shaken about and soaked, Pazair felt useless. Kem took him into the cabin, while two experienced sailors dived to check the condition of the hull. As luck would have it, it had not suffered too badly; as soon as the Nile's anger was stilled, they could resume their journey.

'The crew are worried,' said the big Nubian. 'Before we left, the captain forgot to repaint the magic eyes on either side of the prow. His forgetfulness might cause a shipwreck, because the boat is blind.'

Pazair took his writing-materials from his travelling-bag. He prepared some very black, almost indelible ink, and restored the protective eyes with his own steady hand.

Alerted by the captain of Princess Hattusa's fruit and vegetable boat, five bodyguards from her harem, stationed a day's march to the north of Thebes, waited for the boat carrying Judge Pazair to pass by. Their mission was simple: to stop it by any means necessary. If they succeeded, they would each receive a parcel of land, two cows, a donkey, ten sacks of wheat and five jars of wine.

They were delighted by the storm, for it meant that a shipwreck and death by drowning were thoroughly plausible. For a judge, being absorbed by the Nile would be a fine end. The legend ran that those who drowned gained direct access to paradise, if they were godly men.

On board their fast skiff, the five attackers were planning to take advantage of the weather and the sky laden with black clouds to approach their prey, which was still immobilized near the sandbank. They stopped a little way from it, threw themselves into the water, swam to the boat and climbed on to the deck with ease. Their leader, armed with a mallet, felled the guard on watch. The other river guards were asleep on their mats, rolled up in their blankets, so all that remained was to force open the cabin door, seize the judge and drown him. They would be innocent; it was the Nile that would kill him. Barefoot, moving soundlessly, they halted before the closed door. Two watched the sailors, three would take care of Pazair.

A black shape leapt from the roof of the cabin and landed on the leader's shoulders. He howled with pain as the baboon's teeth sank into him. Flinging open the light wooden door of the cabin, Kem charged at the intruders, a dagger in either hand, and mortally wounded two of them. The two others, terrified, tried in vain to escape, but the guards, now awake and alert, pinned them to the deck.

Killer did not slacken his grip until Kem gave the order. By then, the leader of the raiding-party was drenched in blood and almost unconsicous.

'Who sent you?' demanded Kem.

The wounded man said nothing.

'If you refuse to speak, my baboon will interrogate you.'

'Princess Hattusa,' he gasped.

As before, Pazair was amazed by the harem. Canals, maintained to perfection, served vast gardens where the great ladies of Thebes liked to walk, coming to take the air in the shade and show off their latest dresses. There was abundant water, flowers in harmonious colours were planted everywhere, and bands of female musicians practised the pieces they would play at forthcoming banquets. Hard work went on in the weaving and pottery workshops, but in surroundings that were both comfortable and relaxing. Experts in enamel and rare woods started on their masterpieces at sunrise, while bearers loaded jars of scented oil on to a trading-ship.

In accordance with tradition, Princess Hattusa's harem was a little town where exceptionally talented craft workers took the necessary time to experience beauty in their hearts and hands, so as to pass it on in flawless objects and products.

Pazair could have strolled for hours on end through this ordered world, where no work seemed burdensome, could have wandered along the sandy paths, conversed with the gardeners as they weeded, sampled the fruit while talking to the elderly widows who had chosen to live here. But, alas, in his capacity as Judge of the Porch he had requested an audience with the princess.

The head steward showed him into the reception-hall, where Princess Hattusa sat in state, flanked by two scribes.

Pazair bowed.

'I am extremely busy,' said Hattusa, 'so please be brief.'

'I should like to speak with you privately.'

'The official nature of your action forbids it.'

'On the contrary, I think it demands it.' Pazair unrolled a papyrus. 'Do you wish your scribes to register the charges?'

With an irritated wave of her hand, the princess dismissed them.

'Are you aware of what you are saying?' she said when they had gone.

'Princess Hattusa, I accuse you of stealing foodstuffs and of arranging an attempt on my life.'

The beautiful dark eyes flamed. 'How dare you!'

'I have proof, witness statements and written depositions. I therefore consider you guilty. Before arranging your trial, I call on you to explain your actions.'

'No one has ever spoken to me like this!'

'No royal wife has ever committed such crimes.'

'Ramses will destroy you.'

'Pharaoh is the son and servant of Ma'at. Since truth gives life to my words, he will not stifle them. Your rank cannot keep your crimes secret.'

Hattusa stood up and walked away from her throne. 'You hate me because I am a Hittite.'

'You know perfectly well that that is not so. No resentment guides my steps, even though you ordered my death.'

'To stop your boat and prevent you from arriving in Thebes – that's what I told them to do.'

'Then they misunderstood you.'

'No one in Egypt would ever take the risk of killing a judge. The court will reject your theory and regard your witnesses as liars.'

'That defence is skilful, but how can you justify the theft of food?'

'If your so-called proof is as convincing as your allegations, my good faith will be obvious to all.'

'Princess, be good enough to read this document.'

Hattusa read the papyrus. Her face fell, and her long hands clenched. 'I shall deny it.'

'The witnesses go into great detail, and the facts are over-whelming.'

She defied him, magnificent as ever. 'I am the wife of Pharaoh.'

'Your word has no more worth than that of the humblest peasant. Your position makes your actions even more inexcusable.'

'I shall prevent you from holding a trial.'

'Tjaty Bagey will preside over it.'

She sank down on to one of the steps before the throne. 'Why do you want to ruin me?'

'What are you hoping to achieve, Princess?'

'Do you really want to know, Judge of Egypt?'

Nervously, Pazair met her passionate gaze.

'I hate your country, I hate its king, its glory and its power. Seeing the Egyptians starving to death, the children moaning, the animals dying, would be my greatest happiness. By keeping me prisoner in this false paradise, Ramses thought my rage would ebb away, but all it does is grow. I have suffered injustice, and I will no longer endure it. May Egypt die, may it be invaded by my people, or by one of the barbarian tribes. I shall be the greatest supporter of Pharaoh's enemies. And believe me, Judge Pazair, their numbers are growing every day.'

'Denes the ship-owner, for example?'

The princess anger was suddenly stilled. 'I have not said so.'

'You fell into a trap, didn't you?'

'I told you the truth – that famous truth which Egypt loves so much.'

27

As usual, the reception had been a dazzling success. Nenophar had paraded in a sumptuous dress, delightedly accepting her guests' eager compliments. Denes had concluded several advantageous agreements, and was pleased with the continued growth of a shipping business which compelled the admiration of everyone who mattered in Egypt. No one knew that he held supreme power in his hands. Free of impatience, though edgy, he was growing more and more excited about the future: anyone who had criticized him would be cast down lower than the ground, and those who had supported him would be rewarded. Time was on his side.

When the last guests had left, Nenophar said she was tired and withdrew to her apartments. Denes went out into the orchard, to check that no fruit had been stolen.

A woman suddenly emerged from the darkness.

'Princess Hattusa!' he exclaimed. 'What are you doing in Memphis?'

'You are never to speak my name again. I am still awaiting your delivery.'

'I don't understand.'

'The sky-iron.'

'I beg you to be patient, my lady.'

'That's impossible. I need it immediately.'

'Why?'

'You have led me into madness.'

'No one will trace things back to you.'

'Judge Pazair already has.'

'He is just trying to intimidate you.'

'He has laid charges against me, and intends to make me appear before a court, as the accused.'

'That's merely an idle boast,' said Denes scornfully.

'You do not know him.'

'He has no evidence.'

'On the contrary, he has not only evidence but witnesses' statements and depositions.'

'Ramses will intervene.'

'Pazair is entrusting the case to Tjaty Bagey; the king must submit to the law. I shall be convicted, Denes, stripped of all my lands and, at best, shut away in some provincial palace. The penalty may even be heavier.'

'That is indeed worrying.'

'I want the sky-iron.'

'I haven't got it yet.'

'By tomorrow at the latest. Otherwise . . .'

'Otherwise?'

'I shall denounce you to Judge Pazair. He suspects you, but does not know that you were behind the thefts of food. The jurors will believe me: I know how to be convincing.'

'It will take longer than a day to get it.'

'In two days' time the moon will be full and the sky-iron will make my magic effective. Tomorrow evening, Denes, or you will be destroyed with me.'

Watched with astonishment by Mischief, Brave took a bath. The dog first dipped a cautious paw into the lotus-pool to check that the water was to his liking.

Today was the servants' rest day, and Neferet went herself to lift the water-jar from the bottom of the well. Her mouth was like a lotus-bud, her breasts like love-apples; Pazair watched her go to and fro, placing flowers on an offering-table in memory of Branir, feeding the animals, raising her eyes to the swallows that, every evening, flew in circles over their home. Among them was the survivor, its wings spread wide.

Neferet checked the sycamore fruit; they were a pretty shade of yellow at the moment, but would become red as they ripened. In May she would open them on the tree to empty them of the insects that had chosen to live inside them. The sweet, fleshy fruit would then be edible.

'I have re-read the Hattusa case,' said Pazair, 'and my scribes have checked that it is properly formulated. I can send it to the tjaty with my findings.'

'The princess may not be afraid of him.'

'True, but she knows how determined I am.'

'What will she do?'

'It doesn't matter. It is up to Bagey to conduct the trial, and nothing she does will stop him doing so.'

'Even if Pharaoh asks you to withdraw the case?'

'He can dismiss me, but I'll never give up. If I did, my heart would be tainted for ever – even you couldn't cleanse it.'

Neferet came and sat down on a mat beside her husband's chair. 'Kem told me there was a third attempt on your life.'

'Yes, but this time they were Hattusa's men and they hoped to kill me by drowning me. Previously it was one man on his own and he wanted to cripple me.'

'Has Kem identified him yet?'

'Not yet. The fellow seems particularly cunning and skilful, and Kem's informants are saying nothing. But enough of that. What has the council of doctors decided?'

'The election has been delayed and new candidates have been invited to put themselves forward. Qadash is continuing with his application and is paying endless visits to the members of the council.' She leant her head against him. 'Whatever happens, we shall have known happiness.'

Pazair set his seal on the judgement of a provincial court, sentencing a village headman to twenty strokes of the rod and a heavy fine, for slanderous denunciation. The headman would probably appeal; if his conviction was confirmed, the punishment would be doubled.

Shortly before noon, the judge received a visit from the lady Tapeni. Small and slender, with jet-black hair, she knew how to use her charms and had persuaded hard-headed scribes to let her into the Judge of the Porch's office.

'What can I do for you?' he asked.

'You know very well.'

'I'm afraid I don't.'

'I want to know the hiding-place of your friend Suti, who is also my husband.'

Pazair had not expected this. It seemed that Tapeni, as well as Panther, was far from indifferent to the adventurer's fate.

'He has left Memphis.'

'Why?'

'He's on an official mission.'

'And of course you will not tell me the nature of his mission.'

'That is prohibited.'

'Is it dangerous?' asked Tapeni.

'He trusts in his good luck.'

'Suti had better come back. I am not the kind of woman who lets herself be forgotten and abandoned.' Her voice contained as much menace as tenderness.

Pazair tried an experiment. 'Have any great ladies been causing you problems recently?'

'Given my position, they're always demanding the finest fabrics.'

'Nothing more serious?'

'I don't understand.'

'The lady Nenophar, for example. Has she by any chance demanded your silence?'

Tapeni looked troubled. 'I told Suti about her, because she's a superb needlewoman.'

'She isn't the only one in Memphis. Why did you throw her name into the ring?'

'Your questions are annoying me.'

'I regret that, but they are extremely important.'

'Why?'

'I am investigating a serious crime.'

A strange smile floated about Tapeni's lips. 'Is Nenophar involved?'

'What exactly do you know?'

'You have no right to keep me here.' Quick as a flash, she made for the door. 'I may know a great deal, Judge Pazair, but why should I trust you with my secrets?'

Running a good hospital afforded little respite. As soon as one patient was cured, another replaced him and the battle began again. Neferet never tired of treating the sick; relieving suffering gave her endless joy. The staff helped her unflaggingly, and the scribes ensured that the hospital was properly run, so she was able to devote herself to her art, improving old remedies and trying to find new ones. Her work was full of variety: she might have to operate to remove a malignant growth, or set a broken limb, or comfort patients who were incurably sick. Some of her team of doctors were experienced, some were beginners. They obeyed her gladly, and she never so much as had to raise her voice to them.

Today had been particularly demanding. Neferet had saved a forty-year-old man, who was suffering from a blockage in his intestines. Tired, she was drinking some cool water when Qadash burst into the room where the doctors washed and changed.

He said loudly, 'I want to see the list of drugs the hospital possesses.'

'Why?'

'I am a candidate for the post of principal doctor, and I need that list.'

'What do you intend to do with it?'

'I must know all the drugs used in the country.'

'Why? As a tooth-doctor, you use only specific remedies.'

'Give me that list at once.'

'There's no reason why you should see it. You don't work at this hospital.'

'You don't understand, Neferet. I must prove my skills. Without a list of the drugs, my application will be incomplete.'

'Only the kingdom's principal doctor could compel me to give it to you.'

'I am the future principal doctor.'

'Nebamon has not yet been replaced, so far as I know.'

'Do as I say – you won't regret it.'

'Certainly not.'

'If I have to, I'll break down the door of your workshop.'

'You would be severely punished.'

'Do not resist me any longer. Very soon I shall be your superior. If you refuse to cooperate, I shall dismiss you from your post.'

Several doctors, alerted by the raised voices, came to Neferet's support.

'Your mob doesn't impress me,' sneered Qadash.

'Get out of here,' ordered a young doctor.

'You are ill advised to speak to me in that tone of voice.'

'And your behaviour is unworthy of a doctor.'

'This is an emergency,' declared Qadash.

'Only from your point of view,' Neferet corrected him.

'The post of principal doctor must be given to a man of experience. All of you here like me. Why do we have to argue like this? We all work with the same wish to serve others.'

Qadash pleaded his cause with emotion and conviction. He pointed to his long career, his devotion to the sick, his wish to be useful to the country without being hampered by ridiculous administrative procedures.

But Neferet stood firm. If Qadash wanted the list of poisons and drugs, he must justify its use. Until Nebamon's successor had been appointed, she would guard it closely.

The head of Asher's general staff was very sorry, but his superior was absent.

Pazair persisted. 'This is not a courtesy visit. I must question him.'

'The general has left the barracks.'

'When?'

'Yesterday evening.'

'Where was he going?'

'I don't know.'

'Don't the regulations require him to inform you as to his movements?'

'Yes.'

'Then why did he not do so?'

'I cannot tell, Judge.'

'This is thoroughly unsatisfactory.'

'Search the barracks if you wish.'

Pazair questioned two other officers, but learnt nothing more. According to several witnesses, the general had left by chariot, heading south. Suspecting a ruse, the judge then went to the Foreign Affairs secretariat: no troops had been sent to Asia.

Pazair asked Kem to find the general as quickly as possible. The commander soon confirmed that he had gone south, but could not be more precise. Asher had been careful to cover his tracks.

The tjaty was annoyed. 'Are you not exaggerating, Judge Pazair?'

'I have been trying to find Asher for a week.'

'Have you been to the barracks?'

'There is no trace of him there.'

'What about the Foreign Affairs secretariat?'

'It has not sent him on a mission – unless it is a secret one.'

'In that case I would have been informed, and I have not been.'

'Then we can reach only one conclusion: the general has disappeared.'

'That is outrageous. His office forbids such dereliction of duty.'

'He has tried to escape the net that was closing around him.'

'Have your constant attacks worn him down?'

'To my mind, he was afraid you would take action against him.'

'That means the law would have convicted him.'

'His friends have probably deserted him.'

'Why should they do that?' asked Bagey.

'Asher realized he was being used.'

'But for a soldier to run away!'

'He is a coward and a murderer.'

'If your accusations are correct, why did he not head for Asia and join his real allies there?'

'He may have only pretended to go towards the South.'

'I shall give the order to close the borders. Asher will not leave Egypt.'

If he had no help, Asher would not escape the net. And no one would dare help a disgraced general and disobey an order made by the tjaty.

Pazair ought to have been delighted by this formidable victory. The general could not justify his desertion; betrayed by traitors, he would betray them in turn during his second trial. He had probably tried to take revenge on Denes and Sheshi and then, when he failed, had chosen to run away.

'I shall send the provincial governors a decree ordering Asher's immediate arrest. Have Kem pass it on to the guards' commanders in all the cities.'

The system for sending urgent messages was so efficient that Asher would be sought everywhere in less than four days.

'Your work is not yet done,' continued the tjaty. 'If the general is indeed only a cat's-paw, you must trace the head of the plot.'

'That is indeed what I intend to do,' confirmed Pazair, whose thoughts were turning to Suti.

Denes took Princess Hattusa to the secret forge where Sheshi was working. Located in a working-class district, it was hidden behind an open-air kitchen run by some of Denes's employees. Sheshi was experimenting with combinations of metals, and testing the effects of vegetable acids on copper and iron.

The heat in the forge was unbearable. Hattusa took off her cloak and hood.

'My friend, you have a royal visitor,' announced Denes delightedly.

Sheshi did not look up. He was concentrating on a delicate operation, a solder incorporating gold, silver and copper.

'This is to be the hilt of a dagger,' he explained. 'It will belong to the future king, when the tyrant has gone.'

With one foot, Sheshi pumped regularly on a pair of bellows, to bring the fire to white heat. He handled the metal with bronze pincers, and had to work very quickly, for the pincers melted at the same temperature as the gold.

Hattusa was impatient. 'I'm not interested in your experiments. I want the sky-iron I paid for.'

'You paid for only part of it,' said Denes.

'Deliver it to me, and you shall have the balance.'

'So you're still in a hurry?'

'Don't be insolent! Show me what is due to me.'

'You will have to wait.'

'That is enough, Denes! Have you lied to me?'

'Not altogether.'

'Does the sky-iron not belong to you?'

'I shall soon get it back.'

'You have made a fool of me!'

'No, Princess, you're mistaken there. It was a simple matter of anticipation. We are working together for Ramses' ruin, isn't that the important thing?'

'You are nothing but a thief.'

'It is pointless to be angry. We have no choice but to go on working together.' Denes's expression betrayed his contempt.

'You are wrong, Denes. I shall do without your help.'

'It would be most unwise to break our agreement.'

'Open that door and let me leave.'

'Will you keep silent about what you know?'

'I shall act in my own interests.'

'I require your word.'

'Stand aside.'

As Denes did not move, Hattusa pushed him out of the way. In fury, he pushed her back and she fell against the red-hot pincers, which Sheshi had laid on a stone. She screamed, stumbled, and fell into the hearth. Her dress caught fire instantly.

Neither Denes nor Sheshi went to her aid, Sheshi awaiting instructions from his master. When Denes opened the door and fled, Sheshi followed him. The forge burst into flames.

28

Before presiding over the court's ordinary session, to be held in front of the porch of the Temple of Ptah, Pazair had written a coded message to Suti: '*Asher is lost. Take no further risks. Come back immediately.*'

The judge entrusted the document to a messenger vouched for by Kem; as soon as the man reached Kebet, he would hand it to the desert guards, who were in charge of passing messages to the miners.

The court was judging a series of minor offences, from the non-payment of a debt to an unjustified absence from work. The guilty parties admitted they were at fault, and the jurors were lenient. Among the latter was Denes.

At the end of the hearing, he approached the judge. 'I am not your enemy, Pazair.'

'I am not your friend.'

'Precisely. You should be wary of those who claim to be your friends.'

'What are you insinuating?'

'Your trust is sometimes misplaced. Suti, for example, certainly doesn't deserve it. He sold me information about your investigation and about you yourself, in exchange for money.'

'My office forbids me to hit you, but I might forget myself and do it.'

'One day you'll be grateful to me.'

As soon as she arrived at the hospital, Neferet was asked for help by several doctors who had been toiling since the middle of the night, trying to save the life of a woman who had been badly burnt. The fire had occurred in a working-class district where an unauthorised furnace had caught fire. The unfortunate victim must have been careless; her chances of survival were non-existent.

The doctor in charge had treated the injured flesh by applying black mud and the cattle-dung, heated and crushed into fermented beer. Neferet reduced some grilled barley and colocynth to powder, mixed them with dried acacia-resin, and soaked the mixture in oil; then she made greasy poultices which she applied to the burns. She treated the least serious of the burns with yellow ochre crushed in sycamore-sap, colocynth and honey.

'That will ease the pain,' she said.

'How can we feed her?' asked an assistant.

'We can't at the moment.'

'We must give her water.'

'Slide a reed between her lips and feed copper-water through it, one drop at a time. Watch her all the time. If anything at all happens, however minor, let me know.'

'What about the poultices?'

'Change them every three hours. Tomorrow we'll use a mixture of wax, cooked beef-fat, papyrus and carob. Make sure there is a supply of very fine bandages in her room.'

'Do you hold out any hope, then?'

'To be honest, no.' Neferet turned to the hospital's head steward, who was waiting to talk to her. 'Do we know who she is? We must inform her family.'

The steward had been afraid Neferet would say that. He led her into an empty room nearby.

'I'm afraid, Doctor, there may be complications. Our patient is no ordinary person.'

'What is her name?'

He showed her a magnificent silver bracelet. On the inside was engraved the owner's name, which the flames had not erased: '*Hattusa, wife of Ramses*'.

A hot wind from Nubia set everyone's nerves on edge. It whipped up the desert sand, covering the houses with it. People conscientiously blocked up every aperture, but a fine yellow dust got in everywhere and obliged the housewives to clean constantly. Many people complained of breathing difficulties, causing the doctors a great deal of work. Pazair was not spared. A course of drops soothed his sore eyes, but he struggled against all-consuming fatigue. Kem, on the other hand, seemed as impervious to the heat and wind as Killer was.

The two men and the baboon were taking the air in the shade of a sycamore, near the lotus-pool. Brave, at first hesitant, had eventually settled at his master's feet, but he did not take his eyes off Killer for a second.

'There's still no news of Asher,' said Kem.

'He won't be able to get out of the country,' said Pazair.

'He can go to earth for weeks, but if he does his supporters will drift away and someone will probably denounce him. The tjaty's orders are quite clear. Why do you think Asher's done this?'

'Because he knew that this time he'd lose his case.'

'So his allies deserted him?'

'They didn't need him any more.'

'What conclusion have you come to?'

'That there is no military conspiracy, no attempted invasion.'

'But Princess Hattusa came to Memphis.'

'Like Asher, she's been eliminated because the conspirators don't need her any more. What have you found out about the fire?'

'The forge didn't belong to anyone, but the open-air kitchen was run by employees of Denes.'

'That's very interesting,' said Pazair.

'There's nothing to incriminate him explicitly.'

'No, but at each step we come up against him. And the fire was a serious crime.'

'People were seen running away, but the witnesses differ as to how many and have given only vague descriptions.'

'A forge ... Sheshi must have been working there.'

'Could he have lured Hattusa there to kill her?'

'I can't believe that anyone would burn a woman alive. Unless, of course, we are dealing with monsters.'

'If we are, we'd better prepare ourselves for some tough battles.'

'I assume it's no use asking you to lift the protective measures around me?'

'Even if I weren't commander of the guards, and even if you gave me orders to the contrary, I'd maintain the watch over you.'

Pazair would never decipher the mystery of Kem. Cold, distant, always in control of himself, he disapproved of the judge's actions but helped him without a second thought. The Nubian would never have any confidant but Killer; damaged physically, he was even more damaged in his soul. To him, justice was only an illusion. But Pazair believed in it, and Kem trusted Pazair.

'Have you told the tjaty about the fire?' asked Kem.

'Yes, I've sent him a detailed report. Hattusa hadn't told anyone she was coming to Memphis, it seems. Neferet is watching over her day and night.'

On the fifth day, Neferet ground colocynth, yellow ochre and copper particles to an oily paste and applied it to Hattusa's burns, which she bandaged with infinite gentleness. Despite the pain, Hattusa tried to resist.

On the sixth day, the look in the princess's eyes changed. She seemed to emerge from a long sleep.

'Hold firm. You are in the main hospital at Memphis. The most difficult stage is over. Now each hour that passes brings you closer to healing.'

The once-beautiful Hittite was horribly disfigured. No matter what ointments and lotions she used, her superb skin would never be more than a series of pinkish scars.

Hattusa raised a hand and gripped Neferet's wrist.

'Princess, yours is a sickness I know and can cure,' she promised.

Neferet had at last consented to rest for a while. She had fought fiercely to save Hattusa, with her own hands preparing the bandages and remedies which, little by little, were healing the appalling burns.

Pazair lay beside his wife and watched her as she slept. His love for her grew and blossomed like the crown of a palmtree. Each dawn brought a new colour, undreamt-of and sublime; Neferet had the gift of making life smile and lighting up the darkest night. If Pazair was went on fighting with undimmed enthusiasm, it was only so that he might continue to charm her and prove to her that she had not made a mistake in marrying him. Beyond his weaknesses blazed the certainty of a union which not time nor custom nor ordeals could ever wear away.

A ray of sunshine lit up the bedroom and touched Neferet's face. She stirred gently.

'Hattusa is saved,' she murmured.

'You've been neglecting me, for the benefit of your patient.'

She snuggled up to him. 'She was young, and so beautiful. How will she ever be able to accept what has happened to her?'

'Has there been any word from Ramses?'

'Yes, through the palace's head steward. As soon as she's well enough to be moved, she'll be taken there to be cared for.'

'Unless her confession means that she's denied such a privileged position.'

Troubled by those words, Neferet sat up in bed. 'Hasn't she been punished enough?'

'Forgive me, but I must question her.'

'She hasn't yet said a single word.'

'As soon as she's well enough to speak, let me know.'

Hattusa drank her barley broth and carob-juice. Her life-force was returning, but her gaze was still vacant, as if she were lost in a nightmare.

'How did it happen?' asked Neferet.

'He pushed me. I wanted to leave the forge, and he stopped me.'

The words came slowly and painfully. Neferet dared not ask her patient any more questions.

'The bronze tongs . . . they burnt my dress, a flame flared up, I fell against the forge, the fire caught me.' The voice became strident. 'They ran away, they abandoned me!'

Wild-eyed, Hattusa tried to regain the past and wipe away the tragedy that had destroyed her beauty and her youth. She slumped back, exhausted and defeated.

Suddenly, she sat up straight again and screamed her pain. 'They ran away, curse them, Denes and Sheshi!'

Neferet quickly administered a calming draught, and stayed with the princess until she fell asleep.

As she was leaving the hospital, the head steward of the Mother of Pharaoh's house approached her and said, 'Her Majesty wishes to see you immediately.'

Neferet was invited to take her place in a chair carried by bearers. The men hurried.

Tuya received her without ceremony.

When the greetings were over, Neferet asked, 'How is your health, Majesty?'

'Thanks to your treatment, it is excellent. Have you been informed of the decision taken by the council of doctors?'

'No.'

'The situation is becoming intolerable, so the kingdom's principal doctor will be appointed next week. A single name must emerge from the council's deliberations.'

'That is surely a necessity?'

'Qadash's only rivals will be puppets, because he has been able to deter all his worthy opponents. The former friends of Nebamon, the weak and the undecided will vote for him.' The queen's anger accentuated her natural gravity.

'I refuse to accept that as inevitable,' she went on. 'Qadash is incompetent, wholly unworthy to hold such an important office. I have always been concerned with the people's health. Measures must be taken to improve their well-being, to promote cleanliness so that epidemics are prevented. This man Qadash makes a mockery of such things. He wants power and glory, nothing else. He is worse than Nebamon. You must help me.'

'But how, Majesty?'

'By standing against him.'

Neferet gave Pazair permission to enter the room where Princess Hattusa was resting. Her face and limbs were still heavily bandaged – even her eyes were covered by very fine linen. To prevent gangrene and infection, the doctor had treated the wounds with a lotion reserved for the most serious cases. Copper particles, chrysocolla, fresh terebinth resin, cumin, natron, asafoetida, wax, cinnamon, bryony, oil and honey had been finely crushed and reduced to an oily mass.

'May I speak with you, Princess?' asked Pazair.

'Who are you?'

'Judge Pazair.

'Who permitted you to—'

'Doctor Neferet, my wife.'

'She's my enemy, too.'

'My request was official. I am investigating the fire.'

'The fire . . .'

'I want to identify the culprits.'

'What culprits?'

'Didn't you mention the names Denes and Sheshi?'

'No, you're mistaken.'

'Why did you go to the forge?'

'Do you really want to know?'

'If you will consent to tell me.'

'I went there to get sky-iron to use in magic against Ramses.'

'You ought to have been more wary of Sheshi.'

'I was alone.'

'How do you explain—'

'It was an accident. Judge Pazair, a simple accident.'

'Why are you lying?'

'I hate Egypt, its civilization and its values.'

'So much that you will not even testify against the men who did this to you?'

'Whoever tries to destroy Ramses has my sympathy. Your country rejects the only truth: war. Only war excites the passions and reveals human nature. My people were wrong to make peace with you, and I'm paying for that mistake. I wanted to awaken the Hittites, show them the right way . . . Now I shall be shut away in one of those palaces I loathe. But others will succeed, I'm convinced of that. And you won't even have the pleasure of putting me on trial. You aren't cruel enough to torture a sick woman still further.'

'Denes and Sheshi are criminals. They would laugh at your ideals.'

'My mind is made up. Not one word shall I say.'

As Judge of the Porch, Pazair ratified Neferet's candidacy for the post of principal doctor of the kingdom of Egypt. She had all the necessary qualifications and experience. Moreover, her position as director of the hospital, the official support of the king's mother, and the warm encouragement of many of her colleagues, gave substantial weight to her application.

She dreaded this unsought-for ordeal – Qadash would use the vilest methods to deter her. All she wanted was to heal; she certainly did not want honours and responsibilities.

Pazair could not comfort her. He himself was shaken by Hattusa's madness, knowing that she was doomed to the most desperate loneliness. Her testimony would have brought about the conviction of Denes and Sheshi, but once again they had escaped punishment.

He felt as though he had come up against an insurmountable wall. An evil spirit was protecting the conspirators and guaranteeing their impunity. Knowing that Asher had vanished, and being assured that no military conspiracy threatened Egypt, ought to have reassured him, but a dull anguish persisted. He could not understand the motive for so many crimes and the contemptuous assurance of a man like Denes, whom apparently no blow could shake. Did Denes and his acolytes have some secret weapon, beyond the judge's reach?

Aware of each other's distress, Pazair and Neferet each thought of the other before themselves. As they made love, they saw the birth of a new dawn.

29

When the All-Seeing Ones and their dogs returned from dangerous areas in the eastern desert, they allowed themselves a day's rest before setting off again on patrol. They used the time to bind up their wounds, have a massage and go to the ale-house, where meek, welcoming girls sold them their bodies for a night. The guards exchanged information they had gathered during raids and took to prison any sand-travellers and other raiders they had captured.

The big guard who oversaw the recruitment of miners attended to his dogs, then went to see the scribe in charge of messages.

'Anything for my lot?'

'Ten or so.'

The guard read the names on the scrolls. 'Well, well, there's one for Suti. He's a strange fellow. He doesn't seem like a miner.'

'That's nothing to do with me,' retorted the scribe. 'Sign here to acknowledge receipt.'

The guard distributed the messages himself; he always asked the recipients about the people who had written to them. Three miners were missing from the roll-call, two old hands, who were working in a copper mine, and Suti. The guard checked, and found that Ephraim's expedition had returned to Kebet the previous evening, so he went to the ale-house, visited the inns, and inspected the encampments. No luck: the mining-office informed him that Ephraim, Suti and five other men had failed to report to the scribe charged with noting down all comings and goings.

He set a thorough search in motion. Still nothing: the seven men had disappeared. Others before them had tried to make off with precious stones, but they had all been caught and severely punished. Why had an experienced man like Ephraim embarked on such a mad venture?

Forgetting their rest and relaxation, the All-Seeing Ones got organized at once. They had the souls of hunters, and nothing pleased them more than worthy game. The big guard would lead the search.

With the agreement of the messages scribe, and because of the circumstances, the guard opened the letter to Suti. The hieroglyphs, though individually readable, meant nothing when taken together. Clearly, it was in code. So he was right: Suti was not a miner like the others. But what master did Suti serve?

The seven men had taken a difficult route, leading south-east. All equally strong, they walked at a regular pace, ate little, and took long stops at the water-sources, whose locations only Ephraim knew. He had demanded absolute obedience, and permitted no questions about their destination. At the end of their journey, he said, a fortune awaited them.

'Over there – a guard!' The miner pointed towards a strange, motionless form.

'Keep going, fool,' ordered Ephraim. 'That's just a wool-tree.'

Twice the height of a man, the tree had bluish, grooved bark; its broad, green and pink leaves were reminiscent of the material used to make winter cloaks. The fugitives used the wood to light a fire and cook a gazelle they had killed that morning. Ephraim knew that the wool-tree's sap was not poisonous. He gathered some leaves, kneaded them, ground them to powder and shared them with his companions.

'A good purgative,' he commented, 'and a very effective remedy for venereal disease. When you're rich, you'll be able to afford gorgeous women.'

'Yes, but it won't be in Egypt,' mourned a miner.

'Asian women are warm and yielding. They'll soon make you forget your provincial girls.'

Their bellies full and their thirst slaked, the little band resumed their journey.

One of the miners was bitten on the ankle by a sand viper, and died in agonizing convulsions.

'Idiot,' muttered Ephraim. 'The desert doesn't forgive carelessness.'

The dead man's best friend said furiously, 'You're leading us all to our deaths. No one can escape those creatures.'

'I can, and so can those who tread where I do.'

'I want to know where we're going.'

'A loose-tongued man like you would talk to the wind and betray us.'

'Tell me.'

'Do you want me to break your head?'

The miner looked around: the endless desert was full of death-traps. He gave up, and collected his equipment.

'If attempts like ours have failed,' said Ephraim, 'it wasn't by chance.

It was because a spy infiltrated the group, and managed to let the guards know about his movements. I've taken special precautions, but I can't be certain there isn't an informer among us.'

'Whom do you suspect?'

'You and everyone else – any one of you could have been bought. If there is a spy, he'll give himself away sooner or later. And I shall enjoy that.'

The All-Seeing Ones began their search from the last known position of Ephraim and his group, and calculated how far they could have travelled if they were moving fast. Messengers alerted their colleagues in the north and south regarding these dangerous criminals and their quest for valuable metals. As ever, the manhunt would be crowned with complete success.

Ephraim knew the tracks, water-sources and mines as well as the guards did, and might well guess what the guards would do. So the big guard, who was to lead the patrol, abandoned the usual plan, and trusted to his instinct. In Ephraim's place, he would have tried to reach the area full of abandoned mines. There was no water, the heat was unbearable, there were snakes everywhere, and there were no mines there . . . Who would venture into that hell? In fact, it was an admirable hiding-place, and perhaps more than that, assuming the seams were not completely exhausted. As regulations demanded, the big guard took two experienced men and four dogs with him. By cutting across the usual routes, he could intercept the fugitives in the hilly area where a few wool-trees grew.

Kem was bound hand and foot. He longed to set off on the trail of General Asher, who had still not been found, but he had to stay in Memphis to protect Pazair. None of his men would be vigilant enough.

He could tell from Killer's edginess that danger was not far away. After two failures, the shadow-eater would have to take extra care so as not to be spotted. Now that the element of surprise had been lost, arranging an accident would be far more difficult, but he would surely try to take strong, decisive action.

Keeping Pazair safe had become the main goal of Kem's life. To him, the judge embodied an impossible form of life which must be preserved at all costs. Never, in all the long years when Kem had suffered so much, had he met anyone like this. He would never admit to Pazair how much he admired him, for fear of feeding that creeping, unctuous beast called vanity, which was so swift to rot hearts.

Killer awoke. Kem gave him some dried meat and sweet beer, then leant back against the low wall of the terrace from which they kept watch on the judge's house. Now it was his turn to sleep, while the baboon stood guard.

The shadow-eater cursed his bad luck. He had been wrong to accept this job; it was outside his special expertise, which was killing quickly and leaving no trace. For a moment he felt like giving up, but if he did his employers would denounce him, and his word would carry no weight against theirs. Moreover, he had set himself a challenge. Up till now, his career had not been marred by a single failure; he took extraordinary pleasure in the fact that his finest victim would be a judge.

Unfortunately, Pazair was guarded closely and efficiently. Kem and Killer were worthy opponents, and it would be extremely difficult to beat their vigilance. Since the panther episode, Kem had never been more than a pace away from the judge, and he had strengthened that protection by using several of his best men.

The shadow-eater's patience was infinite. He could wait for the smallest chink in the armour, the slightest slip in alertness. As he was walking through the market at Memphis, where sellers were displaying exotic products from Nubia, an idea came to him. An idea which might well eliminate his opponent's main line of defence.

'It's late, my darling,' said Neferet.

A dozen unrolled papyri lay in front of Pazair, who was seated on the floor, flanked by two tall pedestal lamps. 'After reading these scrolls, I'm not tired any more.'

'What are they?'

'Denes's accounts.'

'Where did you get them?'

'From the Treasury.'

'You didn't steal them, did you?' she asked with a smile.

'I made an official request to Bel-Tran, and he responded at once by giving me these.'

'What have you discovered?'

'A number of irregularities. Denes has failed to pay certain duties, and seems to have cheated over the tax on his revenues.'

'What penalty does he face, apart from a fine?'

'With the help of my comments, Bel-Tran will be able to ruffle Denes's financial peace.'

'Denes again – you're becoming obsessed with him.'

'Why, why, why is he so sure of himself? I must somehow find a way of piercing his shell.'

Neferet sighed, and changed the subject. 'Any news of Suti?'

'No. He should have sent me a message through the desert guards.'

'He must have been prevented from doing so.'

'Yes . . . he must have.'

His hesitation surprised Neferet. 'What do you think has happened?'

'Nothing.'

'The truth, Judge Pazair!'

'During the last court session, Denes alleged that Suti had betrayed me.'

'And you're letting yourself wonder if it's true?'

'May Suti forgive me.'

'Two in the right-hand gallery, the others in the left,' ordered Ephraim. 'Suti and I will take the middle one.'

The miners were uneasy.

'They're in very bad condition,' said one of them. 'The props are half rotten, and if they collapse we won't get out alive.'

'I brought you to this hell because the desert guards think it's worked-out. No water and only worked-out mines, that's what they say in Kebet. I've shown you the ancient well; you can find the treasure in these galleries yourselves.'

'Too risky,' decided one miner. 'I'm not going in.'

Ephraim went over to him. 'Us inside, you on your own outside? I don't like the idea of that.'

'Too bad.'

Ephraim's fist smashed down on the man's skull with such incredible force that he crumpled to the ground.

One of his colleagues bent over him, then straightened up, his eyes wide. 'You've killed him!'

'One suspect the less. Let's get into the galleries.'

Suti went ahead of Ephraim.

'Go carefully, little man. Feel the beams above your head.'

Suti crawled along the red, stony ground. The slope was gentle, but the ceiling very low. Ephraim held the torch.

A white gleam sprang out of the darkness. Suti reached out and felt it. The metal was soft and cool.

'It's silver – gold-bearing silver!'

Ephraim passed him some tools. 'A whole seam of it, little man. Get it out without damaging it.'

Under the pale silver gleamed gold. The precious silver was used to cover the flagged floors of certain temple rooms and sacred objects which stood on the floor, so as to preserve their purity. Indeed, the dawn was made up of silver stones which radiated the original light from the dawn of creation.

'Is there any gold further down?' asked Suti.

'Not here, little man. This mine's only a first step.'

The four dogs guided the three desert guards. For two hours, they had detected a human presence in the area around the abandoned mines. The guards kept their satisfaction in check; without a word, they readied their bows and arrows.

Flat on their bellies at the top of a hill, their tongues lolling out, the dogs watched the miners removing several big chunks of pure silver from the galleries. A veritable fortune.

When the thieves assembled to celebrate their triumph, the guards fired their arrows and released the dogs. Two miners were brought down by arrows, and a third by the dogs. Suti took refuge in a deep gallery, and was soon followed by Ephraim, who had strangled a dog with one hand, and by the last survivor from his team.

'Go deeper!' roared Ephraim.

'We'll suffocate,' objected Suti.

'Do as you're told.'

Ephraim led the way. Seizing a stone, he broke through the ceiling of the gallery at its end. Heedless of the dust and fragments of stone which fell on him, he created a chimney in the crumbling rock. Feet braced against the walls, he dragged up Suti, who helped his companion. The three men managed to get out of the mine and, once outside, gulped in the fresh air greedily.

'We can't stay here – the guards won't give up this easily. We'll have to walk for at least two days, without water.'

The big guard stroked the dogs, while his men dug trenches for the bodies. The first part of the operation had been a success: they had killed most of the fugitives and recovered a large quantity of silver. But three men were still on the run.

The guards conferred. Their leader decided to go on alone, with the strongest dog and some food and water, while the other two took the silver back to Kebet. The fugitives had no chance. Knowing they were being hunted by men armed with bows and arrows and by a ferocious hound, they would have to force their pace. There was no water within a three-day march. Heading south, they would inevitably run into a guard patrol.

The patrol-leader and his dog would take no risks, and would be content to bring down their quarry by cutting off all lines of retreat. Once more, the All-Seeing Ones would have defeated the criminals.

*

On the morning of the second day, the three fugitives licked up the dew that had collected on the stones along the way. The surviving miner wore round his neck his leather purse, which contained fragments of silver, and clutched it constantly. He was the first to break. His legs buckled, and he fell to his knees on the scree.

'Don't leave me,' he begged.

Suti turned and went back.

'If you try to help him,' warned Ephraim, 'you'll both die. Follow me, little man.'

If he carried the miner on his back, Suti would soon be left behind. They would become lost in this torrid desert, where only Ephraim knew the way.

His chest on fire, his lips cracked, the young man followed Ephraim.

The dog wagged its tail eagerly when it found the miner's body. The guard praised the dog, and turned the body over with his foot. The man had not been dead for long. He was still clutching his leather purse, so tightly that the guard had to cut his hands off to recover the silver.

The guard sat down, worked out the value of the silver, gave his dog food and water, and then had some himself. Used to interminable marches, neither of them felt the sun's bite. They were careful to rest regularly, and wasted no energy at all.

Now it was two against two, and the distance between guard and thieves was getting smaller all the time.

He turned round. Several times he had had the feeling he was being followed; but the dog was pulling in the direction of his quarry, and did not signal anything amiss.

He cleaned his dagger in the sand, moistened his lips, and resumed the hunt.

'Just one more effort, little man. There's a seep-well near the mine.'

'Are you sure it won't have run dry?'

Ephraim did not reply. So much suffering must not be in vain.

A circle of stones marked the site of the well. Ephraim dug with his bare hands, and Suti soon joined him. At first there was nothing but sand and pebbles; then softer, almost damp earth; finally, a sort of mud, wet fingers – and water, water rising up from the underground Nile.

The guard and his dog watched. An hour ago they had caught up with the fugitives, but they had kept their distance. They heard the pair sing out, saw them gulp down water, congratulate themselves, then head for the abandoned mine, which was not shown on any map.

Ephraim had played his game astutely. He had not confided in anyone at all, keeping strictly to himself a secret he must have extracted from an old miner.

The guard checked his bow and arrows, took a swig of water and prepared to end the hunt.

'This is where the gold is, little man, in the last seam in a forgotten gallery. Enough gold to enable two good friends to live out happy lives in Asia.'

'Are there any other places like this?'

'A few.'

'Why don't we mine them?'

'There's no time. We've got to get away – and so has our employer.'

'Who is he?'

'The man who's waiting for us here at the mine. The three of us will get the gold out and transport it on sleds to the sea. Then a boat will take us to a desert area where chariots are hidden.'

'Have you stolen a lot of gold for him?'

'He won't like it if you ask questions. Look, there he is.'

A small man with thick legs and a ratlike face came towards them. Despite the burning sun, Suti's blood ran cold.

'The guards are hot on our heels,' said Ephraim. 'Let's dig the gold out and get away from here.'

'You've brought me a very unexpected companion,' said General Asher in astonishment.

With his last shreds of strength, Suti fled towards the desert. He had no chance of beating Ephraim and Asher – the latter was armed with a sword. First he must escape from them, then he would have to think.

A guard and his dog barred his way. Suti recognized the big man who oversaw the recruitment of miners. The guard drew his bow; one word from him and the dog would go for Suti's throat.

'Not a step further, my lad.'

'Thank be to the gods that you're here!'

'You can pray to the gods before you die.'

'Don't shoot the wrong man. I'm on an official mission.'

'On whose orders?'

'Judge Pazair's. I had to prove that General Asher was mixed up in smuggling precious metals. And now I've got that proof. The two of us can arrest him.'

'You're a brave lad, but you're out of luck. I work for General Asher.'

30

Neferet lifted the double lid of her face-paint box, which was divided into compartments decorated with red flowers. It contained pots of lotion, ointment, face- and eye-paint, pumice stone and perfumes. While the household, including the monkey and the dog, was still asleep, she liked to make herself beautiful, then walk barefoot in the dew to hear the first song of the tits and the hoopoes.

The dawn was her time, the time when life was reborn, the awakening of a nature whose every sound was filled with the divine word. The sun had just overcome the darkness, after a long and perilous battle; its triumph nourished creation, its light was transformed into joy, making the birds dance in the sky and the fish jump in the river.

Neferet treasured the happiness the gods had granted her, which she must give them in return. It did not belong to her, but passed through her like a flow of energy, coming from and returning to the source. Anyone who tried to take possession of the otherworld's gifts condemned themself to drying out like a dead branch.

Kneeling before the lakeside offering-table, the young woman laid a lotus-flower on it. It embodied the new day, in which eternity would be accomplished in a moment. The entire garden was meditating, the leaves of the trees bowing beneath the morning breeze.

When Brave licked her hand, Neferet knew that the sacred rite was at an end. The dog was hungry.

'Thank you for seeing me before you go to the hospital,' said Silkis. 'The pain is unbearable – it kept me awake all last night.'

'Lean your head back.' Neferet examined her patient's left eye.

Silkis was so anxious that she could not keep still.

'This is a sickness I know and can cure,' said Neferet.

'Your eyelashes are so tightly curled that they're touching the eye and irritating it.'

'Is it serious?'

'No, only painful. Would you like me to deal with it immediately?'

'If it doesn't hurt too much.'

'It's a simple procedure.'

'Nebamon hurt me terribly when he altered my body.'

'This will be far less severe than that.'

'I trust you.'

'Stay seated, and relax.'

Eye complaints were so common that Neferet always kept her private store of remedies stocked with plenty of ingredients, even rare ones like bat's blood, which she mixed with frankincense to produce a sticky lotion. This she spread over the offending eyelashes, after drawing them out straight. As they dried, she held them rigid and was able to pull them easily out by the roots. To stop them growing back, she applied a second lotion consisting of chrysocolla and galenite.

'There you are,' she said. 'All better.'

Silkis smiled with relief. 'You have such a gentle touch – I didn't feel anything at all.'

'I'm glad to hear it.'

'Will I need any other treatment?'

'No, the cure's permanent.'

'I do wish you could cure my husband. His skin condition worries me a lot – he's so busy that he never thinks about his health. I hardly see him any more. He leaves early in the morning and comes back late in the evening, laden with papyri which he reads half the night.'

'Perhaps this overwork will be over soon.'

'I'm afraid it won't. At the palace they all praise his skill, and at the Treasury they can't manage without him.'

'That's rather good news, isn't it?'

'At first sight, yes, but for our family life, which he and I value so much . . . The future frightens me. People are talking about Bel-Tran as a future director of the Double House. Egypt's finances in his hands – what a crushing responsibility!'

'Aren't you proud of him?'

'I'm afraid the distance between us will grow even greater, but what can I do? I admire him so much.'

Every day, the fishermen laid out their catch before Mentmose, who was now overseer of Delta fisheries in a little town near to the coast. Fat, heavy and slow, Mentmose was sinking deeper into boredom every day. He hated his miserable official house, loathed having to deal with the fishermen and fish-sellers, and flew into a rage over the most insignificant detail. How could he get out of this dead-end town? He never saw a single courtier any more.

When he saw Denes appear at the end of the quay, he thought he was hallucinating. Forgetting all about the fishermen, he stared at the ship-owner's massive form, his square face, his fringe of fine white beard. It really was him, one of the wealthiest, most influential men in Memphis.

'Get out of here,' Mentmose ordered a fisherman who wanted him to authorize the sale of the fish.

Denes observed the scene with an ironic smile. 'You're a long way from the Memphis city guards' operations, my friend.'

'Are you laughing at my misfortune?'

'Not at all. I'd like to lighten your burden.'

During his career Mentmose had lied a great deal. When it came to trickery, dissimulation and setting snares, he considered himself an expert, but he had to admit that the ship-owner ran him close.

'Who sent you, Denes?' he asked.

'No one – it was my own idea. Tell me, would you like to get your revenge?'

'Revenge . . .' said Mentmose in a high voice.

'Afer all, we have a common enemy.'

'Pazair, Judge Pazair!'

'An inconvenient individual,' observed Denes. 'His position as Judge of the Porch hasn't cooled his ardour in the least.'

Mentomose clenched his fists in fury. 'Replacing me with that damned Nubian, who's even more savage than his baboon!'

'You're right: it was unjust and stupid. Shall we rectify the error?'

'What are you planning to do?'

'To tarnish Pazair's reputation.'

'But he's beyond reproach, isn't he?'

'He only seems so, my friend. Every man has his weaknesses, and if not we'll invent some. Do you recognize this?' Denes held out his right hand, in the palm of which lay a seal-ring. 'He uses it to authorize documents.'

'Did you steal it?'

'I had it made. It's a copy of one I was given by a scribe on his staff. We'll use it on a rather compromising document, to put an end to Judge Pazair's career and restore you to your rightful position.'

The air was laden with a strong smell of fish, but to Mentmose it smelt very sweet.

Pazair placed the ebony box between Neferet and himself. He slid open the drawer, and took out the varnished terracotta playing pieces, which he placed on the thirty bone squares. Neferet made the first move. The rule was to move a pawn of the darkness towards the light, trying not to let it fall into one of the traps laid in its path, and passing through numerous doors.

Pazair made a mistake on his third move.

'You aren't paying attention,' said Neferet.

'I still haven't heard from Suti.'

'Is that really so surprising?'

'Yes, I'm afraid it is.'

'How could he possibly get in touch with you from the middle of the desert?'

The judge's mood did not lighten.

'Are you daring to think he really has betrayed you?'

'He should at least give me a sign that he's alive.'

'Are you thinking the worst?'

Pazair got to his feet, forgetting the game.

'You're wrong,' said Neferet. 'Suti's alive.'

The rumour had all the effect of a thunderclap: after being a principal official of the Treasury and overseer of granaries, Bel-Tran had been appointed director of the Double House, in charge not only of the country's money but also of its trade, and answerable only to the tjaty and Pharaoh. It was his job to receive and draw up registers of minerals and precious materials, the tools destined for the temple workshops and for specialist craftsmen, sarcophagi, ointments, fabrics, amulets and ritual objects. He would pay peasants for their harvests and set taxes, assisted by a large number of scribes.

Once the surprise was over, nobody challenged his appointment. Many court officials had recommended Bel-Tran to the tjaty. Although his rise to power was too rapid for certain people's tastes, and although he had a difficult personality and a marked tendency towards authoritarianism, he was remarkably skilled and efficient. He had proved that in the way he had reorganized the secretariats, producing greater efficiency and better control of expenditure. Beside him, the former overseer cut a poor figure: soft and slow, he had become bogged down in routine, with a foolish obstinacy which had discouraged his remaining supporters.

Once appointed to this coveted post as a reward for his tireless work, Bel-Tran made no secret of his intention to leave the well-trodden pathways and give the Double House more prestige and authority. Ordinarily impervious to choruses of praise, Tjaty Bagey had been impressed by the sheer number of people who had spoken in Bel-Tran's favour.

Bel-Tran's huge new offices were right in the heart of Memphis. At the entrance, two guards checked all visitors. Neferet explained who she was, and waited until her summons was confirmed. She walked past an enclosure for animals and a poultry-yard where accounting-scribes received taxes paid in kind. A stairway led to granaries which were emptied and re-filled according to contributions. An army of scribes, seated on daises, occupied one floor of the building. The head produce-receiver kept a permanent watch on the entrance to the shops where the peasants deposited fruit and vegetables.

Neferet went into another building and passed through a chamber where senior scribes were drawing up lawsuits. A secretary showed her into a vast hall with six pillars, where Bel-Tran received important visitors. The new director of the Double House was issuing instructions to three scribes; he spoke quickly, darting from one idea to another, dealing with several different matters at the same time.

As soon as he had finished he dismissed them and turned to her. 'Thank you for coming, Doctor.'

'Your health is now a concern of the state.'

'It mustn't hinder my work.' He showed her his left leg, on which there was a red patch a hand-span across, edged with white spots.

'Your liver is overtaxed and your kidneys aren't working properly. You must rub the red patch with a lotion made of acacia-flowers and egg-whites, and several times a day you must drink ten drops of aloe-juice, as well as your usual remedies. Be patient, and treat yourself regularly.'

'I confess I often forget.'

'This condition may become serious if you don't take care.'

'I do wish I could deal with everything, but I can't. I hardly ever even get the chance to see my son. I'd love to see him more often, make him understand that he'll be my heir, make him aware of what his responsibilities will be.'

'Silkis complains that you're never at home.'

'My dear, sweet Silkis! She understands how important my work is. And how is Pazair?'

'The tjaty has just summoned him, no doubt to speak to him about the arrest of General Asher.'

'I admire your husband enormously. In my opinion, he was predestined for greatness; there is a strength of will in him which cannot be diverted from its path by anything or anyone.'

When Pazair arrived, Bagey was engrossed in a legal scroll concerning free travel on ferries for people of slender means. Shoulders rounded, back bent, the tjaty was clearly feeling the weight of his years. He did not raise his head, merely said, 'I expected you earlier.'

Pazair was surprised at such curtness.

'Sit down, Judge. I must finish this work.'

Pazair, who thought he had won Bagey's friendship, was suddenly the object of cold anger, and had no idea why.

'The Judge of the Porch's behaviour must be beyond reproach,' the tjaty went on in a hoarse voice.

Pazair nodded. 'I have myself fought in the past to ensure that the office was not tainted by any irregularities.'

'And now you occupy that office.'

'Are you accusing me of something?'

'Worse than that, Pazair. How can you possibly justify what you have done?'

'What am I accused of?'

'At least be honest and admit what you have done.'

'Am I to be condemned yet again without proper grounds?'

The tjaty rose angrily to his feet. 'You forget to whom you are speaking.'

'I abhor injustice, wherever it comes from.'

Bagey snatched up a wooden tablet covered in hieroglyphs, and thrust it in front of Pazair. 'Do you recognize this seal?'

'Of course – it's mine.'

'Read the tablet.'

'It concerns the delivery of best-quality fish to a storehouse in Memphis.'

'A delivery you yourself ordered. But that storehouse does not exist. You diverted the fish from its proper destination, the city market. The boxes were found in outbuildings at your house.'

'The investigation was remarkably prompt.'

'You were denounced.'

'By whom?'

'The letter was anonymous but all the details were accurate. In Kem's absence, the checks were carried out by one of his subordinates.'

'Who is a former colleague of Mentmose, no doubt.'

Bagey looked embarrassed. 'That's correct.'

'Did it not occur to you that someone was trying to deceive you?'

'Of course it did. All the signs point in that direction: the fact that Mentmose is in now employed in the fisheries, that the checks were made by a man loyal to him, his longing for revenge . . . But that does not change the fact that your seal has been used on a compromising document.' The look in the tjaty's eyes had changed; Pazair saw that he hoped to be shown that the truth was very different.

'I have conclusive proof of my innocence.'

'Nothing would please me more.'

'I always take one or two simple precautions,' explained Pazair. 'I learnt a lot from my previous ordeal – I'm less stupid than I used to be. Every bearer of a seal ought to take precautions. I suspected that some day my enemies would use mine, so on all official documents

I place a small red dot after the ninth and twenty-first words, and beneath my seal I draw a tiny five-pointed star, almost drowned in the ink but visible if you look very closely. Please examine this tablet, and check whether those signs are there.'

The tjaty stood up, went to a window and held the tablet in the sunlight.

'They are not there,' he said.

Bagey left nothing to chance. He himself checked a large number of the documents signed by Pazair, and found that every one all had the red dots and the little star. Rather than share this secret, he advised the Judge of the Porch to alter his mark and not to speak of it to anyone.

On the tjaty's orders, Kem questioned the guard who had received the denunciation but omitted to inform his commander. The man soon broke, and confessed that he had been bribed and had had an assurance from Mentmose that Judge Pazair would be found guilty. Kem instantly sent a detachment of five footsoldiers to the coast. They brought Mentmose back to Memphis in a very short time.

'I am receiving you in private,' said Pazair, 'in order to spare you a trial.'

'I'm innocent,' protested Mentmose hotly. 'I've been slandered.'

'Your accomplice has confessed.'

Mentmose's bald head turned pink. With great difficulty, he contained his rising anger. He, who had held so many destinies in the palm of his hand, had no influence over this judge. So he became unctuous. 'The weight of misfortune overwhelms me, and evil tongues are attacking me. How can I defend myself?'

'Give up and admit your guilt.'

Mentmose was having difficulty breathing. 'What fate have you in store for me?'

'You aren't worthy of any position of authority. The poison flowing through your veins rots everything you touch. I am sending you far away from Egypt, to Byblos in Canaan. You will be one of a team of men maintaining our ships.'

'Working with my hands?'

'Is there any greater happiness?'

Mentmose's nasal voice filled with anger. 'I'm not the only one responsible. It was Denes who prompted me to do it.'

'How can I believe you? Lying was always your favourite pastime.'

'Don't say I didn't warn you.'

'Strange that you should suddenly show goodness.'

Mentmose sniggered. 'Goodness? It's nothing of the sort, Judge

Pazair. It's delight in seeing you struck by lightning, drowned in the Nile's flood, buried beneath a hail of stones. Good fortune will desert you, and you'll have more and more enemies.'

'Your boat leaves in an hour. Don't be late.'

31

'Get up,' ordered Ephraim.

Suti struggled to his feet. He was naked, with a wooden collar round his neck and his arms tied behind him at the elbows. Ephraim dragged him forward by a rope bound tightly round his waist.

'A spy, a filthy spy! I was wrong about you, little man.'

'Why did you join the team of miners?' asked General Asher softly.

Suti's lips were dry, his body covered in bruises from punches and kicks, his hair full of sand and blood, but he still defied his enemy. His eyes were lit by a flame of intense hatred.

'Let me teach him a lesson,' said the guard.

'Later,' said Asher. 'His resistance amuses me. You were hoping to catch me red-handed, and prove that I'm the head of a gold-smuggling ring, weren't you? Well, you're right. A senior officer's pay wasn't enough for me. I can't change Egypt's government, so I decided to make the most of my fortune.'

'Are we heading back north?' asked Ephraim.

'Certainly not. The army's waiting for us at the edge of the Delta. We'll go south, skirt Elephantine and fork off towards the western desert, where we'll join Adafi.'

With chariots, food and water, thought Suti, Asher would probably succeed.

'I have the map of the wells,' said Asher. 'Have you loaded the gold?'

Ephraim smiled. 'This time the mine really is worked out. But what about the spy? Shouldn't we get rid of him?'

'No. Instead, we'll conduct an interesting experiment: how long will he survive, walking all day, on only two mouthfuls of water? Suti's very strong, and the results will be useful when we are training the Libyan troops.'

'All the same, I'd like to question him again,' persisted the guard.

'Be patient. He won't be stubborn for much longer.'

*

Aggression. An aggression which was part of his body, imprinted on each muscle, in each step. Because of it, Suti would fight until his heart refused to speak in his limbs. Held prisoner by the three plotters, he'd had no chance of escape. At the very moment when he had Asher in his grasp at last, his victory had been transformed into disaster. There was no way of letting Pazair know what he'd discovered. All his efforts had been in vain, and he'd die far from his friend, from Memphis, the Nile, the gardens and the women.

Dying was stupid. Suti didn't want to go back under the earth, to talk to jackal-headed Anubis, to confront Osiris and the scales of judgment. He wanted to fall in love, fight his enemies, gallop in the desert wind, get richer than the richest noble in all Egypt, just for the fun of it. But the collar felt heavier and heavier.

He walked on, dragged by a rope attached to the back of Asher's chariot. It pulled tight as soon as he moved his legs, and tore at the flesh of his hips, his back and his belly. The chariot went slowly, because it could not leave the narrow track in case it sank into the sand, but to Suti it seemed to go faster and faster, forcing him to use up his very last resources. He was close to giving up, but somewhere he found new energy to keep himself alive. One more step, and then another.

And the day passed, dragging its way through his battered body.

The chariot halted. Suti stood for a long time, motionless, as if he no longer knew how to sit down. Then his knees bent, and he sank down, backside resting on his heels.

'Are you thirsty, little man?' Sarcastically, Ephraim swung a water-skin under his nose. 'You're as strong as a wild animal, but you won't last more than three days. I've got a bet with the guard, and I hate losing.'

He gave Suti a drink. The cool water moistened Suti's lips and spread through his entire being.

The guard aimed a kick at him, knocking him down in the sand. 'My friends are going to rest; I'm standing watch, and I'm going to interrogate you.'

'We've got a bet on,' objected Ephraim. 'You mustn't damage him.'

Suti stayed stretched out on his back, his eyes closed. Ephraim went away, and the guard walked round his prisoner.

'Tomorrow, you'll die, but before then you'll talk. I've broken tougher miners than you.'

Suti barely heard the sound of the man's footsteps in the sand.

'You told us about your mission,' the guard went on, 'but I want to be absolutely sure. How were you keeping in contact with Judge Pazair?'

Suti smiled faintly. 'He'll come and find me. All three of you will
be convicted.'

The guard sat down by Suti's head. 'You're alone, and you haven't
managed to get word to the judge. No one's coming to find you, no
one's going to help you.'

'Thinking that will be your last mistake.'

'The sun's making you mad.'

'The more treacherous you are, the more you lose touch with
reality.'

The guard hit him. 'Don't annoy me any more, or I'll give you to
my dog as a toy.'

The sun was low in the sky to the west, and the heat began to ease.
It would soon be dark.

'Don't go to sleep just yet,' said the guard. 'Until you talk, my
dagger will be at your throat.'

'I've told you everything.'

'No you haven't. Why did you run head first into our ambush?'

'Because I'm a fool.'

The guard stabbed his dagger into the ground beside Suti's head.
'All right, then, my lad, sleep if you can. Tomorrow will be your last
day.'

Despite his exhaustion, Suti could not even doze. Out of the corner
of his eye, he saw the guard run his finger over the point of his
dagger, then the blade. When the man lay down, he put it beside
him. Suti knew he would use it before dawn. As soon as he sensed
Suti weakening, he'd cut his throat, only too happy to rid himself of
a dead weight. He'd have no difficulty justifying himself to General
Asher.

Suti gritted his teeth. He wasn't going to die in a surprise attack.
When the guard attacked him, he'd spit in his face.

The moon, the sovereign warrior, pointed its curved knife at the summit
of the sky. Suti begged it to come down and kill him, to cut short his
suffering. He might not be very devout, but couldn't the gods grant
him this one little favour?

The only reason he was still alive was his love of of the desert. In
sympathy with the power of desolation, aridity and solitude, he breathed
according to its rhythm. The ocean of sand and stone was becoming
his ally. Instead of exhausting him, it gave him back his strength. This
winding-sheet, sunburnt and windswept, pleased him more than any
noble's tomb.

The guard sat nearby, watching for the prisoner to weaken. As soon
as Suti closed his eyes, the killer would slip into his sleep, like the

raptor death, and steal his soul. Nourished by the sun, his thirst slaked by the moon, Suti would hold firm.

Suddenly, the guard gave a choked shout. He waved his arms like a wounded bird, tried to stand up, and fell backwards.

Emerging from the night, the goddess of death appeared.

Suti's head cleared for a moment, and he knew he must be dying. He was passing through the fearsome space between the worlds, where monstrous creatures attacked the dead.

'Help me,' commanded the goddess. 'We must turn the body over.'

Suti rolled on to his side. 'Panther! But how—'

'Later. We must hurry. I have to recover the dagger I stuck in his neck.'

The Libyan helped her lover struggle to his feet, and they pushed the body over, she with her hands, he with his feet. Panther pulled out the weapon, cut Suti's bonds, took off the wooden collar and held him close.

'It's so good to feel you,' she murmured. 'It was Pazair who really saved you. He told me that you'd left from Kebet, with the miners. I found out that you'd disappeared, and I followed the guards – they were boasting that they'd soon find you. But before long the only one left was this one. We Libyans know how to survive without difficulty in this hell. Come, you must drink some water.'

She led him behind a sand-dune, from where she had watched the camp and the chariots without being seen. Incredibly, she had carried all through the desert two big water-skins, which she had filled at each watering-place, a sack of dried meat, a bow and some arrows.

'What about Asher and Ephraim?' asked Suti.

'They're asleep in the chariots, along with an enormous dog. It would be useless trying to attack them.'

Suti was close to fainting, but Panther covered him with kisses.

'No,' he croaked, 'not now.'

She helped him to lie down, lay beside him, and began to caress him. Despite his extreme weakness, she was delighted to find his virility stirring.

'I love you, Suti, and I'm going to save you.'

A frightened shriek tore Neferet from her sleep. Pazair moved, but did not wake. She put on a robe and went out into the garden.

She found a servant-girl, who had brought fresh milk, standing by the stone threshold in tears. She had dropped her pots, and the contents were spread out all over the ground.

'There,' she whimpered, pointing at threshold.

Neferet crouched down. She saw the shattered fragments of red vases, which had borne the name of Judge Pazair, painted with a brush in black ink, followed by incomprehensible magic incantations.

'The evil eye!' cried the servant. 'We must leave this house at once.'

'The power of Ma'at is more powerful than the power of darkness, isn't it?' said Neferet, taking the girl by the shoulders.

'But the judge's life will be shattered like the vases.'

'Do you think he doesn't know how to defend himself? Watch these fragments for a minute – I'm going to the workshop.'

Neferet returned with a pot of glue, of the sort used by vase-menders. With the servant's help, she spread out all the pieces of the puzzle and, without hurrying, fitted them back together. Before gluing them in place, she removed the inscriptions.

'You are to give these vases to the washerman,' she told the girl. 'As they hold the water which washes away the soiling, they will themselves be purified.'

The servant kissed Neferet's hands. 'Judge Pazair is very lucky. Ma'at protects him well.'

'Will you bring us some fresh milk?'

'I'll go and milk my best cow straight away,' said the girl, and she ran off.

The peasant drove a post twice his own height into the soft earth, and attached a long, flexible pole to the top. To the thicker end he attached a clay counterweight, and to the thinner end a rope holding a pottery jar. Hundreds of times every day, he would slowly pull the rope so that the jar dipped into the canal water, then slacken his grip so that the counterweight raised the pot to the level of the pole, then rotate the pole and empty the jar's contents on to his plot of land. In an hour, he could transfer enough water to irrigate all his crops. By means of this system, water was carried to high ground which the Nile flood did not reach.

He had barely started work when he heard a deep, most unusual sound, almost like an animal roaring. Clutching the rope, he listened hard. The roar grew louder. He grew more worried. He abandoned his watering, climbed a nearby hillock and looked around.

Stupefied, he saw a raging flood racing towards him, laying waste everything in its path. Upstream, the built-up canal bank had been breached; men and animals were drowning, struggling in vain against the muddy torrent.

Pazair was the first official to arrive on the scene. Ten dead, half a herd of cattle lost, fifteen watering-machines destroyed: the toll was heavy. Already, workmen were rebuilding the bank, helped by army artificers; but the water reserves had been lost. The state, in the person of the Judge of the Porch, who had assembled the population in the square of the nearest village, undertook to compensate and feed them. But everyone wanted to know who was responsible for the incident; so Pazair questioned – at great length – the two local officials in charge of maintaining the canals, reservoirs and dams. He could find no fault with their work: regular inspections had been carried out according to regulations, and had shown nothing amiss. The judge exonerated them at a public audience.

Everyone named the only possible culprit: the evil eye. A curse had fallen upon the dam, before reaching the village, then the province, and then the entire country.

Pharaoh was no longer exercising his protective role. If he did not celebrate his festival of regeneration within the year, what would become of Egypt? The people still trusted him. Their voices and their demands would reach the village headmen, town mayors, provincial governors, court dignitaries, and Ramses himself. Everyone knew that the king travelled a lot, and there was nothing he did not know about his subjects' aspirations. Faced with difficulty, sometimes lost in the turmoil, he had always taken the right path.

The shadow-eater had at last seen a way out of the stalemate. To get close enough to Pazair to cause an 'accident', he must first eliminate the judge's protectors. The most dangerous was not Kem but Killer, whose canine teeth were longer than a panther's, and who could bring down any wild animal. However, the shadow-eater had unearthed the right adversary, albeit at a high price.

Killer would not be able to hold out against another male baboon which was larger and more powerfully built. The shadow-eater had found one, chained it, muzzled it, and left it unfed for two days while he waited for the right moment. That moment came at midday, when Kem fed Killer. At the far end of the terrace from which the Nubian was watching Pazair's house, the judge was dining alone with his wife. Killer picked up a piece of beef and began to eat it.

The shadow-eater unchained his baboon and carefully removed its muzzle. Attracted by the smell of the meat, it climbed silently along the white housefront and stood up in front of its fellow baboon. Ears red with anger, eyes bloodshot, buttocks flushing purple, the attacker showed its teeth, ready to bite. Killer abandoned his meal and did likewise. The attempt at intimidation had failed; each recognized the same desire to fight in the other's eyes. Not a sound had been made.

By the time Kem's instinct told him to turn round, it was too late. The two baboons roared, and charged in to attack.

It was impossible to separate them or strike down the enemy; the baboons formed a single mass, constantly moving; rolling to right and left. With incredible ferocity, they tore at each other, screaming and howling.

The battle did not last long. The shapeless mass grew still. Kem did not dare go near.

Very slowly, an arm emerged and pushed away the loser's corpse.

'Killer!' Kem ran to him and supported him as he collapsed, covered in blood. He had succeeded in ripping out the attacker's throat, though it had cost him deep wounds.

The shadow-eater spat with rage and slunk away.

Killer stared fixedly at Neferet while she cleaned his wounds, before spreading Nile mud over them.

'Is he in much pain?' asked Kem anxiously.

'Few humans would be so brave.'

'Can you save him?'

'Oh yes, certainly. His heart is as strong as a rock, but he'll have to accept bandages and must stay relatively still for a few days.'

'He'll do it if I tell him to.'

'For the next week, he mustn't eat too much. And if there's any problem at all, let me know at once.'

Killer laid a paw on the doctor's hand. Eternal gratitude filled his eyes.

The council of doctors was meeting for the tenth time.

In Qadash's favour were his age, reputation, experience, and ability as a tooth-doctor – Pharaoh much appreciated this last. On the other hand, Neferet had exceptional healing powers, demonstrated her skill daily at the hospital, was admired by many other doctors, and had the support of Queen Tuya.

'My dear colleagues,' said the oldest council member, 'the situation is becoming scandalous.'

'Well, let us elect Qadash, then,' cut in Nebamon's former assistant. 'He would be a sound, safe choice.'

'What have you against Neferet?'

'She's too young.'

'Ordinarily I'd agree with you,' said another doctor, 'but she runs the hospital remarkably well and efficiently.'

'The office of principal doctor demands a representative, level-headed man,' persisted Nebamon's man, 'not a young woman, however gifted she may be.'

'I think you're wrong. She has plenty of energy and stamina, whereas Qadash hasn't any longer.'

'Speaking like that about our esteemed colleague is insulting.'

'Esteemed? Not by everyone, by any means! Don't forget, he was mixed up in illegal trafficking, and was found out by Judge Pazair.'

'Who, I remind you, is Neferet's husband.'

The argument grew more and more acrimonious, and the tone more and more shrill.

'My dear colleagues,' protested the oldest council member, 'have a little dignity!'

'Let us put an end to this, and proclaim Qadash's election.'

'Never! It must be Neferet – no one else.'

Despite all the promises, the situation ended as it had begun. One firm decision was taken: at the council's next meeting, the kingdom's new principal doctor would be appointed.

Bel-Tran had brought his son to visit his country estate. The little boy played with the papyri, jumped over the folding stools, and broke a scribe's brush.

'That's enough,' said his father sternly. 'You must respect those things – you'll use them yourself when you're a senior official.'

'I want to be like you and order other people about, but not do any work.'

'Unless you work, and work hard, you won't even be a field scribe.'

'I'd rather be rich and own lots of land.'

Pazair's arrival interrupted the conversation. Bel-Tran handed his son over to a servant, who took him to the stableyard; he was learning to ride.

'You look worried, my friend,' said Bel-Tran.

'I still don't know what's happened to Suti.'

'What about Asher?'

'There's been no trace of him in Egypt, and the border posts haven't reported anything.'

'That's strange.'

'And then there's Denes. What did you make of his accounts?'

'They're full of irregularities – indeed, they're full of intentional "mistakes" and malpractice.'

'Enough, taken together, to incriminate him?'

'You're nearing your goal, Pazair.'

It was a warm night. Brave, who had been pelting round and round the lotus-pool, fell asleep at his master's feet. Exhausted after a long day at the hospital, Neferet had dozed off. The judge was drawing up the charge-sheet by the light of two lamps.

Asher had condemned himself by his flight, giving irrefutable substance to the charges laid against him at his previous trial. Denes had committed fraud, theft and bribery. Sheshi led a group of smugglers. Qadash, though only an accomplice, could not be unaware of these activities. Many precise points and damning statements, both written and oral, would be presented to the jurors.

The four men would find their reputations destroyed, and would be sentenced to punishments of varying severity. The judge would have liked to destroy the whole conspiracy, but he still had to find Suti and continue his quest for the truth: along the path that led to Branir's murderer.

32

The ostrich halted, sensing danger. It flapped its wings frantically but of course could not take off, so it executed a little dance hailing the rising sun, and then hurtled off into the dunes.

Suti tried in vain to draw his bow. His muscles hurt, and he was still too weak to do much. Panther massaged him, and rubbed his limbs with ointment from a phial which hung from her belt.

'How many times have you been unfaithful to me?' she asked.

Suti gave an exasperated sigh.

'If you don't tell me, I'll leave you here – and don't forget that I've got the water and food.'

'All that effort, and it comes down to this.'

'When you want the truth, there's nothing you can't do. Judge Pazair convinced me of that.'

Her words made Suti feel a bit better, but he knew that Ephraim and Asher would soon find the dead guard and set off in search of their prisoner.

'We must get away from here as quickly as possible,' he said.

'Answer me first.' The dagger-blade stroked Suti's chest. 'If you've betrayed me, I'll turn you into a eunuch.'

'You know about my marriage to Tapeni.'

'I shall strangle her with my bare hands. Any others?'

'Of course not.'

'Not even at Kebet, that town of every luxury?'

'I signed on as a miner, and after that I was in the desert.'

'At Kebet, nobody stays chaste.'

'Well, I did.'

'I ought to have killed you the moment I found you.'

'Quiet!' hissed Suti. 'Look.' He pointed.

Ephraim had discovered the guard's body. He loosed the dog. It sniffed the wind, but would not leave its master. Ephraim conferred with Asher. After a while, they got into their chariots and drove off. It seemed that escaping from Egypt with the gold was more important than hunting down their prisoner. Now that the guard was dead, there were only two of them to share the spoils.

'They've gone,' said Panther.

'Let's follow them.'

'Have you lost your mind?'

'I'm not going to let Asher get away.'

'Aren't you forgetting the state you're in?'

'Thanks to you, it's improving by the hour. Walking will help me get better.'

Panther shook her head. 'I'm in love with a madman.'

Seated on the terrace of his house, Pazair gazed eastwards. Unable to sleep, he had left the bedchamber in order to immerse himself in the starry night. The sky was so clear that he could make out the shapes of the pyramids at Giza, draped in a dark blue tinged with the first blood of the dawn. Anchored in a thousand years of peace, built of stone, love and truth, Egypt lay spread out in the mystery of the day that was about to be born. Pazair was no longer the Judge of the Porch, not even a judge at all; he tried to forget himself, to become absorbed into the immensity where the impossible marriage between the invisible and the visible was celebrated, in communion with the spirits of the ancestors, whose presence remained tangible in every murmur of its earth.

Barefoot and silent, Neferet appeared beside him.

'It's very early – you should still be asleep,' he said.

'This is my favourite time of day. In a few moments, gold will illuminate the fringe of the mountains and the Nile will come back to life.' She stroked his hair. 'What's troubling you?'

How could he admit to her that he, the judge who was so sure of his truths, was in the grip of doubt? People thought him unshakeable, impervious to events, whereas the least of them marked him, sometimes like a wound. Pazair could not accept the existence of evil and had not become inured to crime. Time had not wiped away the death of Branir, which he had been unable to avenge.

'I want to give up, Neferet.'

'You're exhausted, otherwise you wouldn't say that.'

'I agree with Kem: justice, if it even exists, cannot be applied.'

'Are you afraid you may fail?'

'My cases are solid, my accusations well founded, my arguments irrefutable. But Denes, or one of his acolytes, can still use a legal weapon and destroy what I have patiently built up. If that happens, what would be the point of going on?'

'This feeling will pass.'

'The ideal of Egypt is sublime, but it doesn't stop men like Asher existing.'

'But you put a stop to his activities, didn't you?'

'After him there'll be another, and then another ... Is it worth caring any more?' He took her hands tenderly. 'I'm unworthy of my office.'

'Pointless words are an insult to Ma'at.'

'Would a true judge doubt the law?'

'The only thing you doubt is yourself.'

The young sun bathed them in light which was at once fierce and caressing.

'It is our life that's in the balance, Neferet.'

'We aren't fighting for ourselves,' she said. 'We're fighting so the light that unites us can grow. To deviate from that path would be a crime.'

'You're stronger than I am.'

She smiled in amusement. 'Tomorrow you'll agree with me.'

United, they experienced the rebirth of the day.

Pazair was due to see the tjaty, but he kept sneezing and complained of a sharp pain in the back of his neck. Neferet calmly gave him a drink made from the willow-tree's leaves and bark, a remedy she often used to combat fever and several other illnesses.[*]

The medicine worked quickly. Pazair was breathing more easily and looking much better by the time he was shown into Bagey's office.

'Tjaty,' he said, 'here is the complete file regarding General Asher, Denes the ship-owner, Sheshi the inventor, and Qadash the tooth-doctor. As Judge of the Porch, I ask you to hold a public trial: the charges are high treason, damage to the kingdom's security, attempted murder, perjury and fraud. Certain points are well established, others are still somewhat vague. The charges are, nevertheless, such that I feel there is no point in waiting any longer.'

'This is an exceptionally serious matter.'

'I am aware of that.'

'The accused are persons of considerable standing.'

'That makes their crimes all the more abhorrent.'

'You are right,' said Bagey. 'Even though Asher has not yet been found, I shall open the trial after the Festival of Opet.'[†]

---

[*] Willow contains the substance that forms the essential component of aspirin, which was thus 'invented' and used more than four thousand years ago.

[†] The hippopotamus-goddess, who symbolized fertility, both spiritual and material.

'Suti is still missing, too.'

'I share your anxiety about him, so I have ordered a division of footsoldiers to search the desert around Kebet, together with special desert guards. Now tell me, in your findings do you identify Branir's murderer?'

'No, Tjaty,' said Pazair despondently. 'I have failed. I cannot be certain.'

'I want his name.'

'I shall never give up the investigation.'

'And there's another point. Neferet's candidacy for the post of principal doctor is awkward. Those with sharp minds will not fail to point out that Qadash's conviction would free the way for her, your wife, to be appointed, and they will try to discredit her.'

'I have thought of that.'

'What does Neferet herself think?'

'That if Qadash is guilty he must be punished.'

'You must not fail. Neither Denes nor Sheshi is an easy target, and I fear the possibility of a reversal of the situation, of the kind Asher specializes in. The traitors have a particular talent for justifying their crimes.'

'I shall place my hopes in your court. Therein, falsehood will be destroyed.'

Bagey laid a hand on the copper heart he wore round his neck. The gesture signified that he was placing the awareness of his duty before everything.

The conspirators had gathered at the abandoned farm where they met in emergencies. Denes, usually so confident and sure of himself, seemed worried.

'We must act at once,' he said. 'Pazair has handed his files to Bagey.'

'Is that just a rumour, or do you know it for a fact?'

'The matter has been lodged with the tjaty's court and will be heard after the Festival of Opet. It's good that Asher's implicated, but I don't want my own reputation compromised.'

'I thought the shadow-eater was supposed to incapacitate Pazair?'

'He's had a run of bad luck, but he won't give up.'

'That's all very well, but it hasn't prevented you from being charged.'

'We're the masters of the game – don't forget that. All we have to do is use a little of our power.'

'Without coming out into the open?'

'That won't be necessary. A simple letter will do it.'

Denes's plan was accepted.

'To avoid any more problems like this,' he added, 'I suggest we bring forward one of the phases of our plan: the replacement of the tjaty. That way, it won't matter what Pazair does in future.'

'Isn't it a bit too soon to do that?'

'You must face the facts: the time has become propitious.'

Watched in astonishment by Asher and Ephraim, the dog leapt out of the chariot and charged up a small hillock covered in scree.

'Since his master's death,' said Ephraim, 'it's as if he has gone mad.'

'We don't need him,' said the general. 'I'm sure now that we've escaped the patrols. The way is open.'

The dog raced about with foam-flecked lips. It seemed to fly from rock to rock, paying no heed to the sharp flints. Suti forced Panther to lie down flat in the sand and drew his bow. When the dog was within bowshot, it halted.

Man and animal stared defiantly into each other's eyes. Well aware that he must not miss his target, Suti waited for the attack; he did not like the idea of killing a dog. Suddenly, the animal gave a howl of despair and crouched down in the manner of a sphinx. Suti laid his bow aside and went towards it. Submissively, the dog let itself be stroked. There was exhaustion and anguish in its eyes. It had been freed from a cruel master, but would it be accepted by a new one?

'Come,' said Suti, and the dog's tail wagged joyfully. Suti realized he had a new ally.

Qadash staggered drunkenly into the ale-house. The forthcoming trial terrified him, despite Denes's assurances and the solid foundations of the conspiracy. He was afraid that he would be unable to stand up to Judge Pazair and that, if he was found guilty, the post of principal doctor would be lost to him for ever. So he felt an irresistible urge to dull his senses; wine had not given enough relief, so he was planning to relax his nerves in the lap of a prostitute.

Sababu was once again running the largest establishment in Memphis, and maintaining its good reputation. Her girls recited poems, danced and played music before offering their erotic skills to an elegant, wealthy clientele.

Qadash bumped into the door-keeper, pushed aside a flute-player and charged at a very young Nubian servant-girl, who was carrying a dish of pastries. He threw her on to a pile of cushions and tried to rape her. The girl's cries of distress alerted Sababu, who beat him away with a hearty punch.

'I want her,' he demanded.

'This little one is only a servant.'

'I want her all the same.'

'Leave this house at once.'

The girl took refuge in Sababu's arms.

'I'll pay whatever I have to.'

'Keep your money – just go.'

'I'll have her, I swear I will.'

Qadash did not go far from the ale-house. Crouching in the shadows, he kept watch as the employees left. A little after dawn, the Nubian girl and other young serving-wenches came out of the ale-house and set off home.

Qadash followed his prey. As soon as he saw a deserted alleyway, he seized her by the waist and clamped a hand over her mouth. The girl struggled, but he was half crazed and far too strong for her to fight off. He tore off her dress, threw himself on her, and raped her.

'My dear colleagues,' announced the oldest member of the doctors' council, 'we can defer the appointment of the kingdom's principal doctor no longer. Since no other candidates have presented themselves, we must choose between Neferet and Qadash. We shall continue our deliberations until the decision has been taken.'

This line of action received general approval. Each member of the council spoke, sometimes calmly, sometimes vehemently. Qadash's supporters were virulently against Neferet. She, they said, was taking advantage of her husband's position to have Qadash found guilty, thus clearing the path for herself. Slandering a well-reputed doctor and soiling his reputation were scandalous tactics, which ought to disqualify her.

A retired doctor added that Ramses was suffering more and more often from toothache, and he would like to have an experienced tooth-doctor at hand. Should they not think first and foremost of Pharaoh, on whom the country's prosperity depended? No one opposed the argument.

After four hours of debate, the votes were cast.

'Qadash will be the next principal doctor,' announced the oldest council member.

Two wasps buzzed round Suti and attacked the dog, which was chewing a piece of dried meat. The young man watched them, hoping to spot their nest buried in the ground nearby.

'My luck has returned,' he said. 'Get undressed.'

Panther was glad of the invitation. When she was naked, she rubbed herself against Suti.

He shook his head. 'We'll make love later.'

'Then why . . . ?'

'Every single bit of my body must be covered. I'm going to dig up part of the nest and put it in a water-skin.'

'If you're stung, you'll die. Those wasps are ferocious.'

'I intend to live until I'm very old.'

'To sleep with other women?'

'Cover my head.'

As soon as he had located the nest, Suti began to dig. The wasps' stings did not penetrate the fabric, despite the fury of their attacks. Suti thrust a good portion of the buzzing horde into the water-skin.

'What are you going to do with it?' asked Panther.

'That's a military secret.'

'Stop laughing at me.'

'Trust me.

She laid her hand on his chest.

'Asher mustn't get away,' he said.

'Don't worry, I know the desert.'

'If we lose his trail . . .'

She knelt down and stroked the tops of his thighs, so diabolically slowly that Suti was unable to resist her. Between a nest of maddened wasps and a dozing hound, they revelled in their youth with an insatiable passion.

Neferet was very upset.

The young Nubian girl had been weeping ever since her admission to the hospital. Wounded in her soul as well as her flesh, she clung to the doctor as though she were drowning. The savage who had raped and deflowered her had fled, but several people had given fairly good descriptions. However, only the victim's direct testimony could lead to a formal accusation.

Neferet treated the girl's internal injuries and gave her remedies to calm her. Eventually the girl began to shake less violently, and she accepted a drink of water.

'Would you like to talk to me?' asked Neferet.

The child's lost gaze fixed on her protector. 'Will I get better?'

'I promise you will.'

'There are vultures in my head, they're devouring my belly . . . I don't want a child by that vile monster.'

'You won't have one.'

'But suppose I'm pregnant?'

'I will carry out the abortion myself.'

The little Nubian burst into tears again. 'He was old,' she revealed between sobs, 'and he stank of wine. When he attacked me in the ale-house, I noticed he had red hands, prominent cheekbones and a big nose, covered in purple veins. He was a demon, a real demon with white hair.'

'Do you know his name?'

'No, but Sababu does.'

It was the first time Neferet had ventured into a house of pleasure. The wall-paintings and perfumes were heady and suggestive, for they had to create an atmosphere conducive to the abandonment of good sense. The courtesans must be able easily to seduce visitors in search of love.

Neferet was not kept waiting, for she had treated Sababu in Thebes.

'I'm happy to welcome you,' said Sababu, 'but aren't you worried about what people will say?'

'Not in the least.'

'You've cured me, Neferet. Since I've been following your treatment to the letter, my rheumatism has almost disappeared. But you look tense, worried . . . Does this place offend you?'

'No, it's nothing like that. I've bad news for you, I'm afraid. One of your servant-girls has been raped savagely.'

'I thought that crime no longer existed in Egypt.'

'She's a little Nubian girl, whom I have been treating at the hospital. Her body will recover, but it may never forget. She gave me a description of the attacker, and said you know his name.'

'If I tell you, will I have to give evidence at the trial?'

'Of course.'

'In this business, discretion has to be my only religion.'

'As you wish.' Neferet turned away.

'No, wait. Please try to understand, Neferet. If I give evidence, people will realize that I am in an illegal situation.'

'All that matters to me is the look in that little girl's eyes.'

Sababu bit her lip. 'Will your husband help me keep this house?'

'I can't promise that.'

'The criminal's name is Qadash. He almost assaulted the child right in here. He was drunk – and very violent.'

Sombre and withdrawn, Pazair paced up and down. 'I don't know how to tell you the bad news, Neferet.'

'Is it that bad?'

'Yes. It's an injustice, a monstrous injustice.'

'I must speak to you about a monster, too. You must arrest him at once.'

He went to her and took her face in his hands. 'You've been crying.'

'This is very serious, Pazair. I've begun the investigation; now you must finish it.'

'Qadash has been elected principal doctor of the kingdom. I have just been officially informed.'

'Qadash is a criminal of the vilest kind: he has raped a young virgin.'

33

Ephraim and Asher rested before skirting Elephantine and crossing the southern border. They found a cave big enough to hide the chariot, and spent a peaceful night there. The general knew where the garrisons were, and how to slip through the holes in the net. He was looking forward to enjoying his wealth in Libya with his friend Adafi, and to training sand-travellers to attack Egypt. The future was rosy; it was a good time to plan an invasion of the Delta and the acquisition of the best lands in the north-west.

Asher lived only to take his revenge on Egypt. By forcing him to flee, Judge Pazair had created an enemy whose cunning and obstinacy would be more destructive than an entire army.

Eventually the general fell asleep, while his accomplice stood guard.

The water-skin of wasps clutched in one hand, Suti climbed on to the rock that overhung the entrance to the cave. He edged forward with difficulty, taking care not to knock down any pebbles and betray his presence. Panther watched anxiously. Would he be quick enough to extract the nest without being stung, skilful enough to throw it into the cave? He would not get a second chance.

Reaching the edge of the overhang, he concentrated. Flat on his belly, he held his breath and listened intently. Not a sound. High in the sky, a falcon was circling. Suti took out the stopper, swung his arm like a pendulum, and flung the water-skin into his enemies' lair.

An infuriated buzzing filled the calm air of the desert. Ephraim came staggering and lurching out of the cave, surrounded by enraged wasps which he tried in vain to wave them away. Stung a hundred times, he crumpled, clutched his throat, and suffocated to death.

Asher had reacted more quickly: he dived under the chariot and kept very still. When the wasps had gone, he emerged from the cave, sword in hand.

In front of him were Suti, Panther and the dog.

'Three against one?' sneered the general. 'Very brave!'

'What would a coward like you know about bravery?' retorted Suti.

'I have a great deal of gold. Aren't you two interested?'

'I'm going to kill you, Asher, and then I shall take it all.'

'You're dreaming. That dog has lost all his fierceness, and you haven't got a weapon.'

'Wrong again, General,' said Suti, and Panther picked up the bow and arrows and handed them to him.

Asher retreated, his ratlike face tensing. 'If you kill me, you'll get lost in the desert.'

'Panther's an excellent guide, and I'm getting used to the place. We'll survive, you can be sure of that.'

'It is wrong for a human being to raise his hand against another human being: that is our law. You wouldn't dare kill me.'

'You no longer count as a human being.'

'Vengence taints the soul. If you make yourself guilty of murder, you'll be condemned by the gods.'

'You don't believe that any more than I do. If they exist, they'll be grateful to me for having killed the most poisonous snake in Egypt.'

'The load on this chariot is only a small part of my treasure. Why don't you come with me? I can make you richer than a Theban noble.'

'Come with you where?'

'To Adafi's lands, in Libya.'

'He'd kill me.'

'I shall introduce you as my most faithful friend.'

Panther was behind Suti. He heard her coming closer. Libya, her country! Wouldn't General Asher's proposition seduce her? To take Suti to her homeland, have him all to herself, live in luxury . . . How could she resist all those temptations? But he did not turn round. Traitors prefer to strike from behind.

Panther handed him an arrow.

'You're wrong,' Asher hissed. 'We were born to understand each other. You're an adventurer, like me; Egypt suffocates us – we need broader horizons.'

'I saw you torture an Egyptian, a defenceless man, to death. You showed him no mercy.'

'I wanted him to tell me the truth – I knew he was planning to denounce me. You'd have done what I did.'

Suti drew his bow and fired. The arrow found its mark between the general's eyes.

Panther flung her arms round her lover's neck. 'I love you – and we're rich!'

*

Kem arrested Qadash at his home, at midday. He read him the charge-sheet and bound his hands. The tooth-doctor protested only feebly; his head felt heavy and his vision was blurred.

He was taken immediately to Judge Pazair.

'Do you confess your guilt?' asked the judge.

'Of course not.'

'Witnesses have identified you.'

'I went to Sababu's ale-house, met some disagreeable girls and left almost at once. I didn't like any of them.'

'Sababu's statement is very different.'

'Who will believe that old prostitute?'

'You raped a young Nubian girl, a servant in Sababu's house.'

'That's slander! That liar wouldn't dare say such a thing to my face.'

'Your judges will decide.'

'You surely don't intend to—'

'The trial will take place tomorrow.'

'I want to go home.'

'I shall not allow you to go free in the meantime: you might attack another child. Kem will ensure your safety at the guard-post.'

'My . . . safety?'

'That entire district of the city wishes to kill you.'

Qadash clung to the judge. 'You have a duty to protect me!'

'That is, alas, true.'

Nenophar went to the weaving-shed with the firm intention of obtaining the best fabrics, as usual, and making her rivals white with rage. She looked forward to many enjoyable hours making elaborate dresses which she would wear with incomparable elegance.

Tapeni irritated her, with her mutinous eyes and her air of superiority; but she knew her craft to perfection and procured flawless fabrics. Thanks to her, Nenophar was always ahead of fashion.

Tapeni wore a curious smile.

'I want some finest-quality linen,' demanded Nenophar.

'That will be difficult.'

'I beg your pardon?'

'To tell you the truth, it won't be possible.'

'What has got into you, Tapeni?'

'You're very rich, and I'm not.'

'I've always paid you, haven't I?'

'I want more now.'

'A price increase in the middle of the year? That is hardly correct, but I'll agree.'

'It isn't fabric that I want to sell you.'

'Then what is it?'

'Your husband is a well-known man, a very well-known man.'

'Denes?'

'He must be above reproach.'

'What are you insinuating?'

'High society is cruel. If one of its members is found guilty of immorality, he soon loses his influence – and even his fortune.'

'Just what do you mean by that?'

'Don't lose your temper, Nenophar. If you're reasonable and generous, your position won't be threatened. All you have to do is buy my silence.'

'What do you know that is so compromising?'

'Denes is unfaithful to you.'

Nenophar thought the roof of the workshop had fallen on her head. If Tapeni had proof of what she was alleging, and if she spread the story throughout the Theban nobility, Nenophar would become a laughing-stock and would never dare reappear at court or at any social event.

'You . . . you're making it up!'

'No, I'm not. I know everything.'

Nenophar did not argue. Her spotless reputation was her most precious possession. 'What do you want in exchange for your silence?'

'The revenues from one of your farms and, as soon as possible, a fine house in Memphis.'

'That's outrageous!'

'Can you imagine yourself as a scorned wife, with the name of Denes's mistress on everyone's lips?'

Nenophar closed her eyes in panic.

Tapeni felt a savage joy. Sharing Denes's bed just once – he was a dull and selfish lover – had opened the road to riches. Soon she would be a great lady.

Qadash was in a rage. Certain that Denes would already have smoothed the way, he demanded to be freed immediately. Now that he was sober again, he kept boasting about his new appointment in an effort to get out of his cell.

'Calm down,' ordered Kem.

'Show some respect, my friend! Do you know whom you are speaking to?'

'To a rapist.'

'There's no need to use that word.'

'It is the simple and horrible truth, Qadash.'

'If you don't let me go, you'll be in serious trouble.'

Kem smiled. 'I'm just about to unlock the cell door.'

'At last! You aren't stupid – and you'll find that I can be grateful.'

Just as Qadash took a breath of air in the street, the Nubian gripped him by the shoulder.

'Good news, Qadash: Judge Pazair has been able to assemble the jurors more quickly than he expected. I'm taking you to court.'

When Qadash saw Denes among the jury, he knew he was saved. A sombre, tense atmosphere reigned over the porch in front of the Temple of Ptah, where Pazair had convened the court. A large crowd, alerted by word of mouth, was eager to attend the trial. The guards kept them outside the wooden building, which comprised a roof and thin pillars; inside were the witnesses and the jurors, six men and six women of varying ages and social situations.

Pazair, wearing an old-style kilt and short wig, seemed to be in the grip of intense emotion. After placing the proceedings under the protection of Ma'at, he read out the charges.

'Qadash the tooth-doctor, principal doctor of the kingdom, residing at Memphis, is accused of having raped a young Nubian girl, who works as a servant in the house of the lady Sababu, yesterday morning at dawn. The victim, who is in hospital, does not wish to appear and will be represented by Doctor Neferet.'

Qadash was relieved. He could not have hoped for better. He was confronting his judges, whereas the servant was running away from them. He knew three members of the jury besides Denes, and they were all influential people who would plead in his favour. Not only would he emerge from the court completely exonerated but he would attack Sababu and obtain compensation.

'Do you acknowledge the facts?' asked Pazair.

'I deny them.'

'Let the lady Sababu give her testimony.'

All eyes fell on the famous owner of the best-known ale-house in Egypt. Some had thought she was dead, others in prison. A little too heavily made-up, but with her head held proudly high, she stepped forward with confidence.

'I remind you,' said Pazair, 'that false testimony is subject to serious punishment.'

'Qadash the tooth-doctor was drunk. He forced open my door and threw himself at the youngest of my Nubian servant-girls, whose only task is to offer pastries and drinks to the clients. If I had not intervened and had him thrown out, he would have done violence to the child.'

'Are you certain of that?'

'Do you consider an erect penis sufficient proof?'

A murmur ran through the assembled throng. The coarse language shocked the jury.

Qadash asked and was given permission to speak.

'This person runs an illegal business,' he said. 'Every day she soils the good name of Memphis. Why do the city guards and the courts not deal with this prostitute?'

'We are not here to try Sababu, we are here to try you. Moreover, your morality did not prevent you from going to her ale-house and attacking a little girl.'

'It was just a moment of madness – everyone's felt that that at some time.'

'Was the Nubian child raped in your ale-house?' Pazair asked Sababu. 'No.'

'What happened after this first attack?'

'I calmed the child down and she went back to work. At dawn she left, as usual, to go home.'

Sababu was followed by Neferet, who described the girl's physical state after the rape. She did not spare the assembly any of the details, and they were horrified by such savagery.

Qadash broke in again. 'I do not question my excellent colleague's observations, and I deplore this young girl's misfortune, but how am I involved?'

'I would remind you,' Pazair declared solemnly, 'that the only punishment applicable to rape is the pain of death. Doctor Neferet, have you firm proof that Qadash is the guilty party?'

'He exactly fits the victim's description of her attacker.'

'And I would remind the court,' cut in Qadash, 'that Doctor Neferet tried to obtain the post of principal doctor. She failed, and must now feel a certain resentment. Moreover, it is not up to her to carry out an investigation. Has Judge Pazair recorded the girl's own statement?'

That argument carried weight.

The Judge of the Porch called two river boatmen who had seen the tooth-doctor run away after the crime. They both identified him as the rapist.

'I was drunk,' he protested. 'I must have fallen asleep there. Is that reason to accuse me of such an appalling crime, for which, if I was a juror myself, I would apply the law without hesitation?'

Qadash's defence made a good impression. The girl had been raped, the tooth-doctor had indeed been in the vicinity, and had tried to attack her earlier that night: taken together, the evidence tended to mark him out as the rapist, but, out of respect for the rule of Ma'at, Judge Pazair could not venture beyond a strong presumption. His links with Neferet weakened her testimony, on which Qadash had succeeded in throwing suspicion.

However, the Judge of the Porch asked her to speak again in the girl's name, before giving his conclusions and presiding over the jury's deliberations.

A trembling hand slipped into Neferet's.

'Come with me,' begged the Nubian girl, clinging to the doctor. 'I will speak, but not alone.'

Hesitating, stumbling over each word, she spoke of the violence she had suffered, the terrible pain, the despair. When her deposition was over, a heavy silence fell over the porch.

His throat dry, the judge asked her the decisive question. 'Do you see, anywhere in the court, the man who raped you?'

The girl pointed to Qadash. 'That's him.'

The deliberations did not last long. The jurors applied the ancient law, which was such a strong deterrent that no rapes had been committed in Egypt for many years. Because of his eminent position in his profession and his office of principal doctor, Qadash would not enjoy the benefit of any extenuating circumstances. The jury unanimously sentenced him to death.

34

'I shall appeal,' declared Qadash.

'I have already set things in motion,' said Pazair. 'Beyond the court of the porch, there is only the tjaty's court.'

'He will overturn this unjust verdict.'

'Have no illusions. Bagey will confirm the sentence if your victim confirms her accusations, which have been duly registered.'

'She wouldn't dare!'

'Don't deceive yourself.'

The tooth-doctor did not seem unduly shaken. 'Do you really think I'll be punished? Poor judge! You'll soon sing a different song.'

Qadash laughed darkly as Pazair left the cell.

It was the end of September, the second month of a mediocre annual flood, and Egypt was fervently celebrating the festival of the goddess Opet, symbol of fertility and generosity. For the twenty or so days while the floodwaters receded, leaving behind the fertile silt, the people haunted the riverbanks, where travelling vendors sold melons and watermelons, grapes, pomegranates, bread, cakes, grilled poultry and beer. Open-air kitchens served good, cheap meals, while female musicians and professional dancing-girls delighted the ear and the eye. Everyone knew that the temples were celebrating the rebirth of the creative energy; it had been exhausted in the course of a long year during which the gods had made the earth fertile. To prevent them leaving the world of men, they must be offered the joy and gratitude of an entire land, in which no one died of hunger or thirst. The Nile would thus retain its original power, which it drew from the ocean of energy in which the universe was bathed.

At the height of the celebrations, Kani, High Priest of Amon, opened the innermost shrine in the temple; it contained the statue of the god, whose true form was for ever inaccessible. Covered with a veil, it was placed in a gilded wooden boat carried by twenty-four shaven-headed priests dressed in long linen robes. Amon emerged from the temple accompanied by his wife, Mut, the divine mother, and their son, Khonsu, who traversed the celestial spaces in the form of the moon. Two processions left for the temple at Luxor, one travelling by river and the other by land.

Dozens of vessels escorted the divine trinity's enormous, gold-covered boat, while girls playing tambourines, sistra and flutes hailed its progress towards the southern shrine. Pazair, as Judge of the Porch, had been invited to the ceremony that took place in the great courtyard of the temple of Luxor. Outside, everyone was celebrating, but behind the temple's high walls all was silence and contemplation.

Kani offered flowers to the divine trinity and poured a libation in their honour. Then the ranks of courtiers parted to allow the Pharaoh of Egypt to pass through, and all bowed in unison. The king's innate nobility and seriousness impressed Pazair deeply. A man of medium height, very robust, with a hooked nose, broad forehead, and red hair hidden beneath the Blue Crown, he did not so much as glance at anyone, but gazed intently at the statue of Amon, the image of the creation mystery that Pharaoh embodied.

Kani read out a text singing of the many forms of the god, who could take form in the wind, in stone or in the ram with curled horns, without being reduced to any of these manifestations. Then the High Priest withdrew, leaving the king to cross the threshold of the covered shrine alone.

The food at the feast given by Pharaoh to celebrate the Festival of Opet included fifteen thousand loaves, two thousand cakes, a hundred baskets of dried meat, two hundred of fresh vegetables, seventy jars of wine and five hundred of beer, and fruit in profusion. More than a hundred floral arrangements decorated the tables where the revellers extolled the merits of Ramses' government and of Egyptian peace.

Pazair and Neferet received the warmest congratulations from the members of the court, the judge by reason of his courage in the Qadash affair, and Neferet because she had just been appointed – by unanimous vote of the council – the kingdom's principal doctor, following the rapist's dismissal. People tried to forget the flight of General Asher, who was still being hunted, and the murder of Branir, which was still unsolved, as were the mysterious deaths of the honour-guard. The judge remained impervious to these demonstrations of friendship; Neferet, whose charm and beauty enchanted the most cynical observers, paid them no more heed than he did. She could not forget the terrified face of a little girl whose wounds would never heal.

Kem, as commander of the city guards, was in charge of security at the feast. Flanked by Killer, he watched everyone who went near the judge, ready to take instant action if he or Killer sensed the slightest danger.

'You are the couple of the year,' declared Denes. 'Convicting a leading citizen like Qadash is a remarkable achievement, which honours our legal system. And seeing a woman as outstanding as Neferet rising to lead our doctors shows that our medical system, too, is excellent.'

Pazair smiled slightly. 'Don't be too lavish with your compliments.'

'You both have the ability to overcome any and all ordeals.'

Neferet had been looking around. 'I cannot see the lady Nenophar,' she said in surprise.

'She isn't well,' said Denes.

'Permit me to wish her a speedy recovery.'

'She will much appreciate your kind words. Now, may I deprive you of your husband for a few moments?'

Denes led Pazair into the shade of a canopy where cool beer and grape-juice were being served.

'My friend Qadash is a fine man. Becoming principal doctor turned his head, and that's why he got drunk and behaved so deplorably.'

'Not a single juror pleaded for mercy,' Pazair reminded him. 'You yourself kept silent and voted for the death penalty.'

'The law is explicit, but it takes account of remorse.'

'Qadash has shown none.'

'Is he not in deep despair?'

'Quite the contrary: he boasts and swaggers and issues threats.'

'He really has lost his head.'

'He's convinced that he'll escape the supreme penalty.'

'Has the date of his execution been set?'

'The tjaty's court has rejected his appeal and confirmed the sentence. In three days, Kem will give the poison to the condemned man.'

'Didn't you use the word "threats"?'

'If he were driven to suicide, Qadash would not sink into the abyss alone. He has promised me a confession before taking the poison.'

'Poor Qadash,' said Denes. 'To climb so high and sink so low . . . How can one not feel sadness and regret in the face of his fall? Soften his last hours, I beg you.'

'Kem is no torturer. Qadash is being treated properly.'

'Only a miracle can save him.'

'Who would pardon such a crime?'

'I shall see you presently, Judge Pazair.'

The council of doctors received Neferet. Her opponents asked her a thousand questions about abstruse details in the most varied fields. She made hardly any mistakes, and her election was confirmed.

Since Nebamon's death, many files relating to public health had remained in suspense. Neferet asked for a transitional period during which she could train her successor at the hospital. Her new duties seemed so overwhelmingly heavy that she wanted to run away, to take refuge in a post as a country doctor, to stay with the sick and appreciate every moment of their recovery. Nothing had prepared her to head a body of experienced doctors and influential courtiers, and an army of scribes overseeing the making and distribution of remedies, or to take decisions ensuring the population's health and well-being. Before, she had taken care of a village; now it was a kingdom so powerful that it forced the admiration of its enemies as well as its allies. Neferet dreamt of leaving with Pazair, hiding in a little house in Upper Egypt, at the edge of the farmed area, facing the Peak of the West, and savouring the wisdom of mornings and evenings there.

She would have liked to confide in Pazair, but when he returned from his office he wore an expression of utter dismay.

'Read this decree,' he said, handing her a fine-quality papyrus, marked with Pharaoh's seal. 'Please read it aloud.'

She did so. "*'I, Ramses, desire that heaven and earth should be joyful. May those who were in hiding emerge, may no man suffer by reason of his past faults, may the prisoners be freed, may the troublemakers be pacified, may the people sing and dance in the streets.*" An amnesty?'

'A general amnesty.'

'Isn't that highly unusual?'

'I know of no other example.'

'Why has Pharaoh decided to do this?'

'I don't know.'

'But it means Qadash will go free.'

'A general amnesty,' repeated Pazair, still shocked. 'Qadash's crime is wiped away, General Asher is no longer to be hunted down, the murders are forgotten, the case against Denes has been abandoned.'

'Aren't you being too gloomy?'

'This is failure, Neferet. Total, final failure.'

'Why don't you appeal to the tjaty?'

Kem opened the cell door.

Qadash seemed unworried. 'Are you freeing me?'

'How do you know that?'

'It was inevitable. A good man always triumphs.'

'You are benefiting from a general amnesty.'

Qadash recoiled from the fury in the Nubian's eyes. 'Don't lay a hand on me, Kem! You wouldn't benefit from any amnesty.'

'When you appear before Osiris, he will close your mouth. Demons armed with knives will slice open your flesh for all eternity.'

'Keep your childish stories to yourself. You have treated me with contempt, and insulted me. It's a pity ... You missed your chance, like your friend Pazair. Make the most of your position; you won't command the guards for much longer.'

Tjaty Bagey was late. His legs and feet were swollen, and his shoulders bowed; and because of his exhausted state he had agreed to be brought to his office in a chair, by bearers. Just as they did every day, crowds of senior officials wished to speak with him, present him with difficulties they had come up against, and learn his opinion.

Although Pazair did not have an appointment, the tjaty received him first.

The judge could not contain his anger. 'This amnesty is unacceptable.'

'Be careful what you say, Judge of the Porch. The decree emanates from Pharaoh himself.'

'I cannot believe that.'

'It is, however, the truth.'

'Have you seen the king?'

'He dictated the text to me himself.'

'And what did you say?'

'I made him aware of my astonishment and incomprehension,' said Bagey.

'But could not sway him?'

'Ramses would brook no discussion.'

'It is appalling that a monster like Qadash should escape punishment!'

'The amnesty is a general one, Judge Pazair.'

'I refuse to apply it.'

'You must obey, as must I.'

'How can one condone such injustice?'

'I am old, you are young. My career is drawing to a close, yours is just beginning. Whatever my opinion may be, I am obliged to remain silent. You must not do anything foolish.'

'My mind is made up – I don't care what the consequences will be.'

'Qadash has been freed, and his trial cancelled.'

'Will Asher be given his job back, too?'

'His crime has been wiped out. If he can provide a plausible explanation, he will.'

'So only Branir's murderer escapes the pardon, because he hasn't been identified.'

'I am as bitter as you, but Ramses must surely not have acted lightly.'

'His motives do not matter to me.'

'He who rebels against Pharaoh rebels against life.'

'You are right, Tjaty Bagey. For that reason, I cannot continue my work any longer. You will have my resignation this very day. From now on, consider me no longer Judge of the Porch.'

'Think about this, Pazair.'

'In my place, would you have done otherwise?'

Bagey did not reply.

'There is one last favour I should like to ask of you,' said Pazair.

'As long as I am tjaty, my door will be open to you.'

'Free access would be contrary to the justice you and I love with all our hearts. I would ask you to keep Kem at the head of the city guards.'

'I have every intention of doing so.'

'And what will happen about Neferet?'

'Qadash will invoke his previous election and begin court proceedings to regain his title of principal doctor.'

'He need not trouble himself: Neferet has no wish to fight him. She and I are going to leave Memphis.'

'This is a terrible mess,' said Bagey wearily.

Pazair imagined Denes making merry with his friends. Pharaoh's astonishing decree had given them back their utterly unhoped-for purity. All they had to do was keep from making any more stupid mistakes, and they would remain respectable citizens and be able to continue their conspiracy, whose nature was still a mystery and, for Pazair, out of reach for ever. General Asher would soon reappear and no doubt produce an explanation to justify his absence. But what role had Suti played and where was he, assuming he was still alive?

Broken, sick at heart, the judge looked up and saw ten swallows fly overhead. A second group joined the first, then a third, then several others. A hundred birds brushed past him giving cries of joy, all along his way. Were they thanking him for saving one of their kind? Passers-by were moved by the sight. Everyone knew the proverb: 'He who has the swallow's favour has also the king's.' Swift, graceful, light of heart, the birds with their bluish, softly rustling wings accompanied Pazair to the door of his house.

Neferet was seated beside the lotus-pond where the tits were playing. She wore only a short, transparent dress, which left her breasts bare. As he approached, Pazair was enveloped by sweet scents.

'We have just received some fresh ingredients,' she explained, 'and I'm preparing the ointments and perfumed oils for us to use in the coming months. If you didn't have any in the mornings, I fear you'd be angry with me.' Her voice was full of humour.

Pazair kissed his wife on the neck, took off his kilt, and sat down on the grass. At Neferet's feet were stone vases. They contained frankincense, a translucent brown resin from incense trees; myrrh, stuck together in little red masses, gathered in the land of Punt; green galbanum gum resin imported from Persia; dark ladanum resin bought in Greece and Minoa. Phials contained several flower-essences. Neferet would use olive-oil, honey and wine to create subtle mixtures.

'I have resigned,' said Pazair. 'At least I no longer have anything to fear, since I no longer have any power.'

'What is the tjaty's opinion?'

'The only worthwhile one: a royal decree cannot be challenged.'

'As soon as Qadash reclaims his post as principal doctor, we'll leave Memphis. He'll have the law on his side, won't he?'

'I'm afraid so.'

'Don't be sad, my love. Our destiny is in God's hands, not in our own. It is his wishes that are being accomplished, not our desires. We can build our own happiness. I'm glad. To live with you under the shelter of a hundred-year-old palm-tree, to heal humble folk, to take the time to love each other – what destiny could be better than that?'

'How can we forget Branir? And Suti . . . I can't stop thinking about him. My heart is on fire, and I balk like a donkey.'

'Whatever happens, don't ever change.'

'I shan't be able to give you a big house and such beautiful dresses any more.'

'I shall do very well without them. In fact, I might as well take this one off right away.'

Neferet slipped the straps down over her shoulders. Naked, she lay down beside Pazair. Their bodies understood each other perfectly; their lips united in such a passionate ardour that they shivered, despite the warmth of the sunset. Neferet's satin skin was a paradise in which only pleasure had the force of law. Pazair lost himself in it, intoxicated, communing with the wave that bore them away.

'More wine!' bellowed Qadash.

The servant hurried to obey.

Since his return, Qadash had been celebrating with two young Syrian lads – he would never touch a girl again. Before his misadventure, he had felt only a moderate taste for boys, but from now on he would be content with handsome foreign ones, whom he would denounce to the guards once he had tired of them.

In the evening, he would go to the conspirators' meeting summoned by Denes. Their anonymous letter to Ramses had had the results they had predicted. Caught in their net, the king had had to yield to their demands and proclaim a general amnesty in which Denes's case was wiped out along with the others. There was only one dark cloud on the horizon: the inevitable return of General Asher, who was now of no use to them whatever. But Denes would know how to get rid of him.

The shadow-eater entered Qadash's estate through the garden. He walked on the stone borders so as to leave no trace of his progress along the sandy path, and slunk stealthily off towards the kitchen. Crouching under the window, he listened to the two servants' conversation.

'I'm taking them a third pitcher of wine.'

'Should I open a fourth?'

'You'd better. The old fellow and the two young ones drink more than a thirsty regiment. I'm going, otherwise he'll fly into a rage.'

The wine-steward removed the stopper from a jar originating from the town of Imau, in the Delta and bearing the label 'Fifth year of Ramses'. A fine red wine, which lingered on the palate and banished inhibitions. His work done, the man left the kitchen and went outside to relieve himself against one of the garden walls.

The shadow-eater took advantage of the moment to fulfil his mission. Into the jar, he poured a poison based on plant extracts and snake-venom. Writhing in convulsions, Qadash would suffocate and die, together with his two foreign lovers, who would probably be accused of the crime. No one would have any interest in making this sordid story public.

After a death-agony lasting several minutes, Qadash gave up his soul to the god of hell. At that moment Denes was enjoying the caresses of a beautiful Nubian girl with plump buttocks and heavy breasts. He would never see her again, but intended to enjoy her with his customary brutality. To him, women were little more than beasts created for men's satisfaction.

Denes would miss his friend Qadash. Denes had treated him extremely well, even obtaining him the post of principal doctor, which had been promised to him since the beginning of the conspiracy. Unfortunately, though, the tooth-doctor had got old. On the verge of senility, making one mistake after another, he had become dangerous. By threatening to confess everything to Judge Pazair, Qadash had condemned himself to death: at Denes's suggestion, the conspirators had asked the shadow-eater to see to him. True, they regretted losing control of the post of principal doctor, but Judge Pazair's swift resignation had surpassed their wildest dreams. No one now would oppose their success.

The final stages were approaching: first they would seize the post of tjaty, then they would take supreme power.

35

A strong wind swept through the burial-ground at Memphis, where Pazair and Neferet were wending their way towards Branir's house of eternity. Before leaving the great city for the South, they wanted to pay homage to their dead master and assure him that, despite their slender means, they would keep trying to identify the murderer until their last breath.

Neferet was wearing the beaded amethyst belt Pazair had given her. Feeling the cold, the former Judge of the Porch had wrapped himself in a shawl and a woollen cloak. They met the conscientious old priest charged with the upkeep of the tomb and its garden; he received the proper fee from Memphis for seeing that the tomb was kept in perfect condition and for renewing the offerings.

In the shade of a palm-tree, the dead man's soul, in the form of a bird, came to slake its thirst in a pool of cool water after drawing the energy of resurrection from the light. Each day, it walked in the grounds of the shrine to breathe in the scents of the flowers.

Pazair and Neferet shared bread and wine in memory of their master, linking him to their meal, whose echo resounded in the invisible world.

'Be patient,' urged Bel-Tran. 'I can't bear to see you leave Memphis.'

'All Neferet and I want,' said Pazair, 'is to live a simple, calm life.'

'But neither of you has given your full measure,' argued Silkis.

'Opposing destiny is mere vanity.'

For their last evening in Memphis, Pazair and Neferet had accepted an invitation from Bel-Tran and Silkis. Bel-Tran, who was suffering from an attack of urticaria, had been persuaded by Neferet to let her treat his swollen liver and to adopt a healthier way of life. His leg-wound was weeping more and more frequently.

'Drink more water,' advised the doctor, 'and insist that your next doctor gives you something to ensure that your kidneys work properly – they don't at the moment.'

'One day perhaps I'll have time to take care of myself. The Treasury is drowning me in demands which must be dealt with immediately – but I mustn't lose sight of the overall picture.'

Bel-Tran's son and daughter came running in. The boy accused his sister of stealing the brush with which he was learning to draw beautiful hieroglyphs in order to become as rich as his father. The little red-haired girl, furious at the accusation, however right it might be, promptly slapped him and he burst into tears. Ever the attentive mother, Silkis took the children away and tried to put an end to the quarrel.

'You see,' said Bel-Tran, 'we badly need a judge!'

Pazair smiled. 'That investigation would be much too difficult for me.'

'You seem detached, almost pleased,' observed Bel-Tran in surprise.

'That's only how I seem; without Neferet, I'd have given up and despaired. This amnesty has ruined all my hopes of seeing justice triumph.'

'And I'm not looking forward to finding myself up against Denes again – which I'm bound to do without you as Judge of the Porch.'

'Trust Tjaty Bagey. He won't appoint anyone who cannot do the job.'

'There are rumours that he's preparing to leave office to enjoy a well-deserved retirement.'

'The king's decision has shaken him as much as me, and he's hardly in glowing health. But why has Ramses done this?'

'Perhaps he believes in the virtues of clemency.'

'It's done nothing to strengthen his popularity,' said Pazair. 'The people fear that his magical power is weakening and that, little by little, he's losing contact with the heavens. Giving criminals their freedom is not worthy of a king.'

'And yet his reign has been exemplary until now.'

'Can you understand his decision, and do you accept it?'

'Pharaoh sees further than we do.'

'That's what I thought, before the amnesty.'

'Return to work,' said Bel-Tran earnestly. 'Egypt needs you, and you, too, Neferet.'

'I'm afraid I'm as stubborn as my husband,' said Neferet.

'Will nothing persuade you to change your minds?'

'Only the re-establishment of justice.'

Bel-Tran himself refilled the cups with cool wine.

'After we've gone,' Pazair asked him, 'would you be good enough to carry on the search for Suti? Kem will help.'

'I'll approach the authorities straight away. But wouldn't it be better if you stayed in Memphis and worked with me? Neferet's reputation is so firmly established that she'll never lack for patients.'

'My financial skills are very limited,' confessed Pazair. 'You'd soon find me incompetent and a hindrance.'

'What are your plans, Doctor?'

'To settle in a village on the west bank of Thebes.'

Silkis, who had put the children to bed, came back into the room just in time to hear Neferet's answer.

She said, 'Give up the idea, I beg you! You can't just abandon your patients.'

'Memphis is bursting with excellent doctors.'

'Yes, but you're my doctor, and I don't want to change.'

'Between ourselves,' said Bel-Tran gravely, 'there must be no material difficulties. Whatever your needs may be, Silkis and I promise to meet them.'

'We're deeply grateful,' said Pazair, 'but I can no longer occupy a high post in the law. My ideals have been destroyed, and all I want is to enter into silence. The earth and animals don't tell lies; and I hope that Neferet's love will make the darkness less impenetrable.'

The solemnity of his words put an end to the discussion. The two couples talked about the beauty of the garden, the delicacy of the flowers and the excellent food, forgetting the difficulties that lay ahead.

'How are you feeling, my darling?' Denes asked Nenophar, who was reclining on a pile of cushions.

'Very well.'

'What did the doctor find?'

'Nothing, because I'm not ill.'

'I don't understand.'

'Do you know the fable of the lion and the rat? The lion caught the rat and was about to eat it. The rat begged for mercy: it was so small that it wouldn't nearly satisfy the lion's appetite, whereas if the lion let it live it might one day help him out of a sticky situation. The lion let it go. A few weeks later, hunters captured the lion and trussed him up in a net. The rat gnawed through the mesh, freed the lion and climbed up into its mane, and the two of them escaped.'

'Every schoolboy knows that story.'

'You should have remembered it before you slept with Tapeni.'

Denes's square face suddenly looked strained. 'Whatever are you talking about?'

Nenophar rose haughtily to her feet, full of icy anger. 'Because she was your mistress, that slut is behaving like the rat in the fable. But she's also the hunter. She's the only one who can free you from the net she's caught you in: blackmail. That's what we're facing – and all because of your infidelity.'

'You're exaggerating.'

'No, my loving husband. Respectability is a very expensive possession. Your mistress's tongue is hanging out so far that she may very well ruin our reputation.'

'I'll make her keep quiet.'

'You underestimate her. It would be better to give her what she wants, or we'll both be made to look ridiculous.'

Denes paced nervously up and down the room.

Nenophar went on, 'You seem to forget, my dear, that adultery is a serious offence, a vice punishable by law.'

'This was only a minor aberration.'

'Really? How often has it been repeated?'

'You're imagining things.'

'A noble lady on your arm for social occasions, and young girls in your bed the rest of the time. It's too much, Denes. I want a divorce.'

'You're mad!'

'On the contrary, I'm completely sane. I shall keep this house, my personal fortune, the inheritance I brought with me and my lands. Because of your disgraceful behaviour, the court will sentence you to pay me a food pension, and you'll be fined as well.'

Denes clenched his teeth. 'That isn't funny.'

'Your future is likely to be difficult, my darling.'

'You have no right to destroy our life like this. After all, we've spent our best years together.'

'Surely you aren't suddenly having tender feelings?'

'We've been partners for a long time.'

'You're the one who's dissolved the partnership. Divorce is the only solution.'

'Can you imagine the scandal?'

'Better that than ridicule. Besides, you'll be affected by it but I shan't. I shall be seen, quite rightly, as a victim.'

'This course of action is crazy. Accept my sincere apologies, and let us continue to put on a good front.'

'You betrayed me, Denes.'

'I didn't mean to, you know that. We're bound together, my dear. If you ruin me, you'll ruin yourself, too. Our affairs are so intermingled that a clean break is impossible.'

'I know them better than you do. You spend your time posturing, I spend mine working.'

'You forget that I'm destined for great things. Don't you want to share them?'

'Be more specific.'

'This is only a passing storm, my dear – every couple goes through them.'

'I thought I was sheltered from such intemperate behaviour.'

'Let's declare a truce, and not act too hastily – that would be damaging, because a rat like that woman Tapeni would be only too happy to undermine what we've built up so patiently.'

'Well, you'll have to deal with her.'

'I was going to ask if I might.'

Way-Finder had already climbed aboard the boat for Thebes; he was munching fresh fodder and gazing at the river. Mischief had escaped from her mistress and climbed to the top of the mast. Brave, who was more reserved and rather uneasy at the prospect of a long crossing, pressed against Pazair's legs. The dog did not care for rolling and pitching, though he would follow his master on to even the stormiest of seas.

The move had been arranged quickly. Pazair had left the official house and its furniture for his successor, though Bagey had so far refused to appoint one, preferring to perform the office himself until some suitable candidates could be found. This was the old tjaty's way of showing his regard for Pazair, who, in his eyes, had lost none of his merit.

The judge carried the mat he had had since the beginning of his career, and Neferet her medical equipment. All around them were chests full of with jars and pots. Their companions on the voyage were some loud-voiced merchants, who were practising boasting about the wares they hoped to sell in the great market at Thebes.

For Pazair there was only one disappointment: Kem had not come to say goodbye. He supposed the Nubian disapproved of what they were doing.

'Neferet, Neferet! Don't go!' called a woman's voice.

The doctor turned round.

A breathless Silkis caught her arm. 'It's Qadash. He's dead!'

'What happened?'

'Something horrible. Come over here.'

Pazair led Way-Finder off the boat and called Mischief. Seeing her mistress walking away, the monkey jumped down on to the quayside. Brave retraced his steps with relief.

'Qadash and his two young foreign lovers have been murdered, poisoned, and a servant told Kem, who's gone to the scene of the crime, and one of his men told Bel-Tran – and here I am,' said Silkis all in one breath. 'Everything's in chaos, Neferet, but the vote making you principal doctor has the force of law again. And you can go on caring for me.'

'Are you sure that—'

'Bel-Tran says your appointment can't be called into question. You're staying in Memphis.'

'We no longer have a house, we—'

'My husband's already found you another one.'

Neferet took Pazair's hand hesitantly.

'You have no choice,' he said.

Brave barked in a most unusual way, signifying not anger but a kind of stunned joy. That was his way of welcoming the arrival of a two-masted boat from Elephantine.

In the prow stood a long-haired young man and a beautiful woman.

'Suti!' yelled Pazair.

The feast given by Bel-Tran and Silkis was improvised but lavish. It celebrated both Neferet's restoration to her post and Suti's safe return.

The hero held the stage, describing his exploits, which everyone wanted to hear about in detail. He told of how he had joined the miners, of the journey through the burning hell of the desert, the All-Seeing One's betrayal, his encounter with Asher, Asher's departure for an unknown destination, and his own miraculous escape thanks to Panther. The Libyan girl grew almost intoxicated with laughter, but she never once took her eyes off her lover.

As promised, Bel-Tran had given Pazair the use of a house, a small one in the northern part of the city, until Neferet was allocated an official residence. The couple were happy to welcome Suti and Panther, who could stay as long as they wanted.

When they got home, the Libyan collapsed on to her bed and fell asleep instantly, and Neferet withdrew into her bed-chamber. The two men climbed up to the roof terrace.

'The wind's cool,' said Suti pensively. 'Some nights in the desert it was icy.'

'I waited and waited for a message from you.'

'It was impossible to get one to you, and if you sent me one it didn't reach me. But never mind that. Did my ears deceive me or did I really hear during dinner that Neferet is now the kingdom's principal doctor and that you've resigned as Judge of the Porch?'

'Your hearing is as good as ever.'

'Were you forced out?'

'No, not at all. I left of my own accord.'

'Why? Have you despaired of this world?'

'Ramses has decreed a general amnesty.'

'So every murderer will be exonerated.'

'It could not be put better.'

'Your beautiful legal system is in tatters,' said Suti sardonically.

'No one understands the king's decision.'

'All that matters is the result.'

'I have a confession to make.'

'A serious one?'

'I doubted you. I thought you'd sold me out.'

Suti stiffened, ready to strike. 'I'm going to break your head, Pazair.'

'And I deserve it – but so do you.'

'Why?'

'Because you lied to me.'

'This is the first chance we've had to talk freely. I was hardly going to tell the truth to that fellow Bel-Tran and his simpering wife. I might have known I couldn't deceive you.'

'I don't believe you abandoned the hunt for Asher. Your story was true until you met him, but after that I don't believe it.'

'Asher and his henchmen tortured me, with the intention of slowly burning me alive. But the desert became my ally, and Panther was my good spirit. And the thought of our friendship saved me when my courage almost failed.'

'Once you were able to move freely, you followed the general's trail. What was his plan?'

'To reach Libya via the South.'

'That was shrewd. Did he have any accomplices?'

'The dishonest All-Seeing One and an experienced miner.'

'What happened to them? Are they dead?'

'The desert is cruel,' said Suti.

'What was Asher looking for in those desolate places?'

'Gold. He was planning to enjoy the fortune he had amassed, and do it in safety in the land of his friend Adafi.'

'You killed him, didn't you?'

'His cowardice and weakness were unlimited.'

'Was Panther a witness?'

'More than that. She sentenced him, by handing me the arrow I fired.'

'Did you bury him?'

'The sand is quite good enough for his coffin.'

'You gave him no chance at all, did you?'

'He didn't deserve one.'

'So the celebrated general won't benefit from the amnesty . . .'

'Asher had already been judged. I merely carried out the sentence that ought to have been pronounced, and did it according to the law of the desert.'

'That's a rather brutal way of looking at it.'

'I feel lighter. In my dreams, the face of the man Asher tortured and murdered looks peaceful at last.'

'What became of the gold?'

Suti smiled. 'Spoils of war.'

'Aren't you worried that there'll be an investigation?'

'It won't be you who carries it out.'

'No, it will be Kem. He's an honest man and can't be bought or used. Besides, he lost his nose because he was falsely accused of stealing gold.'

'But he's your man, isn't he?'

Pazair shook his head. 'I'm nothing any more.'

'But I am. I'm rich. Letting a chance like that pass me by would have been stupid.'

'Gold is reserved for the gods.'

'They can spare some – they've got plenty.'

'You're embarking on a very dangerous adventure.'

'The most difficult part is behind me.'

'Will you leave Egypt?'

'I don't intend to, and I want to help you.'

'I'm now merely a little country judge with no power, just like I was before.'

'You can't mean you're giving up your quest?'

'I no longer have any means of continuing it.'

'Are you going to trample all your ideals underfoot? Can you really forget Branir's murder?'

'Denes's trial was about to begin. It would have been a decisive step towards the truth.'

'The charges laid out in your file have been erased, but what about the others?'

'What do you mean?'

Suti grinned. 'My friend Sababu keeps a private – very private – journal. I'm sure it contains some interesting details, and you might find just what you need in it.'

'I'll bear it in mind,' said Pazair. 'But now, my brother, what about you? Before Neferet is locked up in meetings and administration, get her to examine you. Your health must have been affected by what you've been through.'

'I was indeed planning to ask her.'

'What about Panther?'

'She's a daughter of the Libyan desert, and as indestructible as a scorpion. May the gods grant that she leaves me soon!'

'But love—'

'—wears out faster than copper, and anyway I prefer gold.'

'If you gave it back to the Temple at Kebet, you'd get a reward.'

'You're joking! It would be a pittance compared to what I've got in my chariot, and Panther wants to be very rich. To have followed the gold road and come back victorious ... could anything be more amazing?

'But let's change the subject,' Suti went on. 'Your punishment for doubting me is going to be very severe.'

Pazair smiled. 'I'm ready.'

'You and I are going to disappear for two days and go fishing in the Delta. I want to see some water, swim, roll in lush fields of green grass, go boating in the marshes.'

'But Neferet's being installed as—'

'I know her: she'll let you go.'

'Will Panther?'

'If you're with me, she'll trust me. She'll help Neferet to prepare for the ceremony – she's very skilful at dressing hair and preparing wigs. And we'll come back with some enormous fish.'

36

Doctors and remedy-makers practising in every field of medicine gathered to witness Neferet's instalment as principal doctor. They were admitted to the great open-air courtyard of the Temple of Sekhmet, the goddess who caused illnesses while also revealing the remedies that would cure them. Tjaty Bagey presided over the ceremony; everyone noticed how tired he looked. That a woman should fill the highest post in medicine did not shock the Egyptians, even if her male colleagues did allow themselves a few criticisms relating to her lack of physical strength and of authority.

Panther had worked with great skill. Not only had she dressed Neferet's hair but she had also attended to her clothes. The young doctor wore a long linen robe of immaculate whiteness, with a broad necklace of cornelians, lapis-lazuli bracelets at her wrists and ankles, and a striped wig. Her regal bearing made a strong impression on the audience, despite her gentle eyes and the delicate beauty of her slender body.

The most senior member of the doctors' council draped Neferet in a panther-skin to signify that her duty, like that of the priest charged with giving life to the royal mummy during the resurrection rites, was to instil a constant flow of energy into the immense body that was Egypt. Then he handed her the principal doctor's seal, which gave her authority over all the doctors in the kingdom, and the writing-desk on which she would draw up decrees concerning public health before submitting them to the tjaty.

The official speech was brief; it set out Neferet's duties and called upon her to respect the will of the gods in order to preserve the happiness of mankind. When his wife took the oath, Judge Pazair hid his face and wept.

Despite suffering pain so excruciating that only Kem could understand it, Killer had recovered all his strength. Thanks to Neferet's treatment, he would suffer no lasting consequences from his wounds. He had got his normal appetite back, and had resumed his guard patrols.

Pazair stroked Killer and made much of him. 'I shall never forget that I owe him my life,' he told Kem.

'Don't spoil him too much or he'll get soft, and that would be dangerous for him. Anything to report?'

'No. Now that I've resigned, I'm not at risk any more.'

'How do you see your future?'

'An appointment to an outlying district, I hope, where I can serve humble people to the best of my ability. If a difficult case arises, I'll let you know.'

'Do you still believe in the law?'

'To prove you right breaks my heart in two.'

'I want to resign, too.'

'No, stay in your post, I beg you. At least you can arrest criminals and guarantee the citizens' safety.'

'Yes – until the next amnesty. Nothing surprises me any more, but I'm very sorry about you.'

'There's not much we can do in this situation – in fact, our room for action is pathetic – but let's do the right thing. My greatest fear, Kem, was that I might not get your agreement.'

'I cursed the fact that I was delayed at Qadash's house, instead of greeting you on the quayside.'

'What are your conclusions about his death?'

'A triple poisoning. But whose idea was it? The two youngsters were sons of a travelling actor. The funeral ceremonies took place most discreetly, without anyone present apart from the specialist priests. It's the most sordid affair I've ever had to deal with. The bodies won't rest in Egypt; they've been handed over to the Libyans, because Qadash was of Libyan origin.'

'Could it have been murder, committed by a fourth person?' asked Pazair.

'Are you thinking of the man who kept attacking you?'

'During the Festival of Opet, Denes asked me about Qadash. I didn't hide the fact that Qadash had promised me to confess before he was executed.'

'Hmmm,' said Kem thoughtfully. 'It's more than possible that Denes wanted to get rid of an dangerous witness.'

'But why use so much violence?'

'Extremely powerful interests must be involved. Of course, Denes would have used the services of a creature of the shadows. I'll keep trying to identify him. Now that Killer's fully recovered, we shall resume our inquiries.'

'There's one thing that puzzles me: Qadash seemed absolutely certain that he wouldn't be executed.'

'He probably believed Denes would buy him his freedom.'

'Yes, probably, but ... He behaved with such arrogance, as if he knew there was going to be an amnesty.'

'Someone might have been indiscreet,' said Kem.

'I'd have got wind of it.'

'Don't deceive yourself – you'd have been the last to know. The court knows how unbending you are and knew that Denes's trial would have had tremendous repercussions.'

Pazair rejected the horrible suspicion that tormented him: collusion between Ramses and Denes, corruption at the very pinnacle of state, the beloved land of the gods delivered up to squalid appetites.

Kem saw that the judge was troubled, and said, 'We need facts – nothing but facts will enlighten us. So I'm planning to go back over a trail which will lead us to your attacker. His confession will be full of interest.'

'Then it's your turn to be careful,' said Pazair.

The man with the limp was one of the best sellers in the secret market at Memphis. He stood on a disused quay as cargo-boats arrived, laden with produce of every kind. The guards kept one eye on these practices; the taxation scribes levied the taxes without rancour. The man with the limp could have retired long ago to his house by the river – he was sixty – but he enjoyed conducting long negotiations and fooling gullible people. His latest victim had been a scribe from the Treasury, who fancied himself knowledgeable about ebony. Flattering his vanity, the man with the limp had sold him a piece of furniture made from ordinary dark wood at the price of ebony, which had been imitated very cleverly.

Another fine deal was in prospect: a man who had recently come into a lot of money wanted to acquire a collection of Nubian shields belonging to one of the most warlike tribes. A tinge of danger, while one was well protected in a city house, was a delicious sensation, which merited spending serious money. In league with some excellent craftsmen, the dealer had ordered counterfeit shields, much more impressive than the real ones. He would damage them himself so that they bore the traces of furious 'battles'.

His warehouse was full of similar marvels, which he produced sparingly and with consummate skill. Only the biggest prey interested him, people whose stupidity and selfimportance he found irresistible. As he drew back the bolt on the warehouse door, he laughed aloud at the thought of the next day.

An animal hide, black and covered in hair, fell on to his shoulders as he pushed the door open. Entangled in the disgusting pelt, the man gave a shout, fell over, and called for help.

'Don't make so much noise,' ordered Kem, allowing him a little air.

'Oh, it's you, Commander. What's got into you?'

'Do you recognize this hide?'

The dealer peered at it. 'No.'

'Don't lie.'

'I'm honesty itself.'

'You're one of my best informants,' conceded the Nubian, 'but it's the dealer I'm questioning. You recently sold a large male baboon. Who bought it?'

'I don't trade in animals.'

'A fine big creature like this ought to have been enlisted in the city guards. Only a scoundrel like you could have arranged to have it smuggled here.'

'Do you really think I'd do something like that?'

'I know how greedy you are.'

'I didn't do it.'

'You're making Killer angry,' warned Kem.

'But I don't know anything.'

'Perhaps you'll find him more persuasive than me.'

The dealer looked at Killer, and gave up. 'I heard that an enormous baboon had been captured near Elephantine. Yes, his sale would make someone a lot of money, but it wasn't my sort of deal. On the other hand, I could arrange the transport . . .'

'At a fat profit, I expect.'

'Bribes and expenses, mainly.'

'Don't try to make me feel sorry for you. I'm interested in only one thing: who bought the baboon?'

'It's very delicate . . .'

Killer stared fixedly at him, scratching the ground with an impatient paw.

'Do you promise to keep my name out of it?'

'Is Killer loose-tongued?'

'No one must know that I told you. Go and see Short-Thighs.'

The man certainly deserved his nickname. He had a large head, a hairy body and legs which were too short, but thick and sturdy. Since childhood, he had carried huge numbers of chests and boxes; now that he had become his own boss, he ruled over a hundred small producers, whose fruit and vegetables he sold. Alongside these official activities, Short-Thighs dabbled in assorted illegal trades, some more profitable than others.

The sight of Kem and Killer gave him no pleasure at all.

'Everything's fully in order here,' he said.

'You don't like the guards much, do you?' said Kem.

'No – and less than ever since you've been in charge.'

'Why? Have you got a guilty conscience?'

'Ask your questions.'

'Are you in such a hurry to talk?'

'Your baboon will force me to, so we might as well get it over with.'

'Actually, it's a baboon I want to talk to you about.'

'I hate the monsters.'

'And yet you bought one from the man with the limp.'

Short-Thighs looked uncomfortable, and pretended to arrange his packing-cases. 'I had an order for one.'

'From whom?'

'A strange fellow.'

'What's his name?'

'I don't know.'

'Describe him.'

'I can't.'

'How surprising,' said Kem sarcastically.

'Yes, it is,' retorted Short-Thighs, 'because I'm usually pretty observant. But the man who ordered the baboon was a sort of shadow, with no substance or distinguishing features. He wore a wig pulled down low over his forehead, almost covering his eyes, and a tunic which hid the shape of his body. I wouldn't recognise him, especially as our meeting was only brief – he didn't even haggle over the price.'

'What was his voice like?'

'Peculiar. I think he was disguising it. He probably had fruit-stones between his cheeks and his jaw.'

'Have you seen him again since then?'

'No.'

The trail ended there. The murderer's mission had no doubt ended with the fall of Pazair and the death of Qadash.

Sababu was pinning up her coiled hair. 'This is a most unexpected visit, Judge Pazair,' she said with amusement. 'Please allow me to finish doing my hair. Do you really need my services so early in the morning?'

'Not your services, no; I need to talk to you.'

The place was ostentatiously luxurious, filled with costly perfumes which made the head spin. Pazair looked for a window, but in vain.

'Does your wife know what you're doing?'

'I hide nothing from her.'

'So much the better. She's an exceptional person and an excellent doctor.'

'You keep a private journal, don't you?'

'In what capacity are you questioning me? You're no longer Judge of the Porch.'

'A small judge without any pretensions. You're quite free not to answer.'

'Who told you about my journal?'

'Suti. He thinks it may contain evidence against Denes.'

'Suti ... a wonderful boy and a splendid lover. For his sake I'll make a small gesture.' The voluptuous Sababu stood up and disappeared for a few moments behind a hanging. She reappeared carrying a papyrus.

'Here's the scroll in which I've noted my best clients' foibles, their perversions and the desires they don't dare admit to. Reading through it again, it's disappointing. Taken as a whole, the nobility of this country are healthy. They make love in natural ways, without physical or mental cruelty. There's nothing here of use to you, Judge. This past deserves only oblivion.' She tore the papyrus into shreds. 'You didn't try to stop me. Suppose I was lying?'

'I trust you.'

Sababu looked at the judge seriously. 'I can't help you, or love you, and I'm sorry for that. Make Neferet happy, think only of her happiness, and you'll live the most beautiful of lives.'

Panther slid back up Suti's naked body, more supple than a papyrus-stalk dancing in the wind. She stopped, kissed him, and resumed her inexorable progress towards her lover's lips. Tired of being passive, he put an end to her tender exploration, and threw her on to her side. Their legs intertwined, they embraced each other with the turbulence of a Nile flood, and shared a blazing pleasure at the very same moment. Both knew that they were bound together by this perfect desire and its accomplishment, but neither would admit it.

Panther was so passionate that a single bout was not enough for her; she easily reawakened Suti's ardour with intimate caresses. The young man called her his 'Libyan she-cat', evoking the goddess of love, who had left and gone into the western desert in the form of a lioness and returned, soft and seductive, in the form of a cat, domesticated but never completely tamed. Panther's slightest movement aroused passion, shimmering and painful; she played Suti like a lyre, making him resound in harmony with her own sensuality.

'I shall take you into town for our midday meal,' said Suti. 'A Hellene has just opened a tavern where he serves vine-leaves stuffed with meat, and white wine from his country.'

'When are we going to fetch the gold?'

'As soon as I'm fully fit again.'

'You seem virtually recovered to me.'

'Making love to you is easier, if no less exhausting, than walking for several days in the desert. I'm not strong enough yet.'

'I'm going with you – you couldn't do it on your own.'

'Who can we sell it to without being denounced?'

'The Libyans? They'd certainly buy it.'

'Never. Let's try to find someone in Memphis. If we can't, we'll have to stay in Thebes and look for an outlet. It'll be risky.'

'And exciting! Wealth has to be earned.'

'Tell me, Panther, what did you feel when you killed the guard?'

'Fear that I might miss.'

'Had you killed anyone before?'

'I wanted to save you, and I did. I'll kill you, too, if you ever try to leave me again.'

Suti sampled the atmosphere of Memphis with astonishment. It disconcerted him, felt almost foreign, after his long spell in the desert. At the heart of the Sycamore district, a colourful crowd was milling around the Temple of Hathor to hear a crier announce the dates of the next festival. Recruits were heading towards the military area to receive their equipment. Merchants were driving donkeys and chariots towards the storehouses, where they would obtain their allocations of cereals and fresh produce. At the 'Good Journey' port, boats were manoeuvring as they prepared to unload, the sailors loudly singing the traditional homecoming songs.

The Greek had opened his tavern in a narrow street in the southern district, not far from Judge Pazair's first office. As Panther and Suti were walking along it, they heard someone screaming in fear.

A chariot, drawn by a maddened horse, was thundering along the tiny street. Its terrified driver had let go of the reins. The left wheel hit the front of a house, the chariot lurched, and the driver was thrown out on to the ground. Some other passers-by managed to stop the horse.

Suti ran up and bent over the victim.

It was a woman – the lady Nenophar! Her head was covered in blood, and she was not breathing.

Initial treatment was given at the scene, then Nenophar was taken to the hospital. She had multiple bruises, a triple fracture of the left leg, a broken rib, and a deep wound on her neck. Her survival was something of a miracle. Neferet and two other doctors operated on her immediately. Thanks to her robust constitution, Nenophar would live, but she would walk on crutches for the rest of her life.

As soon as she was able to speak, Kem was given permission to question her, together with Pazair.

'The judge is accompanying me as a witness,' explained Kem. 'I think it advisable to have a magistrate present at our interview.'

'Why?'

'Because I cannot establish the cause of the accident.'

'The horse simply lost its head – I couldn't control it.'

'Do you usually drive a chariot?' asked Pazair.

'Of course not.'

'Then what happened?'

'I got in first, and a servant was supposed to get in and take the reins. But something – a stone, probably – hit the mare. She neighed, reared and bolted.'

'That sounds as though someone tried to kill you.'

Nenophar turned her bandaged head, and let her eyes wander. 'That isn't very likely.'

'I suspect your husband.'

'That's a hateful thing to say!'

'Am I wrong? Behind his apparently honourable nature, there hides a vain, vile creature, concerned only with his own interests.'

Nenophar seemed shaken.

Pazair widened the breach. 'Other suspicions attach to you yourself.'

'To me?'

'Branir was stabbed with a mother-of-pearl needle. You use a needle exactly like that one, and with remarkable skill.'

Nenophar sat bolt upright, white-faced. 'That's horrible. How dare you accuse me of such a thing!'

'At the trial that was cancelled because of the amnesty, you would have been incriminated in an illegal trade in fabrics, dresses and sheets. One crime may well have led to another.'

'Why are you attacking me like this?'

'Because your husband is at the centre of a criminal conspiracy. Who better than you to be his accomplice?'

A sad smile twisted Nenophar's lips. 'You've been misinformed, Judge. Before the accident, I was intending to get a divorce.'

'Have you changed your mind?'

'It was Denes who, through me, was the target. I shan't desert him in the midst of the storm.'

'Forgive my brutality. I wish you a speedy recovery.'

The two men sat down on a stone bench. Killer was calm, so they knew they were not being watched.

'What do you think?' asked Pazair.

'A notable case of chronic, incurable stupidity,' said Kem. 'She simply cannot understand that her husband tried to get rid of her because the divorce would have reduced him to penury – it's Nenophar who has all the money. Denes didn't realize that he held a winning hand whatever the outcome of the murder attempt. Either Nenophar would die in the accident or she'd become his loyal ally again. Difficult to find a more idiotic woman of her social standing.'

'Short and to the point,' commented Pazair, 'but persuasive. One fact, I feel, has been established: she is not Branir's murderer.'

37

In the depths of a winter which was proving colder than usual, Ramses celebrated the festivals of the resurrection of Osiris. After the fertility of the Nile, which was seen by all, came the fecundity of the spirit, gaining victory over death; in each shrine lamps were lit, so that the eternal light of rebirth might shine forth.

The king went to Saqqara. For an entire day, he meditated before the Step Pyramid, then before the statue of its builder, his illustrious predecessor Pharaoh Djoser.

The single open gate in the curtain-wall could be passed through only by the soul of the dead pharaoh or by the reigning king, during his festival of regeneration, in the presence of the gods of heaven and earth.

Ramses called upon his ancestors, who had become stars in the heavens, to inspire him and show him how to escape from the dark chasm into which his invisible enemies had cast him. The majesty of the place, consecrated to the radiant silence of transfigured life, restored his serenity; it filled his gaze with the play of light, bringing to life the giant stone staircase at the centre of the immense burial-ground.

At sunset, the answer was born in his heart.

Kem was not a man who enjoyed working in an office, so he questioned Suti as they walked along beside the Nile.

'You had an extraordinary adventure. To get out of the desert alive is no mean feat.'

'My good luck protects me better than any god could.'

'She's a fickle friend – don't make too many demands on her.'

'Caution bores me.'

'Ephraim was an unmitigated scoundrel. His death can't have grieved you much.'

'He fled with Asher.'

'Despite intensive searches by the desert patrols, they still haven't been found.'

'I saw how clever they were at avoiding the guards as they moved about.'

'You're a magician,' said Kem.

'Is that a compliment or a criticism?'

'Escaping from Asher's claws was an almost supernatural achievement. Why did he let you go?'

'I don't know – I can't understand it.'

'He ought to have killed you, you must admit. Another strange point: what did he hope to achieve by hiding in a mining area?'

'When you arrest him, he can tell you,' said Suti.

'Gold is the supreme wealth, the inaccessible dream. Like you, Asher cared nothing for the gods; all he wanted was wealth. Ephraim knew about the abandoned mines, and told him where they were. By acquiring all that gold, the general made sure he need not fear the future.'

'Perhaps. He didn't confide in me.'

'Didn't you want to follow him?'

'I was injured, at the end of my strength.'

'I believe you killed him. You hated him enough to try anything.'

'He was too strong for me in the state I was in.'

'I've been in a situation like that myself. The will can dictate to even the most exhausted body.'

'When Asher comes back, he'll benefit from the amnesty, won't he?'

'He isn't going to come back. The vultures and the rodents have eaten his flesh, and the wind will disperse his bones. Where have you hidden the gold?'

'All I've got is my good luck.'

'Stealing it is an unforgivable crime. No one has ever succeeded in keeping gold stolen from the belly of the mountains. Give it back, before your good luck deserts you.'

'You've become a real guards commander,' said Suti sarcastically.

'I like order. A country is happy and prosperous when people and things are in their proper places. The place for gold is inside the temple. Take your hoard back to Kebet, and I'll say not a word about it. If you don't, you can consider me your enemy.'

Neferet refused to live in the house that had belonged to Nebamon, beause it was impregnated with too many harmful vibrations. She preferred to wait until the government allocated her another house, and was content with modest lodgings, where she got what sleep she could at night.

On the very first day after her installation, the various councils concerned with the country's health all requested audiences, eager to show their dedication to their work. Neferet calmed their anxieties and restrained their impatience; before dealing with future promotions, she must attend to the needs of the people. So she summoned the officials in charge of distributing water and of ensuring that no village went short; then she examined the list of hospitals and remedy-stores, noting that some provinces lacked necessary facilities. The division of specialist and general doctors between the South and the North was unsatisfactory. Finally, among the most urgent matters, she must respond to the foreign countries that were asking for Egyptian doctors to treat illustrious patients.

She was beginning to grasp the full extent of her task. To this was added the polite hostility of the doctors who had been caring for Ramses since Nebamon's death. They all boasted of their abilities and claimed that the king was pleased with their treatment.

Walking in the streets refreshed her. So few people knew her face, particularly in the areas near the palace, that she could stroll at her ease, after a day of stressful conversations in which everyone she spoke to put her to the test.

When Suti fell into step beside her, she was astonished.

'I must speak with you alone,' he said.

'Without Pazair?'

'For the moment, yes.'

'What are you afraid of?'

'My suspicions are too vague and so terrible . . . He'd get carried away for all the wrong reasons. I'd rather talk to you first; you shall be the judge.'

'Is it about Panther?'

'How did you guess?'

'She occupies a certain place in your life . . . and you seem very much in love.'

'Don't deceive yourself. Our understanding is a purely sensual one. But Panther . . .' He hesitated.

Neferet, who liked to walk quickly, slowed her pace.

'Remember the circumstances of Branir's murder,' he went on, after a few moments.

'A mother-of-pearl needle was plunged into his neck, with such accuracy that it killed him instantly.'

'Panther killed the guard exactly like that, using a dagger. And he was a huge man.'

'It's just coincidence.'

'I hope so, Neferet, I hope so with all my heart.'

'Don't torture yourself any more. Branir's soul is so close to me, so alive, that your accusation, if there were any truth in it, would have awoken an immediate certainty within me. Panther is innocent.'

Neferet and Pazair hid nothing from each other. Since the moment when love had united them, a complicity reigned which daily life could not wear down and which no arguments ever shattered. When the judge came to bed, late that night, she woke up and told him of Suti's anxieties.

'He felt guilty at the idea of living with the woman who might have assassinated Branir,' she said.

'How did he get this mad idea?'

'From a nightmare.'

'It's absurd. Panther didn't even know Branir.'

'Somone might have used her dangerous gifts.'

'She killed the guard out of love; reassure Suti about that, will you?'

'You seem sure of yourself.'

'I am sure of her, and of him.'

'So am I.'

The visit by Ramses' mother threw the order of the audiences into disarray. Governors of provinces, who had come to request health equipment, bowed as Tuya passed by.

She kissed Neferet. 'Here you are, in your proper place.'

'I miss my village in Upper Egypt.'

'No regrets, no remorse: they are futile. All that matters is your mission, in the service of the country.'

'How is your health, Majesty?'

'Excellent.'

'I must give you a routine examination.'

'Only to reassure yourself.'

Despite the queen's age and previous infections, her sight was satisfactory. Nevertheless, Neferet asked her to continue following the treatment strictly.

'Your work will not be easy,' said the queen. 'Nebamon had the art of putting off urgent matters and burying files, and he surrounded himself with loyal supporters who never questioned anything he did. They are weak, narrow-minded, hidebound people, and they will oppose any changes you wish to make. Inertia is difficult to combat, but do not lose heart.'

'How is Pharaoh?'

'He is away in the North, inspecting the garrisons there. I have a feeling that he is preoccupied with General Asher's disappearance.'

'Can you share his thoughts once more, Majesty?'

'Unfortunately, no. If I could, I would have asked him the reason for that contemptible amnesty of which our people disapprove so much. Ramses is tired, and his power is wearing out. The High Priests of Iunu, Memphis and Thebes will lose no time in arranging the festival of regeneration that everyone rightly believes is necessary.'

'The country will rejoice.'

'Ramses will once again be filled with the fire that enabled him to defeat his most formidable enemies. Do not hesitate to ask me for help; our relationship now has an official nature.'

Such encouragement increased Neferet's energy tenfold.

After the weavers had left, Tapeni inspected the workshop. Her practised eye could detect even the smallest theft; neither a tool nor a piece of cloth must disappear from her domain, on pain of immediate punishment. Only the utmost strictness could ensure constant quality in the work.

A man came in.

'Denes!' she exclaimed. 'What do you want?'

He closed the door behind him. His massive frame advanced slowly, his expression grim.

'Why are you here?' she asked. 'You said we ought not to see each other again.'

'That's right.'

'You made a mistake. I'm not a woman you can use and then abandon.'

'You made another mistake. I'm not a man to be blackmailed.'

'Either you give in or I'll ruin your reputation.'

'My wife's just had a serious accident. If it weren't for the gods' mercy, she'd be dead.'

'That changes nothing in the agreements I made with her.'

'No agreements have been made.'

With one hand, Denes seized Tapeni by the throat and flattened her against a wall. 'If you go on bothering me, you'll have an accident, too. Your disgusting methods won't work with me. Don't try to make use of my wife, and forget all about our little affair. Be content with your craft if you want to live until you're old. Goodbye.'

Freed from his ruthless grip, Tapeni gulped in air.

Suti checked that he was not being followed. Since Kem's interrogation, he feared he might be being watched. The Nubian's warning must not be taken lightly: even Pazair would not be able to protect his friend if Kem proved him guilty.

Fortunately, his suspicions about Panther had been dispelled, but the two of them must leave Memphis without Kem's knowledge. Making the best use of their fabulous wealth would be a delicate enterprise, and they could not do it alone, so Suti contacted a few dubious characters, mostly established dealers in stolen goods. He did not tell them about the gold, of course, but merely said it would be a sizeable transaction, and that he would need to transport the material a long way.

Short-Thighs struck him as useful. The dealer asked no questions, and agreed to provide Suti with strong donkeys, dried meat and water-skins, at a place of his choosing. Bringing the gold back from the cave to the great city, hiding it, buying a luxurious house and leading a grand life would entail taking a lot of risks, but Suti thoroughly enjoyed playing on his luck. He was sure it would not desert him just when he was about to become rich.

In three days' time, he and Panther would take a boat to Elephantine. Armed with the wooden tablet on which Short-Thighs had written his instructions, they would collect the donkeys and supplies in a village where nobody knew them. Then they would retrieve part of the gold from its hiding-place, and come back to Memphis in the hope of trading it in a parallel market which Greeks, Libyans and Syrians were trying to establish. The gold's market value was so high, and it was so rarely available, that Suti was sure to find a buyer.

He was risking life imprisonment, if not death. But when he owned the finest estate in all Egypt, he would organize magnificent parties at which the guests of honour would be Pazair and Neferet. He would burn his wealth like straw, so that a fire of joy rose to the heavens, where the non-existent gods would laugh with him.

The tjaty's voice was hoarse, his face drawn. 'Judge Pazair,' he said, 'I have summoned you here to address your recent conduct.'

'What have I done wrong?'

'Your opposition to the amnesty is too open. You never miss an opportunity to declare it.'

'To keep silent would be dishonest.'

'What you are doing is extremely foolish.'

'But you yourself, Tjaty, made your opposition known to the king.'

'I am an old tjaty, you are a young judge.'

'How could Pharaoh be offended by the opinion of an insignificant district judge?'

'You used to be Judge of the Porch. Keep your thoughts to yourself.'

'Will my next appointment depend on my silence?'

'You are intelligent enough to answer that question yourself,' said Bagey. 'A judge who challenges the law is not fit to practise.'

'If that is so, I renounce my office.'

'But your work is your whole reason for living.'

'The wound will never heal, I know, but better that than hypocrisy.'

'You are being too unyielding.'

Pazair smiled. 'Coming from you, that is a compliment.'

'I detest pomposity, but I believe this country needs you.'

'By remaining faithful to my ideal, I hope to be in harmony with the Egypt of the pyramids, the Peak of the West and the undying suns. That Egypt did not recognize the amnesty. If I'm wrong, justice will follow its course without me.'

'Hello, Suti.'

The young man put down his cup of cool beer. 'Tapeni!'

'It's taken me a long time to find you. This tavern is a bit sordid, but you seem to like it.'

'How are you?'

'I've been rather lonely since you left.'

'A pretty woman needn't ever be lonely.'

'Have you lost your memory? You're my husband.'

'When I left your house, our divorce was consummated.'

'You're wrong, darling. I regard your escape as a mere . . . absence for a while.'

'Our marriage took place because it was necessary for my investigation. The amnesty put an end to it.'

'I take our marriage seriously.'

'Stop joking, Tapeni.'

'You're the husband I've always dreamt of.'

'Oh, really, I—'

'I order you to get rid of your Libyan whore and return to our matrimonial home.'

'That's crazy.'

'I don't want to lose everything. Do as I say, or you'll regret it.'

Suti shrugged, and emptied his cup in a single draught.

Brave was romping about in front of Pazair and Neferet. The dog looked at the canal water, but kept well away from it. The little green monkey clung to her mistress's shoulder.

'Bagey disagrees with my decision,' said Pazair, 'but I shall hold to it.'

'Where will you work? In the provinces?'

'Nowhere. I'm not a judge any more, because I oppose an unjust decision.'

'If only we'd been able to go to Thebes,' sighed Neferet.

'Your colleagues would have brought you back.'

'My position isn't as strong as it looks. A few influential members of the court are unhappy at having a woman as principal doctor. If I make even a tiny mistake, they'll demand my resignation.'

'I'm going to fulfil an old dream, and become a gardener. In our future home, my work will be useful.'

'Pazair . . .'

'We'll live together in utter happiness. You'll work for the health of Egypt, and I'll care for the flowers and trees.'

Pazair's eyes did not deceive him. He had indeed received a summons from the principal judge in the sacred town of Iunu, to the north of Memphis. Iunu had no trade or agricultural importance to speak of, and consisted only of temples built around an immense obelisk, a petrified ray of sunlight.

'I'm being offered a post as a judge dealing with religious affairs,' he told Neferet. 'Nothing ever happens in Iunu, so I won't exactly be overworked. Usually the tjaty sends elderly or frail judges there.'

'Bagey has intervened in your favour,' she said. 'At least you'll keep your title.'

'He's getting me away from civil matters – very shrewd of him.'

'Don't refuse the offer.'

'If anyone tries to impose constraints on me, however small, or if they try to make me accept the amnesty, my stay in Iunu will be a short one.'

Iunu was home to the writers of the sacred texts, rituals and mythological tales designed to pass on the wisdom of the ancients. Within the temples, which were surrounded by high walls, a modest number of priests celebrated the cult of energy in the form of light.

Pazair found a silent town, without merchants or market-stalls. In the small white houses lived the priests and also craftsmen whose job was to create or maintain ritual objects. The commotion of the outside world did not reach them.

Pazair reported to the office of the principal judge, where a white-haired old scribe greeted him with obvious annoyance. After examining the summons, he withdrew.

The place was calm, almost sleepy, so unlike the bustle of Memphis that Pazair could scarcely believe men worked here.

Two guards armed with clubs suddenly entered the room. 'Judge Pazair?'

'What do you want?'

'Follow us.'

'Why?'

'Orders from above.'

'I refuse.'

'There's no point trying to resist. We'll use force if we have to.'

Pazair realized that he had fallen into a trap. Anyone who defied Ramses paid the price. He was going to be given not a post as a judge but a place in the burial-ground of oblivion.

38

Flanked by the two guards, Pazair was taken to the door of an oblong building adjoining the curtain-wall of the Temple of Ra.

The door opened to reveal an old, shaven-headed priest with lined skin and black eyes, dressed in a panther skin.

'Judge Pazair?' he said.

'Detaining me like this is illegal.'

'Instead of talking nonsense, come in, wash your hands and feet, and pray.'

Surprised, Pazair obeyed. The two guards took up positions outside, and the door closed again.

'Where am I?' asked the judge.

'In the House of Life at Iunu.'

The judge was astounded. It was here, in a place forbidden to outsiders, that the sages of past times had composed the pyramid texts, which revealed the changes of the soul and the process of rebirth. The people knew that the most famous mages had been trained in this mysterious school; only a few were called to it, and they never knew the day or the hour when the call would come.

'Purify yourself.'

Nervously, Pazair did so.

'My name is Hairless,' said the priest. 'I guard this door and keep out all harmful elements.'

'But I was summoned—'

'Don't bother me with useless words.' Hairless had an authority which made Pazair's protests stick in his throat. 'Take off your kilt and put on this white robe.'

Pazair felt he was being transported into another world, where there were no landmarks. Light entered the House of Life only through narrow slits near the tops of the stone walls, which were plain and without inscription.

'I am also called "the Slaughterman",' said Hairless, 'because I behead the enemies of Osiris. Here are kept the annals of the gods, the books of knowledge, and the rituals of the mysteries. You may never speak to anyone of what you will see and hear. Destiny strikes down the loose-tongued.'

Hairless led Pazair down a long passageway which ended in a sandy courtyard. In the centre, a mound of sand housed a mummy of Osiris, the receptacle of life in its most secret aspect. Called the Divine Stone, it was spread with precious ointments and covered with a ram's skin.

'Within it, the energy that creates Egypt dies and is reborn,' explained Hairless.

All round the courtyard were libraries and workshops for the craftsmen who were allowed to work in the enclosure.

'What do you see, Pazair?'

'A mound of sand.'

'This is how life takes form. Energy springs from the ocean where the worlds are contained as seeds; it materializes in the form of a mound. Seek the highest, most vital element, and you will approach the very beginning.' He pointed to a closed door. 'We shall enter that chamber, and you shall appear before your judge.'

The judge was seated on a gilded wooden throne; he wore a curled wig which covered his ears, and a long tunic. On his chest was a broad knot; in his right hand, he held a sceptre of command; in his left, a long cane. Behind him was a set of golden scales. This formidable man was charged with the secrets of the House of Life and the distribution of offerings, and was guardian of the primordial stone.

He surveyed Pazair for a moment or two, then said, 'You claim to be an honest judge.'

'I try to be.'

'Why do you refuse to apply the amnesty decreed by Pharaoh?'

'Because it is unjust.'

'In this enclosed place, before these scales, far from the eyes of outsiders, do you dare to maintain that opinion?'

'I do.'

'I can do no more for you.'

Hairless seized Pazair by the shoulder and dragged him out of the chamber.

So, thought Pazair, all those fine words were merely part of the trap. The priests' goal was to break his resistance. Persuasion had failed, so now they would use violence.

'Enter here.' Hairless knocked on a bronze door.

A single lamp lit the small, windowless room. Two channels, hollowed out of the thick walls, brought in vital air.

A man sat on a gilded throne, looking at Pazair. A man with red hair, a broad forehead and a hooked nose. On his wrists were gold and lapis-lazuli bracelets, the upper parts of which were decorated with the heads of two wild ducks. The favourite jewellery of King Ramses.

'You are ...' Pazair dared not speak the word – 'Pharaoh' – that burnt on his lips.

'And you are Pazair, who resigned from his post as Judge of the Porch and has openly criticized my amnesty decree.' The king's voice was full of anger and reproach.

Pazair's heart raced. Face to face with the most powerful ruler on earth, he could think of nothing to say.

'Well, answer me. Have I been told lies about you?'

'No, Majesty.'

The judge realized that he had forgotten to kneel. He dropped to his knees on the ground.

'Get up. Since you defy your king, at least behave like a warrior.'

Nettled, Pazair stood up. 'I shall not recant.'

'Why do you oppose the amnesty?'

'Exonerating guilty men and freeing criminals are insults to the gods and marks of contempt for human suffering. If you follow this dangerous road, you will end by accusing the victims.'

'Do you claim to be infallible?'

'No, Majesty. I have made many mistakes – but not to the detriment of innocent people.'

'And are you incorruptible?'

'My soul is not for sale.'

'Disrespect for the throne is itself a crime,' Pharaoh pointed out.

'I respect the Rule of Ma'at.'

'Do you think you know it better than I, who am her son?'

'The amnesty is a grave injustice, and upsets the country's balance.'

'Do you think you can speak to your king like this, and live?'

'If I die, I shall at least have had the pleasure of telling you my true thoughts.'

Ramses' tone changed. Instead of being angry, his words were slow and serious. 'Since your arrival in Memphis, I have been watching you. Branir was a wise man, who never acted lightly. He chose you because of your integrity; his other pupil was Neferet, who is today the kingdom's principal doctor.'

'She has succeeded, I have failed.'

'You have succeeded equally, for you are the only honest judge in Egypt.'

Pazair was speechless.

'Despite much opposition, including my own, your opinion has not changed. You have held your own against the King of Egypt, in the name of justice. You are my last hope. I am alone, Pazair, caught in an appalling dilemma. Will you help me, or do you prefer your quiet life?'

Pazair bowed low. 'I am your servant, Majesty.'

'Are those the words of a courtier, or do you mean what you say?'

'My actions will answer for me.'

'For that reason, I am placing the future of Egypt in your hands.'

'I . . . I don't understand.'

'We are in a safe place here, and no one will hear what I am about to reveal to you. Think hard, Pazair; you can still draw back. When I have spoken, you will be charged with the most difficult mission ever entrusted to a judge.'

'The vocation Branir awakened in me cannot be stifled.'

'Judge Pazair, I appoint you tjaty of Egypt.'

'But, Majesty, Tjaty Ba—'

'Bagey is old and tired. Several times in the last few months he has asked me to replace him. Your refusal to accept the amnesty enabled me to find his successor, despite the advice of those close to me, who had other men in mind.'

'Why can Bagey not undertake the task you wish to entrust to me?'

'On one hand, he is no longer strong and energetic enough to carry out the investigation; on the other, there would be gossip among the members of his government, who have been in place too long. If the slightest hint of the truth should filter through, the country would fall into the hands of demons from the darkness. Soon you will be the most important person in the kingdom after Pharaoh, but you will be alone, friendless and without support. Do not confide in anyone. Get rid of many of the existing ministers and surround yourself with new men, but do not trust them.'

'Majesty, you spoke of an investigation . . . ?'

'This is the truth, Pazair. The sacred insignia of kingship, which legitimize the reign of each pharaoh, were housed within the Great Pyramid. The pyramid was broken into and violated, and the insignia were stolen. Without them, I cannot celebrate the festival of regeneration that the High Priests are rightly demanding in the name of our people. In less than a year, when the Nile flood is reborn, I shall be compelled to abdicate, to the benefit of a thief and a criminal who is lurking in the shadows.'

'So the amnesty decree was forced on you.'

'For the first time, I was obliged to act contrary to justice. I faced threats that the theft from the pyramid would be revealed and my downfall brought about.'

'Why did the enemy not do that a long time ago?'

'Because he is not ready; seizing the throne cannot be done hastily. The moment of my abdication will be the most favourable one, and the usurper will accede to power peacefully. I agreed to the demands of the anonymous message, in order to see who, if anyone, who would dare stand against the amnesty. Apart from Bagey and yourself, no one has challenged it. The old tjaty has more than earned his rest. You, as his successor, will identify the criminals, or else we shall fall together.'

Pazair thought back over his investigation, right from the crucial moment when he had been the grain of sand that disrupted the evil machine, by refusing to authorize the transfer of a member of the honour-guard.

Ramses went on, 'Never has Egypt seen such a wave of murders. I am convinced that they are linked to this monstrous conspiracy. Why were the honour-guard killed? Because the Sphinx is near the Great Pyramid, and the soldiers were blocking the looters' way. They had to get rid of them in order to enter the pyramid without being seen.'

'How did they get in?'

'By an underground passageway which I thought had been sealed. You must inspect it – there may still be clues there. For a long time I have believed General Asher to be at the centre of the plot.'

'No, Majesty, he only seemed to be.'

'If we still cannot find him, it is because he is in Libya, uniting the tribes against Egypt.'

'Asher is dead.'

'Have you proof of that?'

'My friend Suti told me.'

'Did he kill him?'

Pazair hesitated.

'You are my tjaty. There must be no shadows between us: the truth shall be our bond.'

'Yes, Suti killed him. Suti hated Asher because he saw the general torturing and killing an Egyptian soldier.'

'For a long time I believed in Asher's good faith, but I was mistaken.'

'If Denes's trial had taken place, his guilt would have been proved.'

'That upstart ship-owner!'

'He and his friends Qadash and Sheshi made a formidable trio. Qadash wanted to be principal doctor, while Sheshi said he was working on a way of making unbreakable weapons. Sheshi and Denes were probably responsible for Princess Hattusa's accident.'

'Are those three the only ones in the plot, or are there others?'

'I do not know.'

'Find out.'

'I have been wandering in the dark, Majesty. Now I must know everything. What are the sacred objects that were stolen from the Great Pyramid?'

'The first is a small adze made of sky-iron, used to open the mummy's mouth during the resurrection ritual.'

'It is safe, Majesty. It is in the hands of the High Priest of the Temple of Ptah, in Memphis.'

'And some lapis-lazuli amulets.'

'Sheshi was smuggling amulets. I am sure they are safe at Karnak, with the High Priest.'

'A gold scarab.'

'Kani has that, too!' Pazair felt a mad hope for a moment: had he saved the pyramid's treasures without realizing it?

'The looters,' Ramses went on, 'tore off Khufu's gold mask and collar.'

Those words instantly dashed Pazair's hopes. He could not answer.

'If they have behaved like the profaners of the past, we shall never recover them, nor the gold cubit dedicated to Ma'at. They will have melted them down and turned them into gold bars which they will have sold abroad.'

Pazair was close to tears. How could people be vile enough to destroy such beauty?

He asked, 'If some of the items have been saved and the rest destroyed, what have our enemies still got?'

'The most vital thing of all,' replied Ramses, 'the Testament of the Gods. My goldsmiths have the skill to make another cubit, but the Testament is unique, passed on from pharaoh to pharaoh. During the festival of regeneration, I shall have to show it to the gods, to the High Priests, to the Friends of Pharaoh and to the people of Egypt. Such is the will of the rule of kings; it was so yesterday and will be so tomorrow, and I shall submit to it.

'In the months we have left before the festival, our enemies will not be idle. They will try to weaken me, to corrupt and undermine my power. It is up to you to find the strength to thwart their plans. If you fail, I fear that the civilization of our fathers will be destroyed. Murderers bold enough to desecrate our most sacred shrine clearly have only contempt for the fundamental values by which we live. With so much at stake, my person does not matter. My throne, though, is the symbol of a thousand-year-old dynasty and of the traditions upon which this country is built. I love Egypt as you do, beyond life, beyond time. It is her light that they wish to extinguish. You must save it, Tjaty Pazair.'

39

For a whole night Pazair meditated, seated on the ground before a statue of Thoth, which depicted him in the form of a baboon crowned with the moon's disc. The temple lay silent; on the roof, the star-watchers were at work. Still in shock from his conversation with Pharaoh, he treasured these few last hours of peace before his enthronement, before crossing the threshold of a new life he had never wished for.

He thought of the happy moment when Neferet, Brave, Way-Finder, Mischief and he had prepared to embark for Thebes, of peaceful days in a little village in Upper Egypt, of his wife's gentle sweetness, the regular cycle of the seasons, far from affairs of state and human ambition. But that was now no more than a fading dream, far out of reach.

Two priests led Pazair to the House of Life, where he was greeted by Hairless. The future tjaty knelt down on a mat; Hairless placed a wooden rule on his head, then offered him water and bread.

'Drink and eat,' he ordered. 'Be vigilant in all circumstances, or this food and water will become bitter. May pain be transformed into joy by your actions.'

Washed, shaven and perfumed, Pazair put on an old-fashioned kilt, a linen robe, and a short wig. The priests guided him to the royal palace, around which huge crowds had gathered in response to the announcement the previous evening that a new tjaty had been appointed.

Calm now, and indifferent to the clamour, Pazair entered the great audience chamber where Pharaoh sat upon his throne, wearing the White and Red Crowns fitted together to symbolize the union of Upper and Lower Egypt. On either side of the king sat the Friends of Pharaoh, including Bagey and Bel-Tran. Many courtiers and dignitaries were gathered between the pillars of the hall; among them, Pazair immediately made out the kingdom's principal doctor. At once serious and smiling, Neferet did not take her eyes off him for a moment.

Pazair remained standing, facing the king. In front of him, the bearer of the Rule unrolled the papyrus on which the spirit of the laws was written.

'I, Ramses, Pharaoh of Egypt, appoint Pazair tjaty, servant of the law, and support of the country. In truth, it is not a favour which I grant you, for your office is neither sweet nor agreeable, but more bitter than bile. Act in accordance with the Rule, no matter what subject you are dealing with; give justice to all, no matter what their condition. Act so that you are respected because of your wisdom and your calm words. When you give orders, take care to persuade; offend no one, and reject violence. Do not take refuge in silence, confront difficulties, do not bow your head before senior officials. May your way of judging be transparent, without dissimulation, and may everyone perceive that it is right; the water and the wind will carry your words and your acts to the people. May none accuse you of having been unjust towards them by failing to listen. Never act according to your preferences; judge those you know in the same way as those you do not know, do not seek to be liked or disliked, do not show favour to anyone, but do not be excessively rigorous or intransigent. Punish rebels, the arrogant and the loose-tongued, for they sow trouble and destruction. Your only refuge is the Rule of Ma'at, which has not altered since the time of the gods and which will still endure when mankind has ceased to exist. Your only way of life is righteousness.'

Bagey bowed before Pharaoh, laid his hand upon the copper heart he wore at his throat, and began to take it off to return it to the king.

'Keep that symbol,' decreed Ramses. 'You have shown yourself worthy of it for so many years that you have acquired the right to bear it with you into the afterlife. For now, live a happy and peaceful old age, but do not forget to counsel your successor.'

The former tjaty and the new one embraced, then Pharaoh bestowed on Pazair a superb new copper heart, made in the royal workshops.

'You are the master of justice,' proclaimed Ramses. 'Watch over the happiness of Egypt and her people. You are the copper that protects the gold, the tjaty protecting Pharaoh. Act in accordance with my orders, but be neither weak nor servile, and have the skill to extend my thoughts. Each day, you shall give me an account of your work.'

The members of the court hailed the new tjaty with deference.

The provincial leaders, governors of estates, scribes, judges, craftsmen, and the men and women of Egypt all sang the praises of the new tjaty.

At the state's expense, feasts in his honour were held everywhere, offering the best food and beer.

What destiny could be more enviable than the tjaty's? Servants hurried to satisfy his every whim, he travelled in a cedar-wood boat, the dishes served at his table were succulent, he drank rare wines while musicians played charming airs, the keeper of his vines brought him purple grapes, his steward brought poultry grilled and flavoured with herbs, and fish with delicate flesh. The tjaty sat on ebony-wood seats and slept in a gilded wooden bed with a comfortable mattress; and masseurs soothed away his tiredness.

But all that luxury was just an illusion. The work would be 'more bitter than bile', as the enthronement ritual had stated.

Neferet was principal doctor, Kani was High Priest of Karkak, Kem was commander of the guards . . . The gods had chosen to favour the just, by permitting them to offer their lives to Egypt. The heavens ought to have been bright and people's hearts filled with celebration, but Pazair was sombre and tormented.

In less than a year, would the gods' beloved land be covered in darkness?

Neferet put her arms round Pazair and hugged him. He had told her every word of his conversation with Ramses; united in the secret, they shared its weight. They gazed up into the lapis-blue sky, where the soul of Branir shone among the stars.

Pazair had accepted the house, garden and lands with which Pharaoh endowed his tjaty. Guards handpicked by Kem were posted at the entrance to the vast, walled estate, and others kept it under permanent watch from neighbouring houses. No one could get near without showing a safe-conduct pass or a properly drawn-up summons. Situated not far from the royal palace, the estate formed an island of greenery where five hundred trees flourished, including seventy sycamores, thirty perseas, a hundred and seventy date-palms, a hundred doum-palms, ten fig-trees, nine willows and ten tamarisks. Rare species, imported from Nubia and Asia, were represented by just one example of each. A shimmering vine provided wine reserved for the tjaty. Neferet's monkey was enchanted, imagining a thousand and one climbs and just as many feasts.

Twenty gardeners tended the estate; the cultivated part was divided into squares criss-crossed by irrigation channels. A procession of water-carriers watered lettuces, leeks, onions and cucumbers, which were grown on terraces.

In the centre of the garden was a well. A gently sloping ramp gave access to a hut, sheltered from the wind, where the tjaty might enjoy the winter sun. On the opposite side was a rectangular bathing-pool, with another hut beside it, in the shade of the tallest trees; the hut gave shelter from the north wind in winter.

Pazair had refused to part with the mat he had used as a provincial judge, although there was enough fine furniture in the house to satisfy the most demanding tastes. Neferet was reassured by the many brushes and brooms, concerned as she was to keep such a large house clean.

'The bathing-room is splendid,' said Pazair.

'The barber is waiting for you; he will be at your service every morning.'

'So will your hairdresser.'

'Shall we manage to escape, from time to time?'

He took her in his arms. 'Less than a year, Neferet. We have less than a year to save Ramses.'

Denes disliked having to mark time. Still, he once again had the unconditional support of his wife, who had been bedridden for a long time and would be frail for the rest of her life. By avoiding a divorce, he had both safeguarded his wealth and neutralized Tapeni's threats. But with Pazair's unexpected appointment as tjaty the horizon had grown suddenly dark. Cracks had appeared in the fabric of the conspirators' plot; nevertheless, they were certain to succeed, because they had the Testament of the Gods.

Sheshi was nervous and advised proceeding with the utmost caution. After losing the post of principal doctor and failing to gain that of tjaty, the plotters must stay in the shadows and make use of their infallible weapon, time. The High Priests of the most important temples had just announced the date of the king's festival of regeneration, the first day of the new year, in the month of July, when the star Sopdet's appearance in the crablike group of stars announced the Nile flood. On the eve of his abdication, Ramses would know the name of his successor and hand over power to him in plain sight of the whole country.

'Has the king confided in Pazair?' asked Denes.

'Of course not,' said Sheshi. 'He cannot tell anyone at all – if he confides in even one person, he weakens himself. Pazair's no more virtuous than any other man. He'd immediately gather a group of supporters and move against the king.'

'Why did Ramses choose him?'

'Because the little judge is cunning and ambitious. He must have tricked Ramses into thinking him a man of integrity.'

'You're right. The king's making an enormous mistake.'

'But we must be wary of Pazair – we've seen how dangerous he can be.'

'Having so much power will soon corrupt him. If he weren't stupid, he'd have joined us.'

'Too late. He's playing his own game.'

'We must make sure he gets no chance at all to incriminate us.'

'Let's pay him homage and shower him with gifts. Then he'll think we fully accept him as tjaty.'

Suti waited patiently for the explosion of anger to end. Panther had broken crockery and stools, torn up clothes, and even trampled an expensive wig underfoot. The little house was in a state of utter chaos, but the Libyan still showed no signs of calming down.

'I won't!' she said.

'Be patient for just a little while.'

'You said we'd be leaving tomorrow.'

'Pazair wasn't about to be appointed tjaty when I said that,' retorted Suti.

'I don't care.'

'Well I do.'

'Why do you want to wait? He's already forgotten all about you. Let's leave, as we agreed.'

'There's no hurry.'

'I want to get our gold back.'

'It won't run away.'

'Yesterday, all you talked about was our journey.'

'I must see Pazair and find out what his plans are.'

'Pazair, Pazair, always Pazair! Are we never going to be rid of him?'

'Be quiet.'

'I'm not your slave.'

'Tapeni's ordered me to send you away.'

'You dared see that she-devil again!'

'She tracked me down in a tavern. She regards herself as my legal wife.'

'Stupid woman.'

'The tjaty's protection will be useful.'

Pazair's first guest was his predecessor. Despite his bent back and the pains in his legs, Bagey walked without a stick. The two men went out into the garden and sat down in the hut by the pool.

'You throughly deserve your promotion,' said Bagey. 'I could not have dreamt of a better tjaty.'

'I shall try to continue your work as you would have done yourself.'

'My last year was difficult and disappointing. It was time for me to go, and fortunately the king listened to me. Your youth will not be a handicap for long; the office soon brings a man to maturity.'

'What advice would you give me?'

'Ignore gossip, keep your distance from courtiers, study each case in depth, and always be extremely thorough in everything you do. I'll introduce you to my closest colleagues, and you shall test their skills.'

The sun broke through the clouds and bathed the hut in light. Seeing that Bagey was uncomfortable, Pazair put up a palm-frond shade.

'Do you like this house?' asked Bagey.

'I haven't yet had time to explore it.'

'It was too big for me, and the garden was nothing but trouble. I prefer my quarters in town.'

'I shan't be able to do the work without your help. Will you stay at my side and advise me?'

'That is my duty. All the same, give me some time to attend to my son.'

'Is he having difficulties?'

'His employer isn't happy with him. I'm worried that he may be dismissed, and my wife is anxious.'

'If there's anything I can do . . .'

'No, I cannot accept any help from you: giving me or my family special treatment would be a serious offence. Shall we set to work?'

Pazair and Suti embraced.

Suti looked around. 'I like your estate. I want one just like it, and I shall use it to stage unforgettable parties.'

'Would you like to be tjaty?'

'Certainly not! Work disagrees with me. Why did you accept such an heavy burden?'

'It was made impossible for me to refuse.'

'I'm hugely rich now. Escape from all this, and we'll enjoy life to the full.'

Pazair shook his head. 'I can't.'

'Don't you trust me?'

'Pharaoh has entrusted a vital mission to me.'

'Well, don't end up as one of those stuffy senior officials full of their own importance.'

'Are you criticizing me for becoming tjaty?'

'Are you criticizing the way I made my fortune?'

'Won't you stay here and work with me?'

'Letting this chance pass me by would be a crime.'

'If you commit a real crime, I shan't be able to protect you.'

'Then our friendship's finished,' said Suti.

'No. You're my friend and you always will be.'

'A friend doesn't issue threats.'

'I want to stop you making a disastrous mistake,' said Pazair. 'Kem won't give up, and he'll be merciless.'

'We're evenly matched.'

'Don't provoke him, Suti.'

'Don't tell me how to behave.'

'Stay here – please. If you knew the real importance of my work, you wouldn't hesitate for a moment.'

'Defending the law? What fanciful nonsense! If I'd respected it, Asher would still be alive.'

'I didn't testify against you,' Pazair reminded him.

'You're tense and worried. What are you hiding from me?'

'We've dismantled one plot, but that was only the first stage. Let's go on together.'

'I prefer my gold.'

'Give it back to the temple.'

'Will you inform on me?'

Pazair did not reply.

'The role of tjaty eclipses that of friend, doesn't it?'

'Don't go back to the desert, Suti.'

'It's a beautiful and hostile world. When you're disillusioned with power, you'll join me there.'

'I don't want power. I want to safeguard our country, ourselves, our faith.'

'Good luck, Tjaty. I'm taking the gold road again.'

The young man left the beautiful garden without a backward glance. He hadn't mentioned Tapeni's demands, but what did that matter?

Before Suti had crossed the threshold of his home, four guards surrounded him and bound his hands behind his back.

Alerted by the sounds of the struggle, Panther rushed out with a knife in her hand, and tried to free him. She wounded one guard and knocked over another, but was eventually overcome and bound.

The guards immediately took the pair to the court, where they were accused of flagrant adultery. Tapeni was jubilant: this was a far better result than she'd hoped for. The adultery was made worse by their having resisted the guards. Tapeni's testimony – she spoke of having been been seduced and then deserted – pleased the judges, whereas Panther insulted them, and Suti's arguments seemed unconvincing.

Tapeni asked the jury to be lenient, so Panther was sentenced only to immediate expulsion from Egypt, and Suti to a year's imprisonment, at the end of which he would have to get a job and earn the compensation he owed his rejected wife.

40

Pazair looked at the Sphinx. The giant statue's eyes gazed at the rising sun, confident of its victory over the forces of destruction, won after a hard fight in the underworld. The watchful guardian of the plateau where the pyramids of Khufu, Khafra and Menkaura stood, it took part in the eternal struggle on which the survival of humanity depended.

The tjaty ordered a team of quarrymen to move the great stele that stood between the Sphinx's paws. This revealed a sealed vase and a flagstone with a ring. Two men lifted the flagstone, revealing the entrance to a narrow, low-ceilinged passageway.

Armed with a torch, the tjaty entered first. Not far from the entrance, his foot struck a dolerite cup. He picked it up and, stooping, continued on his way. A wall blocked his path. By the light of the flame he noticed that several stones had been worked free; a complete row pivoted. On the other side was the basement chamber of the Great Pyramid.

The tjaty walked along the route that the thieves had taken several times, then examined the cup. The dolerite, one of the hardest forms of granite and very difficult to work, bore traces of a very oily substance.

Intrigued, Pazair left the pyramid and took the cup to the workshop at the Temple of Ptah, where the specialists identified the substance as stone-oil,* whose use was forbidden in Egypt. As it burnt, the oil dirtied the walls of tombs and clogged up the craftsmen's lungs.

The tjaty demanded a swift investigation of the miners of the western desert and of the secretariat in charge of wicks and lamp-oils. Then, for the first time, he entered the audience chamber where his principal colleagues had gathered.

The tjaty was Pharaoh's overseer of works, the leader of the teams of craftsmen and trade bodies, charged with putting every man in his rightful place by teaching him his duties and ensuring his well-being. He was also in charge of the archives and the country's government,

*Petroleum.

the most senior scribe, the head of the army, and guarantor of civil peace and security. As such, the tjaty must speak clearly, weigh his thoughts, calm people's passions, remain unmoved when storms raged, and see that justice was done in matters both great and small.

His official garb consisted of a long, starched apron made from thick fabric and reaching up to the chest; two straps, passing behind the neck, held it up. On his kilt, which had a panel at the front, was a panther skin, a reminder that the first citizen of the empire, after Pharaoh, must act with speed. A heavy wig hid his hair, and a broad collar covered the upper part of his torso.

Wearing sandals with straps and carrying a sceptre in his right hand, Pazair walked between two rows of scribes, climbed the steps leading to a dais where a high-backed chair stood, then turned to face his subordinates. At his feet was a piece of red cloth, on which were laid forty staffs of command designed to punish the guilty. When the tjaty hung a figurine of Ma'at on his thin gold chain, the audience began.

Pazair said, 'Pharaoh has clearly set out the duties of the tjaty, which have not varied since the day when our forefathers built this country. We live by the same truth as Pharaoh, and shall together continue to hand down justice without differentiating between rich and poor. Our glory lies in spreading justice across the land, so that men breathed it in and it drives evil from their bodies. Let us protect the weak from the strong, refuse to listen to flatterers, oppose disorder and brutality. Each of you owes it to himself to be an example; anyone who derives personal profit from his office will lose his title and his post. No one will gain my trust by way of fine words; only by fine deeds.'

The brevity of the speech, the rigorous nature of its content, and the calmness of the new tjaty's voice, surprised the officials. Those who had been planning to take advantage of his youth and inexperience to lengthen their rest periods abandoned their plans immediately; those who had hoped to profit from Bagey's departure were disappointed.

Everyone wondered what the tjaty's first public order would be, because it would set the tone of his administration. Some of his predecessors had been preoccupied first and foremost with the army, some with irrigation, others with taxes.

'Bring me the scribe in charge of honey production.'

An icy wind blew over the desert around Khargeh oasis. The old bee-keeper sentenced to life imprisonment thought of his hives, large jars where the bees built their combs. He had harvested the honey without protection, for he was not afraid of them and could always tell if they were getting angry. The bee was one of Pharaoh's symbols, a tireless worker, an alchemist capable of creating edible gold. The old bee-keeper had harvested a hundred types of honey, from the reddest to the most transparent, until the day when an envious scribe had accused him of theft. Stealing honey, whose transport was overseen by the guards, was a serious crime. Never again would he pour it into little vessels, sealed with wax and numbered, never again would he hear the buzzing of the swarm, his favourite music. When the sun had wept, a few tears had been transformed into bees as they hit the ground. Born out of divine light, they had built nature. But Ra's light now illuminated only the emaciated body of a prisoner, who cooked revolting meals for his comrades in misfortune.

There was a commotion near the prison gates. Abandoning his ovens, he followed the other prisoners.

A veritable expedition was approaching: fifty soldiers, chariots, horses and carts. Were the Libyans attacking? He rubbed his eyes and made out Egyptian footsoldiers. The prison guards bowed before a man who walked, without hesitation, towards the kitchen.

Astounded, the old man recognized Pazair. 'You . . . you survived!'

'You gave me good advice.'

'Why have you come back?'

'I haven't forgotten my promise.'

'Run away, quickly! They'll lock you up again.'

'Don't worry, I am the one who gives the guards their orders.'

'Does that mean you've become a judge again?'

'Pharaoh has appointed me tjaty.'

'Don't make fun of an old man.'

Two soldiers brought over a fat scribe with a double chin.

'Do you recognize him?' asked Pazair.

'That's him!' exclaimed the bee-keeper. 'That's the liar who got me convicted!'

'I propose an exchange: he'll take your place in prison, and you'll take his as head of the secretariat of honey supplies.'

The old bee-keeper fainted clean away. The tjaty caught him as he fell.

The report was clear and concise: Pazair congratulated the scribe. Stone-oil, which was found in large quantities in the western desert, was of enormous interest to the Libyans. They had tried several times to extract it for commercial purposes, but Pharaoh's army had intervened. Egyptian scholars considered stone-oil a harmful and dangerous product.

Only one specialist, at court, was in charge of studying it, in order to identify its properties. He alone had access to the stock kept in a state warehouse, under military control. When he read the man's name, the tjaty thanked the gods and went immediately to the royal palace.

'Majesty,' said Pazair, 'I explored the underground passage leading from the Sphinx to the chamber beneath the Great Pyramid.'

'Have the entrance sealed for ever,' ordered Ramses.

'The stonemasons are already at work.'

'What clues did you find?'

'A dolerite cup in which stone-oil had been burnt to provide light.'

'Who could have procured the oil?'

'Only the specialist charged with studying it.'

'What is his name?'

'Sheshi the inventor, slave and scapegoat of Denes.'

'Do you know where to find him?'

'He's hiding at Denes's house, according to Kem.'

'Do they have accomplices or are they the core of the conspiracy?'

'I shall find out, Majesty.'

Tapeni prevented the tjaty's chariot from pulling away.

'I want to speak to you,' she said.

The officer whose job was to drive the vehicle and ensure Pazair's safety raised his whip, but the tjaty restrained him and asked, 'Is it very urgent?'

Tapeni smiled. 'You will be glad to hear what I have to say.'

He got down from the chariot. 'Be brief.'

'You're the embodiment of justice, are you not? Well, you'll be proud of me. A deceived, abused woman who has been dragged through the mud is a victim, isn't she?'

'Indeed.'

'My husband deserted me, and the court punished him.'

'Your husband . . .'

'Yes, your friend Suti. His Libyan whore has been deported, and he's been sentenced to a year in prison. Actually, it's a very light sentence, and a mild imprisonment: the court sent him to Tjaru in Nubia, where he'll serve in the garrison. The place is not very welcoming, apparently, but Suti will have the privilege of helping defend his country against the barbarians. When he comes back, he'll enlist in a body of messengers and will pay me a pension in food.'

'You were going to separate amicably.'

'I changed my mind; I love him, as it happens, and I won't tolerate being abandoned. If you intervened in his favour, you'd be violating the rule of Ma'at, and I'd make sure he knew it.' Her smile was menacing.

'Suti will serve his sentence,' agreed the tjaty, hiding his anger. 'But on his return—'

'If he attacks me, he'll be accused of attempted murder and sent to a much harsher prison. He's my slave – for ever. I am his future.'

'The investigation into Branir's murder is not closed.'

'It's up to you to find the murderer.'

'That is my dearest wish. You told me once that you knew important secrets.'

'That was just boasting.'

'Or was it carelessness? You're an excellent needle-woman, are you not?'

Tapeni looked wary. 'In my trade, that's essential.'

'Perhaps, but I can't help wondering whether the murderer isn't very close to me at this precise moment.'

The pretty brunette could not meet the tjaty's eyes. She turned on her heel and walked rapidly away.

Pazair ought to have gone to see Kem, but he chose instead to check the truth of Tapeni's words. So he went to his office and had the account of the trial brought to him, together with the judgement concerning Suti. The documents confirmed the facts. The tjaty was in the worst of positions. How could he help his friend without betraying the law of which he was the guarantor?

Sombre, indifferent to the gathering storm, he went out again and climbed back into his chariot. With Kem's help, he must work out a plan of action.

Neferet had taken a few minutes from her overcrowded schedule to treat Silkis's indigestion. Despite her youth, Bel-Tran's wife put on weight quickly as soon as greed grew stronger than her wish to be slender.

'I think a two-day fast is necessary,' said Neferet.

'I thought I was going to die,' said Silkis. 'I could hardly breathe for the waves of nausea.'

'They relieve your stomach.'

'I'm so tired – but I'm ashamed to say that to you. All I do is care for my children and my husband.'

'How is Bel-Tran?'

'He's delighted to be working under Pazair – he admires him so much. With their respective qualities, the two of them will ensure the country's prosperity. But he spends so much time working . . . I miss him and I get lonely. Don't you?'

'Well, the answer is to see each other every day and talk freely.'

'Forgive me for asking, but . . . wouldn't you like to have a child?'

'Not before we've caught Branir's murderer. We made a vow before the gods, and we shall keep it.'

A dark veil covered Memphis. Thick clouds hung over the city because there was no wind, and all the dogs were howling. The light had got so dim that Denes lit several lamps. His wife had taken a soothing draught and was asleep. All Nenophar's famous energy had faded, to be replaced by a permanent lassitude. Now docile and submissive, she would cause him no more trouble.

He went out into the garden, and joined Sheshi in the workshop where the inventor spent his time sharpening the blades of knives and swords; it helped him work off his nervous tension.

Denes handed him a cup of beer. 'Rest for a while.'

'Is there any news of Pazair?'

'He's busy with the honey harvest. His speech impressed the senior scribes, but that was only words, after all. The factions will soon start tearing each other apart, and he won't have the stature to survive.'

'You're an optimist.'

'Patience is a valuable quality. If Qadash had understood that, he'd still be alive today. While the new tjaty works and works, we'll enjoy life and look forward to the pleasures of absolute power.'

'All I want is to live to be a few months older,' said Sheshi.

'You're discreet, efficient and tireless, and you're going to be an outstanding statesman. Thanks to you, Egyptian knowledge will take a gigantic leap forward.'

'Stone-oil, drugs, metals . . . this country doesn't make proper use of its resources. By developing methods and skills Ramses has disdained, we'll rid ourselves of tradition.'

All at once, Sheshi's excitement died. 'There's someone outside,' he said.

'I didn't hear anything.'

'I'm going to check.'

'It's probably a gardener.'

'They don't come anywhere near the workshop.' Sheshi stared suspiciously at Denes. 'Have you called on the services of the shadow-eater?'

The ship-owner's face hardened. 'It was Qadash who stepped out of line, not you.'

A flash of lightning zig-zagged across the sky, and the thunder rolled. Sheshi went out of the workshop, took a few steps towards the house, then turned and ran back inside. Denes had never seen him look so pale, and his teeth were chattering.

'It's a ghost!' he quavered.

'Calm down.'

'I saw it – a shape blacker than the night, with a flame instead of a face!'

'Pull yourself together and come with me.'

Reluctantly, Sheshi agreed.

The left wing of the house was on fire.

'Water, quickly!' Denes rushed forward, but a black shape seemed to spring out of the flames, and it barred his way.

The ship-owner recoiled. 'Who are you?'

The ghost was brandishing a torch.

Recovering a little of his courage, Sheshi seized a dagger from the workshop and bore down on the strange figure. It went badly for him, for the spectre thrust the torch into his face. Flesh sizzling, Sheshi howled and fell to his knees, trying to force away the instrument of his torture. The creature picked up the dagger he had dropped, and cut his throat.

Horrified, Denes ran towards the house.

The ghost's voice stopped him in his tracks. 'Do you still want to know who I am?'

He turned round. It was a human being, not a demon from the otherworld, who was threatening him. Curiosity replaced fear.

'Look, Denes. Look at your work and Sheshi's.'

It was so dark that he had to go closer.

In the distance, he heard shouts. People had started to notice the fire.

The ghost unveiled itself. The fine-featured face was no more than a mass of scars.

'Don't you recognize me?'

'Princess Hattusa!'

'You destroyed me, and now I'm destroying you.'

'You murdered Sheshi!'

'I punished my torturer. A killer's crime seizes him and takes possession of him.' She thrust her dagger deep into the flames, as though her hand was impervious to them. 'You won't run away, Denes.'

She advanced on him, the blade glowing red.

He could have charged at her and knocked her over, but her madness frightened him: the guards could have the job of arresting her.

Lightning tore across the sky, thunder rolled over the house, and a tongue of fire leapt out of the wall, which crumbled and set fire to Denes's clothing. He staggered, and rolled on the ground to put out the flames.

He did not see the figure bearing down on him, the ghost with the dead face.

41

The caravan advanced slowly; Kem watched it as far as the border. Hattusa, seated in the back of a chariot, was as inert as a soulless statue. When he had come upon her at the scene of the crime, she had offered no resistance. Servants, who had run up to put out the fire, had seen her dragging the bodies of Sheshi and Denes into the flames. Torrential rain had fallen on Memphis, putting out the flames and washing the blood from the princess's hands.

She had not answered any of the questions put to her by the tjaty, who was so overwhelmed that his voice shook. As soon as he reported the facts to Ramses, the king had ordered the embalmers to give the bodies of the two conspirators a cursory preparation, then bury them somewhere remote, far from a burial-ground, without any rites. Through Hattusa, evil had struck down the men of darkness.

With the tjaty's agreement, the king had decided to send the princess back to her own country. However, even the announcement of her liberation, which she had so longed for, did not produce a reaction. Broken, her gaze empty, Hattusa wandered in worlds which were inaccessible to anyone but herself.

The official document that Kem handed to a Hittite officer spoke of an untreatable illness, and the necessary return of the princess to her family. The honour of the Hittite emperor was safe, and no diplomatic incident would trouble the peace that had been so dearly bought.

Under Pazair's watchful eye, workmen searched the remains of Denes's house, and gathered together their meagre finds. Ramses himself examined them. It was thought that this was the king's way of showing his interest in the tragic deaths of the ship-owner and the inventor, whereas he was in fact searching for a trace of the Testament of the Gods.

In vain: the disappointment was a cruel one.

'Are all the conspirators dead?' he asked Pazair.

'I do not know, Majesty.'

'Whom do you suspect?'

'Denes seemed to me to be their leader. He tried to make use of General Asher and Princess Hattusa, in order to establish links with foreign powers. No doubt he envisaged a change of policy, based on trade.'

'Sacrificing the spirit of Egypt to an all-pervading greed ... What a pernicious plan! Did his wife help him?'

'No, Majesty. She does not even realize that her husband tried to kill her. Her servants saved her, and she has left Memphis and is living with her parents in the north of the Delta. According to the doctors who examined her, she has lost her reason.'

'Neither she nor Denes had the necessary stature to attack the throne.'

'Supposing that he did indeed hold the Testament at his house, would it not have been burnt in the fire? If no one – neither you nor your enemies – can produce it at the festival of regeneration, what will happen?'

A glimmer of hope showed in Ramses' eyes. He said, 'As tjaty, you will bring together the country's authorities and explain the situation to them; then you will address the people. As for me, I shall celebrate an era of renewed births, marked by the drawing up of a new pact with the gods. Perhaps I shall fail, for the process is long and difficult; but at least a man of darkness will not take power. Let us hope you are right, Pazair, and that Denes was the instigator of the conspiracy.'

As they did every evening, the swallows were dancing over the garden where Pazair and Neferet met after a day of hard work. The birds flew low over their heads, giving shrill, joyful cries, swooping round at top speed, describing enormous curves in the blue winter sky.

Brave and Mischief had called a truce. The dog was sleeping at his master's feet, the little green monkey under her mistress's chair.

The tjaty was suffering from a cold and breathing difficulties, and had been examined thoroughly by the principal doctor.

'My poor health ought to bar me from being tjaty,' he said.

'It's a gift from the gods,' said Neferet, 'because it makes you think, instead of rushing in blindly like a ram with more enthusiasm than good sense. Besides, it doesn't diminish your energy at all.'

'You look worried.'

'In a week's time, I shall present the council of doctors with the measures to be taken to improve public health. Some measures will be unpopular, but I believe they are vital. It will be a hard-fought battle.'

'The date of the festival of regeneration has been proclaimed throughout the land,' said Pazair. 'At the time of the next flood, Ramses will be reborn.'

'Have any other conspirators shown themselves since the deaths of Denes and Sheshi?'

'No.'

'Then the Testament of the Gods must have been destroyed in the fire.'

'That seems more and more likely.'

'And yet you still have doubts.'

'To keep such a valuable thing in his house seems senseless to me. But then Denes was so over-confident that he thought he was invulnerable.'

'And what about Suti?'

'The judgement was correctly handed down; there were no procedural irregularities.'

'What can be done?'

'I can see no legal solution.'

'If you organize his escape,' said Neferet, 'make it a masterstroke.'

'You read my thoughts too well. This time Kem won't help me. If the tjaty did something like that, Ramses would be tarnished and the prestige of Egypt with him. But Suti's my friend, and we swore to help each other, no matter what.'

'Let's think about it together. At least let him know you aren't abandoning him.'

Alone and weaponless, with several days' walking ahead of her, and only one water-skin and a few dried fish to sustain her. Panther had little chance of survival. The Egyptian guards had left her at the border with Libya, ordering her to go back to her country and never to return to the land of the Pharaohs, on pain of heavy punishment.

At best, she would be spotted by a band of rapacious sand-travellers and raped. They'd keep her alive only until the first lines appeared on her face.

The beautiful Libyan turned her back on the land of her birth.

She would never abandon Suti. It would be a long and dangerous journey from the north-western Delta to the Nubian fort where her lover was locked away. She would have to take bad roads, find water and food, escape wandering brigands. But she was determined that Tapeni would not emerge victorious from their long-distance battle.

'Soldier Suti?'

The young man did not answer the officer.

'A year's disciplinary regime in my fortress. The judges gave you a fine present, my lad. You must show yourself worthy of it. On your knees.'

Suti stared him straight in the eyes.

'A stubborn one – I like that. Don't you like this place?'

The prisoner looked around. The banks of the turbulent Nile, the desert, sun-scorched hills, an intensely blue sky, a pelican catching fish, a crocodile lazing on a rock.

'Tjaru isn't altogether lacking in charm. Your presence is an insult to it.'

'A joker, too,' said the officer. 'And the son of a rich family, I suppose?'

'You cannot imagine how rich.'

'You impress me.'

'That's only a beginning.'

'On your knees. When you address the commander of this fortress, you will be polite.'

Two soldiers hit Suti on the back, knocking him face down on the ground.

'That's better,' said the officer. 'But you aren't here to rest, my lad. First thing tomorrow, you'll stand guard at our most forward position – unarmed, of course. If a Nubian tribe attacks, you'll warn us. Their tortures are so agonizing that the victim's screams can be heard a long way away.'

Rejected by Pazair, separated for ever from Panther, forgotten by everyone, Suti would not get out of Tjaru alive, unless hatred gave him the strength he needed.

His gold awaited him, and so did Tapeni.

Bak was eighteen years old. The son and grandson of army officers, he was rather small, but hard-working and courageous. He had black hair, finely drawn features, and a strong, musical voice. After wavering between becoming a soldier or a scribe, he had entered the archives secretariat, just before Pazair's appointment. To the most recent arrival fell the most thankless tasks, notably the filing of scrolls used by the tjaty when studying a case. That was why Bak had the ones concerning stone-oil; now that Sheshi was dead, they were no longer of interest.

Meticulously, he arranged them in a wooden box which the tjaty would seal himself, and which would be reopened only on his orders. It should have been quick to do, but Bak took care to examine each papyrus. It was just as well he did. One of them was missing the tjaty's annotation, so he could not have read it. The detail seemed unimportant, since the matter was filed for no further action; nevertheless, the young scribe noted it down and handed the note to his superior, so that it might follow the proper administrative path.

Pazair insisted on reading all the remarks, observations and criticisms written by his subordinates, no matter what how junior, so he found Bak's note.

Towards the end of the morning, he summoned the young scribe and asked him, 'What did you notice that was unusual?'

'Your seal is missing from a report by a Treasury employee who was dismissed.'

'Show me.'

Indeed, Pazair found a document he had not read. No doubt a scribe from his own office had omitted to include it in the case of papyri relating to stone-oil.

'One grain of sand in a device,' thought the tjaty, thinking of a little provincial judge who, simply through his concern that a job should be done well, had detected a cancer aiming to destroy Egypt.

'From tomorrow, you will take charge of the archives and inform me directly of any anomalies. We shall meet each day, at the start of the morning.'

After he left the tjaty's office, Bak ran towards the street. Once in the open air, he gave a shout of joy.

'This conversation seems rather formal,' remarked Bel-Tran easily. 'We could have had it over the midday meal at my house.'

'Without wishing to stand on ceremony,' said Pazair, 'I think we must both submit to the dignity of our respective offices.'

'You're the tjaty, and I'm director of the White House and in charge of the country's trade and money. According to the order of precedence, I must obey you. Have I read your mind right?'

'Like this, we shall work in harmony.'

Bel-Tran had put on weight, and his round face was becoming positively moonlike. Despite the skill of his weaving-women, his kilt was always too tight.

Pazair went on, 'You're a specialist in trade and finance, and I'm not. Your advice will be most welcome.'

'Advice or instructions?'

'The economy must not come before the art of governing, for men don't live on material possessions alone. Egypt's greatness is born of its vision of the world, not from its economic power.'

Bel-Tran's lips pursed, but he did not answer.

'One minor matter worries me. Have you been involved at all with a dangerous product, stone-oil?'

'Who's accusing me?'

'That's putting it too strongly. A report by a scribe you dismissed implicates you.'

'What is his complaint?'

'That, for a short period, you lifted the ban on exploiting stone-oil in a clearly designated area of the western desert and authorized a trade from which you deducted a large commission. It was a brief but extremely lucrative operation. There was nothing illegal, in fact, because you had the agreement of the specialist concerned, Sheshi. But Sheshi was a criminal, involved in a conspiracy against the state.'

'What are you insinuating?'

'That connection makes me uneasy. I'm sure it's just an unfortunate coincidence, but as a friend I'd like an explanation.'

Bel-Tran got to his feet. His expression was transformed so completely that Pazair was speechless. The warm, friendly face was replaced by one full of hatred and arrogance. The voice, usually quiet but measured, was brimming with anger and violence.

'An explanation as a friend? What naivety! How long it's taken you to understand, my dear Pazair, tjaty of straw! Qadash, Sheshi and Denes my accomplices? Rather my devoted servants, whether or not they realized it. If I supported you against them, it was only because of Denes's stupid ambition – he wanted to be director of the White House and control the country's finances. I was the only one fit to be director. It should have been a simple step from there to seizing the post of tjaty, but you stole it from me. The whole government recognized me as the most suitable candidate, the members of the court all suggested me when Pharaoh consulted them, and yet it was you, an obscure, disgraced judge, whom the king chose. A clever manoeuvre, my dear fellow; you surprised me.'

'You're mistaken.'

'Not about myself, Pazair. The past doesn't interest me. Either you play your own game and lose everything, or else you obey me and become very rich, without having the cares of a power you are not competent to wield.'

'I am the tjaty of Egypt.'

'You're nothing, because Pharaoh is finished.'

'Does that mean you've got the Testament of the Gods?'

A sneer of satisfaction twisted Bel-Tran's face. 'So Ramses did confide in you. How stupid of him. He really isn't worthy to reign any more. But enough of this talk, my dear friend. Are you with me or against me?'

'I've never been so disgusted in all my life.'

'I'm not interested in your emotions.'

'How can you bear your own hypocrisy?'

'It's a more useful weapon than your ridiculous honesty.'

'Don't you know that greed is the most deadly of all evils and that it will deprive you of a tomb?'

Bel-Tran burst out laughing. 'Your morality is that of a backward child. Gods, temples, houses of eternity, rituals – all that stupid, outworn stuff. You have no understanding at all of the new world we're entering. I have great plans, Pazair. Even before driving Ramses out, I shall put them into practice. Open your eyes, see the future!'

'Give back the things you stole from the Great Pyramid.'

'Gold is a rare and extremely valuable metal. Why should it be frozen into ritual objects which only a dead man can see? My people melted them down. I have enough money to buy a lot of consciences.'

'I can have you arrested within the hour.'

'No, you can't. With one gesture I shall bring Ramses down, and you with him. But I shall do it at my chosen time, and according to the plan. Imprisoning or killing me wouldn't stop it. You and your king are bound hand and foot. Give up following a man who's more dead than alive, and place yourself at my service. I shall grant you one last chance, Pazair. Take it.'

'I shall fight you to my last breath.'

'In less than a year your name will be obliterated from the annals. Make the most of your pretty wife, because soon everything will crumble around you. Your universe is worm-eaten – I've eaten away the posts that supported it. Too bad for you, tjaty of Egypt. You'll regret underestimating me.'

Pharaoh and his tjaty spoke in the secret room of the House of Life in Memphis, far from prying eyes and ears.

Pazair revealed the truth to Ramses.

'Bel-Tran the papyrus-maker,' said Ramses, 'the man in charge of distributing the great texts, the man responsible for the country's money and trade . . . I knew he was ambitious and acquisitive, but I never imagined that he was a traitor, a destroyer.'

'He has had time to weave his web, to create a network of accomplices in all classes of society, to poison the government.'

'Will you dismiss him immediately?'

'No, Majesty. Evil has at last shown its face. We must now try to work out what his plan is, so that we can fight it.'

'But he has the Testament of the Gods.'

'He probably isn't working alone, so killing him would not ensure our victory.'

'Nine months, Pazair; we have nine months left, the length of a pregnancy. Go to war, identify Bel-Tran's allies, dismantle his fortresses, disarm the soldiers of darkness.'

'Majesty, we should remember the words of the old sage Ptah-hotep: "Great is the Rule, lasting its effectiveness; it has not been disrupted since the time of Osiris. Iniquity is capable of gaining possession of the many, but evil will never bring its undertakings to fruition. Have no part in any plot against the human race, for God punishes such actions."'

'He lived in the time of the great pyramids and was a tjaty, like you. Let us hope he was right.'

'His words have endured through time.'

'It is not my throne that is at stake, but tomorrow's civilization. Either treason will bear it away, or justice will be done.'

From Branir's tomb, Pazair and Neferet gazed out over the huge burial-ground at Saqqara, which was overlooked by the Step Pyramid of Pharaoh Djoser. The priests of the *ka*, servants of the immortal soul, tended the gardens of the tombs and laid offerings on the stone tables of the shrines, which were open to pilgrims. Stone-cutters were restoring an ancient pyramid, while others were excavating a tomb. The city of the dead lived a life of serenity.

'What have you decided?' Neferet asked Pazair.

'To fight. To fight to the end.'

'We shall find Branir's murderer.'

'He has already been punished, don't you think? Denes, Sheshi and Qadash died in horrible circumstances, and the law of the desert sentenced General Asher.'

'The murderer is still at large,' she said. 'When our master's soul at last knows peace, a new star will appear.'

She laid her head gently on Pazair's shoulder. Nourished by her strength and love, the Egyptian judge would fight a battle which was lost before it began, in the hope that the happiness of the divine land would not disappear from the memory of the Nile, from granite and from light.

Shadow of the Sphinx

Let the whole rejoice!
Justice has been restored to its rightful place;
All ye righteous ones, come and gaze upon it.
Justice has triumphed over evil,
The wicked have fallen on their faces,
The greedy have been condemned.

Sallier Papyrus I
British Museum 1018, recto VIII.7.

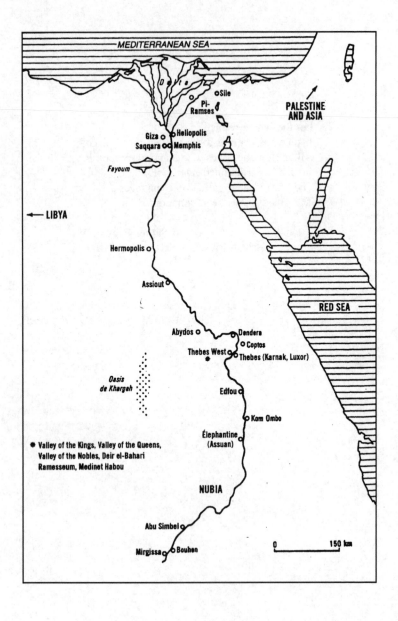

MEDITERRANEAN SEA

Delta

○ Sile

Pi-
Ramses

PALESTINE
AND ASIA

Giza ○ ○ Heliopolis
Saqqara ○○ Memphis

Fayoum

← LIBYA

RED SEA

Hermopolis ○

Assiout ○

Abydos ○ ○ Dendera
○ Coptos
Thebes West ○
⚹ ○ Thebes (Karnak, Luxor)

*Oasis
de Khargah*

Edfou ○

Kom Ombo ○

Éléphantine
(Assuan)

⚹ Valley of the Kings, Valley of the Queens,
Valley of the Nobles, Deir el-Bahari
Ramesseum, Medinet Habou

NUBIA

Abu Simbel ○

Mirgissa ○ ○ Bouhen

0   150 km

1

Treason was showing a healthy profit: Iarrot had grown red-faced, chubby-cheeked and flabby. He gulped down a third cup of white wine, congratulating himself on his choice. When he had been clerk to Judge Pazair, who was now Ramses II's tjaty, he had worked too hard and earned little. Since he had entered the service of Bel-Tran, the tjaty's worst enemy, his life had improved vastly; he was paid for each piece of information on Pazair's habits. With Bel-Tran's support and the false testimony of one of his henchmen, Iarrot was hoping to obtain a divorce from his wife and custody of his daughter, a future dancer.

The former clerk had risen before dawn with a pounding headache, while darkness still reigned over Memphis, Egypt's economic capital, which stood at the junction of the Delta and the Nile Valley.

From the narrow street outside, which was usually quiet and calm, he heard the sound of whispering.

Iarrot put down his cup. Since he had begun betraying Pazair, he had been drinking more and more, not out of remorse but because he could at last afford the finest wines and beers. His throat constantly burnt with an unquenchable thirst.

He pushed open the shutter and glanced outside. There was no one in sight.

Muttering to himself, he thought of the splendid day in prospect. Thanks to Bel-Tran, he was leaving the city outskirts to live in one of the best districts, close to the centre. This very evening, he was going to move into a house with five rooms and a little garden; the next day, he would take up a post as inspector of taxes, reporting to the ministry that Bel-Tran headed.

Only one thing annoyed him: despite the quality of the information he had given to Bel-Tran, Pazair had not yet been eliminated – it was as if the gods were protecting him. Still, luck would eventually turn against him.

Outside, someone was sniggering.

Perturbed, Iarrot put his ear to the door that led to the street. Suddenly, he realized what it was: that band of urchins again, who enjoyed scrawling on the fronts of the houses with an ochre stone.

Furious, he wrenched the door open.

And was confronted with the open mouth of a hyena. An enormous female with saliva on its lips, and eyes which glowed red. It let out a cry like laughter from beyond the grave, and leapt at his throat.

Ordinarily, hyenas cleansed the desert by eating carrion and they avoided areas of human settlement. Very unusually, ten of them had ventured into the outskirts of Memphis and had killed a former clerk, Iarrot, a drunkard whose neighbours detested him. Armed with sticks, the inhabitants of the district had put the hyenas to flight, but everyone interpreted the drama as a bad omen for the future of Pharaoh Ramses, whose authority had never been contested up to now. At the port of Memphis, in the weapons stores, on the quays, in the barracks, in the districts called Sycamore, Crocodile Wall and College of Medicine, in the markets, and in the craftsmen's shops, the same words were on everybody's lips: 'the year of the hyenas'.

The country would grow weak. The Nile's annual flood would be meagre and the earth barren, the orchards would wither, there would be a shortage of fruit, vegetables, clothes and ointments. Sand-travellers would attack the farms in the Delta. Pharaoh's throne would grow shaky. The year of the hyenas: the shattering of harmony, the breach into which the forces of evil would pour.

It was whispered that Ramses had been unable to prevent this disaster. True, in nine months' time the festival of regeneration would take place, giving the king back the power necessary to confront adversity and overcome it. But would the celebration be in time? Pazair, the new tjaty, was young and inexperienced. Entering office during the year of the hyenas meant he was bound to fail.

If the king did not protect his people, he and they alike would perish in darkness's voracious maw.

It was the middle of winter, and an icy wind swept through the burial-ground at Saqqara, which was dominated by Pharaoh Djoser's stepped pyramid, a gigantic staircase to the heavens. No one would have recognized the couple who, warmly clad in thick, long-sleeved tunics made of strips of fabric sewn together, were meditating before the shrine at the tomb of the sage Branir. Pazair and Neferet silently read the hieroglyphs engraved on a beautiful piece of limestone: '*You who live upon the earth and pass by this tomb, you who love life and hate death, speak my name that I may live, pronounce the offertory words for my sake.*'

Branir had been Pazair and Neferet's spiritual master, and due to become High Priest of Karnak, but he had been murdered, stabbed in the neck with a mother-of-pearl needle, and Pazair had been accused of his murder. Although the investigation to find the real murderer had become bogged down, the couple had sworn to uncover the truth, whatever risks they might run.

A thin man with thick, black eyebrows which joined above the nose, thin lips, very long hands and thin legs, approached the shrine. Djui the embalmer spent most of his time preparing corpses to transform them into Osiris.

'Do you wish to see the location of your tomb?' he asked Pazair.

'Yes, show me.'

Tjaty Pazair had been entrusted by Ramses with the mission of saving Egypt from an evil conspiracy which threatened the throne. When still a minor provincial judge just transferred to Memphis, the young Pazair – whose name meant 'the Seer', 'He Who Sees Far into the Distance' – had refused to sanction an administrative irregularity, and that small deed had led to the uncovering of an appalling series of events, whose key had been given to him by the king himself.

Conspirators had killed the honour-guard of the Great Sphinx at Giza, in order to gain access to a passageway that began between the gigantic statue's paws and ended inside the Great Pyramid of Pharaoh Kufu, the spiritual and energy centre of the country. They had violated Khufu's sarcophagus and stolen the Testament of the Gods, which legitimized each pharaoh's power. If Ramses could not show it to the priests, the court and the people at the festival of regeneration, which was to take place in the summer, on the first day of the new year, Ramses would be forced to abdicate and hand over the ship of state to a creature of the darkness.

Because the young judge had shown that he would never betray justice, even if his career and his life were at stake, Ramses had put his trust in Pazair, and appointed him tjaty: supreme magistrate, keeper of the king's seal, guardian of secrets, director of Pharaoh's works, first minister of Egypt. Pazair must try everything to save the country from disaster.

As they walked along between the tombs, he gazed at his wife, Neferet, whose beauty enchanted him more every day. With her summer-blue eyes, fair hair and exquisite face with its gentle features, to him she embodied happiness and the joy of living. Without her, he would long since have succumbed to the blows fate had dealt him.

Neferet had become the kingdom's principal doctor after a long series of ordeals. She loved to heal. From Branir, a doctor and dowser, she had inherited the gift of identifying the nature of illnesses and rooting them out. At her throat, she wore a turquoise her master had given her, in order to ward off misfortune.

Neither Pazair nor Neferet had wanted to occupy such important offices. Their dearest wish was to retire to a village in the Theban region and to live out their days in happiness under the sun of Upper Egypt; but the gods had decided otherwise. The couple were the only people who knew Pharaoh's secret, and they would never retreat from the fight, even if the power at their disposal seemed illusory.

'Here's where it will be,' said Djui, indicating a place near the tomb of a former tjaty. 'The stone-cutters will begin work first thing tomorrow.'

Pazair nodded. In accordance with his rank, his first duty was to have his house of eternity built. There he would dwell in company with his wife.

The embalmer went away, his walk slow and weary.

'We may never lie here in this burial-ground,' said Pazair in a sombre voice. 'Ramses' enemies have clearly proclaimed their will to abandon the traditional rites. It is a whole world they want to destroy, not one man.'

The couple headed towards the great open-air courtyard in front of the Step Pyramid. There, at the height of the festival of regeneration, Ramses must hold aloft the Testament of the Gods – which he no longer possessed.

Pazair was sure that Branir's murder was linked to the conspiracy; identifying the murderer would put him on the trail of the thieves and might enable him to spring open the jaws of the trap. Unfortunately, he had been deprived of the irreplaceable help of his friend and spiritual brother Suti, who had been found guilty of infidelity to his wife and sentenced to a year's service in a Nubian fortress. Pazair had thought of many ways to free him, but the tjaty, master of justice, could not show favouritism to someone close to him, on pain of being dismissed from his office.

The great courtyard of Saqqara epitomized the unequalled grandeur of the age of the pyramids. Here the pharaohs' spiritual adventure had taken flesh, here north and south had been united, forming a radiant, powerful kingdom whose inheritance Ramses had taken on. Tenderly, Pazair put his arm round Neferet's waist; awed, they marvelled at the austere structure, which was visible from everywhere in the burial-ground.

Behind them came the sound of footsteps. They turned round.

The man approaching them was of medium height, with a round face and heavy bones; his hair was black, his hands and feet plump. He was walking quickly and seemed nervous.

Incredulously, Pazair and Neferet looked at each other. It was indeed Bel-Tran, their sworn enemy, the heart of the conspiracy.

Bel-Tran had begun at the bottom of the social ladder, as a mere papyrus-maker. But by working hard and by using his prodigious skill in calculations, he had risen to become first principal overseer of all the country's grain-stores, and then head of the Double White House, the minister for Egypt's trade and finances. At first he had pretended to support Pazair, the better to control his actions, but when Pazair had unexpectedly become tjaty Bel-Tran shed his mask of friendship. Pazair could still see his grimacing face and hear his threats: 'Your morality is that of a backward child. Gods, temples, houses of eternity, rituals – all that stupid, outworn stuff. You have no understanding at all of the new world we're entering. Your universe is worm-eaten – I've eaten away the posts that supported it.'

Pazair had not thought it wise to arrest Bel-Tran. First he must destroy the web the traitor had woven, dismantle his networks of spies, and recover the Testament of the Gods. Had Bel-Tran been boasting or had he really corrupted the whole country?

When he reached them Bel-Tran said in a sugary voice, 'We misunderstood each other, and I regret my strong words. Forgive my hot-headedness, my dear Pazair. I deeply respect and admire you. On reflection, I am convinced that we understand each other on the really vital matters. Egypt needs a good tjaty, and that is what you are.'

'What is behind this flattery?' asked Pazair.

'Why should we tear each other to pieces, when an alliance would prevent many . . . inconveniences? Ramses and his regime are doomed – you know that. Let us move in the direction of progress, you and I.'

A peregrine falcon drew circles in the azure blue of the winter sky, above the great courtyard of Saqqara.

'Your regrets are nothing but hypocrisy,' cut in Neferet. 'Do not hope for an alliance with us – ever.'

Anger filled Bel-Tran's eyes. 'This is your last chance, Pazair. Either you submit, or I shall destroy you.'

'Leave this place immediately. Its light cannot agree with you.'

In fury, Bel-Tran turned on his heel and marched away.

Hand in hand, Pazair and Neferet gazed up at the falcon as it flew south.

2

All the dignitaries of the kingdom of Egypt were present in the tjaty's hall of justice, a vast pillared chamber with unpainted walls. At the back was a dais on which Pazair would take his place; on the steps were forty staves of command covered in leather, symbolizing the application of the law. With their right hands on their left shoulders, ten scribes in short wigs and kilts stood guard over the precious staves.

In the front row, seated on a gilded wooden throne, was sixty-year-old Tuya, the Mother of Pharaoh, a thin, haughty woman with piercing eyes. She wore a long linen robe, fringed with gold, and a magnificent wig of human hair whose long tresses fell midway down her back. At her side was Neferet, clad in the official dress of principal doctor: a panther-skin over a linen gown, a striped wig, a cornelian collar, and lapis-lazuli bracelets at her wrists and ankles. In her right hand, she held her seal; in her left, a writing-box. The two women greatly respected each other; Neferet had cured Tuya of serious eye complaints, and the Mother of Pharaoh had fought successfully against Neferet's enemies and facilitated her accession to the highest medical post in the land.

Behind Neferet was one of Pazair's greatest allies, Kem, a Nubian. As a young man, Kem had been wrongly convicted of theft and had had his nose cut off; he now wore a false one made of painted wood. While serving as a security guard in Memphis, he had got to know and like the young, inexperienced judge, who was in love with a justice in which Kem no longer believed. After many adventures, and at Pazair's request, the Nubian had been given command of the forces who maintained order in Memphis. So it was not without pride that he grasped the emblem of his office, an ivory hand of justice decorated with a wide-open eye, to detect evil, and the head of a lion, evoking vigilance. At his side, held on a leash, was his huge, immensely strong guard-baboon, Killer. Killer had just been promoted in recognition of his remarkable service in the guards. His main role was to watch over Pazair, whose life had been threatened several times.

A good distance away from the baboon was Pazair's predecessor as tjaty, Bagey, whose stooping back showed the weight of the years he bore. Bagey was tall, pale and stern-looking, his long face dominated by a prominent nose. As tjaty he had been both feared and celebrated for his inflexible character. Now he was enjoying a peaceful retirement in a small house in Memphis, while continuing to advise his successor.

Half hidden behind a pillar Silkis, Bel-Tran's wife, stood smiling at her neighbours. A child-woman, she had resorted to the doctor's knife so that she would continue to be attractive to her husband. Her greed, especially for rich cakes and pastries, had made her fat, and she was obsessed with her weight. She often suffered from severe headaches, but no longer dared consult Neferet since Bel-Tran had declared war on the tjaty. Discreetly, she dabbed on her temples a lotion made from juniper, pine-sap and laurel-leaves; ostentatiously, she adjusted her blue porcelain necklace and played with her delicate bracelets made from pieces of red fabric joined by little cords in the form of lotus-flowers in full bloom.

Her husband was with her. Although Bel-Tran obtained his clothes from the best kilt-maker in Memphis, they never seemed to fit properly: either they looked too small for him or else he was swamped by them. At this moment of worrying gravity, he forgot his pretensions to elegance and anxiously awaited the tjaty's arrival. No one knew the reason for the solemn judgment that Pazair had decided to proclaim.

When the tjaty appeared, all talk ceased. Only his shoulders were visible above a stiff gown made from thick fabric, which enveloped the rest of his body; the garment was weighted down, as if it strove to emphasize the difficulties of the office. Accentuating still further the austerity and simplicity of his costume, Pazair had contented himself with a short wig in the old style.

He hooked a figurine of the goddess Ma'at* on to a small gold chain which hung round his neck, signifying that the court was in session.

'May we distinguish truth from falsehood and protect the weak to save them from the powerful,' declared the tjaty, using the ritual words on which each judge, from the lowliest to the most high, must base his rule of life.

Ordinarily, forty scribes formed a line on either side of the central aisle along which the accused, the plaintiffs and witnesses passed as they were ushered in by guards. This time, the tjaty simply sat down

---

*Ma'at was the goddess of justice, whose name meant 'She Who Is Straight', 'She Who Gives the Right Direction'. Embodying the universal rule, which will live on after the human race is gone, she was symbolized by a seated woman holding an ostrich feather.

on a low-backed chair and gazed for a long time at the forty staves of command laid out before him.

'Egypt is in great danger,' revealed Pazair. 'Dark forces are trying to unleash themselves upon the country. That is why I must hand down justice, in order to punish the guilty parties who have been identified.'

Silkis clutched her husband's arm. Would the tjaty dare to attack powerful Bel-Tran head on, despite having no proof against him?

'Five former soldiers who formed the honour-guard of the Great Sphinx at Giza were murdered,' Pazair went on. 'This horrible deed resulted from a conspiracy to which Qadash the tooth-doctor, Sheshi the inventor and Denes the ship-owner belonged. By reason of their various crimes, which have been well established through official inquiries, they must receive capital punishment.'

A scribe asked for and received permission to speak. 'But, Tjaty, they are all dead.'

'Indeed, but they have not been judged. The fact that destiny has struck them down does not remove the duty of this court. Death does not enable a criminal to escape from justice.'

Although those present were astonished, they had to agree that the tjaty was respecting the law. The charges were read out, detailing the crimes of Bel-Tran's three accomplices; his name, though, was not mentioned.

No one contested the facts, no voice was raised to defend the accused.

'The three guilty parties will be devoured by the fire of the royal cobra in the afterlife,' declared the tjaty. 'They will not lie in the burial-ground, will receive no offerings or libations, and will be offered up to the knives of the slaughterers who stand at the gates of the underworld. There they will die a second time, of hunger and thirst.'

Silkis shivered. Bel-Tran remained imperturbable. Cracks appeared in Kem's scepticism; the baboon's eyes widened, as if it was satisfied with this posthumous condemnation. Neferet, overwhelmed, had the feeling that the spoken words had taken on the power of reality.

'Any king, any head of state, who offers an amnesty to the condemned,' concluded the tjaty, repeating ancient words, 'will lose both crown and power.'

3

The sun had been up for almost an hour when Pazair arrived at the gate of the royal palace. Pharaoh's guards bowed before the tjaty, and admitted him.

He walked down a corridor whose walls were decorated with delicate paintings depicting lotus-flowers, papyrus and poppies, crossed a pillared hall containing a pool full of playful fish, and reached the sovereign's office.

Ramses' personal scribe greeted Pazair. 'His Majesty is expecting you.'

This morning, as every morning, the tjaty must give an account of his actions to the Lord of the Two Lands, Upper and Lower Egypt. The place was idyllic: a vast, light-filled room, with windows opening on to the Nile and the palace gardens, porcelain floor-tiles decorated with blue lotus-flowers, bowls of flowers on gilded pedestals. On a low table lay unrolled papyri and writing-materials.

The king was gazing eastwards, deep in contemplation. He wore a simple white kilt, and his only items of jewellery were some gold and lapis-lazuli bracelets, whose upper part was shaped like the heads of two wild ducks. A strongly built man of medium height, with reddish hair, a broad forehead and a hooked nose, he gave the impression of power. As a young boy he had been linked to the throne by his father, the remarkable Seti I, who had built Karnak and Abydos. Since succeeding to the throne, Ramses had led his people to peace with the Hittites and to a prosperity which many other countries envied.

'Pazair, at last! How did the trial proceed?'

'The guilty men were condemned, Majesty.'

'How did Bel-Tran react?'

'He was tense and nervous, but he stood firm. Majesty, I wish that I could say to you the customary words: "All is in order, the kingdom's affairs are proceeding well," but I cannot lie.'

Ramses seemed troubled. 'What are your conclusions?' he asked.

'As regards Branir's murder, I am certain of very little, but with Kem's help I am planning to explore several leads.'

'Will you be investigating the lady Silkis?'

'She heads the list of suspects.'

'One of the conspirators was a woman.'

'I have not forgotten that, Majesty. Three of them are dead; it remains for us to identify their accomplices.'

'Bel-Tran and Silkis, it would appear.'

'That is probable, Majesty, but I have no proof.'

'But did Bel-Tran not unmask himself to you?'

'Indeed, but he has many important supporters.'

'What have you discovered?'

'I am working night and day with those in charge of the various government departments. Dozens of officials have sent me written reports, I have listened to senior scribes, departmental heads and junior employees. The situation is more serious than I thought.'

'Explain that.'

'Bel-Tran has bought a good many consciences. Blackmail, threats, promises, lies – there are no depths he will not stoop to. He and his friends know precisely what they want to do: take over the country's trade and finances, and fight and destroy our ancestral values.'

'How?'

'I do not yet know, Majesty. But arresting Bel-Tran would be a mistake, because I could not be certain of cutting off all the monster's heads and identifying the many snares he has laid for us.'

'On the first day of the new year,' said Ramses, 'when Sopdet appears in the crablike group of stars, signifying the beginning of the Nile's annual flood, I must show the people the Testament of the Gods. If I cannot, I shall have to abdicate and offer the throne to Bel-Tran. Will you have time, in the few months until then, to render him powerless?'

'Only the gods can answer that question, Majesty.'

'It was the gods who created royalty, Pazair, in order to build monuments to their glory, to make men happy and to drive away the envious. The gods gave us the most precious of riches, this light whose guardian I am and which I must spread around me. Humans are not equals; that is why pharaohs offer support to the weak. For as long as Egypt builds temples where the energy of light is preserved, her lands will flourish, her ways will be secure, the child will sleep peacefully in its mother's arms, the widow will be protected, the canals will be maintained, and justice will be done. Our lives do not matter at all; it is this harmony which must be preserved.'

'My life belongs to you, Majesty.'

Ramses smiled and laid his hands on Pazair's shoulders. 'I have the feeling that I have chosen my tjaty well, even if his task is a most arduous one. You have become my only friend. Do you know these words one of my predecessors wrote? *"Trust no one; you shall have neither brother nor sister. It is the one to whom you have given much who will betray you, the poor man you have made wealthy who will strike you in the back, he to whom you have stretched out your hand who will foment unrest. Be wary of your subordinates and those close to you. Rely only upon yourself. No one will help you, on the day of misfortune."**

'But, Majesty, does the text not add that the pharaoh who is wise in his choice of those around him shall preserve his own greatness and that of Egypt, too?'

'You know the words of the sages well. I have not made you wealthy, Tjaty. I have weighed you down with a burden which a reasonable man would have refused. Never forget that Bel-Tran is more dangerous than a sand viper. He was able to outwit the vigilance of those close to me, allay their mistrust, infiltrate himself into the government like a worm into fruit. He pretended to be your friend so that he might destroy you more easily. Now his hatred will grow constantly, and he will never again leave you in peace. He will attack where you least expect, will cloak himself in shadows, will wield the weapons of traitors and liars. Are you still willing to face all that?'

'Once one's word is given, it cannot be taken back.'

'If we fail, you and Neferet must submit to the law of Bel-Tran.'

'Only cowards submit. We shall resist to the end.'

Ramses sat down on a gilded wooden chair, facing the rising sun. 'What is your plan?'

'To wait.'

The king could not hide his astonishment. 'Time is not our ally!'

'Bel-Tran will think I am desperate and will move forward across conquered territory; he will remove other masks, and I shall respond in an appropriate manner. In order to persuade him that I have lost my way, I shall direct my efforts into a secondary area.'

'Those are risky tactics.'

'They would be less risky, Majesty, if I had an additional ally at my side.'

'Whom do you mean?'

'My friend Suti.'

'Why is he not with you? Did he prove disloyal?'

'He was sentenced to a year in a Nubian fortress for marital infidelity. The judgement was in accordance with the law.'

---

*The quotation is from *The Teachings of Merykara*.

'So neither you nor I can overturn it.'

'But if he were to escape, should our soldiers not devote themselves to guarding the border, rather than to pursuing a fugitive?'

Ramses smiled. 'It is possible that they will receive an order telling them not to venture outside the fortress because an attack by some of the Nubian tribes is expected.'

'Human nature is changeable, Majesty, particularly that of nomads. Perhaps, in your wisdom, you knew intuitively that a rebellion was imminent.'

'But it will not take place . . .'

'The Nubians will give up the idea when they see that our garrison is on its guard.'

'Draw up that order, Tjaty Pazair; but in no way facilitate your friend's escape.'

Pazair bowed. 'Destiny will provide for that.'

4

Panther was hiding in a shepherd's hut in the middle of a field. The man had been following her for two hours. He was tall, pot-bellied and dirty, a papyrus-gatherer who spent most of his time in the mud cutting the precious stems. He had been spying on her while she bathed, naked, and had crawled towards her.

Always on the alert, the beautiful young Libyan had spotted him and run away, though she had been forced to abandon her shawl, which she would need against the cold of the night. Panther had been expelled from Egypt because of her open liaison with a married man, Suti, but she refused to accept her fate. She was determined not to abandon her lover, because she feared he might be unfaithful to her – after all, during their affair he had married the lady Tapeni. Panther had resolved to travel to Nubia in order to free him from his prison and live with him again. Never again would she be deprived of his strength and his passionate caresses, never again would she let him wallow in another woman's bed.

The vast distance to Nubia did not daunt her. Making full use of her charms, she had travelled on cargo-boats from port to port, until she reached Elephantine and the First Cataract. Once past the mass of rocks that prevented vessels from passing through, she had allowed herself a moment's relaxation in a water-course which snaked away into a farming area. It was then that the papyrus-gatherer had seen her.

She would not be able to shake him off. He knew every cubit of the terrain, and would soon find her hiding-place. The thought of being taken by force did not frighten Panther; before meeting Suti, she had belonged to a band of looters and had fought Egyptian soldiers. She adored love-making, its violence and its ecstasy. But this man was disgusting – and she had no time to lose.

When the papyrus-gatherer slipped into the hut, he saw Panther lying on the ground, naked and asleep. Her fair hair, which was spread across her shoulders, her generous breasts, her golden womanhood with its luxuriant curls, made him throw caution to the winds and pounce on his prey. His feet were instantly caught in a noose laid out on the floor, and he fell heavily. In the blink of an eye, Panther leapt on to his back and strangled him. As soon as his eyes rolled up in their sockets, she stopped squeezing, undressed him so as to have something warm to wear at night, and continued her journey towards the Great South.

The commander of the fortress of Tjaru, deep in Nubia, pushed away the revolting broth his cook had served him.

'A month in the cells for that incompetent fool,' he decreed.

A cup of palm wine consoled him for his disappointment. So far from Egypt, it was difficult to eat well; but occupying a post like this would bring him promotion and a better retirement. Here, in this desolate, arid land, where the desert constantly threatened the few fields and where the Nile sometimes raged violently, he played host to men who had been sentenced to periods of exile varying from one to three years. Usually, he was rather lenient with them and assigned them domestic tasks which were far from exhausting. Most of the poor fellows had committed only minor crimes, and would take advantage of their enforced stay to reflect on their past.

With the prisoner called Suti, however, the situation had gone rapidly downhill. That fellow would not accept authority and refused to submit. So the commander, whose main duty was to keep watch on the Nubian tribes so as to foresee and forestall any rebellion, had placed his recalcitrant charge well out in the front line, unarmed. Suti would act as bait, and experience a few salutary minutes of fear. Of course, the garrison would rush to his aid if there was an attack; the commander liked to free his guests in good condition and keep his record clean.

A junior officer brought him a sealed papyrus. 'Special message from Memphis, sir.'

'It's the tjaty's seal!' Intrigued, the commander cut the strings and broke the seal.

The officer awaited orders.

'The Information secretariats fear there may be trouble brewing in Nubia. We must be doubly alert and check our defences thoroughly.'

'Yes, sir. Should we close the gates of the fortress and see that no one leaves?'

'Pass the order immediately.'

'What about prisoner Suti?'

The commander hesitated. 'What do you think?'

'The whole garrison loathes that fellow – he's been nothing but trouble. At least he's useful where he is now.'

'Yes, but if something were to happen . . .'

'We would report, sir, that there had been an unfortunate accident.'

Suti was a strong, fine-looking man, with a long face, a frank, direct gaze, and long black hair; he moved with great suppleness and elegance. After escaping from the great scribes' school in Memphis, where his studies had bored him deeply, he had lived the adventurous life he had always dreamt of. He had known beautiful women, and had become a hero of Egypt by identifying a corrupt general and helping his friend and blood-brother, Pazair. Despite his youth, Suti had had many brushes with death: without Neferet's skill, he would have died in Asia, of wounds inflicted by a bear which had struck him down in single combat.*

Seated on a rock in the middle of the Nile, and attached to it by a heavy chain, he could do nothing but gaze into the distance, at the mysterious, disturbing South, whence hordes of formidably brave Nubian warriors emerged from time to time. He, as the advance sentry, would have to sound the alert by shouting at the top of his voice. The air was so clear that the lookouts at the fortress could not fail to hear him.

But Suti would not shout; he would not give the commander and his underlings that satisfaction. Although he had not the slightest wish to die, he would not humiliate himself. He thought of the marvellous moment when he had killed that traitor and criminal General Asher, who had tried to escape from justice, taking with him his stolen gold.

Suti and Panther had found the gold, taken it back with them and hidden it with great care. It was worth a fortune, and would have enabled them to revel in every pleasure they could think of. But he was chained to this rock, and she had been banished to her native Libya, forbidden ever to set foot on Egyptian soil again. She had probably already forgotten him, and was enjoying herself in someone else's arms.

As for Pazair, his position as tjaty tied his hands; intervention in Suti's favour would be punished, and in any case would not lead to his friend's being freed. Suti thought his exile doubly unjust, because the only reason he had married the pretty and spirited Tapeni was to further the judge's investigations. He had thought it would be easy to get a divorce once Tapeni had given him the information he wanted, but he had underestimated her possessiveness. The hussy had accused him of adultery with Panther, taken her case to court, and had him sentenced to a year in the fortress. And when he returned to Egypt he

*See *Beneath the Pyramid*.

would still have to work for her, to provide her with money for when she was old.

In fury, Suti punched the rock and wrenched at his chain. He had done so a thousand times, in the hope that it would eventually break, but this prison without walls or bars had proved unyielding.

Women, his happiness and his misfortune . . . But he had no regrets. Perhaps a tall Nubian girl with high-set breasts, firm and round, would lead the rebels, perhaps she would be taken with him, perhaps she would free him instead of cutting his throat. To die like this, after so many adventures, conquests and victories, was too stupid.

The sun was past its zenith, and beginning its descent towards the horizon. A soldier ought to have brought him something to eat and drink long ago. Lying down, he scooped up some river water in his hands and slaked his thirst; with skill and a little luck, he could catch a fish and so would not die of hunger. But why this sudden change of routine?

When the next day dawned and still no one had come, he was obliged to conclude that he had been abandoned to his fate. If the garrison were staying huddled inside the fortress, it must be because they expected a raid by the Nubians. Sometimes, after a drunken festival, a troop of warriors with a longing for a fight had the mad idea of invading Egypt and set off in quest of a massacre.

Unfortunately, he was directly in their path.

He must break this chain, get away from here before the attack; but he did not even have a hard stone. His mind empty, rage in his heart, he let out a roar.

When evening fell, turning the Nile to blood, Suti's practised eye detected an unexpected movement behind the bushes that lined the bank.

Someone was spying on him.

5

Bel-Tran applied pomade made from acacia-flowers and egg-white to the area of red, scaly skin, bordered by spots, that had spread across his left leg. Then he drank a few drops of aloe juice, without much hope of a spectacular cure. He refused to admit that his kidneys were not functioning properly and that his liver was congested; anyway, the head of the Double White House had no time to look after himself.

His best remedy was constant activity. Perpetually charged with irresistible energy, sure of himself, talkative to the point of wearing out those who heard him, he was like an unstoppable torrent. He was only a few months away from the goal that the conspirators had set themselves, supreme power, and a few petty ailments were not going to interrupt his triumphal march.

Right from the beginning of the conspiracy, Bel-Tran had followed the plan laid down, and he had made not even the smallest mistake. Everyone thought he was a faithful servant of Pharaoh, that his dynamism was being deployed to the benefit of Ramses' Egypt, that his powerful capacity for work was worthy to be compared to that of the great sages who worked for the temple and not for themselves.

True, three of his allies were dead; but he still had plenty of others. The dead men had been second-rate and often stupid – he would have had to get rid of them anyway, sooner or later. Even the death of the corrupt clerk Iarrot hardly troubled him, for his source of information had threatened to dry up. The hyenas had solved a problem for him.

Bel-Tran smiled as he mused that he had succeeded in deceiving the whole government and in spinning his strong web without any members of Pharaoh's entourage noticing. Pazair might be trying to fight him, but it was too late.

He constantly travelled around the large towns and provincial capitals to reassure his accomplices that a revolution was going to occur soon and that, thanks to him, they would become rich and powerful, beyond anything they had imagined in their wildest dreams. The appeal to human greed, upheld by cogent arguments, never failed to strike a chord.

The minister for trade and resources massaged his podgy ankles with a paste of crushed acacia-leaves, mixed with beef-fat; it eased tiredness and pain. He chewed two pastilles designed to sweeten the breath; olibanum, scented grasses, terebinth resin and Phoenician reeds mixed with honey produced an extremely smooth mixture. While he chewed, he gazed out of the window with satisfaction.

A huge house, at the centre of a garden enclosed by walls; a stone gateway, its lintel decorated with palm-fronds; a façade regularly punctuated by tall, thin pillars imitating papyrus stems, of which he was the principal producer; an entrance hall and reception rooms whose splendour deeply impressed his visitors, ten bedchambers, dressing-chambers with dozens of linen chests, two kitchens, a bakery, stone privies, a well, grain-stores, stables, a large garden with a pool fringed by palm-trees, sycamores, jujube-trees, perseas, pomegranates and tamarisks. Only a rich man could own such a dwelling, especially in Memphis.

He was proud of what he had achieved, he, once an insignificant employee, an upstart whom senior officials had disdained – before they came to fear him and submit to his law. Wealth and material possessions: no other lasting happiness or success existed. Temples, gods and rites were nothing but illusions and daydreams. That was why Bel-Tran and his allies had decided to wrest Egypt out of an outdated past and make her set forth on the path to progress, in which all that would count was the truth of money. In that realm, no one could equal him; Ramses and Pazair could only endure the blows and then die.

Bel-Tran picked up a jar set into a hole in a raised plank and sealed with a stopper made from silt; covered in clay, it preserved beer marvellously well. Taking out the stopper, he inserted a pipe linked to a filter, which removed any impurities, and savoured a drink that was cool and aided digestion.

Suddenly, he felt a desire to see his wife. He had succeeded in transforming a rather awkward, plain little provincial girl into a great lady of Memphis, decked in finery of such magnificence that it drove her rivals wild with jealousy. The doctors had charged high prices for the operations, but Silkis's pretty new face and the disappearance of her rolls of fat were worth it. In many ways she was still a child-woman: her moods were changeable, and she sometimes suffered from attacks of hysteria, which only the dream-interpreter could soothe; but she obeyed him without question. At today's receptions, and tomorrow's official meetings, she would appear at his side as a suitable consort, her duties to keep silent and look ravishingly beautiful.

He found her in her bedchamber, rubbing her skin with oil of fenugreek and powdered alabaster. When that was done, she applied a preparation composed of honey, red natron and northern salt, then painted her lips with red ochre, and lined her eyes with green kohl.

Bel-Tran smiled. 'You look delectable, my darling.'

'Would you hand me my best wig?'

Bel-Tran turned the mother-of-pearl button on an old chest made of cedarwood from Phoenicia, and took out a wig made with human hair. Silkis opened a jewellery box and selected a pearl bracelet and an acacia-wood comb.

'How are you feeling this morning?' he asked as he set the wig on her head.

'Still very fragile; I'm taking carob beer mixed with oil and honey.'

'If that doesn't help, consult a doctor.'

'Neferet would cure me.'

'You are not to mention Neferet's name!'

'But she's such a good doctor.'

'She is our enemy, like Pazair, and she'll be destroyed with him.'

'Couldn't you save her . . . for my sake?'

'We shall see. But enough of that. I've brought you something.'

'A surprise!'

'Some juniper oil for your delicate skin.'

She leapt up and threw her arms round his neck. 'Are you staying at home today?'

'Unfortunately, no.'

'Our son and daughter would like to talk to you.'

'Let them obey their teacher; that is more important. Soon, they will be among the most important people in the kingdom.'

'Aren't you afraid that—'

'No, Silkis, I'm not afraid of anything, because I'm untouchable. And no one knows what a powerful weapon I have.'

A servant interrupted them. 'A man is asking to see the master.'

'What is his name?'

'Mentmose, my lord.'

Mentmose, the former head of Memphis's security guards, who had been replaced by Kem. Mentmose, who had tried to get rid of Pazair by accusing him of murder and sending him to a prison camp. Although he did not belong to the circle of conspirators, he had served his future masters well. Bel-Tran thought he had disappeared for ever, exiled to Byblos in Phoenicia, and reduced to the rank of a workman in a boatyard where warships were built.

'Show him into the lotus room, next to the garden,' said Bel-Tran, 'and serve him some beer. I shall be there directly.'

Silkis was anxious. 'What can he want? I don't like him.'

'Don't worry.'

'Will you be travelling again tomorrow?'

'I have to.'

'And what am I to do?'

'Go on being pretty, and don't speak to anyone without my permission.'

'I'd like a third child with you.'

'You shall have one.'

Now aged over fifty, Mentmose had got fat. He had a bald red scalp, a pointed nose and a nasal voice which became shrill and piercing when he was angry. He was a cunning man who had built a brilliant career by using other people's failings. Never could he have imagined falling into an abyss like this, for he had taken a thousand precautions. But Judge Pazair had wrecked his system and brought his incompetence to light. Now that his enemy had become tjaty, Mentmose had no chance of regaining his lost splendour. Bel-Tran was his last hope.

Bel-Tran's opening words were not promising. 'Aren't you forbidden to set foot in Egypt?'

'I am here illegally, it's true.'

'Why have you taken such a risk?'

'I still have a few relations in high positions – all Pazair has is friends.'

'What do you expect from me?'

'I have come to offer you my services.'

Bel-Tran seemed doubtful.

'When Pazair was arrested,' Mentmose reminded him, 'he denied having murdered Branir. I did not believe for a second that he was guilty and I was aware I was being used, but that situation suited me. Someone sent me a warning message, so that I could catch Pazair red-handed when he was bending over his master's corpse. I've had time to reflect on that episode. Who was it that warned me, if not you yourself or one of your allies? Qadash, Denes and Sheshi are dead; you are not.'

'How do you know they were my allies?'

'A few tongues are wagging, and they say you're the future master of Egypt. I hate Pazair as much as you do, and I have some information which may prove embarrassing.'

'What is it?'

'The judge said he ran to Branir's house because he'd had a written message saying, "Branir is in danger. Come quickly." Suppose that, contrary to what I said at the time, I didn't destroy that document, and that the writing could be identified? And suppose I kept the murder weapon, the mother-of-pearl needle, and it belonged to someone dear to you?'

Bel-Tran thought for a moment. 'What do you want?'

'Rent me a house in the city, let me work against Pazair, and give me a post in your future government.'

'Nothing else?'

'I am convinced that you are the future.'

'Your requests seem reasonable to me.'

Mentmose bowed before Bel-Tran. All that remained was for him to take his revenge on Pazair.

6

As Neferet had been called urgently to the main hospital in Memphis for a difficult operation, Pazair was feeding Mischief, his wife's little green monkey. Although the wretched creature spent her time annoying the servants and stealing from the kitchens, Pazair had a great weakness for her. When he had met Neferet for the first time, it was only because Mischief had splashed water over Brave, his dog, that he had dared speak to his future wife.

Brave put his forepaw on the tjaty's wrist. Long-legged with a long tail and drooping ears that pricked up at meal times, the sand-coloured dog wore a pink and white leather collar bearing the legend '*Brave, companion of Pazair*'. While Mischief peeled and ate palm-nuts, the dog feasted on mashed vegetables. Fortunately, peace had been established between the two animals. Brave had agreed to have his tail pulled ten times a day, and in return Mischief left him alone when he curled up to sleep on Pazair's old mat, which had been the young judge's only valuable possession when he arrived in Memphis. It was indeed a fine item, which could serve as bed, table, floor-covering and, if the need arose, coffin. Pazair had sworn to keep it for ever, no matter how rich he became, and since Brave had adopted it, disdaining cushions and soft chairs, he knew his mat would be well guarded.

A gentle winter sun awoke the dozens of trees and flowerbeds that made the tjaty's great dwelling look like one of the eternal paradises where the righteous dwelt. Pazair walked a little way along a garden path, enjoying the subtle scents that arose from the dew-moistened earth. A friendly muzzle touched his elbow: his faithful donkey, Way-Finder, was greeting him in his usual way. A fine animal, with gentle eyes and an acute intelligence, he had an astonishing sense of direction – which the tjaty himself lacked utterly. Pazair was delighted to be able to offer Way-Finder a life in which he no longer had to carry heavy loads.

The donkey lifted his head. He had detected an unexpected presence at the main gateway, and set off rapidly towards it. Pazair followed.

Kem and Killer were waiting for the tjaty. Kem was impervious to both cold and heat, and despised luxury: he was wearing only a short kilt, like any ordinary man of modest standing. At his belt was a wooden case containing a dagger, a gift from the tjaty, with a bronze blade, and a hilt made from a mixture of gold and silver, with marquetry rosettes in lapis-lazuli and green feldspar. The big Nubian preferred this splendid weapon to the ivory hand he was obliged to carry at official ceremonies. He loathed the atmosphere of offices, and continued, as in the past, to patrol the streets of Memphis and work on the ground.

Killer had a massive head, a band of rough hairs running from the top of his back to his tail, and a red cape on his shoulders. He was calm now, but when he was enraged and unleashed his full strength he was capable of felling a lion. The only creature that had ever dared fight him in that state was another baboon of the same size and strength, sent by an unknown assassin who wanted to kill him so as to be able to attack Pazair. Killer had defeated and killed his attacker, but had been gravely wounded. Neferet had treated him, and soon put him back on his feet, and he felt undying gratitude to her.

When Pazair and Kem had exchanged greetings, Kem said, 'There's no visible sign of danger, and no one's been watching you these last few days.'

'I owe you my life.'

'And I owe you mine. However, since it seems our destinies are linked, let's not waste our breath thanking each other. Our quarry is in the nest – I've checked.'

As if he had divined the tjaty's intentions, Way-Finder immediately set off in the right direction. He trotted composedly through the streets of Memphis, a few paces in front of the baboon and the two men. Killer liked to walk upright and gaze all around him; as he passed, everything instantly went quiet.

There was a cheerful bustle in front of the main weaving-workshop in Memphis; weaving-women were chattering, and men were delivering bales of linen thread, which a female overseer checked minutely before accepting them. The donkey halted before a heap of forage, and Pazair, Kem and Killer entered the workshop where the looms were set up.

They headed for the office of the weavers' overseer, the lady Tapeni. Her appearance was deceptive: she might be a small, lively, seductive thirty-year-old with black hair and green eyes, but they knew she ran the workshop with an iron hand and thought of nothing but her career.

The trio's appearance seemed to disconcert her. 'You . . . you want to see me?'

'I believe you can help us,' said Pazair in a firm voice.

Already, rumours were flying round the workshop. The tjaty of

Egypt himself and the head of Memphis's security guards were in Tapeni's office! Was she about to be suddenly promoted, or had she committed a serious crime? Kem's presence rather implied the latter.

'I must remind you,' Pazair continued, 'that Branir was murdered with a mother-of-pearl needle. Using what you had told me, I formed several hypotheses, but unfortunately none of them bore fruit. Now, you claimed to have conclusive information. It is time you revealed it.'

'I was boasting.'

'Among the conspirators who murdered the Sphinx's guards, there was a woman – and she was as cruel and determined as her accomplices.'

Killer's red eyes fixed on the pretty brunette, who was increasingly nervous.

'Suppose,' Pazair went on, 'that this woman was also an excellent needlewoman and that she was ordered to kill Branir so as to stop his investigation in its tracks.'

'All this is nothing to do with me.'

'I should like to gain your confidence.'

'No!' she shouted, on the verge of hysteria. 'You want revenge because I had your friend Suti sentenced, but he was in the wrong and I was in the right. Don't threaten me any more or I'll lodge a complaint against you. Get out of here!'

'You should speak more respectfully,' warned Kem. 'You are addressing the tjaty of Egypt.'

Trembling, Tapeni lowered her voice. 'You have no evidence against me.'

'We shall obtain some eventually. I wish you good health, Lady Tapeni.'

The two men bowed and left.

When they were outside, Kem asked, 'Well, are you satisfied?'

'Indeed I am.'

'We may have stirred up a hornets' nest.'

'That young woman is very nervous. She attaches great importance to her social success, and our visit doesn't bode well for her reputation.'

'So she's likely to react.'

Pazair nodded. 'Straight away.'

'Do you think she's guilty?'

'Of iniquity and meanness, certainly, but . . .'

'Then who do you think is? Surely you can't mean Silkis?'

'A childish woman can, like a child, become a criminal on a mere whim. Besides, she's an excellent needlewoman.'

'But she's said to be very timid,' Kem objected.

'She bends to her husband's slightest wish. If he told her to act as bait, she'd obey him. And if the head of the Sphinx's guard saw her suddenly appear in the middle of the night, he wouldn't have been able to think clearly.'

'Committing a crime . . .'

'I shan't make a formal accusation until I have proof.'

'But what if you never get it?'

'Let us trust in the work.'

Kem looked closely at his friend. 'You're keeping something important from me, aren't you?'

'I must – I have no choice. But you should know that we're fighting for Egypt's very survival.'

'Working with you isn't exactly restful.'

'All I want is to live quietly in the country, with Neferet, my dog and my donkey.'

'Then you'll have to be patient, Tjaty Pazair.'

Tapeni could not sit still. She knew how stubborn Pazair was, how determined he was to uncover the truth, and how unshakeable was his friendship with Suti. Perhaps she had dealt too harshly with her husband, but he had married her and she would not tolerate his being unfaithful to her. He would pay for his affair with that Libyan bitch.

But now, in the light of what the tjaty had said, she knew she must find a protector at once. If recent rumours were to be believed, there could be no doubt to whom she must apply.

Tapeni hurried to the offices of the Treasury secretariat, and asked the guards if she might wait. After only half an hour an empty travelling-chair arrived in front of the offices. It had a high back, a footstool and broad armrests, and woven palm-fronds shaded the user from the sun's rays. Twenty bearers, under the command of a leader with a powerful voice, ensured that it travelled quickly. They hired out their services at a high price, and would not take on journeys that were too long.

A few minutes later, Bel-Tran came out of the secretariat's main door and hurried towards his chair.

Tapeni barred his way. 'I must speak with you.'

'Lady Tapeni! Are there problems at your workshop?'

'The tjaty is bothering me.'

'He sees himself as a righter of wrongs.'

'But he's accusing me of having committed a crime.'

'You?'

'He suspects me of having murdered Branir.'

'What evidence has he got?'

'None, but he's threatening me.'

'An innocent woman has nothing to fear,' said Bel-Tran smoothly.

'It wasn't just Pazair. Kem and his baboon were there, too, and I'm afraid. I need your help.'

'I can't see how I—'

'You're rich and powerful, and people say that you'll rise to still greater power. I'd like to become your ally.'

'In what way?'

'I control the trade in fabrics, and noble ladies like yours have a passion for them. I know how to contrive the best conditions for buying and selling – believe me, the benefit to you wouldn't be negligible.'

'Is there a great deal of such trade?'

'Yes, and with your qualities you'll easily be able to make it grow still further. As a bonus, I promise to do harm to the tjaty – may he be accursed.'

Bel-Tran's eyes narrowed. 'Have you a specific plan in mind?'

'Not yet, but you can rely on me.'

'Very well, Tapeni, you may consider yourself under my protection.'

7

The shadow-eater* was a perfectionist. So far his attempts to destroy Pazair had come to nothing, but he was determined to succeed in the end. After following his trail for a long time, Kem had resigned himself to failure. Working alone, without help, the murderer would never be identified. Thanks to all the gold he had been paid for crimes committed in the conspirators' service, he would soon be the owner of a house in the country, where he would enjoy a peaceful retirement.

The shadow-eater no longer had any contact with his employers; three were dead, and Bel-Tran and Silkis had made themselves inaccessible. However, Silkis had not been exactly shy at their last encounter, when she had passed on the order for him to disable Pazair. She had neither screamed nor called for help when she submitted to his lust. Soon Bel-Tran and Silkis would mount the throne of Egypt, so the shadow-eater felt obliged to present them with the head of the tjaty, their worst enemy.

He had learnt from his previous failures, and would no longer attack head-on; Kem and Killer had proved too effective for that. The baboon always sensed danger, and the Nubian constantly watched over Pazair. The shadow-eater would act indirectly, by setting traps.

In the middle of the night, he climbed the wall of the main hospital in Memphis, crawled on to the roof, and slipped inside the building by means of a ladder. Setting off along a corridor full of the smells of healing ointments and pomades, he made for the rooms where dangerous substances were kept. In several workshops the saliva, excrement and urine of toads and bats were stored, along with the venom of snakes, scorpions and wasps, and other toxic substances derived from plants, from which the remedy-makers prepared very effective medicines.

The presence of a watchman did not hamper the shadow-eater in the least. He struck the man unconscious with a blow to the base of

---

*A literal translation of the Egyptian expression used for an assassin.

the neck, then seized a phial of poison and a black viper imprisoned in a basket.

Aghast, Neferet enquired after the watchman's condition before she even inspected the workshops, and was relieved to hear he was not seriously injured.

'Has anything been stolen?' she asked the hospital's head doctor.

'Almost nothing. Only a black viper in a basket.'

'No poisons?'

'It's difficult to say. We received a new batch yesterday evening, and I was going to enter them in the records this morning. But the thief didn't break anything.'

'From tonight, the guard is to be doubled. I shall inform Commander Kem of the break-in myself.'

Anxiously, the young woman thought of the attempts to murder her husband. Might this odd incident be the prelude to a new threat?

Having crossed the security barriers that prevented unauthorized persons from entering the Treasury district, the tjaty arrived at the door of the Treasury, together with Kem and Killer. For the first time since his investiture, Pazair was inspecting Egypt's reserves of precious metals. He felt as though his mind were still half asleep. He and Neferet had been woken before dawn by a messenger from the hospital, and had not even had time to exchange a few thoughts before Neferet dashed off to the scene of the break-in. Unable to get back to sleep, Pazair had risen very early, taken a burning-hot shower, and then set off for the centre of Memphis.

The tjaty placed his seal on the register handed to him by the guardian of the Treasury, an elderly, slow and meticulous scribe. Although he knew Pazair's face, he checked that the imprint matched the one that had been sent to him by the palace when the new tjaty was appointed.

'What do you wish to see?' the scribe asked.

'All the reserves.'

'That will take a long time.'

'It is part of my duties.'

'I am at your disposal, Tjaty.'

Pazair began with the immense building in which were stored ingots of gold and silver from the Nubian mines and the eastern desert. Each ingot had been given an order number, and their arrangement was impeccable. A consignment was due to leave soon for the temple at Karnak, where the goldsmiths would work the precious metal into ornamentation for two great gates.

Once he recovered from his initial bedazzlement, Pazair saw that the strong-rooms were half empty.

'Our reserves are the lowest they've ever been,' said the scribe.

'Why is that?'

'Orders from above.'

'Where exactly?'

'The Double White House.'

'Show me the documents.'

The scribe was not mistaken: for several months, gold and silver ingots, as well as large quantities of other rare minerals, had been regularly leaving the reserves on Bel-Tran's orders.

Waiting was no longer an option.

Walking fast, Pazair, Kem and Killer soon reached the Double White House, a collection of two-storey buildings housing offices separated by small gardens. As usual, it was as busy as an anthill. Since Bel-Tran had been placed at the head of the great body of state, he had stamped out laxity, and he ruled like a tyrant over an army of busy scribes.

In a large enclosure were fat oxen destined for the temple; specialists were examining the animals, which had been received as payment of taxes. In a shed surrounded by a brick wall and protected by soldiers, accounting-scribes were weighing gold ingots before placing them in chests. The internal message system was in operation from dawn till dusk; young men with strong legs ran from one place to another, carrying instructions which had to be carried out immediately. Stewards took charge of tools, the making of bread and beer, receiving and distributing ointments, materials for the great construction sites, amulets and religious items. One whole department was devoted to scribes' palettes, reed pens, papyri, and clay and wooden tablets.

While Kem and Killer waited in the entrance-hall, Pazair made his way though pillared halls where dozens of officials were writing notes and reports. As he went, the tjaty began to realize the full extent of the system Bel-Tran had come to control. Little by little the man had learnt about its various components, and he had not pushed himself to the forefront until he had mastered them all.

The leaders of the teams of scribes bowed before the tjaty, while their employees continued to work; they seemed to fear their master far more than the first minister of Egypt. A steward led Pazair to the threshold of a vast hall where Bel-Tran was pacing up and down, dictating his instructions to three scribes, who were obliged to write with remarkable speed and dexterity.

The tjaty observed his sworn enemy. Ambition and lust for power impregnated every fibre of his being, every word he spoke; the man had no doubts about his own qualities, or about his ultimate triumph.

When he spotted Pazair, he stopped, tersely dismissed the scribes and ordered them to close the wooden door behind them. 'Tjaty, your visit is an honour,' he said.

'Don't waste your breath on hypocritical words.'

'Did you take the time to admire my administration? Hard work is its abiding law. You could dismiss me and appoint another minister, but the system would take hold and you would be its first victim. You would need more than a year to take back the rudder of this heavy vessel, and you have only a few months before the appointment of the new pharaoh. Give up, Pazair, and submit.'

'Why have you emptied our reserves of precious metals?'

Bel-Tran gave a smug smile. 'Have you inspected them, by any chance?'

'That is my duty.'

'And I'm sure you were very thorough.'

'I demand an explanation.'

'The higher interest of Egypt! We had to keep our friends and vassals happy – the Libyans, Phoenicians, Syrians, Hittites, Canaanites and many others – in order to maintain good relations and preserve the peace. Their governments like presents, especially gold from our deserts.'

'You have hugely exceeded the usual quantities.'

'In certain circumstances, one has to show generosity.'

'Not one speck more of precious metal is to leave the Treasury without my authorization.'

Bel-Tran smiled again. 'As you wish. But everything was done legally and correctly. I can see what you're wondering: did I use a legal procedure in order to misappropriate wealth for my own benefit? A shrewd idea, I admit. Allow me to leave you in doubt, with just one certainty: you cannot prove anything.'

8

From his rock in the middle of the Nile, Suti peered through the darkness at the bushes on the bank where the Nubian spy was hiding, watching him. Wisely, the spy kept absolutely still, probably suspicious of a trap: Suti was too easy a target.

The bushes rustled again; the spy must have decided to attack. No doubt an excellent swimmer, like all his race, he would swim underwater and try to take Suti by surprise.

With the rage of despair, Suti wrenched at his chain; it groaned and grated, but did not break. He was going to die here, stupidly, without even a chance to defend himself. Turning round, he tried to work out where the attack would come from; the night was dark, the waters of the river impenetrable.

A slender shape darted up out of the water, very close to him. He charged, head down, stretching the chain to its maximum. The figure dodged out of the way, slipped on the wet rock, fell into the water and came up again.

'Keep quiet, you fool!' it hissed.

That voice . . . He would have recognized it in the kingdom of the underworld! 'Panther? Is it really you?'

'Who else would come to your aid?'

Naked, her fair hair tumbling over her shoulders, she came towards him, bathed in a ray of moonlight. Her beauty and her sensuality entranced him yet again.

She pressed herself against him, put her arms round him and kissed him passionately. 'I've missed you a lot,' she whispered.

'I'm chained up.'

'At least you haven't been unfaithful to me.'

Panther grew hot with passion, and Suti did not resist this unexpected assault. Under the Nubian sky, lulled by the song of the river, they gave themselves to each other lustily.

When passion was spent, she stretched out beside him, overwhelmed with pleasure, and he gently stroked her hair.

'Fortunately,' she said, 'your strength hasn't been sapped. If it had been, I'd have abandoned you.'

'How did you get here?'

'Boats, chariots, carts, on foot, donkeys . . . I knew I'd find you in the end.'

'Did you have any problems?'

'Rapists and thieves here and there, but nothing really dangerous. Egypt's a peaceful country.'

'Let's get out of this place – fast.'

'I like it here.'

'If the Nubians attack, you'll soon change your mind.'

Panther got up, dived into the river, and surfaced with two sharp-edged stones. With strength and accuracy, she attacked. one of the links in the chain, while Suti smashed the metal ring encircling his wrist.

At last, their efforts were crowned with success. Mad with joy at being free again, Suti seized Panther and hoisted her up; the Libyan wound her legs round her lover's back and his manhood reawoke. He slipped on the wet rock and, joined together, they fell into the river, overcome with laughter. Their bodies were still united as they rolled on to the bank. Intoxicated with each other, they found a new energy in their embrace.

At last the cold of dawn calmed them down. 'We must go,' said Suti, suddenly serious.

'Go where?'

'South.'

'But that's unknown territory, and there'll be wild animals and the Nubians . . .'

'We must get away from the fortress and its soldiers. When they realize I've escaped, they'll send out patrols and alert their spies. We must hide until their vigilance dies down.'

'What about our gold?'

'We'll get it back, never fear.'

Panther frowned. 'It won't be easy.'

'Together, we'll succeed.'

'If you ever deceive me again with that woman Tapeni, I'll kill you.'

'Kill her first – it would be a relief.'

'You're the one responsible for that marriage. You obeyed your friend Pazair, and then he abandoned you, and look where we are now!'

'I shall settle all my accounts,' said Suti grimly.

'If we escape from the desert.'

'It doesn't frighten me. Have you got any water?'

'Two full skins. I hung them on a branch of a tamarisk.'

They hurried down a narrow track, between sun-scorched rocks and hostile cliffs. Then Panther led the way along a dry riverbed, where they found and ate a few tufts of grass. By mid-morning the sand burnt their feet, and white-necked vultures circled overhead.

For two days, they did not meet a living soul. At noon on the third day they heard horses galloping, and hastily took shelter behind an outcrop of granite rocks eroded by the wind. Two Nubian horsemen appeared, dragging behind them a naked boy. He was clinging to a rope attached to one horse's tail, and was breathless from running. The riders stopped, and ochre-coloured dust rose up into the azure sky. One cut the prisoner's throat, the other sliced off his testicles. Laughing merrily, they abandoned the corpse, and headed back towards their camp.

Panther had watched unflinchingly. 'You see what awaits us, my sweet one,' she said. 'Nubian bandits know no pity.'

'Then we'd better make sure we don't fall into their hands.'

'This place is hardly suitable for a happy retirement. Let's go on.'

As they went, they fed on palm-shoots which they found growing wild in the lonely black rocks. A lugubrious moaning accompanied them: a strong wind had begun to blow, and clouds of sand soon hid the horizon. They staggered and fell, holding each other tightly, and waited for the storm to end.

A slight shiver ran over Suti's skin. He awoke, and shook the sand out of his nose and ears.

Panther lay motionless.

'Get up,' he said. 'The storm's over.'

She did not move.

'Panther!' In panic, Suti lifted her up. She lay limp in his arms. 'Wake up, I beg you!'

'Do you love me, just a little bit?' she asked in a sultry voice.

'You were play-acting!'

'When you're in danger of becoming enslaved to a faithless lover, you have to put him to the test.'

Suti set her on her feet. 'We've no water left,' he said. 'We must go on.'

Panther walked ahead, scanning the sand for traces of moisture. When night fell, she managed to kill a rodent. She stuck two pieces of palm-leaf rib into the ground and held them firmly with her knees, then between them she rubbed a length of very dry wood, holding it in both hands; vigorous repetition produced sawdust, which caught fire. The cooked meat, little though there was, gave them back some strength.

As soon as the sun rose, the modest meal and the relative cool of the night were forgotten; they must find a well, and soon, or they would die. But how could they do that? There was not a single oasis in sight, not even a few tufts of grass or thickets of thorn bushes, which sometimes revealed the presence of water.

'Only one sign can save us,' said Panther. 'Let's sit down and watch for it. There's no use walking any further.'

Suti acquiesced. He did not fear the desert or the sun; dying free, at the heart of this ocean of fire, held no terrors for him. The light danced on the rocks, time dissolved in the heat, eternity imposed itself, burning and indomitable. In Panther's company, he felt a form of happiness which was as precious as the gold of the mountains.

'Over there,' she suddenly whispered in his ear, 'on your right.'

Suti turned his head slowly. On the summit of a sand-dune, he saw an oryx stag: at once proud and wary, it was sniffing the air. It weighed at least as much as two men, and its long horns could run a lion through. He knew that these animals could tolerate unbearable heat, wandering in the desert even when the sun beat down vertically.

'We must follow it,' decreed Panther.

A slight breeze lifted the black hairs on the tail of the oryx, whose breathing grew faster as the heat intensified. The animal of the god Set, lord of storms and incarnation of nature's extremes, the oryx knew how to capture the smallest breath of air in order to refresh the circulation of its blood. The stag made a mark in the sand with its hoof, and then set off southwards along the dunes, surefootedly avoiding the areas of soft sand.

The couple waited a few minutes before going to examine the mark. It was like an X, the hieroglyph signifying 'to pass'. Was the oryx showing them a way of getting out of this great barren waste? They followed it, staying a safe distance behind.

Suti marvelled at Panther. She never complained, never balked at even the most strenuous effort; she fought for survival with the same determination as a wild animal.

Just before sunset, the oryx began to walk faster and disappeared behind an enormous dune. Suti helped Panther to climb the slope, which gave way beneath their feet. She fell, he lifted her up, and fell in his turn. Lungs aflame, legs aching, they crawled to the summit.

The desert was tinged with ochre. The heat came not from the sky but from the sand and the stones. The mild warmth of the wind could not cool their burning lips and throats.

The oryx had disappeared.

'It's tireless,' said Panther. 'We have no hope of catching up with it. If it scents greenery, it'll carry on without stopping, for days on end, if need be.'

Suti was staring at something in the far distance. 'I think I can see . . . No, it's a mirage.'

Panther looked, too, but her sight was clouded.

'Come on,' said Suti, 'keep going forward.'

They forced their legs to move again, despite the pain. If Suti was wrong, they would have to drink their own urine before dying of thirst.

'Look!' panted Suti. 'The oryx's tracks.'

After a succession of leaps, the antelope had settled back into a slow walk towards the mirage that had cast a spell on Suti. In her turn, Panther began to hope: could she make out a minuscule patch of green?

They forgot their exhaustion, and followed in the animal's tracks. And the green dot grew and grew, until it became a grove of acacia-trees.

Under the tree with the broadest canopy, the oryx was resting. It watched the new arrivals carefully. They admired its long horns, its fawn pelt, its black and white face. Suti knew it would not flinch in the face of danger; sure of its own power, it would gore them if it believed itself under threat.

'The hairs of its beard,' croaked Panther. 'They're wet!'

The oryx had finished drinking. It was eating acacia-pods, a good part of which would pass, undigested, into its droppings and would result in the growth of new trees wherever it went.

'The earth is soft,' Suti observed.

They walked very slowly past the animal and entered the heart of the grove, which was bigger than it seemed. Between two date-palms lay the mouth of a well, surrounded by flat stones.

Suti and Panther embraced, before running to the well and slaking their thirst.

'This is a real paradise,' declared Suti.

9

Anxiety reigned in the narrow street where Bagey, Pazair's predecessor as tjaty, lived in retirement: the old man was gravely ill.

In his time as tjaty, Bagey had been known as a cold, intransigent, austere man, who was impervious to flattery and who hated sloppiness; he had ruled his subordinates with an iron fist. Eventually, worn out by his burdens of office, he had asked Ramses to release him from his duties so that he might end his days in peace in his little house in Memphis.

Pharaoh, who had closely watched Pazair's career and his clashes with certain eminent persons, had put his faith in the young judge's sincere desire for truth and determination to unravel the conspiracy menacing Egypt. Bagey had approved of that decision. Pazair had proved honest in the pursuit of his investigation and had unfailingly fulfilled his duties as a judge, so Bagey told Ramses that, though he himself was no longer strong enough to fight, the younger man had his full support.

Bagey's wife, a plain, brown-haired woman, had alerted their neighbours as soon as her husband's illness worsened. Usually he rose early, went for a walk in the great city, and came back a little before the midday meal. But this morning he had complained of a terrible pain in his back. Despite his wife's insistence, Bagey refused to call a doctor, convinced that the pain would soon ease. But it had not, and in the end he had been compelled to see reason.

The neighbours had gathered in the street, advocating a thousand and one remedies, accusing all kinds of demons of having caused Bagey's illness. Silence fell with the arrival of Neferet, the kingdom's principal doctor, accompanied by Way-Finder, whose job was to carry her medical equipment. He walked straight through the crowd and headed for Bagey's house, where he halted before the door. The housewives in the crowd called out greetings and congratulations to Neferet, who was very popular, but she was in a hurry and answered only with smiles.

Bagey's wife was put out. She had been expecting a proper doctor, not this radiantly beautiful, alluring creature in a long linen gown. 'You should not have troubled,' she said.

'Your husband helped mine at a difficult time. I shall always be grateful to him for that.'

The two women went into the little white, two-storey house, crossed a drab entrance-hall devoid of ornament, and climbed the narrow staircase to the upper floor.

Bagey was lying down in a somewhat airless room, which had not been repainted in a long time.

'You!' he exclaimed when he saw Neferet. 'Your time is too valuable to—'

'Didn't I cure you once before?'

'You even saved my life. Without your treatment, my portal vein would have killed me.'[*]

'Don't you trust me any more?'

'Of course I do.'

Bagey sat up, his back propped up against the wall, and looked at his wife. 'Leave us.'

'Don't you need anything?'

'The doctor's going to examine me.'

His wife withdrew, with a heavy, hostile tread.

Neferet took her patient's pulse in various places, and consulted the portable clock she carried on her wrist, in order to calculate the reaction times of the organs and their proper rhythm. She listened to the voice of the heart, and checked that the hot and cold currents were circulating correctly.

Bagey remained calm, almost indifferent. 'What is your diagnosis?'

'One moment.'

Neferet took a thin, strong cord at the end of which swung a fragment of granite, and passed her pendulum over the different parts of the patient's body. Twice, the granite described wide circles.

'Tell me the truth,' commanded Bagey.

'This is a sickness I know and can treat. Are your feet always so swollen?'

'Quite often. I soak them in tepid salted water.'

'Does that bring relief?'

'Yes, but these days it doesn't last long.'

'Your liver is congested again: the blood is thick. Too much fatty cooking, I expect.'

[*]See *Beneath the Pyramid*.

'My wife has her ways; it's too late to change them.'

'Take more chicory, and drink a potion made of bryony, fig-juice, grape-juice, and the fruits of the persea and sycamore. You must urinate more.'

'I'd forgotten that remedy. But there's something else wrong, I'm sure.'

'Try to stand up.'

With difficulty, Bagey did so. Neferet brought forward a wooden seat with transverse supports and a concave frame on which lay a cover of cords plaited like fish scales. The old man sat down stiffly, and the seat creaked under his weight.

Neferet used her pendulum again.

When she had finished, she said, 'You're suffering from the early stages of kidney disease. Four times a day you must drink a mixture of water, beer leaven and the juice of fresh dates. Keep it in an ordinary terracotta jar, which must be closed with a stopper of dried earth covered with cloth. It's a simple but effective remedy; if it doesn't work quickly, and if you have difficulty passing water, tell me at once.'

'I shall owe my recovery to you again.'

'You certainly won't if you hide part of the truth from me.'

'Why do you say that?'

'I can sense that you're deeply worried, and I must identify the cause.'

'You're a remarkable doctor,' said Bagey.

'Will you tell me?'

Bagey hesitated, then said, 'As you know, I have two children. My son has given me cause for worry from time to time, but he seems to like his work checking baked bricks. But my daughter . . .' He looked down at his feet. 'She spent only a short time in the temple – the rituals bored her. She has become an accounting-scribe on a farm, and the owner seems pleased with her work.'

'Are you angry with her for doing that?'

'Indeed not – my children's happiness comes before all else, and I respect their choices. She wants to start a family, and I am encouraging her to do so.'

'Then what is it that's worrying you?'

'It is stupid, deplorable! My daughter has been given bad advice, and has started proceedings against me in order to obtain her inheritance before the appropriate time. But I have nothing to give her except this house.'

Neferet smiled. 'I cannot cure an ill like that, but I know someone who has proven skill.'

*

Brave begged for a pastry, and Pazair gave in.

Bagey was seated on a comfortable chair, which he had told the servants to put in the shade: he disliked the sun's fierce rays.

'This garden is much too big, Pazair,' he said. 'Even devoted gardeners would have trouble keeping it up. I prefer my little house in the town.'

'The dog and the donkey enjoy the space.'

'How have your first days as tjaty been?'

'It all seems almost impossibly difficult.'

'The words of the investiture rite should have put you on your guard: it is a task "more bitter than bile". You are young, so don't try to go too far too fast; you have time to learn.'

Pazair longed to confide in the old man and tell him he was much mistaken. Instead, he said, 'The less I master the situation, the more the country's balance will be compromised.'

'Why are you so gloomy?'

'More than half of our reserves of precious metals have been squandered,' said Pazair.

Bagey sat bolt upright. 'What? More than half? That's impossible! My last checks did not reveal anything of the kind.'

'Bel-Tran used – perfectly legally – all the administrative resources at his disposal, and transferred a good part of the Treasury abroad.'

'What justification did he offer?'

'To ensure peace with our neighbours and our vassals.'

'The argument is not without weight. I should have been more wary of that upstart.'

'He has deceived the whole government. He has always worked hard and shown the will to succeed, an obsessive desire to serve his country. Why should anyone have doubted his sincerity?'

'He's taught us a harsh lesson.' Bagey was downcast.

'At least we are now aware of the danger.'

'You are right,' agreed Bagey. 'Of course, no one can replace Branir, but I may perhaps be able to help you.'

'My vanity made me assume I would get the measure of my office quite quickly, but Bel-Tran has locked many doors. I fear that my power may be an illusion.'

'If your subordinates think that, your position will rapidly become untenable. You are the tjaty: you must lead.'

'Bel-Tran's henchmen will block my decisions.'

'Go round the obstacle.'

'How?'

'In each government secretariat,' said Bagey, 'there is always one especially important, experienced man – not necessarily the one in the highest position. Find him and cultivate his acquaintance: you'll soon understand the subtleties of how the different components of that secretariat work.' He gave Pazair names and details. 'Be absolutely scrupulous,' he warned, 'when you attest your actions before Pharaoh. Ramses is highly perceptive, and if you try to deceive him you will fail.'

'In case of difficulty, may I consult you?'

'You will always be welcome, even if my hospitality is not as lavish as yours.'

'The heart matters more than appearances. But now tell me, are you in better health now?'

'Your wife is an excellent doctor, but I am sometimes an undisciplined patient.'

'You must take care of yourself.'

Bagey smiled. 'I am a little tired. Will you allow me to retire?'

'Before you are escorted home, I have something to confess: I met your daughter.'

'Then you know . . .'

'Neferet asked me to see her, and there was nothing wrong in my doing so.'

Bagey frowned angrily.

'It was not a misuse of privilege,' insisted Pazair. 'A former tjaty deserves due consideration. It was my duty to resolve this disagreement.'

'What did my daughter say?'

'There will be no court case. You will keep your house, and she will build her own, using a loan which I have guaranteed. Now that her dearest wish is being met, harmony will reign in your family again. Oh, and you can expect to be a grandfather soon.'

Bagey's stern demeanour crumbled; he could not hide his emotion. 'You have given me many joys at once, Tjaty Pazair.'

'It is a small thing compared with the help you have given me.'

10

The great market in Memphis was a daily festival, in which as many words were exchanged as goods. The traders, who included women with an inexhaustible gift for talking, had their own allocated places. Barter was practised, along with the necessary haggling and gesticulations. The tone became heated from time to time, but transactions always ended in good humour.

Kem, always accompanied by Killer, liked walking through the main square. Killer's mere presence prevented thefts, while his master listened to snatches of conversation reflecting the people's state of mind, and, using a secret code, discreetly questioned his informants.

The big Nubian paused in front of a stall selling preserved food; he was hoping to find a trussed goose which was ready for roasting, having been dried, salted and put in a jar. The stallholder was sitting on a mat, his head hanging low.

'What's the matter?' asked Kem. 'Are you ill?'

'It's much worse than that.'

'Have you been robbed?'

'Look at my goods, then you'll understand.'

The jars used for preserving food were very efficient. They were also attractive, being made of clay from Middle Egypt, decorated with garlands of flowers and glazed with luminous blue. Kem examined the inscriptions of those on the stall: water, wine, but no meat at all.

'I didn't receive my deliveries,' lamented the trader. 'It's a disaster.'

'Have you been given any explanation?'

'None at all. The ship sailed empty – I've never known such misfortune!'

'Has it happened to anyone else?'

'To everyone. Some traders have stocks in reserve, but no one has received fresh supplies.'

'Perhaps it's simply that they've been delayed.'

'If we don't get our deliveries tomorrow, there'll be a riot, I promise you.'

Kem did not take the matter lightly; no one, rich or poor, would accept such disruption. Well-off people demanded meat for their banquets, more humble people needed dried fish.

So he went to the warehouse where jars of meat were stored centrally. When he arrived, he found the scribe in charge standing outside gazing at the Nile, hands folded behind his back.

'What's going on?' demanded Kem. 'Why aren't you working?'

'Nothing's arrived for a week.'

'And you didn't tell anyone?'

'Of course I did.'

'Whom?'

'The scribe I'm responsible to: the man in charge of salting.'

'Where can I find him?'

'In his workshop, near the Temple of Ptah's butcheries.'

The butchers were talking and drinking sweet beer. At this time of day, they would normally have been busy plucking geese and ducks hung on a long pole, gutting them, salting them, and putting them into large, clearly labelled preserving-jars.

'Why aren't you working?' asked Kem for the second time.

'We've got the birds and the jars,' replied one of them, 'but no salt. That's all we know. You'd better go and see the scribe in charge of salting.'

The scribe was a small man, entirely round and almost bald; he was playing dice with his assistant. The appearance of Kem and Killer instantly banished his desire for amusement.

'It's not my fault,' he declared in a shaky voice.

'Did I accuse you of anything?'

'If you're here—'

'Why haven't you given the butchers the salt they need?'

'Because I haven't got any.'

'Why is that?'

'I have two sources of supply, the Nile Valley and the oases. After the great heat of summer, the foam of the god Set solidifies on the surface of the soil near to the river, so that the earth is covered with a white sheet. This salt contains fire which is a danger to the temple stones, so it's collected at once and stored. At Memphis we also use salt gathered from the oases, because we preserve a great many different kinds of food. But as of today we have none left.'

'Why not?'

'The salt warehouses on the Nile have been placed under lock and key and the caravans are no longer arriving from the oases.'

With Killer at his heels, Kem hurried to the tjaty's office, which, he found, had been invaded by ten angry senior scribes. Each was trying to speak louder than the others, with the result that a deplorable cacophony had taken the place of a discussion. Eventually, after a firm instruction from Pazair, they spoke in turn.

'The same price is paid for an untreated skin and a treated skin. The craftsmen are threatening to stop work unless you take action to re-establish the difference.'

'Not only are the hoes delivered to the farm-workers on the estate of the goddess Hathor of poor quality, but their price has doubled: four *deben** instead of two.'

'The humblest pair of sandals costs three *deben*, which is three times their normal price – and I'm not talking about luxury items.'

'A ewe costs ten *deben* instead of five; a fat ox two hundred instead of one hundred. If this madness goes on, we shan't be able to feed ourselves any more.'

'Haunch of bull will soon be unaffordable, even for the rich.'

'And I'm not talking about dishes or vases made of bronze or copper. One will soon have to barter an entire wardrobe for a single dish.'

Pazair got to his feet. 'Please, calm yourselves.'

'Tjaty, this explosion of prices is intolerable.'

'I agree, but who is behind it?'

The scribes looked at each other.

The one who had been angriest spoke up. 'But . . . you did.'

'Did the directives to that effect bear my seal?'

'No, but they bore the seal of the Double White House. And no one has ever heard of a tjaty being at odds with his minister for finance and trade.'

Pazair could see their point. Bel-Tran's plan, he reflected, was a cunning one: artificial price-rises, discontent among the population, and the tjaty accused of being responsible.

'I made a mistake, and I shall rectify it. Prepare a scale of prices conforming to the normal one, and I shall ratify it. Excessive increases will be punished.'

'Shouldn't the value of the *deben* be altered?'

'That will not be necessary.'

'The traders won't like it. Your mistake was making them a lot of money.'

'Their prosperity does not seem compromised to me. Pray make

---

* One *deben* was the equivalent of 91 grams of copper; it was a reference value used to calculate the value of products.

haste. First thing tomorrow, my messengers will go into the towns and villages to proclaim my decisions.'

The scribes bowed and withdrew.

Kem looked around the large office, which was filled with shelves groaning under the weight of papyri and tablets.

'If I understand rightly,' he said, 'we've had a narrow escape.'

'I found out only yesterday evening what was going on,' said Pazair, 'and I worked all night to stem this devastating tide. Bel-Tran is trying to make everyone discontented, to show that I'm carrying out a disastrous policy and that Pharaoh no longer runs the country. We've escaped disaster this time, but he'll try again, concentrating on particular trades. His goal is to divide the country, setting the rich against the poor, spreading hatred, and turning those destructive forces to his own advantage. We shall have to be constantly on the alert.' Pazair sighed. 'I hope you've brought me some good news?'

'I'm afraid not.'

'Has something else happened?'

'Salt is no longer being delivered.'

Pazair turned pale. There was a danger that people would run out of staple food like dried meat and fish. 'How can that be?' he asked. 'Ample supplies were gathered.'

'Seals have been placed on the doors of the warehouses.'

'Let us go and remove them.'

The seals were in the name of the Double White House; in the presence of Kem and two scribes, the tjaty broke them. A deed was immediately drawn up, signed and dated.

The scribe in charge of salt opened the doors himself.

'But the salt's all damp!' he cried in dismay.

'It was wrongly collected and stored,' said Kem. 'It was moistened with stagnant water.'

'It must be washed in clean water and filtered,' ordered Pazair.

'Hardly anything will be saved.'

In fury, Pazair turned on the scribe. 'Who spoilt this salt?'

'I don't know. When Bel-Tran examined it, he judged it unsuitable for consumption and for preserving food. Legal documents were drawn up, in good and due form.'

The scribe trembled under Killer's piercing gaze, but stood his ground; he truly knew nothing else.

The secretariat in charge of trade with the oases was an annexe of the Foreign Affairs secretariat. Although the oases had belonged to Egypt since the time of the earliest pharaohs, these far-off lands remained mysterious in the eyes of those who lived in the Nile Valley. But they produced natron, which was vital for cleanliness and mummification, and salt of excellent quality. Caravans of donkeys travelled the routes ceaselessly, bearing heavy and precious loads.

A former hunter of sand-travellers who looted caravans – his face was still brown and lined from the desert sun – had been placed in charge of the oases secretariat. He had a square head and powerful chest, and it was immediately clear that he knew the value of hard work and danger. All the same, Killer made him uneasy.

'Put that baboon on a leash,' he said. 'Baboons are dangerous when they're angry.'

'Killer has taken an oath,' replied Kem. 'He has sworn to attack only people who are doing wrong.'

The former hunter turned purple. 'No one has ever doubted my honesty.'

'Haven't you forgotten to greet the tjaty of Egypt properly?' said Kem.

The man did so, his back stiff.

'How much salt is there in your storehouses?' asked Pazair.

'Very little. The donkeys from the oases have delivered nothing for several weeks, neither to us nor to Thebes.'

'Weren't you surprised by that?'

'No. I'm the one who gave the order to halt all trade.'

'Were you acting on your own initiative?'

'I had received instructions.'

'From Bel-Tran?'

'Yes, that's right.'

'What reasons did he give?'

'To bring down prices. The people of the oases refused point blank to obey, because they were sure the Double White House would back down. But now the whole situation has become a morass. My demands for more supplies of salt go unanswered – fortunately, we have the salt from the Valley.'

'Fortunately,' repeated Pazair, aghast.

Clean-shaven, wearing a wig which covered half his forehead, and dressed in a long tunic, the shadow-eater was unrecognizable. Leading two donkeys by a long rope, he arrived at the gate of Pazair's estate that gave access to the kitchens.

He presented the steward with a basket of soft cheeses, creamy fermented milk in a jar, and curds with alum. When the steward bent over the basket, the shadow-eater knocked him unconscious and dragged his body inside the gate.

At last he could get down to work.

11

The shadow-eater had a map of the tjaty's villa and grounds. Leaving nothing to chance, he had established that at this time of day the servants were busy in the kitchen, where the gardeners were eating their midday meal. The absence of Kem and Killer, who were with Pazair in the town, meant that he could act with the minimum of risk.

Although usually impervious to the beauties of nature, the murderer was amazed by the garden's luxuriance. A hundred cubits long and two hundred wide,* it had terraced fields, squares interlaced with water-channels, and a kitchen garden. In addition, it contained a well, an ornamental lake, where blue lotuses were in flower, a hut providing shelter from the wind, a line of shrubs shaped into cones along the edge of the Nile, a double row of palm-trees, a shady path, an arbour, clumps of flowers dominated by cornflowers and mandragora, a vine, fig-trees, sycamores, tamarisks, date-palms, perseas and rare species imported from Asia to charm the eye and the nose. But the man of darkness did not linger in this enchanting place. Carefully carrying the black viper in its basket, he walked along one side of the lake until he reached the house, then stopped and crouched down, on the alert for the faintest sound.

Neither the dog nor the donkey had detected his presence, for they were eating their midday meal, too, on the other side of the estate. According to the map, he was outside the bedchambers used for guests. He climbed through a low window into a rectangular room furnished with a bed and storage chests. He kept tight hold of the handle of the basket; the black viper was thrashing about.

Emerging from the room, he discovered, as he had expected, a fine hall with four painted pillars. The painter had depicted, in vivid colours, ten species of birds frolicking in a garden. The shadow-eater decided he would have this sort of decoration in his future home.

Suddenly, he stopped in his tracks.

*About 5,400 square metres.

He heard snatches of conversation coming from his right, from a bathing-room where a serving-girl was pouring warm, scented water over Neferet's naked body. The mistress of the house was listening to her servant's worries about her family problems, and trying to suggest solutions. The shadow-eater would have liked to gaze at the young woman, whose beauty fascinated him, but pleasure would have to wait until his mission was accomplished. He retraced his steps, and opened another door. It was that of a large bedroom. Vases filled with hollyhocks, cornflowers and lilies stood on pedestal tables, and the two beds had gilded wooden headrests; this was where Pazair and Neferet slept.

His first task accomplished, the shadow-eater recrossed the four-pillared hall, passed the bathing-room, and entered an oblong room full of different-sized phials made of wood, ivory, many-coloured glass and alabaster, and taking such varied shapes as a pomegranate, a lotus, a papyrus stem and a duck. This was Neferet's private workshop. Each remedy was identified by its name, with the corresponding instructions for treatment. He had no difficulty in finding the one he was looking for.

Once again he heard the sound of female voices, and the song of cascading water; the sounds were coming from the next room. At the top left-hand corner of the wall, he noticed a hole which the plasterer had not yet blocked. Unable to bear it any longer, he climbed on to a stool and stretched up.

He saw her.

Neferet was standing up, receiving the delicious water poured by her servant, stood on a raised brick bench. Her ablutions done, Neferet lay down on a stone bench. Still complaining about her husband and children, the serving-girl gently smoothed lotion into her mistress's back. The shadow-eater drooled at the sight. The last woman he had taken, Silkis, with her opulent curves, was an ugly bitch beside Neferet. For a moment, he thought about rushing into the bathroom, strangling the servant and raping the tjaty's beautiful wife; but time was getting on.

From a box shaped like a swimming girl pushing a duck before her, the servant scooped up a little pomade and spread it over Neferet's lower back to soothe tiredness and ease muscle spasms. The shadow-eater contained his desire and left the house.

When the tjaty crossed the threshold of his house, a little before sunset, his steward rushed up to him.

'Master, I was attacked this morning! It was the time when the travelling sellers come by . . . The man said he was a cheesemonger.

I was wary, because I didn't know him, but his cheeses seemed of very good quality. He knocked me unconscious.'

'Did you tell Neferet?'

'I thought it better not to alarm her. Instead, I carried out my own investigation.'

'What did you find out?'

'Nothing worrying. No one saw the man anywhere on the estate – he must have left straight after knocking me out. He probably planned to steal something, but saw that that was impossible.'

'And how do you feel now?' asked Pazair.

'Still a bit shaken.'

'Go and rest.'

Pazair did not share his steward's optimism. If the attacker was the mysterious assassin who had tried several times to kill him, he had probably got into the house. What had he intended to do?

Tired after a long, hard day, during which he'd hardly had time to draw breath, the tjaty put the problem aside for the moment, intent on joining Neferet. He walked quickly down the main garden path, beneath the branches of the sycamores and the palm-trees, admiring the way the leaves undulated in the wind. He liked the taste of the water from his well, and of his dates and his figs. The rustling of the sycamores reminded him of the sweetness of honey; the fruit of the persea looked like a heart. The gods had granted him the privilege of enjoying these marvels and, moreover, of sharing them with the woman he had loved with all his heart since the first moment he set eyes on her.

Seated under a pomegranate tree, Neferet was playing a portable seven-stringed harp. Like her, the tree kept its beauty all year long, for as soon as one flower fell another opened. In her pure, high voice full of gentle emotion, she was singing an ancient song telling of the happiness of lovers who were faithful for ever. He went to her and kissed her neck, in the place where the touch of his lips always made her shiver.

'I love you, Pazair.'

'I love you more.'

'You don't – that's impossible.'

They kissed with the fervour of youth.

'You don't look well,' she observed.

'My cold and cough are coming back.'

'That's because you work too hard and worry too much.'

'These last few days have been exhausting. We came close to two major disasters.'

'Because of Bel-Tran?' asked Neferet.

'There's no doubt about it. He organized a rise in prices in order to sow discontent among the population, and cut off the trade in salt.'

'So that's why our steward couldn't find any preserved geese. And what about dried fish?'

'Stocks in Memphis are exhausted.'

'You'll be held responsible, won't you?' said Neferet worriedly.

'That is the rule.'

'What are you going to do?'

'Get things back to normal straight away.'

'As regards the prices, a decree will be enough. But what about the salt?'

'Not all the stores were spoilt by damp, and the caravans will soon start leaving the oases again. Besides, I've opened up Pharaoh's reserves, in the Delta, at Memphis, and at Thebes. We shan't be without preserved food for long, and in order to reassure people the royal granaries will distribute free food for several days, as in periods of famine.'

'What about the merchants?'

'They will receive fabrics as compensation.'

'So harmony has been restored.'

'Only until Bel-Tran's next attack – he'll never stop harassing me.'

'But can you not bring a case against him? Surely what he did was illegal?'

'He can claim to have acted in the interests of the Double White House, and therefore in Pharaoh's. Raising food prices and making the salt vendors lower theirs would have enriched the Treasury.'

'And made the people poor,' said Neferet angrily.

'Bel-Tran doesn't care about them. He's only interested making allies of the rich, whose support will be vital if he takes power. To my mind, these were only skirmishes, intended to test my reactions. He has far greater control of the country's trade and finances than I have, so his next attack may well be decisive.'

'Don't be so gloomy. It's tiredness making you feel like that – and a good doctor will cure you of it.'

'Do you know a remedy?'

'The massage room.'

Pazair let himself be led, as though this was the first time he had been there. After washing his feet and his hands, he took off his official robe and his kilt, then lay down on a stone bench. Neferet massaged him gently, smoothing away the ache from his back and the stiffness from his neck. When he turned on to his side, Pazair gazed at Neferet. Her gossamer-fine linen dress scarcely concealed her curves, and her body was perfumed.

He drew her towards him. 'I have no right to lie to you, even by omission. Our steward was attacked this morning, by a man pretending to be a cheese-seller. He couldn't identify his attacker, and nobody saw the man afterwards.'

'Do you think he was the man who's tried to kill you, the one Kem hasn't yet tracked down?'

'Probably.'

'We shall eat different dishes from the ones planned for this evening,' decided Neferet. 'He tried to kill you with poisonous fish, once, remember?'

Pazair admired his wife's composure; and his rising desire made him forget the worries and the dangers.

'Have you changed the flowers in our bedchamber?' he asked.

'Yes. Would you like to see them?'

'I'd like nothing better.'

They walked down the passage between the massage room and the bedchamber, and went into their room.

Pazair undressed Neferet very slowly, covering her with fevered kisses. Each time they made love, he gazed at her soft lips, her slender neck, her firm, round breasts, her shapely hips, her slim legs, and thanked heaven for granting him such insane happiness. Neferet responded to his ardour, and together they experienced the secret joy that the goddess Hathor, queen of love, granted to her faithful worshippers.

The huge house was silent. Pazair and Neferet lay side by side, hand in hand.

A strange noise caught Pazair's attention. 'Can you hear something that sounds like a stick tapping?'

Neferet listened for a moment. The sound was repeated, then silence fell again. She concentrated; distant memories were slowly surfacing.

'It's coming from over there, on my right,' said Pazair.

Neferet lit an oil-lamp. A chest containing Pazair's linen kilts stood where he was pointing. He got out of bed and went over to it.

He was about to lift the lid when a horrible scene rushed back into Neferet's memory. She caught him by the arm and pulled him back.

'Call a servant,' she said, 'and tell him to bring a stick and a knife. I know what the false cheesemonger came to do.'

She was reliving each moment of the ordeal during which she had had to catch a snake and extract its venom to prepare a remedy. When its tail tapped against the sides of the basket in which it was contained, it made a sound exactly like the one she and Pazair had just heard.

Pazair put on his kilt and went to fetch the steward and a gardener. When he returned with them, the steward carried a long stick, and the gardener a very sharp knife.

'Take great care,' advised Neferet. 'There's an angry snake in this chest.'

The steward opened the lid with the end of his stick – and with a hiss the black viper's head instantly appeared. The gardener, used to dealing with this sort of undesirable visitor, chopped the snake in two.

Pazair sneezed several times and was overcome by a fit of coughing.

'I shall go and fetch your medicine,' said Neferet.

Neither of them had touched the delicious grilled lamb their cook had prepared; Brave, on the other hand, had done ample justice to it. Replete, his chin resting on his crossed paws, he was enjoying a well-deserved rest at his master's feet.

From her workshop, Neferet fetched a phial of bryony-based potion, which would clear Pazair's breathing-passages.

'First thing tomorrow,' he said, 'I shall tell Kem that from now on our house must be guarded by some of his most reliable men. This kind of thing won't happen again.'

Neferet put ten drops of potion in a cup, and added water. 'Drink this,' she said, 'and you are to take the same quantity again in an hour's time.'

Thoughtfully, Pazair took the cup. 'The killer must be in Bel-Tran's pay. Was he one of the conspirators who violated the Great Pyramid? No, I don't think so. He's an element outside the conspiracy proper. Which leads me to suppose there are others—'

Brave growled and bared his teeth.

This astounded the couple: he had never behaved to them like that.

'Be quiet,' ordered Pazair.

Brave stood up on his hind legs, and growled more loudly.

'Whatever has got into him?' said Pazair.

The mongrel leapt up and bit Pazair's wrist.

Stunned, he dropped the cup and shook his fist.

White-faced, Neferet blocked his way. 'Don't hit him! I think I understand.'

His eyes filled with love, Brave licked his master's hand.

Her voice shaking, Neferet said, 'That isn't the smell of bryony tincture. The assassin replaced your usual medicine with a poison he stole from the hospital. In treating you, I was meant to kill you.'

12

Panther set a hare to roast, while Suti put the finishing touches to a bow he had made from acacia-wood. It looked much like his favourite bow, which was capable of shooting arrows sixty paces in a straight line, and more than a hundred and fifty in a curved trajectory. Since adolescence, Suti had shown an exceptional gift for hitting the very centre of small targets, even from a long way away.

King of this small oasis, which was rich in pure water, succulent dates and game that came there to drink, Suti was happy. He and Panther lived naked, sheltering from the sun at the hottest times of day and enjoying the shade of the date-palms and the greenery. When desire took hold of them, their bodies united with an ever-renewing passion.

Suti loved the desert, its power, its all-consuming fire which led a man's thoughts towards infinity. For long hours, he gazed at the sunrise and sunset, the imperceptible movements of the dunes, the dance of the sand, its rhythm set by the wind. Immersing himself in silence, he communed with the burning immensity over which the sun reigned unchallenged. Suti had the feeling that he was touching the absolute, beyond the gods. Was it really necessary to leave this unknown patch of earth, forgotten by men?

'When are we leaving?' asked Panther, snuggling up against him.

'Perhaps never.'

'Are you planning to put down roots here?'

'Why not?'

'It's a hellish place, Suti!'

'What do we need that we haven't got?'

'What about our gold?'

'Aren't you happy?'

'This sort of happiness isn't enough for me,' said Panther. 'I want to be rich and command an army of servants, on a vast estate. You will pour me out the finest wines, and rub my legs with perfumed oil, and I shall sing you songs of love.'

'There's no vaster estate than the desert.'

'Where are the gardeners, the ornamental lakes, the musicians, the banqueting-halls, the—'

'All things we don't need.'

'Speak for yourself!' retorted Panther. 'I loathe living like a pauper. I didn't get you out of your Nubian prison just to rot away in this one.'

'We've never been freer. Look around you: no one to bother us, no parasites, only the world in all its beauty and its truth. Why should we leave such splendour?'

'Your imprisonment has weakened your brain, my poor darling.'

'Don't pour scorn on what I said. I've fallen in love with the desert.'

'And what about me? Don't I matter any more?'

'You're not only a fugitive from justice but a Libyan, Egypt's hereditary enemy.'

'Monster! Tyrant!' She rained blows on him with her fists.

Suti seized her arms and threw her down on to her back. Panther struggled, but he was the stronger.

'Either you become my slave of the sands, or I'll throw you out.'

'You have no rights over me – I'd rather die than obey you. You still think about your slut of a wife, Tapeni, don't you?'

'Well, yes, I admit I do occasionally.'

'You're unfaithful to me in your thoughts.'

'Don't you believe it. If I had the lady Tapeni to hand, I'd deliver her to the demons of the desert.'

Panther frowned, suddenly anxious. 'Have you seen them?'

'At night, while you're asleep, I watch the summit of the great dune – that's where they appear. One has the body of a lion and the head of a snake, another has the body of a winged lion and the head of a falcon, and there's a third with a pointed nose, long ears and a forked tail.* No arrow can reach them, no rope can capture them, no dog can pursue them.'

'You're making fun of me.'

'Those demons protect us, because you and I belong to their race – we're as unyielding and ferocious as they are.'

'You were dreaming,' scoffed Panther. 'Those creatures don't exist.'

'You do.'

'Get off me. You're too heavy.'

'Are you sure about that?' He started caressing her.

'No!' she shouted, shoving him hard to one side.

---

*The fantastic animals believed to people the desert are depicted, notably, in the tombs of the nobles in the burial-ground at Beni-Hassan, in Middle Egypt.

A hatchet-blade sliced into the ground a hair's breadth from where they had been a second before; it was so close that it brushed Suti's forehead. Out of the corner of his eye, he glimpsed the attacker, a tall Nubian who retrieved his weapon and, with a dancer's leap, placed himself in front of his prey.

Their eyes met, each filled with the other's death; talk was futile.

The Nubian swung his hatchet in circles. He was smiling, sure of his strength and his skill, obliging his opponent to back away.

Suti's back met the trunk of an acacia-tree. The Nubian raised his weapon, but Panther seized him round the neck. Underestimating her strength, he tried to push her away by elbowing her in the chest. Indifferent to pain, she put out one of his eyes with a stick. Roaring in agony, he brought down the hatchet, but Panther had let go, dropped to the ground and rolled clear.

Head first, Suti butted the man in the belly and knocked him flat on his back.

Panther instantly straddled his chest and forced her stick down across his throat. The Nubian's arms flailed, but he could not free himself. Suti allowed his mistress to finish her victory alone. Their enemy suffocated to death, his larynx crushed.

'Do you think he was on his own?' she asked anxiously.

Suti shook his head. 'Nubians usually hunt in groups.'

'I fear your beloved oasis may be about to become a battlefield.'

'You really are a demon – you're the one who's shattered my peace by attracting them here.'

'Shouldn't we leave as quickly as possible?'

'But supposing he was alone?'

'You said just the opposite a minute ago. Give up your illusions and let's go.'

'Go where?'

'North.'

'The Egyptian soldiers would arrest us – they must be deployed all over the region.'

'If you follow me, we'll avoid them and we'll get our our gold back, too.' In her excitement, Panther flung her arms round her lover. 'They'll have forgotten you. They'll think you're lost, or perhaps dead. We'll cross their lines, avoid the fortresses and get rich!'

The danger had excited the Libyan girl; only Suti's arms would calm her. He would gladly have answered her expectations, if he hadn't seen an unexpected movement at the summit of the great dune.

'Here are the others,' he whispered.

'How many?'

'I don't know; they're crawling forward.'

'Let's take the oryx's path.'

Panther was brought down to earth when she saw several Nubians crouching behind the rocks on the rounded summit. 'Then we'll head south.'

But that direction was blocked, too: the enemy had encircled the oasis.

'I've made only twenty arrows,' Suti reminded her, 'and that won't be enough.'

Panther's expression grew hard. 'I don't want to die.'

He held her close. 'I'll kill as many as I can, by climbing to the top of the tallest acacia-tree and shooting from there. I'll let one enter the oasis, then you kill him with the hatchet, take his quiver and bring it to me.'

'We haven't a chance of winning.'

'I trust you.' Suti kissed her, then quickly climbed his chosen tree.

From his perch up there, he could see the Nubians clearly. There were about fifty of them, some armed with clubs, others with bows and arrows. Escaping from them would be impossible. He would fight to the end and kill Panther before she could be raped and tortured. His last arrow would be for her.

Far behind the Nubians, on the crest of a dune, he spotted the oryx that had guided them. It was struggling against an increasingly fierce wind; tongues of sand were detaching themselves from the little mountain and flying up into the sky. Suddenly, the animal disappeared.

Three black warriors ran forward, roaring. Suti drew his bow, aimed instinctively and fired three times. The men fell, face forward, hit in the chest.

Three others followed them.

Suti hit two; the third, mad with rage, entered the oasis. He fired an arrow at Suti, but missed his target by a long way. Panther hurled herself on him, and the two entangled bodies tumbled out of Suti's field of vision. Not a single cry was uttered.

The trunk moved; someone was climbing up. Suti readied his bow.

A hand emerged from the leaves, holding a quiver full of arrows.

'I've got it!' cried Panther.

Suti hauled her up beside him, and found that she was shaking. 'Are you hurt?' he asked.

'I was faster than he was.'

They had no time to congratulate each other; another attack was being launched. Despite his rudimentary bow, Suti shot with great accuracy. But to Panther's surprise it took him two shots to hit an archer who was aiming at him.

'The wind's deflecting my arrows,' he explained.

The branches began to toss in the growing storm. The sky became copper-coloured, the air filled with dust. An ibis, caught by the wind, was almost flattened to the ground.

'Climb down,' ordered Suti.

The trees groaned and made sinister cracking noises; uprooted palms were being sucked up into a yellow whirlpool of sand.

When Suti reached the ground, a Nubian charged at him, axe raised.

The desert's breath was so powerful that it held back the attacker's arm, but even so the blade sank into the left shoulder of the Egyptian who, with his clenched fists, broke his enemy's nose. The raging wind tore them apart, and the Nubian disappeared.

Suti seized Panther's hand; if they escaped the Nubians, the desert's terrifying anger would not spare them.

In waves of unheard-of violence, the sand burnt their eyes and rooted them to the spot. Panther dropped her hatchet, Suti his bow; they crouched at the foot of a palm-tree, whose trunk they could scarcely make out. Neither they nor their attackers could move any further.

The wind howled, the ground shifted beneath their feet, the sky had disappeared. Clasped together, already covered with a winding-sheet of golden grains which whipped their skin, Suti and Panther felt as if they were lost in the middle of a furious ocean.

Closing his eyes, Suti thought of Pazair, his blood-brother. Why had he not come to his aid?

13

Kem walked along the quays in the port of Memphis, watching the unloading of merchandise and the loading of cargos of food for Upper Egypt, the Delta or foreign countries. The deliveries of salt had recommenced, and the people's rising anger had been appeased. Nevertheless, the big Nubian was still uneasy: there were strange and persistent rumours about Ramses' failing health and the country's decline.

He was also furious with himself. Why had he failed to identify the man who was trying to kill Pazair? At least the murderer could no longer get inside the tjaty's estate, which from now on would be under strict guard day and night, but Kem had no leads at all, and none of his informants had given him any useful clues. The criminal worked alone, without help, trusting no one. When would he at last make a mistake? When would he leave a significant trace behind him?

Unlike Kem, Killer was calm, though his sharp eyes took in every detail of the scenes unfolding around him. In front of the Pine House, the buildings that housed the scribes in charge of the transport of wood, Killer halted. Sensitive to the baboon's smallest reactions, Kem did not hurry him along.

Killer's red eyes fixed on a tall man dressed in a red woollen cloak who was hurrying aboard a large boat, her cargo protected by sheets of tough cloth. The man was obviously on edge: he was haranguing the sailors, ordering them to hurry up. It was an odd attitude to take at the start of a long voyage. Why was he irritating the dockmen instead of celebrating the rites of departure?

Kem entered the central building of the Pine House, where scribes were registering on wooden tablets all the details of the cargos and the movements of the boats. He made for one of his friends, a man from the Delta who enjoyed the good things in life.

'Where is that big boat over there going?' asked Kem.

'To Phoenicia.'

'What's she carrying?'

'Water-jars and water-skins.

'Is that the captain, the one who's in such a hurry?'

'Who do you mean?'

'The man in the red cloak.'

'He's the ship-owner.'

'Is he always so nervous?'

'No, he's usually a rather quiet fellow. Your baboon must have frightened him.'

'To whom does he report?'

'The Double White House.'

Kem left the Pine House, and saw that Killer had taken up position at the foot of the gangplank, preventing the owner from leaving the ship. The man tried to escape by jumping on to the quayside, at the risk of breaking his neck, but Killer seized him by the throat and flattened him out on the dock.

'Why are you so afraid?' asked Kem.

'He's going to strangle me!'

'Not if you answer my questions.'

'This boat isn't mine. Let me go.'

'You're responsible for the cargo. Why are you loading jars and water-skins in the Pine House sector?'

'All the other quays are full.'

'No, they aren't.'

Killer twisted the ship-owner's ear.

'Killer hates liars,' said Kem.

'The cargo covers . . . Roll them back.'

While Killer guarded his prisoner, Kem did so. He made a most surprising discovery: trunks of pine and cedar, planks of acacia wood and sycamore.

Kem felt a surge of joy: at last, Bel-Tran had put a foot wrong.

Neferet was resting on the terrace. Little by little she was recovering from the terrible shock she had suffered, though she still had nightmares about it. She had checked and rechecked the contents of her private workshop, terrified that the assassin might have poisoned other phials, too; but he had restricted himself to the one intended for Pazair.

The tjaty, closely shaven by an excellent barber, came out of the house. He kissed his wife tenderly, and asked, 'How do you feel this morning?'

'Much better. I'm going back to the hospital.'

'I've just had a message from Kem. He says he has good news.'

Neferet put her arms round his neck. 'Please, let yourself be guarded while you are travelling from place to place.'

'Don't worry. Kem's sent Killer to protect me.'

When Pazair got to his office, Kem was waiting for him. The big Nubian had lost his legendary calm, and was fingering his wooden nose in unheard-of agitation.

'We are holding Bel-Tran,' he told Pazair. 'I took the liberty of summoning him immediately. Five of my men are bringing him here.'

'Is there a solid case against him?'

'The evidence of my own eyes.'

Pazair was well versed in the laws regulating the trade in wood. Bel-Tran had indeed committed a serious offence, and one which carried a severe penalty.

However, Bel-Tran's quietly ironic manner betrayed no sign of anxiety. 'Why such a show of force?' he asked with astonishment. 'I'm not a bandit, as far as I know.'

'Sit down,' suggested Pazair.

'I can't – there's a mountain of work waiting for me.'

'Kem has just seized a cargo boat destined for Phoenicia. She was chartered by a ship-owner who reports to the Double White House – in other words, to you.'

'A lot of people do.'

'According to custom, cargos for Phoenicia consist of alabaster vases, crockery, pieces of linen, oxhides, rolls of papyrus, ropes, lentils and dried fish. In exchange, the Phoenicians send us the wood we lack.'

'You are not telling me anything new.'

'This boat would have carried cedar- and pine-trunks, and even planks cut from our acacias and sycamores, whose export is forbidden. In other words, you would have sent out again wood we had paid for, and we would have been short of wood for our buildings, for the masts set up before the doorways of our temples, and for our sarcophagi.'

Bel-Tran did not lose his composure. 'You know nothing about this affair. The planks were ordered by the Prince of Byblos for the coffins of his courtiers, because he admires the quality of our acacias and our sycamores. After all, Egyptian material is a guarantee of eternity, isn't it? To refuse him this gift would have been a grave insult and a political error, with many harmful consequences.'

'And what about the cedar-and pine-trunks?

'Being young, Tjaty, you are probably unfamiliar with the subtleties of our trade exchanges. Phoenicia undertakes to provide us with varieties which are resistant to fungi and insects. These are not, so I ordered the consignment to be sent back. Specialists have confirmed those facts; the documents are at your disposal.'

'Experts from the Double White House, I presume.'

'By common consent, they are the best. May I leave now?'

'I am not a fool, Bel-Tran. You organized an illegal trade with Phoenicia, hoping to make big profits and to benefit from the support of one of our most important trading partners. I am cutting off that branch. From now on, imports of wood will come solely within my remit.'

'As you wish. But if you go on like this you'll soon collapse under the weight of all your responsibilities. Now, call me a travelling-chair, please. I'm in a hurry.'

Kem was devastated. 'I made you look a fool – I'm very sorry indeed.'

'Not all,' said Pazair. 'Thanks to you, we've taken away one of his powers.'

'The monster has so many heads . . . How many must we cut off before we weaken it?'

'As many as necessary. I'm drawing up a decree calling upon the heads of all the provinces to plant dozens of trees so that people can rest in their shade. Moreover, no tree is to be cut down without my authorization.'

'What are you hoping for?

'To restore confidence to the people, who are being deluged by rumours, and to indicate to them that the future is as bright as a tree's foliage.'

'Do you believe that yourself?'

'Do you doubt it?'

'Being tjaty of Egypt, you can't lie. Bel-Tran is eyeing the throne, isn't he?'

Pazair did not answer.

'I understand that your lips are sealed, but you can't stop me heeding my own intuition. You're fighting a battle to the death – and you stand no chance of winning. Right from the beginning this affair has been rotten, and we're bound hand and foot. I don't know why, but I'll go on fighting beside you.'

On his way home, Bel-Tran congratulated himself on his foresight. He had surrounded himself with strong defences, and had bribed enough officials to ensure that he could not be toppled, no matter who attacked, no matter how. The tjaty had failed, and would fail again. Even if he did manage to uncover some of Bel-Tran's schemes, he would win only paltry victories.

Bel-Tran was followed by three servants bearing gifts for Silkis: a costly ointment for oiling and perfuming the hair of her wigs; another, made from powdered alabaster, honey and red natron, which would make her skin very soft; and a large quantity of the best-quality cumin, a remedy for indigestion and colic.

When he reached home, he was met not by his wife but by her personal maid. The girl looked concerned: it was Silkis who should have welcomed him and massaged his feet.

'Where is my wife?' he asked.

'She is in bed, my lord.'

'What's the matter with her now?'

'She has pains in her belly.'

'What have you given her?'

'What she asked for, my lord: a little pyramid stuffed with dates, and an infusion of coriander. But they don't seem to be working.'

The bedchamber had been ventilated and fumigated. Silkis, who was very pale, was twisting and turning in pain. When she saw her husband, she tried to smile.

He did not smile back. 'Have you been overeating again?'

'No, really – all I had was one tiny pastry. But the pain's getting worse, darling.'

'Tomorrow evening, you must be out of bed and in your best looks. I have invited several provincial leaders here, and you must do me honour.'

'Neferet would make me better.'

'I told you to forget about that woman.'

'But you promised me—'

'I promised you nothing. Pazair won't give up: he's fighting as fiercely as ever – that puppet! Asking his wife for help would be a show of weakness on our part, and I won't do it.'

'Not even to save me?'

'You aren't very ill – it's just a temporary indisposition. I shall send for the doctors at once. In the meantime, concentrate on getting well for tomorrow so that you can use your charms on our guests.'

Neferet was sitting in the garden, talking with a voluble old man with sun-browned, deeply furrowed skin. He presented her with a terracotta jar, and she bent over it with interest.

As he went towards them, Pazair recognised the old bee-keeper who had been unjustly sentenced to prison and who had helped Pazair escape.

The old man stood up and greeted him. 'Tjaty of Egypt! What a pleasure to see you again. Getting in here wasn't easy, I must say. I was asked a thousand questions, my identity was checked, and they even inspected my pots of honey.'

'How are your bees?'

'Extremely well – that's why I am here. Just you taste this.'

The gods, who were often made bitter by humans' behaviour, recovered their gaiety by eating honey, according to storytellers. When Ra's tears fell to earth, they had been transformed into bees, magicians who could transform pollen into edible gold.

The flavour astonished Pazair.

'Never seen a harvest like it,' said the bee-keeper, 'for quantity and quality.'

'The hospitals will all be supplied,' put in Neferet, 'and we'll still have plenty in reserve.'

A gentle substance, honey was used in eye treatments and to treat blood-vessels and the lungs; it was also used for women's problems, and was incorporated into numerous medicines. And was used in most dressings.

'I only hope the kingdom's principal doctor won't be cruelly disappointed,' the old man went on.

'Why do you say that?' asked Pazair.

'News travels fast. Since word of the amazing harvest got round, the area of the desert where I and my assistants work hasn't been as peaceful as it used to be. We're secretly watched while we take the liquid sunshine out of the hives, put it in jars and seal the jars with wax. When all the honey's been collected, I think it's going to be stolen.'

'Aren't there guards watching over you?'

'Yes, but there aren't enough of them. My honey's worth an absolute fortune, and they won't be able to protect it.'

Of course, thought Pazair: Bel-Tran must have been told about the exceptional yield of honey. Depriving the hospitals of such a vital ingredient of medicine would lead to a grave crisis.

'I shall inform Kem – the delivery will take place in complete safety.'

'Do you know what day it is?' asked Neferet.

Pazair said nothing.

'It's the eve of the Garden Festival.'

The tjaty's face lit up. 'Hathor speaks through you. We shall give much happiness.'

On the morning of the Garden Festival, every betrothed girl and young wife planted a sycamore-tree in her garden. In town and village squares, and beside the river, gifts of cakes and bunches of flowers were exchanged, and everyone drank beer. After rubbing themselves with scented lotion, the beautiful girls danced to the sound of flutes, harps and tambourines. Boys and girls talked of love, and the old folk turned a blind eye.

When scribes handed the mayors jars of honey, the names of the tjaty and the king were hailed: the bee was one of the symbols of Pharaoh. For most families the edible gold was unaffordable, an almost impossible dream, but that dream would be realized and relished on this festival day, which was being celebrated under Ramses' protection.

From their terrace, Neferet and Pazair listened in delight to the echoes of the songs and dances. The armed thieves who had been preparing to attack the honey caravans had been ambushed and captured. The old bee-keeper was feasting with his friends, proclaiming loudly that the country was well governed and that the festival honey would ward off bad luck.

14

The oasis had been utterly destroyed. The palm-trees had been decapitated, the acacias torn apart, their trunks split and their branches ripped off; the well was blocked, the dunes disembowelled, and little mountains of sand covered the paths. All around was desolation.

When Suti forced his eyes open, he recognized nothing of his haven of peace. So much yellow dust was floating in the air that the light could not shine through, and he wondered at first if he had descended to the shadowy realms that the sun never reached.

Pain awoke in his left shoulder, where the hatchet-blade had caught it. He stretched his legs, which were so painful that he thought they were broken – fortunately, they were only scratched. Beside him lay the bodies of two Nubians, who had been crushed by the trunk of a palm tree. One of them, stiff as a board, was still brandishing his dagger.

Panther! Although his thoughts were confused, Suti remembered the Nubians' attack, the beginning of the storm, the ferocity of the wind, the desert's sudden madness. One minute she had been beside him, the next a savage gust of wind had separated them. Where was she? On all fours, gasping for breath, he began digging.

He could not find her. But he refused to give up. He would not leave this cursed place without the woman to whom he had given back her freedom.

He searched every corner of the oasis, often having to push aside other Nubian corpses. Then, at last, he heaved aside the crown of a big palm-tree, and saw her. Panther looked like a young girl sleeping, dreaming of a handsome suitor. There was no trace of injury on her naked body, but she had a huge lump on the back of her neck. Suti rubbed her eyes and gently brought her back to consciousness.

'Suti,' she said faintly. 'Thanks be to the gods that you're alive.'

'Don't worry, you're not badly hurt, just stunned.'

'My arms, my legs!'

'They hurt, I know, but they aren't broken.'

She threw her arms round him, like a child. 'Let's get away from here, quickly.'

'We can't, not without water.'

For long hours, Suti and Panther toiled to unblock the well, and in the end they had enough silty, bitter-tasting water to fill two water-skins; then they made a new bow and fifty arrows from the wood of the broken trees. After a restorative sleep, wrapped against the night cold in faded finery taken from the corpses, they set off northwards, under the protection of the starry night.

Panther's resilience amazed Suti. Their narrow escape from death had given her a new energy, a determination to win back her gold and become a rich woman, respectable and respected, able to satisfy all her wishes. She believed in no destiny but the one she made for herself, moment after moment, and gleefully tore off the fabric of her existence, proclaiming the nakedness of her soul with perfect shamelessness. She feared nothing except her own fear, which she stifled ruthlesssly.

She permitted only brief stops, kept a close watch on the water rations, and chose their direction and paths, which led through a jumble of rocks and dunes. Suti let himself be guided, enthralled by the chaotic landscape; it acted on him like an enchantment and filled him with its magic. Resisting it was pointless; wind, sun and heat created a land whose every line and curve he loved.

Panther was constantly on the alert, and as they got closer to the Egyptian lines she redoubled her vigilance. Suti, though, grew uneasy: he was moving further and further away from his true freedom, the immensity where he loved to live with the nobility of the oryx.

As they were filling their water-skins at a well marked by a circle of stones, more than fifty Nubian warriors, armed with clubs, short swords, bows and slings suddenly appeared in a circle round the well. Panther and Suti were horrified: neither had heard them approach.

Panther clenched her fists. She could not bear to fail like this. 'Let's fight,' she murmured.

'It's hopeless.'

'Then what do you suggest?'

Suti look slowly around. If they tried to run for it, they'd stand no chance – he wouldn't even have time to draw his bow.

He said, 'The gods forbid suicide, but if you like I'll strangle you before they smash my head. If they take you alive, they'll all rape you in the vilest way.'

'I'll kill them all.'

The circle round them tightened.

Suti decided to charge at two huge warriors who were advancing side by side; at least he'd die fighting.

Before he could move, an old Nubian addressed him. 'Was it you who wiped out our brothers?'

'I, and the desert.'

'They were brave men.'

'So am I.'

'How did you do it?'

'My bow saved me.'

'You're lying.'

'Try me – I'll soon show you.'

'Who are you?' asked the old Nubian.

'My name is Suti.'

'Are you Egyptian?'

'Yes.'

'What are you doing here in our land?'

'I escaped from the fortress at Tjaru.'

'Escaped?'

'I was a prisoner there.'

'You're lying again.'

'I was chained to a rock in the middle of the Nile, to act as bait for men like you.'

'You're a spy, aren't you?' said the Nubian angrily.

'No, I'm not. I was hiding in the oasis when your men attacked it.'

'If the great storm hadn't come, they'd have defeated you.'

'But they're dead, and I'm still alive.'

'Proud of yourself, aren't you?'

'If I could fight you one by one, I'd prove my pride is justified.'

The Nubian looked around at his fellow countrymen. 'This defiance is contemptible, and you'll pay for it. You killed our leader at the oasis, and I, an old man, have had to take the head of our tribe.'

'Let me fight your best warrior, and give me back my freedom if I win.'

'Fight them all.'

'You're a coward,' sneered Suti.

A stone from a slingshot whizzed through the air and hit Suti on the temple; semi-conscious, he collapsed. The two big Nubians went over to Panther, who glared at them defiantly and did not move a muscle. They tore off her clothes and the strip of fabric concealing her hair.

Stunned, they drew back.

Panther did not try to conceal her breasts, or the golden curls of her sex. Arms hanging loosely at her sides, she walked forward as regally as a queen.

The Nubians bowed.

The rites in honour of the golden-haired goddess lasted all night. The Nubians had recognized the terrifying creature whose power had been spoken of by the ancestors. She came from far-off Libya, and if angered she could spread disease, cataclysms and famine. To appease her, the Nubians offered her date-wine, snake cooked on hot coals, and fresh garlic, which would protect against snakebite and scorpion stings. They danced round Panther, who had been crowned with palm-leaves and anointed with scented oil; prayers passed down from age to age were addressed to her.

Suti was forgotten. Like the others, he was merely the servant of the goddess, which part Panther played to perfection.

When the celebrations were over, she took command of the little band, and immediately gave orders that they should circle round the fortress of Tjaru and follow a track towards the north. As they neared Tjaru she sent out scouts who, with great surprise, reported that the Egyptian soldiers had gone to earth behind their walls and had sent out no patrols for several days.

They halted at the foot of a rocky peak, which offered shelter from the sun and the wind, and Panther stepped down from her travelling-chair, which was carried by four enthusiastic fellows.

Suti went over to her and bowed. 'I daren't raise my eyes to look at you.'

'Just as well – they'd disembowel you.'

'I can't bear this situation.'

'We're on the right road.'

'But not in the right way.'

'Just be patient.'

'That's not in my nature.'

'A taste of slavery will improve your nature a lot.'

'Don't count on it.'

Panther smiled. 'No one can escape the power of the golden-haired goddess.'

Furious, Suti withdrew.

After some thought, he decided to learn the use of the slingshot from his new companions as they travelled. He soon became very skilful, and thus earned their respect. A few sessions of unarmed combat, which he won, confirmed their good opinion, and it was firmly established by a demonstration of his prowess at archery. A friendship between warriors was born.

Most evenings were passed the same way: after their meal, the Nubians talked about the golden goddess, who had come to teach them music, dancing and the joys of love. One evening, though, while the storytellers were embroidering the myth, Suti saw two men go apart from the main group and light a fire. He went over to watch. Over the fire they hung a pot containing glue made from antelope fat. When it was hot enough, the glue became runny. The first man dipped in a brush, and the second handed him an ebony waist-plate, which the first meticulously brushed with glue. Suti yawned. Just as he was walking away, something gleamed in the darkness. Intrigued, he retraced his steps. The man with the brush, who was concentrating hard, was applying something to the buckle.

Suti bent closer. His eyes had not deceived him: it really was gold leaf.

'Where did you get that?' he asked.

'It was a present from our chief.'

'And where did he get it?

'When he came back from the Lost City, he brought back jewels and thin sheets of gold like this.'

'Do you know where the Lost City is?'

'I don't, but our leader does.'

Suti woke the old man, and made him draw a map in the sand. Then he gathered the whole band together round the fire.

'Listen to me, all of you,' he said. 'I was a chariot officer in the Egyptian army. I know how to use the great bow, and I have killed dozens of sand-travellers and meted out justice by killing a treacherous general. But my country showed me no gratitude for any of that, so now all I want is to become rich and powerful. This tribe needs a chief, a man who is battle-hardened and a proven victor. I am that man. If you follow me, the gods will smile on you.'

Suti's impassioned face, his long hair, his height and his bearing impressed the Nubians, but before they could react the old warrior cut in: 'You killed our chief.'

'I was stronger than he. The law of the desert does not spare the weak.'

'It is up to us to choose our next chief.'

'I shall lead you to the Lost City, and we'll kill anyone who tries to stop us. You have no right to keep this secret for yourself. Soon our tribe will be the most respected in the whole of Nubia.'

'Our chief went to the city alone.'

'We shall go together,' countered Suti, 'and you'll all have plenty of gold.'

Suti's supporters and opponents began to debate. The old man's influence was such that Suti thought defeat looked certain. So he seized Panther and, with a brutal gesture, tore off her clothes. The flames lit up her fair hair.

'See?' he shouted. 'She doesn't resist me. I'm the only one who can be her lover. Unless you accept me as chief, she will unleash a new sandstorm, and you'll all die.'

Suti knew the Libyan girl held his fate in her hands. If she rejected him, the Nubians would know he was boasting and would slaughter him. Now that she had been raised to the rank of goddess, had she grown drunk with vanity?

Panther pulled free. The Nubians warriors pointed their arrows and daggers at Suti.

He cursed silently. He'd been wrong to trust a Libyan. Still, at least he would die gazing at a beautiful woman.

With the grace of a wild cat, Panther lay down beside the fire and held out her arms to him.

'Come,' she said, smiling.

15

Pazair awoke with a jolt. He had been dreaming about a monster with a hundred heads and with countless clawed feet which cut into the stones of the Great Pyramid and tried to topple it over. Its belly was a human face: that of Bel-Tran. Covered in sweat despite the chill of the winter night, the tjaty fingered the wooden frame of his bed, with its base made from plaited vegetable ropes, and its feet in the form of lions' heads.

He turned towards Neferet's bed. It was empty.

Pushing back the fine mesh that kept mosquitoes off, he stood up, put on a cloak and opened the window that looked out on to the garden. The gentle sun was awakening trees and flowers, and birds were singing. He saw Neferet, wrapped in a thick blanket, standing barefoot in the dew.

She blended into the dawn, surrounded by its light. Two falcons, soaring up from the ship of Ra, flew around her when she laid an offering of lotus-flowers on the ancestors' altar, in memory of Branir. Making the space fertile, linking Egypt to the celestial ship, the birds of prey flew back to its prow, beyond the sight of men.

When the rite was over, Pazair went out into the garden and put an arm round his wife.

'You are the star of the morning, at the dawn of a happy day. No woman has a radiance like yours, and your eyes are as soft as your lips. Why are you so beautiful? Your hair has captured the brightness of Hathor herself. I love you, Neferet, as no one has ever loved before.'

In the amorous dawn, they made love.

Standing at the prow of the boat as she headed towards Karnak, Pazair looked admiringly out across his country, where the marriage rites of the sun and the water were celebrated with such splendour.

On the banks, the peasants were maintaining the irrigation channels while a body of specialists was cleaning out the canals, Egypt's vital arteries. The crowns of the palm-trees offered generous shade to the men lovingly bending over the black, fertile earth. Seeing the tjaty's boat pass by, the children ran along the banks and towpaths, shouting and waving enthusiastically.

Killer sat on the roof of the central cabin, guarding Pazair. Kem brought the tjaty some fresh onions.

Pazair thanked him and asked, 'Anything new on the shadow-eater?'

'No, nothing.'

'What about Tapeni?'

'She had a meeting with Bel-Tran.'

'So she's found a new ally . . .'

'We should be wary of her,' said Kem. 'She could do you more than a little harm.'

Pazair sighed. 'Yet another enemy.'

'Does that worry you?'

'Thanks to the gods, ignorance serves me as courage.'

'It would be fairer to say that you have no choice.'

Pazair shook his head, and changed the subject. 'I take it all is quiet at the hospital?'

'Yes – your wife can work in peace.'

'She must reform the system of caring for the people's health as quickly as possible. Nebamon cared little about it, and serious inequalities have opened up.' He sighed again. 'Neferet's office and mine are sometimes very burdensome, and we weren't properly prepared for them.'

'Prepared?' said Kem. 'How do you think I feel, becoming commander of the very guards who cut off my nose?'

The wind was blowing hard, and was against the current, so sometimes the sailors used their oars, though they did not take down the mast or the rectangular sail, which was tall and narrow. The captain, who was well used to sailing on the Nile all year round, knew its dangers and how to use the weakest breeze to convey his illustrious travellers swiftly. The vessel's design, with its keel-less hull and raised bow and stern, had been perfected by Pharaoh's shipwrights so that it would glide easily over the waves.

'My friend,' said Kem, 'I can't help wondering when the assassin will strike again.'

'Don't worry about it.'

'But I do. It's become a personal matter – that demon is soiling my honour.'

'Well, have had you any news of Suti?'

'The order to sound the alert definitely reached Tjaru. The soldiers are taking refuge in the fortress until further orders.'

'Was he able to escape?'

'According to the official reports no one's missing, but I have had some rather odd information. A hot-headed prisoner had apparently been chained to a rock in the middle of the Nile, to serve as a lure for Nubian looters.'

'It must have been Suti.'

'In that case, don't be hopeful.'

'He'll find a way out of his situation – he'd escape from the kingdom of darkness itself.'

The tjaty's thoughts flew to his spiritual brother, then communed with the magnificent Theban landscape. The cultivated strip on either side of the river was the widest and the most luxuriant in the Nile Valley. More than seventy villages worked for the immense Temple of Karnak, which employed no fewer than eighty thousand people – priests, craftsmen and peasants. But even those riches were as nothing before the majesty of the area consecrated to Amon, which was surrounded by a brick curtain-wall that undulated like a wave.

When the boat reached Karnak, the High Priest's head steward and other senior household officials greeted the tjaty at the landing-stage. After formal greetings had been exchanged, they offered to escort Pazair to the office of High Priest Kani. However, Pazair said he would rather go alone, and he set off along the central aisle of the vast pillared hall, which only those initiated into the great mysteries might enter. Kem and Killer stayed outside the great double golden doors, which were opened on the occasion of great festivals, when Amon's ship left the shrine to flood the earth with its light.

Pazair meditated for a long time before a sublime depiction of the god Thoth, whose elongated arms provided the basic measurement used by the overseer of works. He read the columns of hieroglyphs and deciphered the message of the god of knowledge: it urged his worshippers to respect the proportions that presided over the birth of all life.

It was this harmony that the tjaty must maintain in daily life, so that Egypt might be the mirror of heaven; it was this harmony that the conspirators wanted to destroy, replacing it with an ice-cold monster ready to torture men the better to gorge itself on material goods. In truth, Bel-Tran and his allies were a new race, more fearsome than the cruellest invaders.

Pazair left the pillared hall, and allowed himself a moment to enjoy the perfect blue of the sky over Karnak. He paused in the little open-air courtyard, at the centre of which a granite offering-table marked the birth of the temple, many years before. Sacred above all others, it was constantly covered with flowers. Why must he tear himself away from this profound, otherworldly peace?

'I am happy to see you again, Tjaty.' Shaven-headed and carrying a golden cane, Kani bowed to Pazair.

'It is I who should bow to you,' protested Pazair.

'No so, Tjaty. I owe you respect, for the tjaty is the eyes and ears of Pharaoh.'

'May they see and hear acutely.'

'You look troubled.'

'I have come to ask for help from the High Priest of Karnak.'

Kani's face fell. 'I was going to beg you for yours.'

'What is happening?'

'Grave problems, I fear. I would like to show you the temple, which has just been restored.'

Kani and Pazair passed through one of the gates into the enclosure of Amon, walked along the curtain-wall, greeted painters and sculptors at work, and went into a modest sandstone shrine to Ma'at. It contained two stone benches where the tjaty sat when judging a senior priest or priestess.

As soon as they were inside, Kani said, 'I am a simple man. I have not forgotten that it was your master, Branir, who should have reigned over Karnak.'

'Branir was murdered, and Pharaoh chose you.'

'He may have made a bad choice.'

Never had Pazair seen the old man so dejected. Before being raised to the dignity of supreme ruler of the biggest city-temple in Egypt, Kani had been a gardener, accustomed to dealing with the caprices of nature and the pitiless realities of the earth. Despite his humble origins, he had nevertheless imposed himself upon his subordinates and the college of priests, and he enjoyed general respect.

Kani went on, 'I am unworthy of my office, but I shall not try to escape from my responsibilities. Before long I shall appear in this very place before your court, and you will have to condemn me.'

'This trial is proceeding far too quickly!' said Pazair. 'Will you allow me to investigate?'

Kani sat down on one of the benches. 'You won't have much difficulty. All you need do is consult the recent archives: in only a few months, I have brought Karnak close to ruin.'

'How?'

'Just examine the returns for cereals, dairy produce, fruit . . . Where food is concerned, my management of our resources has been an appalling failure.'

Pazair was troubled. 'Could someone be deceiving you about it?'

'No, the reports are accurate.'

'What has the weather been like?'

'The annual flood was abundant, and there were no plagues of insects to destroy the crops.'

'Then what has caused this disaster?'

'My incompetence,' said Kani. 'I wanted to tell you straight away, so that you can alert the king.'

'There is no hurry.'

'The truth will come out. As you can see, my help will be no use to you. I shall soon be nothing but an old, despised man.'

The tjaty shut himself away in the archive chamber of the Temple of Karnak and compared Kani's records with those of his predecessors. The difference shattered him.

He soon became certain of one thing: someone was trying to ruin Kani's reputation and force him to resign. His replacement was bound to be someone hostile to Ramses – and without Karnak's support it would be impossible to control Egypt. But who would have dreamt that Bel-Tran and his underlings would dare attack a High Priest whose integrity was so widely known? The consequences would be devasting: Kani would be universally blamed, and Karnak, Luxor and the temples of the west bank would soon find themselves short of offerings. The rites would be poorly celebrated, and everywhere people would shout the name of the man responsible, Kani the incompetent.

Despair overwhelmed Pazair. He had come to ask a friend for help, but instead would be forced to incriminate him.

He jumped as someone tapped him on the shoulder.

'Stop poring over your papyri,' advised Kem, 'and let's get out into the fields.'

The first villages they inspected, those nearest the great temple, were living their normal, peaceful lives, following the eternal rhythm of the seasons. The two men questioned the village headmen and field scribes, but learnt of nothing abnormal. After three days of fruitless investigations, the tjaty's thoughts returned to the evidence. He must go back to Memphis and explain the situation to the king, before opening the trial of High Priest Kani. Reluctantly, he told Kem of his decision.

But the wind was so strong that it would have been unsafe to sail. Kem suggested that they spend the extra day investigating and the two men, the baboon and their escort went to a village at some distance from the temple, on the far edge of the province of Kebet.

When they arrived, they found that here, as elsewhere, the peasants were getting on with their livelihoods, while their wives took care of the children and prepared the meals. On the banks of the Nile, a washerman was at work; in the shade of a sycamore, a country doctor was seeing his patients. Everything seemed normal.

But Killer became edgy; his nostrils quivered, and he scratched at the ground.

'What has he detected?' asked Pazair.

'Harmful energies,' said Kem. 'We haven't made the journey for nothing.'

16

The village headman was a pot-bellied man of around fifty, the father of five children. He was affable and courteous when he performed the duties of his office, which he had inherited from his father.

He was informed at once of the arrival of a small group of strangers, and regretfully interrupted his afternoon nap. Accompanied by a servant carrying a fan of palm-leaves to protect his bald head from the sun, he went to meet the unexpected visitors.

When his gaze encountered that of an enormous, red-eyed baboon, he stopped in his tracks.

'Greetings, my friends,' he said uncertainly.

'And greetings to you,' said a tall, imposing Nubian.

'Is that monkey tame?'

'He is an official member of Memphis's security guards.'

'Ah . . . and you are?'

'I am Kem, commander of the guards, and this is Pazair, tjaty of Egypt.'

Dumbfounded, the headman pulled in his stomach and bowed as low as he could, hands stretched out before him in a sign of veneration.

'What an honour,' he gabbled, 'what an honour! Such a humble village, welcoming the tjaty . . . What an honour!'

As he straightened up, the headman began a flow of sugary compliments, which stopped abruptly when Killer growled.

'Commander, are you absolutely sure you can keep that animal under control?'

'Except when he smells an evildoer.'

'Fortunately, there aren't any in my little village.'

The tall, deep-voiced Nubian seemed as fearsome as his baboon. The headman had heard stories about this strange commander: he had little or no interest in administrative work, but was so close to the common people that no criminal ever escaped him for long. Seeing him here, on the headman's own territory, was a decidedly unpleasant surprise. And the tjaty! Too young, too serious – and bound to be too inquisitive. Pazair's natural dignity, his direct, piercing look, the straightness which which he held himself: these things did not bode well.

'Forgive my astonishment,' said the headman, 'but such eminent persons in this insignificant little village . . .'

'Your fields extend as far as the eye can see,' observed Kem, 'and they are extremely well irrigated.'

'Please do not judge by appearances, Commander. In this area the earth is very hard, so it's difficult to work – my poor ploughmen break their backs.'

'Why? Last year's flood was excellent.'

'We were unlucky. It was too strong here, and our irrigation pools were in poor condition.'

'But you had an excellent harvest, from what I hear.'

'Alas, I'm afraid you have been misinformed. It was much smaller than the year before.'

'What about the vines?'

'Oh, such a disappointment! Clouds of insects attacked both the leaves and the grapes.'

'No other villages in this area shared your bad luck,' said Pazair.

The tjaty's voice was heavy with suspicion; the headman had not expected such a tone.

'Perhaps my colleagues were boasting?' he said. 'Perhaps my poor village was the victim of fate?'

'What about livestock?'

'A lot died of sicknesses. An animal-doctor did come, but it was too late. This place is very remote, and—'

'The earthen road is in excellent condition,' objected Kem. 'The officials appointed by Karnak see that it is well maintained.'

The headman hastily changed the subject. 'Although our resources are meagre, it is an immense privilege to invite you to eat your midday meal with us. I am sure you will forgive the frugal fare – it comes with our heartfelt welcome.'

No one could violate the laws of hospitality. Kem accepted in the tjaty's name, and the headman sent his servant to inform the cook.

As the headman escorted them to his house, Pazair noted that the village looked very prosperous: several white housefronts had just been repainted, the cattle and donkeys had shining coats and plump bellies, the children wore new clothes. At the corners of the pleasantly clean streets, there were statuettes of the gods; in the main square, opposite the headman's office, were a fine bread oven and a large mill, which was obviously almost new.

'Congratulations on the way you run things,' said Pazair. 'Your people lack for nothing, and this is the prettiest village I have had the privilege of seeing in a long time.'

'You honour us too much, too much! Please, come in.'

The house's size, number of rooms and decoration would have befitted a Memphis noble. The important visitors were greeted by the headman's wife, who bowed her head and laid her right hand on her chest – she had hastily painted her face and put on an elegant dress – and by all five children.

They sat down on best-quality mats and ate sweet onions, cucumbers, beans, leeks, dried fish, grilled beef ribs, goat's cheese, watermelon and cakes topped with carob paste. Red wine with a delicious aroma accompanied the food. The headman tucked into each dish with gusto.

'That was a delicious meal and a notable welcome,' said Pazair when they had finished eating.

'Oh, my lord,' said the headman, 'it's such an honour to have you here.'

'May we consult the field scribe?'

'I'm sorry, my lord, but he's away. He's visiting his family, to the north of Memphis, and won't be back for a week.'

'His records must be accessible.'

'I'm afraid not. He has locked his office, and of course I cannot—'

'Well I can.'

'You are the tjaty, of course, but would it not be a—' The headman broke off, afraid of saying something highly inappropriate. 'My lord, it's a long way to Thebes, and the sun sets early at this time of year. Consulting those boring scrolls might delay you till after dark.'

Killer, who had been sitting gnawing a rib of beef, broke the bone; the crack made the headman jump.

'Where are they?' insisted Pazair.

'Well . . . I don't know now. The scribe must have taken them with him.'

Killer stood up. On his feet, he looked even bigger and more dangerous, and his red eyes glared at the headman, whose hands began to shake.

'Please, Commander, tie him up,' he quavered.

'The archives,' ordered Kem, 'or I can't answer for his actions.'

The headman's wife fell to her knees in front of her husband. 'Tell them the truth, I beg you!'

'I . . . I have the scrolls here,' he admitted. 'I'll go and get them.'

'Killer and I will accompany you. We can help you carry them.'

The three soon returned and set a heap of papyri on the table in front of Pazair.

The headman unrolled some of them. 'Everything's in order, my lord,' he muttered, 'and the observations were all made on the correct dates – the reports are very dull.'

'Let me read in peace,' demanded Pazair.

Looking feverish, the headman went back to his seat; his wife left the room.

The pernickety field scribe had gone over the numbers of livestock and sacks of cereals several times. He had given not only the names of the owners but also those of the animals, plus their weight and their state of health. The sections concerning fruit and vegetables were just as detailed. General conclusions were written in red: in every area of production the results were excellent, much better than average.

Perplexed, the tjaty did a simple calculation. The area of agricultural land was such that its wealth almost made up for the deficit Kani would be accused of, so why did it not feature in his records?

'I attach great importance to respect for other people,' he declared.

The headman nodded.

'But if those other people persist in concealing the truth, they are no longer worthy of respect. Is that not true of you?'

'I've told you everything, my lord.'

'I dislike using harsh methods, but in certain circumstances, when urgency demands it, a judge must force himself to do so.'

As if he had read the tjaty's thoughts, Killer leapt at the headman, took him by the throat and pulled his head back.

'Stop him! He's breaking my neck!'

'Where are the rest of the scrolls?' asked Kem calmly.

'I haven't got anything else – nothing at all!'

Kem turned to Pazair. 'I suggest we go for a walk while Killer conducts the interrogation as he sees fit.'

'Don't leave me!' gasped the headman.

'The rest of the scrolls,' repeated Kem.

'Tell him to take his hands off me first.'

The baboon relaxed its grip, and the headman rubbed his painful neck.

'You're behaving like savages,' he complained. 'I reject this arbitrary judgment, and I condemn this unspeakable act, this torture inflicted on a village headman.'

'I shall formally charge you with concealing official documents,' said Pazair.

The threat made the headman blanch. 'If I give you the rest, I demand that you recognize my innocence.'

'What crime have you committed?'

'I acted for the common good.'

From a chest used to store plates and dishes, the headman took a sealed papyrus. His expression had changed: it was no longer afraid but fierce and cold. 'Very well, look!'

The scroll indicated that the village's riches had been delivered to the capital of the Kebet province. The field scribe had signed and dated it.

'But this village is part of the Karnak estate,' Pazair reminded him.

'You have been misinformed, Tjaty.'

'It is shown in the list of the High Priest's properties.'

'Old Kani's as ignorant as you are. His list doesn't show the real state of affairs, the land register does. Go to Thebes and look at it, and you'll see that my village comes under the jurisdiction of Kebet, not the Temple of Karnak. The boundaries prove it. I'm going to lay a complaint against you for causing me bodily harm – you'll have to arrange your own trial, Tjaty Pazair.'

17

The guard at the land registry office in Thebes was awoken with a start by an unusual sound. At first he thought he must have been dreaming, but then he heard someone hammering on the door.

'Who is it?' he shouted.

'The commander of the Memphis security guards, accompanied by the tjaty,' said a deep voice.

'I hate practical jokes, especially in the middle of the night. Go away, or you'll regret it.'

'You'd do better to open up at once.'

'Go away, or I'll call my colleagues.'

'By all means do so. They can help us break down the door.'

The guard wondered; he looked out of a window with stone cross-pieces and, by the light of the full moon, made out the shapes of a huge Nubian man and an enormous baboon. It must be Kem and Killer! He had heard all about that fearsome pair: their reputation had spread throughout Egypt. Then the man coming forward to join them must be the tjaty himself!

He slid the bolt open. 'Forgive me, but this is so unexpected . . .'

'Light the lamps,' ordered Kem. 'The tjaty wishes to examine the maps.'

'I think I had better inform the director.'

'Yes, do. Bring him here.'

When he arrived, the director's face was screwed up in anger, but he soon calmed down when he realized that the guard had not been lying. The tjaty, Egypt's first minister, really was there, in his registry, even if it was at an unexpected hour of the night! He suddenly became obsequious and eager to help.

'Which maps do you wish to consult?' he asked.

'Those showing the properties belonging to the Temple of Karnak,' said Pazair.

'My lord, I warn you, they're enormous.'

'Let's start with the most distant villages.'

'To the north or the south?'

'The north.'

'Small or large?'

'The largest.'

The director spread out the maps on long wooden tables. The land registry scribes had shown the boundaries of each piece of land, the canals, and the settlements.

But Pazair looked in vain for the village he had just visited. 'Are these plans up to date?' he asked.

'Of course, my lord,' said the director.

'Have they been altered recently?'

'Yes, at the request of three village headmen.'

'Why?'

'The Nile flood had swept away the boundary stones, so a new survey was needed. An experienced man carried out the work, and my scribes took account of his observations.'

'He has cut off the Karnak estate,' Pazair pointed out.

'That is not for me to judge. I confine myself to registering land.'

'Did you by any chance forget to inform High Priest Kani?'

The director moved away from the lamp, so that his face was hidden in the shadows. 'I was just about to send him a full report.'

'And why has there been such a deplorable delay?'

'My lord, I'm very short of staff, and—'

'What is the name of the scribe who did the survey?'

'Sumenu.'

'Where does he live?'

The director hesitated, then said, 'He isn't from here.'

'Not from Thebes?'

'No, he came here from Memphis.'

'Who sent him?'

'My lord, it was the royal palace, of course.'

On the processional route leading to the Temple of Karnak, pink and white laurels provided walkers with an enchanting sight, whose gentle sweetness lessened the austerity of the monumental wall that encircled the sacred area. High Priest Kani had agreed to leave his retreat to speak with Pazair. The two most powerful men in Egypt after Pharaoh walked slowly between the two lines of protective sphinxes.

'My investigation is progressing,' said Pazair.

'What good will it do?'

'It will show that you are innocent.'

'But I'm not.'

'You were deceived.'

Kani shook his head. 'I deceived myself about my abilities.'

'No, you didn't. The three villages furthest away from the temple delivered their produce to Kebet. That's why it doesn't show in your records.'

'Do they come under Karnak's jurisdiction?'

'The land register was altered after the last flood.'

'Without consulting me?'

'At the instigation of a surveyor from Memphis.'

'That's inconceivable!'

'A messenger has just left for Memphis with orders to bring back the person responsible, a scribe named Sumenu.'

'But what can be done, if it was Ramses himself who took the villages away from me?'

Meditating on the banks of the sacred lake, taking part in the dawn, noon and sunset rites, observing the star-watchers at work on the temple roof, reading the old myths and guides to the afterlife, and conversing with great dignitaries who had withdrawn into the enclosure sacred to Amon: these were Pazair's main occupations during his retreat. He felt the radiant eternity engraved in the stone, listened to the voices of the gods and the pharaohs who had adorned the structure over the course of the dynasties, and steeped himself in the immutable life that inhabited the relief carvings and sculptures.

Several times, he meditated before the statue of Branir, who was depicted as an aged scribe kneeling down and was unrolling a papyrus bearing a hymn to creation.

When Kem brought him the information he was awaiting, Pazair went immediately to the land registry. The director was extremely gratified: receiving another visit from the tjaty would confer an unhoped-for importance upon him.

'Remind me of the name of the surveyor from Memphis,' said Pazair.

'Sumenu, my lord.'

'Are you sure about that?'

'Yes – at least, that's the name he gave me.'

'I have checked.'

'There was no need for that, my lord. Everything's in order.'

'Ever since I was a minor provincial judge, I have had a mania for checking everything. It often takes a long time, but it's extremely useful. Sumenu, you said?'

'Well, I might be mistaken. I—'

'Sumenu, the surveyor attached to the royal palace, died two years ago. And you yourself replaced him.'

The director's lips parted, but he could not utter a sound.

'Altering the land register is a crime,' said Pazair sternly. 'And you appear to have forgotten that the assignment of villages and lands to any particular jurisdiction is the responsibility of the tjaty. Whoever bribed you was relying on the High Priest of Karnak's inexperience and on my own. He was wrong.'

'My lord, you are talking nonsense.'

'We shall soon know. I have requested an immediate second opinion from the leader of the guild of the blind in Thebes.'

The guild's leader was an imposing man with a broad forehead and a heavy jaw. After the annual flood, if the river had swept away the boundary stones, thus erasing the marks of ownership, the government called upon him and his colleagues to adjudicate in disputes. He was the earth's memory; from many years of criss-crossing the fields and cultivated areas, his feet knew their exact dimensions.

He was eating dried figs under his vine, when he heard footsteps.

'There are three of you,' he said, 'a very big man, a man of average height, and a baboon. Could it be Commander Kem and his famous baboon, Killer? And might the third be—'

'Tjaty Pazair,' cut in Kem.

'So this must be an affair of state. Which lands has somebody tried to steal? No, don't say anything! My judgement must be completely objective. Which is the area concerned?'

'The rich northern villages bordering the province of Kebet.'

'The farmers complain a lot in that area – they say the worms eat their harvests, the hippos trample on them, and mice, grasshoppers and sparrows eat what's left. They're incorrigible liars. Their lands are excellent, and the year was fruitful.'

'Who is the recorder of those estates?'

'I am – I was born and grew up there. The boundaries have not altered for twenty years.' He smiled. 'I won't offer you figs or beer, for I assume you are in a hurry.'

In his hand the blind man held a cane whose top was shaped like the head of an animal with a pointed snout and long ears.* At his side, a surveyor uncoiled a rope, according to his instructions.

Not once did the blind man hesitate. He accurately identified the four corners of each field, re-established the locations of the boundary stones, the statues of the gods – notably the cobra that protected the

---

*This ritual staff was identical to the *was* sceptre, which only the gods, with this almost sole exception, could carry, for its head was that of the animal of the god Set, master of the storm, of thunder and of celestial fire.

harvests – and the stelae, a gift from Pharaoh, that marked the limits of the Karnak estates. Scribes noted everything down, made maps and drew up lists.

Once the process was over, there could be no doubt about it: the land register had been wrongly altered, and rich lands belonging to Karnak had been assigned to Kebet.

"'It is the tjaty's responsibility to draw the borders of each province, to oversee the offerings, and to bring before him anyone who has illegally seized a piece of land": is that indeed the order Pharaoh gave me, as each pharaoh gives it to each tjaty on his enthronement?'

The governor of Kebet province went pale.

'Answer,' ordered Pazair. 'You were present at the ceremony.'

'Yes . . . the king did indeed say those words.'

'Then why did you accept riches that did not belong to you?'

'The land register had altered—'

'The alteration was a forgery, which did not bear my seal or that of the High Priest of Karnak,' said Pazair coldly. 'You should have alerted me. What were you hoping for? That the months would pass quickly, that Kani would resign, that I would be dismissed, and that the position would be given to one of your accomplices?'

'Tjaty, I cannot permit you to—'

'You gave aid to conspirators and murderers. Bel-Tran will have been shrewd enough to leave no trace of a link between you and the Double White House, so I cannot prove your allegiance to him. But your dishonesty is sufficient: you are unworthy to govern a province. Consider your dismissal final.'

The tjaty convened his court at Thebes, before the great gate of the Temple of Karnak, where a wooden shelter had been built. Despite Kem's advice to be careful, Pazair had refused to hold the trial without an audience, as the accused had requested; a large crowd had gathered.

The tjaty read out the charges, after summarizing the principal stages in his investigation; the witnesses appeared and the court scribes noted down their testimony. The jury, composed of two priests from Karnak, the mayor of Thebes, the wife of a noble, a midwife and a senior army officer, delivered a verdict which Pazair judged was in accordance with both the spirit and the letter of the law.

The erstwhile governor of Kebet was sentenced to serve fifteen years in prison and to pay enormous compensation to the temple. The three guilty headmen were found guilty of falsehood and stealing food, and would henceforth work as agricultural labourers. Their land would be shared out among the humblest folk. The head of the Thebes land registry would spend ten years in a labour camp.

The tjaty did not ask for the penalties to be increased; none of those convicted sought to appeal.

One of Bel-Tran's networks had been wiped out.

18

'Look at the desert sky,' the old Nubian warrior urged Suti. 'That is where precious stones are born. It gives birth to the stars, and from the stars metals are born. If you know how to speak to them, and if you can hear their voices, you will learn the secret of gold and silver.'

'And do you know their language?'

'I reared livestock before I left with the tribe on the road to nowhere. My children and my wife died in a year of great drought, so I left my village and entrusted my footsteps to faceless tomorrows. What do I care about the shore from which no one returns?'

'Isn't the Lost City just a dream?'

'Our former chief went there several times and brought back gold each time: that is the truth.'

'And is this the right road?'

'If you're a real warrior, you ought to know that.'

With his regular, unflagging stride, the old man resumed his place at the head of the tribe; they were in a region so arid and desolate that they had not seen even an antelope for several hours.

Suti moved back to join Panther, who was reclining on a rudimentary travelling-chair carried by six Nubians, all delighted to be bearing the golden goddess.

'Put me down,' she said. 'I wish to walk.'

The warriors obeyed, then roared out a war-song, promising that they would cut their enemies into thin strips and devour their magic power.

Panther was sulking.

'Why are you angry?' asked Suti.

'This adventure is stupid.'

'Don't you want to get rich?'

'We know where our own gold is. Why chase a mirage and probably die of thirst doing so?'

'Nubians don't die of thirst, and I'm not chasing a mirage. Are those promises enough for you?'

'Swear that we'll go and fetch our gold from its hiding-place in the cave.'

'Why are you so stubborn?'

'You almost died for that gold,' Panther reminded him. 'I saved you, and you killed that traitor, General Asher, to get it. You mustn't defy destiny any more.'

Suti smiled. Panther was expressing a very personal vision of those events. Suti had not coveted the traitor's gold, but had applied the law of the desert by killing a liar and murderer who was trying to escape the tjaty's justice. The fact that fortune had smiled upon him proved that his deed had been just.

He said, 'Supposing the Lost City's full of gold and—'

'I don't care about your crazy plans! Promise me we'll go back to the cave.'

'You have my word.'

Satisfied, the golden goddess got back on to her travelling-chair.

The track stopped at the foot of a mountain whose slopes were dotted with blackish rocks. The wind swept across the desert; neither falcon nor vulture circled in the stifling sky.

The old warrior sat down; his companions did likewise.

'We will go no further,' he told Suti.

'What are you afraid of?'

'Our old chief used to talk to the stars, but we can't do that. Beyond this mountain, there is not a single source of water. Everyone who has tried to find the Lost City has disappeared, swallowed up by the sands.'

'Your chief didn't.'

'The stars guided him, but his secret has been lost. We shall not go any further.'

'But you said you're in search of death.'

'Not that death.'

'Didn't the chief give you any clues?'

'A chief doesn't talk, he acts.'

'How long did his journey last?'

'The moon rose three times.'

'The golden goddess will protect me.'

The old man shook his head. 'She will stay with us.'

'Are you defying my authority?'

'If you want to die in the desert, you're free to do so. We shall stay here until the fifth moonrise, then we shall leave for the oasis.'

Suti went across to Panther, who was more beautiful than ever. The wind and sun had turned her skin an amber hue, made her hair golden, and emphasized her wild, indomitable nature.

'I'm leaving,' he told her.

'Your city doesn't exist.'

'Yes, it does, and it's full of gold. I'm not going to my death. I'm going to another life, the life I have been dreaming about ever since I was shut away in the scribes' school in Memphis. Not only does this city exist, but it will belong to us as well.'

'Our gold is enough for me.'

'I see things on a grander scale, much grander! Just suppose the soul of the Nubian chief I killed has passed into me and is guiding me towards a fabulous treasure ... Who'd be mad enough to reject such an adventure?'

'Who'd be mad enough to try it?' snorted Panther.

'Kiss me, golden goddess. You'll bring me luck.'

Her lips were hot as the southern wind.

'Since you're determined to go, I suppose I must wish you good luck,' she said.

Suti took two skins filled with brackish water, some dried fish, a bow, arrows and a dagger. He had not lied to Panther: the soul of his defeated enemy would show him the way.

From the top of the mountain, he looked out over a landscape of unusual power. A gorge with reddish soil wound between two steep cliffs and then joined another desert, which stretched to the horizon. Suti set off into it, like a swimmer sliding into a wave. He felt the call of an unknown land, whose luminous essence called to him irresistibly.

He crossed the gorge without difficulty. There was not a single bird, animal or reptile: it was as if no life at all existed there. Quenching his thirst with small sips, he rested in the shade of a rock until night fell.

When the stars appeared, he raised his eyes to the sky and tried to decipher their message. They drew strange shapes; in his mind, he linked them with lines. Suddenly, a shooting-star flashed through the heavens, tracing a path which Suti engraved in his memory. That was the direction he would take.

Despite his instinctive collusion with the desert, the heat became almost unbearable, each step painful; but he followed the invisible star, as if he were somehow outside his pain-racked body. Before long, thirst forced him to empty his water-skins.

Eventually, Suti fell to his knees. In the distance was a red mountain, but it was far out of reach and anyway he would not have the strength to explore it in search of water. And yet he was certain he had not been mistaken. He wished he were an oryx, capable of bounding towards the sun and forgetting his exhaustion.

He dragged himself to his feet again, to prove to the desert that its strength was nourishing him. Slowly he advanced, his legs moved by the fire that ran across the sand. When he fell again, his knee broke a fragment of pottery.

Incredulously, he picked up the fragments of a jar. Men had lived here; probably it had been a nomads' encampment. As he staggered forward, the ground gave beneath his feet. Everywhere there were the remains of pots, vases and jars, so many that they formed small hills which barred his way. Although his body was increasingly heavy, he climbed one of the hills.

Down below, he saw the Lost City.

A guard-post built of brick, half-collapsed, gutted houses, a roofless temple whose walls were threatening to fall into ruin . . . And the red mountain was pierced with galleries, tanks to collect the winter rainwater, sloping stone tables for washing gold, stone huts where the miners had stored their tools. Everywhere, reddish sand.

Suti ran towards a water-tank, demanding a final effort from his failing legs; he gripped the stone rim, and let himself drop down inside. The water was lukewarm, divine; every pore of his skin drank it in while he quenched his thirst.

No longer parched, and filled with an unknown intoxication, he explored the city.

He found not a single human or animal bone. The entire population had suddenly abandoned the site, leaving behind an enormous mining operation. In each house there were jewels, cups, vases, amulets made from solid gold and silver; these alone were worth a vast fortune.

Suti wanted to check that the seams of ore could still be mined, so he went into one of the deep galleries that ran into the heart of the mountain. By hand and eye, he identified long veins, easy to work. The quantity of metal exceeded his wildest dreams.

He would teach the Nubians how to extract the incredible treasure. With a little discipline, they would be excellent miners.

That morning, as the Nubian sun decked the red mountain in magnificent radiance, Suti became master of the world, confidant of the desert, as rich as a king. He explored the narrow streets of the city of gold, of *his* city, until, suddenly, he caught sight of its guardian.

At the entrance to the city sat a lion with a flaming mane, watching the explorer. With one blow from its paw, it could tear open his chest or his belly. The legend said that the lion always kept its eyes open and never slept. If that was true, how could Suti overcome its vigilance?

He drew his bow.

The lion stood up. Slowly and majestically, it entered a ruined building. Suti ought to have passed it at a distance, but his curiosity was too strong.

Ready to let loose an arrow, he followed the lion into the ruins.

It had disappeared. In the half-light, he saw ingots of gold. A forgotten reserve, a treasure offering him the spirit of the place, which had appeared in the form of a wild animal before returning to the realms of the Invisible.

Panther was astounded. So many marvels, such riches – Suti had succeeded! The city of gold belonged to them.

While she examined the city's treasures, her lover directed a team of Nubians who were skilled at extracting metals from rock. They attacked the quartz with hammers and pick-axes, shattered the rock, then washed it before separating out the metal; brilliant yellow, dark yellow, tinged with red, Nubian gold was decked in admirable hues.

In several galleries they found gold-bearing silver which thoroughly deserved its name of 'luminous stone', because it was capable of lighting up the darkness; it was valuable as gold. According to custom, the Nubians would transport it in the form of nuggets or rings.

Suti joined Panther in the old temple whose walls were threatening to collapse. She could not have cared less about the danger, engrossed as she was in trying on collars, earrings and bracelets.

'We shall restore this place,' he declared. 'Can you imagine it with golden gates, a silver floor, and statues decked with precious stones?'

'I'll never live here,' said Panther. 'There's a curse on the place: it drove its inhabitants away.'

'I'm not afraid of the curse.'

'Don't try your luck too far.'

'Then what do you suggest we do?'

'Take with us as much as we can carry, get our gold back, and then settle down somewhere peaceful.'

'You'd soon get bored.'

Panther pouted; Suti knew that he had hit home.

He said, 'You've dreamt of ruling an empire, not a village. Wouldn't you like to be a great lady, reigning over an army of serving-women?'

She turned away.

'Where could you wear collars like those, except in a palace, in front of a sea of admiring, envious noblewomen? But I can make you still more beautiful.'

With a fragment of perfectly polished gold, he rubbed her arm and her neck.

'How gentle that is . . . Go on.'

He moved down to her breasts, then her back, and finally more intimate places.

'Am I going to turn into gold?' she asked.

Panther swayed to Suti's rhythm. At the contact of this precious metal, this flesh of the gods which so few mortals had the chance to touch, perhaps she was indeed becoming the golden goddess the Nubians revered.

Suti forgot not one inch of his mistress's body. The gold acted like smooth balm, and drew delectable shivers from her.

She lay down on the floor of the temple, fragments of gold glittering all around her; he lay down beside her.

'As long as Tapeni lives, you won't belong to me,' she said bitterly.

'Forget her.'

'I shall burn her to ashes.'

'What? A future queen lowering herself to such vulgar work?'

'Are you trying to defend her?'

'She's much too clever for me to argue with.'

'Will you fight Egypt at my side?'

'I could strangle you.'

'The Nubians would slaughter you.'

'I'm their chief, and—'

'And I am their goddess! Egypt has rejected you, and Pazair has betrayed you. Let's take our revenge.'

Suti suddenly cried out in pain, and threw himself to one side. Panther saw the attacker: a black scorpion, hiding under a stone.

The young man bit the sting, which was on his wrist, until he drew blood, sucked out the venom, and spat it out.

'You'll be the richest sham widow in the world,' he said.

19

Pazair held Neferet close. Her tenderness wiped away the tiredness of the journey and gave him back his taste for the fight. He explained to her how he had saved Kani and foiled one of Bel-Tran's plans. But he sensed that, despite her joy, she was weighed down with cares.

'There's been news from Tjaru,' she said.

'Suti!'

'He's been reported missing.'

'What happened?'

'According to the commander's report, he escaped. The garrison had had orders to stay inside the fortress, so no patrols went after him.'

Pazair raised his eyes to the heavens. 'He'll come back, Neferet, and he'll help us. But you look anxious. What is it?'

'It's only tiredness.'

'Tell me, I beg you. Don't carry the burden alone.'

'Bel-Tran has begun a campaign of defamation against you. He eats his midday and evening meals with high dignitaries, senior officials and provincial governors; Silkis smiles and keeps quiet. Your inexperience, your uncontrolled zeal, your insane demands, your incompetence, your ignorance of how the ministries really work, your ignorance of the realities of the present time, your devotion to outdated values ... those are his favourite themes.'

'Talking too much will only do him harm.'

'But it's you he's harming – day after day after day.'

'Don't trouble yourself with it.'

'I can't bear to hear you slandered like that.'

Pazair smiled. 'Actually, it's rather a good sign. If Bel-Tran is acting like that, it's because he still isn't certain of success. The blows I've just dealt him may have been more painful than I thought. Yes, it really is an interesting reaction, and it encourages me to continue.'

'There's something else,' said Neferet. 'The Overseer of Writings has asked several times to see you.'

'Why?

'He won't tell anyone but you.'

'Have there been any other visitors of note?'

'The Director of Secret Missions and the Overseer of the Fields. They want to see you, too, and they deplored your absence.'

The three men belonged to the Brotherhood of the Nine Friends of Pharaoh, the most influential group in the kingdom, and were therefore accustomed to making and unmaking reputations. This was the first time they had intervened since Pazair's appointment.

'Why don't I invite them to to join us for our midday meal?' he suggested.

The Overseer of Writings, the Overseer of the Fields and the Director of Secret Missions had foregathered. Mature men, profound thinkers, with grave voices and solemn bearing, they had climbed the ladder of the scribes' hierarchy and given the king full satisfaction in their work. Wearing wigs, and linen tunics over shirts with long, pleated sleeves, they arrived together at the gate of the tjaty's estate, where Kem and Killer identified them.

Neferet came to the gate to greet them, and led them through the garden towards the house. They admired the ornamental lake, the vine, and the rare plants imported from Asia, and congratulated her on the flowers. At the house, she took them to the winter dining-chamber, where Pazair was conversing with Bagey; the three visitors were surprised to find the former tjaty there.

Neferet withdrew.

'We would like to see you alone, Tjaty,' said the Overseer of Writings.

'I assume you are here because of concerns about the way I am fulfilling my duties. Why should my predecessor not help me? His advice may be valuable.'

Bagey glared sternly at the newcomers. 'Until recently we worked together; do you now consider me a stranger?'

'Of course not,' replied the Overseer of the Fields.

'In that case,' said Pazair, 'the matter is decided. All five of us shall eat together.'

They took their places on their allotted chairs; before each stood a low table on which the servants placed trays laden with food. The cook had prepared succulent pieces of beef cooked in an earthenware cauldron with a rounded base, and poultry roasted on the spit; peas and courgettes in sauce accompanied the meat. To one side were plates of fresh bread, and of butter made with fenugreek and caraway, without water or salt, and kept in a cool cellar in order to avoid browning.

A cup-bearer poured red wine from the Delta, set the jar down on a wooden stand, and left the room, closing the door behind him.

The Director of Secret Missions said, 'We speak in the name of the highest authorities in the land—'

'With the exception of Pharaoh and myself,' cut in Pazair.

The director looked offended. 'Such objections seem pointless to me.'

'Your tone is extremely unpleasant,' said Bagey. 'Whatever your rank and age, you must respect the tjaty Pharaoh appointed.'

'Our conscience forbids us to spare him deserved reprimands and criticism.'

Annoyed, Bagey got to his feet. 'I do not accept such a course of action.'

'It is neither unfitting nor illegal,' the director pointed out.

'I disagree. Your role is to serve the tjaty and to obey him.'

'Not when his actions compromise Egypt's well-being.'

'I will not hear another word,' snapped Bagey. 'You shall eat your lunch without me,' and he stalked out of the room.

Taken aback by the fierceness of the attack and by Bagey's reaction, Pazair felt very alone. The meat and vegetables grew cold, the fine wine was undrunk in the cups.

'We have spoken at length with the head of the Double White House,' said the Overseer of Fields, 'and his worries seem to us to be justified.'

'Why is he not with you?'

'We did not tell him what we were going to do. He is a young and impulsive man, who might get carried away over such a serious matter. Indeed, there is a risk that your own youth will lead you into an impasse, unless reason wins through.'

Pazair had had enough. 'You all occupy important posts in which unnecessary words are inappropriate. My time is as precious as yours, so you will oblige me by coming straight to the point.'

'That is just the sort of attitude we mean. Governing Egypt requires much greater flexibility.'

'Pharaoh governs, I see that Ma'at is respected.'

'Daily life sometimes lags far behind the ideal.'

'If that is how Egypt's most senior scribes think,' said Pazair, 'the country is heading for ruin.'

'You are inexperienced,' said the Overseer of Fields, 'and you blindly follow old ideas which no longer have any real substance.'

'I think differently.'

'Was it in the name of those old ideals that you sentenced the governor of Kebet, heir to a noble and famous family?'

'The law was applied, without taking account of his rank.'

'Are you planning to dismiss many more respected, highly skilled officials like that?'

'If they plot against their country, they will be charged and tried.'

'You are confusing serious offences with the necessities of power.'

'Falsifying the land register is hardly a minor offence, is it?'

'We all recognize your integrity,' said the Overseer of Writings soothingly. 'Ever since the start of your career, you have demonstrated your commitment to justice and your love for the truth – no one is contesting that. The people greatly respect and admire you. But is that enough to avert a disaster?'

'What are you reprimanding me about?'

'Perhaps nothing, if you can reassure us.'

The opening skirmishes were over; now the real battle was beginning.

These three men knew everything about power, the system of government and the mechanisms of society. If Bel-Tran had managed to convince them of the rightness of his views, Pazair would have little chance of overcoming their opposition. Isolated and disowned, he would surely be as easily broken as a child's toy.

'My departments,' said the Overseer of Fields, 'have drawn up a list of landowners and farmers, re-counted the heads of livestock, and assessed the harvests. They have also set the year's taxes, taking account of the peasants' opinions, but all this work will result in wholly inadequate revenue. The taxes on fodder and cattle should be doubled.'

'I refuse.'

'Why?'

'In the event of difficulty, increasing taxes is the worst of all solutions. It seems to me more urgent to eliminate injustice – our food reserves are quite sufficient to see us though several bad harvests.'

'Besides, the arrangements are too favourable to country-dwellers. If a tax demand is unjust, some living in a town has only three days to lodge an appeal, while someone who lives in the provinces has three months.'

'As I know very well – I was myself a victim of that ruling,' Pazair reminded him. 'I shall lengthen the appeal period for town-dwellers.'

'At least increase taxes on the rich!'

'The highest-taxed person in Egypt, the governor of Elephantine, pays the Treasury the equivalent of four gold ingots. The governor of a medium-sized province pays a thousand loaves, as well as calves, oxen, honey and sacks of grain. There is no need to demand more, because they maintain extensive households and look after the well-being of the villages they control.'

'Then do you intend to target the craftsmen?'

'Certainly not. Their houses will remain exempt from taxes, and I shall maintain the ban on seizing their tools.'

'Then will you give way on the wood tax? It should be extended to all the provinces.'

'I have closely studied the wood centres and how they receive brushwood, palm-fibres and small pieces of wood. During the cold season, distribution was carried out correctly. Why alter the work of teams whose rotation is satisfactory?'

'You do not understand the situation,' said the Director of Secret Missions. 'The way our trade and finances are is organized no longer meets the demands of the day. Production must be increased, and profits—'

'Those are words Bel-Tran is fond of.'

'Of course he is – he is the head of the Double White House! If you are at odds with your minister for the economy, how can you carry out a coherent policy? You might as well get rid of him – and get rid of us too!'

'We shall continue to work together, according to Egypt's traditional laws. The country is rich, the Nile provides us with abundant food, and prosperity will endure as long as we struggle each day against injustice.'

'Are you sure your views have not been distorted by your own past? The economy—'

'The day the economy takes precedence over justice, disastrous misfortune will be unleashed upon this earth.'

'Very well. But at least the importance of the temples' role should be reduced,' suggested the Overseer of Writings.

'Why do you say that?' asked Pazair.

'They gather in almost all of the agricultural produce and other items, and then distribute them according to the people's needs. Would a more direct route not be preferable?'

'It would be contrary to the rule of Ma'at and would destroy Egypt in a few years. The temples are our energy-regulators, and the priests, shut away behind their walls, have no concern but harmony. Through the temples, we are linked to the Invisible and to the vital forces of the universe. Their schools and workshops produce people who have been fashioning our country for centuries. Do you wish to cut off its head?'

'You are twisting my words.'

'I fear your thoughts resemble a twisted staff.'

'You insult me!'

'You are turning your back on the values upon which Egypt was founded.'

'You are too single-minded, Pazair – a fanatic.'

'If that is what you think, do not hesitate to ask the king for my head.'

'You benefit from the support of Kani, whose opinion Ramses values. But his favour will not outlast your popularity. Resign, Pazair. That would be the best solution, for you and for Egypt.'

20

The head gardener of the Temple of Iunu was devastated. Sitting at the foot of an olive tree, he was in tears. Pazair, who had been summoned urgently by Kem, shivered: a cold wind was gusting, turning over the silver-backed leaves.

'Tell me what happened,' he said to the gardener.

'I oversaw the harvest myself . . . The oldest olive trees in Egypt! What a tragedy! And why? Why this vandalism?'

The gardener could not say any more. Pazair abandoned him to his sadness, after assuring him that he did not consider him responsible, and followed Kem into the largest storehouse of the Temple of Ra, where the country's best lamp-oil was kept.

The floor was a viscous lake.

Not one jar had been spared: every single stopper had been removed, and the contents emptied out.

'What have you found out?' asked Pazair.

'It was one man acting alone,' replied the Nubian. 'He got in through the storehouse roof.'

'Just as he did at the hospital.'

'It was the man who's trying to kill you, I'm certain of it. But why should he carry out this destruction?'

'The temples stand in Bel-Tran's way. Destroying the lamp-oil will slow the work of the scribes and priests, because they won't be able to work after dark. Send out messages immediately: guards must be set to watch all oil reserves. In the Memphis region, we'll use the palace reserves. Not one lamp shall go unfilled.'

Bel-Tran's reaction to the tjaty's firm stance had not been long in coming.

Every single serving-man was wielding a broom made from long, stiff fibres bundled together, every single serving-maid was armed with a brush of reeds held together by a ring: the tjaty's household was zealously sweeping the floors. A delicious smell of incense and cinnamon floated in the air; the smoke from the burning essences would purify the great house and cleanse it of insects and other undesirable guests.

'Where is my wife?' Pazair asked his head steward.

'In the grain-store, my lord.'

Pazair found Neferet on her knees, pushing cloves of garlic, dried fish* and natron into a corner.

'What's hiding in there?' he asked.

'It may be a snake. If it is, these things will suffocate it.'

'Why all this cleaning?'

'I'm worried that the murderer may have left other traces of his visit.'

'Why? Have you had some unpleasant surprises?'

'Not so far, no, but I'm not going to leave a single suspicious place untouched. But tell me, what did Pharaoh say?'

Pazair helped her to her feet.

'He was surprised at the Friends' attitude, which proved to him that the country is gravely sick. I fear I may not be as effective a doctor as you are.'

'What will his answer to them be?'

'It is up to me to deal with their requests.'

'Did they demand your resignation?'

'It was just a suggestion.'

'So Bel-Tran is still spreading his lies.'

'He has his weaknesses – it's up to us to find them.' The tjaty sneezed uncontrollably, and began to shiver. 'I need a doctor.'

Pazair's cold pounded in his skull; it felt as though his bones were being shattered and his brain hollowed out. Neferet gave him onion juice, considered very effective against chills, purged his nostrils with palm-juice, made him inhale the steam of a potion containing sulphur of arsenic, which doctors called 'that which makes the heart open', and prescribed mother-tincture of bryony to prevent lung problems. She treated his cough with a decoction of the roots of marshmallow and fresh colocinth. Copper-water would soon finish off the infection for good.

Delighted to have his master at home, Brave slept at the foot of his bed, enjoying a soft blanket and, into the bargain, a spoonful of honey.

Despite his fever, Pazair consulted the papyri brought to him by Kem, the only intermediary between the tjaty and his office. The more time passed, the more the tjaty was mastering his job. This period of withdrawal was in fact an advantage, because he noticed that the large

---

* To be precise the fish called *bulti* [*Tilapia nilotica*].

temples, in both the north and the south, were not under Bel-Tran's control. They regulated matters according to the teachings of the ancients, and oversaw the distribution of supplies from their store-houses. Thanks to Kani and to the other High Priests – who were in full agreement with their colleague at Karnak – the tjaty could maintain the stability of the ship of state, at least until the fatal day when Ramses would have to abdicate.

When the tall Nubian fingered his wooden nose, Pazair knew his friend had some important information.

'First,' said Kem, 'a worrying piece of news: Mentmose, my predecessor of sad memory, has left Byblos, where he was living in exile.'

'He's taking an enormous risk. When you catch him, he'll be sent to a prison camp.'

'He knows that, which is why his disappearance doesn't bode well.'

'Is Bel-Tran behind it?'

'Possibly.'

'Or has Mentmose simply run away?'

'I'd like to think so, but he hates you as much as Bel-Tran does. You fascinate both of them, because they don't understand your honesty or your love of justice. So long as you were merely a junior judge, it didn't matter. But you as tjaty? That's intolerable. Mentmose doesn't want to live out his life in peace. He wants revenge.'

'And is there still no progress on Branir's murder?'

'Not directly, but . . .'

'But?'

'I believe that the man's who's been trying to kill you is the one who killed Branir. He came from nowhere, and has disappeared again, faster than a greyhound.'

'Are you telling me he's a ghost?'

'Not a ghost, no . . . But a shadow-eater the like of whom I've never come across before. He's a monster – he's in love with death.'

'Has he at last made the mistake you were hoping for?'

'Yes, when he attacked Killer. That's the only time he's had to use outside help, and therefore to make contact with others. I was afraid this thread might be cut off, but fortunately one of my best informants, a man called Short-Thighs, has a few problems at the moment. A judge has just increased the amount of the food contribution he has to give his former wife, so his memory seems to have been jogged.'

'And does he know who the shadow-eater is?'

'If he does, he'll ask for an enormous reward.'

'It's granted. When are you seeing him?'

'This evening, behind the docks.'

'I'll come with you.'

'Not in your state of health, you won't.'

Neferet had summoned the principal suppliers of rare and expensive ingredients used in the medical workshops. Although stocks were by no means exhausted, she judged it wise to replenish them as quickly as possible, because of the difficulties of harvesting and delivery.

'Let us begin with myrrh,' she said. 'When is it planned to send the next caravan to the land of Punt?'

The man responsible coughed. 'I don't know.'

'Why not?'

'No date has been set.'

'It's up to you to set it, I should have thought.'

'I have no boats or crews at my disposal.'

'And why is that?'

'I am awaiting the goodwill of foreign countries.'

'Have you consulted the tjaty?' asked Neferet.

'No. I applied to the usual secretariats.'

'You should have told me about this problem.'

'There was no hurry . . .'

'But there is now – it's urgent.'

'I'd have to have a written order.'

'You will have it today.'

Neferet turned to another trader. 'Have you ordered green gum resin of galbanum?'*

'Yes, but it won't arrive for some time.'

'Why won't it?'

'It comes from Asia, and we're dependent on the whim of the gatherers and sellers. The government scribes strongly advised me not to bother them. Apparently, our relations with those countries are rather strained, because of certain incidents – the details escape me. But as soon as it's possible . . .'

'And what about the dark ladanum resin?' Neferet asked the third supplier. 'I know it comes from Greece and Minoa, and they are always ready to trade.'

'Not at the moment, I'm afraid. The harvest was poor, so they've decided not to sell any to other countries.'

Neferet did not even ask the other merchants. It was clear from their embarrassment that they would also answer in the negative.

---

*These gum resins [*galbanum* and *ladanum*], extracted from trees or shrubs, and still used today in perfumery, were considered medicinal.

'Who receives these products when they reach Egyptian soil?' she asked the myrrh-supplier.

'The border trade-control guards and scribes.'

'To which secretariat do they report?'

The man stammered, 'To ... to the Double White House.'

Neferet's eyes, usually so gentle, filled with anger and revulsion. 'By becoming henchmen of Bel-Tran,' she said coldly, 'you are betraying Egypt. As the kingdom's principal doctor, I shall ask that you be charged with damaging the people's health.'

'That certainly isn't our intention, but the circumstances ... You must admit that the world is changing and Egypt must change, too. Our way of doing business is altering: Bel-Tran holds the key to our future. However, if you were to increase our profits, and review our margins, deliveries could start again quite quickly.'

'That's blackmail!' said Neferet furiously. 'Blackmail which compromises the health of your fellow countrymen!'

'That's putting it much too strongly. We have open minds, and in well-conducted negotiations—'

'Given that this is a matter of urgency, I shall ask the tjaty for a requisition order and I shall deal with our foreign partners myself.'

'You wouldn't dare!'

'Greed is an incurable disease, which I cannot treat. Ask Bel-Tran for new jobs. You no longer work for the medical services.'

21

Fever did not stop Pazair signing the requisition order enabling Neferet to ensure the acquisition of the ingredients the doctors needed. Armed with the papyrus, Neferet left immediately for the Foreign Affairs secretariat. There, she would personally oversee the drafting of the documents ordering the caravans to set out.

Her favourite patient's condition gave her no cause for concern, but he must stay in his bedchamber for two or three more days, to avoid any risk of a relapse.

The tjaty did not allow himself to rest. Surrounded by papyri and wooden tablets sent by scribes in different ministries and departments, he searched for weak points which Bel-Tran would be sure to exploit. He tried to imagine his enemy's plans, and took measures to counter them, but he did not delude himself: Bel-Tran and his allies would soon find other means of attack.

The head steward came in and told his master someone was requesting an audience. When Pazair heard the visitor's name he could hardly believe his ears. Despite his astonishment, he agreed to see him.

Full of confidence, fashionably dressed in a luxurious linen robe that was too tight at the waist, Bel-Tran greeted the tjaty warmly.

'I have brought you a jar of white wine dating from year two of the reign of Seti II, father of our illustrious king. It's a virtually unobtainable vintage – I'm sure you'll enjoy it.' Without waiting for an invitation, he took a chair and sat down opposite Pazair. 'I heard you were ill. Nothing serious, I hope?'

'I shall soon be on my feet again.'

'It is true that you benefit from the skills of the best doctor in the kingdom, but, all the same, I think this attack of fatigue is significant. The burden of being tjaty is almost impossible to bear.'

'Except for shoulders as broad as yours.'

'There are a lot of rumours circulating at court. Everyone knows you're having great difficulty performing your duties properly.'

'That's true. I am.'

Bel-Tran smiled.

'In fact, I'm not sure I shall ever succeed,' added Pazair.

'My friend, this illness is doing you a world of good.'

'Enlighten me about something. Since you have the decisive weapon, and since you're certain of gaining supreme power, how can what I do be a hindrance to you?'

'It's like being bitten by a mosquito all the time – unpleasant. However, if you agree to obey me and to follow the way of progress at last, I shall allow you to remain tjaty. You are, after all, popular with the people, and they admire your capacity for work, your upright character, your clear-sightedness . . . You'd be useful in carrying out my policies.'

'High Priest Kani would disapprove of my doing that.'

'It's up to you to deceive him. You foiled my plan to acquire a good part of the temple's lands, so you certainly owe me that much. The temples' power over Egypt's trade and resources is archaic, Pazair. The production of wealth must not be held back and restricted – we must encourage continued growth.'

'Will it ensure the happiness of men and the balance between peoples?'

'Oh, that doesn't matter. Money gives power to whoever controls it.'

'Perhaps. But I can't stop thinking about my master, Branir.'

Bel-Tran made an airy gesture. 'He was a man of the past.'

'According to the annals of the past, no crime went unpunished then.'

'Forget that wretched story and turn your thoughts to the future.'

'Kem is still investigating, and he thinks he has identified the murderer.'

Bel-Tran kept his composure, but there was alarm in his eyes.

'However, my hypothesis differs from Kem's. Several times, I've come close to charging your wife with the killing.'

'Silkis? But . . .'

'I believe she is the woman who lured the commander of the honour-guard aside, and distracted him from his duty. Right from the beginning of the conspiracy, she's obeyed you unquestioningly. In addition, she's an excellent weaver, and handles needles better than anyone else. There's no one more dangerous than a child-woman, according to the old sages. I believe she's quite capable of having murdered Branir by stabbing him in the neck with one of her mother-of-pearl needles.'

'I was wrong. Your fever's doing you harm, not good.'

'Silkis needs your wealth, but you're her slave, too – much more than you think. It's only evil that binds you together.'

'That's enough of your miserable thoughts! Will you at last submit?'

'Thinking I might betrays a clear lack of lucidity on your part.'

Bel-Tran stood up. 'Don't try to take action against Silkis, or against me. You and your king have lost: the Testament of the Gods is out of your reach for ever.'

That evening the wind heralded the coming of spring: warm and scented, it bore with it the soul of the far-away desert. People went to bed later, chatted in one another's houses, discussed the day's events.

Kem waited until the last lamps had been extinguished, then he and Killer stole out into the narrow lanes leading to the docks. Killer moved forward slowly, looking up and down, and from right to left, as if he sensed danger. Edgily, he sometimes retraced his steps, then suddenly increased his pace. Kem respected the baboon's instinct; in the darkness, it was a valuable guide.

The docks area was silent; guards were keeping watch outside the storehouses. Kem and Short-Thighs had agreed to meet behind an abandoned building which was due to be rebuilt. Short-Thighs often conducted his illicit dealings there, and Kem turned a blind eye to them in exchange for the sort of information that an office-bound guard would never be able to get.

Short-Thighs had left the path of truth virtually from the moment of his birth. He was a dedicated trafficker, whose only pleasure was his next theft, and the little folk of Memphis could keep no secrets from him. Ever since the start of his inquiry, Kem had thought the thief would probably be the only one likely to give him firm information about the assassin, but he also knew he must not push too hard, or he would come up against a wall of silence.

Killer halted, on the alert. His hearing was much better than a man's, and his time in the guards had developed his faculties. Clouds hid the first quarter of the moon; darkness extended over the abandoned, doorless warehouse. He started moving forward again.

Short-Thighs' goodwill derived from a legal problem. Acting on shrewd advice, his ex-wife was stripping him of the small fortune he had amassed, so he had resolved to sell his most precious possession: the identity of the shadow-eater. What would he demand in exchange? wondered Kem. Gold, certainly, and Kem's silence on a bigger smuggling deal than usual: a cargo of jars of wine. Kem would soon find out.

Killer gave an ear-splitting howl. Kem thought he was hurt, but a swift examination showed that all was well. Killer agreed to continue and walked round the warehouse.

There was no one at the agreed meeting-place.

Kem sat down beside Killer, who was now calm. Had Short-Thighs changed his mind? The Nubian thought not: the man was in urgent need of money.

The night passed.

A little before dawn, Killer took Kem by the hand and led him inside the warehouse. Abandoned baskets, broken chests, the remains of tools ... Killer forced a path through this chaos, halted before a pile of grain sacks and howled as he had done a few hours earlier.

Kem quickly pulled away the sacks.

Propped up against a wooden pillar, Short-Thighs had indeed come to the meeting. But, as the shadow-eater had broken his neck, he would not be selling his big secret.

Pazair did his best to reassure Kem. 'Short-Thighs' death is entirely my responsibility,' he said.

'Of course it isn't. It was he who contacted you.'

'I should have had him protected.'

'How?'

'I don't know, I—'

'Stop blaming yourself,' said Kem. 'The shadow-eater must have got wind of Short-Thighs' intention, followed him and killed him.'

'Or else Short-Thighs tried to blackmail him,' suggested Pazair.

'He was greedy enough to do something as mad as that. And now the trail has gone cold again. Of course, I am maintaining the watch over you.'

'Do what's necessary. We're leaving tomorrow for Middle Egypt.' Pazair's voice had darkened.

'Is something wrong?'

'I've had worrying reports from several provincial governors.'

'What about?'

'Water.'

'What's happened?'

'The worst.'

Neferet had carried out a long and delicate operation on a young craftsman who had fallen from the roof of a house, breaking his skull and cracking several neck-bones; one of his temples was stove in. Fortunately, though, he had been brought to the hospital straight away, so she was confident he would live.

Worn out, she had fallen asleep in a rest-chamber.

One of her assistants woke her. 'I'm sorry, but I need you.'

'Ask another doctor; I haven't the strength to operate again.'

'It is a strange case – we really do need you to look at the patient.'

Wearily, Neferet got up and followed her assistant.

The patient was a woman aged about forty. She wore an expensive dress; that and her well-cared-for hands and feet showed that she belonged to a wealthy family. Her eyes were open, but staring blankly.

'She was found lying in an alleyway in the northern district,' explained the assistant, 'but the people living there didn't recognize her. She looks as though she's been numbed for an operation.'

Neferet listened to the voice of the woman's heart in her arteries, then examined her eyes. 'She has been drugged,' she concluded, 'with extract of pink poppy – which should be used only in hospital.* I shall ask that an investigation be begun immediately.'

In the face of his wife's insistence, Pazair had delayed his departure for Middle Egypt and asked Kem to investigate the case of the drugged woman. She had died without regaining consciousness.

Thanks to Killer, tongues were loosening. The unfortunate woman had gone three times to the alleyway, where a man had been waiting for her. He was a Greek, Kem was told, a seller of precious vases, who lived in a beautiful house.

When Kem arrived there, the suspect was not at home. A serving-woman asked him to take a seat in the receiving-chamber and brought him some cool beer. The vase-seller had gone to deal with a business matter at the quayside, she said, and would soon be back.

When he returned, the Greek, a tall, thin man with a beard, took flight the moment he saw his visitor. Kem did not move, confident that Killer would see to things. He was right: the baboon dived at the fugitive's legs and brought him down on his face on the tiled floor.

Kem pulled him up by his tunic.

'I haven't done anything!' protested the Greek.

'You killed a woman.'

'I sell vases, that's all.'

For a moment, Kem wondered if he was holding the shadow-eater; but the man had been much too easy to catch. He said, 'Unless you tell me what I want to know, you'll be sentenced to death.'

The Greek's voice turned into a sob. 'Have pity! I'm only a go-between.'

'From whom do you buy the drug?'

'From Greece – from people who grow the plants there.'

'They are beyond my reach. You, however, are not.'

Killer's red eyes signalled his full agreement.

---

*From the *shepen* or pink poppy, opium and morphine were extracted for use as sedatives and analgesics.

'I'll tell you their names,' said the vase-seller.

'Tell me the names of your customers.'

'No, not that!'

Killer's hairy hand came down on the man's shoulder. He shivered with fear, and began to speak volubly, naming officials, merchants and a few nobles.

Among them was the lady Silkis.

22

On the morning of his departure, while Pazair and Neferet were in the garden, sitting in the shade of a persea, an invitation arrived. It was from Bel-Tran. At the end of winter, it was incumbent upon the head of the Double White House to host a magnificent reception and banquet, attended by all the principal court dignitaries, senior officials and several provincial governors. And it was customary for the tjaty to honour the reception with his presence.

'He is laughing at us,' said Neferet.

'Bel-Tran bows to tradition when it is useful to him.'

'Are we really obliged to take part in this masquerade?'

'I'm afraid so.'

'Charging Silkis would cause a fine scandal.'

'I shall try to be discreet.'

'Has the drugs traffic been halted?'

'Kem has been spendidly efficient. The Greek's accomplices were arrested on the quayside, and so were all their customers – except Silkis.'

'But you can't move against her, can you?'

'Bel-Tran's threats won't stop me.'

'The important thing is to have put an end to this horror. What good would it do to imprison her now, today?'

Pazair put his arm round his wife. 'It would be justice.'

'But isn't the moment when a deed is done more important than the deed itself?

'Are you advising me to wait? The days and weeks are passing; Pharaoh's abdication is not far off.'

'We must fight clear-headedly right up to the last second,' insisted Neferet.

'The darkness is so dense! Sometimes, I—'

She hushed him by putting a finger to his lips. 'A tjaty of Egypt never gives up,' she said.

*

Pazair loved the countryside of Middle Egypt, the white cliffs bordering the Nile, the vast green plains and the bright hills where the nobles built their houses of eternity. The region possessed neither the lofty character of Memphis nor the sun-drenched splendour of Thebes, but it retained the secrets of the country-dwellers' soul, which had withdrawn into middle-sized farms run by families jealous of their traditions.

During the voyage, Killer gave no warning of danger. The spring air was growing more and more gentle, and he seemed to delight in it, though without ever softening the fierce energy in his eyes.

The province of the Oryx was proud of its water management. For centuries, it had ensured its inhabitants' prosperity, driving away the spectre of famine and drawing no distinction between great and small. In years of low annual floods, skilfully built ponds held enough water to irrigate the land. Canals, sluice-gates and earthen retaining-banks were watched constantly by dedicated specialists, especially during the crucial period following the floodwaters' retreat. At that time, many fields remained flooded, absorbing the precious silt that had given rise to Egypt's nickname of 'Black Earth', and the villages, perched on mounds which rose clear of the water, were alive with songs honouring the Nile's fertilizing energy.

Every ten days, the tjaty received a detailed report on the country's water reserves, and he often went, without warning, to check the local scribes' work. Now, as he travelled towards the capital of the Oryx province, Pazair felt less anxious. The retaining-banks were in excellent condition, the pools lining the way were full, and men were at work maintaining the canals – it was all a reassuring sight.

The tjaty's arrival caused a happy tumult. Everyone wanted to see the great man, present a petition to him, ask for justice. There was no hostility; quite the opposite. The people's esteem and trust moved Pazair to the bottom of his heart and filled him with new strength. For these people's sake, he must safeguard the country and prevent the kingdom from falling apart. He called upon the sky, the Nile, and the fertile land; he implored the creative powers to open his spirit so that he might save Pharaoh.

The governor of the province was descended from a long line of officials of the province. A rotund sixty-year-old who enjoyed good living, he was called Iau, meaning 'the Fat Ox'.

He hastily summoned to his fine white-painted house his principal colleagues: the overseers of retaining-banks and canals, the distributor of water reserves, the official land-surveyor and the recruiter of seasonal workers. Pazair was surprised to find that they all looked sombre. They bowed before the tjaty, to whom Iau at once ceded his place and the leadership of the gathering.

'This visit is a great honour for me,' Iau declared, 'and a great honour for my province.'

'Your reports alerted me. Do you stand by them?'

The bluntness of the question surprised Iau, but did not shock him. Tjaties, overburdened with work, seldom had time for polite formalities.

'I initiated them.'

'Several provinces share your anxiety. I have chosen to come to yours because of its exemplary record over several generations.'

'I shall be blunt, too,' said Iau. 'We no longer understand the orders from central government. Usually I am left free to run the province, and my results have never disappointed Pharaoh. Now, since the end of the last flood, we're being ordered to do things which make no sense.'

'Explain.'

'This year, as every other year, our surveyor calculated the volume of earth to be moved and piled up to make the retaining-walls impermeable. But his figures have been revised downwards. If we accept the correction, the walls won't be strong enough – they'll be destroyed by the tides.'

'Where did this correction come from?'

'From the Surveying secretariat in Memphis. But that isn't all. Our recruiter of seasonal workers knows exactly how many men he needs to carry out the maintenance work, when the retaining-banks are repaired and sealed. But the Employment secretariat will let him have only half that number, and refuses to say why.

'More serious still is the question of the irrigation pools. Nobody knows better than we do how long water takes to pass from a pool upstream to a pool downstream, according to the needs of the kinds of plants to be grown. But the Double White House wants to impose on us dates which are incompatible with the demands of nature. And I haven't even mentioned the increase in taxes that will result from the increase in production. Whatever is going on in the minds of those people in Memphis?'

'Show me these documents,' requested Pazair.

Iau called for the papyri.

Pazair looked at them closely. All the signatories were scribes either from the Double White House itself or from departments which Bel-Tran controlled more or less directly.

He said, 'Give me writing-materials.'

A scribe presented him with a palette, fresh ink and a writing-brush. In his swift, precise hand, Pazair cancelled the orders. Then he affixed his seal to each papyrus.

'These errors have been put right,' he announced. 'Take no notice of these out-of-date orders, and follow your usual procedures.'

Stunned into silence, the provincial administrators exchanged looks. Eventually, Iau found his voice. 'Are we to understand—'

'From now on, only directives bearing my seal will be valid.'

Delighted by the tjaty's unexpected and rapid intervention, the administrators applauded him and went cheerfully back to their daily tasks.

But Iau still looked careworn.

Pazair said, 'Is there something else worrying you?'

'Doesn't your attitude rather imply an open conflict with Bel-Tran?'

'One of my ministers can make a mistake.'

'In that case, why do you retain him in his position?'

Pazair had been afraid that question would be asked. Up to now, the skirmishes had been fairly discreet, but this matter of the water had brought into the open the serious disagreements between the tjaty and the head of the Double White House.

'Bel-Tran has a great capacity for work,' he said.

'Do you know that he is taking steps to convince the provincial governors that his policies are the right ones? My colleagues and I have been wondering, are you the tjaty or is he?'

'You have just had your answer.'

Iau smiled. 'That's very reassuring – I didn't like his offer.'

'What was it?'

'An important post in Memphis, a tempting increase in pay, fewer responsibilities . . .'

'Why didn't you accept?'

'Because I'm satisfied with what I have – but Bel-Tran can't seem to accept that ambition may be limited. I love this region and I loathe large cities. I'm respected here; in Memphis, I'd be nobody.'

'Have you officially refused the offer?'

'That man frightens me, I admit, so I preferred to play at being hesitant. But other governors have agreed to help him – as if you didn't even exist. It looks as though you have taken a snake into your house.'

'If I have, it is up to me to put things right.'

Iau did not hide his concern. 'From what you say, I think the country is likely to face difficult times. As you have preserved my province's integrity, I pledge you my full support.'

Kem and Killer were sitting on the threshold of Iau's beautiful house. Killer was eating dates, and Kem was watching the street, obsessed by the shadow-eater and convinced that the man of darkness was thinking about him with the same intensity.

As soon as Pazair came out of the house, Kem stood up.

'Is everything all right, Tjaty?' he asked.

'Another disaster narrowly averted. We must inspect several other provinces.'

Iau caught up with them, on the road back to the landing-stage.

'Tjaty,' he said, 'there's something I forgot to ask. Was it really you who sent me a man to check the drinking-water?'

'Absolutely not. Describe him to me.'

'About sixty, medium height, with a bald, red pate he scratches a lot, very irritable, with a nasal voice and a peremptory tone.'

'Mentmose,' murmured Kem.

'What did he do?' asked Pazair.

'He carried out a routine inspection,' said Iau.

'Take me to the drinking-water stores.'

The most beneficial drinking-water was collected a few days after the start of the flood. Rich in mineral salts, it helped digestion and also promoted fertility in women. Being turbid and muddy, it had to be filtered, after which it was stored in large jars which preserved it wonderfully well for four or five years. The Oryx province sometimes exported it to the South, in years of great heat.

A guard drew back the heavy wooden bolts and opened the heavy wooden door of the largest storehouse.

The breath fled from Iau's body when he saw the disaster: the stopper had been removed from every single jar, and all the water had been spilt on the ground.

23

How could a woman be so beautiful? wondered Pazair as he gazed at Neferet, who was decked in her finery for Bel-Tran's banquet. She was wearing the seven-stringed collar of cornelian beads, embellished with Nubian gold, that the Mother of Pharaoh had given her; hidden beneath it was her gift from Branir, a turquoise a designed to ward off evil. Her wig's fine plaits and ringlets showed off her beautiful face, with its clear, radiant complexion. Bracelets of small beads encircled her wrists and ankles, and a belt of amethysts, a gift from Pazair, emphasized the slenderness of her waist.

'It is time for you to get dressed,' she remarked.

'Just one last report to read.'

'About the reserves of drinking-water?'

'Mentmose destroyed ten; the others are protected, for the time being. The heralds are proclaiming the criminal's description, so either he'll fall into the hands of the security guards or he'll be forced to go to ground.'

'How many of the governors have sold themselves to Bel-Tran?'

'A third, perhaps. But the work to maintain the retaining-banks will be carried out correctly. I have given orders to that effect, with a ban on reducing the number of workmen involved.'

Neferet sat down on his knee, to stop him working. 'It really is time for you to put on your best kilt, a traditional wig and a collar worthy of your rank.'

As commander of Memphis's guards, Kem had had an invitation to the banquet. The Nubian was very ill at ease at this sort of affair, and his only jewellery was his dagger with the gold-and-silver alloy hilt, with inlaid rosettes of lapislazuli and green feldspar. Standing inconspicuously in a corner of the great pillared hall where Bel-Tran and Silkis received their guests, he watched the tjaty, who was surrounded by people. Killer had taken up a position on the roof of the house, from where he kept watch on the area around.

Garlands of flowers decorated the pillars; the guests, the cream of Memphis's nobility were dressed in their most splendid clothes; roast geese and grilled beef were brought in on dishes of silver, and the finest wines were poured into cups imported from Greece. Some guests sat on cushions, others chose chairs. A constant stream of servants frequently changed the guests' alabaster plates.

The tjaty and his wife sat in state behind a well-laden table; servants washed their hands with perfumed water and hung necklaces of cornflowers about their necks. Each female guest received a lotus-flower, which she set in her wig.

Girls playing harps, lutes and tambourines enchanted their listeners. Bel-Tran had hired the best players in the city, demanding new melodies from them, which music-lovers would appreciate for their true worth.

One very old courtier, who could no longer walk, was enjoying the benefit of a comfortable commode, which enabled him to participate in the evening. After use, a servant removed the earthenware jar from under the seat, and replaced it with another, filled with perfumed sand.

Bel-Tran's cook was a genius with fine herbs. For this feast he had united the tastes of rosemary, cumin, sage, anise and cinnamon, which was known as 'truly noble'. Food-lovers were effusive in their congratulations, while everyone extolled the generosity of the head of the Double White House and his wife.

At last, Bel-Tran stood up and called for silence.

'My friends,' he said, 'on this wonderful evening, which your presence makes still more beautiful, I should like to pay homage to a man whose benevolent authority we all respect: Tjaty Pazair. The post of tjaty is a sacred institution, and through it the will of Pharaoh is expressed. Despite his youth, our dear Pazair has given evidence of a remarkable and surprising maturity. He has earned the people's love, he takes decisions quickly, and he works every day to preserve the greatness of our country. In your name, and as a sign of homage, we present him with this modest gift.'

The steward placed before Pazair a glazed blue earthenware cup, the bottom of which was decorated with a four-petalled lotus.

'My thanks to you,' said Pazair, 'and I hope you will permit me to present this beautiful work of art to the Temple of Ptah, the god of craftsmen. We must never forget that the temples have a duty to collect food and other resources, and to redistribute them according to the people's needs. Who would ever dare to lessen their role, thus damaging the country's harmony and destroying the balance created since the days of our earliest pharaohs? If food is nourishing, if the earth is fertile, if our society rests on the duties of the man and not on his rights, it is because Ma'at, the eternal Rule of life, is our guide. Whoever betrays her, whoever attacks her, is a criminal to whom no mercy must be shown. As long as justice is our central value, Egypt will live in peace and have cause for celebration.'

The tjaty's words were greeted with enthusiasm by one half of the audience and frozen horror by the other. When conversation began again, the two halves clashed in muffled voices, either praising the tjaty's words or criticizing them. Was a banquet an appropriate occasion for such a declaration? While Pazair was speaking, Bel-Tran's face had hardened. The tight smile he wore now deceived no one. After all, was there not talk of a profound divergence of views between the two men? Because of all the contradictory rumours, it was difficult to tell truth from falsehood.

After the meal, the guests took the air in the gardens. Kem doubled his vigilance, assisted by Killer; the tjaty listened to the grievances of a few senior officials who complained, justly, about the slowness of government. Bel-Tran, who was never at a loss for a cheery word, was holding the rapt attention of a group of courtiers.

Near the lake, Silkis came up to Neferet. 'I have been wanting for a long time to talk to you. At last, this evening gives me the chance.'

'Have you decided to get a divorce?' asked Neferet.

'But I love Bel-Tran so much – he's a wonderful husband. Besides, if I intervene on your behalf, perhaps the worst can be averted.'

'What do you mean by that?'

'Bel-Tran feels real esteem for Pazair. Why can't your husband be more reasonable? Together, the two of them could do wonderful work.'

'The tjaty doesn't believe that.'

'He's wrong. Can't you make to change his mind?' Silkis spoke in the naive, sugar-sweet voice of a child-woman.

'Pazair doesn't comfort himself with illusions.'

'There's so little time left – soon it will be too late. Surely the tjaty's obstinacy is a bad counsellor?'

'Compromise would be considerably worse.'

'And what about you? Rising to the position of principal doctor was far from easy. Why wreck your career?'

'Curing the sick is not a career,' said Neferet firmly.

'In that case, you won't refuse to treat me.'

'Yes I shall – I do.'

'A doctor can't choose her patients!'

'In the present circumstances, I can.'

'Why? What have I done wrong?'

'Are you daring to say you aren't a criminal?'

Silkis turned away. 'I don't understand . . . To accuse me, and . . .'

'Unburden your conscience and confess. That's the best remedy in the world.'

'What am I supposed to have done?'

'At the very least, you have taken illegal drugs.'

Silkis closed her eyes and hid her face in her hands. 'Stop saying these horrible things!'

'The tjaty has proof of your guilt.'

Close to an attack of hysteria, Silkis ran to hide in her apartments. Neferet rejoined Pazair. 'I'm afraid I was clumsy,' she said.

'Judging by Silkis's reaction, I'm sure you weren't.'

Bel-Tran cut in on them. 'What's happened?' he asked irritably. 'You—'

Neferet's gaze choked the words in his throat. It showed no hatred, no violence, but was full of a light which pierced him through and through. Bel-Tran felt himself laid bare, stripped of his lies, his connivings and his plots. His soul burnt, and a spasm clenched his chest. Feeling as though he were going to be sick, he withdrew from the fight and left the great pillared hall.

His part in the reception was at an end.

Followed discreetly by Kem, Pazair and Neferet moved to a quiet place, near the house, where they could talk privately.

'You are surely a sorceress,' said Pazair.

'One can't fight a sickness like that without magic. In fact, Bel-Tran looked inward, upon his true self. What he saw doesn't seem to have made him very happy.'

The gentle warmth of the night delighted them. For a few moments, as they strolled in the garden, they forgot that the passage of time was against them. They began to dream that Egypt would never change, that the scent of jasmine would always fill the garden, that the Nile flood would for all eternity nourish a people united in the love of their king.

The slight figure of a woman leapt out of a clump of bushes in front of them. She screamed in fear when, with an enormous bound, Killer leapt from the roof and landed between her and the couple, freezing her where she stood. With his mouth open and his nostrils dilated, he was obviously ready to attack.

'Stop him, please!'

'Lady Tapeni!' said Pazair in astonishment, laying a hand on Killer's shoulder. 'What an extraordinary way to approach me. You might have been badly hurt.'

Killer calmed down and went over to Kem, who had also leapt to the couple's defence, but Tapeni went on shaking for some time.

'I must search you, my lady,' said Kem.

'Get back!'

'If you refuse, I'll ask Killer to do it.'

Tapeni gave in. Pazair concluded that the priest who had given her her name, which meant 'the Mouse', had clearly detected her true nature: vivacious, nervous and sly.

Kem had hoped to find a mother-of-pearl pearl needle, proof of her wish to attack the tjaty, and of her guilt of Branir's murder, but she was carrying no weapons or tools.

When Kem had finished, Pazair asked her, 'What do you want to speak to me about?'

'Soon you won't be questioning anyone any more.'

'How do you know that? Are you a seer?'

She bit her lip.

'Once again, Tapeni, you have said both too much and too little.'

'No one in the whole of Egypt supports your rigorous government. The king will have to dismiss you.'

'That is for Pharaoh to decide. Is that all you have to say?'

'I've heard that Suti escaped from the fortress where he was serving his sentence.'

'You're well informed,' said Pazair.

'Don't hope that he'll come back.'

'I shall see him alive again – and so will you.'

'No one survives the harsh Nubian desert. He'll die of thirst there.'

'The law of the desert is in his favour. No only will he survive but he'll settle his accounts.'

'That flies in the face of justice.'

'I'm afraid that's true, but I cannot control him.'

'You must ensure my safety.'

'As I must the safety of all the inhabitants of this country.'

'You must have Suti hunted down and arrested.'

'In the Nubian desert? That's impossible. We shall just have to be patient and wait until he reappears. I wish you good night, Tapeni.'

Hidden behind the enormous trunk of a sycamore, ears straining, the shadow-eater saw the tjaty pass by, with Neferet, Kem and that damned Killer. After his recent failure, the assassin had wanted to try again during the reception. But Kem had been watching inside, and Killer outside. He might, through mere vanity, have wasted several years of success on trying to prove that no one, not even a tjaty, could escape him.

He must keep his nerve. After killing Short-Thighs, the shadow-eater had felt his hands shake for the first time. Killer impressed him no more than before, but not succeeding in killing Pazair exasperated him. Was a strange force protecting the tjaty? No, it was just a Nubian guard and a baboon with a keen intelligence.

The shadow-eater would win the fiercest battle of his career.

24

Suti fingered his lips, his cheeks, his forehead, but did not recognise the contours of his face. It was no more than a puffed-up, painful mass, and his eyelids were so swollen that he couldn't see. Nor could he could move his legs, so he had to be carried on a litter by six sturdy Nubians.

'Are you there, Panther?' he asked.

'Of course,' she replied.

'Then kill me.'

'You'll live. Another few days, and the scorpion's venom will disperse. The fact that you can speak shows that your blood is circulating again. The old warrior can't understand how you've resisted the poison.'

'But my legs . . . they're paralysed.'

'No, just tied to the litter. You were having convulsions – probably because of nightmares – and kept nearly tipping it over. Were you dreaming of Tapeni?'

'Certainly not. I was floating deep in an ocean of light, where no one could bother me.'

'You deserve to be abandoned at the side of the road.'

'How long have I been unconscious?'

'The sun has already risen three times.'

'Have we made any progress?'

'We're still going towards our gold.'

'Have you seen any Egyptian soldiers?'

'We haven't seen anyone, but we're nearing the border now – the Nubians are getting restive.'

'I'm taking back command,' said Suti.

'In your state?'

'Untie me.'

'Do you know how dreadful you are?'

But she told the Nubians to set the litter down, untied him and helped to his feet.

'It's good to feel the earth under my feet again,' he said. 'Quick, give me a staff.'

Leaning on a rough cane, Suti walked to the head of the tribe. Panther was impresssed by his determination.

The band passed to the west of Elephantine and the border post of the first Southern province. A few isolated warriors had joined them during their slow journey northwards. Suti trusted these valuable, experienced fighters: if they encountered desert guards they would not hesitate to take them on.

The Nubians followed the goddess. Laden with gold, they dreamt of conquests and victories, led by Suti, who was stronger than a scorpion. They crossed a barrier of granite by means of narrow paths, walked along the bed of a dried-up river, killed game for food, drank sparingly and made their way without complaint.

Suti's face had recovered its good looks, and the young man his energy. The first to rise, the last to go to bed, he fed greedily on the desert air and became tireless. Panther loved him all the more: he was taking on the stature of a true warrior chief, whose word was law and whose decisions were not open to debate.

The Nubians had made him several bows of varying sizes, which he used to bring down antelopes and a lion. With unerring instinct, as if he had roamed the unexplored tracks all his life, he led his little army to the water-sources.

'A band of desert guards is coming towards us,' one of the warriors warned him.

Suti recognized them at once: the All-Seeing Ones and their ferocious dogs roamed the desert to ensure the safety of caravans and to capture sand-travellers found pillaging. They did not usually venture into these parts.

'Let's attack them,' suggested Panther.

'No,' replied Suti. 'We'll hide, and let them go by.'

The Nubians hid in a massive rocky outcrop while the guards skirted it. The dogs were thirsty and tired, and did not sense their presence. The All-Seeing Ones had nearly finished their patrol, and were heading back to their base in a nearby valley.

'We could easily have killed them,' muttered Panther, lying down beside Suti.

'If they hadn't got back, the post at Elephantine would have raised the alarm.'

'You don't want to kill Egyptians – but I dream of it. You're a pariah, and you're the leader of rebel Nubians whose only trade is war. You'll have to fight soon. It is your nature, Suti, and you can't escape it.'

Panther caressed her lover's chest. Hidden by the granite rocks, oblivious of the danger, they embraced in the midday heat. Covered in gold jewellery from the Lost City, her skin golden and warm, the Libyan girl played her body as if it were a lyre and sang a burning melody whose every note Suti adored.

'This is the place,' said Panther. 'I recognize the countryside.' She gripped Suti's wrist tightly enough to break it. 'Our gold's over there, in that cave. To me it's more precious than any other gold in the world, because you killed an Egyptian general to get it.'

'We don't need it any more.'

'Yes we do! With it, you will be the master of gold.'

Suti could not take his eyes off the cave where he had hidden General Asher's treasure. Panther was right to bring him here. Rejecting that episode in his life and running away from it into oblivion would have been cowardly. Like his friend Pazair, Suti loved justice. If he hadn't struck down the fugitive traitor, no one would ever have done it. The gods had granted him the traitor's gold, which he intended to use to buy a life of peace from the Libyan warlord Adafi.

'Come on,' Panther demanded. 'Come and marvel at our future.'

As she walked forward, blinding flashes of light came from her magnificent collar and her bracelets. The Nubians knelt down, awed by their golden goddess's slow walk towards a shrine which only she knew: she had led them this deep into Egyptian territory in order to increase their magical power and make them invincible. When she and Suti went into the cave, the warriors sang an ancient chant which hailed the return of the far-off betrothed, ready to celebrate her wedding to the soul of her people.

Panther was convinced that taking possession of the gold would seal her destiny by uniting it with Suti's. This moment was the forebear of a thousand brilliant tomorrows.

Suti was reliving his execution of that vile murderer General Asher, who had been intent on escaping the tjaty's court and living to a happy old age in Libya, where he would have stirred up trouble against Egypt. Suti had no regrets about killing him. Engraved on his soul was the righteousness of the desert, where falsehood could not flourish.

The interior of the cave felt cool. Disturbed by their arrival, bats flew in all directions before once again hooking themselves on to the cave roof, their heads hanging down.

'It's gone!' cried Panther. 'It was here, I know it was, but where's the chariot?'

'Let's go further in.'

'There's no point. I remember exactly where we hid it.'

Suti searched every corner, every cranny, of the cave. But it was empty. 'Who could have known? And who would have dared ... ?'

Mad with rage, Panther tore off her golden collar and smashed it
against a rock. 'We'll rip out the belly of this cave of ill fortune!'

Suti picked up a piece of cloth. 'Look at this.'

She bent over the find. 'Dyed wool,' she said. 'Our thieves aren't
demons of the night, they're sand-travellers. When they took the
chariot out, one of them tore his robe on a jagged piece of rock.' All
at once, her hopes revived. 'We must go after them.'

'It wouldn't be any use,' said Suti.

'I'm not giving up.'

'Neither am I.'

'Then what do you suggest?'

'We stay here and wait – they'll come back.'

'Why are you so certain?'

'In our haste to explore the place, we forgot about Asher's body.'

'He's definitely dead.'

'His bones should still be where I killed him.'

'Perhaps the wind . . .'

'No, his friends have taken him away. They're lying in wait for us,
hoping for revenge.'

'Have we fallen into a trap?'

'Lookouts saw us arrive.'

'Supposing we hadn't come back?'

'That was unlikely. They'd have stayed at their posts for a long
time – for several years, if need be – as long as they weren't sure we
were dead. Wouldn't you have done the same in their place? Identifying
us is vital; killing us will be a pleasure.'

'We'll fight them.'

'As long as they give us time to prepare our defence. They've even
taken my old bow – they'd be delighted to shoot me with my own
arrows.'

The two of them left the cave and returned to their companions.

Naked to the waist, her magnificent, firm breasts bare to the sun,
Panther addressed the faithful. She explained to them that sand-travellers
had looted the golden goddess's shrine and stolen her possessions. A
fight looked inevitable, and she was entrusting Suti with the task of
leading them to victory.

No one protested, not even the old warrior. He felt rejuvenated at
the thought of making the sand drink the sand-travellers' blood: the
Nubians would demonstrate their prowess – no one could match them
in hand-to-hand fighting.

Although he agreed with that assessment, Suti had the Nubians
create a well-entrenched camp, using big stones and rocks behind
which their archers would shelter. In the cave, they stored their full

water-skins, food and weapons. Some distance from their position, they dug holes, equal distances apart.

Then the days of waiting began.

Because of the heat, according to the custom which Nubians and Egyptians shared outside towns, they lived naked. Panther never tired of admiring her lover's splendid body, and he responded in kind; their bronzed skin took no harm from the sun, which only intensified their desire. Each day, Panther wore different jewellery; gold emphasized the curves of her body, and made her inaccessible to anyone but Suti.

Suti enjoyed the lull. Sitting cross-legged, at one with the rocks and sand, he listened to the desert's secret songs, to its invisible movements and to the wind's words; he hardly noticed the heat. He feared the clash of weapons much less than the noise and bustle of the city; here, even the smallest action must be in harmony with silence, bearer of the nomads' steps.

Although Pazair had abandoned him, he would have liked to have his friend beside him, to share the moment when his wandering would come to an end. Without saying a word, they would have fed upon the same fire, their gaze lost in the ochre-coloured horizon, the devourer of all things ephemeral.

Catlike, Panther came up behind him and put her arms round him. As softly as a spring breeze, she caressed the nape of his neck.

'Supposing you're wrong?' she said.

'There's no chance of that.'

'Perhaps the looters will be satisfied with stealing our gold.'

'We disrupted their smuggling operation. Getting the gold back won't be enough: they must find out who we are.'

'If the Libyans are allied to the sand-travellers, will you fight them?'

'I shall kill the thieves whoever they are.'

Their kiss was worthy of the immense open spaces, their interlaced bodies rolled in the soft sand as it drifted in the northerly breeze.

The old warrior told Suti that the man sent to fetch water had not come back.

'When did he leave?' asked Suti.

'When the sun leapt above the cave. Judging by its position in the sky now, he should have got back long ago.'

'Perhaps the spring had dried up.'

'No, it would have supplied us for several weeks.'

'Do you trust him?'

'He was my cousin.'

'He might have been attacked by a lion.'

The old man shook his head. 'The wild animals drink at night, and in any case he knew how to avoid being attacked.'

'Shall we go and look for him?

'If he isn't back by sunset, it means he's dead.'

The hours went by. The Nubians no longer talked or sang. Motionless, they stared along the track that led to the spring, the direction from which where their comrade ought to have appeared.

The day-star sank low in the sky, entered the Peak of the West and descended into the ship of night. It would sail across the subterranean spaces, where it would confront the enormous dragon that would try to drink the water of the universe and dry up the Nile.

The track remained empty.

'He is dead,' declared the old warrior.

Suti doubled the guard. Perhaps the attackers would approach the cave. If they were sand-travellers, they wouldn't hesitate to break the rules of war and launch a night attack.

Sitting facing the desert, he wondered without grief if he was living his last hours. If so, would they be imbued with the peaceful gravity of the immemorial rocks, or with the fury of a last battle? He lay down and prepared to sleep.

Panther came and lay down beside him. 'Do you feel ready?'

'As ready as you are.'

'Don't try to die without me – we'll step through the gateway of the afterlife together. But before then we shall be rich and live like kings. If you really want it, we'll succeed. Be a true leader, Suti, and don't waste your energy.'

As he did not answer, she respected his silence and joined him in sleep.

The cold air woke Suti. The desert was grey, the morning light dimmed by thick mist.

Panther opened her eyes and shivered. 'Warm me up.'

He held her to him, but suddenly drew away, his eyes fixed on a point in the distance.

'To your posts,' he shouted to the Nubians.

Dozens of armed men and chariots were emerging out of the mist.

25

The sand-travellers stuck close together. With their straggly hair, unkempt beards, turbans, and long robes with coloured stripes, they did not look impressive. Some of them were starving and had jutting collarbones, hollow shoulders and staring ribs; they carried rolled-up mats on their bent backs.

As one, they drew their bows and let fly a first volley of arrows, but hit no one. When there was no response – Suti had given the order not to return fire – the sand-travellers took heart. Shouting loudly, they came nearer.

The Nubian archers showed that they deserved their reputation: not one missed his target. Moreover, their firing rhythm was rapid and sustained, and, although outnumbered ten to one, they quickly redressed the balance.

The surviving sand-travellers retreated to make way for light chariots, whose platforms were made of criss-crossed leather strips and which were covered with hyena-skin; the outside panels were decorated with the aggressive figure of a horse-god. In each chariot, one man drove the horses, while a second brandished a javelin. All the men had goatee beards and coppery skin.

'They're Libyans,' observed Suti.

'That's impossible!' cried Panther, sickened.

'Libyans allied to sand-travellers: remember your promise.'

'I'll talk to them – they won't attack me.'

'Don't deceive yourself.

'At least let me try.'

'It isn't worth the risk.'

The horses were pawing the ground. Each javelin-thrower raised his shield to chest height; once within range of their opponents, they would throw, their weapons.

Panther stood up and left her shelter. She picked her way through the rocks, and took a few steps across the flat expanse that separated her from the chariots.

'Lie down!' roared Suti.

A javelin was hurled, powerfully and accurately.

Before the Libyan had even finished his throw, Suti's arrow pierced his throat. Flinging herself aside, Panther avoided the lethal javelin. She crawled back towards the rocks.

The Libyans charged forward, while the Nubians, enraged by the attack on their golden goddess, fired arrow after arrow.

Too late, the charioteers saw the holes the Nubians had dug in the sand, and tried to swerve. A few avoided them, but most did not: some overturned, wheels came apart, chariot-shells broke, and their occupants were thrown to the ground. The Nubians charged at them and gave no quarter; they brought back horses and javelins from the field of battle.

When the attackers withdrew, Suti had lost only three men and had inflicted heavy losses on the enemy. The Nubians acclaimed their golden goddess, and the old warrior composed a song to her glory. Despite the lack of palm-wine, the men were drunk on victory; Suti had to shout himself hoarse to stop them leaving their positions. Every man wanted to wipe out the remainder of the enemy single-handed.

A red-painted chariot emerged from a cloud of dust. An unarmed man got out, his arms hanging loosely at his sides. He was haughty, with a curiously large, square head, out of proportion to his body. His harsh voice carried a long way.

'I want to speak to your leader.'

Suti stood up and showed himself. 'Here I am.'

'What is your name?'

'What is yours?'

'They call me Adafi.'

'And I am Suti, an officer of the Egyptian army.'

'Let us move closer together. Shouting is not conducive to a constructive conversation.'

The two men advanced towards each other.

'So,' said Suti, 'you are Adafi, Egypt's sworn enemy, the conspirator, the troublemaker.'

'And it was you who killed my friend General Asher.'

'I had that honour, though the traitor's death was too easy.'

'An Egyptian officer leading a band of Nubian rebels. Doesn't that make you a traitor, too?'

'You stole my gold.'

'It belonged to me. It was the price agreed with the general for his peaceful retirement in my lands.'

'That treasure is mine.'

'By what right?'

'War booty.'

Adafi smiled grimly. 'You aren't timid, are you, young man?'

'I demand what is due to me.'

'What do you know of my dealings with the miners?'

'Your gang was wiped out and you have no support inside Egypt. You'd better withdraw as quickly as possible and hide in some far corner of your barbarous country. Perhaps Pharaoh's anger won't reach you there.'

'If you want your gold, you'll have to earn it.'

'Is it here?'

'It's in my tent. Since you killed Asher, whose bones I buried, why don't we become friends? To seal the pact, I offer you half the gold.'

'I want all of it.'

'You're too greedy.'

'You've already lost a lot of men,' Suti pointed out. 'My warriors are better than yours.'

'That may be true, but I know where your traps are now, and there are more of us.'

'My Nubians will fight to the last man.'

'Who is the woman?'

'Their golden goddess. Because of her, they fear nothing and no one.'

'My sword will soon cut off the head of that superstition.'

'If you live.'

'Unless you join me, I'll kill you.'

'You won't escape, Adafi. You'll be the most notable of my trophies.'

'Pride has turned your head.'

'If you want to spare the lives of your troops, fight me in single combat.'

The Libyan stared at Suti. 'Against me, you don't stand a chance.'

'I'll be the judge of that.'

'You're very young to die.'

'If I win, I shall take back the gold.'

'And if you lose?'

'You can take mine.'

'Yours? What do you mean?'

'My Nubians are carrying a lot of it.'

'You've taken over the general's smuggling ring, have you?'

Suti said nothing.

'You'll die,' prophesied Adafi, his broad forehead furrowed.

'What weapons shall we use?'

'Each unto his own.'

'I demand that a pact is signed, and approved by both camps.'

'The gods will bear witness.'

The ceremony was organized straight away. Three Libyans and three Nubians, including the old warrior, took part. They called upon the spirits of fire, air, water and earth to destroy either man if he committed perjury, then agreed upon a night's rest before the duel.

Near the cave, the Nubians formed a circle round the golden goddess. They implored her protection and begged her to grant victory to their hero. Using crumbling stones, which left red marks on the skin, they decorated Suti's body with signs of war.

'Don't let us be turned into slaves,' they besought him.

The Egyptian sat down facing the sun, deriving from the desert light the strength of the giants of yore, who could move huge granite blocks to build temples in which the Invisible was embodied. Though he had rejected the way of scribes and priests, Suti still felt the presence of a hidden energy in both sky and ground; he absorbed it as he breathed, channelled it as he concentrated on the goal that must be attained.

Panther knelt beside him. 'This is mad,' she said. 'Adafi has never been beaten in single combat.'

'What's his favourite weapon?'

'The javelin.'

'My arrows will fly faster.'

'I don't want to lose you.'

'As you want to be very rich, I've got to take risks. Believe me, there was no alternative. Seeing those Nubians slaughtered sickened me.'

'Does the thought of my being widowed leave you unmoved?'

Suti smiled. 'You're the golden goddess. You'll protect me.'

'When Adafi has killed you, I shall stab him in the belly with my dagger.'

'Then your countrymen will kill you.'

'The Nubians will defend me – and it'll be the massacre you dread.'

'Unless I win.'

'I shall bury you in the desert and then go and burn Tapeni alive.'

'Will you give me permission to light the pyre?'

'I love you when you dream. I love you because you dream.'

The mist had covered the desert again, smothering the dawn light. Suti walked forward; the sand squeaked under his bare feet. In his right hand he carried a medium-range bow, the best he had, and in his left a single arrow: he would not have time to fire another.

Adafi had the reputation of being an invincible fighter, whom no opponent had even come close to beating. As elusive as the mist, he had evaded a number of military forces sent to catch him. His favoured form of action was arming rebels and looters so as to maintain instability in the western provinces of the Delta. His abiding dream was of reigning over the North of Egypt.

Rays of sunlight pierced the grey mist. Very dignified in his red and green robe, his hair hidden by a black turban, Adafi took up position fifty paces from his opponent.

Suti knew he had lost.

Adafi was wielding not a javelin but Suti's own favourite acacia-wood bow, the one he had hidden in the cave. It was of exceptional quality, and could fire an arrow more than seventy paces in a direct shot. The one Suti was using seemed pathetic by comparison. Its accuracy was unpredictable, and it wouldn't enable him to kill the Libyan, only to wound him at most. If he tried to go any nearer, Adafi would fire first, giving Suti no chance to respond.

The Libyan's face had changed: hard and closed, it no longer showed the slightest trace of humanity. Adafi wanted to kill: his entire being embodied death. His eyes were cold, and he was waiting for his victim to start trembling.

Suti suddenly realized why the Libyan always emerged victorious from his duels. Flat on his belly behind a small mound of rocks on the left, a Libyan archer was protecting Adafi. Would the archer shoot before his master? Were they coordinating their efforts?

Suti cursed himself for his stupidity. An open, honest fight, respect for a man's word . . . Adafi hadn't wasted a moment's thought on that. The young Egyptian's first instructor had taught him that sand-travellers and Libyans often stabbed you in the back. Forgetting that warning might well have cost him his life.

Adafi, Suti and the Libyan archer all drew their bows at the same moment. Suti did so progressively, increasing the tension little by little. His behaviour amused Adafi, who had assumed that Suti would first try to kill the man to his left, then fire another arrow at Adafi. But he was armed with only one arrow.

Out of the corner of his eye, Suti saw something which was as quick as it was brutal. Panther snaked out of the rocks behind the archer and cut his throat. Adafi saw, too, and aimed his arrow at Panther, who flattened herself in the sand. Suti took advantage of that mistake, drew the bowstring as far as it would go, put his soul into the arrow and fired.

Aware of having made a mistake, Adafi hurried his shot, and his arrow merely grazed Suti's cheek. The Egyptian's plunged into Adafi's right eye. He dropped to the ground, face down, stone dead.

While the Nubians shouted with joy, Suti cut off the defeated man's right hand and brandished his bow at the heavens.

*

The sand-travellers and the Libyans laid down their arms and prostrated themselves before the embracing couple of Suti and Panther.

The golden goddess was radiant with happiness. Rich, happy, an army at her feet, Libyan soldiers forced to obey her: her wildest dreams were coming true.

'You are free to leave or to submit to me,' Suti told the Libyans. 'If you follow me you'll have a lot of gold, but at the first sign of disobedience I'll kill you with my own hands.'

No one moved. The promised reward would have seduced even the most suspicious of men.

Suti examined the chariots and the horses, and was well satisfied with what he found. With a few well-trained charioteers, and Nubian archers who were better than any rival, he had an effective, unified army at his disposal.

'You are the master of gold,' said Panther joyfully.

'You saved my life again.'

'I've told you before: without me, you won't achieve anything great.'

Suti distributed a first payment, which dispelled any lingering hostility towards him. The Libyans offered the Nubians palm-wine, and their fraternization took the form of a drinking-session punctuated by songs and laughter. Their new chief went off on his own, preferring the silence of the desert.

After a while, Panther joined him. 'Have you forgotten me, in your dream?'

'Of course not. You're the one who inspires me.'

'You have done Egypt an enormous service by killing Adafi and eliminating one of her most tenacious enemies.'

'What am I to do with this victory?'

26

Patchily shaven, and dressed in a shabby kilt and worn-out sandals, Pazair walked through the great market at Memphis, mingling with the crowd – there was no better way of finding out what people were thinking. He noted with satisfaction that all the usual produce was on sale. Boats were circulating freely on the Nile, and food was being delivered regularly. A recent check on the ports and on the artificial lakes, where boats were overhauled twice a year, had shown that the trading-fleet was in an excellent condition.

Pazair noted that bartering was proceeding well, and that exchanges were taking place normally. Prices were under control, and did not penalize the poor. Among the traders were many women who held respected and coveted positions. When barter went on a long time, water-bearers offered the participants a drink. 'I'm very happy with that,' exclaimed a peasant, pleased to have acquired a pitcher in exchange for some juicy figs.

People gathered in curiosity around a magnificent piece of linen which two cloth-merchants were unfolding.

'What a beautiful piece of material,' commented a prosperous-looking woman.

'That's why it's expensive,' said the clothmaker.

'Since the new tjaty was appointed, unseasonal price rises are frowned upon.'

'So much the better. People will come to the market more often and buy better quality. If you take this linen, I'll throw in a scarf.'

While the transaction was being concluded, Pazair moved to another stall, that of a man selling sandals, which hung by strings from a wooden bar supported by two small uprights.

'You'd do well to buy a new pair of shoes, my lad,' commented the seller. 'You've walked too far in the ones you're wearing, and the soles will soon give way.'

'I can't afford it.'

'You have an honest face. I'll give you credit.'

'That's against my principles.'

'The man who has no debts gets rich! All right, I'll mend yours very cheaply.'

Feeling hungry, Pazair ate a honey-cake, while listening to a conversation about preparing the next meal. There was no anxiety in people's words, and no one was contesting the tjaty's actions. And yet Pazair was far from reassured: the name of Ramses was almost never uttered.

Pazair went over to a woman selling ointments, and began haggling over a small phial.

'It's rather expensive,' he said.

'Are you from the city?'

'No, the country, but the stories I heard about Memphis made me want to see it. Ramses has made it the most beautiful city in the world. I'd love to see him. When will he come out of his palace?'

'No one knows. People say he is ill and living at Pi-Ramses, in the Delta.'

'What, Ramses? But he's the healthiest man in Egypt.'

'People are whispering that his magical power is exhausted.'

'Then let it be regenerated.'

'If that's still possible,' said the seller.

'If it isn't there'll have to be a new king.'

The seller shrugged.

'Who will succeed Ramses?' asked Pazair.

'Who knows?'

Suddenly, shouts rang out. The crowd scattered, opening a way for Killer, who in a few bounds was at Pazair's feet. Thinking she was dealing with a thief and that the baboon was going to arrest him, the seller immediately put a rope round the delinquent's neck to stop him getting away. For once, Killer did not bite his victim in the leg, but merely sat in front of her until Kem arrived.

'I arrested him myself!' boasted the seller. 'Am I entitled to a reward?'

'We'll see,' replied Kem, leading Pazair away.

'You look angry,' said the tjaty.

'Why didn't you warn me you were coming here? You've been extremely rash.'

'No one would have recognized me.'

'Killer found you easily.'

'I needed to listen to people.'

'And did you learn any more?'

'The situation is not heartening: Bel-Tran is preparing people for the fall of Ramses.'

*

Neferet was late, despite the importance of the meeting of the doctors' council over which she was to preside. A few people grumbled, accusing her of taking her job lightly, but she had in fact been giving emergency treatment to Mischief, who was suffering from indigestion, Brave, who had coughing spasms, and Way-Finder, who had scorched his foot. Taking care of the household's three good spirits seemed to her to be a priority.

The assembled dignitaries all stood up when she entered, and bowed to her. Neferet's beauty instantly dispelled all criticism; when she spoke, her voice acted like a soothing balm, and the old doctors never tired of that remedy.

Neferet was very surprised to find Bel-Tran present.

'The government has asked me to be the economic spokesman,' he explained. 'Today measures are to be adopted concerning the people's health. I must be sure those measures don't unbalance the state's resources, for which I am responsible to the tjaty.'

The Double White House was usually content to send a delegate. The direct intervention of the director signalled a battle for which Neferet was not prepared.

'I am not satisfied with the number of hospitals in the provincial capitals and the small towns. I propose that ten establishments are created, on the model of the one in Memphis.'

'Objection,' cut in Bel-Tran. 'The cost would be enormous.'

'The provincial governors will finance their construction; the Health secretariat will provide them with skilled doctors and ensure their proper running. We shall not require assistance from the Double White House.'

'It will affect taxes.'

'According to Pharaoh's decree, the governors have a choice: either to pay taxes to your ministry, or to improve health provision. They have chosen the second solution, on my advice, and have done so perfectly legally. We shall continue next year, I hope.'

Bel-Tran was obliged to give way. He had not expected Neferet to act so quickly and skilfully. She was quietly creating solid bonds with local officials.

She said, 'According to the *Book of Protection*, which dates from the times of the founding ancestors, Egypt must not neglect any of her children: it is up to us, as doctors, to heal those who suffer. At the start of his reign, Ramses promised a happy life to the young generations, and for everyone health is an essential element of that happiness. I have therefore decided to train more doctors and nurses, so that everyone, irrespective of where they live, may benefit from the best treatment.'

'I should like to see a change in the medical order,' said Bel-Tran. 'We ought to give much more importance to specialists and much less to ordinary doctors. When Egypt is opened up to the outside world, as she soon will be, not only will the specialists soon grow rich, but we'll be able to profit greatly from sending them to work abroad.'

'So long as I am principal doctor,' declared Neferet, 'we shall follow tradition. If the specialists are given too much power, medicine will lose sight of the most important thing of all: the human being as a whole, the harmony of mind and body.'

'Unless you accept my proposal, the Double White House will actively oppose you.'

'Is this a case of blackmail?'

Bel-Tran stood up and addressed the assembly imperiously. 'Egyptian medicine is the best in the world – many foreign doctors spend time with us to learn the elements of it. But we must reform our methods, and make more profits from this resource. Your skill and learning deserve better, believe me! Let us produce many more remedies, and use the drugs and poisons whose secrets we know. Above all, let us concern ourselves with quantity. That is the future.'

'We reject it,' said Neferet.

'You are wrong. I came here to warn you, you and your colleagues, in a friendly manner. Refusing my help would be a disastrous mistake.'

'Accepting it would mean destroying our vocation.'

'A vocation is not something which can make us money.'

'Neither is health.'

'You're wrong, just like the tjaty. Defending the past will lead nowhere.'

'I cannot cure the disease from which you suffer.'

Bagey had come to consult Neferet because of unbearable pains in his kidneys and blood in his urine. After examining him for more than an hour, she diagnosed the presence of parasites in his blood, and prescribed a preparation made from pine-kernel seeds, grasses, henbane, honey and Nubian earth,* to be taken each evening before retiring. She reassured her patient that the treatment would be highly effective.

'My body is wearing out,' lamented Bagey.

'You're stronger than you think.'

'My hardiness is failing.'

'It's the infection making you feel weak. I promise you'll soon feel better, and will enjoy many more years of good health.'

---

* Two unidentified ingredients, the plant *shames* and the fruit *shasha*, were also added.

'How is your husband?' asked Bagey.

'He'd like to see you again.'

Pazair and Bagey walked in the shade of the tall trees in the garden. Pleased with this unexpected walk, Brave accompanied them, sniffing at the flowerbeds as he passed.

'Bel-Tran is attacking on all fronts,' said Pazair, 'but I'm managing to slow him down.'

'Have you gained the trust of the main government officials?'

'Some of them agree with me and distrust him. Fortunately, his brutality and over-obvious ambition have bothered certain people's consciences. Many scribes are faithful to the ancient wisdom that created this country.'

'I sense that you're calmer, more sure of yourself.'

'I only seem that way. Every day is like a battle, and I cannot predict where the next attack will come from. I wish I had your long experience.'

'Don't deceive yourself. I no longer had the strength for the fight. Pharaoh was right to choose you. Bel-Tran realizes that now: he wasn't expecting such strong resistance on your part.'

Pazair shook his head. 'How can anyone be treacherous as that?'

'Human nature is capable of the worst things imaginable.'

'Sometimes I lose heart. The small victories I win cannot hold back the passage of time. Spring has begun, and people are already talking of the next flood.'

'What does Ramses say?'

'He urges me to keep working. By yielding not a cubit of ground to Bel-Tran, I get the impression that his deadline is being delayed.'

'You've even conquered part of his territory.'

'That is the only thing that gives me hope. By weakening him, perhaps I shall make him begin to doubt himself. If he tried to seize power without enough support, he'd fail. But is there enough time left for me break down the pillars on which his scheme rests?'

'The people like you, Pazair – they fear you, but they like you. You carry out your duties impeccably, in accordance with the duties the king indicated to you. Coming from me, this is not flattery.'

'Bel-Tran would gladly buy my services! When I think back over his demonstrations of friendship, I wonder if he was sincere for a single moment, or if he was playing a part from the very first second, in the hope of including me in his plot.'

'Why should hypocrisy have limits?'

'You have no illusions, have you?'

'I eschew fervour: it is futile and dangerous.'

'I'd like to show you some documents concerning the land registry and surveys. Would you be kind enough to check whether some of the information has been altered?'

'Gladly, particularly as it falls within my original speciality. What are you worried about?'

'That Bel-Tran and his allies are trying to steal land legally.'

The evening was so beautiful and so mild that Pazair allowed himself a brief rest beside the pool in his garden. Sitting on the edge, her feet in the water, the faintest line of green kohl on her eyelids, Neferet was playing a lute whose strings, tuned in unison, were knotted at the base of the neck. Its gentle, mellow tone delighted him, and the melody harmonized with the quiver of the leaves as the northerly breeze stirred them.

Pazair thought of Suti, who would have loved this music. Where was he wandering, and what dangers was he facing? The tjaty was banking on his heroism to wipe away his faults, but he would come up against the ferocity of the lady Tapeni. According to Kem, she was spending less and less time in the weaving-workshop and was running all over the city. How would she try to harm him?

The voice of the lute soothed his anxieties. Eyes closed, Pazair gave himself up himself to the magic of the music.

The shadow-eater decided to act.

There was only one possible observation post near the tjaty's home, a tall date-palm set in the middle of the courtyard of a small house which belonged to a retired couple. The murderer had got inside, knocked them out, then climbed to the top of the tree, armed with his weapon.

Luck was smiling on him. As he had hoped, this beautiful evening, when the declining sun caressed the skin, the tjaty had come home earlier than usual and was relaxing with his wife, in a clear, unobstructed area.

The shadow-eater gripped a curved throwing-stick of the kind used by bird-hunters. Killer was perched on the roof of the tjaty's house, and so would not have time to take action. The throwing-stick, a fearsome weapon when handled skilfully, would break Pazair's neck.

The criminal found himself a stable position, holding on to a branch with his left hand; he concentrated, and worked out the trajectory. Although the distance was considerable, he would not miss: with this weapon he had, from a very young age, displayed exceptional ability. Shattering birds' skulls amused him enormously.

Mischief was constantly on the alert, ready to gather any fruit that fell from the tree, or to play with the first blackbird on the date-palm. When the shadow-eater's arm drew back, she gave a cry of alarm.

Killer reacted with lightning speed. In a split second, he understood the monkey's call, saw the throwing-stick cleave the air, identified its target and hurled himself from the roof in a prodigious leap. He caught the weapon in mid-air, and landed a few paces from the tjaty.

Stunned, Neferet dropped her lute. Brave, who had been dozing, awoke with a start and jumped on to his master's lap.

His body spear-straight, one bloodstained paw firmly holding the throwing-stick, Killer gazed proudly at Egypt's first minister, whom he had just, once again, saved from the jaws of death.

The shadow-eater was already running away down an alley, his mind in turmoil. What god inhabited the soul of that baboon? For the first time in his career, the murderer doubted his own abilities. Pazair was not a man like other men; a supernatural force seemed to protect him. Could it be that the goddess Ma'at, the tjaty's justice, was making him invulnerable?

27

Killer allowed himself to be cosseted. Neferet washed his paw with copper-water, cleaned the wound, and bandaged it. Although she had seen it before, Killer's strength astonished her: despite the heaviness of his fall, the wound was not deep and would quickly scar over. Hardened to pain, he would need only one or two days of relative rest, and would not even stop patrolling.

'It's a fine weapon,' said Kem as he examined the throwing-stick, 'and perhaps the start of a new lead. The shadow-eater was kind enough to leave us an interesting clue. It's a pity you didn't see him.'

'I didn't even have time to be afraid,' confessed Pazair. 'If Mischief hadn't cried out . . .'

The monkey dared approach the enormous baboon and touched him on the nose; Killer did not move a muscle. Growing bolder, Mischief laid her tiny paw on his huge thigh. His gaze seemed to soften.

'I've doubled the guard around your estate,' said Kem, 'and I shall question the makers of throwing-sticks myself. At last we have a chance of identifying the murderer.'

A fierce quarrel had set Silkis against Bel-Tran. Although Bel-Tran admired his son, who was his designated heir, he intended to be master in his own home. But Silkis refused to discipline the little boy, and still less to discipline their daughter, whose lies and insults she accepted without a murmur.

When her husband criticized her for this, Silkis flew into a rage. Losing her temper, she ripped up lengths of costly fabric, smashed a valuable chest and trampled on expensive gowns. Before leaving for his office, Bel-Tran uttered the terrifying words: 'You are mad.'

Mad . . . the word frightened her. She was a normal woman, in love with her husband, the devoted slave of a rich man, and an attentive mother. By taking part in the conspiracy, by distracting the Sphinx's guard commander with her nakedness, she had obeyed Bel-Tran, trusting in his destiny. Before long, he and she would reign over Egypt.

But ghosts haunted her. By letting herself be raped by the shadow-eater, she had plunged into dark shadows which had not melted away. The crimes to which she was party troubled her less than that wantonness, that source of disturbing pleasure. And then there was the break with Neferet . . . Was it madness, falsehood or perversion to want to remain her friend?

Nightmare succeeded nightmare, sleepless night followed sleepless night.

Only one man could save her: the dream-interpreter. He charged exorbitant fees, but he would listen to her and guide her.

Silkis told her maid to bring a veil, to hide her face.

The servant began to cry.

'What's the matter?' asked Silkis.

'Oh, my lady, something terrible's happened. It's dead.'

'What is?'

'Come and see.'

The aloe, a superb shrub crowned with orange, yellow and red flowers, was no more than a dried-up stalk. Not only was it a rare specimen, a gift from Bel-Tran, but also it had produced remedies which Silkis used every day. Oil of aloe, applied to the genitals, prevented inflammation and favoured bodily union. In addition, when applied to the red patches on Bel-Tran's leg, it reduced the itching.

Silkis felt bereft, and the sight of it brought on an atrocious headache. Soon she, too, would wither, like the aloe.

The room where the Syrian dream-interpreter saw his clients was painted black and kept dark to soothe his clientele, which consisted solely of rich noble ladies. Instead of becoming a workman or a trader, he had studied grimoires and keys to dreams, determined to calm the anxieties of a few idle women in exchange for a well-deserved reward. The fish were not easy to catch in a happy, free society, but once in his net they never got out again. To be effective, the treatment must be of unlimited duration. Once that principle had been accepted, all he had to do was interpret his patients' fantasies, more or less roughly. They were unbalanced when they arrived, and unbalanced when they left; but at least he settled them in their madness, be it slight or otherwise, and made a lot of money. Up to now, his only problem had been avoiding the close attention of the taxation scribes, so he paid heavy taxes in order to carry on his activities without trouble. But the appointment of Neferet as Egypt's principal doctor worried him: according to reliable people, she could not be bought and showed no lenience to charlatans like him.

When she arrived, Silkis lay down on a mat, closed her eyes, and prepared to answer his questions.

'Have you had any dreams lately?' he asked.

'I had a horrible one. I was holding a dagger and plunging it into the neck of a bull.'

'What happened?'

'My blade broke, and the bull turned on me and trampled me underfoot.'

'Are your relations with your husband . . . satisfactory?'

'His work takes all his energy. At night he's so tired that he falls asleep straight away. And when he does have time for lovemaking, he's always in a hurry – too much of a hurry.'

'You must tell me everything, Lady Silkis.'

'Yes, yes, I understand.'

'Have you ever in fact wielded a dagger?'

'No.'

'Or anything like that?'

'No, I don't think so.'

'A needle?'

'A needle, yes.'

'A mother-of-pearl needle?'

'Yes, of course. I can weave, and that's my favourite tool.'

'Have you ever used it to attack someone?'

'No, I swear I haven't.'

'A middle-aged man . . . He turns his back on you, you approach soundlessly and plunge the needle into his neck.'

Silkis howled, bit her fingers, and twisted and turned on the mat. Alarmed, the dream-interpreter was on the point of calling for help, but the attack of dementia subsided and Silkis sat up, dripping with sweat.

'I didn't kill anyone,' she declared in a hoarse, hallucinatory voice. 'I didn't have the courage. But if Bel-Tran ever asks me to, I will. To keep him, I'll do it.'

'You are cured, Lady Silkis.'

'What . . . what are you saying?'

'You no longer need my care.'

The donkeys were loaded and ready to leave for the port when Kem approached the dream-interpreter.

'You've finished packing, have you?'

'The boat's waiting for me. I'm going to Greece, where I won't be given any trouble.'

'A wise decision.'

'I have your promise: the trade-control officers won't stop me?'

'That will depend on your goodwill.'

'I questioned the lady Silkis, as you asked me to.'

'Did you ask her the right questions?'

'I didn't understand, but I obeyed you.'

'And what was the result?'

'She didn't kill anyone.'

'Are you absolutely certain of that?'

'Absolutely. I may be a charlatan, but I know that type of woman. If you'd seen her in her delirium, you'd know she wasn't play-acting.'

'Forget all about her – and about Egypt.'

Tapeni was on the verge of tears. Opposite her, in front of a low table covered with unrolled papyri, sat an angry Bel-Tran.

'I've asked everyone in Memphis, I promise you,' she said.

'That makes your failure all the more bitter, dear friend.'

'Pazair is faithful to his wife, he doesn't gamble, has no debts, and isn't involved in anything illegal. It's insane, but the man is irreproachable.'

'I warned you: he is the tjaty.'

'Tjaty or not, I thought that . . .'

'Your greed distorts your thinking, Tapeni. Egypt remains a land apart, whose judges, particularly the most senior ones, adopt honesty as a way of life. It is ridiculous and outdated, I agree, but one must take account of reality. Pazair believes in his office and fulfils it with passion.'

The pretty brunette was nervous, and unsure what to do. 'I was wrong about him.'

'I don't like people who fail. When you work for me, you succeed.'

'If he has a weakness, I'll find it.'

'And what if he hasn't?'

'Then . . . he must be given one – without his knowledge.'

'That's an excellent idea. What do you suggest?'

'I'll have to think. I might—'

'It is all thought out already. I have a simple plan, based on the trade in very special items. Will you still help me?'

'I am at your disposal.'

Bel-Tran gave his instructions. Tapeni's failure had confirmed him in his hatred of women: how right the Greeks were to consider them inferior to men. Egypt granted them too much status. An incompetent like Tapeni would end up becoming an encumbrance. It would be as well to get rid of her as soon as possible, at the same time demonstrating to Pazair that his famous justice was powerless.

*

In the open-air workshop, five men were hard at work. From acacia-wood, sycamore and tamarisk, they were making throwing-sticks, some stronger than others, some more expensive.

Kem was questioning the owner, a squat, heavy-faced fifty-year-old.

'Who are your customers?'

'Bird-catchers and hunters. Does that interest you?'

'Very much.'

'Why?'

'Have you committed any crimes?'

A workman whispered a few words in the owner's ear.

'The commander of the guards in my workshop! Are you looking for someone?'

'Did you make this throwing-stick?'

The owner examined the weapon intended to kill Pazair. 'It's fine work, very good quality. With this, you can hit a target a long way away.'

'Answer my question.'

'No, it wasn't me.'

'Which workshops are capable of making it?'

'I don't know.'

'I find that surprising.'

'Sorry, I can't help you. Another time, perhaps.'

When Kem turned and left the workshop without another word, the owner was much relieved. The commander wasn't as determined as people claimed.

When he shut the workshop at nightfall, he changed his opinion.

The Nubian's huge hand came down on his shoulder. 'You lied to me.'

'No I didn't, I—'

'Don't lie again. Do you not know that I am more savage than my baboon?'

'My workshop's doing well, I have good workers . . . Why are you victimizing me?'

'Tell me about this throwing-stick.'

'All right, I made it.'

'And who bought it?'

'No one. It was stolen.'

'When?'

'The day before yesterday.'

'Why didn't you tell me the truth earlier?'

'When I saw it in your hand, I was afraid it might have been used in some rather dubious affair. Wouldn't you have kept quiet in my place?'

'You've no idea of the thief's identity?'

'None at all. A valuable stick like that . . . I'd very much like to have it back.'

'You'll have to make do with my lenience.'

The trail leading to the shadow-eater had been cut off.

Neferet took charge of difficult cases and carried out delicate operations. Despite her position and her heavy administrative burden, she never refused to help in emergencies.

She was surprised when Sababu came to see her at the hospital, because all Sababu suffered from was rheumatism. Neferet had cured Sababu of an inflamed shoulder which had threatened to cost her the use of her arm, and her patient was profoundly grateful.

'Has your rheumatism worsened?' asked Neferet.

'No, the treatment is still working well. I've come knocking on your door for another reason.'

The beautiful Sababu was still fairly young – she admitted to being thirty – and she ran the most famous ale-house in Memphis, staffed with delectable girls, and worked as a much-sought-after prostitute. Skilfully made up, perfumed to just the right side of excess, knowing how to make the most of her looks, she mocked at convention. But she greatly admired the tjaty and his wife: the truth of their marriage, a union which nothing could damage, gave her confidence in a kind of life she herself would never know. Moreover, she had never detected any hostility or contempt in Neferet, only the wish to heal.

Sababu put a porcelain vase on the table in front of Neferet. 'Break it,' she said.

'Really? A fine vase like this?'

'Please break it.'

Neferet smashed the vase on the stone-paved floor. In the middle of the fragments lay a stone phallus and a lapis-lazuli vulva, both covered in Babylonian magical inscriptions.

'I discovered this smuggling by chance,' explained Sababu, 'but I'd have heard about it sooner or later. These sculptures are designed to reawaken desire in tired people, and to make barren women fertile. It's illegal to bring them into Egypt without declaring them. In other vases like this, I found alum, which is said to increase pleasure and combat impotence. I detest such artificial aids – they make love unnatural. Honour Egypt by halting this loathsome trade.' Despite her activities, Sababu had a certain grandeur.

'Do you know who the smugglers are?' asked Neferet.

'All I know is that the deliveries are made on the western quay at night.'

'I'll see that something is done. Now, tell me, how is your shoulder?'

'I haven't had any more pain.'

'If it comes back, don't hesitate to consult me.'

'What will you do about the smuggling?'

'I shall tell the tjaty about it.'

Waves had formed on the river; they broke on the stones of an abandoned quay, towards which a boat was being rowed. The captain was skilful, and steered the boat gently in to the quay. At once a dozen men ran up, in a hurry to unload the cargo.

Their task was done and they were receiving their pay, in the form of amulets, from a woman when Kem deployed his men and proceeded to make rapid and problem-free arrests. Only the woman struggled and tried to get away.

Kem took a torch from one of his men and held it near her face. 'Lady Tapeni!'

'Let me go.'

'I'm afraid I must lock you up in prison. You are, after all, involved in smuggling.'

'I've got powerful friends – they'll protect me.'

'Who are they?'

'If you don't let me go, you'll regret it.'

'Bring her,' ordered Kem.

Tapeni struggled fiercely, but in vain. 'I take my orders from Bel-Tran.'

As he had hard proof, Pazair made judging the case a priority. Before convening the court, he arranged a confrontation between Tapeni and Bel-Tran.

The pretty brunette was very agitated; as soon as Bel-Tran arrived, she flew at him and demanded, 'Make them set me free, Bel-Tran.'

'If this woman does not calm down,' he said to Pazair, 'I shall leave. Why have I been summoned here?'

'The lady Tapeni accuses you of having employed her in connection with illegal trading.'

'That's ridiculous.'

'What do you mean, ridiculous?' she exclaimed. 'I was to sell those things to important citizens, in order to compromise them.'

'Tjaty, I think the lady Tapeni has lost her reason.'

'Don't use that tone of voice,' she retorted, 'or I'll tell the tjaty everything.'

'As you wish,' said Bel-Tran.

'But that's insane! Do you realize—'

'Your ravings don't interest me.'

'So you're abandoning me, are you? Well, so much the worse for you.' Tapeni turned to the tjaty. 'Among those important people, you were the prime target. What a scandal there'd have been if people had learnt that you and your lovely wife were indulging in distasteful practices. A good way of sullying your reputation, wasn't it? It was Bel-Tran's idea, and he told me to do it.'

'This is mere spiteful rambling,' sneered Bel-Tran.

'It's the truth!'

'Have you even the smallest piece of proof?'

'My word will be enough.'

'No one will doubt that you yourself are the author of this scheme – you were caught red-handed, Lady Tapeni. Your hatred for the tjaty has led you too far. Thanks to the gods, I have suspected you for a long time, and I had the courage to act. I'm proud of having denounced you.'

'Denounced . . .'

'That is correct,' nodded the tjaty. 'Bel-Tran wrote a report warning of your illegal activities. It was sent yesterday to Commander Kem and registered by his scribes.'

'My cooperation with the law is self-evident,' said Bel-Tran. 'I hope the lady Tapeni will be severely punished. Attacking public morality is an abominable crime.'

28

It took Pazair several hours of walking in the countryside, accompanied by Brave and Way-Finder, to calm his anger. Bel-Tran's triumphant smile was an insult to justice, a wound so deep that even Neferet could not heal it.

There was one small consolation: his enemy had lost one of his allies by betraying her. Tapeni had been sentenced to a short period in prison, and stripped of her civic rights. The great beneficiary of this situation was Suti, who, since divorce documents had been drawn up, would not now have to work for his ex-wife. The downfall of the weaver, caught in the trap of her own greed, would give him back his freedom.

The donkey's gentle pace and the dog's happy confidence calmed Pazair's heart, and as he walked the serenity of the countryside and the nobility of the Nile dispelled his distress. At that moment, he would have liked to confront Bel-Tran, man to man, and wring his neck. But that was a childish whim, because Bel-Tran had so arranged matters that if he were killed it would in no way prevent Ramses' downfall and Egypt's descent into a world where materialism ruled as the absolute master.

How defenceless Pazair felt in the face of such a monster! Usually tjaties, even if they were men of age and experience, did not master their work until two or three years had gone by. Now destiny demanded that young Pazair must save Egypt before the next flood – but without giving him any real weapons to use. Knowing the enemy's identity was not enough. Was it worth continuing to fight, when the battle was lost in advance?

Way-Finder's keen eye and Brave's friendly gaze were decisive encouragements. Divine forces were embodied in the donkey and the dog: bearers of the Invisible, they traced the paths of the heart, outside which no life had meaning. With them, he would defend the cause of Ma'at, the frail and luminous goddess of justice.

*

Kem was beside himself. 'With all due respect, Tjaty Pazair, I must tell you that your behaviour was absolutely stupid! Alone like that, in the middle of the countryside—'

'I had an escort.'

'Why in Pharaoh's name did you do something so risky?'

'I could no longer bear my office, the administration, the scribes ... My task is to impose respect for the law, and yet I have to bow before Bel-Tran when he sneers at me, sure of his victory.'

'What has changed, compared to the day of your appointment? You knew all that already.'

Pazair sighed. 'You're right, of course.'

'Instead of feeling sorry for yourself, you ought to be dealing with a worrying affair which has caused turmoil in Abydos province. I'm told that two people have been seriously wounded, and there has been a violent altercation between the priests of the great temple and the emissaries of the state, and a refusal to undertake compulsory work duties – all serious offences. They'll reach your court eventually, but by then it may be too late. I suggest you strike while the iron is hot.'

Spring had brought warmth, at least in the daytime. Though the nights were still cool and conducive to sleep, the midday sun was beginning to burn, while the harvest was just starting. The tjaty's garden was a glorious display: the flowers rivalled each other in beauty, composing a harmonious blend of red, yellow, blue, violet and orange.

When he ventured into this paradise, immediately after he awoke, Pazair headed towards the lake. As he had assumed, Neferet was having her first bathe. She swam naked, effortlessly, ceaselessly reborn in her own movements. He thought of the moment when he had gazed upon her like this, at that blessed hour when love had united them on this earth and for eternity.

'Isn't the water rather cold?'

'For you, yes – you'd catch a chill.'

'I certainly would not.'

When she emerged from the pool, he wrapped her in a linen sheet and kissed her ardently.

After a moment, she drew back a little and said, 'Bel-Tran won't allow new hospitals to be built in the provinces.'

'It doen't matter. Your file will reach me soon, and, as it's so well put together, I can approve it without fear of being accused of favouritism.'

'Yesterday, he left Memphis for Abydos.'

'Are you sure?'

'I was told by a doctor who met him on the quayside. My colleagues are beginning to realize the danger. They no longer sing Bel-Tran's praises, and some of them even think you ought to distance yourself from him.'

'More minor disturbances have broken out in Abydos. I'm going there this very day.'

Nowhere was more magical than Abydos, the vast Temple of Osiris, where the mysteries of the murdered and reborn god were celebrated by a few initiates, including Pharaoh. Like his father, Seti, Ramses had enlarged and improved the site, and he had granted the priests the use of a vast cultivable estate so that they should not suffer from material worries.

When they reached the landing-stage, it was not the High Priest of Abydos who came forward to greet the tjaty, but Kani, from the temple at Karnak. The two men embraced warmly.

'I dared not hope that you would come,' said Kani.

'Kem told me. Is it really that serious?'

'I'm afraid so, but a long investigation would have been necessary before calling on you. You shall lead it yourself. My colleague at Abydos is ill, and he asked for my help in resisting the unreasonable demands being made of him.'

'What demands?'

'The same as are being made of me and the other priests in charge of the sacred places: that we agree to put the craftsmen employed at the temple at the disposal of the state. Since last month, several provincial governors have improperly requisitioned temple craftsmen and have decreed compulsory work duties, while the large workshops only demand support workers from early autumn, after the start of the flood.'

The octopus was continuing to stretch out its tentacles and defy the tjaty. Fortunately, he had already set off back to Memphis, so Pazair might have a chance to lop off a tentacle or two.

'I was told people have been wounded,' cut in Kem.

'That's right: two peasants who refused to obey the guards' orders. Their family has worked for the temple for a thousand years, so they refuse to be transferred to another estate.'

'Who sent the guards?'

'I don't know. There are rumblings of rebellion, Pazair. The peasants are both free men, and they won't let themselves be moved about like pieces on a gaming-board.'

Fomenting unrest by breaking the laws of work: so that was Bel-Tran had now dreamt up. Choosing Abydos as the first seat of rebellion was a clever idea: the region was considered sacred territory, so its economic and social upheavals would be seen as an example in other areas.

The tjaty would have liked to meditate in the awe-inspiring Temple of Osiris, to which his rank gave him access, but the situation was too urgent for that joy.

He hurried to the nearest village. As soon as they arrived, Kem, in his strong voice, called the villagers to assemble in the main square, near the bread oven. The message spread with surprising speed: the fact that the tjaty himself might address the most humble of citizens seemed like a miracle. People ran up from the fields, the granaries, the gardens, anxious not to miss the event.

Pazair began his speech by celebrating the power of Pharaoh: only he could give life, prosperity and health to his people. Then he reminded them that requisitioning workers was illegal, and would be severely punished, according to the ancient law, which was still in force. The guilty parties would lose their posts, receive two hundred strokes of the rod, would themselves carry out the work they had wanted to assign unjustly, and would then be imprisoned.

These words dispelled the villagers' anxiety and anger. A hundred mouths opened and spoke the name of the troublemaker. He was the stable-master Fekty, 'the Shaven One', owner of a big house beside the Nile and a farm where he bred horses, the liveliest of which were destined for the royal stables. He was authoritarian and brutal, but up to now had been content with his ostentatiously comfortable life, and had not bothered the temple workers.

Five men had just been taken to his property by force.

'I know him,' Kem told Pazair, as the two men, accompanied by Killer, neared Fekty's horse-farm. 'He's the officer who sentenced me for a theft I did not commit, and who cut off my nose.'

'And now you're commander of the security guards.'

'Don't worry, I shan't lose my temper.'

'If he's innocent, I can't authorize you to arrest him.'

'Let's hope he's guilty.'

'You represent force, Kem. Let it remain obedient to the law.'

'Shall we go into the house?'

But leaning against one of the columns of the wooden porch was a man armed with a spear. 'No one may pass.'

'Lower your weapon,' ordered Kem.

'Go away, black man, or I'll disembowel you.'

Killer grabbed the spear, wrenched it out of the man's hands and snapped it in two. The man yelled in panic, and rushed off into the estate. Kem, Killer and Pazair ran after him. Two magnificent horses were being put through their paces, but they were terrified when they saw Killer: they reared, threw their riders and bolted into the countryside.

Several guards armed with daggers and spears emerged from a flat-roofed building and barred the way to the intruders. Killer's red eyes began to grow menacing.

A bald man with a powerful chest pushed them aside and squared up to the trio. 'What is the meaning of this intrusion?'

'Are you Fekty?' asked Pazair.

'Yes, and this estate belongs to me. If you don't leave at once, and take your monster with you, you'll get a good thrashing.'

'Do you know the penalty for attacking the tjaty of Egypt?'

'The tjaty . . . Is that a joke?'

'Bring me a piece of limestone.'

Pazair imprinted his seal upon it, and Fekty sulkily ordered his men to disperse.

'The tjaty here,' said Fekty. 'That doesn't make sense. And that tall black man with you, who is that? But wait . . . I know him. It's him, it really is him!'

Fekty turned to run away, but was stopped in his tracks by Killer, who seized him and threw him to the ground.

'Aren't you in the army any more?' asked Kem.

'No. I prefer breeding and training horses. But there's no need to rake up that old story, is there?'

'You're the one who brought it up.'

'I acted in all conscience, you know. Besides, it hasn't stopped you making a career for yourself. You're one of the tjaty's bodyguards, aren't you?'

'I'm commander of Memphis's security guards.'

'You, Kem?'

The Nubian reached out and lifted the sweat-soaked Fekty off his feet. 'Where are you hiding the five artisans you brought here by force?'

'Me? That's slander!'

'Are your men spreading panic by calling themselves security guards?'

'Vicious gossip!'

'We shall make your men face the complainants in court.'

A horrible smile twisted the bald man's mouth out of shape. 'I won't allow it.'

'You are subject to our authority,' Pazair reminded him. 'I consider it is necessary to search your estate – after disarming your men, of course.'

Fekty's men were reluctant to lay down their weapons, but Killer soon encouraged them. Leaping from one to the next, striking a forearm, an elbow or a wrist, he picked up spears and daggers, while Kem made sure that not even the most resentful tried to fight back. The tjaty's presence calmed the men's anger, to the great displeasure of Fekty, who felt betrayed by his own men.

Killer led the tjaty to a grain-store, inside which the five workmen were locked away. They were very talkative when they were freed, and explained that they had been forced, under threats, to restore a wall of the house and repair furniture.

In the presence of the accused, the tjaty himself registered their depositions. Fekty was recognized as guilty of misappropriating public work and of illegal requisitioning.

Kem picked up a heavy stick. 'The tjaty has authorized me to carry out the first part of the sentence.'

'Don't do that!' cried Fekty. 'You'll kill me!'

'It's possible there might be an accident – sometimes I don't know my own strength.'

'What do you want to know?'

'Who put you up to this?'

'No one.'

'You're a very bad liar.' The stick rose.

'No! You're right: I had my orders.'

'From Bel-Tran?'

'What good does it do you to know that? He'll deny it.'

'If that's all you have to say, here are two hundred strokes of the rod in accordance with the law.'

Fekty grovelled at Kem's feet, watched with indifference by Killer. 'If I cooperate, will you take me to prison without beating me?'

'That depends on the tjaty.'

Pazair gave his permission.

'What happened here is nothing,' said Fekty. 'Take a look at the activities of the office that receives foreign workers.'

29

Memphis was dozing under the hot spring sun. In the offices of the secretariat responsible for receiving foreign workers, it was time for the afternoon nap. A dozen or so Greeks, Phoenicians and Syrians were waiting for the scribes to attend to their cases.

When Pazair entered the small room where the foreigners were waiting, they stood up, thinking that here at last was someone in authority; the tjaty did not disabuse them. Interrupting the din and the flood of protests, a young Phoenician appointed himself spokesman.

'We want work,' he said.

'What were you promised?' asked Pazair.

'That we would get it, because all our applications are in order.'

'What is your trade?'

'I'm a good carpenter and I know a workshop ready to take me on.'

'What is it offering you?'

'Beer, bread, dried fish or meat, and vegetables every day; oil, pomade and perfume every ten days; clothes and sandals as and when I need them. Eight days' work and then two days' rest, not counting festivals and legal holidays. No absence without good reason.'

'Those are the conditions that Egyptians accept. Are you satisfied with them?'

'They're much better than in my own country, but I and the others need this office's agreement. Why have we been stuck here for more than a week?'

Pazair questioned the others; they were all in the same position.

'Are you going to give us the authorization?' asked the Phoenician.

'This very day.'

A plump scribe burst into the gathering. 'What's going on here? Kindly sit down and be quiet. Otherwise, as head of this department I shall have you ejected.'

'Your manners are dreadful,' said Pazair.

'And just who may you be?'

'The tjaty of Egypt.'

There was a long silence. The foreigners were torn between hope and fear, while the scribe stared at the seal Pazair set on a scrap of papyrus.

'Forgive me, my lord' he stammered, 'but we were not notified of your visit.'

'Why have you not given these men the authorization they need? Their applications are in order.'

'Overwork, too few staff, the—'

'Nonsense. Before coming here, I examined the workings of your department, and you have all the resources and staff you need. You are well paid, and you pay only one-tenth in tax and receive gratuities you do not have to declare. You have an attractive house, a pleasant garden, a chariot and a boat, and you employ two servants. Am I wrong?'

'No, my lord . . .'

The other scribes had finished their midday meal and came hurrying back to their offices.

'Tell your people to issue the authorizations,' ordered Pazair, 'and come with me.'

The two men went out into the narrow streets of Memphis, where the scribe seemed ill at ease mingling with the common folk.

'Four hours' work in the morning,' said Pazair, 'and four in the afternoon after a long break for your meal. Is that how you are meant to work every day?'

'Indeed.'

'It seems you don't keep to it.'

'We do our best.'

'By doing too little work, and doing it badly, you wrong those who rely on your decisions.'

'That certainly isn't my intention, my lord, I assure you.'

'Nevertheless, the result is deplorable.'

'Oh, my lord, I think you're being rather too severe.'

'On the contrary, I am not being severe enough.'

'Assigning work to foreigners isn't an easy task. They sometimes have a sour disposition, don't speak our language properly, and are slow to adapt to our way of life.'

'I agree, but look around you: a lot of traders and craftsmen are foreigners, or the sons of foreigners, who came to settle here. So long as they respect our laws, they are welcome. I would like to consult your lists.'

The scribe looked most uncomfortable. 'It's a little delicate . . .'

'Why?'

'We are in the middle of reorganizing our files, and it won't be finished for several months. As soon as it's finished, I will notify you.'

'Not good enough. I am in a hurry.'

'But it really is impossible.'

'I shan't be put off by an administrative jumble. Let us go back into your office.' He saw with interest that the scribe's hands began to shake.

The information Pazair had obtained was good, but how could he exploit it? There could be no doubt that the department was involved in widespread illegal activity; but the nature of that activity still had to be determined so that the evil could be rooted out.

The head of the department had not lied: the archives were spread out all over the floors of the oblong rooms in which they were kept. Several scribes were stacking up wooden tablets and numbering papyri.

'When did you begin this task?' asked Pazair.

'Yesterday,' replied the head scribe.

'Who gave you the order?'

The man hesitated, but the tjaty's expression convinced him it would be unwise to lie. 'The Double White House, my lord. According to long-established custom, it wishes to know the names of the immigrants and the nature of their work, in order to set the level of their taxes.'

'Well, then, let us look.'

'My lord, it's impossible, really impossible.'

'That way of thinking reminds me of my early days as a judge in Memphis. You may withdraw. Two volunteers will assist me.'

'My role is to help you, and—'

'Go home. We shall meet again tomorrow.'

Pazair's tone brooked no argument. Two young scribes, employed in the department for a few months, were happy to help the tjaty, who took off his robe and sandals and got down on his knees to sort the documents.

The task seemed insurmountable, but Pazair hoped that chance would grant him a clue, however small, which would set him on the right track.

'It's strange,' remarked the younger scribe. 'Under the old department head, Sechem, we wouldn't have had to do things in such a rush.'

'When was he replaced?' asked Pazair.

'At the beginning of the month.'

'Where does he live?'

'In the garden district, beside the great spring.'

Pazair left the offices.

Kem, who had been standing guard on the threshold, told him, 'Nothing to report. Killer is patrolling around the building.'

'Please apprehend a witness and bring him here.'

Sechem, 'the Faithful One', was an old man, gentle and timid. The summons had frightened him, and his appearance before the tjaty plunged him into visible anguish. Pazair found it difficult to imagine him as a criminal, but he had learnt to distrust appearances.

'Why did you leave your post?' he asked.

'I had orders from above, my lord. I was transferred to a less senior role, controlling the movement of boats.'

'What had you done wrong?'

'As far as I know, nothing,' said Sechem. 'I'd worked in this department for twenty years, and never missed a single day, but I made the mistake of opposing instructions I believed to be wrong.'

'Please be specific.'

'I criticized the delay over issuing authorizations, and still more the absence of checks as regards hired workers.'

'Were you worried that your pay might be reduced?'

'No, my lord! When a foreigner hires out his services to the owner of an estate or an overseer of craftsmen, he commands a good wage, and quite quickly acquires land and a house that he can leave to his descendants. I do not understand why, for the last three months, most applicants have been sent to a war-fleet boatyard under the auspices of the Double White House.'

'Show me the lists.'

'Certainly, my lord – all I have to do is consult the archives.'

'I fear you may have an unpleasant surprise.'

When he saw the state of his former office, Sechem was close to despair. 'This reorganization is pointless.'

'How were the lists of hired persons registered?'

'On sycamore tablets.'

'Will you be able to find them in this mess?'

'I hope so, my lord.'

But fresh disappointment awaited them: after searching fruitlessly until after dark, Sechem gave his verdict. 'They've disappeared. But the drafts should still exist. Even incomplete, they'll be useful.'

The two young scribes removed the relevant limestone fragments from the rubbish heap where they had been thrown. By the light of the torches, Sechem picked out his precious drafts.

The war-fleet boatyard was like a bustling bee-hive. The overseers were snapping out orders to carpenters, who were working on long acacia-wood planks. Specialists were assembling a ship's hull, others were putting a ship's rail in place. With practised skill, they were creating a ship by placing piece upon piece, fastening them together with tenon-and-mortise joints. In another part of the boatyard, workers were caulking boats, while their colleagues were making oars and tillers.

'No entry,' a supervisor told Pazair, who was accompanied by Kem and Killer.

'Not even for the tjaty?'

'You are ... ?'

'Call your superior.'

The man needed no further asking.

A tall, confident man with an assured voice soon arrived at a run. He recognized Kem and Killer, and bowed before the tjaty.

'How may I be of service to you, Tjaty?' he asked.

'I should like to meet the foreigners listed here.' Pazair handed the overseer a papyrus.

The man looked at it, then shook his head. 'I don't know any of them.'

'Think carefully.'

'No, I assure you—'

'I have official documents proving that, over the last three months, you have taken on about fifty foreigners. Where are they?'

The man's reaction was instant. He ran off so quickly towards the street that Killer seemed caught unawares; but the baboon leapt over a low wall and jumped on to the back of the fugitive, forcing his face into the ground.

Kem pulled him up by the hair. 'We're listening, my fine fellow.'

The farm, which lay to the north of Memphis, was enormous. The tjaty and a detachment of Kem's men entered the estate in the middle of the afternoon and hailed a goose-herd.

'Where are the foreigners?' asked Pazair:

The number of guards so alarmed the peasant that he couldn't speak. He pointed at a nearby stable.

When the tjaty went toward it, several men armed with sickles and staves barred his way.

'Do not use violence,' Pazair warned them, 'and give us free access to that building.'

A hot-head brandished his sickle. A dagger thrown by Kem sank into his forearm, and all resistance ceased.

In the stable, they found about fifty foreigners, all in chains, occupied in milking cows and sorting grain. The tjaty ordered that they were to be freed and their guards imprisoned.

*

Bel-Tran laughed about the incident. 'Slaves? Yes, as there are in Greece, and as there soon will be all over the world. Slavery is the future of mankind, my dear Pazair. It provides docile, cheap workers, and with it we shall develop a programme of extremely profitable projects.'

'Must I remind you that slavery is against the law of Ma'at and forbidden in Egypt?'

'If you're hoping to incriminate me, you may as well give up. You won't find any link between me, the boatyard, the farm and the department for foreign workers. Between ourselves, I will confess that I was trying an experiment – you have interrupted it inopportunely, but it was already bearing fruit. Your laws are outdated. When will you understand that the Egypt of Ramses is dead?'

'Why do you hate people so much?'

'Only two races exist: those who dominate and those who are dominated. I belong to the first; the second must obey me. That is the only law in force.'

'Only in your mind, Bel-Tran.'

'Many of our leading citizens agree with me, because they hope to become dominant. Even if their hopes are disappointed, they will have been useful to me.'

'So long as I am tjaty, no one will be a slave on Egyptian soil.'

'This rear-guard action ought to sadden me, but your pointless gestures are rather entertaining. Stop wearing yourself out, Pazair. You know as well as I do that your efforts are ridiculous.'

'I shall fight you to my last breath.'

30

Suti stroked his acacia-wood bow lovingly, and checked the integrity of the wood, the tension of the string and the flexibility of the frame.

'Haven't you anything better to do?' asked Panther affectionately.

'If you want to be a queen, I must have a weapon I can trust.'

'You have an army, so use it.'

'Do you think it can beat the Egyptian troops?'

'First, let's deal with the desert guards and impose our law in the sands. Libyans and Nubians are collaborating under your command – that's a miracle in itself. Tell them to fight, and they'll obey you without question. You are the master of gold, Suti. Conquer the land whose lords we shall be.'

'You really are mad.'

'You want revenge, my love, revenge on your friend Pazair and on your cursed Egypt. With gold and warriors, you will get it.' And she showered him with fiery, passionate kisses.

Convinced that an exciting adventure lay ahead, Suti ran about his camp. The fierce Libyan raiders were equipped with tents and blankets to make life almost pleasant in the middle of the desert. The Nubians, excellent hunters, tracked game.

But the high feeling of the first days was fading away. The Libyans were at last realizing that Adafi really was dead, and that Suti had killed him. They had given their word before the gods, and so had to keep it, but silent opposition began to spread.

At its head was Jossete, a short, stocky, black-haired man; quick and agile, he was an expert with the knife. He had been Adafi's right-hand man, and was growing more and more resentful of Suti's seizure of power.

Suti inspected each encampment and congratulated his men; they were looking after their weapons, training and taking care to keep themselves clean.

Accompanied by five soldiers, Jossete interrupted Suti, who was talking to a group of Libyans on their return from an exercise.

'Where are you taking us?' he asked.

'That is not your concern,' said Suti.

'I don't like that answer.'

'I didn't like your question.'

Jossete's thick eyebrows knitted in a scowl. 'People don't talk to me like that.'

'A good soldier's most important qualities are obedience and respect.'

'Provided he has a good leader.'

'Are you saying I'm not?'

'How dare you compare yourself to Adafi?'

'I didn't lose, he did – even though he cheated.'

'Are you accusing him of dishonesty?'

'You buried the archer yourself.'

With a lightning-swift lunge, Jossete tried to plunge his dagger into Suti's belly, but the Egyptian parried the attack with an elbow in the Libyan's chest, and knocked him over. Before Jossete could get up, Suti stamped his head down into the sand and held it there with his heel.

'Either you obey me, or you suffocate.'

Suti's expression dissuaded the Libyans from helping their comrade. Jossete let go of his knife and punched the ground, in a sign of submission.

'Very well. You may breathe.'

Suti raised his heel. Jossete spat out sand and rolled on to his side.

'Listen to me closely, little traitor,' said Suti. 'The gods enabled me to kill a cheat and to take command of a good army, and I took the chance they gave me. You will keep quiet, and you will fight for me. Otherwise, you can get out.'

Jossete returned to the ranks, his eyes cast down.

Suti's army headed north, along the Nile Valley, keeping well away from inhabited areas and taking the most difficult and least frequented route. With an innate feel for command, the young soldier knew how to share out hard toil and inspire trust in his men; no one challenged his authority.

He and Panther rode on horseback at the head of their troops. She relished every second of this impossible conquest, as if she had become the owner of the inhospitable land around them. Constantly alert, Suti listened to the desert.

'We've outwitted the All-Seeing Ones,' she declared.

'The golden goddess is wrong: they've been on our trail for two days.'

'How do you know?'

'Are you casting doubt on my instinct?'

'Why don't they attack?'

'Because there are too many of us. They'll have to group several patrols together.'

'Let's strike first.'

'No, we'll wait.'

'You don't want to kill Egyptians, do you? That's it, your big idea! To get yourself filled full of arrows by your countrymen.'

'If we can't get rid of them, how can I offer you a kingdom?'

Accompanied by their ferocious dogs, the All-Seeing Ones constantly criss-crossed the expanses of desert, capturing any sand-travellers who resorted to pillage, protecting the caravans and ensuring the miners' safety. Not a single nomad's movements went unnoticed, not a single predator enjoyed his crime for long. For decades, the desert patrols had nipped in the bud the smallest attempt to disturb the established order.

When a lone scout had reported an armed band coming from the south, none of the officers had believed him. It had taken a report – an alarming one – from a full patrol to spur them into action, necessitating the coordination of patrols spread out across a vast area.

Once all their patrols had joined up, the All-Seeing Ones were unsure what to do next. Who were these strange soldiers, who was commanding them, and what did they want? The unexpected alliance of Nubians and Libyans meant that a hard fight lay ahead, but the desert guards were keen to wipe out the intruders without calling on the army for help, so as to boost their reputation and earn a valuable reward.

The enemy had made a serious mistake by camping behind the line of hills from where the All-Seeing Ones would launch their assault; they would attack at nightfall, when the lookouts' attention was waning. First, they would encircle them; next, they would send over a murderous volley of arrows; lastly, they would finish off any remaining resistance by hand-to-hand fighting. The operation would be quick and brutal: any prisoners taken would be made to talk.

When the desert blushed red as the sun set, the wind began to blow, whipping up the sand; the All-Seeing Ones tried in vain to spot the enemy's lookouts. Wary of a trap, they advanced with extreme caution. When they reached the summit of the hills, they had still not seen a single adversary. From their favourable position on the high ground, they surveyed the camp: to their astonishment, it was empty. Abandoned chariots, horses wandering loose, folded tents – all bore witness to the strange army's disarray. Obviously, knowing they had been spotted, the ill-assorted band had chosen to disperse.

It would be an easy victory indeed, and it would be followed by a determined pursuit and the arrest of every single intruder. The desert guards never allowed themselves to loot or pillage. They would draw up a detailed list of everything they seized, and the state would then award them part of it.

Warily, they entered the camp in small groups, covering each other. Some of the boldest men reached the chariots, took off the protective covers and found gold ingots. Immediately they called to their colleagues, who gathered around the treasure. Fascinated, most of them dropped their weapons and stood lost in contemplation of the precious metal.

Suddenly, in a dozen different places, the desert rose up.

Suti and his men had hidden by burying themselves in the sand. Staking their success on the attraction exerted by an empty camp and the cargo of gold, they knew that their ordeal would be short. They charged the All-Seeing Ones from the rear; surrounded, the guards realized that resistance was futile.

Suti climbed up on a chariot and addressed the defeated men.

'If you are reasonable, you'll have nothing to fear. Not only will your lives be spared, but you will get rich, like the Libyans and Nubians are under my command. My name is Suti, and before commanding this army I served as a chariot officer in the Egyptian army. I am the man who rid that army of a stain on its honour by ridding it of the traitor and murderer General Asher. It was I who carried out the sentence laid down by the law of the desert. Today, I am the master of gold.'

Several of the All-Seeing Ones recognized Suti. His reputation had travelled beyond the walls of Memphis, and some already considered him a legendary hero.

'Weren't you imprisoned in the fortress of Tjaru?' asked an officer.

'The garrison tried to kill me by offering me up to the Nubians as a sacrificial victim; but the golden goddess was watching over me.'

Panther came forward, lit by the last rays of the sunset, which set her golden crown, collar and bracelets aflame. Victors and vanquished alike were subjugated by the appearance of the famous goddess, who had at last returned from the mysterious, savage South to bring the joys of love to Egypt.

They submitted, prostrating themselves in the sand.

The celebration was well under way. Men were juggling with gold, drinking, mapping out a splendid future, singing of the beauty of the golden goddess.

'Are you happy?' Panther asked Suti.

'Things could be worse.'

'I was wondering how you'd manage not to kill any Egyptians . . . You're becoming a good general, thanks to me.'

'This coalition is very fragile.'

'It's strong enough for us.'

'What do you want to conquer?'

'Whatever presents itself. Standing still is unbearable – we must move forward, create our own horizon.'

Dagger raised, Jossete emerged from the darkness and charged at Suti. Swift as a cat, Suti leapt aside, dodging the fierce blow. Once her initial fear had passed, Panther was amused by the attack. The difference between the two men's size and strength was such that her lover would have no difficulty breaking the nasty little Libyan.

Suti struck empty air. Encouraged again, Jossete aimed at his heart. Quick reflexes saved the Egyptian, but he lost his balance getting free, and fell backwards.

Panther disarmed the attacker with a kick to his wrist. Murderous rage increased Jossete's strength tenfold. He flung her aside, seized a block of stone and brought it down on Suti's skull. Suti was not quick enough: he twisted so that the stone missed his head, but it landed on his arm and he gave a shout of pain.

Jossete howled with joy. Lifting the bloody stone high over his head, he stood in front of the wounded man. 'Die, you Egyptian dog!'

Eyes staring, mouth open, the Libyan dropped his improvised weapon and collapsed beside Suti, dead before he touched the ground. Panther had aimed well, plunging her dagger into the back of Jossete's neck.

'Why did you defend yourself so badly?' she asked.

'I can't see in the darkness any more . . . I'm blind.'

Panther helped him to his feet.

He grimaced. 'My arm . . . It's broken.'

Panther took him to the old Nubian warrior.

'Lay him on his back,' he ordered two soldiers, 'and place a roll of fabric between his shoulder-blades. You, on the left; you, on the right.'

The two soldiers pulled the wounded man's arms. The old man found the fracture in the forearm and put the bones back in place, ignoring Suti's cries of pain. Two splints padded with linen would aid his recovery.

'It's nothing serious,' pronounced the old man. 'He can march and he can command.'

Despite the pain, Suti got up. 'Take me to my tent,' he whispered in Panther's ear.

He walked slowly, so as not to stumble. She guided him to his tent and helped him to sit down.

'No one must know I'm blind.'

'Go to sleep. I'll keep watch.'

At dawn, the pain awoke Suti. The landscape he gazed upon seemed so wondrous that he soon forgot his pain.

'I can see, Panther, I can see!'

'The light . . . The light has cured you.'

'I know what it was: an attack of night blindness. It will happen again, at random. The only person who can cure me is Neferet.'

'We're a long way from Memphis,' Panther pointed out.

'Come with me.'

Jumping on to his horse, he led her off on a ride. They passed between the dunes, galloped along the bed of a dried-up river and climbed a stony hillside.

From the top, they saw a magnificent view.

'Look, Panther, look at the white city on the horizon. That's Kebet, and that's where we're going.'

31

The intense heat of early summer had plunged the vast burial-ground of Saqqara into a stupor; work on excavating tombs had slowed down, if not stopped. The priests whose task was to maintain the *ka*, the immortal energy, moved about increasingly slowly. Only Djui the embalmer had no chance of sleep: he had been brought three corpses, which must be prepared as quickly as possible for the journey to the otherworld. Although he was pale with fatigue, and still unshaven, he set to work at once. He extracted the entrails and embalmed the bodies more or less elaborately, according to the price paid.

In his few spare minutes, he took flowers to shrines whose owners offered him a small fee for doing so, a useful addition to his salary. One morning, as he was doing so, he met the tjaty and his wife on the path leading to Branir's tomb. Djui bowed deeply to them.

Time had not lessened the pain or healed the wound. Without Branir, Pazair and Neferet felt like orphans; their murdered master could never be replaced. He had been the embodiment of a perfect wisdom, the radiant wisdom of Egypt, which Bel-Tran and his henchmen were trying to destroy.

In venerating Branir's memory, Pazair and Neferet linked themselves to the long line of founding ancestors, who had valued peaceful truth and serene justice on which they had built a land of water and sunshine. Branir had not been annihilated; his invisible presence guided them, his spirit was creating a path they could not yet make out. Only the communion of hearts, beyond the borders of death, could help them follow that path.

The tjaty met the king in secret, in the Temple of Ptah. Officially, Ramses was residing in the beautiful city of Pi-Ramses, at the heart of the Delta, to benefit from the pleasant climate there.

'Our enemies must think me desperate and defeated,' said the king.

'We have less than three months left, Majesty.'

'Have you made any progress?'

'Nothing very satisfactory. I've won some small victories, but they aren't enough to trouble Bel-Tran.'

'What about his accomplices?'

'There are still a lot of them,' said Pazair, 'though I have managed to eliminate a few.'

'As have I. At Pi-Ramses, I have purged the troops in charge of watching the borders with Asia. Some senior officers were taking illicit payments from the Double White House, through several different organizations. Bel-Tran has a twisted mind. To detect the effects of his actions, we must search for the complicated twists and turns of his plotting. Let us continue to erode the ground beneath him.'

Pazair sighed. 'I seem to find new rottenness almost every day.'

'Have you found the Testament of the Gods?'

'No, Majesty, and I still have no leads.'

'And Branir's murderer?'

'Nothing concrete.'

'We must strike hard,' said Ramses, 'and discover the exact limits of Bel-Tran's domain. As time is so short, we shall proceed to a census.'

'But, Majesty, will that not take a long time?'

'Ask Bagey for help, and enlist all the state secretariats – the provincial governors must devote themselves to this task as a priority. In less than a fortnight, we shall have the first results. I want to know the real state of the country and the extent of this conspiracy.'

Bagey was weary and bowed with age, and his legs were swollen, but he nevertheless greeted Pazair amiably. His wife, though, was not best pleased by the visit: she hated seeing her husband being bothered like this and dragged out of his retirement.

Pazair noted that the little town house was getting into a sad state: in some places, the plaster was falling off the walls. He did not say a word, for fear of annoying the old man. He would send a team of workmen to repair and repaint all the houses in the street – including Bagey's, naturally. He would pay for the repairs himself.

'A census?' Bagey was astonished. 'That's an onerous undertaking.'

'The last one was five years ago. I feel it would be useful to have current information.'

'You are right.'

'I'd like to do it quickly.'

'That isn't impossible, provided you have the full support of the king's messengers.'

The messengers were an elite body who distributed instructions from the central government; the speed at which reforms could be implemented depended largely on their efficiency.

'I'll take you to the census secretariat,' said Bagey. 'You'd have understood eventually how it works, but going there now will save you a few days.'

'Please take my travelling-chair.'

'If you insist.'

Every single royal messenger was present. When the tjaty opened the session of his council by hanging a figurine of Ma'at on his gold chain, everyone bowed before the goddess of justice.

Pazair was dressed in the traditional garb of a tjaty: a long, weighted apron cut from thick, stiff material; his body entirely covered with the exception of his shoulders. He sat down on a straight-backed chair.

'I have summoned you, on Pharaoh's orders, to entrust you with an exceptionally important mission: a census as swift as the flight of a bird. I wish to know the names of the owners of fields and cultivable lands, the area they hold, the number of head of livestock and their owners, the nature and quantity of produce and resources, the number of inhabitants. I don't need to remind you that wilful falsehood or lies of omission are serious offences, carrying severe penalties.'

A messenger asked permission to speak. 'The census is usually carried out over several months. Why must this one be done so quickly?'

'I must take decisions concerning trade and resources, and I need to know if the state of the country has changed greatly in the last five years. Afterwards, we shall refine the results.'

'It won't be easy to meet your demands,' said the head of the messengers, 'but we'll manage it if we gather each day's information very quickly. Can you tell us more about your reasons for the census? Is it a matter of preparing a new tax system?'

'No census has ever been taken with that motive. As always, the goal will be full employment and a just sharing out of tasks. You have my word, by the Rule.'

'You shall have the first information within a week.'

At Karnak, the tamarisks were flowering between the sphinxes that denied outsiders access to the temple. The early summer was spreading its sweet scents, the stones of the temple were bedecked in warm colours, and the bronze of the great gates gleamed.

At the Temple of Mut, Neferet was presiding over the annual assembly of the principal towns' head doctors, who had been initiated into the secrets of their craft at the temple. They raised problems of public health and shared major discoveries which would benefit remedy-makers, animal-doctors, tooth-doctors, eye-doctors, 'shepherds of the anus',* 'they who know the humours and the hidden organs', and other specialists. For the most part elderly, they admired their superior's clear face, swanlike neck, slender waist and delicate wrists and ankles. On her head she wore a diadem of lotus-flowers surrounded by small beads. At her throat hung the turquoise amulet Branir had given her, to protect her from harmful influences.

Kani, the High Priest of Karnak, opened the session. His skin was still brown and deeply lined from his years as a gardener, and bore traces of abscesses on his neck from the days when he had had to carry heavy yokes. And he still made no attempt to charm people.

He said, 'Thanks to the gods, this country's doctors are led by an exceptional woman, whose concern is to improve care and not to increase her own prestige. After an unhappy period, we have returned to the righteous tradition taught by Imhotep. Let us never again deviate from it, and Egypt will know health of both body and soul.'

Neferet disliked making speeches and did not now inflict one on her colleagues; instead she invited them so speak. Their statements were brief and worthwhile. They reported improved methods of operating, notably in the fields of child-bearing and eye diseases, and the creation of new remedies based on exotic plants. Several stressed the need to maintain the high level of training for doctors, even if their studies were long and several years of practical experience were required before they were considered fully trained.

Neferet agreed with all these points. But, despite the congenial atmosphere, Kani sensed that she was tense, almost anxious.

'A census is being carried out,' she told her audience, 'and, thanks to the royal messengers' diligence, some results are already known. One of them concerns us directly: the population is growing much too fast in some provinces. If that growth continues unchecked, the people will be reduced to terrible poverty.'†

'What do you wish us to do?'

'Village doctors must advise on methods of preventing pregnancy.'

'Your predecessor ended that policy, because the state had to give out the preventive remedies free of charge.'

'That was both stupid and dangerous. Let us return to giving out remedies based on acacia – the acid in the spines is highly effective.'

'That is true, my lady, but to preserve it it must be ground with dates and honey – and honey is expensive.'

---

*Gastro-enterologists.

†In the era of Ramses II, Egypt's population, according to estimates which are difficult to verify, was about 4 million. Modern Egypt will soon have over 60 million inhabitants.

'Over-large families will ruin the villages; we doctors must convince parents of this reality. As for the honey, I shall ask the tjaty to set aside enough of the harvest for our use.'

At dusk, Neferet set off along the path leading to the Temple of Ptah. Set apart from the great east–west axis, the spine of the immense Karnak complex, the little temple nestled in the heart of an island of trees.

Priests greeted her, and then Neferet went alone into the shrine, where a statue of the lion-goddess Sekhmet stood. Sekhmet was the patron of doctors and the incarnation of the mysterious force that both caused illnesses and produced their remedies. Without her aid, no doctor could heal.

The goddess, who had a woman's body and a fierce lioness's face, was surrounded by darkness. The last ray of the setting sun entered through a slit in the ceiling, lighting up the terrifying deity's face.

The miracle happened again, as it had done on their first encounter: the lioness smiled. Her face softened, and she lowered her gaze to look at her servant. Neferet had come to ask her for her wisdom, and she communed with the spirit of the living stone. Through the goddess's immutable presence, the knowledge of energy was transmitted, an energy of which the human being was only a fleeting form.

The young woman spent the night in prayer; from being a pupil of Sekhmet, she became her sister and confidante. When the clear light of morning rendered the statue fearsome again, Neferet was no longer afraid of it.

A strong rumour had spread across Memphis: the tjaty's audience would be a very special one. Not only had the Nine Friends of Pharaoh been summoned, but also many courtiers were hurrying into the pillared hall so as not to miss the audience. Some speculated that Pazair would announce his resignation, that he had been crushed by the weight of his responsibilities; others said something stunning had happened, with unforeseen consequences.

Contrary to his usual custom, Pazair had not organized a restricted council, but had opened the double doors of the audience chamber. On this beautiful morning, he was confronting the entire court.

'On Pharaoh's orders, I have carried out a census. Thanks to exceptionally good work by the king's messengers, the first stage has already been completed.'

'He's trying to curry favour with a notoriously difficult body of men,' whispered an old courtier.

'And not forgetting to take the credit for their work himself,' added his neighbour.

'I must inform you of the results,' continued Pazair.

An unpleasant shiver ran through the assembled throng. The gravity of his voice made everyone fear that something terrible had happened.

'The population is growing too fast in three Northern and two Southern provinces. This necessitates action by the Health secretariat, which will stop the rise as quickly as possible by educating families.'

No one made an unfavourable comment.

'The possessions of the temples, if they are still intact, are gravely threatened, as are those of the villages. Without direct intervention on my part, the whole landscape of Egypt's trade and resources will soon be thrown into disarray, and you will no longer recognize the land of your ancestors.'

The courtiers began to whisper and exchange looks: they found the declaration exaggerated and unfounded.

'Of course,' Pazair went on, 'this is not merely an opinion but is based on verified facts whose seriousness cannot escape you.'

'I would ask you to set out those facts clearly,' said the Overseer of Fields.

'According to the reports gathered by the royal messengers, about half of all lands have passed into the direct or indirect control of the Double White House. A number of provincial temples are unaware that they will, before long, be deprived of their harvests. Many small and medium-sized farmers have unknowingly got into debt, and will either become tenants or be expelled. The balance between private and state lands is on the point of breaking down. It is the same for livestock and crafts.'

All eyes converged on Bel-Tran, who was sitting near the tjaty, to the right. Surprise and anger mingled in his eyes. Lips pursed, nostrils pinched, neck stiff, he raged silently.

'The policy carried out before my appointment,' said Pazair, 'was heading in a direction of which I disapprove. The census has revealed its excesses, which I intend to curb without delay, through decrees signed by Pharaoh. By respecting her ancestral values Egypt will preserve her greatness and the goodness of her people; so I shall ask the head of the Double White House to follow my instructions faithfully and to cancel injustices.'

Publicly disowned, but charged with a new mission, would Bel-Tran withdraw or submit? Heavy, massive, he advanced and stood before the tjaty.

'You have my loyalty, Tjaty,' he said. 'Command, and I shall obey.'

A murmur of satisfaction showed the court's assent. The crisis had been averted: Bel-Tran had realized the error of his ways, and the tjaty was not condemning him. Pazair's moderation was widely approved: despite his youth, he had subtlety and knew how to be diplomatic, without departing from his irreproachable line of conduct.

'Lastly,' said the tjaty, 'I shall not introduce compulsory registration of births, deaths, marriages and divorces. Such a measure would restrict freedom, by putting in writing events which concern only the interested parties and those close to them, not the state. We must not strangle our society by binding it in archaic and over-rigid modes of government. When Pharaoh is crowned, we do not mention his age, but celebrate his office. Let us preserve that state of mind, which is more concerned with non-temporal truth than with perishable details, and Egypt will remain in harmony, in the heavens' image.'

32

Silkis was afraid, unable to abate her husband's anger. He was suffering from a severe attack of cramps, and had no feeling in his fingers or toes. In his rage, he broke precious vases, tore up new papyri and insulted the gods. Not even his young wife's charms soothed him.

Silkis withdrew into her apartments, where she swallowed a brew of date-juice, leaves of the castor-oil plant and sycamore-milk, designed to ease the fire that burnt in her intestines. One doctor had warned her about the bad state of the veins in her thighs, another had expressed anxiety about the heat she constantly felt in her anus; she had sent them away, before accepting treatment from a specialist who had given her an enema of woman's milk.

Her belly continued to hurt, as if she were paying for her crimes. She longed to confide her nightmares to the dream-interpreter and to ask Neferet to treat her, but the first had left Memphis and the second had become her enemy.

Bel-Tran burst into her bedchamber. 'So you're ill yet again, are you?'

'It isn't my fault. You know a plague's torturing me.'

'I pay for the best doctors to treat you.'

'The only one who can cure me is Neferet.'

'Nonsense!' snapped Bel-Tran. 'She doesn't know any more than the others.'

'You're wrong; she does.'

'Have I made a single mistake since I began rising to power? I've made you one of the richest women in the land, and soon you'll be the richest of all. And I shall hold supreme power, through my puppets.'

'But Pazair frightens you.'

'No, he irritates me, by behaving like the tjaty he thinks he is.'

'His actions have brought him a good deal of sympathy. Some people who used to support you have changed their minds.'

'Fools! They'll regret it. Anyone who hasn't obeyed me to the letter will be reduced to the rank of slave.'

Silkis lay down, exhausted. 'Couldn't you be content with the wealth you already have – and look after me?'

'In ten weeks' time, we shall be the masters of the land – and you want to give up because of your health? You really are mad, my poor Silkis.'

She stood up, and gripped the belt of his kilt. 'Tell me the truth. Have I really still got a place in your heart and your head?'

'What do you mean?'

'I'm young and pretty, but my nerves are fragile and my belly is not always welcoming. Have you chosen someone else to be your future queen?'

He slapped her, forcing her to let go. 'I made you, Silkis, and I shall continue to do so. As long as you carry out my orders, you have nothing to fear.'

She did not cry, and forgot to simper. Her child-woman's face became as cold as Greek marble. 'And suppose I leave you?'

Bel-Tran smiled. 'You love me too much, my darling, and you love your comfort too much. I know your vices. We're inseparable – we've denied the gods together, lied together, overturned the law and the Rule together. There could be no better guarantee of unfailing loyalty.'

'Delicious,' agreed Pazair, emerging from the water.

Neferet was checking the copper band that ran round the inside of the pool and kept it permanently clean. The sun turned her naked skin golden as drops of water trickled down it.

Pazair dived, swam underwater, and took her gently by the waist before surfacing and kissing her on the throat.

'They'll be waiting for me at the hospital,' she said.

'They can wait a little longer.'

'And shouldn't you go to the palace?'

'I don't know any more.'

Her resistance was feigned; languidly, she gave way. Pazair held her close and took her to the stone rim of the pool. Still embracing each other, they lay down on the hot paving stones and gave free rein to their desire.

A raucous voice shattered the peace.

'Way-Finder,' said Neferet.

'That braying means a friend's arrived.'

A few minutes later, Kem came and greeted the tjaty and his wife. Brave, asleep at the foot of a sycamore, opened one eye and went back to sleep, his head resting on his crossed paws.

'Your performance at the council is being praised highly,' he told

Pazair. 'The criticism at court has been silenced, and there's no longer any scepticism. You're regarded as a true first minister again.'

'But what about Bel-Tran?' asked Neferet anxiously.

'He's getting more and more worried. Some leading citizens are refusing his invitations to dinner, and others are closing their doors to him. It is whispered that, if he puts another foot wrong, you'll replace him without warning. You've struck him a mortal blow.'

'I only wish I had,' said Pazair.

'Little by little, you're cutting away his power.'

'That isn't much consolation.'

'Even if he has got a decisive weapon, will he actually be able to use it?'

'Let's not think of that. We must go on as before.'

The Nubian folded his arms. 'To hear you, anyone would think that righteousness is the kingdom's only chance of survival.'

'Don't you believe that?'

'It cost me my nose, and it'll cost you your life.'

Pazair smiled. 'Let's try to prove that prophecy wrong.'

'How much time have we left?'

'I owe you the truth: ten weeks.'

'What about the shadow-eater?' asked Neferet.

'I dare not believe he's given up,' replied Kem, 'but he lost his battles with Killer, so he may have begun to have doubts. If he has, perhaps he's intending to give up the fight.'

'Are you becoming an optimist?

'Don't worry: I shan't lower my guard.'

Smiling, Neferet looked closely at the Nubian. 'This isn't merely a courtesy visit, is it?'

'You know me too well.'

'There's a sparkle in your eyes. Is there a glimmer of hope?'

'We've picked up Mentmose's trail.'

'In Memphis?'

Kem shook his head. 'According to my informant, who saw him leave Bel-Tran's house, he took the road to the North.'

'You could have stopped him,' said Pazair.

'That would have been a mistake – it's better to find out where he's going.'

'So long as we don't lose him.'

'He didn't take a boat, probably so that he could pass unnoticed – he knows my men are looking for him. By taking dirt roads, he'll avoid our checkpoints.'

'Is someone following him?' asked Pazair.

'Yes, my best trackers. As soon as he reaches his goal, I'll be informed.'

'Let me know at once, and I'll go with you.'

'That wouldn't be wise.'

'You'll need a judge to question him, and who better than the tjaty himself?'

Pazair was convinced he would get a decisive result, so Neferet had failed to persuade him to give up a wild escapade which was likely to be dangerous, despite the presence of Kem and Killer.

Surely Mentmose must know more about Branir's murder? The tjaty would not pass up the slightest chance of learning the truth. Mentmose would talk.

While Pazair was waiting for Kem's signal, Neferet and her concerned colleagues were implementing, throughout the country, the programme of enabling families to limit the number of their children. In accordance with the tjaty's decree, the necessary remedies were again to be distributed free of charge. Village doctors, whose office would regain its old importance, would form a permanent information service. From now on, the Health secretariat would oversee controls on birthrates.

Unlike her predecessor, Neferet had not moved into the government buildings set aside for her and her close colleagues. She preferred to remain in her old office at the central hospital in Memphis, so as to stay in contact with the sick and with those who prepared the remedies. She listened, advised and reassured. Each day, she tried to push back the limits of suffering, and each day she suffered defeats from which she drew hope for future victories. She also concerned herself with editing medical writings,* which had been handed down since the time of the pyramids and ceaselessly improved upon; a specialist college of scribes described successful experiments and noted down the treatments.

After carrying out an eye operation, designed to prevent the build-up of pressure in the eye, Neferet was washing her hands when a young doctor told her of an emergency. She was tired, and asked him to deal with it, but he said the patient insisted on seeing Neferet and only Neferet.

The woman was seated, her head covered by a veil.

'What is wrong with you?' asked Neferet.

The patient did not reply.

---

* A few have survived: they deal with gynaecology, the respiratory passages, stomach disorders, the urinary tracts, ophthalmology, cranial surgery and veterinary medicine. Unfortunately, only a tiny part of the art of Egyptian medicine has come down to us.

'I must examine you.'

Silkis lifted her veil. 'Treat me, Neferet, please. If you don't, I shall die.'

'There are excellent doctors here. Consult them.'

'But you're the only one who can cure me – no one else can.'

'You're the wife of a vile and destructive man, a perjurer and a liar. Staying at his side proves your complicity in his crimes. That is what is eating away at your soul and your body.'

'I haven't committed any crimes. I have to obey Bel-Tran – he made me, he—'

'Are you nothing more than an object?'

'You don't understand.'

'No, I don't, and I won't treat you.'

'I'm your friend, Neferet, your loyal and sincere friend. You have my whole-hearted admiration, so won't you trust me?'

'If you leave Bel-Tran, I'll believe you. Otherwise you must stop lying to me and to yourself.'

Silkis said plaintively, 'If you treat me, Bel-Tran will reward you, I swear it! It's the only way to save Pazair.'

'Are you sure of that?'

Silkis relaxed. 'At last you're facing facts.'

'I face them all the time.'

'Bel-Tran is preparing another future, a wonderfully attractive one. It will be like me – beautiful and seductive.'

'You'll be cruelly disappointed.'

Silkis's smile froze. 'Why do you say that?'

'Because you are basing that future on ambition, greed and hatred. It will offer you nothing else unless you give up your madness.'

'So you don't trust me.'

'You are an accomplice to murder, and sooner or later you will appear before the tjaty's court of justice.'

The child-woman went into a fury. 'That was your last chance, Neferet! By linking your destiny to Pazair's, by refusing to treat me, you have condemned yourself to ignominy. The next time we see each other, you will be my slave.'

33

In the words of a popular song, 'Merchants sail up and down the river, busy as flies, transport goods from one city to another, and supply him who has nothing.'

Pazair stood apart from the other passengers on the boat. They were Syrians, Greeks, Cypriots and Phoenicians, all debating, comparing their prices and dividing up their future clientele. No one would have recognized the tjaty of Egypt in this young, plainly dressed man, whose only baggage was the worn-out mat he slept on. On the cabin roof, which was piled high with bundles, Killer kept watch. His calmness meant that the shadow-eater was nowhere near. Kem stayed up at the prow, his head encased in a hood to hide his identity; some of his men, disguised as Greeks and Syrians, mingled with the other passengers. Fortunately, the merchants were too busy adding up their profits to be interested in anyone else.

The boat moved fast, before a brisk wind. The captain and his crew would be paid a good bonus if they reached their destination earlier than expected: the foreign traders were men in a hurry.

An argument broke out between some Syrians and Greeks. The former offered the latter necklaces of semi-precious stones in exchange for vases from Rhodes, but the Greeks scorned the offer, regarding it as inadequate. Their attitude surprised Pazair, for the exchange seemed fair.

The incident calmed the men's trade-fever, and each withdrew into his own thoughts as they moved down the Nile. After taking 'the Great River', which crossed the Delta, the trading-ship left the cape to the east, and took the 'Waters of Ra', a waterway separate from the main course, and headed towards the crossroads of routes serving Canaan and Phoenicia.

The Greeks disembarked during a brief stop in open country. Kem followed them, as did Pazair and Killer. The dilapidated landing-stage looked abandoned; all around were papyrus forests and marshes. Ducks flapped out of the way.

'This is where Mentmose joined a group of Greek traders,' explained Kem. 'They took a dirt track leading south-east. If we follow them, we'll catch up with him.'

The merchants were talking among themselves warily: they were unhappy about the trio's presence.

One of them, who had a slight limp, came over to them. 'What do you want?' he asked.

'Loans,' replied Pazair.

'In this benighted place?'

'At Memphis, no one will give us anything any more.'

'Has your business failed?'

'There are certain things we can't do, because we have too many ideas and not enough money. If we can accompany you, perhaps we'll find some rather more understanding people.'

The Greek seemed satisfied. 'You haven't chosen too badly. But tell me: your baboon, there, is it for sale?'

'Not at the moment,' replied Kem.

'There are a lot of keen collectors.'

'He's a good animal, quiet and docile.'

'He'll do as a guarantee for you – you'll get a good price for him.'

'Will it be a long journey?' asked Pazair.

'Two hours' walk – we've been waiting for the donkeys.'

As soon as the donkeys arrived, the caravan set off, at the donkeys' regular pace. Although they were heavily laden, they neither stumbled not looked unhappy, being used to hard work. The men slaked their thirst several times, and Pazair moistened the donkeys' mouths.

After crossing an abandoned field, they found journey's end: a small town with low houses, protected by a curtain-wall.

'I can't see a temple,' said Pazair in great surprise. 'No great gateways, no monumental gates, no banners fluttering in the wind.'

'There's no need for sacred things here,' said a Greek in amusement. 'The only god this city knows is profit. We all serve him faithfully, and we're doing very well out of him.'

A crowd of donkeys and merchants was entering the main gateway, which was watched by two good-humoured guards. People bumped into each other over, hailed each other, trod on each other's toes, and almost drowned in the continuous tide that invaded the narrow streets. The Canaanites had pointed beards and luxuriant side-whiskers, and wore their thick hair tied on the top of the head with a band. They went barefoot, but proudly wore striped mantles, which they bought from the Phoenicians, past masters of the art of calculating in one's head. Canaanites, Libyans and Syrians bore down on the Greeks' shops, which were bursting with imported products, notably slender, shapely vases and toilet items. Even Hittites were buying honey and wine, as vital to their table as their rituals. Kem's men melted into the crowds to await his signal.

Watching all this activity, Pazair soon noticed something strange: the buyers did not offer anything in exchange for the goods they acquired. At the end of heated negotiations, all they did was shake hands with the seller.

With Kem and Killer at his heels, Pazair went over to a small, talkative Greek with a beard, who was displaying beautiful silver cups.

'I'd like that one,' he said.

'You have good taste. I'm really surprised.'

'Why?'

'That's my favourite. Letting it go would make me sadder than I can say; but, alas, that is the hard law of trade. Touch it, young man, stroke it. Believe me, it's worth it – there's isn't a craftsman alive who could make another like it.'

'How much is it?'

'Feast upon its beauty, imagine it in your home, think of the envious, admiring looks on your friends' faces. First, you will refuse to tell them the name of the trader with whom you made this incredible deal, then you'll confess: who but Pericles sells such works of art?'

'It must be very expensive,' said Pazair.

'What does the price matter, when art reaches such perfection? Make an offer. Pericles is listening.'

'A spotted cow?'

The Greek's expression became one of profound astonishment. 'I don't like that sort of joke.'

'Is it too little?'

'Your humour's getting feeble, and I've no time to waste.' Annoyed, he moved on to another customer.

Pazair was disappointed. He thought he had proposed an exchange in his own disfavour.

The tjaty went to another Greek's stall and the transaction, with a few variations, was repeated. At the crucial moment, Pazair held out his hand. The trader gripped it loosely, then, astounded, withdrew his hand.

'But . . . your hand's empty!'

'What should it contain?'

'Do you think my vases are free? Money, of course.'

'I haven't got any.'

'Then go to an exchange-house and borrow some.'

'Where will I find one?'

'On the main street – there are more than a dozen.'

Bemused, Pazair followed the merchant's instructions.

The street came out on a square bordered by strange shops. Pazair looked at them; they were indeed 'exchange-houses', a term not used in Egypt. He went to the nearest one and joined the queue.

At the entrance were two armed men examined the tjaty from head to foot, and checking that he was not hiding a dagger.

Inside were several very busy people. One of them was placing small, round pieces of metal on a scale, weighing them, then arranging them in different pigeonholes.

'Deposit or withdrawal?' a scribe asked Pazair.

'Deposit.'

'List your possessions.'

'I . . .'

'Hurry up, other customers are waiting.'

'Because of the enormous amount I've brought with me, I should like to discuss its value with the exchange-house's most senior official.'

'He's busy.'

'When may I see him?'

'One moment.'

The scribe returned a few minutes later, and said the meeting was fixed for sunset.

So money, 'the great twisted one', had been introduced into this closed city. Money, in the form of coins in circulation, had been invented by the Greeks decades ago, but had been kept out of Egypt because it would put an end to the economy of barter and lead to the irremediable decay of society.* 'The twisted one' proclaimed the pre-eminence of having lots of money, increased humans' natural greed and made them apply monetary values detached from reality. Tjaties fixed the price of products and foods according to a reference which was not circulated and did not materialize in little circles of silver or copper – they were a veritable prison for individuals.

The director of the exchange-house was a round man with a square face, aged about fifty. Originally from Mycenae, he had recreated the atmosphere of his native house: little terra-cotta statuettes, marble effigies of Greek heroes, the principal passages from the Odyssey on papyrus, long-necked vases decorated with the exploits of Heracles.

'I am told that you are planning to grant us a large deposit,' he said.

'That is correct,' said Pazair.

---

*We note the existence of money in the XXXth dynasty; the monetary system was, however, not yet in force. It did not make its appearance in Egypt until under the Ptolemies, who were Greek.

'Of what kind?'

'I have many possessions.'

'Livestock?'

'Yes.'

'Grain?'

'Yes.'

'Boats?'

'Yes.'

'And other things as well?'

'Many other things.'

The director looked impressed.

'Have you enough coins here?' asked Pazair.

'I think so, but . . .'

'What is it?'

'Your appearance . . . gives no indication of such wealth.'

'When travelling, I prefer not to wear expensive clothes.'

'I understand, but I would like . . .'

'Proof of my wealth?'

The director nodded.

'Give me a clay tablet.'

'I would prefer to register your declaration on papyrus.'

'I have something more reliable to offer you. Give me that tablet.'

Taken aback, the director did so.

Pazair printed his seal deeply in the clay. 'Is this guarantee enough for you?'

The Greek gazed at the tjaty's seal, his eyes bulging. 'What . . . what do you want?'

'A fugitive from justice has visited you.'

'Me? That's impossible!'

'His name is Mentmose, and he used to command Memphis's security guards before he broke the law and was exiled. His presence on Egyptian soil is a major offence, which you ought to have reported.'

'I assure you that—'

'Don't lie,' advised the tjaty. 'I know that Mentmose came here on the orders of the head of the Double White House.'

The director's defences crumbled. 'How could I refuse to see him? He claimed to be from the authorities.'

'What did he want you to do?'

'To extend our exchange activities to the whole of the Delta.'

'Where is he hiding?'

'Not here – he left for the port of Raqote.'

'Have you forgotten that the circulation of money is forbidden and that those guilty of that crime are subject to heavy penalties?'

'My affairs are perfectly legal.'

'Have you received a decree signed by me?'

'Mentmose assured me that exchange-house activities were regarded as an accepted fact, and that they would become widespread in the near future.'

'You have been unwise. In Egypt, law is more than just a word.'

'You won't resist us for long. Progress is founded on exchange-houses, and—'

'It's a kind of progress we do not want.'

'I'm not the only one who says that. All my colleagues—'

'Let us go and meet them. Show me round this town.'

34

Full of hope, the director of the exchange-house presented the tjaty, accompanied by Killer, to his colleagues. They were charged with smuggling in money, controlling their customers' money, fixing the levels of loans and carrying out exchange transactions so as to make as much profit as possible from them. To a man, the directors insisted that their dealings brought great advantages. If a strong state could manipulate the system as it wished, why should it not utilize for its own benefit the possessions its subjects would be obliged to entrust to the exchange-houses?

While the tjaty was listening to the lecture, Kem's men, at a signal from their commander, dispensed with their Greek and Libyan accoutrements, and closed the gates of the city, despite the protests of an anxious crowd. Three men tried to climb a wall and get away, but their plumpness was their undoing: unable to reach the top of the wall, they were arrested and taken to Kem.

The most agitated of them said vehemently, 'Let us go at once.'

'You're guilty of illegally receiving coinage,' said Kem.

'You have no right to judge us.'

'I must take you before a court.'

When the three were in the presence of the tjaty, who listed his title and his offices, their scorn disappeared, and they began to wail.

'Forgive us. It was a mistake on our part, a regrettable mistake. We're honest traders, and we—'

'What are your names and professions?' asked Pazair.

The three men were Egyptians from the Delta, makers of furniture. Part of their production was not declared to the authorities, but was sent to the Greek city.

'It seems that you are piling up illegal profits and so harming your countrymen. Do you contest those facts?'

There were no protests.

'Don't deal harshly with us. We deluded ourselves.'

'I shall be content to apply our laws.'

Pazair set up his court in the main square. The jury was made up of Kem and five Egyptian peasants whom he had brought in from the nearest farm.

The many accused, most of whom were Greeks, did not contest the charges or the proposed sentence. The jury unanimously adopted the punishment that the tjaty wished for: immediate expulsion of the guilty parties and permanent banishment from Egyptian soil. The coins seized would be melted down, and the metal obtained would be given to the temples, where it would be transformed into ritual objects. As for the city, it would still be allowed to house foreign traders, so long as they observed the laws of Egypt.

The leader of the exchange-house directors thanked the tjaty.

'I was afraid the punishment would be more severe,' he confessed. 'They say the prison camp at Khargeh is hell on earth.'

'I survived it.'

'You?' said the man incredulously.

'Mentmose hoped that my bones would whiten in the sand there.'

'In your place, I wouldn't underestimate him – he's cunning and dangerous.'

'I am aware of that.'

'Do you realize that, by putting an end to the development of the monetary system, you will draw down on yourself the hatred of a formidable enemy? You are destroying one of Bel-Tran's main sources of wealth.'

'I am glad to hear it.'

'How long do you hope to remain tjaty?'

'As long as Pharaoh wishes me to.'

Pazair, Kem and Killer took passage on a fast boat bound for the coastal city of Raqote. The tjaty loved the lush greenness of the Delta landscape, where countless canals and streams intersected. The further north one went, the more the waters extended their kingdom. The Nile grew wider, preparing for its wedding with a dreamy, affectionate sea, which would intoxicate the last lands, with their indeterminate shapes. A world died in a bluish infinity and was reborn in the form of waves.

A significant part of Raqote's livelihood was fishing. Many Delta fisheries had set up their main premises in the areas around the little port, where different races mingled. In the open air, at the market or in warehouses, skilled workers washed the fish, gutted them and flattened them out; then they hung them on strips of wood to dry in the sun, or buried them in hot sand or in a cleansing mud. Next, they were salted; the finest pieces were kept in oil, the eggs of grey mullet put on one side for preparing a special delicacy. Rich people enjoyed fresh fish, grilled and covered in a sauce containing cumin, oregano, coriander and pepper; the ordinary people ate dried fish, a daily food as basic as bread. A grey mullet was equivalent in value to a jar of beer, and a basket of Nile perch to a fine amulet.

Pazair was astonished by the quietness in the town: not a song, not a gathering, no passionate bargaining, no caravans of donkeys coming and going. On the wharf, men were sleeping, stretched out on fishing-nets; hardly any boats were moored alongside.

A large, low house with a flat roof contained the secretariats that dealt with the registration of catches and their despatch.

Pazair and Kem went in.

The place was empty. No documents, as if the archives had never existed; not even a scribe's brush or rough notes. Not a clue to indicate that scribes had worked here.

'Mentmose can't be far away,' suggested Kem, gesturing at the baboon, which was getting restive. 'Killer knows he's here somewhere.'

The baboon prowled round the building and set off towards the port; Kem and Pazair followed. When they reached the docks Killer went to one of the few moored boats, a shabby, badly maintained one. At Kem's hail, the crew, five evil-smelling men armed with fish-gutting knives, emerged from their torpor.

'Go away,' said one. 'You're not from these parts.'

'Are you the last inhabitants of Raqote?'

'Go away.'

'I am Kem, commander of Memphis's security guards. Answer me, or you'll be in trouble.'

'Black men belong in the South, not here. Go back where you came from.'

'Will you obey the orders of the tjaty, who's here with me?'

The fisherman burst out laughing. 'The tjaty's lounging in his office in Memphis! In Raqote, we're the law.'

'I want to know what has happened here,' said Pazair sternly.

The man turned to his friends. 'Did you hear that? He thinks he's the great judge. Perhaps he thinks he can frighten us with his monkey.'

Killer had many good qualities and one failing: sensitivity. Being a security guard, he hated hearing people mock the state's power. His sudden bound caught his opponent by surprise, and the baboon disarmed him by biting his wrist. The second man was stunned, before he could move, by a punch on the back of the neck. As for the third, Killer charged at his legs and knocked him over. Kem took care of the last two, who were no match at all for him.

He dragged upright the only fisherman who could still talk, and demanded, 'Why is the town deserted?'

'The tjaty's orders.'

'Passed on by whom?'

'His personal messenger, Mentmose.'

'Have you met him?'

'Everybody here knows him. He's had problems, it seems, but they've been sorted out. Since he's been working with the law again, he's got on very well with the port authorities. There are whispers that he pays them Greek money, metal coins, and that he'll make his friends rich, so they follow his instructions to the letter.'

'What were his instructions?' asked Kem.

'To throw the reserves of smoked fish into the river and then to leave Raqote at once because there was a dangerous disease in the town. The scribes left first, then the ordinary townsfolk, and the workmen followed them.'

'But you didn't?'

'I and my comrades didn't know where to go.'

Killer leapt up and down.

'You're in Mentmose's pay, aren't you?'

'No, we —'

Killer gripped the fisherman's throat tightly; there was fierce anger in his red eyes.

'Yes, yes, we're waiting for him!' gasped the fisherman.

'Where is he hiding?'

'In the marsh, to the west.'

'What is he doing?'

'He's destroying the tablets and papyri we took out of the secretariats.'

'When did he leave?'

'A little after sunrise. When he comes back, we're to take him to the great canal, and we'll go to Memphis with him. He promised each of us a house and a field.'

'And what if he breaks his promise?'

The fisherman raised horrified eyes to Kem's face. 'He couldn't – not a promise like that.'

'Mentmose's word is worth nothing – he's a born liar. For instance, he's never worked for Tjaty Pazair, no matter what he told you. Now, get into this boat and take us to him. If you help us, we'll be lenient with you.'

The boat travelled through expanses which were half water, half grass, where Kem and Pazair would never have been able to find the way. Disturbed, black ibis soared up into the sky, where little round clouds were pushed along by the north wind. All along the hull slithered snakes, as greenish as the opaque water.

In this inhospitable labyrinth, the fisherman made surprisingly good progress.

'I'm taking a shortcut,' he explained. 'Mentmose is some way ahead of us, but we'll catch up with him before he rejoins the main canal where the transport boats ply.'

Kem lent a hand at the oars, Pazair scanned the horizon, and Killer dozed. The time passed too quickly. The tjaty wondered if their guide was tricking them, but Killer's calmness reassured him.

When eventually Killer stood up on his hind legs, the three men began to think that their pursuit had been successful. A few moments later, within sight of the great canal, they spotted another boat. There was only one person aboard, a man with a bald, pink pate which shone in the sunlight.

'Mentmose!' shouted Kem. 'Stop, Mentmose!'

Mentmose speeded up, but the distance between the boats grew inexorably smaller.

Realizing that he could not escape, Mentmose turned to face his pursuers. A javelin, thrown hard and accurately, hit the fisherman in the chest, and the unfortunate man fell overboard and sank into the marsh.

'Get behind me,' Kem ordered the tjaty.

Killer dived into the water.

Mentmose aimed a second javelin at Kem, who ducked at the last moment and dodged it. Pazair, rowing awkwardly, got the boat stuck in a bed of water lilies, prised her free and set off again.

A third javelin in his hand, Mentmose hesitated. Which should he kill first, Pazair or Kem?

Surging up out of the water, Killer gripped the prow of Mentmose's boat and shook it, trying to capsize it, but Mentmose first smashed down on to his paw the stone weight that served as an anchor, and then tried to pierce the paw and nail it to the wood with his javelin. Badly wounded, Killer let go of the prow, just as Kem leapt across from his own boat.

Although he was fat and unused to exercise, Mentmose defended himself with unexpected vigour; his javelin-point grazed Kem's cheek. Unbalanced, Kem fell to the bottom of the boat, while with his forearm he parried a fierce blow; the javelin stuck between two planks. Pazair came alongside Mentmose, who pushed away the tjaty's boat; Kem gripped his adversary's foot, and Mentmose fell into the marsh.

'Stop trying to resist,' ordered Pazair. 'You are our prisoner.'

Mentmose had kept hold of his weapon, and he aimed it at the tjaty. Suddenly, he shrieked in pain, put his hand to his neck, swayed, and sank down into the murky water. Peering over the side of the boat,

Pazair saw a catfish sneak off into the reeds that bordered the canal. He recognized it as of a kind rather rare in the Nile: it sometimes drowned people by rendering them unconscious.[*]

Kem, half mad with worry, spotted Killer struggling against the current. He threw himself into the water and helped him climb back into the boat. With great dignity, the baboon showed him his wound, as if apologizing for failing to arrest the suspect.

'It's a pity,' said Kem. 'But at least Mentmose will never speak again.'

Depressed and shocked, the tjaty was silent as they set off back to Memphis. He had reduced the size of Bel-Tran's secret empire a little more, but at the cost of the fisherman's life, and all lives were precious, even that of Mentmose's accomplice.

Kem examined Killer's wound, which fortunately turned out to be minor. Neferet would oversee his complete recovery.

As he worked, Kem sensed that Pazair was unhappy. He said, 'Mentmose is no loss. He was repulsive, like rotten, worm-eaten fruit.'

'Why do Bel-Tran's people commit so many atrocities? His ambition causes nothing but ill fortune and unhappiness.'

'You're our rampart against the demons. Don't give up.'

'I was expecting to see that justice was respected, not to investigate Branir's murder and live through so many crises. The office of tjaty is "more bitter than bile": that's what the king told me at my enthronement.'

Killer laid his wounded paw on the tjaty's shoulder; he did not remove it until they arrived at Memphis.

With Kem's help, Pazair wrote a long report on recent events. Hardly had they finished when, as they were relaxing in Pazair's garden, a scribe brought him a sealed papyrus. Addressed to the tjaty, it came from Raqote and was marked 'Urgent' and 'Confidential'.

Pazair broke the seal, and perused the astonishing message. He read out to Kem:

I, Mentmose, former commander of Memphis's security guards, who was unjustly condemned, denounce Tjaty Pazair as incompetent, criminal and irresponsible. In front of many witnesses, he threw the reserves of dried fish into the sea, and thus deprived the people of the Delta of their basic food for

---

[*]*Malapterurus electricus* is a sort of electric catfish; when shocked, its victim receives a discharge of around 200 volts.

several weeks. I address this complaint to the tjaty himself; in accordance with the law, he will be forced to convene his own trial.

'So,' said Kem, 'that's why Mentmose destroyed all the fisheries' scrolls at Raqote: so that they couldn't contradict him.'

'He was right about one thing,' said Pazair. 'The accusation may be a shameless lie, but I shall be obliged to prove my innocence through a trial. There will have to be a reconstruction, witnesses will have to be called, and Mentmose's foul dealings proved. And all during that time, Bel-Tran will be able to do as he pleases.'

Kem scratched his wooden nose. 'Sending you that letter wouldn't be enough on its own. Mentmose would also have had to lodge an official complaint through Bel-Tran or a senior official, so that you'd be forced to take account of his accusation.'

'Of course.'

'So all there is at the moment is this papyrus.'

'That's right, but it's enough to initiate the court case.'

'If it didn't exist, this matter wouldn't exist, either, would it?'

'I cannot possibly destroy it.'

'But I can.' Kem snatched the papyrus from Pazair and ripped it into a thousand pieces, which were scattered by the wind.

35

Suti and Panther gazed at the beautiful city of Kebet, capital of the fifth province of Upper Egypt, whose white houses gleamed in the sunshine. It stood on the right bank of the Nile, about two days' journey to the north-west of Karnak. From here, trade caravans left for the Red Sea ports and teams of miners departed for the sites in the eastern desert. It was here that Suti had enlisted as a miner, in order to track down General Asher.

Suti's motley army approached the fort guarding the road to the city's main entrance. It was forbidden to move around the area without authorization, and travellers had to be accompanied by guards who checked their identity and ensured their safety.

The officers at the guard-post could not believe their eyes. Where had this ill-assorted band sprung from? And could it really be made up of Libyans, Nubians and All-Seeing Ones? Anyone would have sworn they were fraternizing, whereas the All-Seeing Ones ought to have been surrounding their securely bound prisoners.

Alone, Suti went towards the guards' commander, who was armed with a sword.

With his long hair, bronzed skin, bare chest decorated with a broad collar of gold, and bracelets emphasizing the strength of his arms, he had the proud bearing of a true general bringing back his men from a victorious campaign.

'My name is Suti, and I am an Egyptian like you. Why should we kill each other?'

'Where have you come from?' asked the commander.

'You can see it: from the desert, which we have conquered.'

'But that's illegal.'

'My law, and that of my men, is the law of the desert: if you defy it, you'll die pointlessly. We're going to take control of this town. Join us – you'll do well out of it.'

The guard hesitated. 'Are those really All-Seeing Ones under your command?'

'They're reasonable people. I offer them more than they could ever hope for elsewhere.' Suti threw a gold ingot at the guard's feet. 'That is a modest gift, to help prevent carnage.'

The man picked up the treasure, his eyes bulging.

'My reserves of gold are inexhaustible,' said Suti. 'Go and alert the military governor of the town. I shall wait for him here.'

Like most Egyptian cities, Kebet did not shelter behind walls, so while the guard was delivering the message Suti ordered his soldiers to surround the town, so as to control the ways in and out.

Panther took her lover tenderly by the left arm, like a faithful wife. Covered in golden jewellery, she truly resembled a goddess, born from the marriage of the sky and the desert.

'Aren't you going to fight, my love?' she asked.

'A bloodless victory would be preferable, wouldn't it?'

'I'm not Egyptian. I'd rather see your countrymen being felled by mine. Libyans aren't afraid to fight.'

'This is not the right moment to provoke me.'

'It's always the right moment.' She kissed him with a conqueror's ardour, excited at the idea of becoming queen of Kebet.

The town's military governor soon arrived. He surveyed Suti with an expert eye: he had had a long career in the army, during which he had fought no less an enemy than the Hittites. Now he was preparing for a comfortable retirement in a village near Karnak; he suffered from painful joints, and so confined himself to routine work, well away from the exercise yards. At Kebet, there was no risk of heavy fighting: because of its strategic position it was protected by a detachment of guards, which discouraged smugglers and thieves. The city was prepared to repel raids by looters, but not to drive away formidable soldiers like these.

Behind Suti were well-equipped chariots; to his right, Nubian archers; to his left, Libyan javelin-throwers; in the distance, standing on rocky outcrops, the All-Seeing Ones. And that superb woman, with the fair hair, the coppery skin and the gold jewellery! Although he did not believe in the legends, the governor thought she really might come from the otherworld, perhaps from the mysterious isles that lay at the ends of the earth.

'What are your demands?' he asked Suti.

'That you hand Kebet over to me, so that I can set up my own administration.'

'That's impossible.'

'I am Egyptian,' said Suti, 'and I served in my country's army. Now I have not only my own army but vast wealth, which I have decided to use to benefit the town of the miners and gold-seekers.'

'Was it really you who accused Asher of treachery and murder?'

'It was.'

'You were right,' said the governor. 'He was a corrupt man, without a shred of honour. May the gods ensure that he never reappears.'

'You need not fear that: the desert has swallowed him up.'

'Justice has been done.'

'I'd like to prevent fighting between brothers.'

'I must ensure that public order is respected.'

'I have no intention of disturbing it.'

'Your army doesn't seem exactly peaceable.'

'Unless there's provocation, it will be.'

'What are your conditions?'

'The mayor of Kebet is a tired old man, with no energy left. Let him yield his place to me.'

'The transfer of power would not be valid without the agreement of the provincial governor and the tjaty.'

'We'll begin by driving out this senile old man,' decreed Panther, 'and then destiny shall decide.'

'Take me to him,' ordered Suti.

The mayor of Kebet was eating juicy olives, while listening to a young and extremely talented harp-player; a lover of music, he spent more and more of his time in leisure pursuits. The administration of Kebet presented few difficulties: strong contingents of desert guards ensured security, the people were well fed, specialists dealt with matters concerning metals and precious minerals, and the temple was testimony to the town's prosperity.

The military governor's visit was an unwelcome interruption, but the mayor agreed to see him.

'This is Suti,' said the soldier.

'Suti? General Asher's accuser?'

'The very same.'

'I am happy to welcome you to Kebet. Would you like some cool beer?'

'Very much,' said Suti.

The harp-player withdrew, and cup-bearers brought cups and the delicious brew.

'We are on the verge of disaster,' declared the military governor.

The mayor started. 'What are you saying?'

'Suti's army has encircled the town. If we fight, many people will be killed or injured.'

'An army? With real soldiers?'

The soldier nodded. 'Nubians, who are excellent archers, Libyans, who excel with the javelin, and ... All-Seeing Ones.'

'That's insane! I demand that these traitors be arrested and beaten.'

'It won't be easy to persuade them,' objected Suti.

'Not easy? Just where do you think you are?'

'In my own town.'

'Have you gone mad?'

'His army looks formidable,' said the soldier.

'Call for reinforcements!'

'I shall attack before they can get here,' said Suti.

'Arrest this man, Governor,' cried the mayor.

'That would be a mistake,' warned Suti. 'The golden goddess would put the town to fire and the sword.'

'The golden goddess?' asked the mayor.

'She has come back from the distant South, with the key to inexhaustible riches. Welcome her, and you'll find happiness and prosperity. Reject her, and destruction will be visited on your city.'

'Are you so sure you'll win?'

'I have nothing to lose; you have.'

'Aren't you afraid of death?'

'It's been my companion for a long time. The Syrian bear, Asher the traitor and the Nubian bandits all failed to kill me. But try, if you like.'

The mayor thought fast. A good mayor had to be a good negotiator: he had to resolve a thousand conflicts by using the weapon of diplomacy.

He said, 'It seems I must take you seriously, Suti.'

'That would be best.'

'What do you propose?'

'That you give up your office and that I become master of this town.'

'That's unrealistic.'

'I know the soul of this city. It will accept us as rulers, the golden goddess and myself.'

'Your seizure of power will be only an illusion. As soon as the news gets out, the army will dislodge you.'

'It will be a fine battle.'

'Disband your troops.'

'I'm going to rejoin the golden goddess,' declared Suti. 'I'll give you an hour to think about it. Either you accept my proposal or we attack.'

Arm in arm, Suti and Panther gazed at Kebet. They thought of the explorers who had set out along dangerous ways, in quest of treasure they had dreamt of a thousand times. How many had been guided by the gazelle of Isis to the right deposit? How many had come back alive, to marvel at the vast easterly curve of the Nile, around the city of the gold-seekers?

The Nubians were chanting, the Libyans were eating, the All-Seeing Ones were checking the chariots. No one spoke, for they were all awaiting the inevitable clash that would soak the roads and the fields with blood. But some were tired of wandering, some aspired to undreamt-of riches, some wanted to fight in order to prove their bravery. All were under the spell of Panther's beauty and Suti's determination.

'Will the city surrender?' she asked.

'It makes little difference to me.'

'You'll never kill your Egyptian brothers.'

'You shall have your town. In Egypt we worship women who can embody goddesses.'

'You won't escape me by dying in battle.'

'You're Libyan, but you love my land. Its magic has conquered you.'

'If it absorbs you, I'll follow you. My sorcery will be the stronger.'

The military governor arrived before the deadline. 'The mayor accepts your terms,' he said.'

Panther smiled; Suti remained impassive.

'On one condition: that you promise not to sack or pillage the town.'

'We've come to give,' said Suti, 'not to take.'

At the head of their army, the couple entered the town.

The news had already spread, and the inhabitants had gathered on the main road and at the crossroads. Suti told the Nubians to take off the sheets of linen covering the chariots.

The gold shone. Never had the Kebetites seen so much.

Little girls threw flowers to the Nubians, little boys ran alongside the soldiers. In less than an hour, the whole town was celebrating the return of the golden goddess, and singing the legend of the hero Suti, defeater of the demons of the night and discoverer of a giant goldmine.

'You look anxious,' Panther said to Suti.

'This may be a trap.'

The procession went to the mayor's house, an attractive house in the centre of the city, surrounded by a garden. Suti looked hard at the roofs: bow in hand, he was ready to launch an arrow at any hidden archer.

But nothing happened. An enthusiastic crowd surged in from the outskirts of town, convinced that a miracle had just happened. The golden goddess's return would make Kebet the wealthiest city in all Egypt.

On the threshold of the house, the serving-women had spread marigolds, forming an orange carpet. Lotus-flowers in their hands, they welcomed the goddess and General Suti. Delighted, Panther gratified them with a smile and set off royally along a path bordered with tamarisks.

'This house is absolutely charming. Look at its white front, the tall, slender pillars, the lintels decorated with palm-fronds . . . I shall feel at home here. And look over there – that's a stable. We shall go riding, before bathing and drinking sweet wine.'

The inside of the house also charmed her. The mayor had good taste: on the walls were paintings of wild ducks in flight and the luxuriant life of a lake. A wild cat was shown climbing along a papyrus stalk to reach a nest full of birds' eggs, a real feast in prospect.

Panther entered the bedchamber, took off her gold collar and lay down on the ebony-wood bed.

'You are a conqueror, Suti. Love me.'

The new master of Kebet could not resist that appeal.

That evening, a great feast was given for the citizens. Even the humblest folk ate roast meat and drank fine wines. Hundreds of lamps lit the streets, where people danced till dawn. The leading citizens promised to obey Suti and Panther and lauded the beauty of the golden goddess, who received their homage graciously.

'Why is the former mayor not here?' Suti asked the military governor.

'He has left the city.'

'Without my permission?'

'Enjoy your reign – it will be a short one. The mayor will alert the army, and the tjaty will re-establish order in the town.'

'Tjaty Pazair?'

'His reputation grows all the time. He is a just man, but stern.'

'The confrontation will be most interesting.'

'If you're wise you'll surrender.'

Suti smiled. 'I'm a madman, Governor, a madman with unpredictable reactions. My law is the law of the desert, which laughs at rules.'

'At least spare the civilians.'

'Death spares no one. Get drunk: tomorrow, we shall drink blood and tears.' Suti put his hands over his eyes. 'Go and find the golden goddess. I wish to speak to her.'

Panther was enjoying the song of a harp-player, who invited the diners to enjoy the present moment while tasting in it the flavour of eternity. An army of admirers were devouring her with their eyes. When the governor gave her Suti's message, she hurried back. She found Suti staring gazing fixedly into the distance.

'I'm blind again,' he whispered. 'Take my arm and lead me to the bedchamber. No one must know what's happened.'

A number of revellers hailed the couple, whose disappearance marked the end of the celebration.

When they reached their bedchamber, Suti lay down on his back.

'Neferet will cure you,' said Panther. 'I shall go and fetch her myself.'

'There won't be time.'

'Why not?'

'Because Tjaty Pazair will send the army to kill us.'

36

Neferet bowed before Tuya, Ramses' mother, and said, 'I am at your service, Majesty.'

'It is I who should bow to Egypt's principal doctor. Your work over these past few months has been remarkable.'

Tuya was a haughty woman, with a thin, straight nose, stern eyes, high cheekbones and an almost square chin. She enjoyed unchallenged moral authority. The head of a large household, with a palace in every large town, she advised rathered than ordered, and made sure people respected the values that had made the Egyptian monarchy secure. The Mother of Pharaoh belonged to a line of eminent women. It was queens of her stamp who had expelled the Hyksos invaders and founded the Theban empire, whose legacy had been inherited by the Ramses dynasty.

However, Tuya was deeply worried: for several months, she had been excluded from her son's confidences. Without actually disowning her, Ramses had distanced himself from her, as if he bore so weighty a secret that he could not confide even in his mother.

'How is your health, Majesty?' asked Neferet.

'Thanks to your treatment, I am marvellously well, although my eyes burn a little.'

'Why did you not consult me sooner?'

'My daily duties . . . But yourself? Are you properly attentive to your own health?'

'I have no time to think about it.'

'Well, Neferet, you must. If you were to fall ill, many patients would sink into despair.'

'Let me examine you, Majesty.'

The reason for the burning was easy to establish: the Mother of Pharaoh was suffering from an irritation of the eye-membrane. Neferet prescribed a remedy made from bat droppings, which would soothe the inflammation without causing any new problems.*

---

*Bat droppings, which are rich in vitamin A, are also an excellent antibiotic; in other words, the modern treatment corresponds to that of the ancient Egyptians.

'You will be cured within a week, Majesty. But please do not forget your usual eye-drops. Your eyes have greatly improved, but the treatment must be continued.'

'I thoroughly dislike having to concern myself with my own health – I would disobey any other doctor. Only Egypt deserves our attention. How is your husband bearing the weight of his office?'

'It is as heavy as a block of granite and as bitter as bile. But he will not give in.'

'I knew that the moment I first met him. At court, he is admired, feared and envied: that is the proof of his skill. His appointment caused great surprise and there has been no shortage of critics, but through what he has done he has silenced his detractors, to the point where Tjaty Bagey has been forgotten. That is no mean achievement.'

'Pazair cares little for the opinions of others.'

'That is all to the good. So long as he remains impervious to blame and praise alike, he will be a good tjaty. The king values his integrity and even grants him his trust. In other words, Pazair knows Ramses' most secret preoccupations, the ones I do not know. And you know them too, Neferet, because you and your husband form a single being. That is the truth, is it not?

'It is the truth.'

'Is the kingdom in danger?'

'Yes, Majesty, great danger.'

'I have known that since Ramses ceased to confide in me – no doubt he feared I might do something too high-handed, and perhaps he was right. However, now it is Pazair who is directing the battle.'

'Our enemies are formidable.'

'That is why it is time I intervened. The tjaty will not dare ask for my direct support, but I must help him. Whom does he fear?'

'Bel-Tran.'

'I detest upstarts,' declared Tuya. 'But fortunately their greed eventually destroys them. I assume he has the support of his wife?'

'Indeed, Majesty. She is his accomplice.'

'You may leave that goose to me. Her way of bobbing her neck when she greets me exasperates me.'

'Please do not underestimate her – she is dangerous.'

'Thanks to you, my sight is still excellent. I shall deal with that little snake.'

'Majesty, I must tell you that Pazair is in great distress at the thought of presiding over the ceremony when foreign tributes are presented. He is hoping that the king will return from Pi-Ramses in time to take that role himself.'

'Tell him there is no hope of it. Pharaoh's mood is increasingly sombre. He no longer leaves his palace, grants no audiences, and leaves the tjaty to take care of all day-to-day matters.'

'Is he ill?'

'His teeth are probably troubling him.'

'Do you wish me to examine him?'

'He has just dismissed his personal tooth-doctor as incompetent. After the ceremony, you shall accompany me to Pi-Ramses.'

A flotilla from the North brought the foreign envoys. No other boat was permitted on the river while the flotilla docked and moored, which process was overseen by the river guards. On the quay, the head of the Foreign Affairs secretariat welcomed Egypt's guests, who were ushered into comfortable travelling-chairs, followed by their retinues. The imposing procession set off for the palace.

Pharaoh's vassals and trading-partners had come, as they did every year, to pay him homage by bringing tributes. This year Memphis had been granted two days' holiday and would celebrate the peace that had been securely established through Ramses' wisdom and resolve.

Seated on a low-backed throne, dressed in the great robe of his office, weighted and stiff, a sceptre in his right hand, the figurine of Ma'at at his throat, Pazair was extremely nervous. Behind him, on his right, was the Mother of Pharaoh; in the first row were the Friends of Pharaoh, including Bel-Tran, who looked exultant. Silkis was wearing a new gown, which made some less wealthy courtiers' wives turn pale with envy. Bagey had agreed to assist his successor by advising him on protocol, and his presence reassured Pazair. The copper heart Bagey wore on his chest would symbolize, in the ambassadors' eyes, the trust that Ramses still had in him, and would prove that the change of tjaty did not mean a break in Egypt's foreign policy.

Pazair was authorized to direct the ceremony in the king's absence; last year, Bagey had performed this duty. The young tjaty would have preferred to remain in the background, but he knew how important the ceremony was: the visitors must leave satisfied, so that relations with their countries remained good. In exchange for the gifts, they hoped for consideration and understanding of their trading situation. The tjaty must tread a path between excessive strength and culpable weakness. One serious mistake by him, and the balance would be destroyed.

This was probably the last time the ancient ritual would take place. Bel-Tran would dispense with it, because it showed no tangible profit. He would ignore the fact that it was on a foundation of reciprocity, discretion and mutual respect that the sages of the time of the pyramids had built a happy civilization.

Bel-Tran's insolent satisfaction troubled Pazair. The closure of the

Greek exchange-houses had dealt him a serious blow, but he seemed hardly to care. Had it come too late to slow his onward march? With less than two months before the festival of regeneration and the king's forced abdication, Bel-Tran might be content to wait, without stirring up any more trouble.

Waiting . . . A tremendous ordeal for an ambitious man whose normal state was feverish activity. Many complaints had reached the tjaty, begging him to replace Bel-Tran with someone calmer and less tyrannical. He tortured his subordinates by refusing to grant them any rest. Under the pretext of urgent work, he overwhelmed them with made-up cases in order to keep a firm hand on them and prevent them from thinking. There had been occasional protests: Bel-Tran's methods were brutal, and he showed no consideration to employees who did not want to be reduced solely to their skills at work. He cared nothing for that: the amount of work a man did was all that counted with him. Anyone who opposed him was dispensed with.

Some of his allies had, with the greatest discretion, opened their hearts to the tjaty. They were tired of Bel-Tran's incessant talk, when he lost himself in interminable speeches in which he promised the moon; they were tiring of his duplicity and his sometimes crude lies. His determination to be regent, no matter what the circumstances, revealed the extent of his rapacity. A few provincial leaders, who at first had been won over, were now displaying polite indifference.

Pazair was making progress. Little by little, he was revealing the man's true character: inconstant and untrustworthy. The danger he represented had not lessened, but his persuasive abilities were fading day by day.

So why did Bel-Tran look so happy?

A priest announced the visitors, and silence fell over the tjaty's audience chamber.

The envoys came from Damascus, Byblos, Palmyra, Aleppo, Ugarit, Qadesh, the Hittite lands, Syria, Phoenicia, Canaan, Minoa, Cyprus, Arabia, Africa and Asia, from ports, trading cities and capitals. Not one came empty-handed.

The delegate from the mysterious land of Punt, an African paradise, was a small man with very dark skin and curly hair. He offered the skins of wild animals, incense, ostrich eggs and feathers. The Nubian envoy was greatly liked by those watching, for his refinement: a kilt cut from a leopard-skin, covered by a pleated skirt, a coloured feather in his hair, silver earrings and wide bracelets. His servants laid jars of oil, shields, gold and incense at the foot of the throne, while cheetahs on leashes and a giraffe filed past.

Minoan fashion provoked amusement: black hair with locks of

unequal length, beardless, straight-nosed faces, low-cut kilts trimmed with braid and decorated with diamond-shapes and rectangles, sandals with turned-up toes. The envoy laid down daggers, swords, animal-headed vases, ewers and cups. He was followed by the envoy from Byblos, a loyal ally of Egypt, who brought ox-hides, rope and rolls of papyrus.

Each envoy bowed before the tjaty and spoke time-honoured words: 'Receive my country's tribute, brought in homage to His Majesty, Pharaoh of Upper and Lower Egypt, in order to seal peace.'

The representative from Asia, where the Egyptian army had fought hard battles in a past that Ramses believed had gone by, arrived accompanied by his wife. He wore a kilt decorated with tassels and a red and blue tunic with long sleeves tied with thongs; she wore a tiered skirt and a striped cape. Their tribute, to the court's astonishment, was the smallest. Usually Asia closed the ceremony by laying before Pharaoh or the tjaty copper ingots, lapis-lazuli, turquoises, lengths of rare wood, jars of ointment, harnesses for horses, bows, quivers full of arrows, and daggers, not to mention bears, lions and bulls for the royal menagerie. This time, all the envoy offered were a few cups, some jars of oil and jewellery of no great value.

When he greeted the tjaty, he showed no emotion. Nevertheless, the message was clear: Asia was addressing grave reproaches to Egypt. If the reasons for the discord were not brought to light and the causes dispelled with all possible speed, the spectre of war would reappear.

While Memphis was feasting, from the docks to the craftsmen's districts, Pazair received the Asian envoy privately. No scribe or other official was present: before declarations were registered and took on a formal nature, attempts must be made to re-establish harmony.

The envoy had lively eyes and an incisive way with words. 'Why did Ramses not preside over the ceremony himself?'

'He is at Pi-Ramses, as he was last year, to oversee the building of a new temple.'

'Has Tjaty Bagey been disowned?'

'By no means – as you saw.'

'His presence and the copper heart he still wears. Yes, I noted those signs that he is still respected. But you are very young, Tjaty Pazair. Why has Ramses entrusted you with this office, one which everyone knows is overwhelming?'

'Bagey felt too tired to continue. He asked permission to retire, and the king granted his request.'

'That does not answer my question.'

'Who can know the secrets of a pharaoh's thoughts?'

'His tjaty,' said the envoy.

'I am not certain that I do.'

'So you are merely a puppet.'

'That is for you to judge.'

'My opinion is based on facts: you were a minor provincial judge and Ramses has made you first minister of Egypt. I have known the king for ten years; he is never wrong about the worth of those around him. You must be an exceptional person, Tjaty Pazair.'

'It is my turn to question you, if you will allow me to.'

'That is your duty.'

'What did the slightness of your tribute signify?'

'Did it seem insufficient?'

'You know what you have done: that it verges on an insult.'

'"Verges on", indeed. It shows my restraint and a last wish for conciliation, following an insult we have suffered.'

'I don't understand.'

'People boast of your love for the truth. Is it only a fable?'

'On the name of Pharaoh, I swear I do not know your grievances.'

The Asian ambassador was shaken; his tone became less acid. 'That is very strange. Have you lost control of your secretariats, and in particular of the Double White House?'

'I disliked certain practices dating from before my appointment, and I proceeded to reform them. Have you been the victim of an offensive act about which I have not been informed?'

'That word is far too weak! It would be more correct to speak of a crime so serious that it could lead to a break in relations between our countries – even to war.'

Pazair tried to mask his anxiety, but his voice was unsteady. 'Will you enlighten me?'

'I have difficulty believing that you are not responsible.'

'As tjaty, I accept the responsibility; but, at the risk of appearing ridiculous, I confirm that I know nothing about it. How can I make amends for this offence if I do not know what it is?'

'Egyptians often mock our taste for cunning and conspiracies. I fear that you may yourself have fallen victim to them. Your youth does not win only friends, it seems.'

'Pray explain.'

'Either you are the most accomplished of actors or you will not be tjaty for much longer. Have you heard tell of our trade exchanges?'

Pazair did not flinch, despite the biting sarcasm. Even if the envoy thought him both incompetent and ignorant, he must learn the truth.

'When we send you our goods,' continued the envoy, 'the Double

White House sends us their equivalent in gold. That is the custom, and has been ever since peace was established.'

'Has the delivery not been made?'

'The ingots arrived, but the gold was of very bad quality, poorly purified and brittle, only good enough to please a few backward nomads. By sending us unusable gold, Egypt made a mockery of us. The integrity of Ramses himself is implicated: we consider that he has broken his word.'

So that was why Bel-Tran had looked so pleased with himself. Destroying Ramses' prestige in Asia would enable him to pose as a saviour, determined to correct the king's misdeeds.

'There has been a mistake,' said Pazair, 'not an attempt to offend you.'

'The Double White House does not act alone, so far as I know! It obeyed orders from above.'

'Consider that you have been the victim of flawed procedures and a lack of coordination between the secretariats I head, but do not see hostility in it. I myself shall inform the king of my own incompetence.'

The envoy regarded him thoughtfully. 'You have been betrayed, have you not?'

'It is up to me to be aware of that and to take the necessary measures. Otherwise, you will soon be dealing with a new tjaty.'

'I would regret that.'

'Will you accept my most sincere apologies?'

'I believe you, but Asia demands reparation, in accordance with custom. Send double the agreed quantity of gold, as soon as possible. If you do not, I fear war is inevitable.'

Pazair and Neferet were preparing to leave for Pi-Ramses when a royal messenger asked to see the tjaty as a matter of urgency.

'Something serious has happened, Tjaty,' he said. 'The mayor of Kebet has been driven from his city by an armed band of Libyans and Nubians.'

'Was anyone injured?'

'No. They seized the town without waging battle. Some of the All-Seeing Ones have joined the rebels, and the military governor dared not resist.'

'Who is in command of the rebels?'

'A man named Suti, aided by a golden goddess who has subjugated the population.'

Immense joy flooded Pazair: Suti was alive – very much alive! It was marvellous news, even if his much-hoped-for reappearance had occurred in rather chaotic circumstances.

'The soldiers stationed in Thebes are ready for action; their commander merely awaits your orders. As soon as you have signed the necessary documents, I shall ensure that they get to him. According to him, order will soon be re-established. Even if the rebels are properly armed, there are too few of them to resist a full-scale attack.'

'As soon as I return from Pi-Ramses, I shall deal with the matter myself. In the meantime, our soldiers are to surround the city and pitch camp in defensive positions. They are to allow through food caravans and merchants, so that the town will not go short of anything. Inform Suti that I shall come to Kebet as soon as possible and that I shall negotiate with him.'

37

From the terrace of the sumptuous house that had been set aside for them, Pazair and Neferet gazed out over Ramses' favourite city, Pi-Ramses, whose name meant 'Domain of Ramses' or 'Temple of Ramses'. It stood not far from Avaris – hated capital of the Hyksos invaders, who had been driven out at the start of the New Kingdom – and at the king's instigation had become the largest city in the Delta, with some hundred thousand inhabitants. It had many temples, dedicated to Amon, Ra, Ptah, the formidable Set, lord of storms, Sekhmet and Astarte, a goddess who had been brought to Egypt by the Hyksos. The army had three barracks; and to the south lay the port, with its many store-houses and workshops. At the centre stood the royal palace, which was surrounded by the houses of the nobles and senior officials, and a large ornamental lake.

In the hot season, Pi-Ramses enjoyed an agreeable climate, for the city lay between two branches of the Nile, 'the Waters of Ra' and 'the Waters of Avaris'; many canals crossed it, and ponds full of fish provided fishermen with an opportunity to indulge in their favourite pursuit.

The site had not been chosen by chance. Pi-Ramses was ideally placed for observing the Delta and Asia, and a perfect departure-point for Pharaoh's soldiers in the event of disturbances in the protectorates. The sons of the nobility vied with one another in their eagerness to serve in the chariot corps or to ride magnificent horses, swift and highly strung. The city's carpenters, boat-builders and metalworkers, who had been provided with excellent equipment, were often visited by the king, who took a keen interest in their work.

'What joy to dwell in Pi-Ramses,' declared a popular song. 'No more beautiful city exists. There, the small is given as much consideration as the great, the acacia and the sycamore dispense their shade to walkers, the palaces dazzle with gold and turquoise, the wind is gentle, the birds play around the pools.'

During an all-too-short morning, the tjaty and his wife had sampled the tranquillity of the orchards and the olive groves, surrounded by vineyards producing a fine wine which was served at festivals and feasts. The grain-stores reached almost to the sky. The fronts of the opulent houses were glazed with blue tiles, which had earned Pi-Ramses its nickname of 'the Turquoise City'. On the threshold of the brick homes built between the great houses, children were eating apples and pomegranates, and playing with wooden dolls. They laughed at the pretentious scribes and cheered the chariot officers.

The dream was but a brief one. Although the fruit might taste like honey and the garden of his house be a paradise, the tjaty was preparing to confront Pharaoh. According to what the Mother of Pharaoh had said in confidence, the king no longer believed in his tjaty's success. His isolation was that of a condemned man, without hope.

Neferet was painting her face. Using small, bulbous-ended sticks, she drew lines round her eyes with kohl. The box in which face-paints were kept bore the significant name of 'That Which Opens the Sight'. Round her waist, Pazair slipped the belt of amethyst beads, including parts in worked gold, that Neferet loved so much.

'Will you come with me to the palace?' he asked.

'My presence there has been requested.'

'I'm afraid, Neferet, afraid of having disappointed the king.'

She leant back, laying her head on Pazair's shoulder. 'My hand will always be in your hand,' she whispered. 'My greatest happiness is to walk with you in a secluded garden, where the only sound is the wind's voice. Your hand will always be in mine, for my heart is drunk with joy when we are together. What more could anyone want, tjaty of Egypt?'

The palace guard was changed three times a month, on the first, eleventh and twenty-first days. Each time they came on duty, they received meat, wine and cakes, plus the normal wage, paid in grain. For the tjaty's arrival, the men formed a guard of honour; his visit would mean a fine bonus for them.

A steward welcomed Pazair and Neferet, and told them, 'Pharaoh awaits you in the garden.' He led them through the summer palace. The entrance hall, with its white walls and coloured flagstones, led to several audience chambers decorated with tiles glazed in yellow and brown, with dots of blue, red and black. In the throne room, cartouches containing the king's name formed friezes. The reception halls reserved for greeting foreign rulers shimmered with pictures: naked girls swimming, birds in flight and turquoise landscapes enchanted the eye.

The ancients had said that Egypt should resemble an immense garden in which the most diverse species lived in peace. Ramses endeavoured to realize that wish by planting many, many trees. When Pazair and

Neferet saw him he was kneeling down, planting an apple tree. On his wrists he wore his favourite gold and lapis-lazuli bracelets, their upper part decorated with wild ducks.

Ten paces away stood Ramses' finest bodyguard: a half-tame lion which had accompanied the young king on the battlefields of Asia at the start of his reign. Named Invincible, it obeyed no one but its master; anyone who approached the king with hostile intentions would have been torn to pieces.

The tjaty stepped forward; Neferet waited inside a shelter near a pond where fish were frolicking.

'How fares the kingdom, Pazair?' The king turned his back on his tjaty.

'As badly as it could, Majesty.'

'Were there problems at the tribute ceremony?'

'The Asian envoy is extremely unhappy.'

'Asia is a permanent danger. Its peoples do not like peace – they take advantage of it to prepare for the next war. I have strengthened the western and eastern frontiers with chains of fortresses; the former will prevent the Libyans from invading us, and the latter the Asians. Archers and footsoldiers have received orders to watch day and night, and to communicate with each other by signals. Here, at Pi-Ramses, I receive daily reports on events in the Asian princedoms, and I also receive reports on the activities of my tjaty.'

The king stood up and turned to face Pazair. 'Some nobles are complaining; some provincial governors are protesting; the court feels slighted. "If the tjaty is wrong," says the Rule, "let him not hide his mistake in darkness. Rather, let him make it public and make it known that he will rectify it."'

'What fault am I guilty of Majesty?'

'Did you not punish dignitaries and senior officials by having them beaten? Those who carried out the base tasks even sang: "Fine gifts for you who have never received the like".'

'I was not aware of that detail, but the law was applied, to the rich as to the poor. The higher the guilty party's rank, the more severe the punishment.'

'Do you deny nothing?'

'Nothing.'

Ramses embraced Pazair. 'Then I am happy. The exercise of power has not changed you.'

'I feared I had disappointed you.'

'The Greek traders sent me a complaint filling an interminable scroll. Did you stop their trade?'

'I put an end to the smuggling of coins and the setting up of exchange-houses on our territory.'

'The mark of Bel-Tran, of course.'

'The culprits have been expelled, and Bel-Tran's main source of wealth has thus been cut off. Some of his friends are disappointed, and have distanced themselves from him.'

'As soon as he takes power, he will introduce the circulation of money.'

'We still have a few weeks left, Majesty.'

'Without the Testament of the Gods, I shall be compelled to abdicate.'

'Will Bel-Tran be able to rule, weakened as he is?'

'He will destroy rather than give up. Men of his type are not rare, but up to now we have succeeded in keeping them away from the throne.'

'Let us still hope.'

'What does Asia accuse us of?' asked Ramses.

'Bel-Tran had poor-quality gold sent to them.'

'The worst insult imaginable! Did the envoy threaten you?'

'There is only one way to prevent war: by sending twice the agreed quantity.'

'Have we enough?'

'No, Majesty. Bel-Tran took care to empty our reserves.'

'Asia will consider that I have broken my word. One more reason to justify my abdication – and Bel-Tran will play at being the country's saviour.'

Pazair said hesitantly, 'We may have one last chance.'

'Do not keep me waiting.'

'Suti is in Kebet, accompanied by a golden goddess. I wonder, might he know the whereabouts of easily accessible treasure?'

'Go and ask him.'

'Majesty, the matter is not so simple.'

'Why not?'

'Because Suti is at the head of an armed band. He has driven out the mayor of Kebet and controls the city.'

'That is insurrection.'

'Our troops have surrounded Kebet, but I have forbidden them to attack. The invasion was peaceful – we have no deaths or injuries to mourn.'

'What are you going to dare ask of me, Pazair?'

'If I succeed in persuading Suti to help us, impunity for him.'

'He escaped from the fortress in Nubia, and he has committed an act of insubordination of exceptional gravity.'

'He was the victim of injustice and has always served Egypt with devotion. Does that not deserve leniency?'

'Put aside your friendship, Tjaty, and conform to the Rule. Let order be re-established.'

Pazair bowed.

Ramses, accompanied by the lion, went to the shelter where Neferet was waiting.

'Well, Neferet, are you ready to torture me?'

Neferet's examination lasted more than an hour. Ramses was suffering from inflammation of the joints, and to control the pain she prescribed daily decoctions of willow bark.* She also found that several fillings in his teeth were in urgent need of replacement. In the palace laboratory, she prepared a mixture of pistachio resin, Nubian earth, honey, crushed grindstone, green eye drops and fragments of copper, with which to fill the king's teeth, and she advised him to give up chewing papyrus-shoots, so as to avoid premature wearing-out of the teeth.

'Are you hopeful, Neferet?'

'To be completely honest, I fear there may be an abscess at the base of an upper left rear tooth – you should receive much more regular checks. However, we shall avoid having to take out the tooth, if you treat your gums with frequent applications of mother-tincture of calendula.'

Neferet washed her hands; Ramses rinsed his mouth with natron.

He said, 'What concerns me is not my future but Egypt's. I know of your ability to detect the invisible: like my father, you sense the lines of power that hide behind appearance. I ask again: are you hopeful?'

'Must I answer you?'

'Does that mean you despair?'

'Branir's soul protects Egypt: his sufferings will not have been in vain. In the very depths of the darkness, a light will be born.'

The Nubians, stationed on the roofs of the houses in Kebet, were keeping watch on the surrounding areas. Every three hours, the old warrior reported to Suti.

This time, he was breathless with haste. 'Hundreds of soldiers – they came up the Nile.'

'Are we surrounded?'

'Yes, though at the moment they're keeping their distance and holding their positions. If they attack, we'll have no chance.'

'Tell your men to rest.'

'I don't trust the Libyans. All they think of is stealing and playing dice.'

'The All-Seeing Ones are watching them.'

'And when will they turn against you?'

---

*From which our modern aspirin is derived.

'When my gold runs out – and it's inexhaustible.'

Sceptical, the old warrior returned to the terrace of the mayor's house, from where he gazed out at the Nile. Already he was tiring of the desert.

Kebet held its breath. Everyone knew the army would soon attack. If Suti's men surrendered, a bloodbath would be averted, but Panther was inflexible and persuaded her faithful to resist or face terrible punishments. The golden goddess had not come back from the distant South to surrender to the first soldiers she encountered. Soon her empire would extend to the sea, and anyone who obeyed her would know limitless joy.

How could they not believe in Suti's power? The light of another world shone within him; his bearing could only be that of a demi-god. A stranger to fear, he gave courage to men who had never had it. The All-Seeing Ones dreamt of a leader like him, who could command without raising his voice, who could draw the sturdiest bow and shatter the skulls of the cowardly. The legend of Suti was growing: he had penetrated the mountains' secret places and extracted the rarest metals from their bellies. Anyone who dared attack him would fall prey to flames which sprang from the bowels of the earth.

'You've cast a spell on this town and its people,' Suti said to Panther, who was lying beside the pool after bathing.

'This is only a start, my darling. Kebet will soon seem too small for us.'

'Your dream's going to turn into a nightmare. We shan't be able to hold out for long against the Egyptian army.'

Panther seized him round the neck and pulled him down beside her. 'Don't you believe in your golden goddess any more?'

'I must be mad. Why else would I listen to you?'

'Because I keep saving your life. Don't concern yourself with this nightmare, but be content with the dream – doesn't it have the colours of gold?'

Suti would have liked to resist her, but had to admit that he was soon overcome. The mere touch of her golden skin, with its exotic scent, awoke a desire as tempestuous as the Nile in flood. He at once took the initiative and intoxicated her with caresses. Consenting, Panther became gentleness itself, before throwing Suti on to his side and falling with him into the lake.

Their bodies were still united when the old warrior interrupted them.

'An Egyptian officer wishes to speak with you. He's at the main entrance, beside the Nile.'

'Is he alone?'

'Alone and unarmed.'

The town fell silent, when Suti met the officer of the Army of Amon, who was dressed in a coloured coat of mail.

'Are you Suti, who drove out the mayor of Kebet?' asked the officer.

'The mayor offered me his position.'

'And do you command the rebels?'

'I have the honour to be the leader of free men.'

'Your lookouts have seen that we came in force. However strong you are in battle, you will be wiped out.'

'In the chariot corps, my best instructor advised me to distrust vanity. What's more, I have never yet yielded to threats.'

'Do you refuse to surrender?'

'Can you doubt it?'

'Any attempt at escape is bound to fail.'

'Attack – we're ready.'

'That decision will be made not by me but by the tjaty. Until he arrives, you will receive provisions as normal.'

'When will he get here?'

'Take advantage of this respite. As soon as Tjaty Pazair disembarks, he will lead us to victory and re-establish order.'

38

Silkis could not wait for Bel-Tran to come home. She rushed round
the house, called conflicting instructions to her servants, ran into the
garden, slapped her daughter, who had stolen a pastry, and let her son
chase a cat, which took refuge up a tree. Then she turned her attention
to the midday meal, told the cook to prepare different dishes, and
lectured her children.

As soon as Bel-Tran arrived she rushed to the door of the house.
'My darling, it's wonderful!'

Scarcely giving him time to get down from his travelling-chair, she
pulled so hard on his linen wrap, which protected his sensitive shoulders
from the sun, that she tore it.

'Be careful! That cost a fortune.'

'Come quickly. I've some incredible news for you. I've poured you
some wine in your favourite cup.'

More child-woman than ever, Silkis simpered all the way through
the brief walk to her bedchamber, and enlivened the way high-pitched
laughter.

'This morning,' she said 'I received a message from the palace.'
From a chest she took a message marked with the king's seal. 'An
invitation from the Mother of Pharaoh – for me! What a triumph!'

'An invitation?'

'To her very own palace! All Memphis shall know of this.'

Puzzled, Bel-Tran read the papyrus. It was written in the Mother
of Pharaoh's own hand. The fact that she had not used the services of
her personal scribe indicated the very marked interest she had in meeting
Silkis.

'Several great ladies of the court have been hoping for this honour
for years – and I have been given it!'

'It's surprising, though.'

'Surprising? Not at all! It is thanks to you, darling. Tuya is an
intelligent woman, and very close to her son. He must have made her
understand that his reign is about to end, and she is preparing for the

future. She will try to become friends with me, so that you will let her keep her prerogatives and privileges.'

'That assumes that Ramses has told her the truth,' said Bel-Tran.

'He may have confined himself to telling her about his abdication. Tiredness, ill health, his failure to introduce new ways to Egypt – whatever reason he gave, Tuya knows change is coming and she's worried about her future. What better way to ingratiate herself with you than by introducing me into her circle of confidantes? The old lady is very cunning, but she knows she's lost. If we're her enemies, she'll lose her palaces, her household and her wealth. At her age, that would be unbearable.'

'Making use of her prestige in the country would not be a bad idea. If she sanctions the new power, it will take root very quickly and there will be very little opposition. I dared not hope for such a gift from destiny.'

'How should I behave?' asked Silkis, very excited.

'With respect and goodwill. Grant all her requests, and make her understand that we accept her help and her submission.'

'And what if she asks about her son's fate?'

'Ramses will withdraw into a temple in Nubia, where he will grow old with the priests. As soon as our new order is in place and there can be no going back, we'll get rid of both mother and son. We cannot let the past encumber us.'

'You're wonderful, my darling.'

Kem was in a bad mood. If Pazair had little taste for worldly things and protocol, Kem positively detested them. Obliged to wear elaborate clothing worthy of his rank, he felt ridiculous. The barber had dressed his hair, put on his wig, and shaved and perfumed him, and a painter had coloured his wooden nose black. For more than an hour he had been waiting in the antechamber, and he resented this waste of time. But he could not refuse to answer a summons from the Mother of Pharaoh.

At last, a steward showed him into Tuya's office, an austere place decorated with maps of the country and stelae dedicated to the ancestors. Although she was much shorter than the Nubian, the Mother of Pharaoh impressed him more than a wild animal about to spring.

'I wanted to test your patience,' she said. 'A commander of soldiers must never lose his head.'

Kem did not know if he ought to remain standing, sit down, answer or keep silent.

'What do you think of Tjaty Pazair?' asked Tuya.

'He is a just man – the only just man I know. If you wish to hear criticisms of him, Majesty, ask someone else.' Kem immediately realized that his blunt answer had been inexcusably lacking in courtesy.

'You have more character than your miserable predecessor, but you practise the art of polite conversation rather less well,' said the queen drily.

'I spoke the truth, Majesty.'

'As a commander should.'

'I care nothing for my rank or my title. I accepted them only in order to help Pazair.'

'The tjaty is fortunate, and I like men who are fortunate. Therefore you shall help him.'

'How?'

'I want to know everything about the lady Silkis.'

As soon as the tjaty's boat was announced, the river guards cleared a path to the main quay of Memphis. The heavy transport ships manoeuvred with the grace of dragonflies, and found their places without colliding.

The shadow-eater had spent the night on the roof of a grain-store between the trade-control office and a papyrus storehouse. Having committed his crime, he would escape by that route. At the port offices all he had had to do was listen, and he had gained detailed information about Pazair's return from Pi-Ramses. The security measures put in place by Kem meant that improvization was out of the question.

The shadow-eater's plan rested on a plausible supposition: to avoid the crowds, Pazair would not take the main road from the port to the palace. Instead, surrounded by guards, he would take the road past the grain-store – it was narrow, but a chariot could just get through.

The very chariot in which he would ride had just halted, right below the shadow-eater.

This time the throwing-stick would not miss its target. The stick was a simple one, from a lot sold off cheaply in the market because they were second-hand. The seller had not noticed the assassin as he mingled with a group of noisy buyers. Like them, he had offered fresh onions in exchange.

Having committed the crime, he would re-establish contact with Bel-Tran. The latter's position was becoming more and more shaky, and many people predicted that he would soon fall from power. By killing Pazair, the shadow-eater would give him back the certainty of victory.

No doubt Bel-Tran would think of killing him, not of rewarding him, so he would take precautions. They would meet in a deserted place, and Bel-Tran would come alone. If they agreed on mutual silence,

Bel-Tran would leave alive and triumphant; if not, the shadow-eater would close his employer's mouth for ever. His demands would not alarm Bel-Tran: more gold, immunity, an official position under another name, and a large house in the Delta. It would be as if the shadow-eater had never existed. And, one day, Bel-Tran would need his services again ... A reign built on murder was being consolidated, thanks to him.

On the quay were Kem and Killer. The shadow-eater's last anxiety was dispelled: the wind was strong, and it was blowing in the right direction. The baboon would not catch his scent and would have no chance of blocking the throwing-stick, which would not fly in a curve but would fall from the sky as swiftly as a bolt of lightning. There was just one difficulty: the narrowness of the angle. But cold rage and the desire to succeed would make the assassin's aim perfectly true.

The tjaty's boat moored. Pazair and Neferet disembarked, and were immediately surrounded by Kem and his men. After greeting the couple by bowing his head, Killer went to the head of the procession.

He avoided the main road and set off along the narrow street. The wind unsettled the baboon, whose nostrils flared in vain.

In a few seconds, the tjaty would halt before his chariot. In the time it took him to step aboard, the throwing-stick would fracture his head.

Arm bent, the shadow-eater concentrated. Kem and Killer stood on either side of the chariot. The Nubian helped Neferet to climb in. Behind her was Pazair. The shadow-eater stood up, saw Pazair's profile and kept hold of his weapon to the last moment, though it was already leaving his hand.

A man stepped in front of Pazair, masking him.

Bel-Tran had just saved the man whose death he so desired.

'I must speak to you at once,' said Bel-Tran, his hurried words and jerky movements made Killer even more unsettled.

'Is it so urgent?' asked Pazair, surprised.

'Your office tells me your meetings have been cancelled for several days.'

'I do not believe I am required to account to you for how I spend my time.'

'The situation is extremely serious: I appeal to you in the name of Ma'at.'

Bel-Tran did not speak those words lightly before several witnesses, including Kem. The declaration was so solemn that the tjaty must accede to the request, provided it was well founded.

'She will answer you by her Rule. Be at my office in two hours.'

The wind died, and Killer raised his eyes to the skyline. The shadow-eater flattened himself against the roof. Wriggling on his belly, he beat a retreat. When he heard the tjaty's chariot moving away, he bit his lips until they bled.

The tjaty congratulated young Bak, who had become his personal scribe. The youth, who was scrupulous and hard-working, permitted no ambiguity in the wording of official documents. Pazair had entrusted to him the task of examining decrees and communications, in order to forestall criticism from officials and the population.

'Your work gives complete satisfaction, Bak, but it would be advisable for you to move to another department.'

The youth blanched. 'What have I done wrong?'

'Nothing.'

'Be honest, I beg you.'

'I repeat, nothing.'

'In that case, why transfer me?' asked Bak.

'For your own good.'

'My own good? But I'm happy here. Have I annoyed somebody?'

'On the contrary, your tact is admired by all the scribes.'

'Tell me the truth.'

'Well, it would be wise to distance yourself from me.'

'I won't do it.'

'My future is very uncertain,' said Pazair, 'and so is that of anyone close to me.'

'It's that man Bel-Tran, isn't it? He's trying to bring about your downfall.'

'It's pointless for you to be dragged down with me. If you move to another department, you'll be safe.'

'Such cowardice would be disgusting. Whatever happens, I want to stay with you.'

'You're very young. Why risk your career?'

'I don't care about my career. You've given me your trust, and I owe you mine.'

'Are you fully aware of how unwise you're being?'

'If you were in my place, would you do otherwise?'

Pazair gave in. 'Check this text concerning a tree plantation in the northern part of Memphis. There must be no argument about the chosen locations.'

Wild with joy, Bak returned to work.

His expression darkened when he showed Bel-Tran into the tjaty's office.

Seated in the scribe's position on the floor, Pazair was writing a letter to the provincial governors regarding the next annual flood; they were to check that the earthen banks and retaining-pools were in good condition, so that the country would gain the full benefit of the fertilizing waters.

Bel-Tran, who was wearing a new robe with exaggerated pleats, remained standing.

'I am listening,' said the tjaty without looking up. 'Would you oblige me by not losing yourself in unnecessary talk?'

'Do you know the extent of your power?'

'I am more concerned with my duties.'

'You occupy a crucial post, Pazair. If grave misdeeds are committed at the highest level of the state, it is up to you to see that justice is done.'

'I dislike insinuations.'

'Then I'll speak plainly. You are the only person who can judge the members of the royal family – even the king himself, if he betrays his country.'

'Do you dare to speak of treason?'

'Ramses is guilty.'

'Who accuses him?'

'I do, so that our moral values may be respected. By sending poor-quality gold to our Asian friends, Ramses endangered Egypt. He must face trial before your court.'

'It was you who sent that gold.'

'Pharaoh does not allow anyone else to handle Asian affairs, and no one will believe that one of his ministers acted against his wishes.'

'As you say, it is up to me to establish the truth. Ramses is not guilty, and I shall prove that.'

'I shall provide evidence against him. As tjaty, you will be obliged to take account of it and to begin the trial process.'

'The preparations will take a very long time.'

Bel-Tran lost his temper. 'Don't you understand that I'm offering you one last chance? By becoming the king's accuser, you will save yourself. The most influential people in the country are rallying to my cause. Ramses is a man alone, abandoned by everyone.'

'He will still have his tjaty.'

'Your successor will convict you of treason.'

'Let us place our trust in Ma'at.'

'You will have deserved your sad fate, Pazair.'

'Our deeds will be weighed on the scales of the afterlife, both mine and yours.'

Scowling, Bel-Tran swept out.

When he had gone, Bak came in handed Pazair a strange missive. 'I think it may be urgent.'

Pazair read the papyrus. 'You were right to show it to me before I left.'

*

The little Theban village ought to have been dozing in the hot sunshine, shaded by the palm-trees. But only the oxen and the donkeys were resting, for the whole population had gathered in the dusty square where the local court sat.

The headman was at last having his revenge on the old shepherd Pepy, a real savage, who lived apart from other people, preferring the company of ibis and crocodiles, and who hid in the papyrus thickets as soon as a taxation scribe appeared. Since he had not paid taxes for years, the headman had decided that his modest piece of land, a few acres beside the river, should become the property of the village.

Leaning on his gnarled staff, the old man had emerged from his lair to defend his cause. The village judge, a peasant who was a friend of the headman and a childhood enemy of Pepy, seemed little disposed to hear the shepherd's arguments, despite several protests.

'Here is the judgement: it is decided that—'

'The investigation was inadequate.'

'Who dares interrupt me?' demanded the judge.

Pazair strode forward. 'The tjaty of Egypt.'

Everyone recognized Pazair, because he had been born in this village and had begun his career as a judge here. Astonished and full of admiration, they bowed.

'According to the law, I shall head this court,' he decreed.

'It's a complicated matter,' grumbled the headman.

'I know that very well, thanks to the documents brought to me by the official in charge of messages.'

'The charges against Pepy—'

'His debts have been settled, therefore the matter is reduced to nothing. The shepherd shall keep the land that was bequeathed to him by his father's father.'

Everyone cheered the tjaty, and brought him beer and flowers.

At last he was alone with the hero of the day.

'I knew you'd come back,' said Pepy. 'You chose your moment well. You aren't a bad fellow at heart, despite your strange profession.'

'As you see, a judge can be just.'

'All the same, I go on distrusting them. Are you coming back to settle here?'

'Unfortunately not. I have to go to Kebet.'

'It's a tough job, being tjaty. Keep everyone happy – that's what people expect from you.'

'Sometimes I think I'll collapse under the weight of my burdens.'

'Be like the palm-tree. The more you pull it downwards, the more you try to bend it, the more it springs up and points towards the sky.'

39

Panther ate a slice of watermelon, bathed, dried herself in the sun, drank some cool beer and snuggled up to Suti, who was staring at the western bank of the Nile.

'What is it?' she asked.

'Why don't they attack?'

'Tjaty's orders, remember.'

'If Pazair comes, we—'

'He won't come – he's deserted you now that you're a rebel and an outlaw. When our nerves are at breaking-point, there will be an explosion of dissent, and soon the Libyans will clash with the Nubians, and the All-Seeing Ones will return to their duties. The army won't even have to fight.'

Suti stroked her hair. 'What do you suggest?'

'Let's break out. While our soldiers still obey us, let's take advantage of their longing for victory.'

'We'll be slaughtered.'

'How do you know? We are accustomed to miracles, you and I. If we win, Thebes will be in prospect. Kebet seems too small now, and this gloominess doesn't suit you.'

He took her by the hips and lifted her up. Her breasts level with her lover's eyes, her head thrown back, her golden hair drowned in sunshine, her arms outstretched, she sighed with contentment.

'Make me die of love,' she begged.

The Nile was beginning to look different. An experienced eye could see that the blue of the river was becoming less bright, as if the first silt, arriving from the far-off South, was beginning to darken it. It was nearly the end of the harvest; in the countryside, threshing was being done.

Guarded by Kem and Killer, Pazair had slept in his own village, beneath the stars. When he was a young judge, he had often enjoyed that pleasure, relishing the scents of the night and the colours of dawn.

'We're going to Kebet,' he told Kem. 'I shall persuade Suti to give up his insane plans.'

'How will you do that?'

'He'll listen to me.'

'You know very well he won't.'

'We're blood-brothers; we understand each other beyond words.'

'I shan't let you face him alone.'

'It's the only way.'

Pazair turned to leave, then stopped in his tracks. He must be dreaming: Neferet had emerged from the palm-grove and was coming towards him. She was ethereal, radiant, her brow decorated with a diadem of lotus-flowers, her turquoise amulet at her throat.

When he took her in his arms, he found that she was close to tears.

'I had a terrible dream,' she explained. 'You were dying, alone, beside the Nile, and calling to me. I have come to thwart fate.'

It would be a huge risk, but the shadow-eater had no choice. The tjaty would never be more vulnerable than at Kebet. In Memphis he was becoming untouchable. In addition to Kem's close protection, luck was helping him. Some might have claimed that the gods were watching over Pazair, but although the idea crossed his mind from time to time the shadow-eater refused to believe it. Success was a capricious thing; it would eventually change sides.

Indiscreet words had filtered through. In the market, there was talk of a band of rebels who had come out of the desert, seized Kebet and were threatening Thebes. Rapid action by the army had reassured the people, but they wondered what punishment the tjaty would inflict on the insurgents. The fact that the tjaty himself had taken charge of re-establishing order was approved of by everyone. Pazair did not behave like an ordinary official, shut away in his office: he was like a man on the ground, swift to act.

The shadow-eater felt a crawling sensation in his fingers. He remembered his first murder, in the service of the conspirators led by Bel-Tran. As he stepped on to the boat that would take him to Kebet, he felt certain that, this time, he would succeed.

'The tjaty!' roared a Nubian lookout.

The inhabitants of Kebet ran out into the streets. People spoke of an attack, a regiment of archers, several wheeled siege-towers, hundreds of chariots.

Suti addressed them from the terrace of the mayor's house, and re-established calm.

'It is indeed Tjaty Pazair,' he announced loudly. 'He is wearing his official robe and he is alone.'

'What about the army?' asked a frightened woman.

'There are no soldiers with him.'

'What are you planning to do?'

'Walk out of the main entrance and go to meet him.'

Panther tried to hold him back. 'It's a trick – you'll be killed by archers.'

'You don't know Pazair very well.'

'But supposing his troops betray him?'

'He'd die with me.'

'Don't listen to him. Don't yield ground in anything.'

'Go and reassure your people, Golden Goddess.'

From the prow of a warship, Neferet, Kem and Killer – who had all been obliged to remain aboard – watched Pazair. Neferet was in mortal fear, while Kem could not stop blaming himself.

'Pazair's being stubborn because he gave his word – I ought to have locked him up,' growled Kem.

'Suti won't hurt him.'

'We don't know how he's changed. The taste for power may have sent him mad. What kind of man will the tjaty find himself up against?'

'He'll be able to persuade him,' said Neferet.

'I can't stay here doing nothing. I'm going after him.'

'No, Kem. You must respect his promise.'

'If anything happens to him, I'll raze this town to the ground.'

The tjaty took the narrow, paved street leading from the landing-stage, which was dotted with small altars where priests laid offerings during processions. He halted a dozen paces from the main entrance to Kebet, on the Nile side. There he waited, arms hanging by his sides, very dignified in his stiff, heavy robe.

Suti appeared. Long-haired and bronzed, his powerful build more pronounced than before, he was wearing a gold collar; at the belt of his kilt hung a dagger with a gold hilt.

'Who's going to approach whom?' asked Suti.

'Do you still respect our hierarchy?'

Suti came forward. The two men were face to face.

'You abandoned me, Pazair.'

'Never – not for one single moment.'

'Do you expect me to believe that?'

'Have I ever lied to you? My position as tjaty forbade me to violate the law by overturning the judgement against you.

The Tjaru garrison didn't pursue you after your escape because I ordered them to remain in the fortress. After that I lost track of you, but I knew you'd come back. I swore I'd be present when you did, and here I am. I'd have preferred you to reappear more discreetly, but I'm content with this.'

'In your eyes, I'm a rebel.'

'I've had no complaints to that effect.'

'I invaded Kebet.'

'No one was killed or wounded, and there was no conflict of any sort.'

'But what about the mayor?'

'He went to the army, which is on manoeuvres near here. From my point of view, nothing irrevocable has been done.'

'You're forgetting that the law condemned me to become Tapeni's slave.'

'Not any more. She's been stripped of her rights as a citizen, as punishment for trying to form an alliance with Bel-Tran. She had no idea of how much he hates women.'

'Which means that . . .'

'That a final divorce will be pronounced if you wish. You could even demand a share of her possessions, but I'd advise against it because it would probably mean a long court case.'

'I don't want her possessions,' said Suti fiercely.

'Has your golden goddess given you so many that you don't need any more?'

'Panther saved my life in Nubia. But she can't come back to Egypt: the court sentenced her to perpetual exile.'

'Ah, but her punishment was linked to yours. Besides, her heroism in saving the life of an Egyptian soldier means I am authorized to review the judgment. Panther is free to move about in our land.'

'Are you telling the truth?'

'As tjaty, I can't do anything else. These decisions, taken in all equity, will be approved by a court.'

'I don't believe it.'

'You should,' said Pazair. 'It isn't only your blood-brother telling you, it's the tjaty of Egypt.'

'Aren't you putting your position at risk?'

'It won't make much difference: as soon as the annual flood begins, I'll be dismissed and imprisoned anyway – Bel-Tran and his allies seem unstoppable. Besides, there's a threat of war.'

'With the Asians?'

'Bel-Tran sent them poor-quality gold, but of course the blame falls on Pharaoh. To mend matters we'd have to offer them double, but Bel-Tran saw to it that our stocks of gold are low, and there isn't time to replenish them – whichever way I turn, the trap springs shut. But at least I can save you and Panther. Enjoy Egypt during these last weeks before Ramses' abdication, and then leave. The country will become a hell, subject to the law of Greek money, profit and the cruellest materialism.'

'I've got gold.'

'The gold that Asher stole and you retrieved?'

'It would be almost enough to pay Egypt's debts.'

Pazair felt hope begin to revive. 'If it were, we could avoid an invasion.'

'You ought to be more curious.'

'Do you mean you refuse?'

'You don't understand,' said Suti. 'I rediscovered the lost City of Gold in the desert. I've got more gold that I can count. To Kebet, I offer a chariot full of ingots; to Egypt, I offer gold in the amount of her debt.'

'But will Panther agree?'

'You'll need a great deal of diplomacy – this is your chance to prove your talent.'

The two friends fell into each other's arms.

During the festivals of Min, its patron god, Kebet threw itself into one of Egypt's most unbridled celebrations. As the power regulating the fecundity of the heavens and the earth, Min incited boys and girls to join in the mutual expression of their desire. When the peace agreement was proclaimed, joy exploded with an excitement worthy of these traditional celebrations.

The tjaty had decided that Kebet should benefit from Suti's gold, which was exempted from taxes. The Libyans were enlisted as footsoldiers in the army corps stationed at Thebes, and the Nubians as elite archers; and the All-Seeing Ones resumed their missions keeping watch over the caravans and miners; none of the groups was punished.

The soldiers of the regular army had no equals in banqueting and joking. In the hot summer night, laughter rang out endlessly, under the protection of the full moon. Suti and Panther received Pazair and Neferet in the mayor's house, which had been officially placed at the tjaty's disposal.

Although bedecked in dazzling gold jewellery, Panther wore a sulky expression. 'I won't leave Kebet. We conquered it – it belongs to us.'

'Stop dreaming,' advised Suti. 'We haven't got any troops any more.'

'No, but we've got enough gold to buy the whole of Egypt.'

'Why not begin by saving her?' suggested Pazair.

'What? Save my hereditary enemy?'

'It's in your interests, too, to prevent an Asian invasion. If it happened, I wouldn't give much for your treasure.'

Panther looked at Neferet, hoping for her approval, but Neferet said, 'I agree with the tjaty. What use will your fortune be if you can't spend it?'

Panther respected Neferet. Assailed by doubt, unsettled, she stood up and paced up and down the big guest hall.

'What are your requirements?' asked Pazair.

'If we're going to save Egypt,' declared Panther haughtily, 'we have the right to be very greedy. Since we are in the presence of the tjaty, we might as well be blunt: what is he prepared to grant us?'

'Nothing.'

She started. 'What do you mean, "nothing"?'

'Both of you will be cleared of all charges and declared innocent before the law, because you haven't committed a crime. The mayor will accept your apologies and the gold that will enrich his city, and Kebet will owe its prosperity and happiness to you. Isn't that worth something?'

Suti burst out laughing. 'My blood-brother's incredible! Justice speaks through his mouth, but he hasn't forgotten diplomacy. Have you by any chance become a real tjaty?'

'I'm doing my best to be one.'

'Ramses was a genius when he chose you. And I'm lucky to be your friend.'

Panther flamed with anger. 'What kingdom will you offer me, Suti?'

'Isn't my life enough for you, Golden Goddess?'

She charged at him and hammered her fists against his chest. 'I ought to have killed you!'

'Don't give up hope – you may yet.' He gained control of her and held her tightly to him. 'Did you really see yourself as a leading provincial citizen?'

Bursting out laughing in her turn, Panther pulled herself out of his arms and picked up a jar of wine. But when she offered it to Suti, instead of taking it he put his hand over his eyes.

'He's night-blind because of a scorpion's sting,' she cried, dropping the jar.

Neferet said soothingly, 'Don't worry. Night-blindness may be rare but I know I can and shall cure it. Wait here while I go to the hospital workshops.'

To Neferet's relief, the workshops had all the necessary ingredients she needed. On her return to the mayor's house she gave Suti a medicine composed of the humour extracted from pigs' eyes, galenite, yellow ochre and fermented honey, crushed and reduced into a compacted mass. Then she administered a decoction of beef liver, which he must take each day for three months in order to be completely cured.

Reassured, Panther soon went to sleep, and Neferet also dozed off. Suti and Pazair went out and walked through the town's quiet streets, followed at a discreet distance by Killer.

Suti gazed up at the stars, feasting his eyes on their light. 'It's miraculous,' he said. 'Neferet's brought me back to life.'

'Your good luck is still with you,' said Pazair.

'How do matters stand for the kingdom?'

'Even with your help, I'm not sure I can save it.'

'Why don't you simply arrest Bel-Tran and throw him into prison?'

'I've often meant to, but that wouldn't tear up the roots of the evil.'

'If the cause is lost, don't sacrifice yourself.'

'So long as there's even a shadow of hope, I shall carry out the duties entrusted to me.'

'Stubbornness is one of your many failings. Why keep hitting your head against a wall? For once, just listen to me. I've got a better idea.'

The two men passed a group of Libyans leaning against the door of a tavern. Drunk on beer, they were snoring.

Suti once again raised his eyes to the sky, only too happy to see the moon and the stars. At that moment Killer gave a warning howl, and Suti spotted an archer standing on a roof, on the point of firing.

Leaping sideways, he put himself in front of Pazair. The arrow took Suti in the chest, just above the heart, and he collapsed. The shadow-eater jumped into a chariot and fled.

40

The operation began at dawn and lasted three hours. Exhausted from lack of sleep, Neferet drew the energy she needed from the very depths of herself, to avoid making a mistake. She was assisted by two Kebet doctors who had experience of treating the All-Seeing Ones' wounds.

Before removing the arrow, Neferet rendered Suti unconscious. At brief intervals, she gave him ten doses of a powder composed of opium, mandragora root and siliceous stone; during the operation, an assistant would mix more of the powder with vinegar and make the patient breathe in the acid vapours that came off it, so that he would not wake. For additional safety, one of the surgeons anointed Suti's body with a balm against pain, whose main component was mandragora root, a powerful sleeping-potion.

Neferet checked that her stone scalpels were sharp enough, then enlarged the wound in order to withdraw the arrowhead. The depth of the wound worried her. Fortunately, the channels of the heart had not been ruptured, but Suti had lost a lot of blood and was still bleeding. Having stopped the bleeding with compresses of linen soaked in honey, with slow, precise movements she repaired the tears; then she bound together the edges of the main wound with fine thread obtained from cattle intestines. For a few moments she hesitated: would it be necessary to seal the wound with skin taken from another part of his body? Trusting in her instinct and in Suti's robust constitution, she decided against. The skin's initial reaction confirmed her in her opinion; so she strengthened the suture points with strips of sticky fabric, covered with fat and honey. Then she bandaged the wounded man's chest with very soft vegetable fibre.

So far the operation had succeeded; but would Suti reawaken?

Ken inspected the roof from which the shadow-eater had fired. He picked up the Nubian bow the assassin had used. Killer had charged off in pursuit of the murderer's chariot, but had not managed to catch up with it. The man had disappeared into the countryside.

In vain, Kem sought reliable witnesses. Some had indeed seen a chariot leaving the city in the middle of the night, but no one could give a detailed description of the driver. Kem felt like tearing off his wooden nose and stamping on it. Only Killer's hand gripping his wrist stopped him.

'Thank you for your help, Killer,' said Kem.

But the baboon did not let go.

'What do you want?'

Killer turned his head to the left.

'Very well, I'll follow you.'

Killer led Kem to the corner of a narrow street and showed him a boundary stone which had been scratched by the passage of a chariot.

'He went that way, you're right, but . . .'

The baboon led him a little further along the street, bent over a pothole in the road, then stepped back, signalling to Kem to look at it. Interested, the Nubian did so. At the bottom of the pothole lay an obsidian knife.

'He must have dropped it without realizing.' Kem fingered the knife. 'Security Guard Killer, I think you've just given us a vital clue.'

When Suti opened his eyes, he saw Neferet smiling down at him.

'You gave me a bad fright,' she confessed.

'An arrow's nothing compared to a bear's claws. You've saved me for the second time.'

'Two finger-breadths lower, and the arrow would have pierced your heart.'

'Will there be any lasting damage?'

'Perhaps a scar, but frequent changes of dressings should prevent that.'

'And how soon will I be back on my feet?'

'Very soon, because you have a strong constitution – in fact, you seem even stronger than when you had your first operation.'

'Death is amusing itself with me.'

Neferet's voice shook with emotion. 'You sacrificed yourself for Pazair . . . I don't know how to thank you.'

Gently, he took her hand. 'Panther steals all the love I have; otherwise, how could I not be madly in love with you? No one will ever separate you and Pazair – even destiny would wear itself out trying. It happened to choose me to shield him last night. I'm proud of that, Neferet, very proud.'

'May Pazair speak to you?'

'If the doctor permits it.'

The tjaty was as moved as his wife. 'You shouldn't have risked your life, Suti.'

'I thought a tjaty didn't tell tall stories.'

'Are you in pain?'

'Neferet is an extraordinary doctor – I feel almost nothing.'

'The shadow-eater interrupted our conversation.'

'I remember,' said Suti.

'Then what's the piece of advice you were about to give me?'

'What, in your opinion, is my dearest wish?'

'According to you, to lead a great life, to love, celebrate, and get drunk with each new sun.'

'And what's yours?'

'You know that: to retire to my village with Neferet, far from the troubles that face me.'

'The desert's changed me, Pazair; that is my future and my real kingdom. I've learnt to share its secrets, to feed on its mystery. When I'm far away from it, I feel heavy and old, but as soon as the soles of my feet touch the sand I'm young and immortal. There's no true law but the law of the desert. You're of the same nature, so join me and let's go away together, leave this world of corruption and lies.'

'A tjaty exists to fight such wickedness and enable righteousness to reign.'

'And are you succeeding?'

'Every day brings its share of victories and defeats, but Ma'at still governs Egypt. If Bel-Tran ascends the throne, though, justice will leave this earth.'

'Don't wait for that to happen.'

'Help me fight this war.'

As if in refusal, Suti turned away, on to his side. 'Leave me to rest. How can I fight if I don't get enough sleep?'

A boat belonging to the Mother of Pharaoh had brought Silkis from Memphis to Pi-Ramses. In her cabin, which was airy and shaded from the fierce sun, she had enjoyed the care of attentive servants. She had been massaged and perfumed, and offered fruit juices and cool cloths to place on her brow and the nape of her neck, so that her journey was a delight.

At the landing-stage, a travelling-chair equipped with two sunshades awaited her. The journey was only brief, for Silkis was taken to the lake at the queen's residence. Two shade-bearers went down with her to the lakeside, and helped her in a blue-painted boat. Smoothly the oarsmen rowed her to an island in the middle of the lake, where Tuya was seated under a wooden canopy, reading poems from the Old Kingdom which celebrated the sublime beauty of the landscape and the respect that men should feel for the gods.

Silkis began to panic. Her linen gown was ostentatiously luxurious, and she wore many of her finest jewels, but would she be able to confront the richest and most influential woman in Egypt?

'Come and sit beside me, Lady Silkis,' said the queen.

To Silkis's great astonishment, the Mother of Pharaoh looked more like a woman of the people than the mother of the great Ramses. Her hair hung free, and she was barefoot, dressed in a simple white robe with straps; she wore no necklaces, no bracelets, not a trace of face-paint. But her voice pierced the soul.

'You must be feeling the heat, my child,' Tuya went on.

Incapable of speech, Silkis sat down on the grass, not thinking of the inevitable green stains on the expensive linen.

'Be at your ease. Swim, if you wish.'

'I . . . I do not wish, thank you, Majesty.'

'Would you like some cool beer?'

Paralysed with nerves, Silkis accepted a long vessel with a fine metal tube though which one sucked up the beer. She drank several mouthfuls, her eyes lowered, unable to meet Tuya's.

'I love these summer months,' said the queen. 'Their light is dazzlingly honest. Does the intense heat upset you?'

'It . . . it dries out the skin.'

'But surely you have a fine array of creams and lotions?'

'Yes, of course.'

'Do you spend a great deal of time making yourself beautiful?'

'Several hours a day – my husband is very demanding.'

'His has been a remarkable career, I am told.'

Silkis raised her head a little: the Mother of Pharaoh had not taken long to approach the expected subject. Her fear lessened: after all, this impressive woman, with her thin, straight nose, pronounced cheekbones and square chin, was soon going to be her obedient slave. Hatred invaded her, like the hatred that had driven her to undress before the head of the honour-guard so that her husband could kill him. Silkis liked submitting to Bel-Tran, but she wanted her entourage to grovel at her feet. The thought of beginning by humiliating the Mother of Pharaoh gave her a feeling of ecstasy.

She said, 'Indeed, Majesty, "remarkable" is exactly the right word.'

'A little accounting-scribe becoming the greatest man in the kingdom – only Egypt allows that kind of rise to power. But it is important not to lose one's humility when one becomes great.'

Silkis frowned. 'Bel-Tran is honest; hardworking, and all he thinks of is the common good.'

'The quest for power engenders conflicts, which I see only from a great distance.'

Silkis was jubilant: the fish was taking the hook! To give herself courage, she drank a little more beer; it was so delicious that she felt quite relaxed.

'At Memphis, Majesty, there are whispers that the king is ill.'

'He is very tired, Lady Silkis – his burdens are crushing.'

'Must he not soon celebrate a festival of regeneration?'

'That is the sacred tradition.'

'And . . . what if the magic ritual were to fail?'

'The gods would thus signify that a new pharaoh is called to reign.'

Silkis's face lit up in a cruel smile. 'Would the gods be the only ones implicated?'

'You are enigmatic.'

'Does Bel-Tran not possess the stuff of a king?'

Pensively, Tuya watched a flock of mallard glide across the blue waters of the lake. 'Who are we, to claim to lift the veil of the future?'

'Bel-Tran can, Majesty.'

'Admirable.'

'He and I were counting on your support. Everyone knows that your judgments are very sure.'

'That is the role of the Mother of Pharaoh: to see and to advise.'

Silkis had won; she felt as light as a bird, as quick as a jackal, as sharp as a dagger-blade. Egypt belonged to her.

'How did your husband build up his fortune?' asked Tuya.

'By developing his papyrus business. Of course, he juggled with the accounts, as he has done everywhere he has been. No accounting-scribe has ever been his equal.'

'Has he ever been dishonest?'

Silkis became talkative. 'Majesty, business is business, is it not? If one wishes to reach the first rank, one must from time to time forget morality. Ordinary people become mired in it, but Bel-Tran has freed himself of that hindrance. In government he has overturned old habits. No one has noticed his misappropriations; the state has done well out of them, but so has he! And now it is too late to accuse him.'

'Has he ensured that you have a personal fortune?'

'Of course.'

'How?'

Silkis was exultant. 'In the most audacious way imaginable.'

'Enlighten me.'

'You will find it hard to believe, Majesty. It concerns an illicit traffic in papyri of the *Book of Going Forth by Day*. As the supplier to a good part of the nobility, he has taken it upon himself to find scribes capable of drawing the scenes and writing the texts relating to the resurrection of the deceased in the otherworld.'

'What is the nature of the deception?'

'It is threefold, First, he delivers papyrus of lower quality than that promised; then he reduces the length of the texts without reducing the price, and while paying the scribe very little; and lastly he does exactly the same thing with the pictures. The dead people's families are always so grief-stricken that they do not think to check. And I also have an enormous number of Greek coins resting in my coffers, awaiting the free circulation of money . . . What a revolution, Majesty! You will no longer recognize this old Egypt, hidebound in pointless traditions and outdated customs.'

'Those are your husband's words, if I am not much mistaken.'

'And the only ones the country should hear.'

'Have you no thoughts of your own?'

The question disconcerted Silkis. 'What do you mean?'

'Murder, theft, falsehood – do they seem to you to provide a good basis for a reign?'

Silkis was too excited for caution. 'If they are necessary, why not? We have gone too far to draw back. I myself am an accomplice of my husband, and as culpable as he is. I only regret not having killed Branir and Tjaty Pazair, the main obstacles to—' A sudden attack of dizziness made her sway; she put her hand to her brow. 'What's happening to me? Why did I confess all that to you?'

'Because you have drunk beer mixed with mandragora. Its taste is bland but it loosens the tongue, and with its help weak minds are freed of their secrets.'

'What did I say? What did I reveal to you?'

'If the mandragora acted so quickly,' said the Mother of Pharaoh, 'it is because you are in the habit of using drugs.'

'My stomach hurts!' Silkis stood up. The island and the sky seemed to move before her eyes. She fell to her knees, and hid her face in her hands.

'The illegal traffic in the *Book of Going Forth by Day* is an abominable crime,' declared Tuya. 'You have profited from the pain of others, with incredible cruelty. I myself shall lodge a complaint before the tjaty's court.'

'It will come to nothing,' said Silkis, raising her head. 'And soon you will be my servant.'

'You will not succeed,' said Tuya, 'for you carry failure within you and will never succeed in becoming a great lady in the land. Your depravity is known to all. No one will accept you, even if you do wield a measure of power. You will soon see that the situation is untenable. More determined women than you have been forced to renounce their ambitions.'

'Bel-Tran will crush you underfoot.'

'I am an old lady and do not fear bandits like him. My ancestors fought against invaders as dangerous as he is, and defeated them. If he was hoping for your support, he will be disappointed: you will be of no use to him at all.'

'I *will* help him, and we *will* succeed.'

'You will be not be able to help him. You have limited intelligence, fragile nerves, and you have no individual personality, only a destructive fire nourished by hatred and hypocrisy. Not only will you harm him, but also, sooner or later, you will betray him.'

Silkis writhed about, beating her clenched fists on the ground.

At a sign from Tuya, the blue boat drew up to the island shore.

'Take this woman back to the port,' Tuya ordered the crew, 'and ensure that she leaves Pi-Ramses immediately.'

Silkis was overwhelmed by a desire for sleep. As soon as she was aboard the boat, she collapsed, her head filled with unbearable buzzing as if bees were devouring her brain.

The Mother of Pharaoh gazed serenely at the peaceful waters of the ornamental lake, above which the swallows danced.

41

Leaning on Pazair's shoulder, Suti took his first steps on the deck of the boat taking them back to Memphis. Neferet watched, and was satisfied with his recovery.

Panther also gazed at her hero, at the same time dreaming of an immense river which would belong to him and of which she would be queen. From North to South and South to North, they would sail on a huge boat laden with gold which they would present to the villages spread out along the banks. If they could not conquer an empire by force, why not try gifts? The day the mines of the Lost City were exhausted, the whole country would celebrate the names of Panther and Suti. Lying on the cabin roof, she surrendered her copper-skinned body to the summer sun's burning caresses.

Neferet changed Suti's bandages. 'The wound looks very good. How do you feel?'

'I'm not strong enough to fight yet, but I can stand upright.'

'Please rest now. If you don't, your flesh will take longer to knit together.'

Suty lay down on a mat, in the shade of a cloth stretched between four poles. Sleep would help restore his strength.

Neferet went to the prow of the boat and looked out over the Nile. Pazair joined her, and put his arm round her.

'Do you think the flood will come early?' he asked.

'The level of the water's rising, but the colour's changing only slowly. We may have the benefit of a few days' respite.'

'When the star Sopdet shines in the sky, Isis will weep, and the energy of resurrection will bring to life the river born in the otherworld. Death will be defeated, as it is every year. And yet the Egypt of our forefathers will die.'

'Every night I call upon Branir's soul. I'm sure it isn't far from us.'

'I've failed completely,' said Pazair dejectedly. 'I've neither identified the assassin nor found the Testament of the Gods.'

Kem came over to them. 'Forgive me for disturbing you, but I'd like to suggest a promotion to you.'

Pazair was surprised. 'You, Kem, taking an interest in promotion?'

'Security Guard Killer has earned it.'

'Of course,' said Pazair. 'I should have thought of it long ago. If it weren't for him, I'd have travelled to the Western shore.'

'Not only did he save your life, but he's given us a means of identifying the shadow-eater. Doesn't that merit promotion and an increase in wages?'

'What means?' asked Pazair.

'Let Killer see his investigation through to the end. I'll help him.'

'Whom do you suspect?

'I still have a few checks to make before I know the murderer's name, but he won't escape us.'

'How long will your investigation take?

'A day at best,' said Kem, 'a week at worst. Killer will identify him as soon as he faces him.'

'You must arrest him so that he can be put on trial.'

'He's committed several murders.'

'Unless you persuade Killer to keep him alive, I shall be obliged to withdraw Killer from the inquiry.'

'The shadow-eater tried to kill him by sending another baboon against him. How could he forget that? Withdrawing him would be unjust.'

'It's vital that we find out if the shadow-eater is responsible for Branir's death, and which master he serves.'

'You will – and that's all I can promise you. If Killer's provoked, I shan't be able to restrain him. If it comes to a choice between the life of a brave creature and that of a monster, I know which I'll choose.'

'Be very careful, both of you.'

When Bel-Tran crossed the threshold of his house, no one came to meet him. Annoyed, he called for his steward. Only a gardener responded.

'Where is the steward?' demanded Bel-Tran.

'He has left, my lord, with two serving-women and your children.'

'What? Are you drunk?'

'He did, my lord, I assure you.'

Furious, Bel-Tran charged into the house and bumped into Silkis's personal handmaid.

'Where are my children?'

'They have gone to your house in the Delta, my lord.'

'On whose orders?'

'Your wife's.'

'And where is she?'

'In her bedchamber, my lord, but . . .'

'Well?'

'She is very unahppy – she hasn't stopped crying since she got back from Pi-Ramses.'

Bel-Tran strode through the house and burst into his wife's private apartments. She was lying motionless in bed, curled up, sobbing.

He shook her but she did not react.

'Why have you sent the children to the country? Answer me!' He twisted her wrists, forcing her to sit up. 'Answer me, I order you.'

'They're in danger.'

'Nonsense.'

'And so am I.'

'What's happened?'

Sobbing, Silkis told him of her meeting with the Mother of Pharaoh, ending, 'That woman's a monster – she broke me.'

Bel-Tran did not take his wife's account lightly. He even made her repeat the accusations Tuya had made.

'Calm yourself, my darling,' he said when she had finished.

'It was a trap – she lured me into a trap.'

'Don't be afraid. Soon she'll have no power left.'

'You don't understand. I no longer have any chance whatever of being admitted to court. Every move I make will be criticized, every opinion challenged. Whatever I do, I shall be reviled. I couldn't bear persecution like that.'

'You must be calm.'

'Calm? When Tuya's ruining my reputation?' Silkis flew into a rage, shouting incomprehensible phrases which mingled the dream-interpreter, the shadow-eater, her children, an inaccessible throne and unbearable stomach pains.

When Bel-Tran left her he was in pensive mood. Tuya was a clear-sighted woman: Silkis's instability meant that she would indeed be unable to fit into the Egyptian court.

Panther was dreaming. The voyage on the Nile with Pazair and Neferet, in complete safety, was proving an unexpected time of peace in her tumultuous life. Without admitting it to Suti, she was dreaming of a big house surrounded by a garden, though she was ashamed of giving up her thirst for conquest, even for a few hours. Neferet's presence calmed the fire that had been burning her ever since she had first had to fight to survive. Panther was discovering the virtues of tenderness, which she had always despised as though it were a shameful disease.

Egypt, the land she hated so much, was becoming her haven of peace.

She went in search of Pazair, and found him in his cabin, sitting on the floor, writing a decree relating to the protection, in each province, of animals it was forbidden to kill and eat.

'I must talk to you,' she declared solemnly.

'I'm listening.'

'Let's go on deck – I like looking at the Nile.'

Leaning on the rail like two awe-struck travellers, the pair watched the river and the life on its banks. On dirt tracks atop low hills, donkeys laden with grain ambled along; around the good-hearted beasts scampered chattering children. In the villages, in the shade of palm-trees, peasants were finishing the threshing to the sound of flutes playing ancient melodies. Everyone was waiting for the flood.

Panther said, 'I'm going to give you my gold, tjaty.'

'Suti and you discovered an abandoned mine; it belongs to you.'

'Keep all this wealth for the gods – they'll make better use of it than mortals would. But let me live here and forget the past.'

'I owe you the truth: in just one month, this country's soul will change utterly. It will undergo such upheavals that you won't recognize it any more.'

'A month's peace? That's a lot.'

'My friends will be hunted down, arrested, perhaps executed,' said Pazair. 'If you help me, you can be sure you'll be denounced.'

'I shan't go back on my decision. Take the gold, and prevent war with Asia.'

She turned and went back to the cabin roof, worshipper of a sun whose violence she had tamed.

Suti took her place beside the tjaty. 'I can walk,' he said, 'and move my left arm. It hurts a bit, but it's healing well. Your wife's a sorceress.'

'So is Panther,' said Pazair.

'She certainly is! The proof is that I haven't yet managed to free myself from her.'

'She's giving your gold to Egypt, to prevent war with the Asians.'

'I've no choice but to agree.'

'She wants to be happy with you. I think Egypt has won her over.'

'What a horrible future! Must I wipe out a regiment of Libyans to give her back her ferocity? But let's not talk about her – you're the one I'm worried about.'

'You know the truth,' said Pazair.

'Only part of it. But I can see that you're being hamstrung by your main failing: respect for other people.'

'That is the law of Ma'at.'

'Rubbish! You're at war, Pazair, and you're taking too many blows without returning them. Thanks to Neferet, in another week I'll be fit for the fight again. Let me act as I see fit and disrupt the enemy's game.'

'Will you step outside the path of the law?'

'When war's declared, one must make one's own path. Otherwise one's likely to fall into an ambush. Bel-Tran's merely an enemy like any other.'

Pazair shook his head. 'No, he isn't. He has a certain weapon against which neither you nor I can do anything.'

'What weapon?'

'I am sworn to silence.'

'You haven't much time left.'

'At the start of the flood, Ramses will abdicate. He will be unable to experience his regeneration.'

'You're being absurd. Up to now, you were probably right to be suspicious of everyone. But now you must bring together the people you trust, and tell them what this weapon is and the real reason why Ramses can't do anything. Together we'll find a way of parrying it.'

'I must ask Pharaoh. Only he can give me permission to tell you. You disembark at Memphis, and I'll go on to Pi-Ramses.'

In the great burial-ground of Saqqara, Neferet went to the tomb of Branir and laid lotus-flowers, cornflowers and lilies on the offering-table of the little shrine that was open to the living. By doing so, she remained in communion with the soul of Branir, whose body of light, summoned to the resurrection of Osiris, lay in a sarcophagus at the heart of the earth-mother.

Through a slit in one wall of the tomb, she looked at the statue of her murdered master. He was shown as if walking, his eyes raised to the sky.

To her surprise, the darkness seemed less profound than usual; she sensed that Branir's gaze was fixed upon her with rare intensity. These were no longer the eyes of a dead man, but those of a living man who had come back from the otherworld to give her a message beyond human words and thoughts.

Overwhelmed, she drove all thoughts out of her mind, so that her heart might perceive the truth of the ineffable. And Branir spoke to her, as he had done when alive, in his solemn, steady voice. He spoke of the Light that nourished the righteous, and of the beauty of paradise, where thought wandered among the stars.

When he fell silent, she knew he had opened a path which the tjaty must take. Evil's victory was not inevitable.

On her way out of the burial-ground, Neferet met Djui the embalmer, who was going back his workshop.

He bowed and said, 'I have cared for Branir's tomb, as you wished.'

'Thank you, Djui.'

'You look upset.'

'It's nothing.'

'Would you like some water?'

'No, thank you, I must go to the hospital. Goodbye.'

On tired feet, the embalmer made his way back, beneath the implacable sun, to a building with tiny windows; against its walls stood several sarcophagi of varying quality. The workshop was in an isolated place; in the distance were pyramids and tombs. A rocky hill blocked the view of the palm-trees and fields that bordered the desert.

Djui pushed the door, which opened with a creak. Once inside, he put on a goatskin apron covered with brownish stains, and unemotionally regarded the corpse he had been brought. He had been paid for a second-rank embalming, which necessitated the use of oils and unguents. Wearily, he picked up an iron hook, with which he would extract the brain of the deceased through the nostrils.

An obsidian knife was flung down at his feet.

'You lost this at Kebet,' said a deep voice behind him.

Very slowly, Djui turned round.

On the threshold of the workshop stood Kem.

'You're mistaken, Commander,' protested Djui.

'This is the knife you use to cut into a corpse's flank.'

'I'm not the only embalmer—'

'You're the only one who's been travelling a lot over the last few months.'

'That isn't a crime.'

'Every time you leave your post you have to make it known, or your colleagues would complain. Now, your movements coincided with those of the tjaty, whom you have several times tried – but failed – to kill.'

'My trade's so difficult that I often need to take a rest.'

'In your trade, people live apart from society and hardly ever leave their workplace. You've no family in Thebes.'

'It's a beautiful region – and I've a right to move around, just like anyone else.'

'You know a lot about poisons, don't you?' said Kem.

'What makes you say that?'

'I consulted your work record. Before becoming an embalmer, you were an assistant in a hospital workshop. Your knowledge of that environment was of great use in your crimes.'

'It isn't forbidden to change one's job.'

'You're also an excellent shot with the throwing-stick – your first trade was as a bird-hunter.'

'Is that, by any chance, a crime?'

'All the evidence agrees: you are the shadow-eater hired to assassinate Tjaty Pazair.'

'That's slander!'

'There's one piece of irrefutable proof: this expensive knife. At its base, it bears a distinctive mark, that of the embalmers, and a number which corresponds to the Saqqara workshop. You shouldn't have tried to use it, Djui, but you wouldn't be separated from it. It's the love of your trade that betrayed you, the love of death.'

'No court will consider that knife sufficient proof.'

'You know very well that it will. And the final confirmation is hidden here, I am sure of it.'

'You want to search my workshop?'

'More than want: I'm going to.'

'I won't let you – I'm innocent.'

'Than what are you afraid of?'

'This is my own domain, and no one has the right to violate it.'

'As commander of the security guards, I have. Now, before showing me your cellar, put down that iron hook. I don't like seeing you with a weapon in your hand.'

The embalmer obeyed.

'Lead the way.'

Djui went down the staircase, with its worn, slippery steps. Two torches, permanently lit, illuminated a huge cellar where sarcophagi were piled up. At the back were some twenty vases destined to receive the liver, lungs, stomach and intestines of the deceased.

'Open them,' ordered Kem.

'That would be sacrilege.'

'I'll risk it.' The Nubian removed a lid with a baboon's head, a second with a dog's and a third with a falcon's. The vases contained only viscera.

In the fourth, whose lid was in the form of a man's head, was a gold ingot. Kem looked further and found two more.

'Are these the price of your murders?'

Arms folded over his chest, Djui seemed almost indifferent. 'How much do you want?' he asked.

'How much are you offering?'

'If you've come without your baboon and without the tjaty, you're here to sell your silence. Will half of my profits be enough?'

'You'll also have to satisfy my curiosity. Who paid you?'

'Bel-Tran and his accomplices. But you and the tjaty have destroyed the band, and now only he and his wife are left to taunt you.' Djui smiled. 'She's a fine filly, believe me. She's the one who gave me my instructions when I had to kill an inconvenient witness.'

'Did you kill Branir?'

'I keep a list of my successes, so that I'll remember them when I'm old. Branir wasn't one of my victims. I wouldn't have balked at killing him, I assure you, but I wasn't asked to do it.'

'Then who did?'

Djui said with a shrug, 'I've no idea, and I don't care. You've done the right thing, Kem – I expected no less from you. I knew that if you identified me you wouldn't tell the tjaty, you'd come and demand your share.'

'Will you leave Pazair in peace now?'

'He'll be my only failure – unless you lend me a hand.'

The Nubian felt the weight of the ingots. 'They're magnificent.'

'Life is short. You have to know how to make the best of it.'

'But you've made two mistakes, Djui.'

'Never mind that. Let's talk about the future.'

'The first is that you underestimated me.'

'You mean you want everything?'

'A whole mountain of gold wouldn't be enough.'

'Are you joking?'

'You second mistake was thinking Killer would forgive you for sending a rival against him, to try to tear him to pieces. Other people might feel sorry for you, but I'm only a black man with unsophisticated feelings and he's a baboon and is over-sensitive and prone to bear grudges. Killer's my friend, and he almost died because of you. When he cries vengeance, I have to listen to him. And he'll see to it that you eat no more shadows.'

Killer appeared at the foot of the stairs.

Kem had never seen him so enraged: his eyes were bright red, his pelt bristled, his teeth were bared, and he gave a blood-curdling growl. No doubt remained as to Djui's guilt.

The shadow-eater backed away. And Killer sprang.

42

'Lie down,' Neferet told Suti.

'The pain has gone.'

'I must still check the channels of the heart and the circulation of energy.'

Neferet took his pulse in several places, while consulting the little water-clock that she wore at her wrist; inside were gradations in the form of dots on twelve vertical lines. She calculated the internal rhythms, compared them with one another, and established that the voice of the heart was powerful and regular.

'If I hadn't operated on you myself,' she said, 'I'd have difficulty believing you'd been wounded recently. The scarring has taken place twice as quickly as normal.'

'Tomorrow I shall practise with my bow – if the kingdom's principal doctor will permit it.'

'Don't ask too much of your muscles. Be patient.'

'I can't. I'd feel as though I were wasting my life. Shouldn't life be like the flight of a bird of prey, strong and unpredictable?'

'Spending time with the sick has made me accept all ways of life. However, I am obliged to re-bandage you in a way that will hamper your activities.'

'When will Pazair be back?'

'Tomorrow, at the latest.'

'I hope he's been persuasive enough. We must shake off this passivity.'

'You're a poor judge of him: since your unfortunate departure for Nubia, he's fought Bel-Tran and his allies day and night.'

'But he hasn't beaten them.'

'He's weakened them.'

'But not killed them.'

'The tjaty is the foremost servant of the law, and he must ensure it is respected.'

'The only law Bel-Tran knows is his own, so Pazair is fighting on uneven ground. When we were young, he took stock of the situation and then I dealt with it. If my target is clearly defined, I don't miss it.'

'Your help will be very valuable.'

'So long as I know everything, the same way you do.'

'There, I've finished bandaging you.'

Pi-Ramses was less joyous than usual. Soldiers had replaced passers-by, chariots were moving about the streets, and the war-fleet filled the port. In the barracks, which were on full alert, the footsoldiers were undertaking combat exercises. The archers were constantly at practice, and senior officers were checking the horses' tack. There was a scent of war in the air.

The palace guard had been doubled. Pazair's visit aroused no enthusiasm, as if his presence set a seal upon a decision everyone feared.

This time, Pazair did not find Pharaoh gardening. He and his generals were studying a large map of Asia laid out on the floor of the council chamber. The soldiers bowed before the tjaty.

'May I consult you, Majesty?'

Ramses dismissed his generals. When they had gone, he said, 'We're ready to fight, Pazair: the Army of Set is already deployed along the border. Our spies confirm that the Asian princedoms are trying to unite in order to mobilize as many soldiers as possible – it will be a fierce battle. My generals advise me to attack, as a preventive measure, but I would prefer to wait. Anyone would swear that the future belonged to me!'

'We can prevent war, Majesty.'

'How? Has there been a miracle?'

'We can use gold from a long-forgotten mine.'

'Is this information reliable?'

'An expedition is already on its way, with a map drawn by Suti.'

'But will the gold be enough?'

'Enough to satisfy Asia, Majesty.'

'And what does Suti want in return?'

'The desert.'

'Are you serious?'

'He is.'

Ramses thought for a moment. 'Would the post of commander of the All-Seeing Ones suit him?'

'I think it possible that all he wants is solitude.'

'Has he any more miracles concealed under his robe?'

'Suti wants to know the truth, Majesty. He suggested that I bring

Christian Jacq

together the few people who have proved their loyalty and tell them the true reasons for your abdication.'

'A secret council . . .'

'A last council of war.'

'What do you think of the idea?'

'I have failed, because I have not recovered the Testament of the Gods. If you grant me permission, I shall mobilize our last forces in order to weaken Bel-Tran as much as possible.'

Silkis was suffering her third attack of hysteria since dawn. Three doctors had attended her bedside in turn, but without much success. The last gave her a sleeping-draught, in the hope that a deep sleep would bring her back to her senses, but as soon as she awoke, in the middle of the afternoon, she became delirious, disturbing the whole house with her cries and her convulsions. Only more of the sleeping-draught could calm her, although the consequences of overuse were serious: a lessening of the brain's faculties and damage to the intestines.

Bel-Tran made the decision that had been forced upon him. He summoned a scribe and dictated to him the list of possessions he was bequeathing to his children, reducing those left to his wife to the absolute minimum required by the law. Contrary to custom, he had drawn up a very detailed marriage contract, which permitted him to manage his wife's fortune should she show a clear inability to do it herself. He had had that inability verified by three doctors, all of whom he had richly rewarded. Armed with these documents, Bel-Tran would have sole parental authority over his children, whose upbringing would be taken out of Silkis's hands.

The Mother of Pharaoh had done him a service by revealing his wife's true nature: an unstable creature, sometimes childish, sometimes cruel, incapable of occupying an important office. After serving him as a beautiful puppet at receptions and banquets, she had become a handicap.

The best place for her to be treated was in a specialized establishment housing the mentally ill. As soon as she was well enough to travel, he would send her to Phoenicia.

All that remained was to draw up the deed of divorce, a vital document since Silkis was still living in the family home. Bel-Tran could not wait for her departure. Once free of her, he would be ready to tackle the last obstacle separating him from the realization of his dream. That was how one travelled the path to power, dispensing with one's useless travelling-companions.

*

All Egypt was invoking the flood. The earth was cracked open, as if dead; scorched, singed, dried out by a burning wind, it was dying of thirst, longing for the nourishing water that would soon climb the banks and push back the desert. A dull tiredness weighed down men and animals alike, dust covered the trees, the last small areas of greenery were shrivelling, exhausted. However, work did not stop. Teams came one after another, cleaning out the canals, repairing the wells and the irrigation systems, strengthening the earthen retaining-banks by scooping back up the soil that had fallen down and stopping up the cracks. The children were set to filling jars with dried fruit, people's main food during the period when the water covered the lands.

As he sailed back from Pi-Ramses, Pazair sensed the suffering and hope of his land. Soon Bel-Tran would attack the water itself, criticizing it for not being present all year. The regime he imposed would shatter the country's alliance with the gods and nature. By destroying the delicate balance that had been respected by nineteen dynasties of pharaohs, he would leave the field open to the forces of evil.

When his boat docked in Memphis, Kem and Killer were waiting on the quay.

'Djui was the shadow-eater,' said Kem.

'Did he kill Branir?'

'No, but he was Bel-Tran's paid assassin. He murdered the surviving members of the honour-guard and Bel-Tran's accomplices. And he's the one who tried to kill you.'

'Have you imprisoned him?'

'Killer did not grant him his forgiveness. I've dictated my testimony to a scribe. It contains charges against Bel-Tran, complete with names and dates. Now you are safe.'

Accompanied by Way-Finder, who carried a full waterskin, Suti came hurrying along the quay. 'Did Ramses agree?' he asked.

'Yes.'

'Convene your council at once. I'm ready to fight.'

'Before that, I'd like to try one last thing.'

'We haven't much time.'

'Messengers bearing my summons have already left. The council will be convened tomorrow.'

'This is your last chance,' warned Suti.

'Egypt's last chance.'

'What is this "last thing"?'

'I shan't take any risks, Suti.'

'Take me with you.'

'And Killer, too,' urged Kem.

'I can't,' replied the tjaty. 'I must be alone.'

Lisht, two days' journey to the south of the burial-ground at Saqqara, was still living in the age of the Middle Kingdom, a time of peace and prosperity. There stood temples and pyramids, dedicated to Amenemhat I and Sesostris I, powerful pharaohs of the dynasty who had made Egypt happy again after a troubled period. Since that far-off era, seven hundred years before the reign of Ramses II, the memory of the illustrious sovereigns had been respected. *Ka* priests celebrated the daily rites, so that the dead kings' souls might remain present on earth and inspire their successors' actions.

Not far from the fields, the pyramid of Sesostris I was being rebuilt, following the collapse of part of its covering of white limestone, which came from the quarry at Tura.

Bel-Tran's chariot, driven by a former army officer, took the road that bordered the desert. It halted at the start of the covered way that led up to the pyramid. Agitatedly, Bel-Tran leapt out of the vehicle and shouted for a priest. His angry voice sounded most incongruous in the silence that pervaded the site.

A shaven-headed priest emerged from a shrine.

'I am Bel-Tran. The tjaty summoned me here.'

'Follow me,' said the priest.

Bel-Tran was uneasy. He liked neither the pyramids nor the ancient shrines whose builders had raised colossal stone blocks, manipulating them with incredible skill. The temples were an obstacle to his plans; destroying them would be a priority of the new regime. As long as men, no matter how few, escaped the universal law of profit, they would hinder a country's development.

The priest led the way down a narrow causeway on whose walls relief carvings showed the king making offerings to the gods. The priest walked slowly, so Bel-Tran had to rein in his pace. He cursed the time he was losing and the summons to this forgotten place.

At the top of the causeway a temple had been built against the wall of the pyramid. The priest turned to the left, crossed a small pillared hall and halted before a flight of stairs.

'Go up,' he said. 'The tjaty awaits you at the top of the pyramid.'

'Why up there?'

'He is overseeing the work.'

'Is the climb dangerous?'

'The steps beneath the covering have been laid bare. If you climb carefully, you'll be safe.'

Bel-Tran did not admit to the priest that he got dizzy in high places;

drawing back would have made him look ridiculous. Against his better judgement, he set off for the top of the pyramid, some sixty cubits above.

He climbed slowly, watched by stone-cutters busy restoring the covering. Eyes glued to the stones, his feet clumsy, he hauled himself to the summit, a platform deprived of its little pyramid. This had been removed and entrusted to the goldsmiths, so that they could cover it with fine gold.

Pazair held out his hand to Bel-Tran and helped him to stand up.

'The landscape is beautiful, isn't it?'

Bel-Tran swayed, closed his eyes, and managed to keep his balance.

'From the top of a pyramid,' the tjaty continued, 'Egypt is unveiled. Have you noticed the abrupt break between the fields and the desert, between the black earth and the red earth, between Horus's domain and Set's? And yet they are indivisible and complementary. The cultivated land shows the eternal dance of the seasons, the desert the fire of that which never changes.'

'Why did you bring me here?'

'Do you know the name of this pyramid?'

'I couldn't care less.'

'It is called "the Watcher of the Two Lands", and in watching them it creates their unity. If the ancients devoted their energies to building monuments like this, if we build temples and houses of eternity, it is because no harmony is possible without them.'

'They're just pointless piles of stones,' sneered Bel-Tran.

'They're the foundation of our society. The world beyond inspires our government, the eternity of our deeds, for day-to-day mundanities are not enough to feed men.'

'That's outdated idealism.'

'Your policy will ruin Egypt, Bel-Tran, and will soil you.'

'I'll hire the finest washermen.'

'The soul cannot be washed so easily.'

'Are you a tjaty or a priest?'

'Both: the tjaty is a priest of Ma'at. Has the goddess of righteousness never won your heart?'

'All things considered, I hate women. If you've nothing else to say, I shall go down.'

'I thought you were my friend when we helped each other. In those days you were only a papyrus-maker and I was a minor judge lost in a great city. I did not even wonder about your sincerity. You seemed animated by a true faith in your work in the service of the country. When I think of that period, I still find it hard to believe that you were lying all the time.'

A strong wind began to blow. Thrown off balance, Bel-Tran grabbed hold of Pazair.

'But you were, weren't you?' Pazair went on. 'You were play-acting right from our first meeting.'

'I was hoping to persuade you and use you – and I confess I was disappointed when I failed. Your stubbornness and your narrow views have often exasperated me, but making use of you wasn't too difficult.'

'What does the past matter? Change your life, Bel-Tran. Use your skills in the service of Pharaoh and the people of Egypt, renounce your over-arching ambition, and you'll know the happiness of righteous people.'

'What ridiculous words ... You don't believe them yourself, I hope?

'Why lead a whole people to disaster?'

'Although you may be tjaty, you know nothing of the taste for power. I know it; this country is rightfully mine, for I am capable of imposing my rule on it.'

The rising wind obliged the two men to speak loudly and distinctly. In the distance, the palm-trees bent, their fronds intermingling, and moaned as though they would break. Whirlwinds of sand rose to attack the pyramid.

'Forget your own interest, Bel-Tran; it will lead you to nothingness.'

'Branir would not have been proud of you and your foolishness. By helping me, you have proved your incompetence; by torturing me like this, your stupidity.'

'Did you kill him?'

'I never dirty my hands, Pazair.'

'Never speak the name of Branir again.'

In Pazair's eyes, Bel-Tran saw his death. In terror, he took a step back and lost his balance.

Pazair caught him by the wrist; his heart pounding, Bel-Tran climbed down the pyramid, gripping every stone tightly.

The tjaty's gaze weighed down on him, as the storm-wind was unleashed.

43

Since the end of spring the Nile waters had been green; now a month later, they were turning brown, laden with mud and silt. In the fields, work stopped; with the end of threshing began a long holiday. Those who wanted to earn more would go to work on the large construction sites, when the annual flood facilitated the transport by boat of enormous stone blocks.

One worry haunted everyone: would the water rise high enough to quench the earth's thirst and make it fertile? To solicit the gods' favour, villagers and town-dwellers offered the river little terracotta or porcelain figurines representing a fat man with pendulous breasts, his head crowned with plants; he symbolized Hapy, the flood's dynamic energy, a formidable power which made the fields grow green.

In about twenty days' time, Hapy would swell to the point of invading the Two Lands and turning Egypt into a kind of immense lake, in which everyone moved between villages in boats. In about twenty days' time, Ramses would abdicate in favour of Bel-Tran.

The tjaty bent down to stroke his dog, who had been treated to a bone which he had chewed, buried and then unearthed from its hiding-place; Brave, too, too was feeling the effects of this period, heavy with fears and uncertainties. Pazair was concerned for the future of his faithful companions: who would take care of the dog and the donkey when he was arrested and deported? Way-Finder, accustomed to his peaceful retirement, would be sent back to the dusty tracks and made to carry heavy loads again. His two companions, friends for so long, would die of broken hearts.

Pazair held his wife close. 'You must leave, Neferet, leave Egypt before it's too late.'

'Are you suggesting that I desert you?'

'Bel-Tran's heart is a dried-out husk. Greed and ambition have replaced all feeling, and nothing can move him any more.'

'That cannot have surprised you.'

'I hoped the voice of the pyramids would reawaken his deadened conscience, but all I did was intensify his thirst for power. Save yourself; save Brave and Way-Finder.'

'As tjaty, would you permit Egypt's principal doctor to abandon her post when a grave sickness has stricken the kingdom? However the adventure may end, we shall experience it together, all of us. Ask Brave and Way-Finder: neither of them will leave you.'

Hand in hand, Pazair and Neferet looked round the garden, where Mischief was frolicking, forever in search of delicacies. So close to the cataclysm, they drank in the scented peace of this place, sheltered from the tumult; that morning, they had bathed in the ornamental lake, before taking a walk in the shade.

'The tjaty's guests have arrived,' said the head steward.

Kem and Killer greeted the guards at the gate, walked along the tamarisk-lined path, meditated before the shrine of the ancestors, washed their hands and feet on the threshold of the house, crossed the entrance hall and took their places in the four-pillared chamber where the tjaty and his wife were seated. Their arrival was soon followed by those of Tuya, Bagey, Kani and Suti.

'With the king's permission,' said Pazair, 'I can reveal to you that the Great Pyramid of Khufu, which Pharaoh alone is permitted to enter, was desecrated by Bel-Tran, his wife and three accomplices, Denes the ship-owner, Qadash the tooth-doctor and Sheshi the inventor, all three of whom are now dead, as you know. The conspirators violated the sarcophagus, and stole the gold mask, the great collar, the adze of sky-iron and the gold cubit. Some of those treasures have been recovered, but the most important one is still missing. It is the Testament of the Gods, contained in the copper case which the king must hold in his right hand during his festival of regeneration, before showing it to the people and the priests. This document, passed down from pharaoh to pharaoh, gives each reigning king his legitimacy. Who could ever have imagined that anyone would commit such a profane act and such a theft?

'My master, Branir, was murdered because he stood in the rebels' way; and Djui the embalmer became a shadow-eater in the pay of Bel-Tran. Kem and Killer have put an end to Djui's criminal activities, but we have still not identified Branir's murderer and we have been unable to recover the Testament of the Gods and return it to the king. On the first day of the New Year, Ramses will be forced to abdicate and offer the throne to Bel-Tran. Bel-Tran will close the temples, introduce the circulation of coins and adopt one law: the law of profit.'

A long and heavy silence followed the tjaty's explanation. The members of the secret council were devastated: as ancient predictions had feared, the heavens were falling upon their heads.*

Suti was the first to react. 'However precious this document may be, it won't be enough to make Bel-Tran a respected pharaoh, truly capable of ruling the country.'

'You're right,' said Pazair. 'That's why he has spent so much time corrupting the country's government and economy, and creating his network of useful alliances.'

'Haven't you tried to dismantle the network?'

'The monster's heads grow back as soon as they're cut off.'

'Your predictions are too gloomy,' said Bagey. 'Many officials will refuse to take orders from a man like Bel-Tran.'

'The Egyptian government has a strong sense of tradition,' objected Pazair, 'and it will obey the pharaoh.'

'Let's start organizing armed resistance,' proposed Suti. 'Between us, we control a lot of territory. The tjaty should coordinate the forces at his disposal.'

Kani asked to speak, and went straight to the heart of the matter. 'The temples will never accept the financial and other upheavals Bel-Tran intends to impose, because they would lead the whole country to misery and civil war. Pharaoh is the servant of the temple in spirit. If he betrayed that prime duty, he would be nothing but a political leader to whom we no longer owed obedience.'

'In that case,' agreed Bagey, 'the government would be freed from its promises. It swore an oath of loyalty to the mediator between heaven and earth, not to a despot.'

'The Health secretariat will stop functioning,' said Neferet. 'It's linked to the temples, so it will reject the new power.'

'With supporters like you,' said the Mother of Pharaoh, her voice full of emotion, 'all is not yet lost. You should know that the court is hostile to Bel-Tran and that it will never accept at its heart the lady Silkis, whose depravities are well known to everyone.'

'That's splendid, Majesty!' exclaimed Suti. 'Have you managed to sow discord between that pair of criminals?'

'I do not know, but that cruel, perverse child-woman has a fragile mind. If I see clearly, Bel-Tran will soon desert her, or else she will betray him. When she came to Pi-Ramses, hoping to ensure my complicity, she seemed certain of success; when she left, her mind had been shipwrecked. One question, Tjaty Pazair: why are only some of the Friends of Pharaoh here?'

---

*According to mythology, the sky rested on four great pillars, and, if the harmony with the gods was broken, might collapse upon the troublemakers, human beings.

'Because neither Pharaoh nor I have identified all Bel-Tran's active or passive supporters. The king decided to conceal the truth, so as to continue the fight as long as possible without letting the enemy know what he was doing.'

'You have dealt Bel-Tran some severe blows.'

'But none has been decisive, unfortunately. Resistance itself won't be easy, because Bel-Tran has infiltrated the transport systems and the army.'

'The security guards will back you,' declared Kem, 'and Suti's prestige with the All-Seeing Ones is so great that he'll have no difficulty mobilizing them.'

'Doesn't Pharaoh control the troops stationed in Pi-Ramses?' asked Suti.

'That is why he is there,' said Pazair.

'The troops based in Thebes will listen to me,' said Kani.

'Appoint me general in Memphis,' said Suti. 'I know how to talk to soldiers.'

This proposition was unanimously approved by the secret council.

'There remains the matter of transport, which the Double White House controls,' Pazair reminded them. 'And I haven't mentioned the irrigation secretariats or the officials in charge of canals, whom Bel-Tran has been trying to bribe and corrupt for several months. As for the provincial governors, some have distanced themselves from him, but others still believe in his promises. I fear there may be civil war, which will result in many deaths.'

'What other solution is there?' asked Tuya. 'Either we all abdicate before Bel-Tran, and the Egypt of Ma'at is dead, or else we reject his tyranny and keep hope alive, even at the cost of our lives.'

After overcoming the opposition of his wife, who resented his taking on all this work, Bagey helped Pazair draw up decrees relating to the management of estates after the flood and the repair of damaged irrigation pools. He set up a programme of major civil and religious works, over a period of three years. These documents would demonstrate that the tjaty was planning to act in the long term and that no upheaval threatened Ramses' reign.

The festival of regeneration was going to be impressive. One after another, the provincial governors, accompanied by the statues of their local gods, were already arriving in Memphis. Housed in the palace, with the consideration due to their rank, they conversed with the tjaty, whose authority and courtesy pleased them. At Saqqara, in the Djoser enclosure, the priests were preparing the great courtyard where Ramses, wearing the Double Crown, would reunite the North and the South in his symbolic being. In this magical space, he would commune with each divine power, in order to regain his strength and be able to go on ruling.

Suti's reputation had spread quickly, and his appointment aroused great enthusiasm in the Memphis barracks. The new general immediately gathered his troops together, and told them that the war in Asia had been averted and that they would receive a special bonus. The young general's fame reached a peak at a banquet thrown for the troops. Who but Ramses could guarantee lasting peace, a prospect which delighted the soldiers?

The guards felt greater and greater admiration for Kem, whose unwavering devotion to the tjaty was known to all. He had no need to give a speech to maintain his men's loyalty.

In every temple in Egypt, on the advice of High Priest Kani, people were preparing for the worst. Nevertheless, the priests who specialized in tending the divine energy changed nothing in the established sequence of days and nights; the dawn, noon and sunset rites were celebrated regularly, as they had been since the earliest days of the pharaohs.

The Mother of Pharaoh granted numerous audiences and spoke with the most influential courtiers, senior government officials attached to the royal household, scribes in charge of educating the elite, and noble ladies responsible for court protocol. Bel-Tran was considered a troublemaker, and Silkis unbalanced: the fact that they wanted to belong to the monarchy's inner circle seemed insane, a matter for laughter.

Bel-Tran was not laughing. The vast offensive Pazair was leading had borne some fruit. In his own government, he was having difficulty making himself obeyed and had to lose his temper more and more often with negligent underlings.

An alarming rumour was spreading: immediately after Ramses' regeneration, the tjaty would appoint a new head of the Double White House, and Bel-Tran – who was too ambitious, too hasty, and would never be anything more than an upstart – would be sent back to his papyrus works in the Delta. Some people were hawking confidential information, suggesting that the Mother of Pharaoh had lodged a complaint with the tjaty about an illegal traffic in the *Book of Going Forth by Day*. Bel-Tran's rise to power had been fast: would his downfall be even faster?

To these difficulties was added the prolonged absence of Silkis, who seldom left her apartments. It was said that she was suffering from an incurable sickness which was preventing her from appearing at the banquets she used to love so much.

Bel-Tran cursed, but continued preparing his vengeance. Whatever opposition might arise would be swept away. Becoming Pharaoh meant holding the sacred power before which the people bowed. Rebellion against the king was the ultimate crime, and therefore attracted the ultimate punishment, so once Bel-Tran was enthroned the faint-hearts would rally to him, and Pazair's support would melt away. Bel-Tran had been a traitor to his word and his oaths for so long that he now distrusted all promises. When force spoke, weakness and evasion answered.

Pazair had the power of a leader, but had lost his way by placing it in the service of an outdated law. A man of the past, attached to old-fashioned values, incapable of understanding the demands of the future, he must die. As the shadow-eater had failed to kill him, Bel-Tran would deal with him in his own way, by having him convicted of negligence and high treason – after all, the tjaty had opposed the necessary reforms and the transformation of the state. There was only a fortnight to wait: a fortnight until his triumph, a fortnight until the downfall of that inflexible, stubborn tjaty.

Bel-Tran, in whom tension was growing greater and greater, no longer went home. Silkis's rapid physical deterioration horrified him; the divorce papers were in order and he had no desire to see that faded woman again.

He remained in his office after the scribes had left, and thought about his plans and the many decisions he would have to take in a short time. He would strike swiftly and hard.

Four smokeless oil-lamps provided sufficient light to work by. Unable to sleep, Bel-Tran spent the night checking the elements of his plans for the economy. Although many of his networks had been dismantled, those which remained would be maintained by the money-exchangers and Greek traders, and would impose his views on the population. It would be easy, because his main weapon, whose nature Pazair would not know until the last moment, would be used with devastating effectiveness.

A sound made Bel-Tran start. At this late hour, the building was deserted.

He stood up and called, 'Who's there?'

The only answer was silence. Reassured, he remembered that the night patrol ensured the offices' safety. He sat back down on the floor and unrolled an accounting-papyrus, a plan of the new taxation system.

A powerful forearm hooked round his neck. Half-strangled, Bel-Tran flailed his arms, trying to break free.

'Keep quiet or I'll stick a dagger in your side.'

Bel-Tran knew that voice.

'What do you want?'

'To ask you a question. If you answer, your life will be spared.'

'Who are you?'

'Knowing that won't be any use to you.'

'I'll never give in to threats.'

'You aren't brave enough to hold out.'

'I know who you are – Suti!'

'General Suti.'

'You won't harm me.'

'Don't be too sure of that.'

'The tjaty will condemn you.'

'He doesn't know what I'm doing. Torturing someone like you doesn't worry me. If that's what the truth costs, I'm willing to pay.'

'Bel-Tran realized that Suti was not joking. 'What is your question?'

'Where is the Testament of the Gods?'

'I don't know.'

'That's enough, Bel-Tran. The time for lies is over.'

'Let me go! I'll talk.'

The stranglehold loosened.

Bel-Tran rubbed his neck and looked at the dagger Suti was brandishing. 'Even if you stick that blade in my belly, you won't learn any more.'

'Let's try.'

The blade pricked Bel-Tran's flesh and, to Suti's astonishment, he smiled.

'Do you want to die?'

'Killing me would be stupid; I don't know where the Testament of the Gods is hidden.'

'You're lying again.'

'Use that dagger and you'll be committing a useless murder.'

In the face of such disturbing self-assurance, Suti hesitated. Bel-Tran ought to have been shaking with fear, almost fainting at the thought of failing so close to his goal because of this brutal intervention.'

'Get out of here, Suti,' said Bel-Tran. 'You're wasting your time.'

44

By the time Suti had finished telling Pazair about his attempt to make Bel-Tran talk he needed a cup of cool beer. He drained the cup, but he was still thirsty.

'It was incredible,' he said, 'unbelievable. But Bel-Tran wasn't lying, I'm sure of that. He really doesn't know where the Testament of the Gods is hidden.'

Neferet brought Suti some more beer. Mischief jumped on to his shoulder, dipped a finger in the cup, leapt up the trunk of the nearest sycamore tree and hid in the foliage.

'I'm afraid he may have deceived you. He's a formidable talker, a past master of the art of dissembling.'

'But this time he was telling the truth, even if it doesn't make sense. Believe me: I was ready to run him through, but that revelation took away my desire to do so. I'm lost. It is up to you to give us direction, Tjaty.'

The gatekeeper came up to them and told Neferet that a woman was at the entrance and insisted on speaking to her. Neferet said he might show her into the garden.

The woman turned out to be Silkis's personal maid, who prostrated herself before Neferet. 'My lady, my mistress is dying. She's asking for you.'

Silkis would never see her children again. When she had read the divorce document, which had been given to her by a scribe without Bel-Tran's knowledge, she had had an attack of hysteria which left her utterly without strength. All around her, everything was soiled; despite treatment by a doctor, her intestinal bleeding had not stopped.

Looking at herself in a mirror, Silkis had been appalled. Who was that witch with swollen eyes, misshapen face and spoilt teeth? Trampling on the mirror had not removed the horror: Silkis could feel the degradation of her body, rapid and unstoppable.

When her legs gave way beneath her, she could not get up. The huge house was almost deserted – only a gardener and a maid remained.

They picked her up and laid her on her bed. She was delirious, howling, then fell into a lethargy, only to become delirious once again. Silkis was rotting away from inside.

In a moment of lucidity, she ordered her servant to fetch Neferet. And Neferet came.

Beautiful, radiant, peaceful, she looked down at Silkis. 'Do you want to be taken to the hospital?'

'It would be no use – I'm going to die. Dare tell me otherwise.'

'I should sound you.'

'You don't need to – your experience will tell you the truth. I'm horrible, aren't I?' Silkis tore at her face with her nails. 'I hate you, Neferet. I hate you because you have everything I've ever dreamt of and will never have.'

'Hasn't Bel-Tran given you all you could want?'

'He's left me because I'm ill and ugly – it's a properly drawn up divorce. I hate you and Pazair!'

'How are we responsible for your unhappiness?'

Silkis leant her head to one side; her hair was sticky with unhealthy sweat. 'I almost won, Neferet, I almost crushed you, you and your tjaty. I was the most hypocritical of women, I made you trust me, I won your friendship – with the sole intention of harming you and defeating you. You'd have been my slave, forced to obey me every moment of the day.'

'Where has your husband hidden the Testament of the Gods?' asked Neferet.

'I don't know.'

'Bel-Tran has perverted you.'

'Don't believe that! We've been in full agreement, ever since the start of the conspiracy – not once have I opposed his decisions. The murder of the honour-guard, the shadow-eater's crimes, the assassination of Pazair . . . I wanted them, approved of them, and congratulated myself on them. I was the one who passed on the orders, and I wrote the message luring Pazair to Branir's house. Pazair in the prison camp, accused of murdering his master – what a victory!'

'Why do you hate us so much?'

'To give Bel-Tran the highest position in the land, so that he'd raise me to his level. I was determined to lie, plot and deceive anyone, in order to achieve that. And now he's left me, because my body has betrayed me.'

'Did the needle that killed Branir belong to you?'

'I didn't kill him. Bel-Tran's wrong to leave me, but the real guilty party is you! If you'd treated me, I'd have kept my husband instead of rotting away here, alone and abandoned.'

'Who murdered Branir?'

An evil smile lit up the misshapen face. 'You and Pazair are on completely the wrong track, and when you understand, it will be too late – much too late. From the depths of hell where demons burn my soul, I shall witness your downfall, beautiful Neferet.' Silkis vomited.

Neferet called the maid. 'Wash her and purge this room with herbal fumes. I shall send you a doctor from the hospital.'

Silkis sat up, madness in her eyes. 'Come back, Bel-Tran, come back! We'll tread them all underfoot, we'll—' Her breath failed. Head flung back, arms flung outwards, she collapsed and lay still.

The coming of Akhet, the time of the flood, affirmed the reign of Isis, queen of the stars, the great sorceress whose generous, inexhaustible bosom gave rise to all forms of life. Women and little girls, evoking her benefits, prepared their most beautiful dresses for the great festival to be held on the first day of the flood. On the island of Philae, the goddess's sacred territory in the extreme South of Egypt, the priestesses were practising musical pieces to be played as the waters rose.

At Saqqara, the priests were ready. In each shrine in the courtyard where the regeneration would take place, a statue of a god had been placed. Pharaoh would climb a stairway and kiss the stone body, brought to life by a supernatural force; it would enter him and rejuvenate him. Fashioned by the divine powers, a masterpiece conceived by the Principle and made concrete by the temple, Pharaoh, the link between the visible and the Invisible, would be filled with the energy necessary to maintain the union of the Two Lands. In this way he would ensure the unity of his people and lead them towards bliss, in this life and in the world beyond.

When Ramses arrived in Memphis, three days before the festival of regeneration, the court was there in full to greet him. The Mother of Pharaoh wished him success in the ritual ordeal, the dignitaries assured him of their confidence. The king stated that the peace with Asia would be lasting and that he would continue, after the festival, to reign according to the eternal law of Ma'at.

As soon as the brief ceremony was over, Ramses shut himself away with his tjaty.

'Anything new?' he asked.

'Yes, Majesty, but it's rather worrying. Despite being handled somewhat roughly by Suti, Bel-Tran says he does not know where the Testament of the Gods is hidden.'

'A crude lie.'

'We must assume not.'

'What conclusions can be drawn from that?'

'That neither you nor anybody else will be able to present the Testament to the priests, the court and the people.'

Ramses was troubled. 'Could our enemies have destroyed it?'

'There is serious dissension among them. Bel-Tran has killed his accomplices and is divorcing his wife.'

'If he has not got the Testament, what is he planning to do?'

'I made a final attempt to appeal to the glimmer of light in his heart, but it was fruitless.'

'So he has not given up.'

'Silkis, in her delirium, claimed that we are wrong.'

'What did she mean?'

'I do not know, Majesty.'

'I shall abdicate before the start of the ritual, and will lay my sceptres and my crowns before the one gate in the sacred enclosure of Saqqara. Instead of my regeneration, the priests will celebrate the coronation of my enemy.'

'The officials who oversee the waters are quite clear: the flood will indeed begin the day after tomorrow.'

'The Nile will flood the land of the pharaohs for the last time, Pazair. When it returns next year, it will nourish a tyrant.'

'Resistance is being organized, Majesty. Bel-Tran's reign is likely to be an extremely difficult one.'

'The title of Pharaoh alone is enough to compel obedience. He will soon regain the ground he has lost.'

'Without the Testament?'

'He did lie to Suti. I am withdrawing into the Temple of Ptah. We shall meet again before the enclosure gate at Saqqara. You were a good tjaty, Pazair, and the country will not forget you.'

'I have failed, Majesty.'

'This evil was wholly unknown to us, so we did not have the means to fight it.'

The news spread from South to North: the flood would be perfect, neither too low nor too high. No province would go short of water, no village would suffer. Pharaoh still enjoyed the gods' favour, because it had been shown that he could still feed his people. Ramses' regeneration would make him the greatest of kings, before whom the entire earth would prostrate itself.

There was bustling activity around all the river-gauges; marks on the stone walls would enable the rate of the waters' rise and the energy of Hapy to be evaluated. The speed of the current and the Nile's brownish colour told people that the annual miracle was about to happen. Joy filled everyone's heart, and the celebration would commence within the hour.

The tjaty's secret council, meeting again, could not hide their near-despair. Tuya felt the weight of her years; Bagey was more and more stooped; Suti's many wounds were hurting; Kem hung his head, as if he were ashamed of his wooden nose; Kani's face had become more deeply lined than ever; Pazair's dignity was steeped in desperation. They had all done their utmost, in their own domains, but they had failed. What would remain of undertakings made here or there, when the new pharaoh dictated his law?

'Don't stay in Memphis,' advised Pazair. 'I shall stay, but I've hired a boat to take my household to the South. From Elephantine it will be easy to reach Nubia, and they can hide there.'

'I have no intention of abandoning my son,' declared Tuya.

'Silkis is dying, Majesty,' said Pazair worriedly. 'Bel-Tran will hold you responsible for her death and will show you no mercy.'

'My mind is made up, Tjaty. I am staying.'

'And so am I,' said Bagey. 'At my age, I am no longer afraid of anything.'

'I am sorry,' said Pazair, 'but I must disagree with you. You embody a tradition whose destruction Bel-Tran demands.'

'He will break his teeth on my old bones. My presence, beside Ramses and the Mother of Pharaoh, might even encourage him to moderation.'

'In the name of myself and all the other High Priests,' said Kani, 'I shall see Bel-Tran as soon as he is enthroned and will emphasize our attachment to the laws and virtues that made Egypt great. He shall know that the temples will not grant their support to a tyrant.'

'Your life will be in danger.'

'That is of no importance.'

'Pazair, I must stay to protect you,' said Suti.

'And so must I,' said Kem. 'I serve the tjaty and no one else.'

Moved to tears, Tjaty Pazair closed his last council with an appeal to Ma'at, whose Rule would survive after the extinction of humanity.

After telling Pazair about her last visit to Branir's tomb, Neferet left for the hospital, to operate on a patient with a broken skull and to give her colleagues final advice. She had confirmed that the communion with her master's soul had not been an illusion. Although she could not translate the message from the otherworld into human words, she was convinced Branir would not abandon them.

Alone before the shrine of the ancestors, Pazair let his thoughts wander in the past. Since he had held the office of tjaty, he had had hardly any time to meditate like this, detached from a reality which had slipped from his grasp. The mind, that mad monkey which must be kept chained up, had been pacified; his thoughts flew free, keen and clear-cut as an ibis's beak.

He went over the facts one by one, from the crucial moment when, refusing to sanction the transfer of the head guard of the Giza sphinx, he had unwittingly thwarted the conspirators' plan. His determined search for the truth had been strewn with traps and dangers, but he had not lost heart. Today, although he knew the identities of most of the conspirators, including Bel-Tran and Silkis, although he had solved parts of the puzzle and knew what the outcome of the plot would be, Pazair felt he had been fooled. Swept up in a whirl of activity, he had not stepped back far enough to see clearly.

Brave lifted his head and growled softly: someone was coming. In the garden, though the moon was still shining, birds were beginning to awake and sing gaily. Someone slipped along the edge of the lotus pond and made for the porch. Pazair held the dog back by the collar.

An emissary from Bel-Tran, charged with killing him? A second shadow-eater, whom Killer had not stopped? The tjaty prepared himself for death. He would be the first to fall beneath the blows delivered by the new master of Egypt, so eager to wipe out his opponents.

There was no sign of Way-Finder. Pazair was afraid the intruder might have slit the donkey's throat. He would beg him, no doubt fruitlessly, to spare Brave.

She appeared in the moonlight, a short sword in her hand, her bare breasts covered with strange signs, her brow decorated with black and white stripes.

'Panther!'

'I must kill Bel-Tran.'

'Is your face painted for war?'

'It was the custom in my tribe. He won't escape my magic.'

'I'm afraid he will,' said Pazair.

'Where is he hiding?'

'In his office at the Double White House, and he's well guarded. After Suti's visit, he's not taking any risks. Don't go there, Panther. You'll be arrested or killed.'

Her mouth took on a sullen pout. 'Then it's all over . . .'

'Persuade Suti to leave Memphis straight away – tonight. Hide in Nubia, work your goldmine, and be happy. Don't be destroyed with me.'

'I promised the demons of the night to kill that monster and I shall keep my promise.'

'Why take such a terrible risk?'

'Because Bel-Tran wants to harm Neferet, and I won't let anyone destroy her happiness.'

Panther ran off across the garden, and Pazair saw her scale the surrounding wall with the grace of a cat.

Brave went back to sleep, and Pazair returned to his thoughts. Odd details came back to him and, so as not to forget them, he noted them down on clay tablets.

As the work progressed, other aspects of his investigation, neglected until now, came to light. Pazair grouped the evidence, drew provisional conclusions and forged strange paths, which reason forbade him to take seriously.

When Neferet came back, at sunrise, Brave and Mischief greeted her joyfully.

Pazair took her in his arms. 'You're exhausted.'

'The operation was difficult, and then I had to put my affairs in order. My successor will have no difficulty continuing my work.'

'Rest now.'

'I'm not sleepy.'

Neferet looked at the scores of clay tablets piled beside him. 'Have you been working all night?'

'I've been stupid.'

'Why do you say such a thing?'

'And not only stupid but blind, because I refused to see the truth. That's an unforgivable sin for a tjaty, a sin which would have plunged Egypt into misfortune. But you were right, and something wonderful happened: the soul of Branir spoke to me.'

'Do you mean . . . ?'

'I know where the Testament of the Gods is.'

45

As the star Sopdet shone in the east, companion of the rising sun, the birth of the flood was proclaimed throughout the land. After several days' anxiety, the new year was surging up out of the restorative tide. The rejoicing would be especially great because the festival would also celebrate Ramses' regeneration.

Demons, miasmas and invisible dangers had been defeated. Thanks to the principal doctor's conjurations, the terrifying Sekhmet had not sent her hordes of diseases against Egypt. Everyone filled a blue porcelain vase with the water of the new year, which held within it the very first light; keeping it in one's home ensured prosperity.

At the palace, there was no deviation from custom. A silver vase containing the precious water was placed at the foot of the throne where Ramses had been sitting since first light.

The king wore no crown, collar or bracelets, merely a simple white kilt in the style of the Old Kingdom.

Pazair bowed before him. 'The year will be happy, Majesty. The flood is perfect.'

'But Egypt will soon know disaster . . .'

'I hope I have accomplished my mission.'

'I do not blame you for anything.'

'I beg you, Majesty, to put on the insignia of power.'

'A futile request, Tjaty. That power no longer exists.'

'It is intact and will remain so.'

'Are you making mock of me, at the very moment when Bel-Tran is about to appear in this throne-room and seize Egypt?'

'He will not come.'

'Have you lost your mind?'

'Bel-Tran is not the leader of the conspirators, Majesty. He led those who violated the Great Pyramid, but the real leader did not take part in the expedition. Kem suggested this idea to me while we were speculating about the number of plotters, but my ears remained closed.

As we discovered the extent of their plan, Bel-Tran imposed himself as their spokesman, while his master remained hidden in the shadows. I believe I know not only that master's name but also the hiding-place of the Testament of the Gods.'

'Shall we find it in time?'

'I am sure that we shall.'

Ramses stood up, put on the great ceremonial gold collar and silver bracelets, set the Blue Crown upon his head, took up the sceptre of command in his right hand and sat down on the throne.

The head steward came in and asked permission to speak: Bagey was requesting an audience.

The king concealed his impatience. 'Would his presence hinder you, Tjaty?'

'No, Majesty.'

The former tjaty approached, his face grim, his gait stiff. The only jewellery he wore was the symbol of his former office, a copper heart attached to a chain about his neck.

'Our defeat is not yet certain,' said the king. 'Pazair thinks that—' He broke off in surprise: Bagey had not bowed before him.

'Majesty, this is the man of whom I spoke,' said Pazair.

The king was stunned. 'You, Bagey? My former tjaty?'

'Give me the sceptre of command,' said Bagey. 'You are no longer fit to rule.'

'What demon has taken hold of your mind? To think that you, of all people, could commit this treachery . . .'

Bagey smiled. 'Bel-Tran persuaded me that he is right. The world he wants, which he and I shall fashion together, suits me. My coronation will not surprise anyone, and will reassure the country. By the time the people notice the transformations Bel-Tran and I have made, it will be too late. Those who do not follow us will fall by the wayside, where their corpses will turn to dried-out husks.'

'You are no longer the man I knew, the honest, incorruptible judge preoccupied with truth.'

'The times are changing, and so are men.'

Pazair cut in, 'Before meeting Bel-Tran, you were content to serve Pharaoh and to apply the law, with an almost excessive severity. But Bel-Tran showed you a new and shimmering horizon, and he was able to buy your conscience because it was for sale.'

Bagey remained icily calm.

'You had to ensure your children's future,' continued Pazair. 'So, although you showed an ostentatious distaste for material possessions, you became the accomplice of a man whose main characteristic is greed. And you are greedy, too, because you covet supreme power.'

'We have talked enough,' said Bagey dryly, holding out his hand. 'The sceptre of command, Majesty, and the crown.'

'We must appear before the high priests and the court.'

'I am glad of it. You shall renounce the throne in my favour.'

Pazair seized Bagey's copper heart, and pulled it towards him so hard that its chain broke. He handed it to the king. 'Open this dead heart, Majesty.'

With his sceptre, Ramses smashed it.

Inside lay the Testament of the Gods.

Bagey stood rooted to the spot.

'Coward among cowards!' exclaimed the king.

Bagey drew back. His cold eyes contemplated Pazair.

'The truth did not appear to me until tonight,' confessed the tjaty in a calm voice. 'I trusted you completely, so to me it was inconceivable that you were in alliance with a creature like Bel-Tran, and still less that you were the rebels' secret leader. You wagered on my credulity and you almost won.

'And yet I ought to have suspected you a long time ago. Who but the tjaty could have ordered the transfer of the Sphinx's head guard, and then laid the responsibility at the door of General Asher, whose treason he knew? Who but the tjaty could pull the strings of government and build such a conspiracy? Who else could so easily have manipulated Mentmose, who was so preoccupied with keeping his job that he obeyed orders without understanding them? Who allowed Bel-Tran to climb the stairway to power without hindrance? If I had not become tjaty myself, I would never have realized the full scope of this office and the range of action it implies.'

'Did you yield to Bel-Tran's threats or to his blackmail?' asked Pharaoh.

Bagey said nothing, so Pazair answered for him.

'Bel-Tran outlined a brilliant future for him, in which he would at last occupy the highest position in Egypt, and Bagey knew how to make use of a crude but all-conquering man. He hid in the shadows, while Bel-Tran showed himself. All his life, Bagey has hidden behind rules and the dryness of the surveyor's maps, for his heart is inhabited only by cowardice. I realized that when, faced with difficult circumstances in which we had to confront enemies together, he preferred to make his escape rather than help me. Sensitivity and love of life are unknown to Bagey. His thoroughness was merely a mask for fanaticism.'

Ramses' eyes blazed with anger. 'And you dared wear the tjaty's heart round your neck, making people believe that you were Pharaoh's conscience!'

Before the king's wrath Bagey drew back a few paces, but he still glared at Pazair.

'Bagey and Bel-Tran,' Pazair went on, 'based their strategy on lies. Their accomplices did not know of Bagey's role – in fact, they even despised him – and that deceived me. When the old tooth-doctor Qadash became a hindrance, Bagey gave the order for him to be killed, and the same fate would have befallen the ship-owner Denes and the inventor Sheshi if Princess Hattusa had not taken her own vengeance.* As for my death, it was to make up for the disappointment of seeing the post of tjaty elude Bel-Tran. When I was unexpectedly appointed, he hoped to corrupt me, and when that failed he tried to discredit me. When that also failed, all he had left was murder.'

No emotion showed on Bagey's face; he seemed indifferent to the enumeration of his crimes.

'Thanks to Bagey, Bel-Tran was progressing safely. No one would ever have thought of looking for the Testament of the Gods in the copper heart, symbol of the tjaty's awareness of his duties, a symbol Pharaoh had permitted Bagey to continue wearing after he retired, in recognition of the services he had rendered. Bagey had foreseen that you would make that generous gesture, Majesty. Leaving nothing to chance, he used it as the best and most inaccessible of hiding-places. Lurking in the shadows, he would not be identified before he seized power. Until the very last moment, we would concentrate on Bel-Tran – and all the while Bagey was a member of my secret council and was informing his accomplice of my decisions.'

As if being close to the throne was becoming intolerable, Bagey moved further away.

'The only point on which I was right,' stated Pazair, 'is the link between Branir's murder and the conspiracy. But how could I have dreamt that you were mixed up in this appalling crime, either directly or indirectly? I was a feeble tjaty, with my legal procedures, my blindness and my trust in your integrity. There again, you calculated right – until the dawn of this wonderful day when Pharaoh Ramses will be regenerated. Branir had to be killed because, as High Priest of Karnak, he would have occupied a powerful position and would have provided me with means of investigation I did not then have. Now, who knew that Branir was to become High Priest? Only five people. Three of them were above suspicion: the king, Branir's predecessor at Karnak, and yourself. The other two, though, were excellent suspects: Nebamon, principal doctor of Egypt, who hoped to kill me and marry Neferet, and his accomplice Commander Mentmose, who did not hesitate to

---

* See *Secrets of the Desert*.

send me to the prison camp, even though he knew I was innocent. For a long time I believed that one or the other was guilty, before I became certain that they had not made any attempt on my master's life. The murder weapon, the mother-of-pearl needle, seemed to indicate a woman. I followed false trails, thinking of Denes's wife, of Tapeni, and of Silkis. That Branir made no attempt to defend himself when the needle was stabbed into his neck meant that the killer must belong to Branir's small inner circle, must be lacking in all sensitivity, must be capable of killing a sage and accepting that he would be damned, and must show perfect accuracy in the murder. Now, the investigation established that the three ladies were not guilty of this crime. Neither was Branir's predecessor, who has not left Karnak since his retirement, and therefore could not have been in Memphis on the day of the murder.'

'Aren't you forgetting the shadow-eater?' asked Bagey.

'Kem's interrogation of him dispelled all my doubts: he did not kill Branir. That leaves only you, Bagey.'

The accused made no denial.

'You were familiar with his home and his habits. On the pretext of congratulating him on becoming High Priest, you visited him at a time when no one would see you. A man of the darkness, you know how to pass unnoticed. He turned his back on you and you stabbed him with a needle you had stolen from Silkis during one of your secret conversations at Bel-Tran's house. Never was a greater act of cowardice committed on this earth.

'After that, your successes came thick and fast: Branir was dead, Mentmose could not identify you, Neferet was under Nebamon's authority, Suti was reduced to impotence, Bel-Tran was soon to be tjaty, and Ramses would be constrained to abdicate in your favour. But you underestimated the power of Branir's soul and forgot the presence of the world beyond. Killing me was not enough: you also had to stop Neferet realizing the truth. You and Bel-Tran have nothing but contempt for women, but you were wrong to overlook her. Without her I would have failed, and you would have become the masters of Egypt.'

'Let me leave the country with my family,' said Bagey in a husky voice. 'My wife and children are innocent.'

'No. You shall be judged,' decreed Pharaoh.

'I served you faithfully for many years, and was never rewarded according to my true worth. Bel-Tran saw that. What was Branir, what is this miserable creature Pazair, beside me and my knowledge?'

'You were a false sage,' said Ramses, 'the worst of all criminals. The monster you nourished within yourself destroyed you.'

*

On this day of celebration, the Double White House was deserted. Worried that Suti might attack him again, Bel-Tran had not stood down the guards, and had even demanded that they increase their vigilance. The people's revelry amused him: they did not yet know that they were cheering a deposed monarch. When the truth became known, no one would be surprised that a discredited Ramses should stand down in favour of Bagey, who was respected by all. They would trust the former tjaty, who have never shown any sign of ambition.

Bel-Tran consulted his water-clock. By now, Ramses would have abdicated, and Bagey, installed on the throne with the sceptre of command in his hand, would have summoned a scribe to note down his first decree: that Pazair be dismissed and imprisoned for treason, and that Bel-Tran be appointed tjaty. In a few minutes, a delegation would come to fetch Bel-Tran and take him to the palace, where he would attend the new monarch's coronation.

Bagey would soon become drunk on a power he did not know how to wield. Bel-Tran would flatter him skilfully for as long as necessary, and would meanwhile do as he pleased. As soon as the state was in his hands, he would get rid of the old man – assuming sickness did not do the job for him.

From his window, Bel-Tran saw Kem coming towards the Double White House at the head of a squadron of guards. Why was the Nubian still in his post? Bagey must have forgotten to replace him. Bel-Tran would not make that kind of mistake: he would at once surround himself with subordinates devoted to his cause.

Kem's martial bearing was strange: he did not look like a defeated man being compelled to carry out an unpleasant order. However, Bagey had assured Bel-Tran there was no risk of failure: no one would ever find the Testament of the Gods.

The Double White House guards lowered their weapons and allowed Kem to pass. Bel-Tran panicked: something had gone wrong. He left his office and ran downstairs to where there was an emergency door, in case of fire. The bolt drew back with a grating noise, and Bel-Tran entered a passageway that led to a garden. Slipping between clumps of flowers, he slid along the surrounding wall.

As he was preparing to knock out the guard posted at the gate opening on to the grounds of the Double White House, something landed on his shoulders and knocked him over. Bel-Tran's face was squashed into the soft earth, which had recently been watered. Killer's fist flattened him to the ground.

Watched by the High Priests of Iunu, Memphis and Karnak, Pharaoh united the North and South, and entered the courtyard of regeneration.

Alone before the gods, he shared the secret of their incarnation, then came back into the world of men, and returned to his palace.

Ramses wore the Double Crown, and held in his right hand the leather case containing the Testament of the Gods. From the palace's 'Window of Appearance', the king showed his people the document that made him a rightful sovereign.

Ibis took to the skies from all four points of the compass to spread the news. From Minoa to Asia, from Phoenicia to Nubia, vassals, allies and enemies would all know that Ramses' reign was continuing.

On the fifteenth day of the flood, the celebrations were at their height.

From the terrace of his palace, Ramses and his tjaty looked out over the city, which was lit up by countless lamps. In the hot summer nights, Egypt thought only of pleasure and the joy of living.

'What a magnificent sight,' said Pharaoh.

'Indeed it is, Majesty. Looking at it, I cannot understand why evil took hold of Bagey.'

'Because evil had dwelt in him since birth. I made a mistake in appointing him tjaty, but the gods enabled me to correct it by choosing you. A man's deepest nature never changes. It is up to us, who are in charge of the people's destiny, and who have inherited a kind of wisdom, to learn how to discern it. Now, justice must be done; upon it, and upon it alone, rest a country's greatness and happiness.'

46

'May we distinguish truth from falsehood,' declared Pharaoh, 'and protect the weak to save them from the powerful.'

The tjaty's court was in session. The three accused, Bagey, Bel-Tran and Silkis, must answer for their crimes before Pazair and a jury made up of Kani, Kem, an overseer, a weaving-woman, and a priestess of Hathor.

The tjaty read out the charges, not omitting a single detail. Bagey showed no emotion and apparently took no interest in the accusations against him. Bel-Tran protested, gesticulated, insulted the judges and claimed that he had acted properly. Silkis had been given permission to remain at home because of her poor health. When Kem had handed her the document concerning her, she had taken refuge in silence.

After a brief deliberation, the jury reached its verdict, which Pazair approved.

'Bagey, Bel-Tran and Silkis, having been found guilty of conspiracy against the king's person, perjury, of crime and complicity in crime, treason and rebellion against Ma'at, are condemned to death, both on this earth and in the afterlife. Henceforth, Bagey shall be called "the Coward", Bel-Tran "the Greedy One", and Silkis "the Hypocrite"; they shall bear these names for all eternity. As they are enemies of the Light, their effigies and their names shall be drawn with fresh ink on pieces of papyrus, which will be attached to wax figures in their image, pierced with a spear, trampled underfoot, then thrown into the fire. In this way, all trace of the three criminals shall be erased, in this world and the next.'

When Kem brought the poison to Silkis, so that she could carry out the sentence herself, the maid informed him that she had died shortly after learning her own and her accomplices' names of infamy. The Hypocrite had expired in a last attack of hysteria; her corpse was burnt.

Bel-Tran had been locked away in the barracks under General Suti's command. He occupied a cell with whitewashed walls, where he paced up and down, his eyes fixed on the phial of poison that Kem had placed in the centre of the room. The Greedy One was so afraid that he could not accept the idea of taking his own life. When the door opened, he thought of charging at the arrival, knocking him down and running away.

But the apparition rooted him to the spot.

Panther, her body covered with war paint, was threatening him with a short sword; in her left hand, she held a leather bag. The young woman's gaze was terrifying. Bel-Tran backed away, until the wall prevented him from going any further.

'Sit,' ordered Panther.

Bel-Tran obeyed.

'Since you're so greedy, eat.'

'Is it poison?'

'No, it's your favourite food.'

Laying her sword-blade against Bel-Tran's neck, she forced him to part his lips and poured the contents of the bag into his mouth: Greek silver coins.

'Stuff yourself, Greedy One! Stuff yourself into nothingness!'

The summer sun was reflecting off the faces of the Great Pyramid of Khufu, covered once more with white limestone from Tura. The whole structure was transformed into a powerful petrified ray of light, so intense that no one could bear to look directly at it.

His legs swollen, his back bent, the Coward followed Ramses with difficulty; the tjaty brought up the rear. The trio crossed the threshold of the great monument and continued along an upward-sloping corridor. Gasping for breath, Branir's murderer moved more and more slowly; climbing the great gallery was torture. When would this climb end?

After bending almost double, he entered a vast chamber with bare walls, whose covering was in the form of nine gigantic granite flagstones. At the far end was an empty sarcophagus.

'This is the place you wished so much to conquer,' said Ramses. 'Your five accomplices, who defiled it, have been punished. You, coward among cowards, gaze upon the energy centre of the country, decipher the secret you wanted to steal.'

The Coward hesitated, suspecting a trap.

'Go,' ordered the king, 'explore the most inaccessible domain in Egypt.'

The Coward grew bolder. He slid along a wall like a thief, searched in vain for an inscription, a hiding-place for precious items, and arrived at the sarcophagus, over which he bent.

'But . . . it's empty.'

'Your accomplices looted it, didn't they? But look more closely.'

'Nothing. There is nothing there.'

'Since you are blind, go.'

'Go?'

'Leave the pyramid. Disappear.'

'You are permitting me to leave?'

Pharaoh remained silent. The Coward entered the low, narrow corridor, and ran down the great gallery.

Ramses turned to Pazair. 'I have not forgotten the sentence of death, Tjaty. For cowards, the most violent poison is the noonday sun. It will strike him as he emerges from the pyramid, and it will utterly destroy him.'

'Are you not the only person permitted to enter this shrine, Majesty?'

'You have become my heart, Pazair. Come to the sarcophagus.'

The two men laid their hands upon Egypt's founding stone.

'I, Ramses, son of the Light, decree that no visible body shall again rest in this sarcophagus. From this void is born the creative energy without which a reign would be nothing but a paltry government of men. Look, tjaty of Egypt, look beyond life, and worship its presence. Do not forget it, when you hand down justice.'

When Pharaoh and his tjaty emerged from the Great Pyramid, they were bathed in the gentle rays of sunset; inside the stone giant, time had been abolished. The guards had long since carried away the charred body of the Coward, who had been struck dead on the threshold of the Temple of Purification.

Suti could not keep still: despite the importance of the ceremony, Panther was late. Although she had refused to tell him why her body was covered in warlike paint-markings, he was convinced that only she would have been cruel enough to suffocate the Greedy One with silver. Kem, content to verify that the condemned man was dead, did not open an investigation. The dead man's body would be burnt, like those of his accomplices.

The whole court had travelled to Karnak. No one wanted to miss the magnificent ceremony during which Ramses would reward the tjaty, whose praises were being sung throughout the Two Lands. In the front row, beside Kem in his ceremonial dress, were Way-Finder, Brave and Killer, who had been raised to the rank of captain. They all wore dignified expressions. Mischief, Neferet's little green monkey, had wisely perched on her mistress's shoulder.

As soon as the festivities were over, Suti would leave for the Great South, in order to restore the Lost City and enable gold and silver to be mined again. At the heart of the desert, he would feast upon sublime dawns.

At last Panther arrived, bedecked with collars and bracelets of lapis-lazuli, compelling admiration from even the most resolutely unimpressed. Her golden hair, the plumes of an indomitable wild creature, aroused a good deal of feminine jealousy. Panther threw hate-filled looks at a few beauties who were gazing too longingly at General Suti's fine figure.

Silence fell when Pharaoh, carrying a gold cubit, walked towards Pazair and Neferet, who were standing side by side in the middle of the sun-filled courtyard.

'You have saved Egypt from chaos, rebellion and ill fortune. Receive this symbol: may it be your goal and your destiny. Through it Ma'at is expressed, the intangible foundation upon which righteous deeds are built. May the goddess of truth never leave your heart.'

Pharaoh himself consecrated the new statue of Branir, which was placed in the secret part of the temple, with those of the other sages who had been admitted to the shrine. The statue showed him as an elderly scribe looking down at an unrolled papyrus, on which were written the ritual words: 'You who see me, greet my *ka*, recite the offertory words for me; pour a libation of water, and the same will be done for you.' Branir's eyes sparkled with life: quartz for the eyelids, rock crystal for the white of the eye, and obsidian for the pupil, produced a gaze filled with eternity.

When the summer night glittered above Karnak, Neferet and Pazair gazed upwards. At the zenith of the celestial vault, a new star had appeared; it crossed the sky and joined with the pole star. Henceforth the soul of Branir, now at peace, would dwell with the gods.

From the banks of the Nile rose up the song of the ancestors: 'May hearts be gentle, O inhabitants of the Two Lands. The time of happiness is come, for justice has resumed its rightful place. Truth drives out falsehood, the greedy are driven back, those who transgress the Rule fall to the ground. The gods are filled with delight, and we are living through wondrous days, in joy and light.'